Acclaim for GISH JEN'S

Mona in the Promised Land

"Gish Jen bravely skewers what we *think* we mean by assimilation, cultural diversity and the uniquely American right to forge a new identity and then patent it. Not only that, now I finally know why Chinese mothers are like Jewish mothers." —Amy Tan

"Gish Jen is . . . a literary force worthy of attention and respect. . . . [This book is] hilarious and touching." —*Newsday*

"Funny, headlong and completely delightful. . . . A light-hearted novel of radiant charm and human warmth." —Cynthia Ozick

"A sublime novel, piquant and deliciously irreverent." —*Elle*

"[Mona] is her own melting pot, her own mosaic, and someone whose life it is satisfying to join for a bit." —*Christian Science Monitor*

"A sparkling, rollicking novel that shuffles the numerous broken contracts of the American dream like a pack of shining cards." —Jayne Anne Phillips

"Hilarious. . . . If a tape is made of this book, with its episodic leaps and energetic humor, it could be marketed as a form of literary aerobics." —*The Nation*

GISH JEN
Mona in the Promised Land

Gish Jen grew up in Scarsdale, New York. Her work has appeared in *The Atlantic Monthly, The New Yorker, Best American Short Stories of the Century,* and many anthologies. The author of three novels and one book of short stories, she lives in Massachusetts with her husband and two children.

Mona in the Promised Land

Mona in the Promised Land

GISH JEN

Vintage Contemporaries

VINTAGE BOOKS

A DIVISION OF RANDOM HOUSE, INC.

NEW YORK

FIRST VINTAGE CONTEMPORARIES EDITION, APRIL 1997

Copyright © 1996 by Gish Jen

All rights reserved under International and Pan-American Copyright Conventions.
Published in the United States by Vintage Books, a division of Random House, Inc.,
New York, and simultaneously in Canada by Random House of Canada Limited,
Toronto. Originally published in the United States in hardcover by Alfred A. Knopf,
Inc., New York, in 1996.

A portion of this work was published in somewhat different form in
The Atlantic Monthly.

The Library of Congress has cataloged the Knopf edition as follows:
Jen, Gish.
Mona in the promised land / by Gish Jen.—1st ed.
p. cm.
ISBN 0-679-44589-7
1. Chinese-American families—New York (State)—Westchester County—Fiction.
2. Chinese Americans—New York (State)—Westchester County—Fiction. 3. Girls—
New York (State)—Westchester County—Fiction. 4. Westchester County (N.Y.)—
Fiction. I. Title.
PS3560.E474M66 1996
813'.54—dc20 95-44447
CIP

Vintage ISBN: 0-679-77650-8

Author photograph © Marion Ettlinger

Random House Web address: http://www.randomhouse.com/

Printed in the United States of America
20 19 18 17 16 15 14 13 12

For my mother,

who sat on her father's lap and read scrolls—

and for my father,

who tucked Tai Shan under his arm, and jumped over the

North Sea

I'm becoming Chinese, I know it.   —Richard Rodriguez

And having grown up next door to Skokie, Illinois—the land
of perpetual spring, a Rosenbloom on every corner—I knew
more Yiddish than Japanese.   —David Mura

. . . all things change. The cosmos itself is flux and motion.
                                                    —Ovid

He dissolves his bond with his group.
Supreme good fortune.
Dispersion leads in turn to accumulation.
This is something that ordinary men do not think of.
                                        —the *I Ching*

I

CHAPTER I

Mona Gets Flipped

There they are, nice Chinese family—father, mother, two born-here girls. Where should they live next? The parents slide the question back and forth like a cup of ginseng neither one wants to drink. Until finally it comes to them: what they really want is a milk shake (chocolate), and to go with it a house in Scarshill. What else? The broker hints patiently, in a big round voice; she could have modeled her elocution on the cannonball. "The neighborhood!" she says, appreciating herself in the visor mirror. Her enunciation is something for someone doing her lips while she talks. Now she smooths her French twist. In smell she is cultivated, this realtor, a real Chanel No. 5; however, she is married to a conspicuously hairy husband, as the minor Changs know via spying skills and nosiness. She powders her nose. "Moneyed! Many delis!" In other words, rich and Jewish, she! for one! would rather live elsewhere!

This is such a nice thing to say, even the Changs know to be offended, they think, on behalf of all three Jewish people they know, even if one of them they're not sure about. Still, someone has sent the parents a list of the top ten schools nationwide, and so *many-deli* or not, they settle into a Dutch colonial on the Bronx River Parkway. For they're the New Jews, after all, a model minority and Great American Success. They know they belong in the promised land.

Or do they? In fact, it's only 1968; the blushing dawn of ethnic awareness has yet to pink up their inky suburban night. They have an idea about the blacks because of poor Martin Luther King. More distantly perceived is that the Jews have become The Jews, on account of the Six Day War; much less that they, the Changs, are The New Jews. They are just smitten with the educational opportunity before them—that golden student-teacher ratio—and also with the dumb majesty of the landscaping. Three giant azaleas they have now, not to say a rhododendron the size of their old bathroom, and in addition a topographical feature of forsythia. Two foothills of the forsythia they are moved to address immediately with hedge clippers (feeling quite hardy and pioneering, Westward ho! and all that), only to discover that to render your forsythia into little can shapes is in this town considered gauche. And so they desist. Leaving an effect, as their nice new neighbor, Mr. 20-20, helpfully points out. Older sister Callie dubs it *Two Small Cans with Wild Mountain Range*.

Still they figure there's much to admire about their house, what with its large brick chimney and considerable wood door, and not to forget its stucco-clad walls. Never mind that when younger sister Mona asks, she discovers stucco to be designer cement. They've never lived in a place *clad* in anything before. Their house is still of the upstanding-citizen type. *Remember the Mayflower!* it seems to whisper, in dulcet tones. They could almost be living on Tory Lane, that's how fetching their road is, how winding. So what if drivers miss their turns, plow up their flower beds, then want to use their telephone? *Of course,* Helen tells them, like it's no big deal, they can replant. They're the type to adjust. The lady drivers weep, Helen gets out the Kleenex for them.

The Changs are a bit down the hill from the private-plane set, in other words. Only in their dreams do their jacket zippers jam, what with all the lift tickets they have stapled to them, Killington on top of Sugarbush on top of Stowe; and they don't even know where the Virgin Islands are—although certain of them do know that virgins are like priests and nuns, which there were more of in the town they just moved from, than here. This is Mona's first understanding of class. In the old neighborhood, everybody knew everything about virgins and nonvirgins, not to say the technicalities of staying in between. Or almost everybody. In their old town, Mona was the laugh-along type. Here, she's an expert.

"You mean the man . . . ?" Pigtailed Barbara Gugelstein spits a mouthful of Tab back into her pop-top can. At this age she has chin-to-chest disease, but even so you can see how riveting are her dewy green eyes. These are not set in regular sockets like your everyday cup and ball, but rather in most exquisite deep hollows, big and thought-provoking as TV dish antennae. Naturally, she does not see this. Naturally, she is obsessed with hair frizz, and what's more is convinced that her nose resembles a half-open sleep sofa. To everyone else she looks like Cleopatra. Ostrich fans, she brings to mind. Languid nights on the Nile.

"That is *so* gross," she says.

Pretty soon Mona's getting popular for a new girl. The only hold-out is Danielle Meyers, who, what with her blue mascara and contact lenses, not to say other attributes, has gone steady with two boys. "How do *you* know?" she starts to ask. Proceeding to edify the eighth grade at large with how she French-kissed one boyfriend and just regular-kissed the other. ("Because, you know, he had braces.") They hear about his rubber bands, how once one popped right into her mouth. Mona begins to realize she needs to find somebody to kiss too. But how? She can't do mascara, her eyelashes stick together. Plus—as Danielle the Great Educator points out—Mona's *Chinese*.

Luckily, she just about then happens to tell Barbara Gugelstein she knows karate. She doesn't know why she tells Barbara this. Her sister Callie's the liar in the family, ask anybody; it's a result of looking exactly like their mother, only with granny glasses instead of regular. Callie's got the kind of beauty that makes you consider where you stand in life, whereas Mona doesn't see why they should have to hold their heads up. But for some reason, Mona tells Barbara she can make her hands like steel by thinking hard. "I'm not supposed to tell anyone," she says.

The way Barbara backs off blinking, Mona could be the burning bush.

"I can't do bricks," Mona says, just to set things straight. "But I can do your arm if you want." She sets her hand in chop position.

"Uh, it's okay," Barbara says. "I know you can—I saw it on TV last night."

That's when Mona recalls that she too saw it on TV last night, in fact at Barbara's house. She rushes on to tell Barbara she knows how to get pregnant with tea.

"With *tea*?"

"That's how they do it in China."

Barbara agrees that China is an ancient and great civilization that ought to be known for more than spaghetti and gunpowder. Mona tells her she knows Chinese. *"Byeh fa-foon,"* she says. *"Shee-veh. Ji-nu."* This is Shanghai dialect, meaning, "Stop acting crazy. Rice gruel. Soy sauce." Barbara's impressed. At lunch the next day, Danielle Meyers and Amy Weinstein and Barbara's crush, Andy Kaplan, are all impressed too. Scarshill is a liberal place, not like their old town, where the Whitman Road Gang used to throw crab-apple mash at Callie and Mona, and tell them it would make their eyes stick shut. Here they're like permanent exchange students. In another ten years, there'll be so many Orientals they'll turn into Asians; a Japanese grocery will buy out that one deli too many.

But for now, the late sixties, what with civil rights on TV, they're not so much accepted as embraced. Especially by the Jewish part of town—which it turns out is not all of town at all, that's just an idea people have, Callie says, and lots of Jews could take them or leave them same as the Christians, who are nice too; Mona shouldn't generalize. So let her not generalize, except to say that pretty soon she's been to so many bar and bas mitzvahs, she can almost say herself whether the kid chants like an angel or like a train conductor. At seder, Mona knows to forget the bricks, get a good pile of that mortar. Also she knows what is schmaltz. Mona knows that she is, no offense, a goy. This is not why people like her, though. People like her because she does not need to use deodorant, as she demonstrates in the locker room, before and after gym. Not to say she can explain to them, for example, what is tofu (*der-voo,* they say at home). Her friends' mothers invite her to taste-test their Chinese cooking.

"Very authentic." She tries to be reassuring. After all, they're nice people, she likes them. "De-lish." She has seconds. On the question of what her family eats, though, Mona has to admit, "Well, no, it's different than that." She has thirds. "What my mom makes is home style, it's not in the cookbooks."

Not in the cookbooks! Everyone's jealous. Meanwhile, the big deal at home is when they have turkey pot pie. Her sister Callie's the one who introduced them—Mrs. Wilder's, they come in this green and brown box—and when the Changs have them, the girls get suddenly interested in helping out in the kitchen. Meaning, they stand in front of the oven, watching the cuckoo clock. Twenty-five minutes. Callie and Mona have a deal, though, to keep this activity secret from school, as everybody else thinks frozen food is gross. The girls consider it a big improvement over authentic Chinese home cooking. Oxtail soup—now, that's gross. Stir-fried beef with tomatoes. One day Mona says, "You know, Ma, I have never seen a stir-fried tomato in any Chinese restaurant we have ever been in, ever."

"In China, we consider tomatoes as delicacy." (With the sun behind her head, Helen looks to be a cross between a saint and an eclipse.)

"Ma," Mona says. "Tomatoes are *Italian*."

"No respect for elders." Helen wags her finger. Having been a reluctant beauty in her youth, Helen could now graduate to the dignified kind if her greater desire were not to try and shame Mona into believing her. She turns, abandoning her halo; sunlight washes with corny radiance her brow, her eyes, her mouth, all beautiful, as she scoots her glasses down and makes a gorilla face. "I'm telling you, tomatoes *invented* in China."

"Ma."

"It's true. Like noodles. Invented in China."

"That's not what they said *in school*."

"In China," Helen says, resorting to facts, "we eat tomatoes like fruit. Just like we eat apples here. Of course, first we drop them in hot water to take the skin off. Because, you know, Chinese people don't like to eat anything with the skin on."

And at this show of authority, Mona reluctantly makes a gorilla face too. For if she ever had to say what means Chinese, it would have to include a predilection for peeling grapes in your mouth without moving your jaw—also for emitting the peels without opening your lips. On the other hand, her mother once admitted that China was such a long time ago, a lot of things she can hardly remember. She said sometimes she has trouble remembering her characters, that sometimes she'll be writing along, and all of a sudden she won't be sure how the strokes go.

"So what do you do then?"

"Oh, I just make a little sloppy."

"You mean you *fudge*?"

Helen laughed then, but another time, when she was showing Mona how to write her name, and Mona said, just kidding, "Are you sure you're not fudging now," she was hurt.

"I mean, of course you're not," Mona said. "I mean, *oy*."

Meanwhile, what Mona knows is that in the eighth grade, people do not want to hear about how Chinese people eat tomatoes without the skin on. For a gross fact, it isn't gross enough. On the other hand, the fact that somewhere in China somebody eats or has eaten or once ate living monkey brains—now, that's conversation.

"They have these special tables," Mona says, "kind of like a giant collar. With, you know, a hole in the middle, for the monkey's neck. They put the monkey in the collar, and then they cut off the top of its head."

"Whaddathey use for cutting?"

Mona thinks. "Scalpels."

"Scalpels?" Andy Kaplan is going to turn out the sort of spatial brilliant that can rotate irregular objects in his head, but for now he's just a pale sprout of a guy with spittle on his braces.

"Kaplan, don't be dense." Barbara Gugelstein straightens as if to lock into firing position her twin early maturities. "The Chinese *invented* scalpels."

Once a friend said to Mona, that everybody is valued for something. This friend explained how some people resented being valued for their looks, others resented being valued for their money. Wasn't it still better to be beautiful and rich than ugly and poor, though? *You should be just glad,* she said, *that you have something people value.* She said it was like having a special talent, like being good at ice-skating, or opera-singing. She said, *You could probably make a career out of it.*

Here's the irony: Mona is.

But to return: Mona is ad-libbing her way through eighth grade, as described. Then comes one bloomy spring day. Scarshill is everywhere azaleas and other understory plants offering year-round interest; even Mona is looking spriggy, what with the bluebell she has tucked behind her ear in the manner of a Honolulu tour bus hostess. This is not so easy on account of her glasses being in the way, and also on account of her having her father's ears—i.e., the fold-out kind that if life were fair would also fold in. These go, somehow, with her blue-ribbon cowlick, and best-of-class freckles; it's no wonder (not to boast) that she has developed some aplomb to go with all these looks. How much aplomb, however, remains to be seen on said bloomy spring day, as she saunters in late to homeroom, only to experience a personal seasonal shock—a new kid in class.

Chinese.

So what should she do—pretend to have to go to the girls' room like Barbara Gugelstein the day Andy Kaplan took his ID bracelet back? She sits down. She is so cool she reminds herself of Paul Newman. First thing she realizes, though, is that no one looking at her is thinking of Paul Newman. The notes fly:

"*I* think he's cute."

"Who?" Mona writes back.

"I don't think he talks English too good. Writes it, either."

"Who?"

"They might have to put him behind a grade, so don't worry."

"He has a crush on you already, you could tell as soon as you walked in—he turned kind of orangish."

Mona hopes she's not turning orangish as she deals with her mail, she could use a secretary. The second round starts:

"What do you mean, who? Don't be weird. Didn't you *see* him??? Straight back over your right shoulder!!!!"

She has to look, what else can she do? She thinks of certain tips she learned in Girl Scouts about poise. She crosses her ankles. She holds a pen in her hand. She sits up as though she has a crown on her head. She swivels her head slowly, repeating to herself, *I* could be Miss America.

"Miss Mona Chang."

Her bluebell falls to the floor. Barbara rescues it for her, but still the blackboard ahead seems to swim with yesterday's homework equations.

"Notes, please."

Mrs. Mandeville's policy is to read all notes aloud.

Mona tries to consider what Miss America would do. She envisions herself, back straight, knees together, crying. Some inspiration. Cool Hand Luke, on the other hand, would quick, eat the evidence. And why not? She should yawn as she stands up, and boom, the notes are gone. All that's left is to explain that it's an old Chinese reflex.

She shuffles up to the front of the room.

"One minute, please," says Mrs. Mandeville.

Doom looms.

Mrs. Mandeville loudly uncrinkles a piece of paper.

And Miss Mona Chang, who got almost straight A's her whole life except for in Math and Conduct, is about to start bawling in front of everyone.

She is delivered out of hot Egypt by the bell. Mrs. Mandeville still has her hand clamped on Mona's shoulder, though, and the next thing Mona knows, she's holding the new boy's schedule. He's standing next to her like a big blank piece of paper.

"This is Sherman," says Mrs. Mandeville.

"Hello," Mona says.

"Non how a," Mona says.

She's glad Barbara Gugelstein isn't there to see her Chinese in action. *"Ji-nu,"* she says. *"Shee-veh."*

Later Mona finds out that Sherman's mother asked if there were any other Orientals in his grade. She had him put in Mona's class on purpose. For now, though, he looks at her as though she's much stranger than anything else he's seen so far. Is this because he understands she's saying *soy sauce rice gruel* to him, or because he doesn't?

"Shah-man," he says finally.

Mona looks at his schedule card. Sherman Matsumoto. What kind of name is that for a nice Chinese boy?

(Later on, people ask her how she can tell Chinese from Japanese. She shrugs. *It's the kind of thing you just kind of know,* she says. Oy!)

Sherman's got the sort of looks Mona thinks of as pretty boy. Monsignor-black hair (not monk-brown like hers), kind of bouncy—not the kind that lies down slick and flat, his is almost bushy. Crayola eyebrows, one with a round bald spot in the middle of it, like a golf hole. She doesn't know how anybody can think of him as orangish. His skin looks white to her, with pink triangles hanging down the front of his cheeks like flags. Kind of delicate-looking, but the only really uncool thing about him is that his spiral notebook has a picture of a kitty cat on it. A big white fluffy one, with blue ribbons above each perky ear. Mona's opportunities to view this are legion, as all the poor kid understands about life in junior high school is that he should follow her everywhere. This is slightly mortifying. On the other hand, he's obviously even more miserable than she is, so she tries not to say anything. Give him a chance to adjust. They communicate by sign language, and by drawing pictures, which he's much more proficient at than she is, although not as fast. He puts in every last detail, even if it takes forever. She calls on her patience.

A week of this. Finally she explains, "You should get a new notebook."

He turns the sort of pink you associate with bubble gum and hyacinths.

"Notebook." She points to his. She shows him hers, which is psychedelic, with big purple and yellow stick-on flowers. She tries to explain he should have one like this, only without the flowers. He nods enigmatically, and the next day brings her a notebook just like his, except that her cat sports pink bows instead of blue.

"Pureety," he says. And, after a moment, "You."

He speaks English! Has he spoken it all this time? *Pretty,* she thinks. *You.* What does that mean? If that's what he said at all. She's assuming he means pretty, but maybe he means pity. *Pity. You.*

"Jeez," Mona says finally.

"You ahh wer-u-come," he says.

She decorates the back of the notebook with stick-on flowers, and holds it so that these show when she walks through the halls. In class, she mostly keeps her book open. After all, the kid's so new, Mona thinks she really ought to have a heart. And for a livelong day, nobody notices.

Then Barbara Gugelstein sidles up. "Matching notebooks, huh?"

Mona's speechless.

"First comes love. Then comes marriage, and then come Chappies in a baby carriage."

"Barbara!"

"Get it?" she says. "Chinese Japs."

"Bar-*bra*," Mona says to get even.

"Just make sure he doesn't give you any *tea*," she says.

Are Sherman and Mona in love? Three days later, Mona hazards that they are. Her thinking proceeds this way: She thinks he's cute, and she thinks he thinks she's cute. On the other hand, they don't kiss and they don't exactly have fantastic conversations. Their talks are improving, though. They started out, "This is a book." "Book-u." "This is a chair." "Chai-a." Advancing to: "What is this?" "Dis is a book-u." Now, for fun, he tests her. "What is dis?" Already he speaks more slowly than he used to, and with less staccato. He throws in fewer extra syllables; he gets his accents in the right place. For actually, his English teacher at home taught him all this before, he just needed to get his mouth to listen. As for Mona, she dutifully answers, "This is a book" when he asks, as if she's the one who has to learn how to talk. He claps. "Good!"

Meanwhile, people ask her all about him, Mona could be his press agent.

"No, he doesn't eat raw fish."

"No, his father wasn't a kamikaze pilot."

"No, he can't do karate."

"Are you sure?" somebody asks.

It turns out he doesn't know karate, but judo he does. She is hurt she's not the one to find this out; the guys know from gym class. They line up to be flipped, he flips them all onto the floor, and after that he quits eating lunch at the girls' table with her. She's pretty much glad. Meaning, when he was there, Mona never knew what to say. Now that he's gone, though, she's still stuck at the *This is a chair* level of conversation. Nobody's interested in China anymore; it's just more and more questions about her and Sherman. "Got me," she's saying all the time. *Are* they going out? They do stuff, it's true. For example, Mona takes him to her family's restaurant, where they spray whipped cream in their mouths and eat fudge sauce straight from the vat. Also she takes him to the department stores. She explains to him who shops in Alexander's, who shops in Saks. She tells him her family's the type that shops in Alexander's. He says he's sorry. In Saks, he gets lost; either that, or else she's the lost one. (It's true Mona finds him calmly waiting at the front door, hands behind his back, like a guard.) She takes him to the candy store. She takes him to the bagel store. Sherman is crazy about bagels. She explains to him Lender's is gross, he should get his bagels from the bagel store. He says thank you.

"Are you going steady?" people want to know.

How can they go steady, when he doesn't have an ID bracelet? On the other hand, he brings her more presents than Mona thinks any girl's ever gotten before. Oranges. Flowers. A little bag of bagels. But what do they mean? Do they mean *thank you, I enjoyed the trip,* do they mean *I like you,* do they mean *I decided I liked the Lender's better even if they are gross, you can have these?* Mona knows at least a couple of items were supposed to go to their teachers; Sherman told her that once and turned red. She figures it still might mean something that he didn't throw them out.

More and more now, they joke. For example, he often mixes up *thinking* with *sinking*—which they both think is so funny that all either one of them has to do is pretend to be drowning, and the other one cracks up. And he tells her things. For example, that there are electric lights everywhere in Tokyo now.

"You mean you didn't have them before?"

"Everywhere now!" He's amazed too. "Since Orympics-u!"

"Olympics?"

Nineteen sixty-four, he reminds her, humming the Olympic theme song. "You know?"

"Sure," Mona says, and hums with him happily, they could be a picture on a Unicef Halloween can. The only problem is that Mona doesn't really get what the Olympics have to do with the moderniza-tion of Japan, any more than she gets this other story he tells her, about that hole in his left eyebrow. This is from some time his father acci-dentally hit him with a lit cigarette—when Sherman was a baby. His father was drunk, having been out carousing, and his mother was very mad, but didn't say anything, just cleaned the whole house. Then his father was so ashamed he bowed to ask her forgiveness.

"Your mother cleaned the house?"

Sherman nods solemnly.

"And your father *bowed*?" Mona finds this more astounding than anything she ever thought to make up. "That is so weird."

"Weird," he agrees. "*Fader* bow to *moder*!"

They shake and shake and shake their heads.

As for the things he asks her, they're not topics Mona ever talked about before. Does she like it here? "Of course I like it here, I was born here," Mona says. Is Mona Jewish? "Jewish!" She laughs. "Oy!" Is she American? "Sure I'm American," Mona says. "Everybody who's born here is American, and also some people who convert from what they were before. You could become American." But he says no, he could never. "Sure you could," Mona says. "You only have to learn some rules and speeches."

"But I Japanese."

"You could become American anyway," Mona says. "Like I *could* become Jewish, if I wanted to. I'd just have to switch, that's all."

He looks at her in alarm.

She thinks maybe he doesn't get what means switch.

She introduces him to turkey pot pies. "Gross-u?" he asks. She says they are, but that she likes them anyway. "Don't tell anybody." He promises. They bake them, eat them, agreeing turkey is just like chicken, only spelt differently. While they're eating, he's drawing her pictures with a pencil stub.

"Dis American," he says, and on a napkin he draws something that looks like John Wayne. "Dis Jewish." He draws something that looks like the Wicked Witch of the West, only male.

"I don't think so," Mona says.

He's undeterred. Partly this is because there is next to no lead in the pencil stub; difficulty seems to bring out in him resolution. "Dis Japanese," he says, and draws a fair rendition of himself. "Dis Chinese," he says, and draws what looks to be another fair rendition of himself.

"How can you tell them apart?"

"Dis way," he says, and puts the napkin of the Chinese so that it is looking at the napkins of the American and the Jew. The Japanese is looking at the wall until Mona finds him a replacement pencil, a red one. Then he draws a color picture of a Japanese flag, so that the Japanese is looking at his flag. "Chinese lost in depart-o-ment-o store," he says. "Japanese know how to go."

"What do you mean?" says Mona.

"Atomic bomb dropped on only one people," Sherman says. "The Japanese do not forget." On the back of an old mimeograph sheet, he draws another Japanese flag, a bigger one, which he puts on the icebox door with daisy magnets. "In school, in ceremony, we dis way," he explains, and bows to the picture.

When Helen comes in, her face is so red that with the white wall behind her, she looks a bit like the Japanese flag herself. Yet Mona gets the feeling she'd better not say so. First her mother doesn't move. Then she snatches the flag off the icebox, so fast the daisy magnets go flying. Two of them land on the stove. She crumples up the paper. She hisses at Sherman, *"This is the U.S. of A., do you hear me!"*

Sherman hears her.

"You call your mother, tell her come pick you up."

He understands perfectly. Mona, on the other hand, is stymied. And how can two people who don't really speak English understand each other better than she can understand them? "But, Ma," Mona says.

"Don't *Ma* me." Helen hands Sherman the telephone. (This she accompanies with Kleenex, out of habit.)

Later on, she explains that World War II was in China too. "Hitler," Mona says. "Nazis. Volkswagens." She knows the Japanese were on the wrong side, because they bombed Pearl Harbor. Helen explains about before that.

"What Napkin Massacre?" says Mona.

"Nan-king."

"Are you sure? In school, they said the War was about putting the Jews in ovens."

"Also about ovens."

"About both?"

"Both."

"That's not what they said in school."

"Just forget about school."

Forget about school? "I thought we moved here for the schools."

"We moved here," says Helen, "for your education."

Sometimes Mona has no idea what her mother is talking about.

"I like Sherman," Mona says, after a while.

"Nice boy." Helen gives the icebox door a quiet slam.

Meaning what? Mona would ask, except that her dad's just come home from the restaurant, which means it's time to start talking about whether they should build a brick wall across the front of the lawn. Recently a car made it almost into their living room, which was so scary that the driver fainted and an ambulance had to come. "We should discuss this problem," Ralph said after that. "Find solution." In appearance, Ralph could be an archetype of himself—his ears still stick out, his hair still sticks up. He is as padded as ever. Also his elbows still tend to rise and float in the air when he talks, as if he is standing in his own private water tank. But internally he is given to abrupt resolutions and real changes of outlook, for example about solving this problem. And so, for about a week, every night they'll be discussing how.

"Are you just friends, or more than just friends?" Barbara Gugelstein is giving Mona the big cross-ex.

"Maybe," Mona says.

"Come on. I told you *everything* about me and Andy."

Mona actually is trying to tell Barbara everything about Sherman, but everything turns out to be nothing. Meaning, she can't locate the conversation in what she has to say. Sherman and she go places, they talk, one time her mom threw him out of the house because of World War II.

"I think we're just friends," Mona says.

"You think"—Barbara pulls up her fishnet stockings—"or you're sure?"

Now that Mona does less of the talking at lunch, she notices more what other people talk about. Who likes who, whether to wear pants to rec night, this place in White Plains to get earrings. On none of these topics is Mona an expert. Of course, she's still friends with Barbara Gugelstein, but Mona notices that Danielle Meyers has spun away to other groups.

Barbara's analysis goes this way: To be popular, you have to have big boobs, a note from your mother that lets you use her Lord & Taylor charge card, and a boyfriend. On the other hand, what's so wrong with being unpopular? "We'll get them in the end," she says. It's what her dad tells her. "Like they'll turn out too dumb to do their own investing," she says. "And then they'll get killed in brokers' fees and have to move to towns where the schools stink."

"I guess," Mona says, shifting her weight a little.

But the next thing Mona knows, she has a true crush on Sherman Matsumoto. *Mis*ter Judo, the guys call him now, with real respect; and the more they call him that, the more Mona doesn't care that he carries a notebook with a cat on it.

Mona sighs. "Sherman."

"I thought you were just friends." Barbara Gugelstein lifts an eyebrow, something she learned to do last week.

"We were." Mona employs her own new air of mystery. For this, she's noticed, is how Danielle Meyers talks. Everything's secret, she only lets out so much; it's obvious she didn't grow up with everybody telling her she had to share.

And here's the funny thing: The more Mona tells people that she and Sherman are more than just friends, the more it seems to be true. It's the old imagination giving reality a prod. When Mona starts to blush, he starts to blush. They get to a point where they can hardly talk at all.

"Well, there's first base with tongue, and first base without," Mona tells Barbara Gugelstein.

In fact, Sherman and Mona have brushed shoulders, which was equivalent to first base, Mona was sure, maybe even second. She felt as though she'd turned into one huge shoulder. That's all she was, one huge shoulder. They not only didn't talk, they didn't breathe. But how can Mona tell Barbara Gugelstein that? So instead she says, "Well, there's second base and second base."

Danielle Meyers is her friend again. She says, blinking bluely, "I know exactly what you mean," just to make Barbara Gugelstein feel bad.

"Like *what* do I mean?" Mona says.

Danielle Meyers blinks bluely some more.

"You know what I think?" Mona tells Barbara the next day. "I think Danielle's giving us a line."

Barbara picks thoughtfully at her split ends.

If Sherman Matsumoto is never going to give Mona an ID to wear, he should at least get up the nerve to hold her hand. Mona doesn't think he sees this. She thinks of the story he told her about his parents, and in a synaptical firestorm realizes they don't see the same things at all.

So one day, when they happen to brush shoulders again, Mona doesn't move away. He doesn't move away either. There they are. Like a pair of bleachers, pushed together but not quite matched up.

After a while, Mona has to breathe, she can't help it. She breathes in such a way that their elbows start to touch too. This is in a crowd, waiting for a bus. They are both wearing short sleeves. She cranes her neck to look at the sign that says where the bus is going. Now their wrists are adjoining. Then it happens: He links his pinky around hers.

Is that holding hands? Later, in bed, Mona wonders all night. One finger, and not even the biggest one.

Sherman is leaving in a month. Already! Mona supposes he will leave and they'll never even kiss. She guesses that's all right. Just when she's resigned herself to it, though, they hold hands all five fingers. Once, when they are at the bagel shop; then once more, in her parents' kitchen. Then one day, when they are at the playground, he kisses the back of her hand. He does it again not long after that, in White Plains. She begins to use mouthwash.

Instead of moving on, though, he kisses the back of her hand again. And again. She tries raising her hand, hoping he'll make the jump from her hand to her cheek. It's like trying to wheedle an inchworm out the window. You know, *This way, this way.*

All over the world, people have their own cultures. That's what they learned in social studies.

If they never kiss, she's not going to take it personally.

It is the end of the school year. There've been parties. Kids've turned in their textbooks. *Hooray!* Outside, the asphalt steams if you spit on it. Sherman isn't leaving for another couple of days, though, and he comes to visit every morning, staying until Callie comes home from her big-deal job as a grocery checkout clerk. Mona and Sherman drink Kool-Aid in the backyard, holding hands until they are sweaty and make smacking noises coming apart. He tells her how busy his parents are, getting ready for the move; his mother in particular is very tired. Mostly he is mournful.

The very last day, he holds Mona's hand and does not let go even when their palms fill up with water like a blister. They talk more than usual. How complicated is his address, whether the Japanese have aerograms too. Then suddenly he asks, looking straight into his Kool-Aid, will she marry him?

I'm only thirteen.

But when old? Sixteen?

If you come back to get me.

I come. Or you come to Japan, be Japanese.

How can I be Japanese?

Like you become American. Switch.

He kisses her on the cheek, again and again and again.

His mother calls to say she's coming to get him. Mona cries. She tells him how she's saved every present he's ever given her—the ruler, the pencils, the bags from the bagels, all the flower petals. She even has the peels from the oranges.

All?

I put them in a jar.

She'd show him, except that they're not allowed to go upstairs to her room. Anyway, something about the orange peels seems to choke him up too. *Mister* Judo, but she's gotten him in a soft spot. They are going together to the bathroom to get some toilet paper to wipe their eyes, when poor tired Mrs. Matsumoto skids up onto the lawn.

"Very sorry!"

They race outside.

"Very sorry!"

Mrs. Matsumoto is so short that about all they can see of her is a green cotton sun hat, with a big brim. It's tied on. The brim is trembling.

Mona hopes her mom's not going to start yelling about World War II.

"It's all right, no trouble," Helen says, suddenly on the steps, behind Mona and Sherman. She's holding the screen door open; when Mona turns, she can see her mother waving. Helen is wearing a dress you would never guess she's mended twice, and she is practically standing on her toes, as if trying to hail a taxi. "No trouble, no trouble!"

"No trouble, no trouble!" Mona twirls a few times with relief. Sherman is blushing; the air smells of summer, which is to say of Mr. 20-20's roses next door.

Mrs. Matsumoto keeps apologizing; Helen keeps insisting she shouldn't feel bad, it was only some grass and a small tree. Crossing the lawn, she insists Mrs. Matsumoto get out of the car, even though it means mushing some lilies of the valley. She insists Mrs. Matsumoto come in for a cup of tea. Then she will not talk about anything unless Mrs. Matsumoto sits down, and unless she lets Helen prepare for her a small snack. The coming in and the tea and the sitting down are settled pretty quickly, but there is more negotiation over the small snack, which Mrs. Matsumoto will not eat unless she can call Mr. Matsumoto. She makes the mistake of linking Mr. Matsumoto with a reparation of some sort. This Helen will not hear of. "Please!" "No no no no." Back and forth it goes. "No no no no." "No no no no." "No no no no." What kind of conversation is that? Mona looks at Sherman, who shrugs. Finally Mr. Matsumoto calls on his own, wondering where his wife is. He comes over in a taxi. A strong-jawed businessman, friendly but brisk, he is not at all a type you could imagine bowing to a lady with a taste for tie-on sun hats. Helen invites him in, as if it's an idea she just that moment thought of. And would he maybe have some tea and a small snack?

Sherman and Mona sneak back outside for another final good-bye, next to the house, behind the forsythia bushes. They hold hands. He kisses her on the cheek again, and then—just when Mona thinks he's finally going to kiss her on the lips—he kisses her on the neck.

Is this first base?

He does it more. Up and down, up and down. First it tickles, and then it doesn't. He has his eyes closed. Mona closes her eyes too. He's hugging her. Up and down. Then down.

He's at her collarbone.

Still at her collarbone. Now his hand is on her ribs. So much for first base. More ribs. The idea of second base would probably make her nervous if he weren't on his way back to Japan, and if Mona really thought they were actually going to get there. As it is, though, Mona isn't in much danger of wrecking her life on the shoals of passion. His unmoving hand feels more like a growth than a boyfriend. He has his whole face pressed to her neck skin so she can't tell his mouth from his nose. She thinks he may be licking her.

From indoors, a burst of far-off laughter. Her eyelids flutter, she can't help it. She starts to try and wiggle such that his hand will maybe budge upward. Does she mean for her top blouse button to come accidentally undone?

He clenches his jaw; and when he opens his eyes, they're fixed on that button like it's a gnat that's been bothering him for more than long enough. He mutters in Japanese. If later in life he were to describe this as a pivotal moment in his youth, Mona would not be surprised. Holding the material as far from her body as possible, he buttons the button. Somehow they've ended up too close to the bushes.

What to tell Barbara Gugelstein? She says, "Tell me what were his last words. He must have said something last."

"I don't want to talk about it."

"Maybe he said good-bye? Sayonara?" She means well.

"I don't want to talk about it."

"Aw, come on. I told you everything about . . ."

Mona says, "Because it's private. Excuse me."

Barbara squints at Mona with her dewy green eyes as though Mona is a distant horizon she's trying to make out. She straightens her back maturely. Then she nods and very lightly places her fingertips on Mona's forearm.

The forsythia seemed to be stabbing them in the eyes. Sherman said, more or less, *You will need to study how to switch.*

And Mona said, *I think you should switch. The way you do everything is weird.*

And he said, turning pink, *You just want to tell everything to your friends. You just want to have boyfriend to become popular.*

Then he flipped her. Two swift moves, and she went sprawling through the late afternoon, a flailing confusion of soft human parts such as had no idea where the ground was.

It is fall, and Mona is in high school, and still he hasn't written. So finally she writes him on her new electric typewriter.

I still have all your gifts. I don't talk so much as I used to. Although I am not exactly a mouse either. I don't care about being popular anymore, I swear. Are you happy to be back in Japan? Jackie Kennedy married a Greek, but neither one of them switched—that's what Barbara says. What do you think about that? I know I ruined everything. I was just trying to be entertaining. I miss you with all my heart, and hope I didn't ruin everything.

He writes back in fountain pen: *You will never be Japanese.*

She throws all the orange peels out that day. Some of them, it turns out, were moldy anyway. She burns the letter with the help of Barbara Gugelstein. She tells her mother she wants to move to Chinatown.

"Chinatown!" Helen says.

Mona doesn't know why she asked.

"What's the matter? Still boy-crazy?"

"No."

"Forget about school."

Later she tells Mona that if she doesn't like school, she doesn't have to go every day. Some days Mona can stay home, like Callie.

"Stay home?" says Mona. In their old town, Callie and Mona used to stay home all the time, but that was because the schools there were *waste of time.*

"No good for a girl be too smart anyway," says Helen.

For a long time, Mona thinks about Sherman. But after a while, she doesn't think about him so much as she just keeps seeing herself flipped onto the ground. Lying there shocked, as the Matsumotos get ready to leave. Her head has hit a rock. Her brains ache as though they've been relocated in her skull. Otherwise, she's okay. She sees the forsythia, all those whippy branches, and can't believe how many leaves there are on a bush, every one green and paniculate and durably itself. And past them, real sky. She tries to remember what makes the sky blue, even though this one's gone the kind of gray you associate with words that end with *nk. Dank. Sunk. Stink.* She smells their neighbor's roses, but also she smells grass. Probably she has grass stains all over her back. She hears Helen calling through the back door, *Mon-a! Everyone leaving now* and *Not coming to say good-bye?* She hears Mr. and Mrs. Matsumoto bowing as they leave—or at least she hears the embarrassment in her mother's voice as they bow. She hears their car start. She hears Mrs. Matsumoto directing Mr. Matsumoto how to back off the lawn so as not to rip any more of it up. She feels the back of her head for blood. Just a little. She hears their *chug-chug* grow fainter and fainter, until it has faded into the *whuzz-whuzz* of all the other cars. She hears her mother singing, *Mon-a! Mon-a!* until her father comes home. Doors open and shut. She sees herself standing up, brushing her shirt off so she'll have less explaining to do if someone comes out to look for her. Grass stains, just like she thought. She sees herself walking around the house, going over to have a look at their churned-up yard. It looks pretty sad—two big brown tracks right through the irises and the lilies of the valley, and that was a new dogwood they'd just planted. Lying there like that. She hears herself thinking about her father, and how he had always considered gardening a waste of time to begin with. *That's for rich guys,* he used to say; sometimes he just wanted to cut everything down with the lawn mower. It was only when he saw her mother out there digging the hole herself that he agreed to help with the dogwood. And now he was going to have to go planting the thing all over again. Adjusting. She thinks how they probably ought to put up that brick wall.

And sure enough, when she goes inside, no one's thinking about her, or that little bit of blood at the back of her head, or the grass stains. That's what they're talking about—that wall. Again. Helen doesn't think it'll do any good, but all these accidents are giving Ralph stomach gas. Should they or shouldn't they? How high? How thick? What will the neighbors say? They have to check about the zoning, Helen claims, but Ralph, eating a danish, seems suddenly to have never heard of such a thing. *Soning? Ah, zoning! Begins with "z."* Mona plops herself down on a hard chair. And all she can think is, they are the complete only family that has to worry about this. If she could, she'd switch everything to be different. But since she can't, she might as well sit here at the table for a while, discussing what she knows how to discuss. She listens and nods to the rest.

CHAPTER 2

Her Life
More Generally

When is a pickle dish more than just a pickle dish? Two years later, Mona ponders this in tenth-grade English class; also pickles in general. She used to love pickles, but now hesitates to bring them to school (even if they are satisfyingly crunchy and low-calorie to boot), for fear of setting off a sublimation lunch—i.e., the kind of lunch where everyone discusses which people are sublimating and, in particular, whether she is. Also if all of life, in reality, is sublimation. If it is, Mona would rather not know about it.

By now, Mona would love to have forgotten about Sherman—to have proven disloyal, impulsive, fickle, a regular *femme fatale*. But though she is in the sweet bloom of her youth, she hasn't exactly had to worry about catching mono like Danielle Meyers. There was that fling with DeWitt Traub freshman year—all forty-eight hours of it before he went back to Farah Liason, the ham radio queen. And it did also transpire once, after a Dead concert, that Mona somehow found herself slow-dancing with one of the roadies—a musician in his own right, it turned out, who used just one name for his first name and last name both. Jupiter. Of course, even he seemed to feel that something was missing, for when he introduced himself, he never said just Jupiter, period, but generally added *like the planet* in such a way that that almost seemed to be his last name. And after the nice warm dance, Mona told him that she had noticed this; which she later thought must have impressed him. For though, like his namesake, he proved to have many moons in orbit, he sent her a postcard a week for a good two and three-quarters months, and almost half of them

were addressed to her, Mona Chang, and not to Pee-pee Vulva, whoever she was.

All the same, her chief hangout is still Barbara Gugelstein, and one
of their chief activities is a game called Wonder What Sherman Is
Doing Right Now. It seems that this is how they have always whiled
away their afternoons—imagining what Sherman is wearing, imagining what Sherman is eating, imagining whether Sherman is thinking
about Mona. Of course, in all their imaginings, he is pining so desperately that his mother keeps having his blood drawn, thinking that
something is the matter. He has decided to return to the U.S. He is
obsessed with student exchange programs. He plays a game with his
friends called Wonder What Mona Is Doing Right Now—only, of
course, in Japanese. Does he, in his wildest imaginings, imagine that
right at that moment, his Mona is actually imagining him, imagining
her? "It kind of like blows your mind," says Barbara Gugelstein.

Other interests: fashion. Mona and Barbara both wear ponchos,
peasant blouses, leotards, bikini underwear. Hip-hugger bell-bottoms.
Water-buffalo sandals. Barbara favors elephant-hair earrings and love
beads; Mona has a necklace with a tear-shaped peace symbol she got
in Greenwich Village. (This, she maintains, looks nothing at all like
a declawed chicken foot.) She wears her hair long and straight and
parted in the middle, as do Barbara and Cybill Shepherd, among other
fashion leaders. At night, Barbara has to roll hers all up on an orange juice can; Mona has her cowlick to contend with. Sometimes
she Dippity-Dos it down, but mostly she leaves it to do its anti-
gravity thing.

A subinterest: fashion design. Mona uses scissors to get the bottom
edge of her hip-hugger bell-bottoms to fray. Also she washes them
a hundred times with bleach. She debates whether under her knee
patches there ought to be real holes. She would cut some, except that
Barbara Gugelstein told her she did that once, and then her jeans really ripped—not only across the front completely, but around the back
too. Mona wonders about this. Didn't the rip get stopped by the side
seams? Still, she doesn't exactly want to risk pedal pushers, given all
the time she spent arguing about her pants with her mom.

"Waste water, waste electricity, waste soap, I don't know what
is the matter with you," Helen kept saying. "You want to wear old

clothes, you can borrow some from your parents. Everything we wear is washed soft already. Save you a lot of work."

"You know, Ma," Mona said, "I'd be happy to pay for the electricity if you want."

To which Helen answered, huffily, "You want to pay for something, you can go stay in hotel."

This, for the record, is not what Barbara Gugelstein's mom would have said. At Barbara's house, the kids get fined if they're incurring costs over and beyond the reasonable. For example, with a bird phase: Somebody gave Barbara a pair of Australian zebra finches, which she decided to try and breed. And this, it turned out, was just like they learned in sex ed. You got the boy bird in the vicinity of a girl bird who hadn't gotten the big talk-to, and before you could say, *Think of your future* there were some hundred birds at least. They took up a whole wall. And these birds were not going to any four-year college, that was obvious. They were just flying around their cages, and kicking their seed out the bars, and generally making such a big delinquent mess that the maid insisted on being paid extra to clean it up.

It was just lucky Barbara could finance this. She got forty-five dollars for helping paint their backyard fence alone (that was fifty cents a picket for two coats plus cleanup). Also she gets paid for things like bringing in the paper and setting the sports section by her dad's cereal. For Barbara is her own separate accounting unit, unlike Mona and Callie.

Mona and Callie, that's to say, are slave labor. Never mind their handy on-call restaurant service. They mow the lawn and don't get paid. They vacuum the living room and don't get paid. They wash the storm windows and don't get paid, Callie especially—Callie's always been the power scrub of the family. But even Mona the mother's favorite helps dry and is not paid, not that it really matters. For even if they did get paid, they couldn't exactly spend the money on hot pants just because it was their money and they'd earned it. After all, this is what it means to be a family member: There is nothing so small but that you've got to ask the parents' permission. Once, Callie and Mona tried to unionize and go on strike, but instead of becoming folk heroes, they turned into Disappointments. "Mom's tired," Helen said, and they could see that she was. Who wouldn't be, working all the time the way she did? Some days she went straight from the restaurant to bed, instead of going grocery shopping and doing the cooking; these were the days she was likely to start brooding about her family in China, wondering whether everyone was dead by now or still being tortured. The Disappointments came home to find their mother in her bathrobe; and then they felt about ready to put on their bathrobes too. For her mood had turned into their mood, it was like a forest fire jumping a ditch.

And so the girls toil on. Helen is always talking about who really suffered, as in "Your aunt Theresa, she really suffered"; from which the girls deduce that women distinguish themselves in life by their misery. Ergo, they strive to be as miserable as possible, Callie especially. For Callie used to want to be a martyr anyway, back when they were in Catholic school; she had that head start. Now she makes people feel sullied by the world, and in need of confession, and this is great, since she's on the school newspaper. "Scoop," everyone calls her, nobody gets the story like she does, she was even asked to be editor in chief. Naturally enough, though, she declined.

For this is the difference between Mona and Callie: Mona would probably have said sure, which is exactly why nobody is asking. Who needs to draw her out? After years of everyone emphasizing the Importance of Class Participation, Mona can finally be counted on to volunteer. With the result that at least one of her teachers, Miss Feeble, has begun to ignore her hand up in the air. *Now, Mona, you have to give someone else a chance to talk.* This she is not supposed to have to say to nice Chinese girls. So what does it mean that she has to say it to Mona?

Miss Feeble has apparently been pondering this question, because one day she asks Mona if she is really Chinese. This is while Miss Feeble pushes desks around, arranging them in a horseshoe.

"Of course I'm Chinese," Mona says, helping out. "I'm Chinese American."

"And your parents?" continues Miss Feeble, pushing. "They're Chinese too?"

"Of course," Mona says. "They're *immigrants*." She knows as she says this, naturally, that her parents would never use that word on themselves. They think it means people who try to bring live chickens on buses and don't own real suitcases.

All the same, it works on Miss Feeble.

"Ah." She repeats the holy word. "Immigrants." It is as if Mona has cut a little window into the fence of a construction site. Sure enough, there it is, the big crane.

The restaurant: This is not the first restaurant Mona's family's owned. The first was a fried chicken palace, to talk about which is now verboten, on account of it all but brought about the untimely demise of Aunt Theresa. How this came to pass is the complicated subject of another whole book. Suffice it to say here that since Theresa was the one who lay on death's doorstep, staring down that old house cat, she is the only one who can crack jokes about it now. Calling the chicken palace the Forbidden Palace, for example. Wondering wherefore the imperial freeze on the subject. It's not as if we staffed it with eunuchs, she'll say.

In response to which, everyone is supposed to laugh politely and not ask what a eunuch is, especially since she's sure to explain. For apparently this is what being plucked from the jaws of eternity will do to you; a certain derangement has to be expected. Now she's up and moved to California, where she strolls around on the beach with Uncle Henry all day—rumor has it, in a two-piece bathing suit and sometimes less, and without having gotten married, either. Leaving this narrator here to report that the one good thing about the chicken palace fiasco was that it forced Ralph and Helen to sell their house. Because that's how it was that they had the cash to go in on the new franchise Uncle Henry's old wife was buying. *One countertop,* Ralph and Helen joked then. But even that was a help to poor Aunt Janis; and with time, they could call more and more of the Formica their own—poor Aunt Janis having moved on to shopping centers.

So that the next thing they knew, they were moving too, out of their old town and into this Dutch colonial with landscape problems, as you've heard. For this is what pancakes can do. It's true the magic's been patchy at times, for example, the day dear old Fernando socked Cedric the new cook in the nose on account of some missing minute steaks. Cedric lifted an eyebrow at an inopportune time; and then it didn't matter who had really been stealing and who had not, Fernando had to be fired for punching.

Which was why he put a curse on the restaurant—sort of like the curse on the house of Atreus, Callie said, except that theirs was a house of pancakes; and hopefully nobody was going to get murdered in the bathroom like poor Agamemnon, who worked so much harder than that Aegisthus ever did. Still everyone was upset for a good long time. There was something in Fernando's voice, hoarse and crazed and serious, that made them wish they still believed in Buddha, or God, or Guan Yin—someone. They would have liked to have burned some money, left some fruit, lit some candles.

Instead they took refuge in the register. *Wha—inng!* They never completely forgot Fernando, or the unnatural strength of the outraged. But in time, it made them appreciate all the more what came quietly together for them. For ever since Helen started helping, the fact has remained: On those light-as-air stacks, the Changs did rebuild their lives.

Nowadays: They don't really have much to complain about, the girls. Except, well, that the pancake house isn't the greatest place for the lovelorn, especially on Saturday nights, when people you know are always coming in with other people you know. Mona dishes them up some extra-big scoops of ice cream, then goes to find herself some side work—unlike Callie, who won't come out of the back at all. She says she doesn't see why they should be working in the family restaurant when everybody else is out going to concerts to begin with. She says it isn't normal, and that she's sick of being Chinese. And with that, she plops herself on their father's red recliner and puts her feet up, as if officially taking a break from it—for which Mona can't blame her. She knows what Callie means, after all, even though neither one of them would ever say so to anybody but themselves.

It's not just the restaurant. It's not just the fact that they have a real brick wall blocking off their lawn. It's everything. For example, if one of them gets their father a bowl of rice before he asks for it, everyone approves. *She knows her father's mind,* say the parents. But if they know their own minds instead, watch out. And no one in their family is allowed to prefer not to eat something. If someone makes a face at, say, the fish, she has to eat the whole thing while everyone else watches.

Plus their father pushed their mother out the window once, and their bathroom doors don't close all the way, and the parents never wash the car. In fact, Mona had never even noticed that other cars got washed until someone wrote in big letters on the side of the Rambler: WASH ME! Now the girls do the car every single week.

Callie would sooner die than have anybody catch her in the dining room. But Mona figures everyone already knows the part about their being abnormal; waiting table isn't going to make any difference. However, Valentine's Day is hard, it's true. It makes Mona weepy to do the doilies and cherubim for the window. Do they have Cupid in Japan? And what about heart-shaped boxes, and funny little rhymes involving thees and thines; and what about long-stem red roses? Something about the long stems seems particularly un-Japanese to her, even though she realizes that to imagine everything in Japan to be short, like the people, is a type of thinking likely to result in low SATs.

Autumn: By this time, Mona has turned sixteen and gotten her learner's permit. This enables her to crash the car into the garage door the very same day that Barbara Gugelstein marches into the pancake house and announces that she's Jewish.

"Oh, really," Mona says, sharp-minded and quick. "Now, this is news. And what were you before?"

Barbara does not answer. Instead she takes out something from her pocket and begins to blow. This is not a harmonica, which would be bad enough. This is something more like a pipe crossed with a fire alarm—operating, it seems, on the principle of naked harassment. Customers spring up. Manny the salad boy glides forth from the kitchen like the priest he almost was; ever so effortlessly, he emanates a composure that spells crisis. Cooks Cedric and Alfred crane their necks behind him.

Mona, a bit sprung herself, says, "Barbara! Whaddayadoing?"

"Ancient Jewish music custom." Barbara starts to let loose another blast.

"Bar-*bra*," Mona pleads. "Most honorable friend."

"Please to give up on old jokes."

"So sorry," Mona says. "I just would fain see so good a personage start forsooth to toot her own horn."

Barbara laughs, tossing her hair.

"Nu?"

"A ram's horn," Barbara says. "It's for making new beginnings." She honks one more time. "Which I am now doing and which you should do too."

"Okay," Mona says. "Uncle. From today on, you are going to be Jewish. So, fine. But what do you want—that I should be Jewish too?"

Barbara laughs and tosses her hair again; it's the sort of instant replay that makes you realize something important must be happening.

And sure enough, next thing you know, they have embarked on a new chapter of their lives.

CHAPTER 3

The New Chapter

Religion? Confirmation? In this anti-establishment age? Mona got confirmed in the Catholic Church, but she did it the way you were supposed to, which is to say with a certain big roll of the eyeballs. How can the classmates be discussing whether G-d is good or just neutral, and whether Judaism is a religion or a culture? Yet they are. Also they talk about what it means to be Jewish, which so far as they've been able to tell mostly seems to be about remembering that you are. Naturally, if you asked a rabbi, there's a lot more to it. But asking Barbara Gugelstein, the message comes back, *Don't forget, don't forget.* Mona tries to imagine what it would be like to forget she's Chinese, which is easy and hard. It is easy because by her lonesome she in fact often does. Out in the world of other people, though, Mona has people like Miss Feeble to keep the subject shiny. So here's the question: Does the fact that Mona remembers all too well who she is make her more Jewish than, say, Barbara Gugelstein?

A most interesting inquiry, especially since before you can say matzoh ball, Mona too is turning Jewish. It happens this way: Barbara gets her driver's license. Her parents buy her a VW van, despite their opinion of the Germans. And pretty soon Mona's tagged along to so many temple car washes and food drives, not to say weekend conclavettes, that she's been named official mascot of the Temple Youth Group. There she is, helping build the sukkah for Sukkoth—knotting up the corners, arranging the roof boughs so as to avoid overt danger to human life and limb. She's even helped give tours to some of the Youth Group members' parents, who have never seen a sukkah before, and want to know what it means. They poke at the shaky walls from the outside. Mona explains edifyingly how the gaps in the roof appear due to faulty construction, but in fact afford a view of the sky symbolic of the desire to live spitting distance from G-d.

"Come Yom Kippur, those kids are going to be swinging chickens around their heads," mutters one, but Mona reassures him.

"How orthodox can they be?" she says. "After all, here I am."

The man works his sinuses as if he is in an Excedrin ad. He slides thumb and forefinger down his nose; he raises his bleary gaze. "Don't you have a home?"

"I do."

"Then what are you doing here?"

Trusty Barbara Gugelstein, rising to Mona's defense, says, "This is her home, you turkey."

"That's right!" chime in some other kids. "You tell him!"

"What?" says the man. "You live here?"

"I guess you could call it my home away from home," Mona says.

"I get it. It's your vacation place. Some people go to Palm Beach, you come here."

Mona shrugs. "Why spend the airfare?"

The man laughs and leaves. But two days later, Mona's still chewing the cud of this conversation. A stranger in a strange land, that's her, she concludes after two more days of rumination. Finally she approaches Rabbi Horowitz, who turns out to be less easygoing than he seems. He looks like a Hasid turned rock star, what with his long black hair and his untrimmed beard, and he doesn't mind being called Rabbi H., or the Big R.H., or even Rabbit H. He is young enough to sit cross-legged; he listens to Crosby, Stills and Nash; he plays the harmonica. He doesn't insist that anyone learn Hebrew, much as he'd like to encourage it. But when it comes to a sixteen-year-old choosing her own faith, what he professes to hear is mainly the reaction of other people. That of her parents, for example. Is she sure she doesn't want to see a school counselor? Rabbi Horowitz connects up his thick flat brows, so that they look just like the road by which one thing leads to another. He worries about her parish priest, who happens to play shortstop in their Batters of Conscience League (their cheer: *Holy Homers!*), and also about the temple board of directors. With the board it seems he is not so popular already, being anti-Vietnam, and also pro things like letting the kids wear what they want at confirmation, including bare feet.

"To tell you the truth, I'm not so sure I'll even be here next year," he finishes, cracking his knuckles.

Isn't that all the less to keep him from helping her?

"Also," he says—and by the way he clears his throat, Mona can tell that he is coming up on his real point—"I have to wonder, excuse me, how serious is this wish."

"You mean, whether this isn't my just wanting to be like my friends?"

"Like your friends, and also, an important factor at your time of life, unlike your parents."

Behind the rabbi's shoulder hangs a full-size human skeleton, with a fedora hat and necktie—something of which his parents would undoubtably approve. Mona does not point this out. Instead she says, "You mean, is this adolescent rebellion? Maybe. But also I like it here at the temple. I like it that you tell everyone to ask, ask, instead of just obey, obey. I like it that people are supposed to be their own rabbi, and do their business directly with G-d. I like it that they're supposed to take charge of their own religion, and that they even get to be general-rabbi-for-a-day when they get bar and bas mitzvahed. In the Catholic church, you know, you're always keeping to your place and talking to God through helpers. I like it that you tell people to make a pain in the neck of themselves."

"Who told you to make a pain in the neck of yourself?"

"Brian Levi." This is the TYG adviser. "And I don't mean to sound conceited, but I figure I'm a natural at that."

"At making a pain in the neck of yourself?"

Mona smiles sweetly.

Rabbi Horowitz's eyebrows come far enough apart for Mona to see what nice laugh lines he has. He wheels back in his chair, rattling Mr. Bones. "Brian is speaking for some Jews," he says. "Other Jews think you should study your whole life before you should dare to make a challenge. Sure you can talk to G-d yourself, and how can you learn if you don't ask questions? But without study, what are you? An ignoramus."

"I am!" agrees Mona. "Although I practically celebrate the High Holy Days already, and know that hamantaschen are supposed to represent the hat of that What's-his-name, may he roast in hell, Haman." As is proper, Mona stamps her feet to drown out the name of the infidel.

Rabbi Horowitz laughs aloud. "There's more to Judaism than that," he says, and the studying begins. Mona finds out for starters that God revealed the Torah in seventy languages (including Chinese), so that everybody could understand it; it just so happened that only the Jews read it through. Also that in Roman times, the Jews did lots of proselytizing. If she'd lived then, she could've probably just signed right up to be a fellow sufferer. But sign 'n' pray went out with the toga. Now the idea seems to be to discourage prospectives three times in theory—in practice, as much as is practical. Rabbi Horowitz assigns so many books that Mona feels like she started on a mud bath, only to end up on a mud swim.

Still she slogs through. A lot she knows already. All about the holidays, for example, and what is a mitzvah—namely a good deed. Also what is rachmones, namely a type of mercy every human should extend to others but sometimes doesn't. That part is easy and fun. It's like watching a home movie, you get that little shiver of recognition. Aha! So that's why they light eight lights at Hanukkah, and not seven or nine. Then there are new parts Mona likes—all the big ancient stories of blood and gore and guile. Rabbi Horowitz makes her glad she never had to put up with those stiffs the Egyptians—what do you expect from people who wore so much eye makeup—or wander around the desert for forty years. She feels concerned for those ten lost tribes of Israel. She wishes she'd been around for the liberation by the Persians and the era of the Great Prophets. She likes debating like a Pharisee faced with a stick-in-the-mud Sadducee. She likes looking at maps, especially now that she's finally getting her real driver's license. What a down-to-earth religion this is! It's not like Catholicism, with people electing to get crucified upside down, as if right side up wasn't bad enough. The whole purpose of Judaism seems to be to avoid these things when possible. And why should rabbis be celibate? It does seem more natural to let them dutifully procreate, that instead of manning their seminal gates, they might sprinkle the earth with useful ideas. Things they can do about the world, for example. How they can help, how they can fix, how they can contribute and illuminate; and how they can stay, forever and ever, Jews.

The last subject is one on which Mona could use a *Guide to the Perplexed*—it's okay to turn into a Jew, but not to turn out of one?—and even harder to take in is not only the Holocaust, but the whole endless history that spirals up to it like a staircase in a nightmare. It winds on and on, a torchlit, hellish thing, bristling with caesars and czars; there's a lot to contemplate about the nature of this sweet world and most noble humanity. Do her happy friends in Scarshill with their patios and lounge chairs really live at the mouth of a stone age tunnel? It was hard to make out at first, but now she can see it plain, their own express lane down the centuries.

It makes her want to dig in her heels and extend them a steadying hand, though in fact, they're more likely to steady her. For while Callie and Mona know what it's like to have rocks thrown at them, this kind of welcome is for their family a novelty. Their group hasn't always been the oppressed. They used to be the oppressors; and that makes them, as a minority, rank amateurs. The Changs don't have their friends' instincts, or reflexes. They don't have their ready alert. They don't have their friends' institutions, or their ways of reminding themselves who they are, that they might not be lulled by a day in the sun. Prescriptions and rituals, holidays and recipes, songs. The Jews have books, they have games, they have tchotchkes. They have catalogs. And soon, G-d willing, so will Mona.

In the meantime, she is not the only one starting anew. Callie is being allowed to go to college, even though Helen found out over the summer that Callie's roommate was named Naomi, which she thought might be a black name. Not, of course, that Helen and Ralph had anything against blacks. In fact, they had a lot of blacks working for them at the restaurant. For example, Alfred the number-two cook. But seeing as how they happened to know someone who had a friend who had a daughter also going to Harvard, they couldn't help but wonder why this nice Chinese girl and Callie couldn't room together. This nice Chinese girl had a roommate too, Helen pointed out. Why couldn't this nice Chinese girl's roommate room with this Naomi? Helen said that she also knew somebody who knew somebody who worked in the financial aid office; maybe she could arrange something. And there was someone who knew someone who knew someone who worked at the Faculty Club. That's where all the professors have lunch, said Helen. Even the president himself eats there.

"Mom, those people can't do anything," argued weary Callie, sewing on name tags. "Especially since there's nothing the matter with a roommate turning out to be black. And anyway, the last thing I want to do is room with some nice Chinese wonk who's going to study all the time."

To which Helen managed to answer both "Not everyone Chinese studies all the time, that's *stereotype*" and "It would be good for you to study all the time with your roommate. Study together is nice."

Now it turns out that Naomi is indeed brownish black as the most serious-looking spines of her considerable personal library. Naomi works on her shelving system; the parents leave Callie to assist. How diligent this Naomi! And how well she speaks English!

The parents appear relaxed. On the way home, though, Mona notices that the car seems unexpectedly empty, a regular rattletrap, even though it is loaded full of Callie's boxes (which she personally collected from dumpsters all over the county). And when they get home, Mona discovers another unexpected thing: that she has her parents all to herself. This is not something she had counted on. In fact, Mona had rather expected they would think of nothing but Callie, their daughter at Harvard. Instead it is as if Mona is suddenly famous, the most interesting person in the room, every day, all day, even when she's asleep. If she goes out, it's only to be replaced by her palpable absence. *Where's Mona? How long has she been gone for? What time is she coming back home?*

Once, when Mona's ballet class was doing *Swan Lake*, her teacher gathered all the young cygnets around her. She described how Anna Pavlova beat her arms, and elongated her neck, just exactly like a real swan, though of course Pavlova never hissed, or bit anyone. And then this teacher described the effect all this beating and elongating had on the audience: *It stirred them,* she said, pulling up her leg warmers. (She knit these herself, with a pattern she copied out for her students for free.) It stirred them so much that the day Pavlova died, nobody could bear the thought of an understudy. Of course, this class would still have understudies, in case somebody got the hiccups, or the mumps, or something. But when Anna Pavlova died, the show went on without anyone. The light was moved around just as if she were there, and the audience pictured her in its mind's eye—pictured her beating her arms and elongating her neck.

And now, as with Anna, so with Mona. Truly: she could up and expire, and her parents would still be moving the beam around. Imagining where she would be if she were there, and in what fine fashion she would flap. This makes it hard to work on turning Jewish. If only Callie would come home! So Mona wishes, most ardently.

Until, all too soon, Callie does.

Thanksgiving already. At temple, Mona has begun to consider with Rabbit H. the holidays, and how very much she unfortunately likes the family Christmas tree. Not that they have always had the tasteful real Scotch pine they have now, with the fresh woodsy scent and the tendency to drip real pitch on the living room carpet. Before they moved, they used to unpack their tree out of a box, and sort out the silvery limbs by size, and poke them into little coded holes in the tree trunk. They had a revolving colored light to shine on it, so that it would turn blue, then red, then yellow, then green, and there was a Styrofoam tree skirt too, all sprinkled with glitter that used to fall off. New Year's Day meant having to vacuum that glitter up. But the Changs liked that tree and its rituals, or at least Mona did—even the vacuuming. If you asked her, she'd have to say that she's only just gotten used to the idea that they now have a new kind of tree, with a fabric skirt—the kind of skirt that matches the kind of people who say, as they do now, "fridge" for "icebox," and "wastebasket" for "garbage." That's to say that it's hard to contemplate moving on—already!—from a basic change of tree to no tree at all.

Yet that seems a distinct possibility, not just because of her conversations with Rabbi Horowitz, but also because of Callie. Is this what it means to be sisters, to come up with the exact same idea, only for opposite reasons?

When Callie first comes home, all's simple hilarity. Callie has changed her hair; she hadn't meant to go so short, but her roommate Naomi was doing the cutting, and though she started at Callie's waist, she ended up above her shoulders. This makes Callie, by the standards of the day, practically bald. But Callie doesn't care. She says at least all her split ends are gone. (Plus it makes her cheekbones stick out, and her lips look swollen up as if they maybe got bit by a bug.) She and Mona and Helen stay up past their bedtimes, way later than they ever have before, giggling on Callie's bed. Helen has her slippers on the wrong feet, and is sitting cross-legged with one of her pajama buttons undone; Mona tells dirty jokes and even Helen laughs, covering her mouth with her hand. They discover that all three of them know what is a diaphragm, even though each of them thought the others couldn't possibly, and only Callie knows how to spell it. With a *g*, she says; they can look it up in a dictionary if they don't believe her. And so they do. A silent *g*! It's almost enough to make Mona want to go to Harvard too, to learn such things. Never mind that Callie insists she didn't learn this at Harvard and wishes Mona would stop saying that. Especially since she isn't even going to Harvard, she's going to Harvard-Radcliffe, and anyway she learned how to spell *diaphragm* from reading *Goodbye, Columbus*. A serious book, she maintains, although under questioning she admits that she originally only read it because the movie version was being filmed over at the high school. And because it had a diaphragm in it.

It is ascertained that for all concerned, a knowledge of reproductive technology is theoretical. The topic swerves to Ping-Pong diplomacy, and how mainland China can join the U.N. when it is not even a proper country but a bunch of leather-eating peasants. "You mean like belts?" Mona asks. "You mean like shoes?" Helen nods. Mona wants to know if they cook them first, and how. With soy sauce? With ginger? "That was only on the Long March," says Callie. "Those Communists eat rats too," says Helen, "and what do you call—you know, on the head? Lice." The night goes on. Did So-and-so really hitchhike all the way to Chicago, just to find So-and-so had completely given up baking? Does So-and-so really bleach her underarms?

The next day, turkey. As a surprise, Ralph has arranged for the head waitress to come serve the meal. Magdalena has had a fight with her family and has nowhere to go, he says. He offered for her to just come and eat, but she insisted she'd rather help out. So what could he say? Of course, he knew from the beginning that she would offer something like this. He claims the real reason he made the offer was so that Helen wouldn't have to run around like crazy the way she usually does.

But Helen knows a gift horse when it kicks her. "Your father just like to act like big shot. He thinks this is China."

A familiar complaint. In fact, one of the lilting refrains of their melodious lives. Sometimes it seems like no one even has to sing;

everyone can hear how annoying it is that Ralph should treat the help like far-flung family—buying them glasses and dentures and shoes, but also expecting them to run errands, or help fix the furnace at home. In general, he is getting better. He is learning to say, *That's your problem.* Also to expect people to say it to him. But from time to time he suffers relapses, and now what to do? Send Magdalena home?

"I always thought you like to sit there, doing nothing, instead of run around, do this, do that," Ralph says, cleaning out his ears. (Though they stick out, he still has to pull at them to get a good angle.) "Act like lady. Join some country club. I thought you sick and tired of work in the restaurant all day, then come home and work again."

"What did you say?" Helen is so stunned by this acknowledgment of her efforts that it seems she needs to clean her ears out too. "You hear that?" She addresses Mona and Callie. "Your father actually noticed that someone works at the restaurant and then comes home and works some more. All these years he acts like the food we eat comes from heaven, but actually he has his big eyes open all the time."

"Of course, I see everything," says Ralph, bugging his eyes first at Mona and then at Callie. They laugh. "And that's why this Thanksgiving, our nice waitress Magdalena coming here to help." He winks and grins, triumphant, only to have Helen set aside her hurt with breathtaking speed.

"This is the U.S. of A.!" she says. "Who has a waitress come to serve at Thanksgiving? Who?" She appeals again to the girls. They shrug obligingly.

But in the end, she doesn't want to fight in front of Magdalena, or to spoil Callie's first visit home, or even to show Ralph up. (It's bad enough the pancake house only started running in the black with her help.) Plus she feels sorry for Magdalena.

And so Magdalena swoops around. She sets Ralph's and Helen's plates down gently in front of them. However, Mona's and Callie's she sends skating down the wood-tone table, the way she would at the restaurant. What a champion she would be at horseshoes! The plates stop just in front of the girls; everyone claps.

She murmurs modestly, in her husky staccato, "I practice every day." She rolls some more *r*'s on request. Then she sits down with the family to eat. Troubles or no, she is sweetly flamboyant, thick-scented as a gardenia farm. Her long hair coils like a black and white snake on her head; she applies makeup with the feathery restraint of a diva. Still, in small things she attends to nicety. For instance, she expresses polite amazement that they stuff the turkey with stir-fried rice stuffing; also that Ralph carves the turkey with a knife and chopsticks.

"Is that your Chinese tradition?" she asks.

Ralph nods gravely. "This is the Chinese tradition when we cannot find the big fork."

No sooner have they sent Magdalena home, though, than the subject of Christmas shopping comes up. This spurs Callie to announce that she doesn't think they should have a tree anymore.

"Naomi says it's a symbol of oppression."

Helen nods amiably. "Did Naomi go home see her family too?"

"Naomi says Christmas trees aren't indigenous to China." Callie says this with an insistence that is rare for her; she is not exactly the type to steer the conversation like a grocery cart. Even Helen has remarked how, though Mona and Callie have identical voices on the phone, you can easily tell who's who once the conversation gets going. If it twists and turns, it's Mona. Callie does not exactly hold forth.

Or at least she didn't use to. Now that she's at practically Harvard, though, she seems to have points to make, ideas to advance, albeit with more doggedness than bravura.

"Indigenous means what?" says Helen.

Callie thinks. "Natural."

"Native," Mona supplies. "I had that on the PSATs, and *natural* wasn't even one of the choices."

"Native." Helen mulls it over.

"Native means what?" asks Ralph, cutting the crust off his second piece of pie.

"Guess," Mona says.

"A kind of Indian people?"

While Helen translates for Ralph, Callie whispers to Mona, annoyed, "I was just trying to define it in a way they would get." Ralph nods; Callie goes on. "Naomi says we should hate them just as much as you hate Panasonic radios. She says you probably didn't have Christmas trees, growing up, why should you have one now? She says we should stick to our guns, like the Jews."

Mona pretends to be choking on her whipped cream.

"But we did have Christmas tree, growing up," says Helen evenly, one hand in her lap. "Every year. Not so a big tree as we have here, but still, we had it. Shanghai, you know, is a big city, we have everything. You know what we eat every morning in Shanghai? Bagels."

"Bagels!" Mona says.

Helen says the bakery used to string them together by the holes the way that people once used to string money. That was a long time ago, she says, when coins had little square holes in the middle.

"It was just because you went to a convent school that you had a tree." Callie is so busy talking that she hasn't eaten one bite of dessert. "The question is why you were going to a convent school to begin with."

"It was run by missionaries," says Helen. "French missionaries. Oh! We played a lot of tricks on them. I remember one nun especially, we used to call her Boat Feet, and when she came down the hall—"

"They were imperialists," says Callie, still not eating. "That's what Naomi says. They were bent on taking over China and saving the heathen. But you weren't heathen. You were civilized."

"Of course we were civilized," says Helen. "Chinese people invented paper. Chinese people invented ink, and gunpowder. We were wearing silk gowns with embroidery before the barbarians even thought maybe they should take a bath, get rid of their smell."

"But is that what the missionaries thought?"

"Oh, the missionaries just wanted to teach us some nice songs in French, and to tell us what nice food they eat in France. Especially they have nice pastries. The Chinese, you know, don't think so much about dessert." Helen looks at Callie, as if to reinforce her point.

"And to convert you, right?"

"Of course," says Helen. "But we don't mind."

"You didn't mind?" So nonplussed is Callie that she picks up her fork by accident. "But didn't you use to be Buddhist?"

"Oh, well, we are still Buddhist after we are baptized," explains Helen. "We are Buddhist, and Taoist, and Catholic. We do however we want." She maintains that her family liked having a Christmas tree, and that it was fun, and that it had nothing to do with oppression. Callie finally eats. Still she insists later that she will have nothing to do with the tree this year. Also she says that in the spring she's going to drop French so that she can take Chinese instead.

Everyone laughs.

Mona expects that when Rabbi Horowitz hears she is in charge of the family Christmas tree, he will tell her that her days as a prospective convert are up. Instead he gives her the kind of nod you associate with deeply significant moments in the movies—column A but column B moments, Mona calls these. In this case, disappointed but understanding.

"It's like an election. Some votes you win, some votes you lose. You're all right so long as you've got more on your side than the other," he says, straightening a pile of books. "Also you must realize that these days a lot of Jews have trees. It's not kosher, but that's the way it is. If they don't have a tree, they have a bush, and at the top they put the Star of David. And for you, please understand there's a lesson in this."

"What kind of lesson?" says Mona.

"The lesson of a lifetime." He gestures at his book-lined study. "What you're discovering is that it's not so easy to become Jewish. As, excuse me, I believe I tried to tell you. You can read and study, study and read, but still it will probably take you your whole life."

"My whole life?" Mona gulps.

And all over Christmas break, while everyone else is eating and opening and trying on and exchanging for credit or cash (including Callie the anti-imperialist), this is what Mona is pondering. Does she want to be converting for the rest of her life, Amen? New Year's Day, she drags around with such a heavy heart that when it comes time to take down the tree, Callie offers to help—also taking this opportunity to comment on how bushy the tree was this year. And why did Mona insist on getting a new star for the top when the old one worked fine?

For a resolution, Mona considers giving up converting. It seems against the spirit of New Year's—who resolves to strive less?—but so what. Rabbi Horowitz is right. Kosher is great, but nonkosher is the way things sometimes happen to be.

Just when she is ready to break the news to him, though, he naturally enough decides he's impressed enough; it's time to order her to her optional mikvah. And so it is that on a melty January morning, Barbara and Mona drive over to the bath. This happens right after Mona's real license arrives in the mail, so that Mona is for her inaugural celebratory spin able to drive herself and Barbara through the fresh-fallen slush to the ceremony—which, it turns out, is not unlike getting baptized by John the Baptist, except with chlorine. It's not so easy to get her hair to submerge; Mona is called upon to employ her best sinking skills. But finally, success. Through a sheet, three witnesses listen solemnly to the dunk. She chants her Shema Israel. She burns her special four-stranded candle. Her three witnesses sign neatly her nice framable certificate. And in this way, she becomes Mona-also-known-as-Ruth, a more or less genuine Catholic Chinese Jew.

Maybe there are people who do not accept her, as Rabbi Horowitz has warned. Also it is tricky to be a solo Jew with no family. Still, it is a promotion to be no longer a mascot. The TYG throws a shindig in her honor; Mona attends happily a host of seminars, slide shows, art exhibits. For orphans she makes caterpillars out of knee socks; for the elderly she makes draft dodgers, also out of knee socks.

The only problem is that she has been unable to break the news to her family. And so it is that when Helen finds out, it is from Saint Callie at Practically Harvard, who you'd think would have better things to talk about. Like what she thinks about the coed bathrooms now that the novelty's worn off, and whether there really is a pool where everybody swims naked. Or what about a recap of how Harvard plays football against Yale every year? Callie told them that already, but Mona knows there were details she left out—for example, how everybody has to sit on concrete to watch, except people who are smart and bring pads. This might not be conversation for everybody. However, her parents, Mona knows, would be captivated.

Instead Callie has to go passing on some high school gossip she heard from somebody who knows somebody who knows somebody.

"Callie told us some surprise." So neatly does Helen fold up her Chinese newspaper, you would think she was planning to return it to the newsstand for credit. "She said you weren't going to tell us. She said you were going to keep it a secret. She said you did it behind our back."

"I guess I forgot to mention it," Mona says.

"Don't tell me that. That's . . . that's . . ." On the wall, the cuckoo clock ticks louder than normal. "That's *crap*."

"Ma! That's no way to talk." Mona wags her finger, expecting her mom to smile.

But Helen looks as though she's about to start crying. Her eyes redden; her face whitens. If she put a carrot on her nose, she would look just like the snowman that happens to adorn her at-home sweater. "A lot of crap!" She takes a drink of her tea. "Who do you think you are, you can lie to your mother like that?"

Mona looks down, penitent.

Helen goes on with a delicate bang of her cup. "You are daughter. *Daughter*. Do you remember what is a daughter?"

"I remember."

"Who are you?"

"I'm your daughter."

It's like being in church, right down to the moment of silence—which Mona takes to be a chance for Helen to turn misty-eyed again, that Mona might feel what a Disappointment she is. Helen swishes around some tea in her mouth, a good sign. Mona makes a gorilla face, and out of habit, her mother almost makes a face back. But in the midst of furrowing her brow, she suddenly starts talking.

"We agree, except what kind of daughter lies to her mother?"

"No kind."

"I have no daughter."

"What about Callie?" Mona means to be comforting.

Helen claps the lid on her teacup. "You know, you bring shame on our family, you act this way. What do you think people think of us?"

Mona contemplates the kitchen table.

"People talk, how do you think I feel? You have no consideration for others. You have no consideration for how other people feel."

Above Helen, the hour is struck. The clock door swings open, but what you see in place of the long-broken cuckoo bird is (courtesy of Callie) a glued-on Statue of Liberty pencil sharpener. *Cuckoo!* this cries. *Cuckoo! Cuckoo!*

Mona shrugs.

"Wiggle your shoulders is not a way to talk. How can you be Jewish? Chinese people don't do such things."

"They don't?" Mona asks this in her smallest, meekest voice—just wanting by this point to say the right thing, the thing that will make Helen look hurt again. Then Mona can feel ashamed, and they can make up, and Mona will be her mother's favorite once more. But what is that thing? Mona thinks and thinks. Still the right thing will not come to her—which must be why she abruptly gives up and says the opposite of what she should. As the Statue of Liberty pencil sharpener retreats, Mona says in her school voice, as if she's talking to Miss Feeble, "I guess I must not be Chinese, then."

"What do you mean, not Chinese?"

And from there on in, they are stuck in the land of words, until they are no longer speaking to each other and are forced onward to the land of deeds.

There was a time when Helen made this trip quietly, if at all. How demure she was! It was Ralph who barreled through life, crackerjack active. But since then they've switched positions, one fading back right when the other came forward, the way the day bird replaced the night bird, back when there were birds in the cuckoo clock. For Helen was so mad when she realized Ralph couldn't take care of her—wasn't that what a husband was for?—that she had what amounted to a personality transformation. She'd gotten used to the idea of helping, of working hard, even of going out of the house to work. But she'd never adjusted to the idea of becoming a main pillar of the family, standing there all by herself like the kind of ruin people went to Greece to see. In a way, she was proud of what she'd learned to do. But in another way, this so wasn't what she'd counted on, growing up in China, that if you pointed out how energizing was her fury, she'd probably give you a nice maternal whack such as would excuse you from gym for a month. Mona knows this because Helen's done it to Callie from time to time—not meaning to, of course. And of course, it's not as if she hasn't been whacked herself. In fact, Ralph can be credited with pioneering the whole tradition.

But whereas he has given up that sort of thing in practice, Helen has given it up in principle. So that in a way, Mona is getting off easy when Helen confiscates her Hebrew dictionary, and her menorah, as well as the mezuzah Barbara made for her out of some parchment and an avocado-green toothbrush holder. She says something about having Ralph take her door down.

Ralph, though, first wants to get the facts straight. He sits Mona down at the kitchen table when he comes home; he turns on all the lights, as if to help him see better. His face is soft with worry, and he has mysteriously equipped himself with a pad of paper, a mechanical pencil, and a slide rule. Also the soles of his feet are planted on the floor, in position to lever him forward. *How do you get this idea? When is the first time you go with your friend? Who is the driver?* She tells him everything—what the traffic was like, what the weather report was, how they had trouble parking. He listens as if he is hoping to discover a clue to her—as if he hopes to find out that one morning Mona ate something fishy, only to come down with this idea in the afternoon.

Of course, he hasn't always been like this, so methodical. It is how he learned to be as a result of his impulsive youth. *Things are not always how they look,* he likes to say now, and *Watch out before you leap.* Has somebody tricked her into turning Jewish? He himself has been tricked, he says, with a slight averting of his face; and Mona knows, naturally, that here he is referring to the disaster that was the chicken palace. Still Mona says, "You? Really?" as if there was no one in the world she could imagine less trickable—which is true in a way. These days he turns every stone, he thinks of all the angles. *In back every wise man is fool,* he likes to say, although he is also quick to point out that not every fool becomes a wise man, and also that it is not easy to tell the fools from the wise men. *For the really wise men, they like to look as if they are fools.* He nods to himself, and with this chestnut, switches the lights back off.

Only to have another light turn on, illuminating the slight crevasse between him and Helen. Is there an icy split between every two people in the world? Anyway, this one is blue and wide and deep, and cold enough, Mona's sure, to freeze a child or two to death, though thankfully there are ways of skipping right over it. It's just a matter of watching where you put your feet, and keeping a certain spring to your step, and figuring a crack's a crack. Helen has to care extra about everything, for example, because he doesn't keep up his end. To wit: He does not even care who really suffered and who didn't. To him, everyone's suffered. To talk about it is just a matter of sitting one person on a little higher branch than another, and what are people doing up in a tree to begin with? He says this with his Ancient Wisdom voice, which to Helen is the voice of someone who isn't even trying anymore. In her opinion, all he does is philosophize—he might as well be a hippie. She thinks that if it weren't for her, who knows, he would probably stop taking baths, which of course matters, seeing as it separates people from rhinoceroses and hippopotamuses and other low-standard animals who consider mud wallowing a proper way of life.

What surprise then that according to Ralph, this whole affair with Mona's converting is nothing to flip your lid over; whereas to Helen it takes absolute top place in an entire escalating series of incomprehensible and distinctly menacing developments, such as Mona's buying a down jacket, and her wanting not only her own car, which she can forget about, but her own telephone line. (Which she can forget about as well.) There is no use in talking to Helen about rachmones, or about her converting too, never mind the act of remembering, which Rabbi Horowitz calls the doorway to wisdom. There is no use in reminding her that Mona is her favorite child, and that she, Helen Chang, likes a lot of American things herself.

For if you asked her, she would say that she signed up for her own house and garage, but not for her children to become big-mouthed separate accounting units, and what is the matter with a regular coat with a nice interlining such as she has worn her whole life? "There's nothing warmer than down," Mona tries to tell her, but all Helen hears is what she wants to ask next—namely, why should Mona need her own telephone line? "So you won't eavesdrop," Mona says. To this Barbara Gugelstein's mother certainly would have said, "I don't eavesdrop," even if Barbara could hear her munching potato chips as she listened in. Once she even broke into the conversation to give some advice; she couldn't resist. Helen, on the other hand, said, "If I like to know what my daughter is up to, I don't see what's wrong about it." It all has to do with the Chinese way versus everyone else's way, as Mona sees it, but Helen doesn't even agree with her on that. "I think I'm very Westernized. I brought you children up without you even speak Chinese." Helen points out that some of her friends make their children all sit together around a big table at night, and study. They work out problems together, and none of them puts the stereo on loud; in fact, they don't even own records. Mark and Carole Louie's kids, for example, have no idea who is Jimi Hendrix. Which sounds like a path to a National Merit Scholarship, except that one of the boys set the curtains on fire, and another one got in trouble for climbing the water tower and throwing rocks from the top. It wasn't a lot of rocks—after all, he had to carry them up in his pockets. But he got a JD card for it just the same. "The way they live is too difficult for the children," Helen said when she heard. "The parents should be like bamboo, bend in the wind. Not stand there stiff, like a telephone pole."

"That's right," Mona says now, during yet another discussion of her religious freedom. "You are the one who brought us up to speak English. You said you would bend like bamboo instead of acting like you were planted by Bell Telephone. You said we weren't pure Chinese anymore, the parents had to accept we would be something else."

"American, not Jewish." Helen assigns Mona a piece of pork to slice while she herself cleans the fish, and it calms them both down to see what a nice job Mona can still do—thin, and across the grain. (Lucky for them, Mona is the reformed kind of Jew that does not observe the many rules regarding fins and hoofs, mollusks and ruminants.)

"Jewish is American," Mona says. "American means being whatever you want, and I happened to pick being Jewish."

"Since when do children pick this, pick that? You tell me. Children are supposed to listen to their parents. Otherwise, the world becomes crazy. Who knows? Tomorrow you'll come home and tell me you want to be black."

"How can I turn black? That's a race, not a religion." (Mona says this even though she knows some kids studying to be Bobby Seale. They call each other brother, and eat soul food instead of subs, and wear their hair in the baddest Afros they can manage.)

"And after that you are going to come home and tell me you want to be a boy instead of a girl."

"Blood, Mom," points out Mona.

Helen glances up at the cuckoo clock as she crooks a knife-nicked finger; she runs it under the faucet while starting to stir-fry the pork with her other hand. After the pork, there is still the fish and also some spinach to do, and then it's time to get back to the pancake house. Behind her, the space heater flares up in ominous fashion. The kitchen used to be the warmest room in the house, but recently they had to turn the radiator off because of a leaking valve. "And after that you are going to come home and tell me you want to be a tree."

"Whoever heard of someone turning into a tree?" Mona tactfully refrains from bringing up this poet Ovid her English class is reading, never mind that he didn't write in English. Instead, she gets her mom a Band-Aid. She goes to sleep thinking that they have had a heart-to-heart communication such as leads to true intergenerational understanding and tolerance.

The next morning, however, Mona discovers her new down jacket outside on the milk box. This is after some searching that Mona finds it, and with some surprise. Did Helen really put it out there to freeze all night? Mad as Helen's been of late, Mona still can't imagine her doing such a thing; and later she finds out that it was in a way her father's idea. If Helen was so upset, he said, why didn't she just throw the jacket out? (That's Ralph for you, always a proponent of the concrete solution.) Except it wasn't so simple, in the end. Outside was dark and cold, and Helen didn't feel like going all the way to the garbage cans.

Now Mona has unmasked her treachery. "How can I wear this? It's freezing."

"Nothing warmer than down," Helen quotes her.

"How could you do this?"

Mona must look really forlorn, because Helen softens. "Oh, not that big a deal, you don't have to cry," she says, and taking the jacket from her daughter, she drapes it on top of the space heater to warm. "There." She says this in a leave-it-to-mommy voice she seems to have learned from TV, even though the Changs don't have a TV. (*The idiot box,* Ralph calls it.)

"Ma," Mona says, "I don't think that's such a good idea."

But Helen is the mother, and Mona is the daughter, which means that Helen knows what is a good idea and what isn't. And so it is that they take the jacket back off the heater really at the first whiff of trouble, before too large a hole has been burnt. Still down goes exploding through the kitchen. Who could believe a couple of jacket baffles could produce such a veritable snowstorm? But it just goes to show what a good value Mona got on her jacket, that so much went into it. There are goose feathers flying everywhere. Mona and Helen have to wave their hands in front of their faces to keep from breathing them; Helen very sensibly closes the door to the dining room while Mona opens the regular window, and the storm window too. Cold air rushes in as she tries to shoo the feathers out. "A broom!" Helen cries, and so they try that. Sweeping at the air with long swings, short swings—they could be the sorcerer's apprentice, it's that effective.

Still they keep on, so that this is what they're doing when Mickey the milkman appears on the other side of the sill.

"Having a problem?" Mickey is a trim man with an ever-moist mustache they have ascribed to nasal drip; Mona stops shooing feathers in his face, for fear one might stick.

"Oh, no," Helen says, nonchalant. "Just helping my daughter with her homework."

"It's a science project," Mona says. "There's a contest at school."

"Well, good luck with it," says Mickey. "God knows, if I had any money I'd put it on you two." He walks away whistling; they hear the gate bang shut then bounce open, an old problem. They sneeze.

CHAPTER 4

Hot Times at the Hot Line

This is Mona's theory about her parents: that Ralph thought they should live in their own little world, whereas Helen thought they should belong to society. Even she never intended that they should be a minority, though, and especially an outspoken one. Mona explains this to Rabbi Horowitz as he gravely cracks his knuckles.

"First of all, they don't like the word *minority*," Mona says. "They say they were never a minority when they were in China, why should they be a minority here."

"But there are few of them, and many of everyone else."

"That's what I said. They said they're just as good as anybody, why should they ask for help? Also they do not want to have to riot. I told them they don't have to riot if they don't want to. I told them they can just march in parades and protest. Or else, if they don't want to go outside, they can write letters, like the Jews. I told them that was one of the reasons I turned Jewish, because I thought writing letters was smarter than standing out in the freezing cold, which I knew was not for them, being from Shanghai and everything. I said I knew how much they worried about catching cold, and that I had recently discovered that they were absolutely right when they said people caught cold through their feet. For instance, when they stood on street corners for hours on that cold concrete. I told them writing letters was much warmer, and also that the kind of letters that worked best were the ones that got sent off to big shots. I thought they would like that, writing letters to big shots and not having to get their feet cold."

"But they didn't like it?"

"No. They said they grew up arranging things. Their friends arranged things for them, they arranged things for their friends."

"And what about the poor people? Who did the arranging for them?"

"Got me." Mona shrugs. "I think that's why they had to have a revolution. But my mom said before that nobody yelled. Yelling just meant you had no self-control. She said in fact people knew what other people meant without their hardly saying anything. They understood each other perfectly by what it was that wasn't said."

Rabbi Horowitz clears his throat. "Well, of course, nobody likes to yell," he says. "But your parents want to be Wasps. They are the only ones who do not have to make themselves heard. That is because they do the hearing. And how is that possible?"

"That's what I said. But my mom said it's possible. She said it's all a matter of manners. You have to know how to stand, how to sit. She said people in Shanghai knew who you were right away, you didn't have to open your mouth."

"And is that true?"

"I think you also had to wear a lot of jewelry. Anyway, I said, we are a minority, like it or not, and if you want to know how to be a minority, there's nobody better at it than the Jews. I said it's our job to ask questions now. We can't just accept everything the way they did in China. We can't just go along."

"And what did she say then?"

"She said that as soon as the Communists leave she is going to take me back to Shanghai, where I won't have so much to say."

Naturally, Helen cannot take Mona back to Shanghai; that is the good news. And so Mona continues to be Jewish. Also she takes up the guitar, which involves growing out the nails of her right hand while keeping the left ones short. Helen points out that there are many instruments that do not require asymmetrical nail-growing—for example, how about going back to the piano? Such a nice instrument after all, and you don't have to tune it yourself, a convenience. But in the fashion of the day, Mona is more interested in symbols of wayfaring than in things associated with living rooms and arm protectors and miracle-fiber carpet. How about the harmonica, Mona says, or the mandolin? She has never actually seen a mandolin, but she knows it is anti-orchestra. Helen knows this too. They move diplomatically on to sports, which Helen considers unladylike except for ice-skating and tennis. Does this explain why Mona takes up rock climbing, which she might have otherwise recognized to be, past the rope and carabiners, a form of crawling?

Over Callie's spring break, she journeys out to watch Mona at the Gunks, even though Mona is officially not speaking to her. Callie attempts to patch things up with sisterly concern.

"It just looks so dangerous," she says.

They are perched on a rocky ledge, becoming acquainted with the brevity of life. Callie puts her arm around a tree; she got her ears pierced at college and is wearing large multipart earrings that do not help her balance. Otherwise, she looks more outdoorsy than you'd expect, on account of her also having gotten herself contact lenses. These mean she can now hold her head at funny angles, not to say let her hair swing around as if she's in a hair conditioner ad. "Mom and Dad would have a canary if they knew."

"But of course they're not going to know." Mona surveys the stratosphere.

Callie answers, "Of course not."

The right answer. But then she goes on, by way of changing the topic, to sweetly wonder if that jittering Mona was doing out there on the rock face is what people call sewing-machine knee. Naturally, she is just making conversation. Mona realizes that Callie would just as soon say nothing, except that to say nothing in this case would be to emphasize how big a fight they are having. The silence might fill up with anger and explode, for instance if Mona had a chance to demand whether Callie realized what she was doing when she decided to squeal to the parents like a low-phylum invertebrate; why doesn't she just admit that she has been lusting her whole life to knock Mona off her throne? Instead Callie elects to bravely forge on in a conversational manner, never mind if it means saying the exact wrong thing. For example, How did such a crazy sport become so fashionable? And is it truly intrinsically enjoyable to clutch at nothing for hours, worrying about gravity? Her tone is full of intellectual inquiry. Mona's has the sweet sibilance of a sibling who has learned to use words but atavistically prefers teeth. She insists her interest in climbing is far more than a matter of fashion, and that she finds it spiritually satisfying to pit herself against unyielding nature. She informs Callie that she expects to be climbing as long as her skeletal and muscle groups allow, and that it is a matter of passion she would not expect a milquetoast to quite comprehend.

This is before Mona is treated to a demonstration of the pulley. One day at the Gunks, she sees a climber fall and fall until, just at the point where he's supposed to arrest and dangle, he keeps falling. His partner, meanwhile, is also in good-paced motion—going up, you might say, like there's no tomorrow.

A hunch comes to her about then that her G-d-given sport talents are better exercised at the temple than at the cliffs. She accordingly trades in her trusty climbing rope for the Youth Group hot line, thanking G-d Callie will not be home to make Ivy League observations until June. Also Mona thanks G-d that the swap has become possible—an offshoot result of confirmation class. For Rabbi Horowitz has talked so much about I-and-Thou and so on, that many people have been elevated, if not up to his level, then at least a rung or two out of the subbasement. Hitherto sacred distinctions between cool and uncool have thus lost their sanctity. They are all the chosen, or at least the as-good-as-chosen-let-us-not-split-hairs.

Barbara Gugelstein and Mona are thus, through the rigor of the special training course (with its extra-heavy rap sessions, and stress interviews, and mock emergency drills), suddenly friends with all manner of people. Some of these are eminently regular types like Rennie Klingenstein, and Hilary Rothschild, and Aaron Apfelbaum, and Eddie Levine—kids who've gone skinny-dipping once or twice and are not strangers to the agony of blackheads. But included too are the distinctly higher likes of Danielle Meyers and Chip Weinstein, not to say exquisite Eloise Ingle with the Rapunzel hair, who everyone thought was Wasp, seeing as how she thought so herself until just recently. That was when she discovered the truth about her dead mother's extraction.

Said extraction being a fact her stepmother had been purposefully hiding in the name of sensitivity—said sensitive stepmother having wanted Eloise to feel on a par with her stepsibs. (It was bad enough that they sat so killingly well on their horses and played such cunning games of tennis and got snapped up by Phillips Andover, which she didn't despite alumni pull.) One day in a temple rap session, she reveals how she discovered her identity from a long-lost cousin; and though Rabbi Horowitz is quick to point out that the stepmother meant well, still the group sympathy flows. Indeed, the class stands with Eloise in a solidarity such as bards will someday sing of, and in the meantime, is happy to fill her in on various points she missed as a child—such as the use and meaning of the dreidel, and who is Elijah, and what to make of his drinking habits. Rabbi Horowitz likes to call on Mona most of all for these details; and if Eloise is taken aback by the breadth and depth of Mona's knowledge, she is too well bred to let it show, except to ask whether Mona also plays tennis and skis.

"Not really," Mona says.

Her stepbrothers sail, Eloise informs her, and of course they all ride, and they summer on an island in Maine. "Mid-coast," she says.

"You mean you have a summer place?" Mona says.

"A cottage," says Eloise. And this seems to be the match point, because Eloise then graciously affords Mona a glimpse of her orthodontic work, and in conclusion says how splendid to see a Chinese girl turn Jewish. Here they are, two newcomers. She just hopes that Mona feels welcome.

Eloise feels less pressed to extend her welcome to anyone else in the class; and after a few weeks, she has no need at all—having decided to go back to being Wasp. This, even though she is actually still a Jew, according to some people (staunch adherents of the what-the-mother-is-the-child-is rule). Others, though, think how she was brought up determines at least as much who she is, if not more. "Think about what she grew up eating," they say. "That's who she is, you can't deny it." "Like an Eskimo who prefers hamburgers to walrus meat is American," says somebody. "That's assuming walrus is what Eskimos eat," says someone else. "And why can't a person be both?" People nod. Yet another person thinks Eloise can be what she wants. Who are they to say what she is actually, because of her blood or her diet, either? Like the Changowitz, says this person, meaning Mona. People nod again. Should Mona take offense, though, that with this the conversation ends?

Eloise remains friends with a few of the temple crowd—especially Danielle Meyers, but also Barbara Gugelstein, whose father, it turns out, works in the same Wall Street house as Eloise's. That's to say, her ghost lingers hauntingly. For example, Mona notices Barbara start to look down, as if putting away some more pressing matter, before turning her head to answer someone; she does this the exact slow way Eloise Ingle does. In fact, once she takes so long that Mona worries Barbara is not going to respond at all. Not that it is necessarily Mona's business. Mona knows herself to be fatally afflicted with excessive concern, it's because of the parents from China. Still Mona taps her friend on the elbow to remind her to say something. *Oh, he just caught me daydreaming.* So says Barbara later. But another time, she accuses Mona of being too nice. She says that if there's one thing she learned from Eloise Ingle, it's that she doesn't owe it to people to listen just because they want to talk.

"But it's rude," Mona argues weakly. "What happened to honoring other people as you would have them honor you?"

Barbara replies that she doesn't expect that people should listen just because she wants to talk, either. But she doesn't look too sure of this, and when Mona doesn't answer, she goes on to say, nonplussed, "Oh, Mona, you really need to think more like an American. You're too polite."

"Doesn't Eloise have manners? And she's American."

Barbara concedes that Mona's right in a way, but she's wrong in a way too. According to El, Barbara says, manners are not about being nice to everybody. In fact, the whole key to manners is to be aware what set you're talking to.

"Very nice," Mona says. "And what set, pray tell, is she?"

She stomps off in self-righteous fashion, feeling the might of the moral—even though, to be honest, Eloise Ingle's way of thinking is not so different from that of Mona's parents. This Mona admits to Rabbi Horowitz.

"So your parents are snobs. That makes you a snob too?" he says.

"It's more like they'd like to be snobs," Mona clarifies. "The trouble is that here in America, they often can't tell what set they're talking to. And they're not sure what set we are, either."

Rabbi Horowitz listens, working his knuckles as usual, only more sporadically. To appease the temple board of directors, he has recently trimmed his beard, so that his Adam's apple shows; as a result, he from time to time leaves off what he calls his wisecracking, in order to cup his hand over this—his naked compromise.

"With their Chinese friends, it's different. There they can, say, make allowances for So-and-so who's Cantonese but has made something of himself here in America. Which of course they need to do partly because they themselves are from Shanghai, which is sort of like being from New York. People in Peking think they're uncultured and slick." Mona stops. "I've always thought that was so Chinese. I mean, to think like that, everyone looking down on everyone else all the time. I've always thought that was so undemocratic, and un-American, and I've always been glad they at least had redeeming character traits, such as being hardworking. I thought they were the only ones."

"But now you discover what." Rabbi Horowitz, uncharacteristically gloomy, tilts back in his chair. The skeleton rattles behind him.

Barbara is teaching Mona to be cool. The first lesson: When in doubt, act like you couldn't care less.

"But what if you do care?" Mona says.

Barbara doesn't answer. Sometimes when Mona calls these days she finds Barbara's line tied up for hours. Also Barbara now attends concerts without warning. ("El called me up on a whim.") There's a new privacy zone around her; she seems always to be burning incense. Indeed the air is thick enough, that by the time Barbara announces where she is going to sit for the PSATs—namely, next to Eloise—Mona has already lumpenly begun to prepare a defense. Barbara maintains that she would sit next to Mona if their last names were alphabetically closer. But as it happens, Mona is glad enough to be conjoined instead with sweet Rachel Cohen.

Sweet Rachel! Such a true heart she is, sincere and gentle, not to say of a composure you might not predict for a dentist's daughter. She does not sweat. She does not swear. She glides where others lumber, blinks feelingly where others moan. In fact, with her large oval face and sweet limpid eyes, she could almost be the heroine of a long Victorian novel—you would just have to add a little salt—and just as she is, she could no kidding be the heroine's dear sister. Which would make her an ace companion for Mona, except that Rachel is ever-so-gently heavy into making jewelry, and truth to tell (though Mona knows it churlish to say so), she stretches the limits of Mona's interest in solder.

"I notice you didn't like the tiger's eye," says Rachel. "What about these?"

Over Helen's objection, Mona gets her ears pierced like Callie's, and soon they hang noisy with creativity. She sounds like Mr. Bojangles, complete with tambourine. During a math exam, the teacher has to ask her to please stop tinkling, so that other people can think.

"Far out," Rachel says when she hears. "Now for some rings."

After the rings come necklaces, and after the necklaces, bracelets. Rachel is not interested in rap sessions. She takes after her grandfather and great-grandfather—scholars who kept to their small world, and found everything there. They were dreamy people, like her father, a dentist whose life goal is to produce a quartet. (Rachel is the viola.) He will stop in the middle of drilling a tooth to hear how a passage of music develops; also he has been trying to make sense of the new music, though this irritates his clientele. Mutiny! they've threatened (being music lovers themselves). At least one patient has climbed out of the chair, bib and all, to change the tape.

Mona laughs to hear this. How wonderful! She too would like to spend her life among the grace notes—and eventually, maybe she will. For now, though, a callow youth, she's not ready to retire. In truth, she deplores but adores the bloody fray. What would life be without developments?

For example, a cool front happens to blow into Eloise just as the Gugelsteins move to a new house—leaving Mona to help Barbara with the adjustment. Not that the Gugelsteins haven't always lived in something nice. But this house is French provincial to begin with, meaning turrets to house the AC ducts in the Norman style. Also there is a pool, and a tennis court, and a greenhouse with automatic vent flaps; there is a circular driveway, and a two-story, four-bay garage, with servants' quarters up above. There is a screening room for showing movies; there is a library with chestnut paneling; there are six bedrooms, each with its own bathroom. There is a plug-in vacuum system, and an intercom; and instead of regular wallpaper with stripes or birds or flocking, there are in the hallways hand-tinted murals of country scenes in France. Barbara points out the milkmaids for Mona. The scenes begin in the fields and end with wheels of cheese, though there also seem to be a number of rafter-hung hams. Barbara and Mona debate whether hams get dried or smoked, and how many hams a regular rafter can support. Also how many hams one nets per dead pig. They agree that when it comes to production, those milkmaids are an inspiration, Henry Ford himself could probably have picked up a tip. They agree too that the house is some house, and that's not even counting its humanitarian side: Barbara claims that in the basement is a real-life entrance for the Underground Railroad.

"The Underground Railroad was a big deal around here," she says. "That's what the realtor said. It's because this area used to be crawling with Quakers."

"I thought the Underground Railroad wasn't really underground," says Mona.

"Some of it had to be. Otherwise, they'd have called it something else, right?" Barbara retwists her French twist, clamping it into position with a leather-and-stick affair decorated with runes, then goes on to say that according to the realtor, the original house was a colonial. The present house was built on the old foundation plus some, who knows why.

The girls descend the basement stairs. Barbara's head is almost on a level with Mona's, even though she's a step lower; Mona keeps slightly back, so as to avoid being poked by the stick of Barbara's hair affair. More steps. And then, sure enough, in a far corner, behold! A wooden panel the size of a short door, soft with rot. The basement walls are dungeonlike, all ancient rock and hairy mortar, you wouldn't be surprised to find a skeleton built into them. And when Mona and Barbara remove the wooden panel, the rough hole is of a similarly creepy feel. It exhales a cool musty air, though its dirt walls are dry; Mona thinks this must be what catacombs are like, the ones where the early Christians hid to get away from the Romans. Or was it the Jews who hid there to get away from the Christians? Anyway, the hole is just high enough for Mona to stand in; when she steps forward, her hair is teased by the gravel-encrusted ceiling.

"It probably doesn't go very far," Barbara says. "The realtor said the tunnels are mostly blocked off."

"I dare you to go in," says Mona.

But Barbara is chicken; Mona bravely ventures into the tremendous dark alone. One step, two. She's not planning on going far. Hard-packed walls to either side of her; she braces her hands against them. More gravel. "See you later!" she calls. "I'm going to Alabama for to see my Susianna!" Her voice seems sluggishly amplified, as if she is singing in a large padded shower.

"Singing Polly Wolly-doodle all the day?" answers Barbara. Her voice is reassuringly close—right at Mona's back. Two steps more. Now this is the heart of darkness, thinks Mona. But before she can remember who wrote that story, much less what *The horror! The horror!* in it was, she bangs into some kind of metal rack. There is more air beyond this; smooth objects stuck into it. She reemerges, heart thudding, with a pair of bottles.

"Bordeaux!" says Barbara. "Wait until my dad sees these! Are there more?"

"Underground Railroad, wine cellar," mutters Mona. "Very easy to get them mixed up."

Better lit is the last stop of the tour, Barbara's new bedroom, which is so enormous that she's positioned her bed center stage, to take up some of the space. It's the sort of thing you associate with bed-and-bath stores. She's placed a night table next to the bed, and there's a blanket chest at its foot, but all around this island, instead of alluring merchandise, there's just space. For wallpaper she's picked a blue and white sprigged print exactly like the one she had before, in her old room; and her hi-fi too is set up just the way it used to be, with the speakers on either side of the turntable. This, even though she now has the space to separate them for realistic stereophonic sound.

"Where are your records?" Mona asks her.

"Under the bed." This is where she always used to keep them in her old room, in her old house.

"Maybe you should keep them standing up now," says Mona.

But Barbara simply shrugs, digging out her Simon and Garfunkel, her Carole King, her Laura Nyro. "They're warped already anyway," she says. And when she puts them on, you can see that indeed the needle surfs most alarmingly up and down, just the same as ever.

Although the hot line begins as a temple activity, in time Gentile classmates are also encouraged to join, provided that they pass the screening and get trained. And some do, such as Jim Magruder, and Jill Spence, and Georgina Elliott. Also Eloise Ingle. And why shouldn't they be allowed to, after all? The Jews are the Chosen People, but they have always invited outsiders to their Sabbath meals. *You shall love strangers, for strangers you were in Egypt.* Plus they are, Jew and Gentile alike, against suicide—although without an attempt every so often, what will staffers do while on duty but eat fruit leather and gossip? And make out, Barbara says—which Mona would not believe herself, except that Jim Magruder and Aaron Apfelbaum have signed up for every night shift available with Danielle Meyers and Eloise Ingle (who Barbara wishes would sign up with her and Mona, but never does). Also Mona discovers a rubber in the bathroom. Unused, it's true, but as Barbara points out, it could have been used, and why was it there unless someone had ideas?

"You mean as in a Big Idea?" Mona says; and this becomes a joke between them. "What an Idea," they say, and "He was keeping his Idea to himself," and "Now, that's an Idea." Still Mona wonders if Barbara's right. Is there hidden within the circle to which they've been admitted, another, smaller circle? It seems like something out of Nancy Drew: *The Secret of the Temple Hot Line.* Until one day, sure enough, Seth Mandel starts signing up as senior counselor for their shift.

Seth Mandel is a shortish, bright-eyed, pony-tailed guy, with big broad shoulders and the surprise domestic side you associate with primates like the silverback gorilla. Not only is he the type to offer people back rubs of surprising penetration, but he'll pick a piece of lint off your sleeve if he sees it, saying, *Excuse me, I can't help it; I'm driven by early training and the force of neurosis.* And then his eyes will crinkle, and a crack will open in his red-brown beard, and you'll know he's smiling his wide crooked smile. He doesn't laugh much—the enigmatic smile is more his style. But once in a while, he'll let out a guffaw, shocking people, and then he will smile to see their reaction. For this is what he likes more than anything, to conduct little experiments— or as he puts it, to send up balloons. *This is how you see the wind. That is, if you are interested in seeing the wind.* He smiles again.

Seth is the youngest of the senior counselors, meaning that he has graduated from high school, but hasn't from college on account of never having gone. Instead he is taking time off to decide whether college is a socializing force to which he can submit. How this came to pass has been a topic of town debate for some time. To some parents, this is obviously related to the war. Humans are generalizing animals, goes this line of reasoning. Once the kids get the idea they can resist the draft, they start to resist whatever they want. Other parents, though, blame the high school social studies curriculum, and especially advanced placement American history. This everyone knows is taught by a radical extremist in half-glasses. He starts the year by explaining how the Constitution had as much to do with economics as with noble ideals; pretty soon the kids think they know everything, it's only just lucky that this doesn't stop them from going to Ivy League schools if they get in. Seth is the exception, probably because he was the star student, and also because he got in everywhere he applied. That gave him an attitude, say some people. Needless to say too, he'd have gone if he had drawn a lower draft number.

But as it is, Mr. Above-It-All is now more or less educating himself. This is easy enough, since he is the kind of guy who compares translations of Dante for the hell of it, and who goes almost only to foreign films. The exception being *Romeo and Juliet* with Olivia Hussey, which he saw thrice in order to ascertain that (*a*) he doesn't think she is so beautiful, and (*b*) he is personally against girls parting their hair in the middle as if to suggest purity when in fact all they have on their minds is popularity. In other words, he's deep.

Is he interested in Barbara or in Mona? In the beginning it is not so clear, and then it is. He is interested in Mona, partly because of her superlative grade point average, but mostly because she is a phenomenon. A Chinese Jew! He says he sees her sometimes in the pancake house, and that he can't believe she is the same person he sees at temple. What a world-spanner!—a regular Yoko Ono. He takes her, in other words, for a high-wire freethinker, perhaps of his own school— no small compliment since he has, at age nineteen, all but broken away from the small-minded bourgeois thinking of his father, a paper-products mogul and in-the-flesh subscriber to *Pulp* magazine. He does not even live in his father's house anymore, but in a teepee in the backyard, except for when it is really cold. (And of course he helps himself to whatever from the fridge, and leaves his laundry for the maid.) *What do you like to read?* he wants to know. Which inquiry, in truth, Mona finds something of a thrill, seeing it as a level up from *Do you speak Chinese?* and *What do you eat at home?* Her mind, her mind! Someone cares about her mind!

A delicious thought for a closet reader—Mona has never admitted how much she reads, figuring, Why act brainier? It was one thing for JFK to speed-read; it's another for people in the sweet bloom of their youth. As it is, people say things like, *Don't you just hate her?* Meaning her. Last year somebody switched out of Mona's math class, saying he didn't want to be on the same curve as she was, even though Mona wasn't the one pulling down the perfect scores, it was Andy Kaplan. Mona always managed to make some little mistake.

Moreover, as Mona tells Seth, she immediately changed her part from the side to the middle after seeing *Romeo and Juliet;* and she is not interested in being a phenomenon (this being a Feeble excuse for a love affair, it seems to her). In addition, she fails to be charmed when he attempts to woo her with a synopsis of *A Critique of Pure Reason,* even if he did distill it himself from a most hefty original with only a small amount of help from a lecture series he's been listening to on tape. *The Great Thoughts Condensed for the Modern Mind,* this is called; and yes, the reel-to-reel tape machine is indeed installed in his teepee. Likewise, a telephone.

Says Mona, "Why didn't Kant just say, 'Thou shalt not use other people'?"

"Because only G-d can issue commandments," says Seth, gesturing with his hands. (He likes to make a kind of cage with them as he listens, each fingertip lightly touching its comrade on the other hand. When he talks, the cage opens, as if to let the truth flap out.) "And Kant wasn't G-d."

"So why didn't he say it was just his suggestion? Why didn't he say it was just his Big Idea?" This is for Barbara's sake. Mona can tell Barbara feels left out by the fact that she's even checked that Kant book out of the library and looked to see how it ends.

Barbara laughs appreciatively.

"Because," sputters Seth.

Another fact, not to be ignored: When Seth is too nonplussed to hold forth any further, Mona feels for him. Is he really so terrible for a pseudointellectual? Plus how can he help but leave Barbara out? After all, he's so in love with Mona, poor fellow.

Still she staunchly defends the status quo that is Barbara and her 4-ever—thereby officially forgiving her friend her E.I.L. (Eloise Ingle lapse). Until after a while, he begins to get the hint. He begins to share with Barbara his synopses and hypotheses and analyses, his assumptions and suppositions. Whereupon, to Mona's confoundment, Barbara goes intellectual. There is suddenly no question like a higher question, and wherefore are there depths to existence, except for to be plumbed?

Creepingly, creepingly, things begin to change. At the outset they all make a show of taking their turn at the phone; and after the calls, they review them as usual. Somehow, though, it begins to transpire that Barbara and Seth happen to have cases requiring extraordinary attention. And so elaborate are the discussions they happen to get involved in while Mona is on the phone, that they are still engrossed in them when the phone rings again; so that it seems only courteous for Mona to answer it. Then it begins to seem only courteous for them to remove themselves and their discussion to the next room, so that they are not disturbing Mona's concentration. And then it seems only courteous that they shut the door.

There being no door between the rooms, they are obliged to move into a large utility closet. This is not such a hospitable place, being full of cleaning supplies and other objects of large utility. Still Mona's friends repair there uncomplainingly, turning out the light so as better to explore the hitherto hidden complexities of this case or that. Every now and then, Mona hears a pail get knocked over, or a mop. And one day, there is a giant crash, which can only be the wet-dry industrial vac. The vac, Mona happens to know, is loaded up with a temple art class project (somebody's still-wet, life-size, papier-mâché armadillo having been sabotaged by felons wielding granola and Gatorade). Is this why the crash is followed by muffled yelling that sounds like "Help! Help!" but could also be "Pulp! Pulp!"? (The latter being a favorite cry in the Mandel household, apparently.)

Mona approaches the closet door but does not knock. "Barbara? Seth? You okay?" The closet door seems to her amazingly wooden.

Silence.

Mona explores with her toe the nub of the indoor-outdoor carpeting. It feels the way it looks, bluish green. "Hey, Kugel Noodle. You vant I should call an ambulance?"

Says Barbara, "I'm fine. But what's that ringing?" Then she says, "Please to go answer it, Polly Wolly," and makes a giggle-like noise.

Was it a giggle? That night, Mona considers this question closely and with tears. "Barbara," Mona says the next time she sees her friend. This is in AP English class. "Barbara."

"That's my name, don't wear it out," she says.

Mona gets up her courage. "What am I, chopped liver, you should do this to me?"

"Wait. What? I'm doing something?"

Mrs. Thompson has left the room. Everyone knows this is because she has a collapsed uterus and needs a bathroom break—during which time, they are supposed to be writing an in-class essay defining irony.

"To you?" Barbara looks honestly puzzled. In fact, so sincerely does she look at Mona with her dewy green eyes, that it is Mona who looks away. Outside the classroom window, the lawn slopes steeply up the road; Mona wonders suddenly who mows that lawn, and whether the person ever feels discouraged. "I thought you didn't want him."

"I didn't, I don't think."

"You were so clear about it, you hurt his feelings. A lot."

"Oh," Mona says, feeling as though she has more to say. But as she doesn't know what it is, she turns her eyes to her page and begins to write.

Mona is waiting, once again, for the hot-line phone to ring. Confirmation class seems for now a light-year away; also Rabbi Horowitz. Mona sees him there at the temple, not preoccupied with his beard length, as he has been of late, but cheerfully snapping one after another of his joints in place. She should shrug too. Instead she thinks about calling him just to say hi, or maybe to ask why it is that now that she's Jewish, she feels like more of a Chinese than ever. Is there some grand explanation—Hegelian perhaps? (Ah, Seth, how you've expanded her wardrobe of trenchant and other thoughts.) All this would tie up the line irresponsibly, though; and so it remains an idle eddying notion, one of life's spin-off ideas that curl to the sides of your mainly rushing existence. It's like wishing that she could call herself up. Or like wishing, when callers are done with themselves, that she could then call them back and tell them how it feels to behold her best friend and erstwhile suitor closeted up with the cleaning appliances. Is this what it means to be your own accounting unit? Mona would ask. And then maybe she would tell them how she's not sure what she thinks about that. In a way she understands that this is how life operates in America, that it's just like the classroom. You have to raise your own hand—no one is going to raise it for you—and then you have to get ready to stand up and give the right answer so that you may gulp down your whole half-cup of approval. But how tempting to stay hunkered down with everyone else, in the comfortable camaraderie of the hungry! After all, you are so tall when you stand up. People look at you with their stomachs rumbling, and you can't help but notice how around you there is so much air.

Of course, this is a foolish way to think. Mona understands that according to the rules, if you don't eat up, someone else will. None of this *nali, nali* Chinese self-effacement. *You've got to look out for number one.* No one sits lumpenly when opportunity knocks—except her, every now and then, and of course Callie, a self-cleaning oven if ever you met one. Is this a matter of their genotypes? Or is it just that other people grew up eating their individual portions from their individual plates; whereas the Changs help themselves from bowls in the middle of the table, and no one can leave until everyone else is done.

A true story: A friend of Helen's comes to visit, some years later, from China. The friend is going to a university, where she will share a room with two other Chinese students. Unfortunately, due to travel and other miseries, she is the last one to arrive. The result: she gets the best bed. No one else would take it! The first to arrive took the worst bed, the second to arrive, the second-worst. And so for an entire year, she is closest to the bathroom and the radiator, farthest from the window opening out onto the fire station. Of course, she tries to make it up to her roommates bit by bit. She brings them fruit, and folding umbrellas, and tickets to the movies. Still she feels the difficulty of her position.

Is this a way to live? Mona ponders the question. Meanwhile, the phone rings—someone calling about her boyfriend. Since he started doing speed, all he will eat is baby food; everything else he suspects. *Trace minerals,* she says he says. *Did you ever think about what they mean by trace minerals?*

The phone rings again. This caller is shook up because in the middle of her parents' divorce, their giant cactus became possessed.

"So I said, Mom, it's moving, I swear, just like in *Rosemary's Baby*. And she said she knew I needed attention, but that she didn't appreciate my trying to get it in this manner, and also that I just wouldn't believe what my papa was putting her through. Even her lawyer had never seen anything like it, and he'd been in the divorce business as long as anybody. Way, way, way before it got popular. So I called up my papa and said, It's moving, I swear. And he said he loved me, but did I have any idea how many times his phone rang an hour? And so the next day, guess what. The whole plant exploded. It turned out it was full of tarantulas hatching, and then there were baby tarantulas everywhere, and they attacked my dog, her name was Sheepie, even though she was a beagle, because that was what I wanted originally, a sheep dog. The vet thought that she would live, but she died, and now they want to bury her, but I won't let them. I told them I didn't want my dog buried by her own murderers, especially since all they care about is who's going to pay for the exterminator, and how long my mom and me are going to have to stay in a hundred-dollar-a-night hotel."

The caller is remarkably poised until she describes how in order to bury the dog someplace her parents don't even know exists, she somehow has to first get Sheepie's body back from the veterinarian. Unfortunately, he won't let her have it because she's a minor. "But she's my dog, I told him. I had her since she was a puppy. I raised her up. I taught her tricks. She slept in my bed." She sobs and sobs. Mona tries to say what Rabbi Horowitz would say. She tries to bear in mind what they were taught in training, which is that everyone is calling out of loneliness, and that their job, on some spiritual level, is to take the caller's side. Is it working, though? Suddenly the caller whispers, "Uh oh, it's my ma," and hangs up. Mona waits, hoping she'll call back, but when the phone rings again, it's someone else.

Luckily, none of the day's callers is code red—meaning that none of them is calling from the train tracks, or from the nether reaches of a hallucinogen. Though Mona has been specially trained to deal with drug overdoses, she is first supposed to try to hand such calls over to the capable senior counselor. As for what is the protocol if the capable senior counselor happens to have his hands full, who knows.

Mona tries, between calls, to ignore the loud quiet emanating from the utility closet. Mona tries, between calls, to read an Irish book called *Dubliners*. This is an assignment for English class, meaning that Mona is supposed to be on the lookout for epiphanies. It turns out there is one at the end of each story. The phone rings again. This is no divorce; neither is it a drug-related, or a parent-related, or a school-related call. And it doesn't seem to be Andy Kaplan, either. The boy identifies himself as Japanese, the son of a businessman, and though his English pronunciation is now textbook clear, there is something familiar about his voice.

If he weren't supposed to be in Japan, Mona would almost believe this to be Sherman Matsumoto.

Or is it? Anyway, if this person is in trouble, he won't say what kind. They exchange pleasantries about the weather, and also about how beautiful an area is Westchester, what with the landscaping and lawns. Mona explains about lime, and turf-builder, and preemergent crabgrass control. He replies that he lived in Scarshill some years ago. Now he is living in a neighboring town, near a duck pond with a willow tree. Is he happy to be back? He is enigmatic about this, and about what moved him to call. All he will say is that he is upset because someone trimmed the willow. He had liked the way the branches reached almost all the way down to the water; in the slightest breeze they would touch the pond, and then it would be as if it had been raining just there, right under the tree. The water would be all shivery where it had been touched—as the caller puts it, *full of spirit*—and the bits of light that reflected back up into the undersides of the leaves would toss and dance wildly.

"Crazy in the leaves," he says. "Everywhere else, it is a nice day, sunny. But in just this one tree—monsoon."

"It sounds beautiful." Mona is amazed at how clearly she can picture this private storm, especially the light-in-the leaves part. It's one of those things you've seen a hundred times without noticing it—how magically the water splatters the sun, like nature's own mirror ball.

"They should not have cut the tree," he says.

"No, they shouldn't have," Mona agrees. "Although did they cut the tree or did they cut the branches?"

"The branches."

"Ah, well. Maybe they'll grow back."

He is suddenly quiet.

"Trees do grow back quickly." Mona tries to take the long view like Rabbi Horowitz, to put things in the comforting context of universal natural principles. "Did they cut a lot or a little?"

Still he says nothing.

"If they cut a lot, it might take a while. If they cut a little, it might be pretty quick."

"It can never grow back," he says with vehemence.

"Are you sure?"

No answer.

"Is there something else you'd like to say?"

The caller hangs up.

Her note in the call log reads this way: *Japanese (?) male calling for (is this prejudiced?) somewhat inscrutable but probably profound reasons. Although who knows, maybe also/just for language practice (English). Good vibes established despite long silences and short sentences. More attention should probably have been paid to drug education. Given caller's depressed state of mind, probably ought also to have explored caller attitude toward hari-kari, even if that's a stereotype. Instead discussed lawn care (fertilizer) and duck pond with tree (willow). Caller disturbed by the pruning of aforementioned tree, which he characterized as full of lights like a monsoon and incapable of ever growing back. All this before suddenly hanging up. A hidden message here? Cultural considerations certainly a factor, perhaps major or minor. Still questions remain.*

For instance: Is this Sherman? Sherman! The idea seems at once impossible and preordained. Are they sixteen already? Here he is, as promised. It's kind of young to get married. All the same, Mona studies up on Japan.

An elongated isle, says one book. *Crowded.*

Mona would not have thought she could become Japanese, but here she is, Jewish, right?

She wonders if she is not getting ahead of herself. Why would she want to be Japanese? What if this caller has nothing to do with her at all? The next week, as soon as she comes in, she checks the log to see if he's called, which he hasn't. She waits to see if he calls while she's there. It's amazing how little it matters to her what goes on in the utility closet now. How reoriented she is! So to speak.

The Japanese caller calls again, with about as much to say as last time. They talk about how he's gone down to visit Monticello, in Virginia, with his parents. She's never been there, but he says it's very beautiful, except with too many sides, and he can't understand why Thomas Jefferson had a slave as his mistress.

"Maybe he loved her," Mona says.

"But he is President of whole United States," he says. "Of course, at that time, the United States is only half the size we see now."

"Love is unpredictable."

"That way he makes everyone unhappy."

"But what if he loved her?"

"If he loved her he should leave her alone. When a nail sticks up, people hammer it down."

"But is that right?"

Silence. "That way brings peace and harmony."

"What about right and wrong? Don't you think that's important too?"

No answer at first. Then, "It can't be helped."

"You know," says Mona, "in America, we don't care so much about peace and harmony."

"Oh, really."

"That's right."

"Then why all the time those peace marches?"

"That's different."

He starts to sing: " 'All they are say-ing / is give peace a chance.' "

"Where'd you learn that?"

He hangs up.

The next times he calls, it's about how he walked right under Niagara Falls, which he thought was worth getting soaked—the first thing he's said that they've agreed on. He says this even though as a result of getting wet, he got so sick he ran a fever. Then he calls about Kentucky, and the horse farms there. He does not think these are fundamentally undemocratic. He thinks they are beautiful. Also he says he wouldn't mind being a horse, even if he had to be shot for breaking a leg, and that he wouldn't mind being bred, either.

In short, a pattern has emerged. He calls, always on her shift, offers two or three comments about scenic spots he has visited, then hangs up so abruptly Mona can't help but wonder if there isn't something he doesn't want to go into. For instance, how it is he travels so much. Doesn't his father work? Doesn't he go to school? Is he making it all up about these adventures of his? The last seems unlikely. If she's being read to from *The Scenic Wonders of America*, it must be some special haiku edition. So much is unspoken that when they get to the end of an entry, she doesn't feel nearly so much like saying *Aah* as *Huh?*

What he's holding back may not be trouble—that occurs to her too. Mona wonders if she shouldn't try on some of those wooden platform shoes, see if she can walk in them. She recalls that once she tried stilts and did okay. Also she's a whiz on a pogo stick. And what about the weather in Japan, and do they have mosquitoes? She can almost believe that they don't. For mosquitoes go with cut-offs and camp shirts, who has ever seen a lady in a kimono swat at her pulse points?

She dreams about Sherman, and about what his life is like in Japan, and she finds that in her dreams it is a lot like her life at home, except that her family is like everyone else's. People read each other's minds. They share their food. Everything is simpler. Of course, the Changs also have to eat their fish raw, and sleep on the floor, and wear socks with their sandals; and what with her cowlick, it is not so easy for Mona to get her hair up into that big breakfast-bun style you see the geishas wear. But life is serene. Her family is an interlocking piece of a vast and complex puzzle. There is no Eloise Ingle, and no Seth Mandel; and it is not like China, either, taken over by leather-eating Communists.

Here is the odd thing, though: In her vision, Mona is always fifteen, and never old enough to drive. In fact, she doesn't even have a learner's permit. This is an unreasonable conception, she knows. She knows that people do drive in Japan, although in smaller cars. Still the next time the caller calls, Mona asks, "Do you mind if I ask you a question about driving?"

"Driving?"

"Driving cars," Mona says. "I was just wondering how old you have to be to drive a car in Japan."

He hesitates in a way that makes her wonder if she is being too personal. But how can the driving age in Japan be too personal? "I don't know," he says finally.

She tries to speak more clearly. "I mean, do you have learner's permits there? Here they have learner's permits, and then you have to do the three-point turn, and then you can take the driving test and get your license."

"I see."

"I've been wondering, that's all."

A long silence. So long, Mona wonders if he's hung up. Then he says, "Are you going to Japan?"

"I'd like to. Someday."

"Why?"

"Oh," Mona says. "I guess I've never been there. Why did you go to Monticello?"

"To see the cherry trees. Of course, they are not so nice as the trees in Japan."

"I see."

"Do you like Japan?"

"Oh," Mona says. "I hear it's very interesting."

"I see."

"Very crowded, and with small cars and earthquake trouble," says Mona. "An elongated island. I've never been in an earthquake. Also with volcanoes, I think."

"Mount Fuji," he says politely.

"That's right," Mona says. "Isn't that the one with snow on it?"

"In the wintertime," he says, "snow falls on many mountains. All over. Just like here."

"I see," Mona says. And then, not knowing what else to do, she pretends to knock the phone over. "Whoops." She hangs up. He does not call back.

Seth and Barbara are having a fight. This is because Seth is interested in free love, whereas Barbara is interested in ownership.

"I can't help it," she says. "I do want to be able to say *my* boyfriend, and I just don't see what capitalism and serfs and the Russian Revolution have to do with it." Seth wants her to read *Das Kapital*. She wants him to read Ann Landers. "He has no idea what real love is about," she says. "Him and his Big Idea." She stops.

"Oh, Barbara," Mona says. "You didn't."

Barbara begins to sob.

"You let him give you his tea?"

"We were stoned. And it's just like everyone says—it ruined everything."

Mona takes her friend's backpack for her. She helps her friend sit down on the grass, well away from a pile of dog doo.

"I thought it meant we were definitely going out with each other. But he said we contributed to the social good by reducing world horniness; he doesn't see why that's not enough. He said that all that mattered was if I liked it too, and if I was acting out of my own free will."

"Were you?"

"I was. That's the worst part, except for what he said. Why should he be just my boyfriend, he said."

"What a shithead!"

"It's just what my mother always warned me. What does he really want, a guy like Seth? A guy like Seth, what he really wants is a shiksa."

Nineteen. Eighteen. They count down the days until Barbara's next period while, outside, the dogwood blooms virginal yet again. May! Most merry month. Seventeen. They discuss abortion. First of all, how lucky that it's legal in New York; second of all, what exactly it is. For this information, Mona calls Callie at college. Who else to ask about the special vacuum cleaner, and whether there are nowadays special coat hangers too? Callie looks up the info in *Our Bodies, Ourselves*, which she seems to have sitting right next to the phone; apparently you need it more in college than a dictionary. She does not lecture unduly, except to suggest that Barbara tell her mom. Barbara would sooner throw herself in front of a commuter train.

Sixteen. Seth wonders why the snap freeze. Even pleads, professing concern. Barbara refuses to address His Ignoramus. "Let him use his higher intellect and figure it out himself," she says. "He who reads Nietzsche and can spell it too," agrees Mona. Fifteen. As if Barbara and Mona don't have enough to worry about, they have to take the SATs. They sharpen their number-two pencils together; they try to avoid Eloise Ingle. Mona still sits with Rachel Cohen, though, and so far is this from the G–R section that Mona does not even witness how Barbara breaks down crying in the middle of the test and has to leave the room. Barbara is bravely philosophical about this later. She says she'll try again in the fall, assuming the special vacuum cleaner works.

Fourteen. They try to gain perspective. They discuss whether entertaining a Big Idea was at least fun. Barbara says it wasn't, although it was exciting. Meaning what? Also she says that it was messy and smelly and sticky, and that she dripped for a whole day afterward and had to take about eighty showers to get rid of the smell of him. "Eighty showers?" says Mona. Barbara concedes this to be a manner of speaking. Still the words haunt Mona, rekindling themselves like trick birthday candles. *Eighty showers. Eighty showers.*

Thirteen. Mona lies in bed and wonders: Will Sherman Matsumoto ever make her need to take eighty showers? She feels guilty wondering this. She thinks she should have thoughts only for Kugel Noodle, her friend in need. At the same time, she figures it can't be that bad to wonder, seeing as how there is so little to wonder about. For how should Sherman make her take anything when she hasn't seen him in years? Also the Japanese in general don't seem as if they smell. Maybe this is a stereotype. Maybe if she saw the statistics for deodorant sales in Japan she would be shocked. But what matter, when there is a yet greater misstep in the analytic march of her thinking? For while Mona is antisublimation and can see herself as almost old enough to get married, she finds that she does not see herself as old enough for sex.

How can this be? Mona was the first one in her entire grade to get her period. Plus she surmises by the population problems of the Far East that she is appropriately equipped. But she doesn't look like, say, Barbara. If her friend is a developed nation, Mona is, sure enough, the third world. Barbara's is the body Mona is still waiting to grow into: Her breasts, for example, are veritable colonies of herself, with a distinct tendency toward independence. Whereas Mona's, in contrast, are anything but wayward. A scant handful each, hers are smooth and innocent—the result, you might think, of eating too much ice cream. They meld into the fat under her arms. Even her nipples seem somehow dietary, smallish brownish nubs—areolaless, perhaps, due to inadequate consumption of true adult drinks such as beer and tonic water. Later Mona will realize how in the popular conception Orientals are supposed to be exotically erotic, and all she'll want to say is, But what about my areolaless nubs? Not to say my sturdy short legs—have you ever seen a calf so hammy? And no billowy, Brillo-y bush, alas. How should she have one when she does not even need to shave her legs? This last a convenience of sorts. Although how can she let her legs go natural when they already are natural? Her underarms too— actually she boasts a few wisps there. If only she didn't have to put her hands on her head for anyone to notice! Hair, hair, hair, she thinks. And especially facial hair, body hair. It's different for the sexes, of course. But in general, these are the dead cells that spell wild-side bohemian. She feels condemned to the straight and narrow.

Of course, this whole train of thought will one day prove not her own train at all, but a train set on track by racist sexist imperialists. She will one day discover that it is great to be nonhairy, and what's more that not all Asians are areolaless, just her and some others. Plus that she is yellow and beautiful—baby boobs, hammy calves, and all. She will ask for an extra print when people take her picture. She will come to recognize, with a little squinting, her goddess within.

But for now all Mona can think is, Oh, that subcutaneous fat! So young she looks; so rounded; so unavoidably, irrevocably cute. Oh, to be angular and gaunt! Oh, to be tall! (How she hates the word *petite*.) Oh, to be leggy and buxom like Barbara Gugelstein, and Oh, to have a crisis with Seth Mandel! It seems so awfully glamorous, except when Mona tries to put herself in Barbara's shoes. Then Mona recalls that she would not be in Barbara's shoes. Because if Mona got pregnant, the baby would be mixed. Meaning what? She's not sure, but something complicated, that's certain, and also something for which she's too young.

Twelve. "Ma," Mona says. "Have you ever seen a mixed baby?"

Helen says that she has, yes, two, and that one was beautiful, but the other looked completely Caucasian. That baby had blue eyes and brown hair, and when she grew up she was as big as a horse.

"And what about her legs?"

"Why do you want to know about her legs?" asks Helen, chopping scallions. But then she answers that the girl's legs looked as though there was something the matter with them. "She was still a nice girl. Very smart, and never give her parents any trouble."

"Like me, you mean."

"You!"

"What do you mean, something the matter with them?" Mona asks, after a moment. "What was the matter with her legs?"

"Too long."

"Hmm. I wish my legs were longer."

"Your trouble is not your legs." Helen adds the scallions to the chicken, which is steaming.

"What if I had a mixed baby?" Mona says. "What if I had a mixed baby, and it looked completely Caucasian?"

"Are you having a baby?"

"No. But what if I did, and it looked completely Caucasian? With a big nose and blue eyes and everything."

"Oh, then I would throw it in the garbage," says Helen, turning the heat down.

That night Mona dreams Helen is having a new baby, a boy, which is also the baby that Mona is having, except that Helen doesn't realize it until she notices how long the baby's legs are. Then she shouts, "This baby is Jewish! Throw it in the garbage!" and will not be appeased until Mona throws herself in the garbage instead. The garbage looks to be mostly paper, but turns out to have eggplant at the bottom, which Mona thinks is Italian. Helen insists it's Chinese, though; and when Mona looks again, she sees that her mother is right. There's no mozzarella. She wakes up sweating and feeling like she needs eighty showers.

Eleven. Barbara is friends with Eloise Ingle again, but things so aren't what they were that Barbara doesn't even tell Eloise she might be pregnant. As for Barbara and Mona, they are able to continue working on the hot line as a result of Seth's diplomacy: Knowing an awkward situation when he's engendered one, he graciously cedes his place to an out-of-work comptroller named Mathilde. "You need any help, why, speak right on up," she says, knitting. Her sweater pattern involves chipmunks in a tree full of letters that are going to spell LUV YA.

Barbara wants to quit. Mona, though, explains about the phone calls from Sherman. "Why didn't you tell me?!" says Barbara then. And she's right, Mona should have told her. First of all, because Barbara is telling Mona everything, but also because she knows something Mona doesn't.

"Oh!" she says. "That Andy Kaplan!"

"Andy Kaplan?"

They review the evidence. Now that they are discussing it, Mona can recall certain weird moments in her conversations with the Japanese caller. Barbara analyzes these incisively; Mona is suddenly the one who wants to quit the hot line, post-haste. In fact, Mona wouldn't mind quitting town, quitting New York, quitting North America. She wishes she were old enough and had good enough eyes for the space program. Barbara, however, absolutely wants to stay. "Aren't you curious, Watson?" Holding up a pretend monocle, Barbara proposes that Mona let her listen in on the next call. After all, aren't they telling each other everything?

Ten. They wait. Nine.

The mystery caller does not call.

Eight. Barbara Gugelstein's theory (advanced as she taste-tests a can of Diet Dr Pepper) is that Andy Kaplan is afraid to call now because he knows she will catch him out. But how can Andy Kaplan know what Barbara is planning? "He doesn't have ESP," says Mona. Whereupon Barbara, opening a second can for Mona, introduces her to the Theory of Blood Knowledge. Barbara says she believes some people are linked by ancestral memory. She believes that there are genes for ways of thinking, and that if you come from the same gene pool, you are likely to have the same genes.

"I even asked Mr. Ed about it," she says. Mr. Ed is their biology teacher—a horse lover who people say is starting to resemble his favorite ride. "And he said it's possible."

"Possible is only possible."

"Andy Kaplan and I have always been on the same wavelength. Even if he did turn cool before I did."

She says this last because ever since Andy grew his hair and took up the electric guitar, he's been considered the cutest guy in their grade. Not that he rose to this summit without hormones; for a long time he was just like anybody else, only shorter. People noticed that he was golden of aspect and had been to a crack orthodontist, also that he was coordinated and musical, not to say the sort of class-A mimic you would definitely want on your side for charades. But after he suddenly grew eleven inches, he became the sort of guy with whom people liked to claim some connection. His mom worked with their mom on the library committee. They used to be on his paper route. Even Seth claims to play chess with Andy now and then; and Mona sometimes imagines a strange vibe between them, on account of his mom staking her prize chrysanthemums with chopsticks. Also the Kaplans have been to Taiwan and Japan; his father is a professor of East Asian civilization. Around their house, people say, are *belly many Buddhas*.

But of everyone, Barbara feels that she knows Andy best. Not only did they get the same thing for their mothers for Mother's Day, they also have the same hiking boots, the same camping stove, the same Kelty backpack.

"Maybe you should get married," Mona says, sipping away, but Barbara says it would be like marrying her brother. Even going out with him would be like going out with her brother. However, every so often they do smoke pot together, and then it's amazing what they share with each other, the depths of their souls; it's only too bad that the next day she can never remember what they found way down there.

"It's kind of like the tie between you and Sherman Matsumoto," she says. "Now, if you guys end up married, I won't be surprised."

But wouldn't that be like Mona marrying her brother? And what kind of tie is it between her and Sherman Matsumoto if Sherman is not Sherman at all, but actually Andy Kaplan?

Seven. Six. Five. Barbara reports feeling fat. Then, finally—a day early!—her period comes. Hooray! She and Mona celebrate with a ritual egg smash. *O ovum, dear ovum,* they intone. *Be thou ever chary!*

"Chary, or wary?" says Barbara. Mona isn't sure. Still they spend their hot-line shift composing an ode with the rhyme scheme *chary/ scary/marry*. They are finagling a way to work in *hari-kari* when, lo and behold, guess who calls?

"Long time no speak," Mona says.

Barbara Gugelstein picks up the other handset. Sherman is talking about a weekend trip to Boston. "Many bricks," he says. "Some of the sidewalks are very hard to walk, and some of the streets have rocks."

No hiking boots? writes Barbara, and passes the note to Mona.

"Those cobblestones," Mona says.

"That's right, cobblestones," he answers, sounding delighted. "All over. Very rough. So hard to drive in Boston! Even we look at the map, we are lost all the time." Still he had fun. He liked the gas lamps, and the swan boats, and the Freedom Trail, although he couldn't understand the Boston Tea Party. Why did the colonists dress up to dump the tea overboard?

"And why they like tea? To drink with their hot dogs?"

Mona explains that in the colonies, there were no hot dogs.

"No hot dogs?" he says, with what seems like real surprise. But then he goes on. "How about hamburgers?"

Ha ha, writes Barbara Gugelstein. *Very funny.*

The caller is generally glad not to have lived through the Revolution. The absence of hot dogs is one reason, but the main reason is that he prefers peace to big fights. On the other hand, he says that he went to Walden Pond and that the man who lived there seemed to him a nut.

He went to Walden Pond too? All in how long?

Mona tries to explain what is a nonconformist.

"Different drummer," Mona explains. "Like in a band."

"If he is in band," the caller says, "the drummer must drum like everyone else."

Get off it! writes Barbara.

The caller goes on to describe how he visited Harvard while he was in Boston, and MIT. (*All in ONE weekend?!*) Both of these he thought very nice, although a little dirty. Also he says the students looked sloppy, and even some of the professors.

"They're just anti-establishment," Mona says.

"What is anti-establishment?"

Mona hesitates. How can he not know what means anti-establishment, when he knows about protest songs?

Ask him what professors wear in Japan, writes Barbara.

"What do professors wear in Japan?"

"What?"

Ask him what he's wearing right now.

"What are you wearing?" Mona asks. "Right now."

"Me? What am I wearing?"

Ask him if he's wearing blue jeans.

"Are you wearing blue jeans?"

How could he not know what he is wearing?

"I am wearing blue jeans," he says finally.

Tell him you are too, with no underwear underneath.

"I'm wearing blue jeans too," Mona says. "Mine have pretty big bells."

More silence. Has he hung up?

"I am so busy these days," he says.

"Schoolwork?" Mona says.

"Sure," he says. "Schoolwork, and sports also."

"Sports!" Mona says. "What sports?"

"Oh," he says. "Some judo, and baseball."

Some judo!!!

"Some judo?" Mona says.

"Judo is very popular sport in Japan."

Did he do it when he lived in America?

"Did you do it when you lived in America?"

"Sure," he says.

Tell him you used to know someone who did judo.

"I used to know someone who did judo," Mona says.

Tell him you were completely in love with him.

"Really," he says.

Tell him you have been saving yourself for him.

"He flipped me on the ground once," Mona says.

"Oh," he says. "You must have done something very bad, that he was so mad at you."

Mona says, "I don't know if it was really that bad."

Now's your chance! Just ask, Do you mind if I ask you a question? Is this Sherman M.?

"Do you mind if I ask you a question?" Mona says.

"Sure," he says.

"I used to know someone named Sherman Matsumoto," Mona says. "Many years ago. Do you know anyone by that name?"

"Sure," he says.

Ask him!

"Are you Sherman?"

Silence.

Or is this Andy Kaplan?

"Or is this Andy Kaplan?"

"Andy?" he says.

"Andy Kaplan," Mona says. "K-A-P-L-A-N."

"Who?" he says. "Kaplan?"

"You heard her," Barbara chimes in. "Give it up!"

"Who's this?" he asks.

"Your friend Barbara," says Barbara.

"Barbara? Not Mona?"

"Also Mona," Mona says.

"Barbara and Mona? What do you mean?"

"Kaplan . . . ," starts Barbara.

"Oh, God. I'm sorry, Sherman," Mona says. "This is Mona. I'm really sorry. It's just that—"

"You will never be Japanese." He hangs up.

CHAPTER 5

A Turn in the Car

Barbara buries her head in her hands. Her hair is not at all frizzy, and so what about the curly commas that most adorably punctuate her forehead? She would be pleased if she could see how well does work her orange juice can. Instead she is upset. "You'll never forgive me."

"You're right," Mona says.

"I'm turning into my mother. It's already happening."

"Seems like you should at least get to go to college first, huh?"

"I hate it when she jumps right into the conversation like that. She's so rude. She just has this urge to fix everything all the time. The other day she started to scrape the dirt out from between the floor and the baseboard with a toothpick. And now I go and do the exact same thing."

"With a toothpick?"

"No, jumping into conversations. I mean, I'm sorry I jumped into yours."

They are sitting on a curb. Mona shrugs; and though Barbara can't see her, she must sense something, because she tosses her hair behind her shoulders, bites a cuticle, and tucks her two hands between her knees as if praying for a bathroom. "Tell me how I can make it up to you." She appeals to Mona with her dewy green eyes.

"It's all right."

"Aren't you mad? Aren't you upset? You know, sometimes I can hardly even tell whether you're upset or not."

Across the street, the trees buzz loudly with assorted winged bugs; Mona has never noticed before how loudly.

"Why don't you just go ahead and yell. I'll tell you what my mom would say if she were in your shoes. If she were in your shoes, my mom would look me right in the eye—"

"Kugel Noodle," Mona says. "I'm not your mother."

Barbara looks back down. "I know how I'll make it up to you," she announces finally. She speaks from behind her hairy curtain like a cross between Cousin It and the Wizard of Oz. "I'll give you my van."

"Okay."

"Or how about you can borrow it for a month? It's the end of the year anyway; I'll only have to walk to school for a bit. Plus I do have a ten-speed."

"Don't worry, I'll give you a ride."

"Thanks," says Barbara. And then to Mona's surprise, she actually hands over the keys. These are still warm from their home in Barbara's pocket; the key fob is a roach clip.

"Don't you need your house key?" says Mona.

"Forsooth! I did forget." Barbara accepts back the key to her house, also the key for the burglar alarm, and the roach clip. Mona puts the keys to the van on her own ring, which is boringly fobless.

"What am I going to tell the 'rents?" says Mona.

"Tell them this is America; anything is possible. And if they don't believe you, tell them the truth."

"Which is?"

Barbara smiles. "This isn't America. You among others are simply confused."

Haight-Ashbury, watch out! In the spirit of the day, they decide to go driving off into madness and anarchy as soon as their shift at the hot line is over. Why the simple fact of Mona driving should put them in mind of the Merry Pranksters is not clear even to them as they tumble reasonless outside, happy for an excuse to fix dandelions in their hair. Never mind that milk leaks from the stems, trickles down behind their ears. The road, the road, the open road! Will they pick up hitchhikers? They decide yes, of course, in fact they'll hunt for them; Barbara knows the streets with the best selection. First, though, they head prankishly for Mona's old hometown, where there is a great new burger place. What a day! Neither one of them has ever noticed before how musty the hot-line office is, though they do notice how twinkly bright and leafy is the rest of the world. They wind their windows all the way down. At stoplights, they lean out of the car and close their eyes, turn their faces to the sun so that their eyelids go red. They count floaters. The light turns, people honk. Barbara laughs and turns and blows kisses while Mona pulls slowly, slowly, maddeningly slowly, into the intersection. Hope they're in a hurry! Barbara giggles. They turn up the radio, they pretend they are Joni Mitchell. At the burger place, the girls prankishly ditch their diets, and down a whole thinga-majig of french fries each. And from there—since it's sort of far to Big Sur—they drive to a certain neighboring town, in search of a pond with a willow.

This town looks a lot like Scarshill, only infinitely more exciting. Old, green, lots of houses, landscaping. Ponds. Mona and Barbara circle these, making their inspection. Are there too many ponds? Too few? What about the willows? They try to look as though they are doing a school project. *Can you believe it?* they're going to say if they actually run into Sherman. *This biology teacher . . .* Et cetera.

Their actual goal is not to talk to Sherman. Their actual goal, what with Barbara in the car, is to spot him and run; they don't want to remind him of the phone call. In fact, Barbara has promised to duck if they see anyone remotely Japanese. She practices squashing herself down into the footwell, though she is hardly a handy fold-up size. But they do not see any Japanese people at all, only many white denizens, engaged in their sundry activities.

"Try the phone book," Barbara suggests finally. They stop at a phone booth. No luck. When they call up directory assistance, though, they find that a Matsumoto is indeed tantalizingly listed, under new listings. If only the operator would give out the address! Mona begs shamelessly. Barbara calls information again, and then again. But the stalwart operators prove dishearteningly true to their operating procedures.

"Call," Barbara urges Mona, holding out a dime.

Mona accepts the coin. In sad truth, though, being sixteen, she believes the boy should call the girl. Moreover, she believes Sherman believes this firmly and without exception—recalling as she does, for example, the button incident of long ago. Of course, that was eighth grade. Still she pockets the coin, climbs back into the van, and heads to the pancake house.

Cedric the cook waves his spatula. "Welcome, welcome to the two human beans."

An old joke; all the same, Mona and Barbara laugh. Being not-so-long-ago-from-China, Cedric has even more *pronounce-trouble* (as he puts it) than Ralph, and mostly it's legitimate. He's been known to ham his problems up, though, as if he considered his job description to include making Ralph's English look good. No one could exactly prove this. However, his pronunciation got noticeably better after he got his green card: He stopped saying "meck" for "make" and "tlaks" for "tracks." Now he yells at the busboys the same as everybody else. "Make tracks!" he says. "Don't give me no jive!"

"What kind beans we have today?" he continues, flipping flapjacks. He turns the hood fan down so he can hear them. "Green beans? Black beans? Soy beans?"

"Dried beans," they say. "Dried up and died beans. Tired of bein' beans."

"Oh," he says, still smiling. "Too bad." He is a round and genial man with a serene shiny face; in his chef's hat, he looks like a Taoist immortal trying to pass for a short-order cook. Today his smile tightens ever so slightly as he turns the fan back up, and Mona wonders if he's thinking about his family in China. Two children he's left behind, and a wife, and his parents, all of whom agreed he should grab his chance to get out. He promised in return that he would get them out when he could. But how is he going to do that, and when, and are they surviving the Cultural Revolution in the meantime? Listening to him has made Helen and Ralph worry anew about their long-lost families—about who is dead and who is alive, and who is being tarred, or stoned, or peed on. Cedric knows things they don't; he knows what to imagine—namely, anything. This Helen and Ralph can't quite do anymore. However, Mona can. When Cedric first arrived, she would regularly describe to him the goriest, grossest things, and ask him if the Red Guards would do that.

But seeing as how he hasn't had a letter in months, she has shut up. Also she knows the answer by now—always yes. There is nothing too gory or gross for the Red Guards. When it comes to torture, they appear to have a gift. And this is why Cedric has gone on sending his family money, even if he doesn't know if they'll get it. Ralph and Helen sent money for a long time too. They had no way of helping Helen's family, but they did know someone in Hong Kong to whom they could send money in the hope it would be sent on to someone else, who they hoped would in turn send the money to Ralph's family. Then one day something happened to the friend in Hong Kong, they never knew what—only that the special bank in Chinatown couldn't wire the money through. The first explanation was that the account was too full. There was no second explanation.

How lucky Cedric seems, to have someplace to send money! And to be able to write to his family! Never mind that they could very well be dead. He says he tells them everything except about his American girlfriend: Wendy, her name is, Mona sees her almost every day. A divorced social worker, white, not young, with a jalopy, and no snow tires in the winter, and three alarming kids. Rats her hair. Cedric says he will never marry this Wendy, and that this Wendy knows that. Still she waits for him to get off work, her motor idling. The kids hang out the windows, yelling, "Uncle Cedric! Uncle Cedric!" What kind of problems can Mona have, compared to what he's seen? Now Cedric rubs his feet together as though he has an itch in his left heel—a private gesture that goes with an even broader, tighter smile. An instant later, though, he seems returned to himself, a genuine friend again.

"Drag my cigarette?" he offers, winking. He nudges an ashtray toward them with his spatula. Barbara takes him up on his offer, and after checking on her dad's whereabouts, Mona does too. Cedric's not supposed to smoke while he cooks—it's against code—but he seems to have a butt going all the time anyway, he doesn't care what kind. When he's a real American, he says, he'll pick a favorite. For now he smokes anything that doesn't explode, which today means unfiltered cigarettes so strong Mona can feel the rush in her fingertips. Her head reels.

"Sit down, have seat," Cedric offers, as if they're guests. They wander out into the busy dining room and settle themselves in a booth. The table is sticky; Mona cannot help but think how she really should talk to the new busboy. First here comes Magdalena, though, with two banana splits so overpiled and goopy that one whole slope of whipped cream avalanches onto the tray.

"And what kind of behavior is this?" demands Magdalena of the ice cream, in her most rapid-fire voice. The ice cream doesn't answer. "Back to the kitchen!"

But Mona will not hear of the sundae going back anywhere, especially since the maraschino cherries have survived—bulwarked, luckily, by the banana halves. There are five cherries on each sundae, their stems sticking more or less into the air; their color bleeds into the whipped cream in a pleasantly psychedelic way. Capturing this effect, though, is no easy matter. Mona has to quick, snatch the sundaes off the tray herself before Magdalena can assert her standards. Magdalena retires in seeming defeat, only to reappear with a whipped-cream gun. "Ready or not," she chortles, exuberantly adding a whole new range of peaks to Mona's mountainside. Barbara's sundae likewise sustains some unexpected geologic activity. The girls agree to restart their diets tomorrow—a life ritual so agreeable that their real aim does not seem to be to lose weight, but rather to sighingly start and gleefully abandon their regimen with a friend.

Barbara leans forward like a school psychologist. "So what's the next step?"

"Nu?"

"*Sherman: The Search Goes On*. Will young Mona Chang ever get the man she deserves?" Barbara searches the ceiling as if the answer might be written on the acoustic tiles.

"*Seth Mandel: Fiend or Friend?*" answers Mona. "Sweet Barbara Gugelstein says that they're through, but can she just kiss him good-bye?"

"That's a book with just one chapter. I was in love; he was having an experience." Barbara's eyes fill with tears—not from the bottom up gradually, but instantly to the point of overflow, as if they have this routine down. Her handkerchief likewise leaps readily to hand. She mops up impatiently, heartily sick of being heartsick, as they review the possibilities in their grade.

"How come there's no one like *him*?" says Barbara, when Alfred the number-two cook comes in for his shift. For besides being a spatula whiz, Alfred is movie-star handsome from the neck up. From the neck down, he is trim, athletic, tall—more than he resembles Tarzan, though, he resembles a two-by-four. No, his fortune is in his head shot. Not only has he got the mysteriously sullen aspect occasionally broken up by the boyish big grin; he has the piercing gaze and steely jaw that put you in mind of dinner jackets and diplomats, maybe even Mount Rushmore, if you can imagine those chalk cliffs, brick brown.

What college does he go to? Mona says he doesn't, meaning that he did, but only for a month. "He said he couldn't see the point of it. He asked this professor what kind of car he drove, and it turned out the professor didn't drive any kind of car at all, he couldn't afford it. So Alfred up and dropped out. He said even he had a two-year-old Chevy with whitewalls, he thought the professor should be studying from him."

"How old is he?" asks Barbara.

"Twenty, twenty-two?" Mona further reports that he wasn't drafted because of something about his hearing. "You'd have to shout your sweet nothings."

Still Barbara moons.

" 'Lady-killer like him don't need to go to war, he notch his belt right here.' That's what they say in the kitchen."

Barbara continues to moon.

"And of course Andy Kaplan is out?"

"I told you before, we have the same backpack. Plus we got our moms the same present for Mother's Day." So Barbara says. But then she looks up, takes two shanks of her long hair, ties them under her chin, and makes a face.

"I see." Mona smiles tactfully.

For her part, Barbara points out that there are many people in whom Mona could be interested if she put her mind to it. "Even if you do end up marrying Sherman Matsumoto, there's no harm in enjoying yourself while he's Sherman Incommunicado, is there?"

Mona concedes that there are other fish in the sea. Benny Meyers, for example, who has a girlfriend, and Alvin Nickelhoff, who might as well have a girlfriend, being so in love with his model T Ford. "What about Chris Allefart?" Barbara says. Mona tries to have an open mind about him even though he's six-foot-four and descended from John Jacob Astor. They are still discussing how many inches true love can surmount when Andy Kaplan saunters in, hand in hand with Eloise Ingle.

Barbara looks to be doing brave battle with her tear ducts. But then Mona whispers, "Can you believe it? You've even been seeing the same person!" and Barbara has to laugh. She, quick, unties her hair before anyone sees.

To go with his height, Andy has developed a lumberjack's stride, and to extend the woodsman theme, he is wearing a red bandana on his head. (A lot of guys do this when they're hiking, to keep out blackflies—never mind that their moms did the same getup for them when they were pirates for Halloween.) Beside him, Eloise scurries. She is pre-Raphaelite as always, and takes what look to be three tripping steps to his one, so that for once her breathlessness seems a matter of breath. When they stop to say hello, though, it is Andy who flushes, as if from her exertion. Eloise coolly turns her front foot out, sits back on her hip, and with a little shake of her mane, lifts and angles her chin. She could be a Degas if the background weren't a franchise dining room.

"Well, if it isn't the Gugelsteiner and her better half." Andy bows. "Most honorable Miss Changowitz."

"Andy! El!" Consciously or unconsciously, Barbara is brandishing a fork in a manner that predates table manners.

"Have a cherry?" Mona says, filling in.

Andy Kaplan gives her a cuff. "Very funny. Where'd you get that wit of yours from anyway?"

"I'm afraid I'm a self-made mouth," Mona says.

Andy laughs.

"How long has this been going on?" Barbara asks finally.

"Oh, maybe a week. Would you say?" Eloise looks to Andy. "Three weeks, at most. I've been meaning to tell you."

"Really," says Barbara.

"But the moment was never quite, oh, how shall I say . . . ?"

"Right to break it to me?" Barbara's eyelashes begin to clump up with tears.

"What's this?" says Andy.

"How could you not have told me?" says Barbara.

"But it was quite impossible," says Eloise. "You . . ."

Andy Kaplan looks off into the air as if to make clear to some important observer that he, the male of the species, is in no way involved in this squabbling.

"I what?" says Barbara. "And what do you mean, impossible?"

"Nothing's impossible," Mona puts in.

Everyone looks at her.

"You just have to put your mind to it," Mona says. "Like the Little Engine That Could. Just repeat to yourself, I think I Chang, I think I Chang."

Andy laughs, Barbara smiles, Eloise is not amused.

"I was brought up to understand that it's rude to interrupt," she observes.

"That's for conversations. The rules are different for catfights."

Eloise glares.

"Uh oh," says Andy Kaplan, astutely observant. "Time to exit left?"

"I wish you would," says Mona, his accomplice. "You're bad for business."

Andy and Eloise turn to leave. Then Eloise pivots. "Will you join us?" she asks Barbara.

Barbara hesitates.

"It was not a catfight," says Eloise. "It was a tiff."

Barbara looks to Mona, who says, "You've got matters to investigate, I know."

And so it is that Barbara leaves Mona at the booth by herself, with more melting glop than one person could possibly get up an appetite for.

Mona is glad to see Barbara's van out in the parking lot, though the sight of it makes her feel even lonelier in a way. It's a good-time car, the kind of car that would talk to everybody at a party instead of standing under a spider plant all night, getting stoned and counting the spiders. She drives over to the temple to see what's up. Rabbi Horowitz is out. Brian Levi is out. Mona methodically reads all the cartoons on Brian's oak-wood door. She takes in the blinking, buzzing death throes of the overhead fluorescent light. Everywhere there are branches: She examines the menorahs in the glass case; the big brass tree full of generous-donor leaves; the mitzvah bush for the kiddies. The halls smell of fresh paint. There's a sign up for an afternoon drop-in rap. She's never gone to any of the drop-ins but figures why not try it.

When people show up, though, there doesn't seem to be anybody she knows very well. Confirmation isn't until next week, but already there's a new crowd, it seems. Has Brian been recruiting? Or maybe these are kids from the next town; the temple sits right on the border. Somebody says to her, "You sure you got the right kind of temple, now?" and though someone else rejoins, "Shut up, jerkface, if you had half a brain your head would tilt," Mona still finds herself examining the finer architectural details of the room. For instance, the all-metal radiator covers, now beaded up with air-conditioning condensation. The talk today centers around things like nose jobs—how the doctor starts with a hammer and breaks the bone, moving on to what he restructures, and where the scars are. It hurts, someone testifies, a lot. They go around the circle talking about why they would want to do such a thing to themselves, a serious subject until they get to her.

"Do Chinese have operations to make their noses bigger?" someone asks.

Mona laughs with everyone else before explaining that actually, yes, there are operations like that. She too envies the aquiline line, she tells them. In fact, she envies even their preoperative noses.

"You can't mean like this schnozz here?" somebody says, exhibiting his profile.

We-l-l, thinks Mona. Still she politely nods.

"Now, that's bad," says someone.

"And your eyes too," Mona explains, scrambling for firmer ground. This much she can say about herself: She knows her good material. She starts to explain how there are also operations to make single-fold eyelids into double-fold lids, then backs up to explain what that means—about how her eyes look the way they do because of subcutaneous fat, and how that's what the Eskimos have. Also how some people think the Chinese evolved for the cold, although Mona herself wonders, seeing as how most of China is hot. She leaves aside the related topic of the shallowness of her eye sockets, along with how tricky it is to wear eye shadow as a result, and how you have to use an eyelash curler to wear mascara. Her turn is going on too long. She fast-forwards to how lids can also be made to look double with Scotch tape (not that she's ever tried this herself); and she ends with a demonstration of her sidelong look. She shows them how, when she looks all the way to the side, one of her eyes appears to be in the corner of her eye, but the other appears to be in the middle.

"Wow," says somebody. "You look like straight out of the Twilight Zone."

"Jesus H. Christ," says somebody else. "How insensitive can you get?"

"I'm just sharing with you my honest reaction," says the first person. "I think you should thank me for contributing in an up-front way instead of—"

Brian Levi intercedes. "Anything else you would like to share with us, Mona?"

She considers a demonstration of how she can hang a spoon on the end of her nose, that's how flat it is. But on further consideration, she decides to save it for the temple talent show.

Barbara's white van shines in the late-June dusk like a truth made manifest. Mona's parked it away from the other cars, to be sure nobody backs into it or opens a door against it; Barbara would sooner die than the Big V should know touch-up paint. And in its solitude it appears even more possessed of some strange coherence—*Mingle not with me*. Of course, this is romantic projection on Mona's part. In fact, the van is only a van. What does it carry besides full replacement insurance?

Mona cranks down the window, and cracks the vent window too. She starts the engine; the radio comes on by itself. Some love song she's never heard before, but she finds that after a couple of bars she can hum along just the same. New song. Then comes the refrain—she could be Janis Joplin reincarnated with straight hair—when suddenly there's a bass accompaniment in the back seat.

She shrieks and stalls out in the crosswalk.

"You sing better than Barbara," says Seth Mandel. "But you let the clutch up too fast."

"What are you doing here?"

"Did Barbara give you her keys?"

"She did." Mona quickly restarts the engine. "She lent me the van. For a month."

"Well, she lent it to me too."

"Are you kidding?"

"I used to surprise her like this all the time."

"She never told me that." Mona glances up to the rearview mirror.

A smile-like opening appears in his beard. "Didn't she ask for the keys back when you broke up?"

"She did. But when I tried to give them to her, she was too mad to take them."

"And you are here today . . . ?"

"To try to give them back again, even though the whole concept of keys is totally bourgeois." He leans forward and gathers Mona's hair into his competent hands, lifting and draping the mass of it over the back of the seat. His forefingers brushing her neck are warm and dry and slightly rough, as though he is too much of a man to use hand lotion.

She shakes her head. "Excuse me."

He slides into the other front seat. "You smell nice."

"I do not smell," she informs him. "If you smell anything, it's yourself."

"Really." He lifts one of his arms as if to sniff his armpit.

"You are grossing me out."

"Just playing my part of the love scene." He winks. "We're into improv now."

"Let me set you straight. I'm not into communal property, and I'm not into free love. I'm into keys. Private property. Private enterprise. Banks. Safe-deposit boxes."

"Being a nice Chinese girl, you mean."

"Exactly."

"What happened to the big rebellion?"

"I had it, and now I'm a nice Jewish girl such as knows kosher from kosher."

"And I'm not?"

"Treif is your middle name."

"Such a nice Jewish girl, but already you are talking about eating me," he observes.

"Seth!" Mona is so embarrassed that she takes a bend wide, bumping the curb. Seth gets thrown against the door.

"We don't have to do this James Bond style," he says. "If you want me to get out, you can just stop and say so."

"Okay."

"We should probably take a look at the tire anyway."

What with the streetlight above them on the blink, it's hard to tell for sure, but the tire looks leakless. Seth feels one suspicious section, then rubs his hands on his thighs. In the poor light his blue jeans look gritty, as if they are some sort of denim-and-newspaper blend.

"I hear you are practically engaged," Seth says.

"Who says that?" Mona is thankful for the dark.

"Barbara."

"And what business is it of yours?"

"None, of course, but if you want to know what I think . . ." Does he leave off midsentence because he realizes she's about to start crying of embarrassment?

"Pray tell."

"I think you're a little young to be entering a bourgeois and bankrupt institution designed for the stultification of life-giving impulses." (At least he says this gently.)

"Thank you for the free advice." Mona takes a breath. "And now may I ask how you are going to get home?"

"It appears that I'm going to run."

He says this with an air of expecting to surprise her, when in fact Mona already knows not only that he runs, but that running is not Seth Mandel's only sport. He is also a cyclist, which according to Barbara does not mean puttering about with your chain falling off every time you try to switch your big gear. No, Seth Mandel will pedal the sort of distances that a Seth Mandel must—id est, eighty or ninety miles a day. He carries his own tool kit, and no one has ever seen him stand on his pedals going uphill. Is this what Nietzsche on tape will do to you? He says he believes that people are enslaved by their cars. In Turtle Wax he foresees the demise of the Holy American Empire. There is no article he holds in greater disdain than a chamois cloth.

So why then does he insist on giving Barbara's keys back in person? Why doesn't he just leave them for her—unless at some level he does not really want to return them? Mona broaches these delicate subjects as he tightens his sneaker laces.

"By introducing a random element to her car use, I help her maintain a level of consciousness about it," he claims. "I keep her from developing at least one of the sorts of habits people use to avoid living their lives."

"How interesting," Mona says. "Though it must also be convenient to have keys to other people's cars."

"That is a competing truth," he admits cheerfully. Then he strides away, ponytail bobbing up and down behind him. This is not a jog he is doing. He opens his legs so that they seem twice their normal length, and there's real gallop to his feet. His white T-shirt floats above his legs; his arms appear the arms of a soloist in *Swan Lake*. How Mona's ballet teacher would approve! Except he's no swan, of course. No—of course, he is Prince Siegfried, all he needs besides a jerkin and tights is to stop rushing the beat. (*Why do we race the music?* her teacher used to say. *Can we beat it and win?*) Mona watches him in the rearview mirror: He disappears into the dark, only to reappear in the next pool of streetlight. Disappear, reappear. Disappear, reappear. Really the sight would be just the thing for a one-year-old. Still Mona backs the van up slowly, watching, keeping pace, until in her absorption she smacks one of the side mirrors on a telephone pole. *Oy!* The mirror looks okay—only jolted enough to remind her that the vehicle she is driving is not her own. She switches gears from backward to forward, and heads home.

Mona means to tell Barbara about Seth. But at the last minute Barbara's parents decide to take a June vacation, and so, though it means doing two research papers without a library, not to say missing confirmation, Barbara is suddenly gone. Probably Mona could have interrupted her friend in her flurry to get ready. However, Mona hesitated, and just like that, her hesitation erupted like a spotty mildew all over her. For what was she thinking at that moment, but of how Barbara and Eloise could possibly be buddy-buddy again, and with Andy Kaplan too?

For the first few days of her van proprietorship, Mona parks her wheels out on the street, around the corner from her house. For the van, it's not that secure a situation, being just too close to the parkway exit ramp. All manner of Homo sapiens pass through—some of whom, Mona knows, have got to have the big eyes for a shiny new mobile. In fact, there have been articles in the Scarshill *Inquirer* all spring about this very subject. MAKE WAY FOR THUGS, read the headlines. PARKWAY

BECOMES LARKWAY. Mona knows she'll be doing some praying on the van's behalf. But what else can she do?

And as it turns out, the only real problem is that Mona sometimes gets it in mind to avail herself of her freedom and mobility, only to discover the van gone—borrowed, it seems, by Seth Mandel to sweat in.

She surmises this because on one occasion, he left a well-used gym towel on the passenger seat. On another, he very generously left his bicycle parked where the van had been; and how did it get there unless under the perspiring tush of philosophic enlightenment? Mona could not help but wonder, as she beheld Seth's black ten-speed, leaned against a tree, what Sherman Matsumoto would think of the sight. Seth had considerately lowered the seat so that Mona could use the bike if she needed to; it was just too bad that what she wanted was the van. Which he did eventually return. She found it at the mercy of the world—unlocked, windows down, all but out of gas.

Granted there were on the driver's seat five dollar bills, also a note explaining how he didn't notice the tank was low until it was too late to fill it up. Still Mona pictures Sherman shaking his head. *Boy, but that schmuck has got you in the bath,* says he. Says she, *Who asked you, and since when did you start with the Yiddish expressions?* Says he, *Bubbela, about the same time as did you.* He shakes his head some more. *Talk about no manners. Talk about no shame. Talk about no consideration for others. What do you see in that Seth that you've forgotten me entirely?* Says she, *I have not forgotten you entirely.* But he continues as if he hasn't heard her. *And what if Seth shows up again? Will you make him run home the way you did before? Or will you give him a ride to wherever he likes?*

With the car, several more incidents of the aforementioned ilk. Then it begins to transpire that Seth does not even return the car sometimes. Sometimes he leaves it wherever he happens to be going—in Scarshill Village, for example, or at temple. One day Mona leaves a note for him. It reads: *This is my car, seeing as how Barbara lent it expressly to me. Would you please knock it off?* He responds: *If you want to discuss it, why don't you call?* He includes the phone number for the teepee.

This is when, against her better judgment, Mona moves the car onto her family's driveway.

Helen notices.

"Barbara lent you her car? How could be?" Helen these days is not so much shocked as irritated—the general trend of their relationship, it seems. "Her parents said okay?"

"I guess they must have."

"How about insurance?"

Mona can tell this is not Helen's real concern. Helen is just stalling for time, trying to figure out what her concern should be. In a world where kids want new clothes to look old, not to say turn suddenly Jewish, it is no easy matter to sort strange out from strange. Still she tries.

Mona makes something up about the insurance.

"Just no more trouble," says Helen.

"Okay."

"Just send the car back to Barbara, say thank you very much. Tell her our family has our own car, practically brand-new. Only break down once in a great while."

"I can't. Barbara's out of town."

Helen helpfully suggests Mona should leave the van on Barbara's driveway until she comes back.

"I can't." How to explain about Seth? "It's not safe."

"What do you mean, not safe?"

Mona tells her there's something the matter with the locks—a calculated risk. Unfortunately, Mona calculates wrong. Helen encourages Mona to show her what's the matter; and sure enough, when Mona tries to demonstrate how the ignition key fails to open the door lock, Helen inquires as to the purpose of the other key on the ring.

"How do you like that," Mona says. The door opens wide, revealing the driver's seat.

Helen says nothing.

"So much for that problem."

Helen says nothing again, only to go on to a related matter—namely, how Mona thought she could get away with such murder. What is she becoming these days? What kind of daughter? Helen does not yell at first. She doesn't have to, in order to make herself clear, for what she means is already clear. And yet the more she articulates, the madder she gets. Pretty soon her eyes flash, and she does not close her mouth right on the last syllable of her last word, but a moment later, as an afterthought. For a moment her jaw hangs open, her lips open and relaxed, though the *er* of *daughter* has already left them; and whatever type of daughter Mona is, this makes an impression—how in her anger her mother has so forgotten herself as to assume the look of a largemouth bass. (*Close your mouth,* Helen always used to say. *Leave your mouth open, the fisherman catch you for supper.* It was one of the reasons she hated gum-chewing, that people not only chomped away, but more often than not did it with their mouth guts showing.)

But here she is, momentarily slack-jawed herself, a lapse. Indoors, her anger is a force of nature, inexorable; but out here in the open, it seems part of the afternoon—an interesting moment such as makes time seem not a forced march after all, but a regular change of scenery designed for one's improved mental health. Mona could be a tour guide: *Today we have the garage and the wall and the house and a mother, mad as all get-out. See how she has closed her mouth finally, though her body still seems to fill; she seems more fleshy than normal, as if her specific gravity is going up. She has of late been bothered by a tic near her eye, but for now it has stopped, and look again as she swallows. She sighs with a little gasp, as if surprised that her magnificence should require so much air. She turns and strides back to the house, leaving footprints in the grass. These are the light green of glowworms and produce a similar feeling of squirmy fascination.*

End of tour. Mona resigns herself to putting the van back out around the corner. In the meantime, though, it does stay for just this one evening on the driveway—Helen thinks it too late to bring the van to Barbara's. Ralph comes home; Helen is duly reminded of the events of the day; Mona has an astoundingly miserable supper in which the driveway is revisited and hostilities are resumed until Mona gets tangled up in the idea that she is indeed an etcetera, not like Callie who got into every college she applied to and then some.

It is the sort of evening when Mona learns for the first time how an unspecified number of colleges actually wrote to Callie and all but begged her to apply. Hinting broadly about what a strong candidate she was. Who is going to write Mona a letter like that? Ralph and Helen want to know. Who? And when a list does not readily spring to mind, they make it clear not only that even they, Mona's very own parents, wouldn't write her a letter like that, but that even they, her very own parents, wouldn't so much as send out an application on request if they knew just what kind of daughter she was. And so on in this tenor, it's the song of songs, you'd have to be deaf not to catch the refrain: *Not like Callie, not like Callie.*

Of course, of the two of them, Mona has always been the mouth. That's because Helen used to laugh at Mona where she would have frowned at Callie and said, *You don't know how to talk.* So that Callie turned long-suffering, as has been described—so well-behaved that people used to remark on the extraordinary way with which she did things like ride her bicycle. Now she rides rounded over à la Gumby like everybody else; those dropped handlebars don't leave you much choice. But she used to ride with the posture of someone who had just come back from ballet class, and was still pretending a string came out of her head. Even her faults were model faults, such as reading in bed with a flashlight, and secretly wanting to be normal instead of perfect. She has never gotten thrown out of class for talking, or otherwise made trouble; and all this because she was never her mother's favorite. Some people might think the exemplary behavior will make her the favorite eventually, and indeed it might. Other people might think it not right to have favorites to begin with.

But the Changs understand the basic structure in life to be the hierarchy. Better and worse, number one and number two, more loved and less. Even now, when they come home, Helen will prepare a dish and say, *For you I cooked shrimp and peas, your favorite,* whether it is your favorite or not. Indeed, whether you have a favorite or not. For you must have a favorite; if you do not, she will simply pick one for you, because this is the sort of fact they live by. And to understand how Callie got into all those colleges, you would have to understand how this sort of fact has kept her running the steeplechase all her life. *I earn my keep,* she said to Mona once. The unmouthed part of the sentence being, *Unlike you.* And these days, Mona can see better how Callie felt. For now Mona's been signed up for the family project too. After all, one generation is supposed to build on the last, ascending and ascending like the steps of a baby bamboo shoot; and how nice indeed for the parents to be able to say, "The girls go to Harvard"! Mona realizes this herself, the misty elegance of the sound—it lingers in the air like something out of a perfume spritzer.

·   ·   ·

Later, she gazes out her open window at the Trouble itself, white and innocent as a bathtub, as Sherman Matsumoto complains. *You've forgotten all about me.* Mona says, *I haven't.* He says, *You could care less about, say, Hershey, Pennsylvania, or wherever it is I've been recently. You don't care how big the chocolate factory is there, or whether chocolate can sweat. You have other adventures in mind.* Mona says, *Like what?* He naturally cannot answer.

Actually, she does wonder about Sherman in a long-distance kind of way. Will he ever call the hot line again? She wonders how she would feel if she were to call him to apologize. Would he say, *Thank you very much, I accept your abject efforts, let me tell you about my trip to the Grand Canyon . . . ?* Or would he say, *Please to go to hell, if I saw you in person I would flip you on the ground all over again . . . ?* In truth, he'd probably hang up. But what if Mona called and called? Wouldn't he finally have to talk to her, if only to keep his mother from asking nosy questions?

Mona sighs. The dark seems like heat to her tonight, a mysterious energy such as can turn one thing into another. Objects seem to be losing their edges and, slowly, their innards too. The van on the driveway begins to seem a hollow affair, more shell than motor, while around it, weird shadows wax energetic. Mona watches these sway with the trees. She listens as they jiggle with the lock.

She sits up. Lock?

A distinctive metallic sound that can only be Seth Mandel.

She has made her stealthy way down the stairs and out the house before she's had a thought. Whatever she's doing, she starts by putting her hands over his eyes.

"Hold it right there," she says.

He twists both her arms behind her back, so hard he's practically dislocated her shoulders.

"Ow," Mona says. "Seth." There's a large hand over her mouth, its fingers smelling of cigarettes; and then there's a patch of moonlight as a cloud blows by. The light is wavery but clear blue and bright enough for her to tell even through a stocking cap that this person is not Seth Mandel.

"Help," she tries to call. She tries to scream, but his hand is clamped tight. She tries to kick, but only manages to jab his kneecap with her heel. She can feel bone meet bone—also the brush of the hair on his legs. He's wearing shorts; Mona wishes she weren't barefoot. She wishes she were wearing shoes, or at least sandals. Her glasses have slipped down her nose; she can feel them slip more as he twists her arms up higher, tighter, forcing her body toward the ground. Her hair is everywhere, she can feel it caught in the crooks of her elbows; the front of her shoulders scream, also her wrists. Mona can feel her hands high against her back—an oddly placed warmth, like the squashy heat of his gut against her side, and now the twin hairy warmths of his legs, straddling one of hers. His thighs sweat, there should be an antiperspirant for legs. He smells of cigarettes, and something else—something thickly personal. Mona fights to crane her neck. She wiggles her nose, trying to work her glasses up closer to her eyes. Everything is a blur, but she thinks she can see her parents turn their light out for the night. She thinks she can see that their window is open. Mona tries to yell, and manages a small noise. She tries to bump her hip against the car, hoping that that will make more. She tries to scrabble her bare feet against the loose gravel on the asphalt.

And sure enough, the bedroom light turns back on. The bathroom light. Mona continues to struggle. Is that someone closing the window? Most anyone else would think it too hot to sleep with the windows closed. But Helen has never liked to sleep in a draft; she says it makes you sick to have something blowing on you. The bathroom light goes out again, and the bedroom light; and the dark that then drapes itself close over the driveway seems like no night Mona has known before. Even the brick wall disappears into it, gone. The man maneuvers her against the car. He rubs himself against her hip in a way she strangely recognizes. It is as though she knows this, what is this sweating thrusting rubbing; she remembers later that she'd seen something like this at the zoo—it was gorillas—and that her classmates all giggled when their teacher tried to explain what was a female in heat. *Oh, she's in heat,* they joked for weeks afterward, dismissing the teary prickliness of certain simple girls. They never considered what state the males were in, what name there was for this. *This is the forest primeval,* Mona thinks—not the right thought, not even quite a thought. She is locked stiff with fear, even as she struggles harder, using her legs. She can feel the warm asphalt crazing her feet. *I still have my clothes on,* Mona thinks, *I still have my clothes.* Even though a nightshirt is not exactly clothes. *I still have my glasses.* Grunting, gasping, then suddenly he lets go. Released, Mona shrieks; she pushes up her glasses and begins to run when she realizes that the man is headed for the brick wall, and that she can stop. For standing over her is who else?—but Seth Mandel, her avenging angel, bicycle pump in hand.

II

CHAPTER 6

Into the Teepee

She doesn't tell the parents. Instead she squirrels the incident away as if she were once again in second grade, drying a doll's dress over the kitchen stove. Back then she held the dress over the flame with a pair of chopsticks; and so satisfying was it to see how the skirt lightened and stiffened, that she almost didn't notice that the hem had caught fire. She threw the dress quick into the sink as it shrank to a one-armed blouse, and from there to a white puff sleeve with still-stretchy elastic; it had glued-on Swiss dots, like the flocking on wallpaper. The flames reached up to the sink faucet, but looked to be shooting out of the faucet instead—not like regular water, but like rust water after a repair's been made and the pipes have been finally turned back on. Which is to say that the flames seemed to start, then stop, then sputter and start again, in a way that seemed to promise better service with time.

This more recent event, of course, is of a whole different order. Still, her reasoning in keeping it to herself is the same. She thinks the parents will punish more than comfort her. She thinks they will prick her all over with questions, that the truth, when they heat her up, may steamily escape. For small example, why did she sneak up to that man? And suppose it had indeed been her crazy friend Seth and not a real live attacker. What was she intending? With no lights on, and the two of them alone but for the bugs. What is she becoming? She does not think they will ask how she saw their lights go on by a miracle but then turn off, or about the ensuing dark—about how strange a night it was, how violet and grainy. Mona thinks they will see instead what they would've seen if they'd known about her little doll's dress, swallowed up by flames—namely, their house burning down.

This, then, becomes a bond between Seth and her, that he knows something nobody else does. She might have told Barbara, if Barbara were around. She might have told Callie, if Callie weren't an automatic door with a big black mat, mouth-wise. She might have told Auntie Theresa in California, if Auntie Theresa were in New York instead. And she might have told Rabbi Horowitz, had he not been fired, it so happened, the very day of the incident. Unfortunately, he was. Fired! The exact same day! Also he disappeared, no one knows where, Seth says. Maybe he went backpacking. Or maybe he moved to Boston, where rumor has it he has been seeing someone with something the matter with her. Not a woman but practically a girl, goes the hearsay. Possibly a shiksa.

Is that why he was fired? Mona is outraged, even as the coincidence of timing between his firing and her attack snags her imagination; she cannot believe it to mean nothing in particular. She believes that out there, somewhere, in the machine rooms of the universe, there exists a small crossed wire. Once there was a short in her parents' car, she says, and guess what? When you turned on the blinker, all the idiot lights blinked too—idiot lights that they were. Everything is connected, weirdly connected. Hasn't Seth ever heard someone else talking on his telephone? A far-off voice, but definitely talking, and not to you?

Seth nods and smiles. *Yes indeedy*. But he goes on with his accounting of the firing, insisting that crossed wires or no, the possibly shiksa girl was only part one of the problem. Part two being the fact of confirmation coming up. The temple board wants a seemly affair, he says. Meaning no bare feet. Also, yes, an end to things like Chinese people turning Jewish, since she asks, but if there is a part three to the problem, it is probably the marriage service Rabbi H. did for a Christian couple. Nobody could exactly divine why two Christians would elect to get married by a rabbi; it had to do with transcending worldly allegiances, and really, everyone thought the ceremony just beautiful/ in the interests of world peace, except for the temple board of directors. Says Seth, arms packed up in front of him like camp-table legs, *You want to know what happened, that's what happened.* He says he's going to write a letter of protest.

"How is it that you know everything," says Mona, hating him for his details. There is nothing more annoying than being contradicted in detail. At the same time, he is not hateful at all. He is gentle, he is patient, she tells him everything. About the hands up her back, the wrenching. "Here?" He kneads her shoulders. He explains about her trapezius, her scapula, her deltoids. He has the warmest hands of any human being Mona has ever known; they could be the broad-palmed touch of the sun itself, except that they reach her in the dark. He says everything will be tender for days, and it is. He says that she'll ache, and she does.

It's the first time anyone's touched her so intently. It's the first time anyone's held her, stroked her, kissed her. She's surprised by the details. How much stretching and shifting of weight and arms, how much limb arranging, how much neck discomfort. Not to say unintended bumping, and mingling of body fluids otherwise thought gross. And how inconveniently placed is the nose! A chaperon to be worked around. Seth sucks and nibbles; he circles her face; he removes her glasses and knows to put them someplace safe. She has never taken her glasses off with someone before. His beard tickles and scratches. He kisses her eyelids, her brow, a pimple she tried to steam out. He returns aimlessly to her mouth, holding her head in his hands. The rest of her attends, attends, even as she wonders about the etiquette of teeth—of teeth clinking in particular, and of teeth exploring also—and is it proper to keep your mouth as wide open as possible, as at the dentist?

She had not known that the hairs on her arms could stand on end. She had not known her mouth to be so engrossing, much less wired to her breasts. Indeed, she had not even known herself to be possessed of erectile tissue. With Seth, lesser play leads quickly to greater. Too quickly to be proper. Her glasses are one thing, her clothes she keeps on. She allows and disallows. A nice girl, recalling all her mother told her—namely, *Don't let anyone touch you down there.*

Still she finds that she owns a whole self inside the self that she knows, someone sharing her skin. It is as if she's discovered that when she gets up each day, another self comes to sleep in her bed, except that her second self does not sleep. Her second self carries on in ways that threaten to bring the police. How common she is! For how else can it be that on early acquaintance, someone can know her so much better than she knows herself? She did not realize how wholly she fit the word *female*, just as she did not realize how partly she fit other words. How she's had to take them up, like the clothes in department stores. *Those are way long.* But everything is, all that matters is how they'll fit after she fixes them. Is she a proper best friend? A proper sister, a proper daughter, a proper student? None of those things. Between her and other people there has always been a moat of explaining, work and explaining, until now.

Some days she doesn't want him to touch her, and he doesn't. Other days they talk about what the man felt like, and what he did, and what she did, and how she felt, and it's like a temple rap session. At first she is shy. But later she boggles herself with the things she can say and do. Seth helps her by reenacting the whole scene. Sometimes they do it over and over, and in the dark, and it's like what happened, except that she can say stop when she wants, and cry. Seth gets shorts like the burglar's; he rubs cigarettes on his fingers; and sometimes the terror comes back. But other times, Mona wants him to go on. Other times, they kiss at the end, or more. She keeps her legs together; they roll together on grass, on carpet; she always knows where her glasses are. She keeps her clothes on, keeps her clothes on. He proves less shy about his. His largeness. She pets him the way she would a gerbil— marshaling up enthusiasm. Poor pinkish-blue thing, so veiny, and with only one eye. She is astounded by his hair. His hair gets caught in his fly zipper, she thinks he really ought to wear underwear. *I'm just talking sanitary.* A word she'd never thought she would need in an intimate situation. She is surprised when it comes out *se-an-i-tree*, she sounds exactly like her sixth-grade gym teacher, only without the bouncing of basketballs in the background.

But this is her prerogative, to use whatever words she wants, just as she can always say stop. She can always say, *Seth, you're becoming the attacker.* The attacker seems more and more to be becoming Seth; she can't remember things so clearly. He ran away, she remembers. She wishes now Seth had run after him, and caught him.

But Seth didn't run. He says he didn't care about vengeance; his care was for her. Anyway, the attacker was bigger than he was. Plus he could have been armed. The real mistake, says Seth, was in not calling the police, they ought to have informed the police. Although the parents would then know about her being out on the driveway, et cetera. They agree it's not great for the attacker to be at large. Should they file a report now? Would she know the attacker if she saw him? At first she isn't sure. Then she is. By the end of the week, she would have to say no. That stocking cap, after all. She could not point him out, no.

Between kissing with tongue their variety of body parts, Mona and Seth go to see movies. These are not the kind of movies Mona is used to. These are movies Seth considers *fine*—movies like *Women in Love*, and *A Clockwork Orange*, and *Claire's Knee*—movies where the people have highly unusual ideas. Some movies Seth likes, you have to go into the city to see. They are not even in color. He explains to her about sadism and voyeurism and onanism and other isms unlikely to be found in the vocabulary section of the SATs. She tells him she knows how to spell *diaphragm*. With a *g*, she says. She says she read a book about it, sort of. Not about how to spell *diaphragm*. A book with a diaphragm in it. He explains about conceptual art and why he hated *Fiddler on the Roof*. She does not tell him that she has the original-cast album and knows every song by heart. He gives her a book, *Notes from Underground*. This, it turns out, is not exactly *Love Story*.

Should she say so to someone who not only went to Woodstock but knows it wasn't in Woodstock at all, and who in addition marched on the Pentagon (never mind it was with his stepmother)? Seth can tell you why Bill Graham closed Fillmore East, not to say what is in napalm, and what they speak in Cambodia, and what you should call people who live in Laos. She thinks about how he got to the end of *Finnegans Wake* and sure enough started reading at the beginning again. She decides, Probably not.

But in the end she does anyway, figuring he'd most likely see through her if she didn't. For he's the type to see through things. Not only does he live in a teepee, for example, he soaps his hair once when he washes it, instead of the twice recommended by your average shampoo label. He claims once is plenty, the wily manufacturers just want you to consume more of their nice capital-producing product. Also he doesn't use regular soap bars, but a kind of peppermint liquid that comes in a squeeze bottle. And he uses just that one kind for everything—hair, underarms, clothes, dishes. (When he does his own clothes and dishes, that is, for example on camping trips.) Soap is soap, he says, the rest is just mind games. He says that if he had a job he wouldn't pay income tax, just like Thoreau. Why support the war machine and a capitalist system that requires ever-expanding markets and control of world resources? He says he doesn't believe the Russians are evil; in fact, sometimes he wonders if they're even Communist. That's just what the newspapers say, he says. Who knows what the truth is, or if Communist even means what we think.

"What else could it mean?" says Mona.

"I'm not sure. That's the point."

"Hmm," says she, admiringly. Only Seth could be so brilliantly ignorant.

As for things he believes in, these are for the most part sweat related. Running, biking. Sex and its warm-ups. Student strikes. Tutoring in Harlem, even right through the summer without air-conditioning. (That wasn't the hard part, he says. The hard part was deciding whether to agree to play Santa at the project Christmas party.) (He did.) Also he believed in Rabbi Horowitz, before the Big R.H. got fired; and though it's heavy on retribution, Seth's liked Judaism so far, what with its radical implications.

"What do you mean, so far?" Mona says. "What kind of way is that for a nice Jewish boy to talk?"

He grins his big crack-in-the-beard grin. "I am afraid I am an authentic inauthentic Jew," he says. "More ethnic than religious. However, in the process of becoming an inauthentic inauthentic Jew."

"Not to be confused with an authentic Jew?" says Mona.

"Exactly." Seth grins.

He says this foray into Judaism is one part of finding out who he is, and that this is why he didn't go to college—because he needs time to see what takes hold in him, what he does with himself. When he looks back on this period of his life, he says, he'll know more. As for his immediate future: He says he once met somebody who was hiking the whole Appalachian Trail, and that he thinks he might try the same thing, as a first step. So to speak.

"By himself?" Mona says. "The person hiked the whole Appalachian Trail by himself?"

"Herself."

"Alone?" A question close to what Mona means. A question she happens to have at hand, that shows interest, and not dismay.

But a few minutes later, when he is talking about the Northern Cascades, and how you can see caribou up there, and spawning salmon, and a starry sky worthy to be called the heavens, he says she should come with him sometime to witness these wonders. And this, she realizes, is as good an answer to her question as any she's likely to get. For Seth, no surprise, does not believe in love, but only in a kind of long-term mutual survival-related imprinting, not unlike what Konrad Lorenz described in geese.

Personal matters: She tells him all about the calls from Sherman Matsumoto, which it turns out he knew about but didn't know about. He listens. They pore over the log so carefully, it could be the Talmud in ballpoint.

"So he flipped you," says Seth finally. "So what? I can flip you too, if you'd like." And he goes on to conjecture what manner of ism that would be.

"That's not the point."

"The guy's not a person, he's an idea. Everyone's first love is an idea."

"Oh, really. And how would you know?"

"It just so happens I do know," he claims vaguely—talking, Mona guesses, about poor Barbara.

The teepee: Seth has a tent too, of course, with a rain flap and a window and a built-in floor, and that's what they would take with them if they went to witness prolific nature in the Northern Cascades. But here in the backyard he prefers the roomy ambience of his authentic canvas teepee, which he inherited from a brother he met at a peace rally. An *Übermensch*, this guy was; he gave a speech so powerful people were hugging total strangers by the end. And yet he was broke. He wanted to go on messing up the establishment, but all he had left in the way of worldly goods was this teepee in Tennessee. Hearing which, Seth gave the Joe—his name really was Joe—all the money he had. He even gave away his emergency traveler's checks, signing the whole wad of them with a fluorescent Magic Marker. Joe, in turn, wrote Seth's address on the inside of his forearm; and lo and behold, a month later, what should arrive in the U.S. mail but most of the teepee, everything but the poles. These the post office apparently refused to accept for shipping, as they were not properly packaged in a sealed and labeled box.

Death to the ornamental birches! Seth hacked down with an ax a clump of innocent paperbarks; the thunder of his efforts echoed through the yard, so loud the neighbors called. Which is how his stepmother Bea found out. (It occurred then even to Seth that maybe he should have consulted her first.) Still he went on to design his own lashings, using his ingenuity. And, voilà, the result: a living, breathing edifice that huffs and luffs like an asthmatic, but has yet to collapse entirely. In cold weather Seth keeps a fire going in the middle, and sleeps in a down mummy bag rated to minus ten; in warmer weather he sleeps right smack on some sheepskins, with nothing whatsoever between him and high heaven. He's talking about upgrading to a heated water bed. Mona, though, likes the sheepskins; she likes their smoky smell and their splat-flat shape, never mind if they're scratchy and reminiscent of roadkill. Also she likes hanging out in a room with a hole at the top. It's like the sukkah, except that in the sukkah there were chairs and other furnishings conducive to normal social conduct. Here there are only books, and a reading lamp, and a tape recorder, and a sky-blue princess telephone, push-button—leaving much room for mingling and commingling, and resultant strange tinglings.

Inner probings: He shows her his amalgam tattoo. *See it? All the way in there?* It's exactly the kind of oddity you can leave it to Seth to know about—that your fillings can leave tattoos in your mouth. Mona wonders if even daughter-of-a-dentist Rachel Cohen knows this. His is from the first filling he ever had, on a way-back molar. Flashlight in hand, Mona beholds with suitable wonder an iron-gray butterfly on his pink pulpy cheek innard.

"You probably have one too," he says. "They're common."

And sure enough, eureka! Hers is not so much a butterfly, though, as a most ghostly leaden egg.

. . .

More sensitive issues: Seth shares with Mona how the family stocks are doing, which is not at all well. Also how his stepmother has the money in the family—his father is not a mogul, actually, but a middle manager with more realizations that prospects. He's learning to keep his mouth shut, reports Seth with disgust. Seth tells her what percentage of the money is liquid, what percentage not, and what liquid means. *For example, stocks. Stocks are liquid.* He explains how his stepmother has gone short where she ought to have gone long, long where she ought to have gone short, and how she took a beating in the stock market crash.

"Crash?" says Mona.

Seth is dumbfounded. "A year, year and a half ago." The Dow-Jones, the price of gold, the devaluation of the dollar. "We almost had to move to Edgewood, where the Catholics live." He winks. "Then the market rebounded."

"Is that what Barbara's dad says isn't going to last? The rebound? Maybe your stepmother should talk to him."

But Seth says he personally wouldn't mind if his stepmother lost everything. It would only go to show that there was some justice in the world.

"Wait, what?" Seth's stepmother Bea seems like a nice lady to Mona, if you can call a lady a lady who does things like march down South for civil rights. To be honest, Mona admires her. Mona thinks it's nice she marched, especially since it's hard to imagine how much fun it could've been, what with the general lack of air-conditioning or even cold drinks out on those roads and bridges.

"At least she didn't have to wear riot gear like the police," Seth says.

"That's what she said."

"That's what she always says. She tells everybody that."

Does that matter?

A scene in Seth's backyard: Seth retires to his teepee for some peace pipe. Meanwhile, Mona (abstaining) chats with the stepmother at the other end of the yard. Said stepmother appears to know the whereabouts of her postadolescent but does not appear to mind. Neither does she appear to mind that this teepee business is sure to leave a big dead spot in the chem-green grass. For her three real sons have had rebellions of their own, and one of her friends has a daughter who moved to Germany—of all places, Germany! for a Jew!—so that to move to a genuine canvas teepee seems tame by comparison. So what about the birches? A tree is just a tree. Never mind that Bea planted those trees herself, and arranged the rocks around them in a ledgy look; this is the official line. "That all kids should leave home by staying home." She shrugs.

Now she swings back and forth on the old swing set. "At least we didn't have to wear riot gear," she says. A skinny-legged woman with a certain mid-body loft, she is soupy-eyed and pouffy-haired, and easily pushed by her ragamuffin granddaughter. "Would we have killed for a glass of ice tea? You bet. But you just don't think about those things." The wrinkled back flap of her sailor shirt balloons.

"You don't?" Mona says.

"Not if your heart is in what you're doing." Bea pumps a little, but her granddaughter protests, *No, Grandma, I push.* Bea relaxes. "What's the difference between a chicken and a pig at breakfast?"

Mona thinks. "One's a big sausage and the other's a yolk?"

"Very good." Bea laughs. "In fact, that's better than what we used to say."

"What did you used to say?"

"That the chicken's involved, but the pig is committed." She starts to pump again, then stops. "It took me a long time to learn that lesson. People think it's brains that makes a pig smart, but that's only part of it. Commitment counts too."

"Commitment counts too," Mona echoes, hanging on to the swing set herself.

What's not to like? It's true that Bea sometimes orders people around. On the one hand, she tells you to help yourself to whatever; on the other, she expects you to put your own dishes in the dishwasher, and while you're at it to give the counter a wipe. But that's just the flip side of her general disregard for what Helen would call the proper way to do things—easy enough to forgive when you think of her out marching. And to think of how she's allergic even to dust up here! Can you imagine the roads down there? Says Mona to Seth, "She must have been living on her inhaler."

Seth answers, "That's a different kind of dust, and in reality she's still a capitalist oppressor, committed to the principle of her own private property."

"Oh, really," says Mona.

"You're just seeing her guilty conscience," he goes on. He's re-lashing his teepee as he talks, using an idea that he got while stuffing kneesock dachshunds at temple. "You've got to understand that every woman like Bea has a cause. They all volunteer. It's part of their life-style, not to say a way of keeping clear of socialism. The great Re-publican way."

"But isn't Bea a Democrat? And I don't see how marching for civil rights is doing away with any government agency."

Seth thinks. "Touché." He smiles. "You got me there. Still, aren't we talking about housewives who just have to let the world know they don't work? Isn't it a status symbol?" He saws off the twine with his Swiss Army knife.

"They could spend all their time playing mah-jongg."

"It would be more honest."

"But not as useful for society, and maybe Bea is doing her best, given that she's no rebel. I think you should be proud of your stepmother that she doesn't mind getting dirty and thinks about higher things. Even if she does have a big house and a stock portfolio. Can't normal people do good, maybe even despite themselves? It's like what Rabbi Horowitz used to talk about, only the opposite. The banality of goodness. I think it's nice of your stepmother. I mean, my parents would never even go marching for themselves, much less for a bunch of blacks."

As soon as Mona says this, she knows she has on her hands a big wet fish.

"They wouldn't?" Seth is so shocked he leaves off his lashing.

"It's hard to explain," says Mona. "You've got to understand. I mean, people they've never even met."

"You mean your parents are *racist*?"

"No," Mona says. "That's not what I mean at all."

That night, though, Mona is party to a discussion about who could replace Cedric, if necessary. For sale in the next town is another fran-chise, a great buy; Auntie Janis is pushing Ralph and Helen to think about how to afford it, instead of how they can't. Price, however, isn't the only problem. There's also been trouble in the other staff, and Mona's parents are wondering—if they can get rid of the trouble-makers—where they're going to find proper replacements.

"Can't Alfred do Cedric's job at the old restaurant while Cedric does Cedric's job at the new?" Mona asks. Alfred Knickerbocker being, after all, the next-best cook.

But her parents dismiss the suggestion. "Cedric, we know who he is." They say this because it so happens Cedric's hometown in China was not far from Ralph's; they speak the same dialect. Moreover, by dint of some highly creative sleuthing, it has been determined that Cedric's uncle went to school with Ralph's second cousin's best friend's youngest brother. "Alfred, who is he?"

"Do you mean you can only trust other Chinese?"

"Not only Chinese. But other Chinese, you talk to them, you get a kind of feeling. More sure."

Make sure, more sure—the endless refrain of her parents' lives. Sometimes Mona wants to say to them, You know, the Chinese revolution was a long time ago; you can get over it now. Okay, you had to hide in the garden and listen to bombs fall out of the sky, also you lost everything you had. And it's true you don't even know what happened to your sisters and brothers and parents, and only wish you could send them some money. But didn't you make it? Aren't you here in America, watching the sale ads, collecting your rain checks? You know what you are now? she wants to say. Now you're smart shoppers. You can forget about *make sure*. But in another way she understands it's like asking the Jews to get over the Holocaust, or like asking the blacks to get over slavery. Once you've lost your house and your family and your country, your devil-may-care is pretty much gone too.

Anyway, there's another reason her parents don't want to have too much to do with blacks—namely, that they don't want to turn into blacks. *Come on, guys,* Mona wants to say. *Really! How can we turn black? Jewish is one thing, that's a religion.* Even her Bobby Seale-nik friends are finding the color row tough hoeing. But Helen's been testier than ever on this count, and all because one day some lady came into the restaurant with a petition. A clinic she wanted to establish. Birth control, prenatal care, treatment for venereal disease—the works, she said, and all for free or just about. A sliding scale depending. *And of course you people would be welcome.*

"Excuse me," said Helen then. She grabbed two menus and showed a party to their table, only to discover there were four of them.

You people, said the lady again, as Helen came back for two menus more. *Common cause.*

"We own this restaurant," Helen said in reply. "We live in Scarshill. You should see our tax bracket." And she very nicely showed the lady out. She didn't slam the door, that would have been rude. However, she let it clap shut by itself on its nice stiff spring, and later, at home, she said, "Can you believe that woman? What is she talking about? Venereal disease! Birth control! She want to lump us with black people!"

"Are you sure?" Mona said.

" 'You people! You people!' What people is she talking about, that's what I want to know. Is she talk like that to her friends?"

"But Mom, she didn't say one thing about blacks."

"You think you know everything," said Helen. "But let me tell you something. She is talk that way, you know who she is talking to? She is talking to us as if we are black! She is talking to us as if we are Negroes! She is talking to us as if we are—"

"Mom!"

"I can talk however I want," Helen said. But she didn't say what Mona thought she was going to say next. "If that lady can talk how she wants, I can talk how I want too. And make no mistake. We are not Negroes. You hear me? Why should we work so hard—so people can talk to us about birth control for free?"

And after that, she makes more observations about general character than Mona has ever heard her make before.

"Those black people, they just want to make trouble," she says. "Those black people, you never know what they are going to do next." And how similar the Chinese are to the Jews, all of a sudden! What with their cultures so ancient, and so much value placed on education. How are classes at the temple? she asks Mona for a change. What is she studying there? Mona explains about how the classes have stopped; it's a boycott on behalf of Rabbi Horowitz. *He was fired,* says Mona. *It wasn't fair.* Ah, Helen says, and is it true that Jewish mothers are just like Chinese mothers, they know how to make their children eat?

Mona, meanwhile, is interested in this clinic. Birth control for free! When will it open? Not that she is planning on sleeping with Seth, however well acquainted she is becoming with his very nice teepee. Other questions: Has Seth lit for her more dark chambers of his heart, explored with her more misty haunts of his soul than he has for/with Barbara Gugelstein? Should Mona care? What will be Barbara's surprised reaction when she comes home? And are Seth's true druthers for free love and an antibourgeois experiment in living?

Mona suspects this last because ever since the incident with the attacker, Seth has been only too glad to keep the van in running order. "You are really selfish," Mona tells him one day in a pizza shop. This is part of an argument about whether Nietzsche would order anchovies if they totally nauseated his companion. And this is early enough in their relationship that she expects him to flinch to hear himself so characterized. She expects this because if someone had called her selfish, instead of enumerating with feeling all the well-meaning ways in which she made life easier for other people at her own considerable and barely mentioned expense, she would have made herself write, *I shall be nice if it kills me,* until the pen ran out of ink.

Instead he wholeheartedly agrees. "I am," he says, and grins with approving satisfaction to see her freethinking.

Is this the same person who used to quote Kant? And is he ever going to move on from Nietzsche?

Once, Mona went with Seth and another couple to a concert, during which he spotted some other friends down in better seats. (This was the kind of concert where a few people were dancing in the aisles but most were dancing in their own paid-for spots.) The friends down below were waving and gesturing: There were two empty seats next to them. So what to do? Mona thought they should stay up in the rafters with the couple they had come with; or, if one couple were going to move down, she thought they should at least draw straws to decide which one. But before she could say so, Seth was asking if it was all right for he and Mona to leave. She could see his reasoning—he was friends with the people down below, whereas the couple they were sitting with were not. And that couple agreed. Still, Mona felt bad, and when she looked up, it seemed to her that the friends they had left felt abandoned. Seth said later that they had increased the social good by moving down, and that to be selfish was to be human. He had simply acknowledged his will to power rather than become a sick animal.

"That's two different arguments," said Mona. Adding that she thought he should try reading Jane Austen, or George Eliot. "Those were people who knew what was right."

"Those were Christian sops who didn't realize that they were enticed with social approval to give themselves away. Plus there is no good and evil, and G-d is dead."

"Why do you go to temple if G-d is dead?" Mona said. "And anyway, this has nothing to do with your philosophic enlightenment. This has to do with the fact that you grew up with a stepmother who assigns her guests chores like cleaning up their own bathroom. As a result of which, you have no manners."

"Manners!"

This is the kind of thing Mona has always believed: that you should never open a present in front of the giver, for example, since the giving is what matters. If someone presents her with a wrapped box, Mona says thank you. Never mind if she is dying to know what's inside. She acts as if she could care less, with the result that she does care less than she otherwise might. For how you act influences how you feel; she believed that completely even before she became a Jew.

Meanwhile, if someone presents Mr. Authentic Self with a box, he says, "What is it?" Then he opens it, and if he likes it, he says, "Oh, wow." Otherwise, he might say, "Oh, man, this is just like the one I got from So-and-so." Which he says is just an honest response, in keeping with what he believes—that between the inside person and the outside person there should be no difference. He does say thanks if he feels thanks, and he says please when making a request—or, more accurately, he says *if you please*, like his father, the most solicitous human being ever to walk a golf green. But whereas Mona worries about the gift-giver's feelings—don't those matter?—he worries that he remain true to himself. *How self-centered,* Mona says. She says what her mother always says—*You have no consideration for others!* But he is simple as a sack of potatoes. There should be no front stage and backstage; to have a private face and a public face is to be two-faced.

"You mean everyone should be up-front," Mona says. "Like Thoreau. Everyone should have one set of clothes."

"If they wear clothes at all."

This is what she will say to him, years later: that that was a nice experiment Thoreau had in the woods. However, in the present-day world there aren't enough ponds to go around. There isn't room enough in this country for everyone to be authentic all day long. We need to have *consideration for others*. Or else what will we have but what we have? Fisticuffs without cease.

For now, though, she just shakes her head, enjoying their anchovy-free pizza.

"People should say what they mean and mean what they say," he says.

"They should let it all hang out, right? This is the age of Wood-stock. We are the stars; we don't believe in shoeshines."

"Very funny." Seth reminds her of how Rabbi Horowitz used to say that the inside of a person should fit the outside like a hand in a glove.

"Rabbi Horowitz was talking about moral action," Mona says. "Remember? All that stuff about the first letter of the Bible, and how *bet* was shaped like a horseshoe laid on its side, and how if you were standing in it, there was nothing to do but go forward." *Do not ask what's above,* he said, *or below, or behind; just go.* "He meant we should act on our beliefs. It had nothing to do with manners."

"Hmm," says Seth.

If only they could ask Rabbi Horowitz himself! (They've written him a letter, care of the board of directors, but who knows if it will be forwarded.) "Where do you think he went?" Mona asks later. "And are we going to picket confirmation?"

"Of course we'll picket," promises Seth.

"Let's have a sit-in too." She drapes herself over his back like a sweatshirt with legs.

"We can organize it together." He knots her arms around his neck.

And so, in a few days, they do.

Another true story: Mona once went to an exhibit on Chinese portraiture, in which only the faces of monks were depicted in all their idiosyncratic detail. Members of society were depicted in terms of their activities and their clothes, which was to say their rank. For these clothes were not about self-expression; these were closer to uniforms. And that was what mattered—not these people's inner selves, but their place in society. At least to the artists who drew them. But what about to the subjects? Mona was with a friend that day, who thought that if the people portrayed had drawn the pictures, they would have presented themselves very differently. Mona wasn't so sure, though. Mona thought they would have liked to be seen in those beautiful gowns and high-status silks. For she understood what mattered most to the people in the pictures as if it still mattered most to her: not that the world would know them for themselves—they would never dare to dream of any such thing—but only that they might know that they belonged, and where.

CHAPTER 7

Social Action Comes to the Pancake House

Barbara Gugelstein is sporting a fine new nose. Straight, this is, and most diminutive, not to say painstakingly fashioned as a baby-grand tchotchke, if a little blue and green. Mona does not gasp with immediate shock, though for support she does lean a bit against the warm and stable van. "Barbara!" she says, in so many words. Mona returns to her friend the van keys, saying, "Thanks so much for the vehicle, which I enjoyed and didn't scratch and just had hot waxed at that place on Central Avenue." In short, she does not immediately say, Barbara, don't you realize you will be excommunicated from the Temple Youth Group just for starters? That is, if Jews do excommunication. Instead she says, "What a surprise. And here I thought you were going to the beach for a suntan." She says, "How nice, and so little swelling." Barbara's face is in places colored to match her nose; Mona admires her friend's nostrils, which are a triumph of judiciousness and taste. Really, it's a shame to think about them used just for breathing. Also Mona notes how much more attractive are small oval nostrils than their large round counterparts—small oval nostrils conveying a certain hairlessness that large round nostrils can never quite attain.

"Don't you think that's true?" Mona presses Barbara to agree or disagree, in any case to talk. In the spirit of friendship, Mona figures she'll back into the truth later and with tact.

Seth arrives on his black bicycle. *How vain,* he says, in not so many words. *How shallow.* His hands sit square on his handlebars, his fingers lined up like a most knuckleheaded jury.

Barbara flees into the garage. This is through a side door, since she does not have handy her remote control opener. Her new nose she cups in her hands.

"It was my mother's idea," she sobs. "She said I should have the tip sculpted, it would be so nice. She said she knew the surgeon, nobody would even notice. Especially with the summer to forget what I looked like. It was only because of a cancel that we could even get in with this guy."

"Oh, Barbara. I almost didn't notice, I swear."

"She duped me!" Barbara's eyes are so puffy, she could be a blow-fish with hives. "My own mother! And now everyone will say how vain I am, and how shallow, just like Seth said."

It turns out that this is all related to her mother not wanting to talk Yiddish, or to vacation on the east coast of Florida, where she claims there are too many Jews. "She said they spent their whole lives getting out of the ghetto, why should they go back for vacation? She's anti-Semitic," Barbara cries. "My own mother!"

Mona locates some Kleenex in one of the cars. These are the boutique kind that come in a cubelike box—a kind Helen would never consider buying even for their best drop-in guests.

"What about bangs?" Mona is thinking *distraction*: Let people sensing something ascribe it to a change of hair. Is this not a helpful idea?

Barbara, though, is not ready for a helpful idea until after lunch. She polishes off some yogurt with granola. Then, with the slightly shiny look of someone new-basted by the brush of divine inspiration, she says, "Bangs."

To the hairdresser! It turns out Barbara has always wanted bangs. She just never had them before because they put too much emphasis on what she calls her proboscis.

"Bangs are feature-enlarging," agrees the hairdresser. A baby doll in a beehive, she sports white lips and go-go boots. "See the new emphasis? How they bring out those baby greens?"

Mona and Barbara drive home singing songs. They discuss how Barbara is going to keep her new bangs from frizzing up. They part two happy friends.

But in the teepee that evening, by the light of a pillar candle with a painted-on peace dove, Mona says, "You were cruel and unfeeling. Barbara will probably never speak to you again, and I can't blame her."

She and Seth rehash their argument about manners. Says he: If you had any respect for Barbara, you'd have told her the truth. Says she: If you'd had any respect for her feelings, you'd have thought twice about hurting them. He calls her liar. She calls him jerk. The head of the peace dove caves in, olive branch and all. Mona slaps at herself, noting how even the mosquitoes choose her over Seth, that is how truly thick of skin and skull he is. For once the lovers do not make up with feeling and fond fondling.

And what happens? A jolt. Three days later, Barbara announces in the privacy of her kitchen that she is once again in love, unfortunately with who else? This is over twin dishes of crunchy peanut butter with vanilla ice cream. Barbara's nose by this time approximates its normal color.

"After what he said to you?" Mona says. "And what about Andy Kaplan?"

"Andy Kaplan," Barbara says vehemently, "is the brother I thankfully never had."

"Really," says Mona.

"He and Eloise broke up."

"Such terrible news."

"Now he's going out with Danielle Meyers."

"Danielle Meyers?" Mona, like Barbara, has always assumed Barbara to be Andy's very close second choice. "But I thought he went to Colorado to do Outward Bound."

"She went too. On purpose, I swear. And you know what all that singing around the campfire leads to. They're going to start a band—get that. She can't even sing on tune, or at least she never did in Concert Choir."

"Maybe she's not going to sing. Maybe she's going to play guitar."

"I hadn't thought of that." Barbara looks even more despondent. In fact, Danielle is such a great guitar player, she's gone on to twelve strings; six weren't enough for her. Mona wishes she'd made some crack about Danielle eating the mike instead. That is, at least, until Barbara says, "I hope you don't mind."

"Mind?" Mona's mouth gloms up with peanut butter. "Mind what?"

"About Seth." Barbara puts her hand behind her waist to feel the ends of her hair.

"He's not my property."

"I don't mean that I should go out with him too."

"You don't?"

"Oh, no," she says, tilting her head back some more, so that her hair falls to her hips. "I wouldn't do that to you. Plus I don't think he's interested in me anymore. He even gave me my car keys back. That's how little he wants to have to do with me, ever since . . ." She straightens, pointing to her nose.

For this is how she talks all the time these days: "ever since . . ." and "before . . ." More than ever too, she seems to be considering who she is, picking out her personality. When they repair upstairs, for example, Mona sees that Barbara has not only moved her records and gotten rid of her bedframe, so that her mattress rests straight on the floor, but also that she's changed the wallpaper. In a hostile manner, her mother has said, and indeed the style does seem antiparent—a Day-Glo-yellow op pattern swirls around so vividly that the walls seem to be pulsing, rolling, heaving in waves. It's a phosphorescent ocean such as you just hope doesn't glow by black light. Mona and Barbara discuss in detail how Barbara had this all hung without her mother knowing; and over the next few days, it becomes apparent that the fluorescent ocean is only one part of a much greater sea change: For every morning now, Barbara looks in the bathroom mirror and just wants her old nose back.

On account of Harvard-Radcliffe getting out so much later than other schools, Callie's had to go straight from exams to her summer job in Rhode Island. As for why she needs to go to Rhode Island to waitress, who knows? Ralph and Helen inquire politely. Why doesn't she waitress at home? But Callie makes so much of how everybody working at this resort is either from Harvard or Yale that they begin to feel she is practically getting a joint degree. And while lots of their friends have kids in Ivy League schools, who has a daughter going to Harvard and Yale both? In truth, there are a lot of waitresses from nearby Brown too; but Callie knows better than to dwell on a hippie school where everything is pass-fail so you can't even tell the A students from the rest. Also not dwelt upon, except literally, is the golden crescent beach with its sparkly azure wavelets. These Mona has heard about from Barbara Gugelstein, who it turns out has stayed at this resort before.

(Not that the Gugelsteins ever went back; Barbara says her dad didn't like it because of the beach towels, which in more generous moods he said appeared to be genuine Yankee heirlooms, passed down through generations and fashioned in the Puritan manner—i.e., without undue use of cotton. In less generous moods he called them Greenwich dishrags—for instance, to the attendant at the bathhouse, from whom he always demanded three of them: one for his overused head, one for his much-abused tush, and one for his foot-to-shin area, which after all were with him on vacation too.) All the same, by the rays of the no doubt mind-improving sun, Mona hopes, perhaps toward the end of the summer, to be illuminated. In the meanwhile, Callie the sophist has been working on her schedule, until finally she has traded enough breakfasts and dinners and buffet luncheons so as to be able to come home and practice her Mandarin for a few days. Of course, she's been speaking it all semester. But she hadn't wanted to unveil her new skills until she felt more confident. She says she still doesn't feel very confident.

However, by day two back in the house, she feels confident enough to tell Chinese from Chinese; it turns out English isn't the only language the parents speak with an accent. "I can hardly understand them," she sighs when they've left the room. "It's because they're from Shanghai. They say *san* for *shan*, *si* for *shi*. Plus I swear they're talking too fast on purpose." And in fact, they are; Mona has noticed this too. In the beginning they seemed just to be having trouble talking as slowly as they needed to. Habit, they said. But now it seems as if they don't exactly mind demonstrating how fluently they still do speak after all, accent or no accent. This is unconscious. They don't intend to put phrases by Callie in the manner of the Harlem Globetrotters. All the same, it's pick 'n' roll and around the back and plain through the legs sometimes, and all because, though Callie's trying not to make a big point of it, they sense that the language she's learning to speak is not their language at all.

"Harvard Chinese," Ralph jokes. "Not like how we speak, right?" He winks. "What Callie learns, every word is standard Chinese. As if she is come from Peking, not some low-class Shanghai guy, all he understands is money. She is speak some real Chinese. Classical stuff."

To which Helen replies, "What do you mean, our Chinese is not real Chinese? Shanghai people are just as good as Peking people."

"That's not how they thinking at Harvard," says Ralph. "You are so-called native speaker, but do they ask you go teach there? The answer is no. Because how we speak, that way is not so standard. You want to know how the correct way sound? You can ask Callie. She can give us lessons." He laughs. "Come on, Callie, you teach us. What means this character here, huh? Can you tell us, please?"

They all laugh, but not too much later, Callie is complaining that instead of speaking too fast, they are now saying a few words and then losing interest. They don't have the patience, she frets. Plus Ralph thinks learning Chinese is basically a waste of time.

"Has no use," he says.

Of course, in good time, even Ralph will be affirming his heritage; in good time, even he will be celebrating diversity in this, our country the melting pot—no, mosaic—no, salad bowl. Mostly this will mean writing checks. He'll be too old for going to unity dinners, and he won't be too sure what everyone is talking about, anyway. Community? What community?

For now, though, he would rather see Callie study engineering. Or accounting: "Even people lose money, they still need make report," he says. "Somebody need to figure out where is the trouble, how much the trouble cost."

Callie tries to explain to him about how Harvard doesn't offer accounting, or engineering either.

"I thought Harvard is supposed to be the number-one school," says Ralph.

Helen explains "what is so-called liberal arts education," and he nods at the end of the explanation. But the fact remains that Callie's best conversational opportunity is still Naomi, who thinks it's great for Callie to be in touch with her ancestry. *Forget your parents,* she says.

"But aren't my parents my ancestors?" says Callie.

"Only if you so choose." Naomi herself claims for her ancestors a number of people not related to her—for example, Harriet Tubman and Sojourner Truth. These are famous people of whom Callie is just now hearing. Luckily, another ancestor is Roberta Flack. Callie and Naomi attempt to discuss in Chinese what a moment it was for Naomi, seeing a natural on an album cover.

"*Zemme shuo* powerful?" says Naomi.

Callie has no idea, either.

"Do you think my fourth tone still sounds wishy-washy?" she asks, and when Naomi answers, she sighs. "I'm never going to speak as well as you," she says. "Let's face it."

For work, Mona is likewise working in a restaurant, only hostessing. And *naturellement* at the pancake house, where to keep herself company, she gets Seth a job waiting table. This is after he gets into a fight with his boss at the gas station—the problem being, according to Seth, that his boss was a fascist. Benito did breath checks on his employees every day; also he inspected their pupil size and kept track of their bathroom breaks. They had to sign in and out, says Seth, and though they were not required to write down what they did in that interval, Seth liked to note a little 1 or 2 next to his times. This baffled Benito at first.

Then Seth was called into the office. "I just thought you'd want a complete record of my activities," he said.

What next? Mona agrees to talk to Ralph about Seth waiting table. In principle they have only waitresses at the restaurant, no waiters, but no sooner does Seth get wind of that than he naturally absolutely has to work out front. Mona tries to talk him into salads, but he claims he has never held an iceberg lettuce without feeling an urge to bounce it off the wall; and such is the power of suggestion that Mona soon finds that she too is having trouble taking iceberg lettuce seriously as a food item. More and more it looks to her like someone's failed agricultural experiment, or like the inside of something else, the zip-out lining of a raincoat trying to pass on its own.

Mona makes Seth's case to Ralph. How useful to have someone with extra-long arms, he'll be able to balance more dishes than anybody, she says. He can specialize in large parties. And when the ice cream barrels run out, he can change them himself instead of complaining until the cooks go nuts. This last, Mona knows, is a particularly potent argument, as sometimes the front freezer ends up all but empty. *Pistachio or nothing,* the waitresses tell the customers. *Take it or leave it.*

But Ralph, though hardly insensible to this problem, is not fooled by its prospective solution. "Is he so-called boyfriend?" he asks suspiciously, feeding a large sheaf of paper into the jaws of his clipboard.

Mona answers, "Sort of"—how to explain?—and braces herself.

The first time Callie brought a guy home, Helen locked the screen door after he left, and then all three door locks, and this just because he asked how old was the bottle of warm beer they offered him. (Also, when they told him ten years, he asked for water.) *Typical American no manners!* said Helen when he left. And Ralph agreed, saying it was a good thing the kid didn't stay for supper; you could tell he was the type who put soy sauce on everything.

But Ralph is, as ever, given to changes of outlook. "In that case, he can work however he wants," he says with a wink. "Just remember: no kiss in front of the customers."

Helen is less sanguine. "That boy good for nothing!" She tells him to cut his hair, he looks like a girl from the back. She tells him to shave his beard off, he looks like a gorilla from the front. And what college is he going to in the fall? Seth says that he's not going to college, he's taking a thirteenth year at Eton instead. This is a joke. He says this expecting Helen to say, "Eton?"

As she does. "Eton?"

But when he starts to explain what is Eton, an explanation that involves a punch line, she says, "That's the place where the gunboats come from." And from then on, she glares at him as if to say she knows an old empire type when she sees one, and cannot be fooled by any amount of hair.

Seth is not the only person Mona gets hired at the pancake house. No sooner is he stomping up and down the aisles in his hair net (complete with bobby pins, this is, a victory for Helen) than Mona manages to get Barbara a real job too. Over this, Barbara is beside herself. Originally slated to spend the summer chez 'rents, she decided on account of the nose incident to stay home by herself. *Think of the beach,* her parents pleaded desperately. *Think of the new outdoor shower.* But when Barbara's cousin Evie volunteered to come live with her, they sighed and gave up. Evie the Responsible, after all; they'd always hoped for a little Evie to rub off on their Barbara. It was just lucky that Evie was coming East for some photography course. Who knew but that they just might return to new wallpaper?

And so it is that Barbara comes to hang out at the pancake house all day. When a waitress quits, Barbara hardly even needs any training to sub in. She already knows a German pancake from a French; she knows how to jiggle open the walk-in door; she knows only a rookie checks the bottoms of the syrup jars by looking, you have to feel them to be sure they are clean. Plus she knows the lingo—who the wheel is, and that she should call him sir. She knows that to order a Denver omelet she should say, *Mile-high city, and make it pretty.*

No sooner does she settle into the official job, though, than it turns out someone is desperately needed on salads: Saint Manny of the holy demeanor has unfortunately decided to move to the city, where his girlfriend lives. (He's going to put her through music school or die, people say, apparently she's some type of genius.) And so Barbara good-naturedly just switches, even though white people generally work out front. Other staff members point out how she isn't going to make as much money in back, but Barbara of the new nose shrugs.

"This is fun too," she says.

"Fun?" says Alfred the number-two cook. "You can't have no fun, girl. This here is your *job.*"

But having any kind of job is fun for her—never mind that she gets to work with Alfred the Handsome. To watch, you would never believe her once under the spell of Eloise Ingle. For Barbara positively thrives on the cutting up of carrots and cucumbers, and yes, even iceberg lettuce; and pretty soon she's thriving on the company too. *Alfred! Cedric! Darryl! Seymour!* Before you know it, she's greeting them like the oldest of friends, even the dishwashers. *Rhumba Rick! Jack of Hearts! Why, if it isn't the Moriarty!* She's lending them records; she's sharing her dope; she knows names for the busboys Mona's never heard before. *Darryl-darryl-do!* for example, and *El Commandante!* She's even making up names, names to which the people addressed duly respond. Can this be old Kugel Noodle, lately of the nose job? The staff calls her Miss B.—not for Miss Barbara, but for Miss Blanco, which sounds like an insult but isn't actually. Mona shakes her head, flabbergasted; Barbara might as well be giving her van away for good this time.

The staff is an assorted bunch, prone in general to changes in life status. They end up in and out of jail; they move out of state without notice; they break their limbs and facial extremities, or have them broken for them. Always there are losses to contend with. They lose their cars, their licenses, their leases, their kids, their welfare, their watches. They lose their willpower, and go back to drugs; they lose their minds, and knock up their girlfriends. They lose their temper. Once, a cook and a busboy cut off another busboy's ear, it was even in the newspaper. (*Those guys rough, that's I can tell you,* said Ralph.) Yet none of this much ruffles Cedric and Magdalena, the unofficial overseers, who expect from their previous life experience to always be pinch-hitting. Whereas Magdalena is an ever-faithful reporter of events, though, Cedric doesn't necessarily tell Ralph about so-called *everyday crazy*— things like Seymour's friends taking up all the parking spots while they wait for him to get off work. For Cedric, these things are like the details of the franchise magic mix. He says Ralph doesn't care what's inside, just so long as when you add water, it works.

Or so Barbara reports from the kitchen. She brings new kinds of cigarettes to the waitresses to try. She explains to the busboys just how rich she is, describing all about her house, and the four-bay garage. She counts up how many gardeners her dad's gone through this year.

Meanwhile, Seth and Mona make out in the pantry. This may well be a step up from the hot-line utility closet, who knows. It most definitely is not the teepee, however, what with all the cans and boxes— *Peaches in Syrup. U.S. Grade A Kidney Beans. Steak Sauce.* There is also the time-to-time threat of getting busted by Helen or Ralph—which prospect, of course, Seth pretty much adores. For him, confrontation is *confrontation!*—while Mona is just glad that the parents are these days engaged, once again, in considering that second restaurant. They had recently definitely decided they absolutely couldn't swing it. But then Auntie Janis found out about a new road going in, practically right up to the welcome mat. Now they're definitely deciding again. This has entailed investigations. Exit ramps, gas stations, preexisting HoJos. Average number of storms a year, and do storms really make people pull off for coffee?

There are all the same a number of false alarms in the pantry, including an avalanche.

"O brave new world, that has so much Jell-O in it," sighs Mona, from under a pile of boxes.

The love doves finally give up, and on their breaks retire to the attic storeroom instead—a spacious if warmish hangout, sumptuously outfitted with a table fan, a netless Ping-Pong table, and crates such as leave your tush most decoratively indented. It reeks so charmingly of cigarette smoke that Mona wonders why anybody bothers to light up. There are no windows; the ceiling slopes. When it rains, the metal roof sounds as if it is being pelted with gum balls.

And yet hanging out there is fun, if only because Barbara's new nose has indeed brought her to life, just as her mother planned, only as a Jew above all. She has decided to go work on a kibbutz with Rachel Cohen next summer; she's saving up to pay for her own airfare. In the meantime, a mitzvah: She is thinking civil rights right here in the restaurant.

Why would she want to go plant trees in a desert? She makes a most careful explanation to her new friends, especially Alfred, who speaks more freely to her than he ever did to Mona. For example, on the subject of how he cannot understand this desert-tree thing, even if the land did look different back at the time of the Bible. That was a long time ago, he points out, and he hasn't heard of nobody getting rid of no cars just because there weren't none at the time of the Bible. However, Alfred can certainly understand Barbara's wanting to get right out of this, our sweet land of liberty.

Seth says, "You mean, like you yourself would like to make like a hockey player and get the puck out of here."

Alfred's laugh seems to come from deep in his chest. "You motherfucking got it, man, how do you like that."

People discuss Israel with more curiosity than animosity, even though they are vaguely pro-Arab. Meaning that what they mainly want to know is, Why do Jews live in the United States, if they already have a homeland? Barbara endeavors to explain among other things how there's a war going on in the homeland, it's not all apple pie. Also she's not sure she'd want to actually move to the homeland, the Law of Return notwithstanding.

"It's like you could probably go back to Africa if you wanted," she says, poised on one corner of her crate. "But what about your friends and everything? Just because a place is your homeland doesn't mean you would feel at home there."

"I know a cat who says we ought to go anyway," observes Alfred. He's stacked two crates together so that they form a kind of stool.

"Hang out with our black brothers and sisters. Because there ain't no way whitey is ever going allow us no elbow room here. That's what my brother Luther says. He says there is only one reason to stay in this here country, and that is to bring down whitey's government. Black power!" He raises his fist.

Some of the other staff raise their fists too, in laid-back solidarity.

"But say you really had to move to Africa," says Barbara. "What then?"

Alfred shrugs. "They speak English there?"

"That's what I mean," Barbara says, tipping her crate so that the back edge leaves the floor. "I don't speak Hebrew. And there's no Holocaust going on now, and I'm not on that ship the *St. Louis*, and this is not the attic Anne Frank got stuck in. I think every Jew should visit Israel, and try a kibbutz, and make a donation. But does that mean everyone should live there?"

She backs up to explain who was Anne Frank, and what was the *St. Louis*, and what is a kibbutz. Alfred breaks out a cigarette, but waits until the fan rotates by him to light up. For an ashtray he is using a banana split boat.

"You've got to be shitting me," he says.

"I shit you not," says Barbara. Also she explains that America is a great country if you forget about Vietnam and maybe some other details. Or at least it's been great for the Jews. For once the Promised Land has turned out more or less as promised.

"So why don't you turn plain American, if this country's so great?" asks Alfred. "Why do you still call yourself an American Jew?" He says this expecting that he has cagily trapped her, and that the truth of her opinion will shortly emerge.

But instead she maintains that there's something special about being Jewish she wouldn't want to give up. Look at all the great people who are—Einstein. Freud. Woody Allen. Sandy Koufax. Einstein rings a bell with her audience, but Freud and Woody Allen do not, even after Barbara explains how they both have to do with sex. Sandy Koufax they recall as that crazy cat who refused to pitch in the opening game of the World Series. Barbara explains about Yom Kippur. Barbara says being Jewish is also great because it's about fighting for freedom. "We're the original Freedom Riders. Just think if everyone in the world were Jewish, how much better off we would be."

"What you talking about, girl?" says Alfred. "How can everybody in the fucking world be Jewish?"

Barbara says she only meant to say what if. But that's not to say that everyone couldn't indeed become Jewish, theoretically. "For instance"—and she points to Exhibit A, namely Mona, who is sitting cross-legged on the soft wooden floor.

"Jewish?" says Alfred, peering down. "You expect me to believe that? Uh uh. Not until you grow your nose, baby. Then you come see old Stepin and see what he say."

"Stepin?" says Mona. "Who's that?"

Alfred smiles mysteriously and winks. "That's me," he says. "Yeah, man. Stepin Fetchit. That's me."

Other staff members laugh. "Now, now. No *making mockery*," says Darryl the busboy, in a vaguely British voice.

Alfred winks again; his dimples lengthen. "Never you mind the riffraff here. Alfred, you can call me, man. Alfred the cook. Once you grow your nose, you come see Alfred the cook, all right? Maybe that day he'll say, All right, now you are a nice Jew-girl indeed, you can have some nice Jew-babies. But you've got to have that nose grown out *big* now, you hear?" He wags his finger at her. "See, I don't want to hear how you got your nose grown out like your friend Barbara here and then stopped. Her nose is some aberration of nature, man, her mama must've kept it in a little nose mold when she was a baby so it would never get to regular size. But now, you hear cook Alfred. A nose like that don't convince nobody of nothing. No, ma'am. See, that there's one unconvincing nose. That nose of yours has got to grow out so big you've got to sneeze in a dish towel. That nose of yours has got to grow out so big you've got to cut your nose hair with hedge clippers."

"Grow your nose," chants Darryl. Jack and Seymour, the dishwashers, chime in. "Grow your nose. Grow your nose."

"Tell them," urges Barbara. "Tell them how it's changed your life, turning Jewish."

"I think you guys are stereotyping," Mona says instead.

"Typing? Stereo? I've never heard of no stereo that could type," says Alfred. "No hi-fi, neither, man. But back at my place, now, I've got me a stereo that can cook." He winks. "That stereo can cook!"

"You tell 'em, Alfred!" Darryl and Jack and Seymour laugh; also Seth.

"Come on, guys," he says to Mona and Barbara. "You're not really offended, are you?"

Barbara looks as though she is going to cry. Still she manages some facsimile of a smile. "Grow your nose," she tells Mona.

"You grow *your* nose," says Mona, gently.

General laughter.

"Seriously, though," starts Barbara.

"Hey, man, we're serious," insists Alfred, winking. "We're most seriously serious."

"Mona is Jewish now, and it's made a big difference in her life."

"You trying to convert us, sister?"

"She's trying to educate you," says Mona. "So you can have a big house and a four-bay garage and a gardener too."

"We're never going to have no big house or no big garage, either," explains Alfred. "We're never going to be Jewish, see, even if we grow our nose like Miss Mona here is planning to do. *We be black motherfuckers.*"

"You can be Jewish too," Barbara says.

"Even Stokely Carmichael originally wanted to go to Brandeis," Seth says. "He learned a lot from the Jews."

"The whole key to Judaism is to ask, ask, instead of just obey, obey," Mona says. "That's what I learned. Also you've got to know your holidays. You've got to know all the ritual, so you know who you are and don't spend your time trying to be Wasp and acting like you don't have anything to complain about. You've got to realize you're a minority."

"Man, but we're asking, all right," says Alfred. "We're asking and asking, but there ain't nobody answering. And nobody is calling us Wasp, man, and nobody is forgetting we're a minority, and if we don't mind our manners, we're like as not to end up doing time in a concrete hotel. We're black, see. We're *Negroes.*" He says this emphatically, but rotates his head as if to judge the reaction, scanning the room like a second table fan. He is wearing a red shirt that glows in the dim light; everyone watches as he stubs out his cigarette. Cedric runs up the stairs.

"Chow time!" Cedric calls, spatula in hand—meaning not that it's time for the staff to eat but that there are hungry customers out in the dining room, waiting to be fed. This is the latest in a series of time-to-get-going orders, all of which have been, usage-wise, slightly odd.

"Crack the whip!" for example, and before that, "Feed the masses!" At one point, he did try a straight-ahead "Back to work," but somehow he didn't realize he'd hit the right phrase, and went on trying others—which so amused the rest of the crew that they allowed him to continue fumbling. Of course, beneath the amusement ran a sneaky current of lower-motive calculation. At least some staffers figured Cedric to be on a path to owning his own place someday; why should they help him? But that wasn't to say there wasn't pillow-time figuring on his side too. Callie once said she thought Cedric softened his position as sub-in boss by getting people to laugh as they stood up. *Otherwise, what?* she said. *Otherwise, wouldn't they grumble about how a Chink happened to choose for a right-hand man another Chink?*

Correctly perceiving the truth, Mona tells Barbara and Seth that evening, in Barbara's kitchen. It's not something Mona planned on telling them, just as she had not planned on smoking so much dope. She's generally a social toker, a real two-puff type, as a result of the Opium War. (Which of course happened a long time ago, you wouldn't necessarily predict that those British gunboats in the Shanghai harbor would have much to do with Mona now. Except that so violent are Helen's feelings about narcotics that they do; who knows if Mona ever even got to properly enjoy her baby bottle.)

Still, here she is, sharing a water pipe in the almost dark. Barbara's turned off the lights, so that all they can see is what they can make out by the moonlight through the window, and words seem to bubble up with the smoke.

Wow, says Barbara, taking a toke.

Wow, says Seth.

Mona feels as though they are engaged in a primitive rite, in a bear-clawed cave, at the dawn of civilization. She relates what her parents said about trusting Alfred.

Wow.

She explains to them too about things that have happened in the past—for example, how Fernando got fired for stealing minute steaks. Which may or may not have had to do with her parents preferring to hire Chinese.

"It was a big deal," says Mona. "He punched Cedric in the mouth. He put a curse on the restaurant."

Wow.

On the other hand, who else was going to hire Cedric? And is Ralph such a bad guy for wanting to keep some China around him, for wanting to *make sure*?

"You're defending him," says Seth, rummaging for munchies.

But Mona says that her father's been through a war and a revolution and an uprooting they can probably never understand. And Mona does think that's relevant. Plus think how hard he works, she says. They all acknowledge this, a fact. For they've seen themselves how he is always there before they are, and is still there when they leave; it's as if he is under some special court order, pancake house arrest. Is it so terrible for him to want as a helper somebody who speaks his first language? Especially since, if he himself were to look for a job, somebody might just prefer not to hire him. His English being what it is.

They talk on (through four bags of Fritos and a six-pack of Tab) about how with the Chinese it's just like with the Jews: Some people get to Scarshill, but a lot get stuck on the Lower East Side, namely Chinatown. And is Cedric really on a path to owning his own place?

"Where's he going to come up with the capital?" says Mona. "He's got some management experience, but he probably doesn't even know that on every street there's a good side and a bad; we wouldn't have known that either if Auntie Janis hadn't told us." Also she bets he has no idea how important it is to have a parking lot you can see. "He probably thinks it's the same thing to have your parking behind the store," Mona says. "Or to have no parking at all."

Wow. Barbara and Seth shake their ponderous heads, taking a few more tokes. Poor Cedric. On the other hand, what about Alfred? They debate which is worse—not speaking English and having no visa and leaving your family behind to be forced to drink their own piss, or having a black face and living in a project and having a great-grandmother who was a slave? Not that all blacks live in projects; they realize they shouldn't generalize. "But not to forget the white great-great-grandfather who was fifteen years old and just trying out his prick," says Seth. He betakes himself to a bean-bag chair, that he may better contemplate the tragedy.

Wow.

On the subject of tragedy, they find that crowding in next—after the auction blocks and the Ku Klux Klan and the fuss over getting even a library card—is, of course, the Holocaust: the hiding and the trains and the ovens and the dentistry. Seth explains about how his mother survived. She luckily fled east from Cracow during the war, he says, so that she ended up in a part of Poland taken by Russians instead of Germans.

"Your mother was almost in the Holocaust?" says Mona. "She spent time in a Siberian refugee camp?"

Seth nods dully. "She was only eight at the time."

"And then what happened?"

"Then she came here and got married and got hit by a drunk in a German car."

Wow. Nobody knows what to say. This is the most Mona has heard of Seth's real mother—besides, of course, that she was nothing like Bea.

"We need a point system," says Barbara finally, getting back to the comparative-tragedy project. And they do indeed start to devise one. But in the end they go to the vote instead, figuring it's as American a way as any to arrive at the shining truth.

Which is how it is that, though it's a tough decision, they finally, generously agree: The Chinese revolution and the Holocaust notwithstanding, by and large, in present-day America, even if there was a black *Hello, Dolly!* on Broadway, it's generally an advantage to look more like Archie Bunker than like Malcolm X.

What to do with this terrible realization? *"Teshuvah,"* says Seth. "We need to think how to undo the harm done." Yet how?

"Let's ask the kitchen gang what to do," suggests Barbara. "Maybe they have a favorite charity. I'm going to give them all of my paycheck."

They agree that this would be most generous of her, since her *tzedakah* would only be ten percent of her net income after taxes. They consider starting a *pushke*—a donation can—for emergency funds.

"That's not enough," Barbara argues. "That's the kind of philanthropy my parents do."

"The stay-out-of-it kind," says Mona.

"Exactly!" says Barbara.

"That's like my parents," says Mona. "Only without the money part."

"My mom says she learned something from the fifties," says Barbara. "She says that Rabbi Horowitz could blab on about how Jews should do this and Jews should do that because he was busy pottytraining when other people were finding out what trouble is."

"But what about Seth's stepmother, Bea?" says Mona. "How come she's still doing this, doing that?"

"Her number didn't come up," says Seth.

Is it that simple? Anyway, Barbara goes on. *Gemilut hassadim,* she says, meaning acts of loving-kindness. She says they must think how to promote black independence, an idea astonishing to Mona. For while Ralph will jump off a bridge for *his boys,* his object is to keep them *his boys.* Why would you want them to simply up and leave? *Waste of time,* he'd have to say if they did, shaking his head mournfully. *Today we have no relationship.*

Meanwhile, Seth couldn't see things more differently. Of course the goal should be independence; let the workers throw off their chains! Wherefore, after all, is there Sabbath rest for everyone, if not to make plain that the proletariat and his oppressors live under the same sky, one as human as the other? The true condition of man being one of equality! He holds forth about Poland, land of his forebears, and how his mother's father refused to learn Hebrew. Yiddish was the language of the workers, said this grandfather, who by the way was not in favor of Israel, either. For why should Israeli workers stand separate from Polish workers? There should be no nations whatsoever, that was his opinion. The oppressed should stand together.

"You mean like us," Mona says, and Barbara and Seth agree. *Like us!* They agree that they are one nation—no, nationless. However, pro-Israel.

Where to go from here? Mona doesn't at first see why they should have to go anywhere, but then she recalls that she is Jewish. So that when Barbara says, "There must be something we can do," Mona does not say, as Helen would, *To do nothing is better than to overdo.* Instead Mona agrees, "There must be something."

But what? They think and think. So solid is their mutual resolve, however, that they cannot seem to get past it. A duet: "What action can we take?" says Barbara. And Seth: "What action is possible?"

"Action," Mona echoes. *Action. Action.* It's like trying to hum along at the opera. Most of the notes are too high for her, but still she can make out the nobility of the enterprise. *Action! What action? They need to take action!*

Two days later, an opportunity. Alfred arrives for his shift in mourning, having lost his apartment. Turns out he'd been fooling around on the side and his wife found out, but that was just the precipitating incident. The real problem being that she couldn't stand his friends, especially one black power type who always had to be out protesting and organizing to prove how much blacker he was than you. A field nigger, he called himself, even though he was one of the lightest Negroes Charlene ever did lay eyes on; almost as light as Charlene herself, who could pass for white easy. People sometimes took her and Alfred for salt-and-pepper, no kidding. Charlene said this troublemaker just didn't know how to appreciate what he had. And she couldn't understand how Alfred could be friends with this cat—his name was Luther the Race Man.

But they hung with the same brothers, and so far as Alfred was concerned, a bro' could wear a dashiki if he wanted, he could wear an Afro if he wanted, he could have a little something on the side if he wanted. See, these sisters have no motherfucking sense of humor, he says, especially when they come home from the night shift at the emergency room. They don't realize it's a free motherfucking country. She said his friends were a bad influence, wanting everything the way they did; that was because her mama and papa were from Jamaica, where Negroes didn't always realize they were Negroes, according to Luther. Some of them got pretty airy; that's what happened when you gave a Negro a lawn and a pool. In fact, Luther said, she wasn't hardly black at all. He used to point out to everybody how you could see the veins in her arms right through her skin. Made her so self-conscious she wore a high-neck long-sleeve shirt even in the summertime around him. And then he had a game he liked to play called Make a Request of Nurse Char-lene. He'd ask her something like, *Hey, Nurse Char-lene, might we have some of your de-licious ribs here? This boy's dying for one of your ribs.* And if she said *I would fix you a bone except that I am saving it for my dog to chew on,* he would wink and mention how on such and such a subject, the white folk had such and such an opinion. And then he would turn to Charlene and ask, *Ain't that right now? Ain't that what the white folk say?* Charlene thought Alfred's friends were a bad influence, but here Alfred had a steady gig and everything, and if he finally got to having a little on the side, why, see, that Charlene drove him to it, man, what with her house nigger ways. And so what if Charlene's doctor daddy was going to be proclaiming how right he was about these American blacks? Charlene shouldn't have had the locks changed, and hidden the car away somewhere, and taken all the money out of their bank account, man. She could've at least left his clothes out on the steps, and how's he going to get back and forth now to keep his steady job? That was a brand-fucking-new Buick he was driving too.

"What am I going to do, man?" he finishes. "I've been shut out like a fucking hound dog."

And just like that, Barbara offers him a room in her house.

"Aw, no," says Alfred, flipping pancakes. "That's right nice of you, Miss B. But see, poor Alfred here can find himself his own house." He grins after a fashion, itching with his forearm his unshaved chin.

Barbara continues to insist, poor Alfred continues to refuse. And later on, Mona tries to point out to Barbara that this is just as well.

"You have to consider how long he might stay," Mona says. "Plus you don't want to get into trouble."

"I'm not in love with him, if that's what you mean."

"And what about your cousin?"

Evie, Barbara claims, has been working so hard on her photography that they barely even see each other. "She's living in a complete other part of the house," Barbara says. "She's got this bathroom she's set up as a darkroom."

"In any case," Mona says, "he's got another place."

"Good," Barbara says, a clear look to her dewy eyes. "He was welcome at mine."

Mona thinks of her friend's words a number of times over the next week or so. In fact, Mona thinks so admiringly of Barbara's spontaneous generosity of spirit, that everything about her own life begins to seem small and self-centered and shrunken up. She feels like a discount troll doll, one that doesn't even come with colored hair.

This is exacerbated by an encounter with Bea in the supermarket, where Bea is stocking up on pineapple rings. A luau, she explains, the proceeds to benefit a halfway house. She is friendly and flatteringly open to advice on several matters Polynesian. Would coconuts make good bowling balls, for example. Bea is thinking of having a bowling competition with coconuts for balls and wooden palm trees for pins.

Mona reassures her that this is very much in the Polynesian spirit. Bea thanks Mona for her contribution to the cause.

"It's nothing," says Mona, and means it. How disappointed Bea would be to know the true her! Mona resolves to be more Jewish, to do Rabbi H. proud.

"You are right," Mona tells Barbara one day. "We should've done what we could have for Alfred."

"We spend so much time protecting our bourgeois interests," Barbara says, standing tall. Her hair falls straight as a plumb line down her back.

Meanwhile, Seth beams; more and more, he has been regarding Barbara with warm approval. True, there was that ice age after her nose. But the thaw that began with Barbara's dialogues with the help has continued steadily, especially since Seth moved his stereo to the teepee. Now he puts "Lay Lady Lay" on every time he and Mona make out. Which Mona wishes he wouldn't. She says she already knows he wants to sleep with her, it's a hard fact to miss. So to speak. He doesn't deny it. Is this why he starts engaging Barbara in higher talk again? One day he even brings in a book for her to read— *Siddhartha* this is, all about how the noble spirit wars with the most ardent body. Barbara accepts this loan with her two hands and two eyes, you would think he was handing her the Torah to kiss.

How can Mona yell at Seth for lending a book to Barbara? What's a little intellectual exchange between friends, and who's to say higher ideas turn lower? Barbara jets up to visit her parents for a week, giving them all time to consider what means friendship.

And so it is that when Alfred falls out with his new girlfriend, Mona is the one who comes to his rescue. Her nose is no bigger than it ever was, she jokes; but she would like to offer him, out of the Jewishness of her heart, refuge in Barbara's garage.

CHAPTER 8

Further Changes of Occupation

Barbara, when she comes home, is as shocked as she is sunburned. However, she quickly says, "How can he stay in the garage?"— and in the process of saying the right thing, is transformed. She is a balm for the weary, a veritable aloe vera rub, especially compared to Mona, who meanly reports how Alfred has a mattress, and a cube fridge, and a Sterno camp stove with little fold-up legs. These are basics she had thought would keep him comfortable. But Barbara, her new nose pinkly peeling, insists he move to the house like a proper indoor guest.

A generous idea, a magnificent idea. Unfortunately, however, he refuses. This is on account of his hoping this Whole Trouble with Charlene is almost over; he's hoping that pretty soon the lights will come up and the credits will roll. Or at least so goes Seth's analysis of the situation. For Seth has read about these things, it turns out—how a person who hopes to return to his old digs might just refuse to get comfortable in his new.

"This is called denial," says Seth.

"A psychological thing," says Barbara.

"Like sublimation," says Mona.

All nod knowingly.

Seth goes on to say that he thinks he knows Alfred's second-choice accommodation, and that is not at Barbara's house, either. Alfred's second-choice accommodation, thinks Seth, is with one of the brothers. But how can he stay with them, when they are the very cats Charlene can't abide?

Mona and Barbara ponder this quandary. "Poor Alfred," they say. They note how these matters psychological seem to bulk up mysteriously, like yeast breads. Still, on Alfred's behalf, they begin to hope what they think he hopes.

But Charlene doesn't call and doesn't call, and then even Alfred starts to see how a hardworking babe like her might not have time for his brand of shit. That's why he finally calls her, only to find out she's changed their phone number to something unlisted. He discovers she's signed up her coworkers to run interference at the hospital. He starts to realize he's never going to get her on the line there, or anywhere. And that's when it comes to him, finally, a subrealization: that she means to take her own sweet time softening up, maybe it wouldn't be such a bad thing to wait out the duration in the house.

Especially since there's also been a discovery regarding the new girlfriend—namely, that the whole time Trixie was seeing Alfred, she was also wrinkling up the sheets with somebody else. Some white dude, no less, who is now claiming he's going to move her into a real house, with real furniture.

"Appliances too," complains Alfred. "A dishwasher. A washing machine. A dryer, and not the bottom of the line, either. No, sir. See, he's going to get her the permanent-press cycle. He's going to get her the stackable if she wants. Of course, first he's got to slip-slide his rich ass out of his correctional institution." Alfred smiles gamely as he shakes his head, but the motion's got no swing; it puddles down like ink into his fine steel chin. "And that's the fucking story, man. My baby done traded me in for a washer-dryer combination."

"How do you know?" Seth asks, cracking his knuckles like Rabbi Horowitz.

"The bitch told me herself, live and in English. I called her up and told her, Trixie, baby, your Alfred's coming on back, and that's when she told me. She said, Alfred Knickerbocker, don't you do nothing of the kind. She said she's got her a dude who's going to do her right for a change. They're going to get married in a motherfucking church. They're going to ride up in a motherfucking limousine. She said she's got the ring already, it's flashing like the roof light on a motherfucking goonmobile. She said this dude, man, he's not like some regular motherfucker. Uh uh. She said he's something else." He laughs loudly. "Yessiree. Sounds like he is something else indeed. And that makes old Alfred the something on the side, except he ain't even on the side no more, man. See, now he's just plain something." He winks a wink reminiscent of a wince.

Practicalities: How to get food to Alfred, and what route would be the best for him to take in and out, and how to be sure Barbara's cousin Evie won't notice. And what about the neighbors? Will they assume he's a much-needed manservant, worth his weight in gold? Or will they turn into sleuthy private eyes, discuss him between rubbers of bridge?

"We don't want them to phone the police or anything," says Barbara, at a meeting around her kitchen countertop. To this everyone agrees. They are perched on their padded stools, with a bowl full of bridge mix, discussing the Problem Most Serious—namely, that Barbara's house so convincingly commands its little knoll. The major sport facilities are hidden behind a hedge, but on account of a Y in the road, the house itself sits in intermittent view of two streets. One side of the property does fetchingly undulate down to a patch of town woods. But even if Alfred comes and goes from that side, how will he manage the fetching undulation? Alfred volunteers to plain hoof it, a time-honored solution. However, Barbara points out that smack across the street lives a boy with a telescope.

Mona spins around on her stool. "How about the Underground Railroad? If it really is a railroad, and not just a wine cellar. Can Alfred go back and forth that way?"

"What a genius idea!" exclaims Barbara. "Except, is there more tunnel back behind the wine rack?"

"And does it go in the right direction?" Mona says this modestly, not wanting to seem as though she too thinks this is a genius idea. "Anyway, it's worth checking out."

"What you talking about, girl?" says Alfred.

"What railroad?" says Seth.

Barbara explains. Seth leaps barefoot from his stool to investigate.

Alfred pushes back more slowly. "Those tunnels are short, man. My grandpa used to say they're something smelly besides. He said his pa came up from Dixie for a stretch that way. Mostly he came up the rivers, see, on account of the dogs. But every now and then he came up a tunnel, and he said they are something noxious, man. He said a body can't hardly breathe down there."

But in the end Alfred too is overtaken by the spirit of exploration. In the basement with Seth, he pries out the wine rack, complete with four more bottles of wine; they could be Lewis and Clark, except that beyond them stretches, not an unsullied continent, begging to be ravished, but instead a long hole, as low as Alfred predicted, and reinforced with bits: bits of brick, bits of stone, bits of wood. Also something that looks to be the tip of a buried bone, but which turns out upon excavation to be a doorknob.

Says Barbara, "That's got to be antique."

They pass it around like a talisman of their tribe. How cool, how smooth, how round. They conclude it to be ceramic. They cradle its heft; they turn it in the air as though it still might unlatch some door, who knows—as if it still might open to them some room, some mystery. Seth tosses it playfully into the air.

"Hey! Don't do that! You're going to break it," says Mona. And for safekeeping she presents it to Alfred.

Seth and Mona repair home to round up proper orienteering equipment; when they reconvene at Barbara's, it is with ropes and shovels, flashlights, water bottles, a first-aid kit. Gorp. A compass. Carabiners. It's clear they all know their way to Eastern Mountain Sports. As for who's going to go in the tunnel, they agree it makes more sense for Seth to go than Alfred, Seth being so much shorter. Mona, for the same reason, is a definite go too. But should Barbara go or stay? It seems to make sense for her to stay, but she wants to go, so that no one can say she chickened out.

"No one's saying anything," says Seth.

Still Barbara insists that she's going, and whatever her intention, Seth is suitably impressed. She ties up her hair to get it out of the way; Mona ties up her hair too. Then they link themselves, expedition style. For this purpose they pick the orange and blue climbing rope that is Mona's old favorite; they argue over the knots, which no one quite remembers, except to be able to tell that they're tied wrong. Alfred shouts into the tunnel, trying to get a sense of the acoustics. If he hears anything that sounds like trouble, he's going to get help, he says. Also if they haven't come back in a half hour. They synchronize their watches.

Equipped with six flashlights—they each have a spare—Mona and Barbara and Seth set off. The tunnel is cool enough that Mona's glasses fog, and so low on headroom that only she can stand up straight. Barbara (behind her) and Seth (in front) have to crouch. For Seth in particular this is not so easy, since he has to walk holding their one big shovel out in front of him; he shuffles like a camper on latrine duty. Twice he stops. He squats all the way down on his heels so that he can at least rest his back, but pretty soon his arms ache too, it's a relief when at one spot he has to stop and shovel. Behind him, Mona and Barbara wait encouragingly; they can feel his efforts via the tug of the rope around their waists. They check the compass. Northwest, they're headed—toward the woods! They whoop it up quietly, not wanting to alarm Alfred. Still they hear him shout to them.

"Everything okay?"

"Yes," they shout back, as clearly as they can.

They note that the tunnel is sloped gently downhill, a good sign. Seth finishes shoveling; they move on bravely, forging the considerable muddy spots. These are caused by the hoses for the in-ground lawn sprinkler system, which cross the tunnel in a number of places, and leak primordially; for sure they'll be growing stalactites in another thousand years. Or is it stalagmites?

Quietly they discuss their worst fears. Mona's is of coming upon a porcupine. She says she is afraid that when it realizes they are coming at it, it will shoot. However, Seth says this fear has nothing to do with porcupines at all; he says it has to do with the war and just goes to show that the nation has been traumatized right down to its deepest subconscious. Is that true? Anyway, Barbara's worst fear is of skunks. She says tomato juice doesn't work; if they get sprayed, they'll have to cut all their hair off. Seth's fear is snakes; he trains his flashlights with disproportionate interest on the floor until Mona points out that snakes could just as well be coming out of the walls. At this, Seth jumps slightly out of his skin, occasioning a head thump. They go on to other fears, agreeing that for all of them, the first-place nonanimal nightmare is a cave-in.

"We could be buried alive!" observes Mona helpfully. "Like in 'The Cask of Amontillado' or something."

" 'The Cask of Amontillado,' " muses Barbara. "Is that a song?"

"It could be," says Mona. And to the tune of "If you're going to

San Francisco," she sings, "If you're going to Amon-till-ado . . ." No one else sings. "Be sure to inter me in an oaken casket there . . ."

The tunnel is very quiet; none of them has ever been in a place so quiet. If Alfred has yelled again to them, they haven't heard him.

"Get it?" says Mona finally. "Oaken casket, open casket?"

"Very punny," says Seth. "Just what we need, a little black humor."

"Jewish humor," says Mona.

"But of course," says Seth. "It's your Jewish heritage speaking."

"Singing," says Mona. "It's my Jewish heritage singing." She clears her throat. "And for my next number, 'Singing in the Grave.' "

Seth laughs and joins in; Barbara checks her compass again— still headed for the woods. They cross another hose line. Another. More mud. They agree that should Alfred truly come to use the tunnel on a regular basis, he will have to wear hiking boots. If he has any, that is.

Finally Seth says, "How are we going to know when we've come far enough?"

"One more hose, and that'll be the edge of the woods," says Barbara. "There are eight sprinklers between the house and the edge of the lawn. I think."

"Plus won't there be tree roots?" says Mona. "If there are trees?"

They soldier on. Until there it is, finally, the eighth hose, bright green and, sure enough, leaking like the others. And just beyond it, an underground forest of tree roots. These are as enormous and ropy as anything in *Babes in Toyland*, you half expect them to start talking.

"Now what?" says Seth.

Later it will turn out that this is not exactly the Underground Railroad. Later it will turn out that this is the Underground Railroad re-made into a passageway for a bomb shelter. But for now the explorers explore as explorers will, which is to say with their feet firmly planted on what they think they know. Back up on the open lawn, by the brilliant light of the sun, they count the water sprinklers. The eighth one to the northwest of the house does indeed skirt the woods; they dig a little here, a little there, starting from the sprinkler, making their way on out along the feeder hose. The ground begins to look like the acorn pantry of a large forgetful squirrel. Until just when they are about to give up, a piece of ground collapses under Barbara's foot. Hooray! They do a little dance, until they realize that the tunnel too has collapsed some, and they are collapsing it more by celebrating.

They stabilize the tunnel with two-by-fours. This takes some enterprise. Also they fashion an entrance, with a stepladder down; the door is a metal garbage can lid laden with mossy camouflage. Worried as they are about the dirt needs of the moss, Mona can hardly lift the lid. However, Alfred can, which is what matters. The moisture in the tunnel they soak up with kitty litter; Alfred they equip with a heavy-duty flashlight. And the next thing they know, it seems the most natural thing in the world for Alfred to be popping in and out of Barbara's basement.

As for his room: Barbara's house having an annex, there is a series of tiny rooms right upstairs from the garage. These were servants' quarters at one point, and now are mostly empty, only the last two still house objects once useful to their occupants. It's as if someone had meant to clean out the whole shebang but for some reason quit three quarters of the way down the hall. With the result that in one room there are lamps and tables; an old phonograph turned into a potter's wheel; some old dresses with perspiration stains; and a beasty mink stole complete with a beady-eyed head and businesslike claws. Also a girdle. Barbara holds this up.

"I came, I held in my stomach, I conquered," says Mona.

Alfred occupies himself with the closet door. "This door's not hung straight," he says. "I bet it doesn't close right, either." He seems pleased when, sure enough, it doesn't. He sits down on a bare gray mattress, bounces a little, trying it out. There's no bounce. "It's all right, I guess," he says.

"You sure?" Barbara sits down too.

Alfred strokes his smooth-shaved jaw, contemplative. They move on to the next room, expecting more of the same. But, surprise: This room is completely furnished, and splendidly. There is a moth-eaten blue velvet chair; also lace curtains. And children's toys—the owner before Barbara's dad had some six or seven kids. But these are small distraction from the lion's head door knocker on the door, and the full two thirds of a fancy-stitch throw on the bed. There is even a mural on the cracked walls (hand drawn in imitation of the ones downstairs), along with a painted fireplace. The fireplace sports a roaring red fire. Who could have lived here? And why did the person leave everything behind? There is a definite atmosphere, as Seth observes, of unplanned departure. As for what could have precipitated this unplanned departure, there are clues. For instance, whereas there are only milkmaids in the mural downstairs, in this one there is a master wielding a whip in one hand while fondling his private parts with the other. The milkmaids by and large pull at their pigtails and cower behind the cows. However, one vengeful lass seems to be taking aim with an udder.

Perfect! Stroking his smooth chin some more, Alfred agrees: This should be his new place of residence.

"Make yourself at home." Barbara proffers Alfred keys to the house and alarm, and when he hesitates, tosses the ring into the air. He catches it, of course—this being reflexive in men, not to let things get by them. "I mean it," she says.

"She really does," offers Mona. "She lent me her van for a month, I swear."

"She's like that," echoes Seth. "Born to give things away."

Barbara flushes. "Anyway, you mostly won't even be using the door. And we haven't been using the alarm, either. You just should have the keys in case."

"Well, now," says Alfred, contemplatively. "I guess a body can't help how they're born, now, can they?" He throws the keys up underhand, then he catches them overhand, easily.

Alfred seems happy enough at first. Living at Barbara's is like camping out for him, not that he's ever gone camping or even considered going camping as a voluntary activity. "That's for white folk," he says. His idea of fun would be closer to the fanciest hotel you could imagine, with push buttons everywhere, and revolving beds and bars, and everything polished up to a bright mirror shine. But if he can't see the fun in the stripped-down life, he can at least see the peace and quiet of it, that's true. Nobody busting in or calling him on the carpet, and no cars or windows or brothers getting smashed up either, the big activity here being the crickets. "Listen," say Barbara and Seth. "They do that by rubbing their legs together." *Chirp, chirp*. And here he'd thought he needed to pop his ears or clean out his wax or blow his nose or something, he says. Being a mite hard of hearing. He explains about how he had so many ear infections as a child that he plain wore the clinic out. So that now he wasn't sure if that noise was inside his head or something automatic about the house, maybe the driveway warmer gone and fried itself up. Barbara laughs when Alfred tells her that, but he says he's being seriously serious. He's heard that before, that there are houses with driveway warmers to melt the snow off in the winter; you can tell which ones in a storm because the flakes die as soon as they hit the asphalt. The little shits be white, he says, but they might as well be black, they never stand a chance.

And let Charlene wonder how come he's not howling like an alley cat at her door—little does she know he's living in a big house on a hill with a free ride to work and all he can eat and no rent to make! This life has its considerable satisfactions. Plus he's never seen so many TVs outside of a department store, or so much furniture either, and he can't believe all the silver; nothing is plain old metal. And all that carpet, wall-to-wall everywhere. He's never lived so fat. Forget high heaven, he says, it's like living in a fucking movie.

On the other hand, it's right quiet. Of course, he understands why he shouldn't play no music, and why he can't turn no lights on at night, and why he can't have no telephone or no television. He understands that he's lucky. He's lucky to be hiding out here like a fugitive. He's lucky to be going back and forth in a tunnel. He's lucky to have a servant's room to live in. Barbara has stuck her neck out for him, and as likely as not will get her head chopped off like a turkey tom if he does not abide by the rules. But the truth is that after a week it begins to feel like prison, the house, except that there are no other inmates. It begins to feel like solitary confinement, only with crickets instead of roaches the size of cigarette lighters and other pet-size vermin. Not that he can't hang out with Mona and Seth and Barbara, getting high and shooting the shit. But what's he going to do the rest of the time—lie in the dark and play with himself? And the more he looks around, the poorer he feels; and the more he looks at Mona and Seth and Barbara, the older he feels too. "Twenty-one, man," he says. That's almost as old as his father was when he croaked. He was getting along fine, had himself a steady job, just like Alfred. But then he croaked.

"Did he get shot?" Mona wants to know.

"Naw, nothing like that." Alfred says he knows people who've gotten shot up, naturally, but that his dad got a pneumonia in his heart. Turned his heart into a bag of worms, and according to the doctor, that's why he died. A bag of worms can't pump. That's when Alfred's mother came down from Hartford. She was headed back to Georgia, to where her people come from: Racist or not, Georgia still was a whole lot friendlier than the North, that was her opinion. *I don't think so*, she liked to say. *I know so*. Also kids didn't go getting ideas down there; they didn't go getting uppity. But she got stuck in New York and had her a stroke, and here's Alfred now, alone; all he had was Charlene.

"You know the difference between you white folk and me?" he says one day in the kitchen. He's talking to Mona and Barbara and Seth, only two of whom are white; Mona thinks she should point this out.

But instead she says, "What?"

"See," he says, "you white folk look at the calendar, and at the end of the year comes Christmastime, and at the beginning of the year comes a whole new year, maybe the year you pack your white ass off to college, maybe the year you go off traveling somewhere nice. Me, I look at that calendar, and at the end of the year there's flapjacks, and at the beginning of the year there's flapjacks, and when I die, man, they're going to cover me with flapjacks, and put the butter and the syrup on top, and they're going to write on the tombstone, He done burnt only a couple of jacks his whole life, and that's when the stove was broke and burning like a hellhole."

He laughs. Mona and Barbara and Seth laugh too.

"So why don't you go back to college?" Mona reaches for a barbecue potato chip.

But if Alfred does anything, he's going to start himself a restaurant. They discuss what kind of restaurant. They discuss social justice. There is nothing about which they do not totally agree.

A few days later, though, Alfred's restless. For one thing, something's disagreeing with his stomach. Maybe it's all that deli Jew-food, he says, he ain't used to it.

"I don't think you should call it Jew-food," Mona says.

"Pastrami is Jew-food, don't tell me no different," he says. (And later on, it turns out Seth and Barbara are unoffended—making Mona, she supposes, too sensitive.) Or maybe it's the fucking crickets that's bothering him, continues Alfred; he wants to go out and kill them. He wants to know if you can just stamp on them or have to do something special.

"Probably you can just stamp," says Mona. "But it's kind of a big lawn."

Alfred gazes out at the acreage. He adjusts the pads of his lounge chair.

"Maybe you can mention it to the gardener." Mona moves into the adjustable shade of the patio umbrella. "His name is Willie."

"The gardener." He lowers his chin. "You got a gardener too?"

"Sure," Mona says.

"He black?"

"She," Mona says.

"She! You got yourself a lady gardener?"

"Sure."

"What for, man, what for? You tell Alfred why you got a lady gardener."

"It just so happens."

"She black or white?"

"I'm not sure."

"In that case, she's black."

"What do you mean?"

"White is white, man. Everything else is black. Half and half is black."

"Are you telling me I'm black?" Mona says.

He looks at her, puzzled, then grins. "Are you pulling poor Alfred's chain again?"

Mona grins back, offering him a beer. "Couldn't help it," she says. "It was hanging right there." For herself she has a diet soda with a loopy straw.

The sun shines.

"How come your daddy don't drive no Caddy-lack yet, all those flapjacks we send singing all day?" asks Alfred. "Why are you the gardener?"

"Ancient Chinese tradition, I guess. No rice paddies to tend, so I mow the lawn instead. Have you ever seen a rice paddy?"

"No, ma'am."

"It looks like a golf course, except actually it's the putting green and water trap all rolled up in one. I've seen pictures."

"How about that," says Alfred. Then he says, "That bitch landed me in prison, man. She got everything."

"You mean Charlene?"

"Who else?"

"Oh, whew. I thought maybe you meant me," says Barbara, sneaking up behind them.

"What? You? Oh, no, I don't mean *you*, Miss B.," says Alfred. "You're one good shit, all right, helping me out." He glances at the sliding door through which Barbara appeared, as if making a mental note. *Keep an eye on that sucker.* "Alfred's just lucky," he goes on, getting up some steam. "The day he dies, he's going to leave everything he ever owned to you. The day he dies, they're going to read his will, and it's going to say, To my main savior, Barbara G., otherwise known as the Blanco, I do leave all my clothes, and my hi-fi if she can get it back from my bitch wife, and maybe even the toaster. If she can fix it, it's hers to burn up her bagels in before she lays on that cream cheese and five-dollar-a-pound lox."

They laugh. The sun shines some more.

Barbara says, "You feel like you're in prison?"

"Oh, no," says Alfred. "It's beautiful here. Like a movie or something."

"Except that he feels like killing the crickets," Mona says.

"Why'd you say that, girl?" says Alfred.

"Because it's true," Mona says. "It's okay, you can tell Barbara. It's too quiet for you here, right?"

He hesitates. "It's on the quiet side."

"And maybe a bit on the lonesome side too?"

"That bitch Charlene," he says. "She got everything, man. How can anybody even call me? After she went and changed the fucking phone number."

"You miss your buddies?" Mona asks.

Alfred takes an elaborately casual swig of his beer.

"Or are you trying to steer clear of them?"

"Ain't steered clear of nobody in my life, man." The veins in his neck stick out.

"So why don't you call them up, then? I know my dad's pretty strict about making calls from work, but maybe he'll make an exception."

"The day the Rice Man makes an exception," snorts Alfred, sitting forward, "is the day the clouds come down from the sky and lay on the ground so as we've got to shovel 'em up." He swings his bare feet down to the hot flagstone, but then quickly returns them to the chair pad.

Meanwhile, Mona's flinching too. "How about the pay phone?" She says this even though the pay phone is right between the bathrooms, everybody can hear every word you say. "Or some other pay phone."

"How're the brothers going to call me back?"

"Do they need to call you back?"

Alfred downs some more beer.

"Is something bothering you?"

He laughs sharply. "What're you talking about, is something bothering Alfred?" He suddenly recalls something he needs to get from his room.

Mona watches him hop across the patio, and when he's out of sight, she discusses this conversation with Barbara. Mona half expects that her generous friend will offer Alfred use of the phone at the house. But what if Evie answers? And what if the phone bill comes and there are all these calls to who knows where? Barbara presents him instead with an AM-FM radio.

"You got to keep it down low," she tells Alfred. "I don't want my cousin to hear."

"Low," he says. "Alfred's going to play this baby so low anybody would think it's just one more little cricket got born—it can hardly make no noise, it's so small."

But a week later, the cricket is getting louder.

"It's growing up," says Barbara, taping her bangs down to dry. She uses special pink tape, and Dippity-Do besides. "What should I do?"

"Did you try talking to him?" says Mona.

"I did. But he has that problem with his ears."

"He can hear crickets."

"I guess that's different."

Back and forth, until finally Mona has another genius idea. They leave a radio on in the kitchen; also they plant a number of other radios and lights around the house, on timers. These slavishly switch themselves on, switch themselves off, and naturally Evie complains in this squeaky voice, you'd swear she cleans her vocal cords with vinegar. But Barbara holds her ground. She insists that the house is giving her the heebie-jeebies. *It's too empty. It's too quiet.* The lights and radios help her relax. Plus they'll scare away burglars.

Evie concedes that she can always shut her door if the commotion bothers her; Barbara and Mona congratulate themselves on their creative social management. They tell Alfred that they want him to feel at home. *We are willing to go the extra yard for you.* He allows that this seems to be true.

Barbara offers him additional proof of their goodwill. She tells him he can use the den TV if he is really, really careful and sure to get out of there by six-thirty at the latest. That's when Evie comes back from her course for dinner. Not every day, but enough days, she says. To which Alfred nods, delighted. He expresses gratitude, he expresses comprehension, and without further ado heads for the set.

Seth, meanwhile, has been arriving late at the restaurant. Ralph has had to yell at him twice; and now here it is, day three, and Seth is late again. Not to say stoned, which means he will do things like serve up the Salisbury steak with a series of forks stuck in it.

"Mysteries of the universe," he told a customer last week, as he set it down. "Stonehenge." The customer was so absorbed in the sports section that he didn't even react until one of the forks fell over with a clink.

"There are forks in my meat!" he exclaimed then, indignant. "Forks!" He put down his paper to express his moral outrage. "Waiter! There are forks! In my meat!"

Seth swooped in. "Oh, my! We'll send this back right away!" And bearing the plate aloft on his fingertips, he disappeared through the swinging kitchen doors. The staff roared and clapped.

"Sett," says Ralph now, sitting at his desk. His feet are planted on the ground, his face is serious. However, he is peeling an orange with a letter opener as he talks. "You late third day in a row now, what's happen?"

Says Seth, blinking, "I guess I got lost or something."

"Lost? How could be?" Ralph continues his peeling. "Every day you coming to the restaurant, suddenly today you are lost? I don't know what you talking these days. Cedric tell me last week you put fork in customer's food. Are you crazy?"

"It was a joke."

"That's how you make joke? Seems like very strange. And you talking some kind funny today. Are you maybe drink some beer before you come?"

"Beer?" Seth starts laughing.

"What you laughing now? Some more joke?"

"Oh, no, man. I mean, I've been known to kill some soldiers every now and then, but—"

"Kill somebody!" says Ralph, jumping up. The naked orange rolls off the desk; Seth catches it, and when Cedric steps in, lobs it to him. Cedric fumbles but recovers. And soon enough, Ralph is eating his orange, everyone is back to work. But Seth isn't satisfied.

"Your old man," he says to Mona at break time, then launches into his worshipful opinion.

"Actually, he has a great sense of humor," Mona says.

Seth goes on. "What does he do besides milk his workers like a capitalist oppressor? Doesn't he have any hobbies?"

Mona tries to explain that while no, Ralph doesn't have any hobbies, this is only because he was an oppressed proletariat not so long ago. Or if not a proletariat, at least oppressed. Or if not oppressed, at least not an oppressor. Ralph might seem like Seth's parents to Seth, she says, but he isn't. She says her family's seen some rough times.

"This pancake house is everything for us." She is lying on her back, squinting up at the attic rafters. "We're not like you. We don't have investments. We don't read the *Wall Street Journal*. I've never even seen a stock certificate." For argument's sake, she omits from mention the new franchise her parents have finally decided to try and finagle a way to afford.

"You've never seen a stock certificate?"

Mona shakes her head.

"Have you ever seen a coupon?"

"You mean, like for cereal?" In fact, Mona knows what kind of coupon he means; she only says this to impress upon him the messy essential truth.

It works. "Excuse me for confusing your class status." Seth emits a quick whistle through his beard before planting on her lips a nice scratchy kiss. Mona kisses back, fondling his ear as she adjusts for him his hair net.

That same evening, seven-thirty. Barbara and Mona saunter into the house, only to behold Alfred watching baseball on the color TV. It's a red-socked team versus a white-socked team, the eighth inning, a tight game, and Alfred's excitement is apparent from the kitchen. They can hear him shouting at the screen. He jumps up. He cheers.

"Is Evie here?" Barbara checks quickly for her cousin. Luckily, Evie's out. Barbara goes to talk to Alfred, but doesn't step all the way into the room. Instead she stalls in the doorway, one hand on the jamb. Mona lines up behind her like someone waiting to use the ladies' room.

"Alfred," Barbara says. "It's seven thirty-three."

He swivels in his BarcaLounger. Mona and Barbara perceive that he is holding a beer.

"I see you are looking at my beverage here," observes Alfred.

"I am not," says Barbara.

"You know who you remind me of, looking at my beverage? My bitch wife Char-lene."

"It's seven thirty-three," Barbara says again. Her voice rises slightly; her fingers curl around the doorjamb so that her fingernails whiten. Mona peeks around her. "You know, I wish you could just stay here, but Evie is going to come home any minute. In fact, she could've come home an hour ago."

"*E*-vie," he says, letting the name roll on his tongue like something delicious. He stretches out the "Eee" and lets it drop down into the "vie" with the spilling acceleration of a ball into a golf hole. He says it like it is all sound and no meaning; and from this, Mona and Barbara can see that he is, as he claims, not drunk. However, he is more than usually relaxed. He grins a Cheshire cat grin as he enunciates again—"Eee-vie." He might as well be tossing an antique soup tureen in the air—catching it with sure hands, but setting everyone on edge all the same.

The red-socks steal a base, the crowd goes wild, but now Alfred doesn't seem to care. He hovers between the world of the TV set and some other world that is not quite the world inhabited by Mona and Barbara.

"Who gives a shit about Evie, man?" He says this, smiling. "Why don't you just tell her to shut her clam?"

"Because I know she won't," says Barbara. "If she doesn't tell my parents, she'll tell my aunt. Evie's always been a tattletale."

"So what," says Alfred. "What's it going to matter, man? What's your Jew-daddy going to do to you? Take away your shiny new au-to-mo-bile?"

Barbara, shocked, backs up a step.

"Her dad," says Mona, bravely, straight into her friend's shoulder blade, "is not a Jew-daddy."

"What you know back there? You're not Jewish, don't give me that shit." Alfred addresses Barbara again. "You know what Luther says about you? He says you're willing to be giving us all those pennies and nickels that be stretching out your pants pockets. He says you're willing to be giving away those nickels and dimes that be hanging down and banging your leg when you walk. But you ain't going to be giving out no quarters without going on about how you be sufferers just like we be sufferers; and how you be our Moses, that is going to lead us out of the desert, so long as we turn off the TV before E-vie come home so's nobody don't get in no trouble and lose any au-to-mo-bile." He smirks, glancing back at the TV. "That's what Luther says, man."

"Jesus Christ," Mona says, as Barbara stalks away. "When'd you see your friend Luther?"

"Called-him-on-the-tel-e-phone," chants Alfred. He laughs a heh-heh laugh. "You hear me? I-done-used-the-tel-e-phone."

"But why, Alfred? Why?"

"I-done-picked-on-up-the-tel-e-phone. I-done-dialed-on-up-the-tel-e-phone, and when the phone stopped ringing, you know what I said? I said, Hey, Luther. This is Alfred. I'm-call-ing-on-the-tel-e-phone."

"But Alfred, why? What are you going to do now? Have you got some other place to stay?"

"I'm moving, all right. I'm moving today, man. See, I'm moving right this minute." He puts his feet up on the BarcaLounger footrest.

"Oh, Alfred," Mona says. "Don't be like this."

"Like what, sugar?"

"Don't be angry."

"Who's angry?" he says. "What for?"

How could he talk to me that way? How could he? I didn't have to let him stay here. I didn't have to stick my neck out for him. I didn't have to do shit for him. This is what Mona expects Barbara to say. And Mona expects to console her: *You've been a mensch. I can't tell you how sorry I am that I invited him to stay at your place to begin with, and without even asking.*

But by the time Mona joins her friend on the hall stairs, she finds to her amazement that Barbara's calmed down.

"Of course he's angry," she says. "He's angry about his whole life. And he's right. Here we are so rich, and we're willing to help him up to a point. But not to the point where we're going to lose some of our own privilege, right?"

So astonished is Mona to hear this that for a moment her voice volume doesn't work. "Barbara," she whispers. "Barbara Heloise Gugelstein!"

Barbara makes a modest wave with her hand, as if trying to tell a hairdresser no hair spray. "I don't think he even really believes I have a cousin. I mean, he hasn't seen her, he hasn't heard her. So far as he's concerned, she's just a phantom. I think he thinks I'm making it up about her."

"So what are you going to do?" says Mona, hanging on the banister. "Introduce them?"

"Such a helpful idea," says Barbara.

But the next evening, Seth too proposes they drop the secrecy. "What are we, the CIA? I think we should just call the elder Gugelsteiner and let him in on the news. Why not be up front? Why not stand up for what we believe?"

"Are you kidding?" Mona says. "If you call Mr. Gugelstein, it's going to be lawyers and police and forcible removal. We'll probably all get JD cards. Our pictures will be on the front page of the paper."

"Let's do it!"

"And what about Alfred?" continues Mona. "What if he ends up in jail? Have you thought about that?"

Could Alfred end up in jail? Anyway, not even Barbara has the stomach for the kind of confrontation Seth has in mind; and so Mona's original idea is resurrected with some seriousness. Why not tell Evie, indeed? For even if Evie blows their cover, there'll be time for Alfred to move out if he has to; and then what can the parents do? Of course, Barbara stands to lose her car and allowance. But she's making her own money now anyway.

"Think of what's to be gained if Evie does keep her mouth shut," she goes on. "No more sneaking around, no more worrying . . ."

And so it is that Barbara and Mona and Seth and Alfred are soon making like hovercraft outside Evie's darkroom door.

"Evie?" says Barbara.

"Just a sec, okay?" says Evie Squeaky Voice. "I'm right in the middle of printing some stuff."

"Okay." They wait outside the darkroom for another five minutes. They watch the red light at the bottom of the door until everywhere else they look, there's a green stripe. "Are you ready yet?" says Barbara.

"Are you still waiting?" says Evie. The phone rings; there's a vertical flash of red as Barbara hands the phone in to her cousin. Evie talks without leaving the darkroom. Barbara and Mona and Seth and Alfred wait.

"When you get a moment, I have something to tell you," says Barbara finally. "It's a big surprise. Why don't you come downstairs when you're ready."

But Evie never does come downstairs, and eventually the gang just calls it a night.

More and more, Alfred does as he likes around the house; and somehow he manages to avoid Evie in a way that begins after a while to feel magical. Then it feels mysterious; and then fraught with higher significance, like Easter Island, or the Bermuda Triangle. *It's a sign,* Seth says, and who could disagree? It's hard to look at the way Alfred and Evie pass without meeting and not say it was ordained. Alfred was meant to live here, unencumbered, and they were meant to relax about it. Indeed, Alfred-and-Evie-watching begins to become a sport. *Sighted, 5:45: Alfred entering via the tunnel. Sighted, 5:49: Evie entering via the front door.* Evie is elfin, and light of foot, and easy to miss as she leafs through the mail in the front hall; she sashays away kitchen bound, just as Alfred heads for the john. Probably he should be more careful. But his hearing, after all; anyway, Evie fails to look up at the sound of the toilet flushing, becomes immersed in a letter as Alfred makes for the den, crossing her line of vision. He, of course, is not exactly elfin, or light of foot either. The gang wonders, *Is she blind?* and it's hard not to laugh at the idea. A blind photographer! Whoever could imagine such a thing? But Barbara says Evie's not blind, she's just not using her eyes because she's concentrating on other things. For example, her photography, and also some love affair she's conducting long-distance. Evie spends a lot of time imagining the Philippines, says Barbara, and of course this immediately becomes a joke. *What's the matter?* says person A. *Are you imagining the Philippines?* To which person B is supposed to answer with suitable intonation, *Yes, behold yon volcano, it explodes, I am full of wonder.* Or, *Yes, there are rice paddies everywhere, oh my dearest, my feet are wet with love.* Or, *No, I ain't imagining no nothing. See, I'm just as deaf and blind as I look.*

This last is Alfred's contribution, which he makes without prompting. For as they relax, he seems to relax too, a true member of the gang. His anger seems to have dissipated; he seems finally to trust that Mona and Barbara and Seth, his friends, are the exception to some general rule. He finally seems, in fact, to feel gratitude. One day he runs smack into Evie outside. He tells her he works for the gardener. She accepts this explanation without apparent surprise.

Mona and Barbara and Seth relax some more, and being relaxed, begin to belatedly realize that it is summer. They begin to notice the way the heat hangs in the air, as if too lazy to move up or down; they notice the thin-stretched sky, and the blunt muzzy glare of certain avenues. Also the way that the trees, which in autumn seem to stand so high and mighty, now seem to have inexplicably lost their dignity. Everything melds together. Everything needs water. How nice it would be to go to the beach, Mona thinks; and Seth, as if reading her mind, agrees.

"Why don't you go visit Callie," he says, massaging her neck. "I'll still be here when you come back."

"What an interesting prediction," says Mona.

Still she is on the fence until she runs into Bea.

"Mona!" trills Bea from her Thunderbird. "Stay right there, I'm pulling over." And pull over she does, in a dazzling U-turn such as blows her sun hat right off.

Mona asks how was the luau; Bea reports how much the guests enjoyed the bowling, not to say how they raced pineapple boats across the country club pool. Only the grass skirts flopped; her theory was that certain women were afraid they would look fat in them.

"So no hula dancing," she says, rescuing her hat from the front passenger seat. "And nobody swam. Maybe it's just as well, after all those piña coladas. Still, can you imagine that? In this weather. You'd think everyone would be dying to get in the water."

"I'm dying to get in the water," says Mona.

"So then why don't you go visit your sister with the resort job?"

"How did you know where my sister is?"

"Anything that doesn't matter, Seth tells me," says Bea.

"Maybe I will go visit Callie at the beach."

"A terrific idea. Need a ride somewhere?"

Mona shakes her head; a car honks; Bea waves. "Aloha!" she cries. "Have a good time!" And with another traffic-stopping U-turn, this time with one hand on her head, she is gone.

CHAPTER 9

The Expressers in Rhode Island

"What are you doing?" Mona finds Callie on the golden crescent beach. It is early morning, so early even the sun's still all zipped up in its nice warm sleeping bag, just as Mona would like to be. Instead she is feeling astonished to have discovered Callie not only up but already into what appears to be her regimen—an enthralling aspect of Callie's grown-up life that Mona might have missed altogether, had she not happened to waken to go to the bathroom, and on the return trip stumbled upon Callie's absence. Now she beholds her sister in what is in their family considered a most compromising state—namely, one in which she's bound to catch a cold. For despite the chill, Callie is barely dressed in an orange swirly-print kimono-like gown, with a fringe at the bottom. Attached to the fringe at random intervals are beads and what look to be rabbit feet, although they could also be some other manner of rodent extremity. Mona holds out the limp hope they may prove synthetic. As for Callie's own feet, they are bare, like her hands, which appear nonetheless objects of intense interest. They drift slowly around her; she scrutinizes them as if for signs of dishpan damage. For this activity, she has put in her contact lenses. Also she has put her hair up—the better to swivel her neck, it seems. She bends and straightens her legs in slow motion, all the while rotating and stretching her back and shoulders as if to demonstrate for a science fair how very remarkable are her many functioning joints. Indeed, Mona has never before appreciated how jointed her sister is, a regular praying mantis.

Callie answers, "Exercises."

"What kind of exercises?" says Mona.

"Chinese exercises."

"But I always thought the Chinese don't believe in exercise." Mona says this because one of Helen's greatest points of life pride has been not only that she has never sweated, but that she has only rarely perspired, and that in times of record high temperature and humidity both. Of course, she owed much in this accomplishment to the aid of talcum powder.

"Well," says Callie, looking at her hands. "That's wrong."

"Don't tell me," guesses Mona. "The Chinese invented exercise."

Callie doesn't answer.

"Table tennis, for example, a game played for thousands of years. Witness the fossil balls unearthed by that world-famous archaeological team, who were they? Ah, yes—Ping and Pong."

"Oh, Mona," says Callie. "The morning was so peaceful without you."

"Just tell me what you're doing, and I'll go back to sleep."

"*Tai qi,*" says Callie.

"Is it for your flab?"

"Please be serious."

"I am. I'm being seriously serious."

"It is not for my flab. It's for my *qi*—my breath. My spirit."

"It's probably good for your flab too. I mean, it can't be bad."

Callie stops.

"I never heard of anybody doing exercises for their spirit, but it sounds like a good idea. I'm surprised, though, that you can't do them in bed. I mean, if they're for your spirit."

Callie puts her hands on her hips—a forbidden gesture their mother has deemed low-class. "Have you thought about going back to sleep?"

"Okay, okay," Mona says. "Just one more question and I'll go, okay? Just one more question?"

"One more question."

"How come you're turning Chinese? I thought you were sick of being Chinese."

It isn't until breakfast that Mona is finally tendered this explanatory sweetmeat: Callie is indeed sick of being Chinese, but there is being Chinese and being Chinese.

"I see," Mona says. "How true."

Instead of Wheaties or an English muffin, Callie is eating *shee-veh*, with assorted pickled and deep-fried condiments, something like what their parents used to eat in China. Of course, Helen and Ralph now prefer raisin bran—less work, they say, and good for your performance. (This last being a delicate reference to their alimentary output.) Still Callie eats on, saying she didn't understand what it meant to be Chinese until she met Naomi.

"Really," Mona says. "And can Naomi teach me to be Chinese too?"

"If you ask her, I'll kill you," says Callie pleasantly.

And so it is that when Naomi and Mona are introduced— really, reintroduced—Mona prepares to ask her immediately. This being, after all, Mona's pesky nature. Her pesky nature is for once checked, though, by her dumbfounded fascination. For Naomi is a formidable presence and certainty such as puts you in mind of somebody like Oliver Wendell Holmes; you just know one day she'll be using three names too. Also her voice does not scrape along like a regular old voice, but somehow seems to resonate with delight and sorrow at the same time. Hers is an outsized, magnificent instrument: the voice of a woman, thinks Mona, and an older woman at that—a woman of amplitude, and bosom.

Naomi, though, looks more the way you might expect, which is to say that she is tall, and loose-limbed, almost hipless, and of completely average shelf size. Her facial addenda have a kind of mythic circularity—round glasses, hoop earrings, basketball Afro; if she were an archaeological ruin, you would surmise circles to be of central significance to her culture. *Large round eyes too!* you might note, the opening lines of your thesis typing themselves before your eyes. But a few paragraphs down, you'd be stumped, for her face is square as a chessboard, and below her fetching dimples and ever-so-pouty mouth juts a jaw of the no-truck type, sweet as the prow of an Arctic icebreaker. No one would dare call her pretty.

And yet you wouldn't call her not beautiful, for she conducts herself like a beauty. She has a beauty's bearing—her circumspection, her poise. She has a beauty's air of restraint. You get the distinct feeling she does not go home from parties feeling like a jerk.

Is this what happens when you take a pom-pom girl from Chicago and set her to reading Lao-tzu in a fancy New England prep school? Mona gathers over the next few days that Naomi grew up on powdered milk, just like her and Callie; but also that Naomi sewed her own clothes and darned her own socks, and had a biggish hand in raising up her brother and sister. Her mom was a car-rental agent, her dad a mechanic. Before she went and got herself that scholarship to prep school, her most daring dream was of a job that did not involve arch supports.

Now she requires a lot of time by herself. She is flattered to hear tell of her most impressive self-possession. However, this surface, she claims, is a mere product of preparation. The way other people get dressed in the morning, she puts herself together—meaning that in the past she has donned like a lift-and-firm foundation a kind of dignity that almost seemed an argument. But now she has *tai qi*, she says; it's all about grounding. "I thought it was about the spirit," Mona says. Naomi, though, just keeps on with her explaining. She's not rufflable, like Callie. She's something closer to Buddhist—meaning that she does meditation, and yoga. She chants, and drinks tea, and makes kites—that's to keep lively her spirit of play. For this has been her experience, she says. The outside world presses in on you, and you have to maintain an equal pressure, in the opposite direction, so as not to implode.

"You make kites? You implode?"

"Spiritually," she says.

Callie nods, basking in reflected wisdom.

"What about jazz?" Mona says. "What about sweet potato pie?"

She blurts this out in stupid fashion; luckily, Naomi likes *all that* too. And later she will discourse a bit about Duke, Monk, Bird, Train. She will tease cool jazz from free jazz, bebop from hard bop. Jazz is definitely one of her interests, and she scarfs down her collard greens with as much gusto as anybody, maybe more. For she also likes Chinese dumplings and diet soda, not to say Scrabble, film noir, star gazing, soccer. She is, in short, a statistical outlier and overcompensator, a Renaissance woman such as Mona would have envied mightily had she not been black.

But as it happens, pretty soon Mona worships her, just like Callie. She does everything Naomi says. She strives to think the way Naomi thinks. In terms of *white folk,* for example. Naomi never says they're out to get your ass, the way Alfred does. She talks about them in a gentler way that makes them seem involuntarily stuck to one another by a special invisible but all-weather glue. This makes Mona and Callie and Naomi stuck together too, by virtue of their being colored folk. Mona has never thought of herself as colored before, though she knew herself not to be white. *Yellow,* says Naomi now. *You are yellow. A yellow person, a yellow girl.* It takes some getting used to, this idea, especially since Mona's summertime color is most definitely brown, and the rest of the year she is not exactly a textbook primary. But then Naomi is not black either; she claims to be closer in color to a paper bag. If she were a cabinet door or a shade of hair dye, people would have a name for her exact shade. But as she is only a person, she is called black, just as Mona and Callie are called yellow. And as yellow is a color, they are colored, which is how it is they are working together on the project.

"What project?"

"Shh," says Callie.

Naomi is more willing to tell her how they are secretly studying the manners and mores of the people at the inn. Naomi and Callie are not sure what exactly they're going to write about these manners and mores, but they know it's going to be a joint project, and for a certain professor; the professor is the type who would probably sign up to be colored if she could. And as she is big on field notes, the project will require what else? Which is why Naomi and Callie are writing down what the guests do, and say, and eat. What sports they play, and at what age they start their children at tennis, at sailing, at skiing. Whether they carry their own luggage. Whenever a guest does something peculiar, such as describe for Callie all about being stationed in the Pacific, or inquire of Naomi whether she might recall the lines of a certain spiritual, Callie and Naomi jot this down; and later they share their tidbits, hooting. There are perhaps fewer of these incidents than they would like. However, the uniform they wear involves a kilt and a polo shirt, clearly a Scottish theme, and both of them do regularly get asked: What part of Scotland are you from? To which Callie answers, the Far Eastern part; and Naomi, that she's not actually from Scotland. She is, she says, from deepest, darkest Wales.

"But what about when they're nice?" Mona says. "Why don't you write down those times?"

"Good point." Naomi smiles. "That can be your job."

And so it is that Mona spends the better part of her holiday eavesdropping. Pen and notebook in hand, she tries to pretend that she's sketching—drawing a picture of one of the outbuildings, or the dock with the seagulls—when actually she's listening to what people say. Much of it is innocuous enough: Who's going to school where, and when they're taking their semester abroad; who married whom, and whether or not it was a shame. They chat with the younger set about what it means to be a good sport; also about agreeable children, by which they mean children who do not contradict their elders. Among themselves, they return to subjects like their board work. Suddenly someone will leap to life on the subject of a particular art foundation, or teen shelter. For the Jews, it turns out, are not the only ones who worry about the world; these people too consider that the problems of society are theirs to fix. They will do right. They will hold forth, saving for later the chat about their boats. Races they have been in, and how they made out. Also where they summer, where they winter. These are verbs Mona always thought were nouns.

Naomi says, "What they're talking about is status."

"Status?" Mona says, as if this is her first word of Chinese.

"Listen more carefully," Naomi says. "Think about what it means to have leisure." And when Mona complains that it's hard to get in hearing range, Naomi says Mona must learn to make herself invisible. "Think wall bug," she says.

This is how it happens that Mona is in the lobby thinking *wall bug*, when through the door saunters sweet Eloise Ingle, her four stepbrothers like a wall of bodyguards behind her. Their bobbing heads ascend the staircase at different rates. Otherwise, they are identifiably Ingle-y, right down to their jockish jocularity. One of them, the most baby-faced, with floppy brown hair and an open demeanor, has resourcefully supplied himself with a walnut to toss around; his several siblings, roused by this ball-like object, are fitfully moved to piracy. Much scuffling, of a good-natured sort that does not threaten the dignity of the lobby but in fact seems to add to its summer fun feel. The family shirt is Lacoste. The family shoe is the scuffed-up Top-Sider.

There is no family sock. They cluster around the tennis sign-up sheet and begin signing up for time before their dad has even checked in, it's the Protestant play ethic. They're going to play singles and doubles, every possible combination of one against the others, starting at 8:00 A.M. That is for tomorrow. For today it turns out that they have called ahead, and reserved some courts already.

Eloise, meanwhile, has brought her dog with her, and although pets are expressly against inn policy, no one at the front desk so much as raises an eyebrow. This, perhaps, is because the dog goes with her outfit. The one family member not busy signing up for tennis, Eloise is nevertheless wearing tennis whites—white sneakers, white socks, white skirt. No love beads, no bell-bottoms, no water-buffalo sandals such as she would be wearing at home; and Mona notices that she has not skimped the way Barbara Gugelstein once told her you can, buying a boys' Lacoste shirt. Instead Eloise has paid extra for the ladies' version, with its several more buttons, closely spaced. White headband. And in her arms, well camouflaged, the white dog—a mini something or other, by the looks of him, part poodle, part hamster, the kind of officious little pompadour that yaps a good game at neighborhood cats but keeps a sensible distance away when the ferocious felines yawn back.

Eloise's pinkish-brown dad is commanding in his Nantucket red pants, though his tennis hat has the lift of something being blown off his head. Has it shrunk in the wash? Gotten mixed up with someone else's? It is a hat that would make Mona's dad look like a boob. So flinty a type is Mr. Ingle, however, what with his thin straight mouth and thin straight nose and thin straight eyebrows, that even thus attired he looks to be throwing care to the wind in a philanthropic manner. He is clearly the sort of man who does not raise his voice. He is clearly the sort of man who uses phrases like *The evidence notwithstanding* and *Make no mistake*, and without having to rehearse them first. They spring from his tongue, natural as daisies. *Make no mistake. This hat notwithstanding, I am no boob.*

Eloise's stepmom, on the other hand, is more meticulously assembled. Her sandy hair is coiffed à la Jackie Onassis; her outfit is whimsically nautical. Anchors abound. Moreover, she is herself tall and spindly as a mast. Proudly she breasts the great lobby, albeit with a slight limp. The family luggage follows behind on a bellboy-powered barge, a leather and canvas heap bristling with rackets. It passes. Mona is espied.

"Mona!"

"Eloise."

"What are you doing here?" says Eloise, and before Mona has a chance to ask back, adds, "I asked first."

"I thought you had a place on an island in Maine," Mona says. "Mid-coast."

Eloise, stiffening, stops petting her dog. "We do," she says, and lifts her chin as if to place it in the sort of face harness eye doctors use to check your retina. "However, this year we were overrun by cousins and had to get away. They were using blueberries for spitballs."

"How awful," Mona says.

"Are you up with your family?"

"I'm spying," Mona almost says, but instead manages: "I'm visiting my sister."

"Your sister?"

"She's working here."

"Working here? You mean as a waitress?"

Mona tries to explain that you have to go to Harvard or Yale or Brown or someplace to get a job here, it's not like being a regular waitress.

But Eloise asks finally, with a toss of her hair mass to disguise her polite horror, "Is Callie putting herself through college?"

"Well," Mona says; and then recalling she's a spy, she for once says the agreeable thing. "Things haven't been so hot at the pancake house."

"Oh, I'm so sorry," Eloise says instantly.

Whereupon Mona looks down the way Lauren Bacall supposedly did when she was terrified of the cameras and the lights; and as this worked on Humphrey Bogart, so it works on Eloise. She hugs her dog close, petting him with long sad strokes, as if not sure how else to express her heart's overflow.

So begins Mona's life as a cause. In temple, Mona knew all the answers, and Eloise was the second most noteworthy convert. Here, Eloise seeks to find diversions for Mona, to brighten up her cheerless little life. Eloise is kindness itself. She is generosity itself. She is self-lessness itself. Mona is a lucky camper who goeth but for the grace of the Fresh Air Fund. Eloise suggests they take a boat out together. She'll teach Mona to sail, she says. And indeed, the bay is balm for the soul. How far the distant shore! They behold the wriggly reflection of the clouds in the water. Unfortunately, when Mona takes over the tiller, the boat jibes wildly; she is beaned but good by the boom. Eloise volunteers to teach her to play shuffleboard, a sport she says you can easily manage even while holding an ice pack to your head.

And so it is that, much too soon, the afternoon draws to a most amiable close. On the line, or out? They debate, they jump up and down. They admire their long shadows. From the top of a certain hill, they can see themselves stretch right down to the water. They are more enormous than enormous; with their shadow arms they can pick up whole boats, the dock, even an islet across the way. And look how thin they are! Twiggy, move over. Tomorrow they will play croquet, says Eloise. A game Mona did not think was played outside of *Alice in Wonderland*. Mona volunteers to give Eloise a tour of the workers' quarters.

They part fondly. At dinner, they wave to each other across the dining room. Eloise's family, naturally, has a table by the window, one of the very best. It's where the inn holds its buffet on Sundays, two steps up from the rest of the dining room. The paned window stretches from kneewall to ceiling there, and curves to form a crescent in which the Ingles command the center spot. As the sun sets over the bay, they seem to be floating, first in the ocean, then in an ocean of light. They shade their eyes—squinting, it seems, at their own tremendous luck. Finally the sky begins to darken. Their feet fall into shadow, their knees. They begin, it appears, to sink. They pass the bread basket. Meanwhile, Mona stands by Callie's station, trying to make herself in-conspicuous. She's waiting for her pass-off; Callie has promised her the world's finest doggie bag.

Team Ingle trains the next morning as scheduled, or so Callie reports. Mona sleeps through the first set and a half.

"How goes the infiltration?" asks Naomi, doing dishes. Mona asks her again what kind of a project this is. Naomi reassures her it's most worthwhile, especially for something as yet half-baked.

"Because I would really rather avoid Eloise altogether. She wasn't exactly my best friend at home," Mona says.

Naomi shakes the water from her hands; the drops hit the metal sink with a patter. "It's your vacation," she says. "Do what you want."

Mona decides that what she wants is to try to call Seth again. This is not so simple, since all the workers share one outdoor pay phone, and since she is not even a worker proper. The evening is impossible, she has tried that already; the day, next to impossible. Still Mona waits in line. No answer at the teepee. No answer at Barbara's house, either. She ponders.

But before she can decide what else it is she wants, she discovers not only that Eloise is engaged in mortal combat with her stepmother, but that into this engagement, she, Mona, has been drafted. At issue is Eloise's trust, a sum of money her stepmother believes to have been left to Eloise as a formality, to avoid taxes. Really it belongs to Eloise's father, believes this stepmother—which is how it is that she, the manager of the household, is managing it. She maintains that Eloise is too young to have her own income, especially since she is threatening to use it to move out of the house. There have been words.

But for now there are none. They do not yell at each other, or argue, or throw things. Instead they are with each other exquisitely brief. Eloise makes herself clear by placing between them on the bench an intermediary mass, namely Mona. A strategy, Mona surmises, that Eloise has used before, for the brothers do not ask who Mona is as they break for water, or switch sides of the court. They glance her way, but seem to realize that she is a statement. Only Eloise addresses Mona, and more and more sporadically. The tension level seems to be growing; Mona can only conclude that she is missing some of the jabs and left hooks. For Eloise's stepmother—her name is Frisky—is apparently making herself clear by doing needlepoint. A hunt scene, very sporting, with a number of dogs. The execution of this is hampered by Eloise's real dog, on account of which animal Mrs. Ingle is obliged to keep her bag of yarns poked into a hole in the chain-link fence. As she is also having a problem with her ankle, she requires Eloise to stand up every now and then, to fetch a bit of yarn for her.

"The Chinese red," says she. "The cerulean blue."

"If you would pass this to Frisk," says Eloise to Mona, as though her stepmother is not just behind her.

The dog, it turns out, is also a statement. Dog, Capital D, his name is in full, exactly because he is not what Mrs. Ingle considers a real dog. Real dogs are large dogs, like setters and retrievers—magnificent dogs with magnificent instincts.

Dog, Capital D, on the other hand, is what Mrs. Ingle considers a Hollywood dog. She says this because the one time he ever had a chance to prove himself with a burglar, he not only did nothing in the way of dissuasion, but actually followed the poor criminal about—wagging his tail and proving so persistent that the burglar finally had to circle back to the house. He was caught trying to coax Dog back into the kitchen. Which to Eloise just proved that the man wasn't a run-of-the-mill burglar. Maybe she was prejudiced about criminals, but she thought that a more typical burglar would have shot Dog or something, and that her father should not have had the guy prosecuted. But her father did anyway. *The law is the law. Social order is threatened on all sides these days,* he said. *Witness the hippies. One has to have a system. For one starts to think twice about things, and what does one find? That in a certain light, things appear one way; but in another light, another.*

And in a way Mona knows what he means. For example, when Mrs. Ingle finally limps off to her room, Mona finds herself sitting quite chummily with Eloise—from which spot she almost can't remember what it was that she didn't like about Eloise back at temple. Was it her popularity? Her hair? The fact that she went out with Andy Kaplan? I must have just been jealous, Mona thinks now. For slowly but surely her entire appraisal of the family is changing; even Eloise's brothers are beginning to seem like four distinct persons. Eloise points out their sports profiles: There is floppy-haired Charlie, with the freckles and the reckless first serve. There is Sumner with the silver glasses, who calls balls out when they're in; everyone would like to assume it's a matter of his prescription. Eliot, with the baritone, puts that ball away; whereas chubby Andrew is more likely to set you up that you may do yourself in. Mona contemplates this education in demolition. And as much as she recognizes tennis to be just the sort of sport Helen admires, she must admit the undeniable truth. The four of them out there playing does make a charming sight. Even more charming is the sight, a little later, of Charlie and Andrew and Sumner practically sitting on their hands so that Eloise can play. Eloise plays well, especially at net, but she can't deal with her brothers' serves. And so they bloop it over to her. Their crosscourts too come hopping sweet as Easter bunnies. Mona thinks how pleasant it must be to be thus indulged on this large parcel of oceanfront property; they are close enough to the water that a ball going over the fence could conceivably end up in the waves. More likely, it would land in the sand. All the same, the Ingles cry, "And it's going, going— out to sea!" if they lose a ball. Not that this happens too often. But so infectious is their enthusiasm that by the third time, Mona finds that she's chanting too, along with them. And when a couple comes to claim the court and is upset to find that they mistook the sheet by the inn desk as the sign-up for today, when in fact it's for tomorrow, Mona is as satisfied as the Ingles are generally that it's the couple's own fault. They should've asked someone if they didn't know what was what.

"We can't play tomorrow, we're going home," wails the woman.

And really, who knows? If she hadn't shaken her racket at them like a madwoman, the Ingles might well have given up their time remaining. But instead they agree that fair is fair. It's what Mr. Ingle always tells the kids is the great lesson of life: *You've got to know how the game is played.*

Mona is invited to have supper with the Ingles. She's to sit with them at the sunset, as their guest, even though she doesn't have proper clothes with her. The dress code calls for tie and jacket for men, the equivalent for women. This does not mean jeans, which is all Mona has brought, and she has a feeling it does not mean Callie's swirly print kimono with the rabbit feet either. Still Eloise thinks Mona should come. She says her father will speak to the maître d'.

Mona is skeptical. "What is he, the Pope? He can arrange a special dispensation?"

"He rowed with the owner in prep school." Eloise says this with a simplicity that would become a Shaker abbess.

Mona hesitates greatly.

But when she next runs into Callie and Naomi, she is dressed in Eloise's continued generosity. A brightly flowered wrap skirt hangs down to her calves, and she is wearing with it a top of a tropical hue.

"And what is this I see before me?" says Naomi. "Do I spy . . . a spy?"

Callie laughs. "Goes great with your peace pendant."

Naomi and Callie are wearing football jerseys and cutoffs.

"So how goes the infiltration?" asks Naomi.

Mona shrugs. "They're not so bad. They just play a lot of games."

"Well, keep up the good work," says Callie.

"Hold down the fort," says Naomi.

"Don't let any flies fly by," says Callie.

"Really," Mona says. "Maybe they're not typical."

But when, after cocktails and chatting in the lounge, time for supper trots around, the first thing that happens is that a new waitress approaches the table. This is not the Ingles' waitress-for-the-week; Ginger, it turns out later, has managed to break her toe swimming. This is a replacement waitress, to whom Mr. Ingle's very first words are, "So what part of Scotland are you from?"

Mona looks up.

"I'm not from Scotland," says Naomi, and winks at Mona.

Mona looks down.

"Oh, really," says Mr. Ingle.

And that is when, to Mona's profound surprise, Naomi looks down too. She does not say she's from deepest, darkest Wales. She looks as though she has never seen Mona before in her life.

Mona admires the sunset for a moment. What a view! It really is something to have a seat like this on the world. All the same, Mona is about to supply the "She's from deepest, darkest Wales," when Naomi says, "Would you like some wine with dinner?"

Mr. Ingle orders. Naomi leaves. Mona peruses the menu. You can order all you want here. You can have an appetizer and a soup and a salad, even two of each, or three. You can have the fruit cup and the shrimp cocktail and the oysters Rockefeller; you can have the salad Niçoise and the chef's salad and the Caesar salad. You can have the clear broth and the clam chowder and the cream of leek; and then you can have the filet mignon and the lobster and the swordfish, with the baked potato and the rice pilaf and the home fries on the side; also the carrots and the broccoli and the sliced beets. For dessert you can have a piece of everything on the cart if you want—you don't even have to say anything, you can just point. But here's the surprise: Nobody orders very much in this family. Mona is the only one to order two of anything. Some of the Ingles don't even order one of each category— for instance, Mrs. Ingle, who goes for one cup of the clear broth and one piece of swordfish. Steamed broccoli on the side, no starch. This is not because she is on a diet. This is because she doesn't much care for eating, actually, just as she doesn't much care for the view. The sun is too much, she says, especially night after night. Charlie thinks she should wear sunglasses if the light bothers her, but she says it simply isn't done.

To order doubles is another thing that *simply is not done*. Mona wishes she had not, as the guest, been asked to order first, so that she would have realized this. It's too late, though. Naomi presents her, at each course, with what seems like more food than the rest of the table has ordered combined. Mona has two dishes before her, where everyone else has one, or none; and to make matters worse, Naomi has seemingly arranged for extra-large helpings. She presents these wordlessly, with a blank look on her face. Mona tries to catch her eye, but Naomi will not look at her; if anything, her chin seems to jut out even farther than usual as she leans over Mona's shoulder. Mona stares at its underside, thinking how this is an aspect of Naomi that she literally has not seen before. Though what did Mona expect? Nobody could invent herself the way Naomi has without also being able to serve a person what she asked for.

What can Mona do but eat? It seems to her that she has to at least sample each thing. She is glad Callie is off tonight, and not there to see her, although she also wonders if for once she couldn't use some sisterly guidance. Would Mona be in this situation if she took *tai qi* more seriously?

"Some of us have an actual pea under the mattress," Mr. Ingle is saying. "Others of us imagine peas where there are only in fact only lumps."

Apropos of what he says this, Mona's not sure. But she can feel herself growing hot, as if he is talking about her, or Callie, or Naomi. Is she being too sensitive? Is she indeed imagining a pea where there is only a lump? She is, Mona thinks, she must be. Although maybe she's not, since following the pea/lump comment, the conversation mysteriously meanders her way.

"Her sister Callie is working her way through college," says Eloise. (Because of her fight with her stepmother, this is the first thing she has volunteered all evening.) "And Mona may well have to do the same."

"Dear, dear," says Mrs. Ingle. "We admire you, young lady." Is that by way of reconciliation? She passes Mona the bread basket—as if Mona is not eating enough already—insisting that the popovers are divine. Mona wonders how she knows.

"Don't have one if you don't want one." Eloise gazes off into the sunset, as if after a departing knight.

Mona diplomatically takes a roll, but does not eat it.

Mrs. Ingle says nothing. Eloise says nothing. Mr. Ingle says nothing. The boys start analyzing people they know on scholarships. All of these people, it turns out, are great athletes. They go through the sports these kids play, they argue about how essential to the team these scholarship kids are. Lacrosse, hockey. Baseball, swimming, tennis. Rugby. Crew. Mona begins to rather regret not only that she ordered so much food, but that the inn has this system at all, where so many little courses are served in so leisurely a manner. And is Naomi purposefully letting the Ingles enjoy a particularly leisurely dinner? It does seem so, as the conversation progresses to the next question of interest—namely, are the scholarship kids self-financing? Charlie maintains that they are not charity cases at all. In fact, they generate so much alumni contribution that he thinks they are a moneymaking proposition.

"I do believe I've had enough of this topic of conversation," says Mrs. Ingle.

"If not all of them, at least the starters," continues Charlie—undeterred by his mother, maybe even pleased to have riled her. "And I bet the school breaks even on the rest."

"So why don't they recruit some more?" says Sumner, sardonically. "Why do they bother to let us in, if these kids are so great."

"Because they generate the contribution, and we contribute the contribution," says Eliot, irrefutably.

"Enough," says Mrs. Ingle again.

The boys exchange glances.

"I wouldn't mind being a scholarship student," says Andrew, flushing. "I think it's a great honor."

The sun goes down and stays down. When the lobster arrives, Mona realizes that everyone else has ordered fish. Besides being the only person thinking how nonkosher is this dish, Mona will be the only person eating with a bib. Eloise volunteers to help her with the crustacean, and, willing to engage in any interaction, Mona agrees. Eloise shows Mona how to use the cracker. She explains to her about the tomalley. Mrs. Ingle points out the roe. Eloise ignores her and points out the roe herself. Unfortunately, in the process of cracking one of the claws, Mona squirts lobster juice across the table and hits Naomi.

Naomi finally looks at Mona. Mona stands to help wipe off her friend. Everyone else watches.

When Mona sits back down, Mrs. Ingle asks, "And where are you from?"

To which Mona answers, surprised, "The same town as you. In fact, Eloise and I are classmates."

Says Mrs. Ingle again, "But where are you from?"

Eloise's brother Andrew glosses this helpfully. "She means where are you from, from."

"Ah," Mona says. And then, with Naomi attending, Mona says, "Deepest, darkest China."

Two of the brothers laugh, but the rest of the family is not sure whether to laugh or not.

"Is that a joke?" says Eloise.

"Yes," Mona says.

And to her credit, Eloise smiles as if with genuine amusement—thrilled, apparently, that Mona has said something fresh to her stepmother.

Mona now seems to be officially in their midst and, as such, fair game. She works on the lobster; they work on her, starting with the astounding fact of Naomi's being Mona's sister's roommate.

"Full scholarship to Harvard." Andrew whistles.

"Harvard-Radcliffe," says Mona.

"Is she on any teams?" Eliot wants to know.

"Basketball?" guesses Sumner.

"Ask her yourselves," Mona says. But they do not talk to Naomi;

when she's serving or clearing, only Mona talks. It's not a lot of conversation, but it's enough that you'd never know anything was ever the matter between them. And when Naomi leaves, Mona talks some more, only now about all things Chinese—her parents, and China, and how many of her relatives are over there, and whether she's been back, and whether she speaks the language. ("Of course she speaks it," says Eliot when Sumner asks. "Open your eyes.") Also whether Mona misses China even though she's never been there.

"That must be so weird," says Andrew. "I mean, to never get a chance to see your own home."

"It's not her home," says Charlie.

"So what is her home?" demands Sumner.

"America," says Charlie. "I think."

They also discuss Chinese art, about which Mona knows nothing and Mrs. Ingle everything, as the latter inadvertently demonstrates by making Mona do the talking. Communism is Mr. Ingle's forte. He discusses the Korean War with Mona, assuming she knows what a parallel is. He discusses Hong Kong, and Formosa, which Mona at least knows is now called Taiwan.

"When did that happen?" Mr. Ingle wants to know.

Then begins a more personal conversation, with special conventions of speech. For example, Mr. Ingle begins introducing his questions with "I'm curious." Mrs. Ingle, on the other hand, tends to "Do you mind my asking?" Mona answers, figuring it's just the cost of dinner. Once or twice she asks them about where they come from, occasioning a general kind of answer. But then they switch the topic, gently but firmly, back to her. For Mona is so much more interesting than they are; they already know all about themselves.

Finally Naomi calls Mr. Ingle away from the table for a telephone call. Everyone seems to have been waiting for this, because the atmosphere in his absence is of hushed anticipation. Mona returns gratefully to her lobster.

"Let's try this," she says to Eloise, and she slides the meat out of the tail by pushing with a fork from the small end. This is an efficient approach Helen taught Mona just a few summers ago, having learned it herself from a clam shack place mat.

"Wow. Did you just figure that out?" says Eloise.

"The Chinese really are going to take over the world," says Eliot. "They really are smarter than everybody else."

Mr. Ingle returns with an inscrutable look on his face.

"Say what you will," says Mrs. Ingle, "it's just not right."

"Have I said something?" says Mr. Ingle.

"That poor man has a family too," says Mrs. Ingle. "In fact, he even has a daughter. . . ."

"Thank you for your opinion," he answers. "If there were a choice, we would choose." Everyone at the table can hear the perfectly round black period at the end of the sentence.

And then it's back to the Far East until the dessert cart wheels over, bearing a strawberry shortcake to die for.

"That's what we do when no one is talking," says Eloise. "We converse."

Eloise and Mona and Naomi and Callie sit on the beach in the dark, using beach towels they filched from the bathhouse. These are just as threadbare and tiny as Mr. Gugelstein maintained, and instantly damp; sitting on one is like sitting on a wet diaper. Only Eloise's dog seems truly comfortable. A white curl on the black sand, he looks like a furry antimoon, except when he leaps up to patrol the strip. He barks at the waves as if to scare them off his property; lucky for him, the tide is going out.

Meanwhile, Eloise continues. "Thou shalt not raise thy voice. It's the first commandment. But I do sometimes, I can't help it. Maybe because I'm half Jewish; that's what my stepmother says. She says I'm a bit . . . *expressive*."

"Is she right?" asks Naomi.

Eloise shrugs. "It must be from watching Woody Allen movies. I'm the only one in my family who even thinks he's funny. Everyone else thinks it's a shame a chap that clever wasn't sent to prep school."

"Might not it have something to do with having your real family broken up and your inheritance stolen?" Naomi says. "That would make one *expressive*, would it not?"

"It would!" Eloise says that according to her stepmother, Eloise does not realize that there are things one does not say—indeed, that one should not have *things to say* to begin with. "If you do, then you haven't been brought up properly."

"Ah—a catch-22: The rules of your set," says Naomi, "are that you should belong without objection to your set."

Manners, reticence, class. They discuss self-hatred, which Mona doesn't exactly understand; also something called antagonistic cooperation, which seems to be a kind of dance you can't stop dancing even if you hate your partner as much as you hate yourself.

"Don't you think Mom and Dad looked down on themselves when they were in China?" says Callie at one point. "Think about those gunboats in the harbor. Don't you think they hated the British but in a way looked up to them too?"

Says Mona, "I never thought about it before."

"But here you are now," says Naomi. "Thinking."

"And here I am too," says Eloise.

"Half Jewish," Mona says.

"Maybe starting to turn part black too," says Naomi.

"Why not?" Eloise raises her fist proudly, the way Miss Montana did in the Miss America pageant one year.

Mona and Callie raise their fists as well. "Black is beautiful!"

"They are the oppressors," says Naomi, her voice extra sonorous. "We are the expressers."

They all laugh.

"Seriously, though," continues Naomi. "If I were you, I would express myself right out of that household."

"Why don't you come stay with us?" Mona looks to Naomi and Callie for approval; they nod with the sort of dignity you associate with beards. "Of course, it's not the Ritz."

"I wouldn't think so." Eloise smiles. However, she doesn't say yes, doesn't say no, just fills her shoes up with sand, then empties them out. Her golden hair ripples silver down her back, a private sea.

Mona spends the morning alone, trying to call Seth. No answer. She tries to call Barbara. No answer there either. In the afternoon, Eloise shows up with Dog, a pile of hotel linen, and some hotel blankets. "I wasn't sure how well supplied you were," she says.

"Actually," says Callie, "we get the new stuff. Pull with the chambermaids, you know." She winks.

Dog sniffs around while Mona sets Eloise up in the corner of the room, away from the ant trail. Also Eloise gets the one lamp, it's the red carpet treatment. However, with no carpet. Mona explains how they are similarly blessed with no air conditioner.

"I've always preferred the sea breeze," says Eloise. She smiles even as Callie explains how they don't actually get a sea breeze; they're not exactly water view. However, they do get some kind of draft as a result of the kitchen exhaust fan.

"Isn't that hot air?" Eloise doesn't actually stop in the middle of pulling a pillowcase onto a pillow, but she does slow down like a self-reversing machine about to self-reverse.

"All that hot air rising pulls the cold air in behind it," says Callie. "And the cold air flows by our windows."

"How lucky!" says Eloise, picking up speed again.

So happy is she, in fact, that pretty soon they are discussing how long a stay makes her an official runaway, and whether she should go back to Scarshill with Mona when she goes. Mona explains all about Alfred, and how Eloise can probably live at Barbara's house too.

"That's the last place in the world I could live," says Eloise.

"But Barbara lives in a great house. It's not like this." Mona explains how the air-conditioning works so well you practically have to wear a sweater. Plus she'll like Alfred, Mona says, and no one hardly ever sees Evie.

"You don't understand," Eloise is saying again, when in strides Naomi. They can hear her in the vestibule; the wooden screen door bangs shut behind her.

"So trouble really did come to stay," she says, entering the room.

"What do you mean?" says Mona. "You said it was okay. And anyway she's probably going to move pretty soon to Barbara Gugelstein's house."

"Of course she's welcome. But she is not your friend Alfred. Nobody cares what happens to Alfred. If Eloise disappears, every policeman on the East Coast is going to be out searching for her."

And sure enough, no sooner does Naomi finish her sentence than there is rapping on the screen door.

Whispers Naomi, "It was in the script. They all go home again."

"Is that true?" Mona says. "I thought . . ."

"They go home changed, that's all," Naomi says. "A variation on the theme, maybe significant, maybe not." She turns to Eloise as the rap is repeated. "So who is it? The police, or just your father?"

"My father." Eloise is glumly lucid; already she is rising to the occasion, even as she sits on the floor. She lifts her head, lets go of her knees. "He wouldn't want any publicity, especially right now."

And she's right: It's her father. Mona opens the door.

"What is the meaning of this?" His voice sends a tremor across the room.

Eloise stands.

"Are you dressed for dinner?" he asks.

"No," she says.

"You're keeping everyone waiting."

And just like that, Eloise scoops up Dog and is gone.

What would have happened if she had stayed? Naomi and Callie and Mona discuss this over supper. It's Naomi and Callie's day off, which means that they have to cook for themselves; and that means Chinese food so genuine Mona finds it an encounter. Naomi, for example, has learned to do an authentic tea-smoked duck that involves burning tea leaves in a wok and smoking the duck in it for sixteen hours. (Mona, meanwhile, shares Helen's most recent favorite duck dish recipe— namely, Peking duck, Westchester style. The whole secret is soaking the duck overnight in Pepsi-Cola.)

But what would have happened?

Says Mona, "I think Eloise would've become a great spy."

Says Naomi, "If Eloise had stayed, she would have gotten bored."

Is that right?

"Eloise was not brought up to participate in someone else's experiment," says Naomi. "There's nothing we could have done."

And with that, a hush falls over their little supper. They eat silently, peacefully, their faces bedewed by the steam from the rice, their chopsticks clicking against their hotel-logo bowls. They will discuss yin and yang, and balance the foods they eat. They will return the linens, with apologies, to the chambermaids. The chambermaids will rib them about going to Harvard; they will discuss how Juanita has back problems, and how Cookie is getting married. They will plan what to make for a shower present. Then they will meditate; and then, when the kitchen exhaust fan finally goes off, they will sleep.

CHAPTER 10

Camp Gugelstein

Back home, it turns out that Seth and Barbara have been going to the beach also. Alone, it turns out—Alfred, claims Seth, is afraid of the water. "I see," Mona says, though what she beholds in her mind's eye is in fact not fearful Alfred at all, but fearless Barbara and Seth, minimally clad. Side by side on beach blankets. Did the blankets touch? Did their selvages overlap? Is that why there was no answer at the teepee? And is this dread jealousy? Last year in English, when they read *Othello*, Mona thought that poor Moor meshugga, but now she wonders if she is not Moorishly afflicted, that she can't get the phrase *thirsty terry* out of her mind. *All that thirsty terry*, Mona thinks, and there they are, Barbara and Seth, thirsty too; it's only natural in the hot New York sun. They quench their thirsts; they cool off in the water together, it's only natural. They body surf, letting the waves carry them to shore like flotsam. Or is it jetsam? What fun, in any case! They are all abandonment. Their bathing suits fill up with sand, they empty their crotches in the water, discreetly. Pretending to be admiring the day. *Get a load of that seagull!* they say as they slightly squat. And then what? The suntan lotion problem. One must consider one's back, especially Barbara, who's never had a tan in her life—though *avant de* peeling there is at least a stage of being evenly, brilliantly burnt. Mona's seen this, it is really quite autumnal. To attempt to avoid which, Seth, with his surprise domestic side and penetrating touch, may give Barbara a little suntan application. It's only natural. As she lies there prone on her thirsty terry. He rolls the bathing suit straps around. A little up, a little down. And then what? Does not force of habit take over? For once you know another person's body, it's hard to forget that you know it. It's like playing a song, one phrase leads to another.

Speaking of which, Mona notices that Seth has a new little jingle: *You put your beep beep in, you pull your beep beep out, you put your beep beep in, and you move it all about. You do the hanky-panky and you turn yourself around. That's what it's all about.* Mona asks him about the circumstances under which this song came to him. He says the highway was his muse.

"All that bumper-to-bumper traffic," Mona says. "Bump bump bump."

He puts his arm around her, and with his fingers plays her upper arm like an accordion. "My dear Changowitz." He calls her this even though he knows it is Andy Kaplan's name for her, and in his opinion Andy is going to grow up to be some muckety-muck's most-valued assistant. (From comments like these Mona gathers that Andy has been beating Seth at chess.) "Are you trying to get at something?"

"Funny," Mona says. "That's what I was about to ask you."

"So ask." His fingers hit a chord.

But Mona can't ask. Instead she says, apropos of nothing, "Barbara said something about an amalgam tattoo."

"How interesting."

"She said you showed her yours, but she didn't say how it was that you were sharing with her the mysteries of your oral cavity."

"And here I thought you told each other everything." Seth resumes playing.

How to explain? Mona pulls away.

"Let me guess," says Seth finally, facing her. "You are wondering are we three contemplating an experiment in living?"

Mona doesn't answer.

He winks. "We could do anything to which Miss Bourgeoisie would agree."

This is another thing he calls her these days. He says that Mona thinks she's no radical, but that she's just denying her true nature. *Ah, yes,* she says. *Just call me Yoko Ono.*

"Are you by any chance falling in *luff*?" he adds, as seriously as he can in a phony German accent.

"*Mit* who?"

"*Mit* yours truly. Or a reasonable facsimile thereof."

Mona snorts credibly. "To quote a certain stubborn eminence: Never, never, never, never, never."

And she smiles, mortified, as they go on to other topics of conversation. For right or wrong, Mona realizes, she is just like Barbara in this way: She is interested in ownership. *My boyfriend.* Seth thinks this is a capitalistic impulse, but she knows it has more to do with *make sure.* As in, Make sure you don't get your heart smashed up.

After the other topics of conversation, she goes for a long walk. This one is full of interesting ritual ablutions—people washing down their driveways, their cars, their dogs. *The more Jewish you become, the more Chinese you'll be*—that's what Rabbi Horowitz told her once. Meaning what? Is Mona on her way home again already? And how is it that she feels she's become part of someone else's experiment?

Mona runs into Alfred on the road to Barbara's house, where it seems she's been headed without thinking about it.

"Hey, Alfred," Mona says. "I hear you're afraid of the water."

Alfred gives her a mock-sheepish look at odds with his stance, which is arms folded, weight forward, legs spread; he looks like Mr. Clean, only with hair and proper clothes. "Yes, ma'am, I am indeedy," he says. "It's a Negro thing. I'm afraid that water is going to rise up and drown old Alfred. I'm terrified of that water, yes ma'am I am. I'm plain terrified." He laughs, looks away, stretches his mouth as if about to yawn.

"You know, Alfred," Mona says, "if you came with us to the beach sometime, you would realize that a lot of black people swim just fine."

"Oh, no, ma'am, I'm too afraid."

"What's with the jive talk, Alfred? And since when have I become ma'am?"

"Since you started trying to tell Alfred what's going down. Ma'am."

"I'm just trying to be encouraging. You never know. You'd be surprised."

"No, no, ma'am, I do know. You'd be surprised yourself." He does not unfold his arms.

And indeedy, Mona is surprised when, a week or so later, she and Seth and Barbara happen to set out for the beach, only to run into so much traffic that they turn around and come home. For that is when they discover Barbara's empty house not to be empty.

"Holy shit," says Seth.

Alfred's friends are mostly in the den—hanging out, watching TV, drinking beer. Also they are smoking cigarettes, so that Mona's first reaction—after the considerable *shtup* of discovery—is vindication. For recently, Mona has noticed a smell of cigarette smoke in the house, even mentioned it to Barbara. Barbara, though, hasn't been able to smell a thing since she had her nose fixed. Of course, the doctor maintains that, medically speaking, she can smell just fine. But the truth is, she could run a manure factory if that were her inclination. Even when Mona insisted the house fairly reeked of tobacco, Barbara thought it must just be Alfred enjoying an occasional puff, or maybe Maria the maid on the sly. For so vigorous a worker is Maria, that the stove knob markings are wearing off. And what do people with that kind of energy do to relax, but smoke?

Alfred's friends are boisterous without being unruly. They are Afro-proud and close-cropped, shiny-faced and gnarled, bearded and clean-shaven—yet there's a relatedness to the way they move. Maybe this is in response to the unexpected advent of Barbara and Seth and Mona: They've grouped themselves so palpably that a person could almost touch their brotherhood. They are to a man deliberately casual. They are ostentatiously unfazed. You don't get the feeling they're looking to make an exit, quite the contrary. They're looking to give you a chance to absent yourself, with decorum or not—your choice. *You like your tail between your legs, that's fine with us,* they seem to say. *You just do what comes natural.*

What seems to come natural, meanwhile, is for Mona and Seth and Barbara to stand there, shrinking. They curl their toes. They remind themselves that this is a clear violation of the house rules. Such a violation would shock them in any case, but it packs a particular whap because of a particular detail that, up to now, has almost been too much to take in—namely, that sweet as a Kmart parakeet, perched on Alfred's lap, in the midst of everyone, is Evie.

"Evie," says Barbara, finally.

"Hiya," says Evie, waving one of her bare feet.

Evie has not only always been smarter than Barbara, but more clearly an aspiring adult. In junior high she won the Betty Crocker Award; now she is the type of do-gooder to whom benches are dedicated. But to make matters worse, Evie has always been nice. When Barbara, at Evie's bench dedication, wanted nothing more than to puke, Evie actually guessed that. "I guess this makes you want to puke," she said, standing there with her perfect elfin features, and nary a blackhead in sight. It was hard to completely hate her. However, Barbara has always considered herself cooler than Evie, who eschews slang and is instead into things like collecting. Candles, rocks, bugs, shells. It has always seemed to be the way she goes about life—labeling things neatly, pulling them from drawers. "Do you think she knows where her hymen is?" Barbara said once, after being compared yet again to her illustrious relative. "She'll probably marry a curio cabinet." Even after Evie got involved with a guy, it was a long-distance relationship. In short, she's been Miss Priss.

Until now. Evie starts to stand up, but when Alfred pulls her back down, she cheerfully swings her legs. She is wearing cutoffs, below which her thighs look white as dug-up tree roots; her knees glow with indecency.

"Howdy do," she says.

Around her break great rolls of laughter. "Howdy do," says one person, and then another, and then another.

"Well," says Seth. "It must be Howdy Doody time," and that makes them all laugh some more. Seth laughs too.

"Evie," says Barbara again.

"You can't really be surprised," says Evie.

Barbara blinks like a green-eyed barn owl.

"I guess we fooled 'em," says Evie to Alfred. She claps her bare feet together.

"They really are just as deaf and blind as they look," agrees Alfred.

Later Mona and Barbara and Seth listen to Alfred's explanations with admiring irritation. He explains how his friends broke into Charlene's place and stole his clothes back for him, and how this was the first and only time they came to Barbara's house, to deliver the clothes. Evie waltzes along with this story, until at some particularly flirty revolution she breaks out laughing. Then Alfred starts laughing too, and they have to admit Alfred's friends have been coming around a lot. How many times altogether? They're not sure, but Evie says it did feel like she and Alfred were cleaning up all the damn time, doing away with the evidence. As for how did they first get together, they describe it all, from day one, beginning with how shocked Evie was one fine evening, when she found Alfred watching TV in the den. Evie had come in to express her amazement that Barbara was watching baseball, and perhaps to watch some herself—her erstwhile boyfriend was a jock who liked it when she watched games for him and gave the details in her letters.

But in the den was Alfred. Evie screamed and ran out of the room; he had to clap his hand over her mouth to calm her down. "I'm Alfred the cook," he said. "I'm a friend of Barbara's, living here on account of I got eighty-sixed by my bitch wife Charlene." Still she wanted to call the police, until finally he said, "You're too upset. Let me call." And he did, he called the police himself. He was already trying to explain how it was that he, the intruder, was calling to report the intrusion, when Evie started to believe him. Then she got on the line and explained to the officer that there had been a mistake. Of course, the police came out to the house anyway; and this was the first joint show that they did, Alfred and Evie. Explaining to the officer how nothing had happened, and how the phone call was a lark, they were sorry. The officer was skeptical. He wanted to see Alfred's driver's license; he wanted to see the parents of the house. He said he knew the Gugelsteins. But had he ever met Mr. Gugelstein's sister, Elaine? asked Evie. The officer thought. Did she drive a gold Cadillac? "That's her!" exclaimed Evie, though in fact her mother drove a third-hand Benz, one of the two-seaters, with an expansive hood and a roof the size of a cafeteria tray. "And this is my boyfriend." In desperation she kissed Alfred, luxuriating in the officer's shock, not to say Alfred's: Knowing a challenge when it Frenched him, Alfred promptly kissed back.

Which did indeed lead to further developments of the lubricious sort, but not so straightaway as a body might think. For first there was a profound intellectual thirst to be slaked. To wit, once the officer left, Evie was curious. How long had Alfred been in residence? How had he escaped her notice? What was his room like? She recognized his radio station; so she wasn't going crazy, she said. She had thought she was going crazy as a result of spending too much time in the darkroom with those chemicals. Either that, or else she thought Barbara was going crazy, what with the radios on all over the house. He didn't like it here, he told her. But why not? A soul-to-soul conversation. Evie had grown up with black help; in fact, she had had her first affair with her nanny's son, it was practically incest. Also she had once tutored in an inner-city school that was just about all black. She told him about the school she'd worked in. The students had to wear their winter jackets to class, that's how cold it was, and of course there weren't enough books; people had to share. Everyone had head lice. Alfred shook his head. And why was she working in a place like that without even getting paid?

"You're just like your cousin Barbara," he told her. "Got to fix the world right up."

They agreed not to say anything to Barbara and Seth and Mona. Evie didn't want Alfred to get in trouble, and Alfred didn't want to get in trouble himself. For how mad would that Miss Blanco be if she heard that he got caught in the den just the way she predicted?

"Evie thought that just the funniest thing," supplies Alfred.

"Thanks a lot," says Barbara.

Says Evie, "You said you wanted to hear everything."

Barbara powwows with Mona and Seth. Would they have been mad if Alfred and Evie had immediately come clean?

"Not as mad," says Barbara finally, "as we are now. For Evie has lied to us, and Alfred has betrayed our trust."

"But I didn't mean to betray nobody," says Alfred.

"So what were you doing, then?"

"I was just having me a piece of—I mean, excuse me." He winks at Evie. "I was just having me a broadening experience."

"It was fun," says Evie. "Seeing what would happen. Seeing whether you'd figure it out."

"It was like an experiment," says Mona.

"That's right," says Alfred. "We didn't mean no harm. We were just hanging out, seeing what came down."

"*Que sera, sera*, right?" says Mona. "Only it was your experiment instead of ours. You didn't want to be in someone else's experiment."

"I guess you could put it that way," allows Alfred.

In any case, by the time Mona and Barbara and Seth set up camp outside the darkroom door, Evie couldn't possibly have come out. She and Alfred would have both started laughing for sure.

"But what do you mean?" says Seth. "Are you saying that it was all right for him to be a kind of pet, even a rambunctious pet, so long as he didn't turn into a normal horny male?"

"I didn't say anything about horny males," says Barbara.

"If he were white, we'd think he was James Bond," says Seth. "He used his head, he kept his wits, he's balling the girl. Instead we think he's a sneaky Negro. It's like what Baldwin says—when white men fight back, they're heroes. When black men fight back, they're savages."

"I never said he was a sneaky anything, or a savage, either," says Barbara. "And the girl is not just a thing you ball or don't ball." She turns the color of spaghetti sauce for a moment, but goes on. "And what do you think the Russians think of James Bond? If a white man had betrayed us, we'd be pissed off too. The problem is that we're the big bad Russians now."

"The big bad Russians as opposed to the Americans, or the big bad Russians as opposed to the serfs?"

"I mean this has nothing to do with race."

"Nothing to do with race!" Seth guffaws. "You may be right about the James Bond part. But how can anything have nothing to do with race?"

Seth and Mona and Barbara sit cross-legged in Seth's teepee. A perfect circle of rain drips into the fire pit; the drops make little thuds as they land.

Says Mona, "I don't see why Alfred should be evicted if this whole affair isn't really his fault."

"Maybe Evie's the one who should be evicted," says Seth.

But is it her fault, either?

"Maybe we should let them go on as before," says Mona.

"They tricked us," complains Barbara.

"Plus, realistically, how can we evict them?" says Mona. "Are we really prepared to kick them out ourselves?"

At this, Barbara of the wounded pride suggests, "My parents could suddenly appear."

Silence.

"Spoken like a true fair-weather radical," says Seth.

"I'll tell you what I am," says Barbara, straightening. "I'm no-body's fool."

More silence. Then advises Seth, gently, "Forget about Evie. Don't let your ego get in the way of your politics."

But Barbara has no intention of forgetting about anybody. Already you can see that she is going to be the kind of person unfazed by dis-count clothes stores where everybody shares one big dressing room. Barbara is going to be the kind who just up and strips. (For she is who she is, as she'll tell you; she never pretended to be a size two.)

"I don't have any politics," she says now, putting on her sandals. "I have feelings, something men in general and you in particular will never understand. I refuse to let them walk all over me. I feel I owe it to myself, not to say to my ancestors who were serfs."

"My grandfather was a Polish worker," objects Seth.

"So you shouldn't let people walk all over you, either," replies Barbara. "Plus wasn't your other granddad a German industrialist? He didn't exactly hail from a shtetl in Galicia."

Seth hangs his head; Barbara stands up, forgetting that she is in a teepee and needs to move to the middle first. As a result, she all but knocks one of the birch poles right out of its hole. The whole tent shud-ders, the circle of rain blurs; and when she's gone, the canvas sags worse than ever.

Alfred's friends continue to hang out. Barbara is not actually anxious to call her parents, and that is one reason. The other is that Alfred's friends have set out to woo her, and, transparent as their efforts are, she is not indifferent to them. "Miss B.," they call her, just like every-one at the restaurant. Nobody puts the moves on her, but they are openly appreciative of her physical endowments. They also appeal to her noble nature; and they do not forget to make Evie look bad. "Not everybody in the world has got such a sense of fair play as you, Miss B.," they say. "Not that's got no horse sense too. For example, that Evie." They lower their voices. "She's got the fair play. You leave her be, she's going to straighten out the whole world so there ain't going to be no more warfare or shit like that. But what's she throwing herself away on that Alfred for, man? She should be humping somebody fine, somebody like that Seth, now." And they wink at Barbara.

Meaning what? Barbara blushes. Seth looks away.

There is a mod squad that comes regularly: Luther the Race Man, Big Benson, Ray, and Professor Estimator. Professor Estimator is the brain of the group, a bookworm who remembers everything about everything and can take a fair guess at the rest. Smooth and shiny as he is above, he is jowly and loose-skinned below, and bespectacled: He wears his glasses tilted so far forward they look to be falling off. However, no one makes comments about this, or asks him why he doesn't just loop the curvy ear wire around his handy ears, or points out how on account of his glasses he is forced to turn his head in slow and level fashion. For he has the sort of giant, directed eyes you would just as soon not have fasten on your temerity. No—better to behold than be beheld. He is a tremendous man, the color of old iron, with an unmistakable center of gravity. He sits square in his chair and arranges his elbows in symmetric fashion, and when he stands he never uses the arms of a chair to help him up. He simply stands, head high, glasses perched, as if he's forsworn even the most pedestrian assistance. By day the Estimator is a produce buyer, but by night he's going to law school, meaning that usually he has no time. This year he's taking the summer off, though; and besides helping him get over some heartache, this is helping stem speculation that he's getting too uppity to run with his people anymore. No one's calling him Oreo. No one's wondering what he does for fun. Now they're ribbing him about how he's going to have a brandy-ass new Cadillac someday, and a fancy new babe to put that bug-eyed Ruth Buzzy to shame—some sister whose idea of a bedtime activity is not reading. His buddies joke that they'll be counting on him to get them out of trouble; he's going to be their secret weapon. When the shit comes down, he's going to send it flying back.

Not that they don't have other means. Big Benson is their very own law enforcement official. He got himself through high school, which was more than enough schooling for him. Now he works on and off in a construction crew. A burly vet the color of gingerbread, with small features set like raisins in his face, he could be a cookie except that he loves demolition. Also he hates to wear a helmet on account of what it does to his Afro. In 'Nam he cut his hand but bad; the doctors were talking amputation. But now he can use it so fine that his whole philosophy of life is based on the experience: *Don't listen to nobody. Just talk your talk and walk your walk.* It's what he tells his kid, who's just like him. Even in the middle of the winter this child won't wear a hat, and he's never been caught anywhere without a pick.

Ray's a vet too, of the peg-legged variety. Yet he's still nimble, a papaya-colored man with two good arms. *Used to be I could lay them brick like any dago, and what with my two good arms I probably still could.* So he says sometimes. Other times, though, he doesn't know what he can do. He can't work, he can't talk. Not about 'Nam; not about anything. Sometimes it seems something got left overseas—besides his leg, that is—and that right there is the problem. Other times it seems he brought too much back. *Got me a new pair of eyes. Didn't ask for 'em but I got 'em just the same.* Like he sees his three kids, and he's not so sure who they are anymore. One of them is his spitting image right down to his extra-long pinkies. The other two, though, have eyes and noses and mouths like nothing he's ever observed in the mirror; if he ever finds out where they came from, he'll probably borrow him a machine gun and go mowing.

Then there's Luther the Race Man—always dressed in Afro tricolors, though he is just as positively cream-colored as Charlene used to claim. He is not as pee-in-your-pants handsome as Alfred. However, he is certainly beguiling, what with his pen-stroke eyebrows, and his dark, dark eyes, and his air of open appraisal. He has a smile full of private meaning, and a temper to match—quick to rise, quick to vanish. But most appealing of all is his taste for disruption. For belying his bulk, he is a winker, a darter. He loves to be putting on white folks, or to be gaming his way into something or another; he is given to sudden appearances and disappearances—often in the nick of time, often too with goods of some salty kind. *That Luther,* his friends are always saying, with disconcerted delight. *That Luther!* He can be nasty too, though, and his personal life is one long tangled yarn of lovers, and children, and miscellaneous husbands gunning for his ass. No one knows where his money comes from; mostly, he is a phenomenon with a theme. As for the theme, that goes race, race, race. Luther attends rallies, and returns blowing black. "That's plain old motherfucking racist bullshit!" he might say. Or else, more equably, "You take that, you won't be no brother of ours no more, man. You take that, you'll be our most dearly beloved sister."

There are also three lesser members of the squad—guys who show up occasionally on account of their work hours, or their wives, or on account of their simply preferring to stay home. Ace, the Hatchet, and Billy. Of all of them, the Hatchet is the only one who puts Mona and Barbara and Seth on edge, and that's mostly because of his moniker. Also he has been known to bear arms. But when a no-firearms rule is instituted, he observes it. From time to time, other squad members kid him about his weapons status, and he always proves clean.

Other issues: They smoke cigarettes in the house and leave the butts all over. Also there are beer cans. Probably no more than there would be after any party, but usually you don't have parties all the time. The personalities concerned talk these things over, and after that there are no more butts and no more beer cans. "Hey, man, pick that up," they tell each other. "Where your manners." And to their hosts: "Our mamas brought us up decent." Easy as it is to get them to pick up certain things, though, it proves less easy to get them not to pick up other things, especially when the people are high. Candlesticks, bowls, silverware.

"It's just not natural to ask people not to touch things," says Seth. "That's why there are guards in museums. They don't need the guards just to keep people from smoking and drinking beer."

"That's easy for you to say," says Barbara. She is trying to be cool, really she likes everyone, but she says one of these days, something is going to be stolen, she just knows it.

In the meantime, it's hash brownies and James Brown, none of this Arlo Guthrie shit, and definitely no Joan Baez. *Pul-eez!* It's Soul Train and the funky chicken and mah-jongg—that's Barbara's idea, Mona's never played before. Checkers—Chinese and regular. Chess—the Estimator and Seth pit pawns. A slow expansion to more spacious activities, some of them outdoors. Basketball, baseball, swimming. (Luckily, the pool, like the tennis court, is behind a hedge.) The squad tries tennis. Badminton. They discuss lot versus lawn sports, which is like debating beer versus ice tea. But don't lawn sports have their charm? *Charm!* Ray and Big Benson laugh. Something they've always looked for in a sport. Rainy days mean billiards. Ping-Pong. Even a little yoga—nothing too elaborate, mostly just sequences where they stretch and let their bodies fill up with light in order that they may lay their eyes on Evie. For Evie runs these sessions, in the living room. The guys push all the furniture back; they sprawl on the royal-blue real-wool carpet, trying to pretzel themselves up the way she does. She is wearing a halter top, so that you can see the skin of her stomach getting twisty; it looks like a towel being wrung out. Also you can see the distinctive hang of her breasts, which are outgoing, in the manner of duck feet. She doesn't have cleavage so much as a bony midchest bowl. Still she holds her own, the centered center of her circle of attention, and this rubs on Alfred. He says she can't think what the brothers are thinking.

The room seems very small; the pile of footwear by the door, large and jumbled.

Seth buys himself a dashiki like Luther's—his camp shirt. On account of this, the guys give him grief. For Christmas, they say, they're going to buy him a tricolor yarmulke. Or not for Christmas, for— what is it?—Hanukkah! Seth laughs.

"Camp Gugelstein will come to order," he says now, when it's time to call a meeting. And as if this has been the ritual all their lives, people obligingly gather round for some sort of discussion. Sometimes this revolves around politics, or drugs, or the war; other times around sports, or cars, or—a surprise favorite—car repair. The transmission, they talk about. The alternator. *You disconnect the positive on the battery and it keep running, that means it was the alternator that was the trouble, not the battery.*

Today, though, the subject is hair.

Explains Professor Estimator, "There's good hair, bad hair, and no hair." He pats his own pate ruefully.

"There's 'fros and 'fros," agrees Big Benson. "Not everybody got the kink to get their natural to good size. Now, Ray, he respectable. He ain't no record-holder, but he respectable. See, he uses that Afrosheen. But now, Alfred here. He just ain't got what it takes. Even that Evie do up his cornrows extra tight, you still got a bro' with no 'fro."

Everyone laughs except Mona and Seth and Barbara.

"What's a cornrow?" asks Mona. Evie rises to give a short demonstration. Outside, it is starting to drizzle lightly. The arm of the turn-table makes its way to the record center; silence falls; the patter of the rain turns to a rush. On other days, such silence has led to continued conversation; and sure enough, as Alfred straightens his neck, signaling the end of the beauty show, the Estimator brings up certain esoteric types of love. Meaning positions and practices, he says, winking. At this, Big Benson seems to eye Barbara.

But the chief position involved turns out to be sitting, and as for the practice, it is turning the other cheek. For the talk of Afros has got the Estimator thinking not only about fashions in hair but also about fashions in the heads that wear the hair, and about ideas falling too quickly out of date—namely, those of Dr. Martin Luther King, Jr. *Satyagraha,* says the Estimator, meaning the force of the truth that is love. *Agape,* meaning love of all humanity. The Estimator sees redemptive love as still alive here, at Camp Gugelstein, but he thinks elsewhere it is on the wane.

Says Luther, "Why we got to translate and explicate when we got words in English everybody understand? Like black power, man. Nobody got to ask what that mean." He grins, lights up a joint.

"There's more disagreement about the definition than you realize," says Professor Estimator, and goes on to discourse about materialism and humanism and free will, and about seeking to win the friendship of one's opponent rather than to destroy or humiliate him.

"That's beautiful, man," says Seth, taking a toke.

"How can you believe in sainthood for Negroes," objects Mona, "when you think George Eliot was a sap?"

"Touché," says Seth. "I reverse my opinion. How Christian. How sappy. How unnatural."

"That's what Elijah Muhammad says," puts in Ray, surprising everyone. "Integration is going to fail."

Says Seth, "I didn't mean *integration* was unnatural."

"Integration is natural for blacks, but how about for you?" says Luther. "You still got to have Israel no matter what, right?"

"And the white domination of blacks that has gone on for six thousand years is coming to an end," continues Ray. "According to Elijah Muhammad. Actually it was supposed to have ended already. In 1914."

"So what happened?" says Seth.

"I guess whitey got an extension." Ray grins as he says this; he's rolling another joint. "But we are the chosen people, you know. You are the white devil, and your empire is falling apart."

"Do you really believe that?" says Mona.

"The empire *is* falling apart," says Ray.

"But here we are, integrated," says Evie. "Is it unnatural?"

"I seen everything, man." Ray shrugs. "This ain't nothing compared to what went on in 'Nam."

Big Benson nods; the Estimator folds his arms. He says a few words about Thurgood Marshall, and how sad he would be to hear this kind of talk. Separatism is just a mimicking of Jim Crow, says the Estimator. He quotes Gandhi: " 'One becomes the thing he hates.' "

At this, Luther, to everyone's surprise, folds his arms too. He does not jump into the conversation; he is waiting on Ray, allowing him room to continue. (*You learn by talking,* that's what he'll say later. *Nobody ever radicalized without they had an audience.*)

But before Ray does continue, Seth takes charge. "Time to focus the energy," he says.

And on cue, with a kind of relief, they all gather in a circle; they could be the actors in *Hair,* except that they have their clothes on. They close their eyes. Later Seth will say that he called for a circle because this is what he's always done, taken charge out of anxiety and fear. Later Luther will proclaim it to be no wonder blacks don't believe in liberals anymore, look at Seth—your typical paternalistic motherfucker who cannot stand blacks talking for themselves, much less acting in their own self-defense.

But for now, no one perceives anything except that it's fun to chant. *Ommmmm. Ommmmm.* They are all sitting cross-legged; they hold hands. The first time they did this, Mona thought they had to be on *Candid Camera;* not having taken Evie's Introduction to Yoga in the living room, she wasn't yet accustomed to communal exhalation. But now she loves to sit next to different people; she loves to close her eyes and feel the different grips. There are warm palms, cool palms, firm grips, loose; and attached to them such an amazing array of humanity, that she can hardly keep from peeking every now and then, to behold the sight: For here is Seth and here is Barbara; and here are Evie, and

Alfred; and here too is a gang who loomed up like strangers not long ago. Now, though, they are friends, plain and simple—already! What are they, besides the most interesting people Mona has ever known? What are they but a bunch of hair-bedeviled buddies?

A flask is missing. In the course of packing for a picnic breakfast, Barbara goes to find a pocket brandy flask she wants to fill with cream. This is necessary because while Seth drinks his coffee with Cremora, Barbara will not. Cremora is gross, she says. She says this Cremora thing is a working-class affectation on Seth's part. Even Big Benson, she points out, now drinks his coffee with cream.

But the flask is nowhere apparent to be found. It is apparently not in the dining room, and it is apparently not in the living room, and it is apparently not in the pantry. It is apparently not in the kitchen, it is apparently not in the storage closet with the stadium blankets and other picnic items. It is apparently not in the attic. It is apparently not in the basement.

"Are you sure your parents didn't take it with them to the Vineyard?" Mona asks.

But Barbara says she's definitely seen it since the summer started. The flask in question is heavy silver plate, with a pierced design of a baskety sort, and she particularly noticed it in the dining room sideboard because it had an inch or so of something left in it. She and Mona go through the sideboard again.

Still confrontation rumbles toward them like a freight train. Barbara is so upset, Seth offers to do the talking for her; but Barbara knows that to say what she means, she has to make her speechy accusations herself. And so she calls everyone to order. No sitting in a circle on the floor, she makes everyone sit on a folding chair. The chairs are in two shortish rows. For a moment Barbara hesitates. Then she speaks her mind clearly, only orating a little. For the occasion, she is wearing a new stature-building fashion, platform shoes.

She is greeted with scuffling and the distinct sliding sound of people slouching. There seems to be a new first row made up entirely of sneakers; everyone seems to be smoking. No one knows anything. Barbara rocks in her shoes, she pushes her bangs off her forehead. Outside, a bright evening haze hovers over the yard like some grass treatment that's evaporating instead of being absorbed. She says that the flask is her dad's absolute favorite. She says it's got sentimental value, and that her mother gave it to him.

"You hear that, man?" Luther laughs in a laid-back manner. "It was a fucking present for her Jew-daddy."

Says Evie, "Luther Pinckney, that's no way to talk."

"What you talking about?" says Luther.

Says Alfred, "She means how would you like it if some cat called you a Jew-daddy."

Says Luther, shrugging, "I talks how I talks." He takes a drag of his cigarette. "In point of fact, I talks like the *niggah* I be, man. And the *niggah* I be knows a Jew-daddy when I see one."

"But you haven't seen Mr. Gugelstein," says Mona from the back row. With everyone slumped down, she has a clear view of Barbara, whose eyes are flashing even as other people speak. "And I'm not sure this has anything to do with being Jewish or black or anything else."

"What you know about it, girl?" Luther says this without even turning around.

"It doesn't," Mona insists, to the back of his head.

"And even if it did, 'someone must have sense enough and morality enough to cut off the chain of hate,'" says Seth, also in the back row.

"Dr. King," glosses the Estimator, turning.

"You tell us, then." Luther turns now too, so that cigarette smoke wafts in Mona's face. "Who own the flask? Who keep picking it up, you got to tell us to put it on down? Who like to steal the flask, who don't got no flask like that at home?" He winks. "I think that flask would look just fine on my fireplace mantel."

"Cut the shit," says Alfred, beside him. "You ain't got no fireplace."

"How you know what I got, man?"

Big Benson shakes his head. "Just got to come on bad. The devil in that boy."

"You got that flask?" says Alfred.

"I don't hear no questions from no boy sleeping white," says Luther.

"He's just got to start some shit," says the Estimator. "He's just got to fan some flames."

"You hot too?" says Seth, pulling at his dashiki.

"Hot as a motherfucker in here," agrees Big Benson. He looks at Barbara, looks at the floor.

"Hot as a hellhole," says Ray.

Professor Estimator looks at Seth. "So what are we doing here?" he says, resignation in his voice. He sweeps the room with his level gaze. "It time to split, or what?"

People look at each other.

"Let's get the hell out of this hellhole," says the Estimator.

"Time to split," says the Hatchet.

"What the hell," says Benson.

"Motherfucking hellhole," echoes Ray.

"A lot of racist bullshit coming down here," says Luther.

And with that, they file out of the house, into the light-orange air. Only Alfred stays. He gives people the high five, but stands stalwartly by his Evie as his friends disappear.

No one has to call the Gugelsteins. The mod squad is gone, and the mod squad does not come back, except for Professor Estimator, the next day, to help Alfred move. The squad has helped Alfred find a new place; they've helped him find a new car. He doesn't have to stay with some white folk like a charity case.

" 'We shall have our manhood,' " quotes the Estimator. " 'We shall have it or the earth will be leveled by our attempts to gain it.' "

"What's this 'we'?" says Seth. "And since when have you become a Representative Black Man instead of Old Estimator, the distinguished thinker and chess player?"

"I was suspected of stealing along with my black brothers. Who distinguished among us then?"

"And since when do you quote Eldridge Cleaver? Has a panther been born of the pacifist?"

" 'Free at last,' " says the Estimator, terse.

" 'Let us not seek to satisfy our thirst for freedom by drinking from the cup of bitterness and hatred.' "

The Estimator softens, but answers, " 'We will not be satisfied until justice rolls down like waters and righteousness like a mighty stream.' "

Alfred invites Evie to come visit anytime. She says she will. "Just don't bring your motherfucking camera," he says, and he drives away with the Estimator. The way the pair of them stick their elbows out the windows, they look from far off like a single large passenger, taking up the whole front seat.

Was all that transpired such a bad thing? In one way Mona and Barbara and Seth can't decide. Camp Gugelstein couldn't go on forever, and at least its breakup didn't involve the law. That's how they see it from afar. From afar, they think their purpose was to help Alfred back on his own feet, and they did. They wanted him to be independent of them, and he is.

From closer in, though, they are devastated, Seth especially. One day Mona finds him sitting in his teepee with his head in his hands, and she is surprised at how much older he looks. This is partly because, though he still has his beard, he's had his ponytail cut off. His hair is much wavier than she'd realized, and it even has a side part now, neat and white—who knows how long that will last. Still he does not look like a defeated youth so much as a defeated man. A defeated youth sets his elbows on his spread knees, and stares intently at the locker room floor; and you know by this that he has lost an important match such as he will never forget. A defeated man, on the other hand, is a crumpled-up thing. He looks as though he doesn't even mind that his mental function is not what it used to be; in truth, he would just as soon forget everything.

"I believed it would work." Seth says this over and over, doggedly, reinforcing the mental-function-is-not-what-it-used-to-be impression. "I wanted it to work."

This is the most prolonged acquaintance Mona has had with the nape of Seth's neck, and she's surprised and oddly touched to behold his most unruly hairline—how his hair whorls up and suddenly down, a haircutter's challenge. She traces the swirl with her finger, thinking how rarely anything like this has happened to him. For how could it? He's so rarely cared about anything, to begin with. Here's a guy who doesn't believe in love, or college, or task-specific soap. But he did buy that dashiki, his first new clothes in years—only now, already, to have to pack it away. Her family has run into so many life knots that they don't think much of it anymore. Boards split, things splinter, what's new? You've got to wear your safety goggles, that's obvious. Seth, though, assumes he misjudged the situation. The more he thinks about what happened, the more he thinks he should have seen everything in advance.

"Like what, a human oracle?" says Mona.

But so fixated is he on the fallibility of his perceptions that he does not hear her. "It was naive to think it could work," he says, his hands hanging limp. And later, "I was naive."

Mona tries to tell him that it wasn't a waste of time to try and live Judaism the way they did. Rabbi Horowitz would still have been proud, plus it was an education. And Alfred is on his feet, and Seth got to play chess, and wasn't it great how they all held hands? For the rest of her life *om* will be a special syllable. Sure, things fell apart and they got called racist bastards. But even she's got the social-action bug now, who knows but that she'll be out getting arrested pretty soon?

She says this cheerily, not as if she is trying to plump a rock pillow. Seth removes her comforting fingers from his neck.

"Yeah, yeah." His hands hang limp again. "But we're not friends."

"Friends?" For a moment Mona wonders if he's not saying something like what Ralph might have said—*Today we have no relationship*. But no, Seth wasn't looking to be a paterfamilias.

"They considered me a racist bastard, and I considered them my friends." He says, "It's so quiet now."

Actually, it's pretty noisy. There's a good stiff wind, and the walls of the teepee are snapping in and—*bang!*—out, loud as a backfiring engine. But Mona knows what he means. It is as if he is just discovering that he grew up an only child, which in a way, he did. His stepbrothers were all but out of the house by the time he came along; and what with his interests, he could practically have been an Old World scholar boy, the kind with cuff links and green skin and no appetite. Even now, she can see him with a piano, and an illuminated globe, and a sliding wooden ladder that he really does need, to get to all his books. Then one day: Enter a group of playmates. And when they leave, the library is a whole different place.

In fact, Seth had lots of friends in high school. But whereas they went willingly off to the slaughter (Mandelese for college), he stayed home. He has truthfully followed his own idiosyncratic heart, and now what? An American affliction.

"But, Seth." Mona is suddenly the one talking with her hands, Seth style; she is suddenly the one trying passionately to persuade. "Alfred and his friends were so different than you."

Still he had thought if he was honest enough, direct enough . . . He had a vision, he says. He woke up one morning, and saw a house with no walls between the rooms.

"Seth," Mona says. "If people lived in houses with no walls between the rooms, there would have to be a lot of rules. I don't think you would like it. You can't have no walls and also have everyone in touch with their feelings. People would have to have manners. They would have to have a public face and a private face."

"I was naive," he says. "I think I've said that already."

He bends his head forward. Mona ruffles his neck hairs some more. He does not protest. The tent heaves as if bent on dismantling itself for the season. Mona wonders, Is Seth going to live out here all winter again?

That is when he turns to her and says something highly unlike anything she ever thought he would say. He says, "This is why you don't want to be a freethinker. You've had enough of being an original."

To which Mona nods a little, as though she sees what he's getting at. But what she sees, actually, is that what Seth has needed all along has been company—and that company is what he had hoped to make of her.

At the restaurant, Alfred too sulks. He's slow at the stove, he's forgetful. It used to be he was proud of how round his pancakes were; and indeed, they never looked to be procreating, like Cedric's. But now they are turning eccentric. They are impossible to stack; they are big and small, wild with irregularity, and lumpy to boot. Usually he's fastidious about clearing the griddle between orders. *You've got to start clean,* he always tells trainees. *You've got to start with nothing if you want to make something.* These days, though, he lets drips of batter fry right up into little blackened knobs, which in turn get embedded in new pancakes. This lends his cuisine an element of crunchy surprise.

"Those black people," complains Cedric. "One day this way, one day that way."

"Just tell him you want him to clear the griddle between orders," Mona says. "And it's not *those black people*. It's Alfred."

"You think he is going listen? I tell you something. Alfred is completely burn some pancakes today. So I say, Alfred, that one too dark, cannot serve to customer. And you know what he say?"

Mona shakes her head.

Cedric imitates Alfred. " 'Black is beautiful, man.' I tell him black is no beautiful, black is burnt, but he don't want listen. He say, 'Fuck the customers.' I say, The customer is king, and you know what he say? He say, 'I the king. The customers are motherfuckers.' I say, What is this motherfucker you always talking about? I say, I look this up in the dictionary, and I find out there is no translation. Maybe I spell wrong. I ask Alfred spell for me. But Alfred, he just laugh. He say, 'Don't tell me there no motherfuckers in China.' I say yes. We have no motherfuckers. I say, Is that some kind of swear word? He say yes. And I say, Maybe you mean something like turtle egg. He say, 'That's a swear word?' I tell him yes, that's a very bad word; you call somebody that, they very mad of you. And what happen? He laugh, that Alfred. He laugh and laugh, until all the pancakes burnt up again."

Mona sighs.

It is Labor Day weekend, and there are almost no customers—everybody's away, it seems, on vacation in New Hampshire or Vermont or Maine or Cape Cod. Mona wishes she were away too. Instead she's home, partly because Ralph and Helen don't believe in vacation. *All Americans think about is vacation,* they like to say, and while in fact they too like to stroll by a lakeside and spend money and do nothing, they don't mind making a deposit to their superiority account instead.

Plus the Changs are still debating whether or not to buy that other restaurant. There was talk of another buyer, and as long as the talk was hot, the Changs were hot to buy too. But when the other buyer got cold feet, so did Ralph. *Where it going lead? It going lead to trouble. That's I can tell you, mister.*

"Janis," starts Helen now.

"Everything Janis says is right," says Ralph, sipping a milk shake. "Janis is one hundred percent smarter than your husband. But dumb as he is, your husband it so happen remember how he made this mistake before. Make a big business. For what? Just give us stomachache. Already we work day and night, day and night. Now what? Time to work harder? We buy another restaurant, you know what we will have? Ulcer." He sips. "Sure thing. That's how Janis say. But I can tell you: There is no *sure thing*. Even our restaurant, standing there so nice, can fall down, good-bye. Forget about *sure thing*. I still believe *make sure*."

Mona sets out the mousetraps. This is her new job, a secret job even though there isn't even a big problem; they've only caught one mouse so far, and it was all of a half size up from a roach.

"You just want to run away, hide from everything," says Helen.

"Hide what? I am not hide anything. I am talk horse sense. Look at Alfred these days. Unreliable like crazy."

"Why does everything come back to Alfred?" Cheese cube in hand, Mona feels like crying. "Why can't you and Mom just have your fight by yourselves?"

"We are not fighting," says Helen.

Says Ralph, "I tell you. Alfred is one day, he care very much what is happen in the restaurant. The next day, for no reason, look like he do not care anymore. To have another restaurant, we need two people like Cedric."

"That's racist!" Mona says.

But Ralph, putting down his shake, insists that the other person like Cedric could be any color. "He could be blue. He could be green. He could be striped like the zebra in the zoo."

"It doesn't matter so long as you know you can trust him," Mona says. "It doesn't matter so long as you know who the person is."

"That's right."

"He could be blue, he could be green. It doesn't matter so long as he's Chinese."

"Not true," says Ralph.

"It is!" cries Mona, upsetting her bag of cheese.

"She is just like this, these days," says Helen. "Crazy."

The Gugelsteins return from their summer away. To prepare for their arrival, Barbara and Mona have gone everywhere, hunting down a flask like the one missing; and, incredibly, they have found its spitting image in a Fifth Avenue store. They have this engraved. Also, to age it, they soak it in Coca-Cola. Someone has told them that Coke will rot anything, that in fact, Russian spies introduced it to America as a way of corroding the guts of the general population. And this may be true. However, on silver plate it does nothing. Luckily, they then enlist the services of Rachel Cohen, who with her jewelry-making know-how oxidizes the flask. The result looks so good that when the Gugelsteins come home, Mona and Barbara want nothing more than to run up and show it to them.

Instead they act as though they've barely noticed anyone's arrived.

"Guess what I have for you," sings Mrs. Gugelstein, and she pulls out a shopping bag full of clothes and accessories for Barbara. There are a lot of things you can get on the Vineyard that you can't get in White Plains, it turns out, and Mrs. Gugelstein has found them all. Moreover, she has made special arrangements with the Vineyard storekeepers to accept returns by mail in case Barbara doesn't like something.

"But I know you'll love it all," she says. "Look at this." She pulls out a liquid silver choker, set with turquoise.

"Hmm," says Barbara, and moves toward a mirror. "What do you think?" she asks Mona. "Is it me?"

"What a question," says her mother. "Who else would it be?"

Is Barbara going to keep on at her job at the pancake house, what with school starting and all? Mona will still be faithfully serving her greater accounting unit, but Barbara might want to, say, study. And what about Seth, who all of a sudden wears nothing but black turtlenecks?

"Aren't you ever going to do something?" Mona asks.

"No," he says. "I've decided to give up on Judaism and be a waitress instead."

"You'll never be a waitress, and you can't give up on Judaism. You're Jewish."

No response. Mr. Authentic Self, but suddenly he has a public face and a private face. For this is the way he's been recently—ornery and sardonic and moody and, most disturbing of all, elliptical.

So why does Mona decide it's finally time to sleep together?

This is what she thinks later: that there are moments when the zippy narrative of your life lets up, and swampy reflection sinks in. There are moments when you begin to feel ending. Maybe it's just seasonal wear and tear. But there are moments when the inexorable shrinking of the days makes you miss people who have not yet left you—people like Barbara, Alfred, Seth. It is as if you have come unmoored from your present—as if you are floating out in the floodplain of your future. So that, out of a sort of nostalgia, you might decide yes. All right. It's time.

Only to have Seth of the black turtleneck sweetly question your motives. "What's come over you? A fit of passion?"

"Very funny," Mona says.

"Don't do anything you're going to blame me for later."

"I thought you believed reducing world horniness increases the social good."

"That presumes two consenting adults."

Mona argues that she is indeed a consenting adult.

"Okay," he says finally. "Let's have a fit of passion, then. Since you insist."

Mona is so annoyed that she almost refuses to go with him to the new almost-free clinic. But they go, and survive the waiting room. What kind of defloration is this? thinks Mona in the drugstore—and again that evening, as they lie in the teepee, inert. Aren't they supposed to be carried away, if not by romance and the meeting of their eternal souls, then at least by the power of their respective hormonal drips?

"I want to be tragically undone by my stampeding youth," she tells Seth.

"Yeah, right," he says.

"Surging tides. Pounding blood. Lusty thighs."

"We're supposed to wait for a whole cycle of pills," says Seth. "If you recall. Plus we talk too much."

"Does that lead to low-lust syndrome?"

Happily, they are soon enough revisited by natural bodily urges. The very day that time is up, they find his penis in. Mona is surprised how uneventfully this happens. After all the diagrams she's seen, she half expected that they would first turn into line drawings, then get split into flesh-toned cross-sections like the poor beings depicted. In real life, she sees a reflection of the sky in Seth's earth-brown eyes; such a grand uniting! His eyes are all the world—no, more: They are the world made twin. His neck is craned up. How much shorter she is than he! She had never noticed before. But groin to groin, there's no denying it. Her chin lies on his hairy chest, on a line with his nipples. Of course, she is on top—everything with Seth has to be counterconventional. Still, she feels so much more than she sees. And in a rush, it occurs to her how nobody told her that—how nobody told her that it would be like discovering yourself to own an extra sense organ. This has nothing whatever to do with seeing; even in daylight, most everything is hidden, like the green-covered pamphlet she keeps between her mattress and boxspring at home. Callie, passing it down, said their mother gave it to her. "*Mom* gave it to you?" That was hard to believe, and even harder was what the pamphlet (*Introducing . . . You!*) had to say. First of all, that girls had three holes! Mona had to sit down immediately to see. Of course, there was more too, much more, in the pamphlet, all about sweating walls, and turgid cells, and items of miraculous elasticity. For all of which, Nature got credit. The pictures featured amounts of pubic hair Mona thought gross. The penises were big as sewage pipes, and about as attractive. Still she read the pages over and over, her body tingling. *When the woman is relaxed and elastic, the man inserts his member, thanks to Nature's ingenuity.*

Is that this sweet, grand entrance? Utterly nonviolent; she didn't know she could be so wet. She did not know she could feel so full. She tightens around him, and is surprised that he can feel this greeting. He flexes a return hello. They laugh, link legs, rock.

"Is this thrusting?" says Mona.

"Shut up," says Seth.

"Yes," says Mona. "Yes I said yes. Yes."

"Shut up," says Seth again, and this time subdues her with mouth kisses. And then they rock some more, until all they wish for is ditto, ditto, ditto.

"Feel the breeze," says Seth—there's a leak in the wall of the tent.

"Shut up," says Mona.

And with this they sink back into themselves, pulsing.

When Mona puts her glasses on, she surmises by the hole at the top of the teepee that the sun is still shining blandly. Into the blank sky float skimmingly puffy, indifferent clouds.

"Are you really a virgin?" Seth asks, propping himself up on an elbow.

And Mona says yes. That is, she was—although there's no blood, to their mutual surprise. Neither of them mentions that Barbara bled so much it was scary, though both know this. "Maybe because of using Tampax?" Mona says. (Helen is against Tampax, but Mona uses them anyway, she just hides them behind some books in her bookcase.)

"And you came," he says—happy, yet there's an odd fall-off to his gladness.

"Why would I lie to you? I can't believe you even care about such things."

"Did I say you were lying?"

"Let's just be happy," Mona says. "Either that or let's do it again."

They do it again. It's harder for Seth to come—he's interested but droopy, and Mona's so slippery from the first time. As for Mona, she's not even sure if she has come or not. Which is not the way it's supposed to be, Mona thinks. Isn't the woman supposed to go on and on? *In bed as in conversation,* she read somewhere. What if she is mono-orgasmic? A sobering life prospect, no doubt related to her subcutaneous fat, hammy calves, et cetera. Still she is exhilarated. And he is happy, in a way. But in another way, he remains the Seth he has been recently—that moody Seth so stuffed full of things he's not saying, he could be some sort of special-edition piñata. *It changes everything,* that's what Barbara said. And maybe it does. But without changing anyone. This dawns on Mona like a big baked brick, and later she counts this realization as her real loss of innocence: All this happy youthful fucking, yet Seth still ails.

Mona ponders for a few more days. She talks things over with Barbara, who blames for the weirdness, of all things, the pill. "Nobody knows what's in those things," she says. Mona begins to regard her neat case with suspicion, even though she's hitherto felt toward it, gratitude—her figure being so greatly enhanced that Barbara has also said, "You know, Polly Wolly, pretty soon we're going to have to call you Polly Golly."

Was this the voice of jealousy? Anyway, Mona begins to consider whether Seth and she shouldn't split up the way Evie and Alfred are doing. "Monkey see, monkey do," says Barbara, studiously uninterested in Seth's prospective availability even as Mona watches, watches.

Seeing how what's done is done. To wit, how you simply avoid the other person until you can hardly conceive how you stood him or her for more than five minutes.

"Evie," says Alfred. "All she wanted was to be fucked by a black man."

"Alfred," says Evie. "All he wanted was a chick even whiter than Charlene."

Could you really sum up what a person wanted, just like that? Mona isn't sure. But she begins to feel as though that is what a relationship is about—getting to know someone well enough to fill in the blank. And then you fill it in, and then you don't care about anything for a while.

For example, if you are Evie, and have on top of everything else broken up with your boyfriend in the Philippines for Alfred, you stop taking pictures, and stop developing pictures, and stop talking about pictures. Instead of putting things back neatly into drawers, you leave them lying all around, in such a state that one day your aunt feels compelled to clean up for you. Which is when she discovers your self-portraits—pictures of you and Alfred, in bed in her house. There are also pictures of the gang hanging out, and the gang getting down, and the gang having a good old time, and every one of these is perfectly focused, with lovely detail. If your aunt were so inclined, she could hang every one of them.

III

The Fall Begins

Evie is packed home to Minneapolis a week early, and as for Alfred, he is of course fired.

"I'm sorry," says Mona, entering the attic storeroom. Alfred is holding his old navy-blue windbreaker, the one with an apple tree logo over the left breast. *Eden Orchards,* reads the caption. *Bite and You Shall Know.* Now he stands in front of his hook as though expecting something more to appear on it, and for the first time Mona realizes how low the hooks are. Alfred's cubby too hangs level with his chest, meaning that he has to stoop just to check that there's nothing in it besides that old doorknob they found in the tunnel. He chucks this in a wastebasket.

"What you sorry for?" he says, without turning. "You're the boss's smartass daughter."

"I'm sorry you got fired."

"You're sorry. I'm fired. If that ain't the oldest story in the world, I must be President of the United States."

"What do you mean?"

"Somebody's going to take the heat, it's got to be the Negroes, right? Who else gets burnt up and keeps walking? Who else gets deep fried and is still talking nice as you please? Except for maybe on occasion calling a motherfucker a motherfucker."

"Nobody," says Mona.

Alfred turns around, his jacket dangling on a finger. His eyes are burning. "Nobody else takes this brand of shit, and you hear me: The day is coming when nobody ain't going take it, neither." His jacket swings in front of him like a hanged man.

. . .

At home that evening, the conversation attains a similar level of peace and satisfaction.

"I don't think you can fire somebody because of where he's been living," Mona says.

Helen keeps stirring the pork. "You people were having parties. There were pictures."

"But is that a reason to fire somebody?"

"Of course." The pork sizzles and spits; Helen does a backbend, trying to avoid the splatter. Also she moves the open sugar bowl out of range. "How do you think we feel? Our cook act like that."

"But he's not your representative. He's your employee."

"He is our cook," says Helen again. "And that girl, she is white, you understand? Barbara's mother called; of course we have to do something. What happens if I see Barbara's mother on the street? Am I going to say hello, how are you, that Alfred still work for us as if nothing happened? You know what kind of insult that is to Barbara's mother? It is as if I stand there in front of Daitch Shopwell and slap her in front of everybody. Our cook make that kind of big trouble, and we say hello, how are you, we do nothing?"

"But aren't there laws?" Mona says.

"Laws!" Helen turns the heat off. The meat's still a little pink; she covers the pan, leaving it to cook some more by itself. Mad as she is, she still cooks with care, it's automatic. The little judgments and adjustments, the split-second coordinating of this with that. Mona has never seen Helen burn anything, she would hate to waste the food; it's only with Mona that she leaves the heat on high. "You invite Alfred to go live in someone's house, now you want talk about laws?"

This is how the conversation goes on their better days. Other days it is less reasonable.

How could you. How could you. Over and over, as if the whole affair was Mona's fault. *What kind of daughter. How could you.*

Mona tries to explain that she wasn't the person behind it all—that really she had help. Also that she did it because she was trying to find herself, which in fact is downright common. Mona tries to hint that some mothers actually try and help their daughters find themselves. For instance, Mrs. Gugelstein, if it's only through clothes and jewelry. But she might as well be trying to talk sense with a store fixture.

"What you talking, find yourself?" says Helen. "And who do you think you are, tell me what to do? Daughter's job is to listen, not to tell mother her big-shot opinion."

"That's the whole problem. I'm not just a daughter. I'm a person."

"A person!"

Outside, a plastic jug moans in the night wind.

"You know what you are?" Helen says. "You are American girl. Only an American girl can do something like that and hide it from her mother. Every day you lied to me." She appears shocked all over again by this recap of the facts. "Every day!" She cannot go on.

"At least I wasn't the one sleeping with Alfred." Mona genuinely means this as a comforting thought.

But it is not comforting. "Sleep with somebody! Alfred!" Helen closes her eyes. "No, no, no." Her mouth trembles. "You do that, I would kill myself."

"But Mom, that's so racist."

"Racist!" Helen springs suddenly back to life, as if it is not night at all, but day, day, day! "Only an American girl would think about her mother killing herself and say oh, that's so racist. A Chinese girl would think whether she should kill herself too. Because that is how much she thinks about her poor mother who worked so hard and suffered so much. She wants to do everything to make the mother happy." And with that, she leaps up as if she's overslept and it's way past time to get going.

The Gugelsteins don't want Mona to visit anymore. She is persona non grata, a real *kochleffl*, such an official bad influence that she is not even allowed to phone; Mrs. Gugelstein is screening all calls. Never mind the many times Mona encouraged her friend to study instead of plain hanging out. She is the mastermind, according to the Gugelsteins. This whole affair is not something their daughter had the brains to dream up.

"What a nice thing to say about you," says Mona to Barbara. "In fact, I think it's an insult."

"I think it's supposed to be an insult to you too."

"Well, insulted I be, I guess." Mona pulls an apple out of her backpack.

They're encamped on the floor of the high school lobby, which is crisscrossed with trails of mud. This is the problem with everyone wearing hiking boots all the time—add a few goats, and the lobby could be a third world train station. It smells of general staleness and dope. But Mona and Barbara don't mind. It's true that Barbara's gotten her car keys taken away, and that Mona is about to break up with Seth. They should be depressed. But in fact, Barbara and Mona are closer again, thanks to the quick-dry glue-all that is common traumatic experience. They're both friendly with Eloise Ingle, but she hasn't been through what they've been through. Barbara and Mona are Laurel and Hardy, Mutt and Jeff, Tweedledee and Tweedledum. A twosome for the ages.

"No more going around being Jewish. That's another thing," says Barbara. "A little Jewish is fine, but my mom says too much is too much—look at what happened in Munich. Not that it's right for terrorists to attack anybody; she's definitely not saying that. And at the Olympics! Of all places. But harping on difference brings trouble, she says; it's human nature. Some people are too Jewish even for other Jews. For example, Rabbi Horowitz. No wonder he got fired and had to move to Massachusetts, where else would people put up with him?"

"Is that where he's living?"

"That's what she heard, plus it figures. Her friends say there are as many communes in Cambridge now as bookstores. Of course, they'll still pay their good money to send their kids to Harvard if they get in; it's still better than Berkeley or Columbia. My mom says if I want to be Jewish like Rabbi Horowitz, I can move to the Lower East Side."

"How far is it from there to Chinatown?"

Barbara laughs. "Do you have relatives there?"

"Not a lot of relatives," says Mona. "In fact, now that you mention it, I don't know a single person who lives in Chinatown."

"And who do I know on the Lower East Side?" Barbara shakes her head.

It is easier to break up with Seth than Mona would have thought, on account of her having filled in the blank for herself.

"All you wanted was for me to be a radical," Mona says. "All you wanted was to make me into company for you."

Seth's cheeks have a papery look Mona has never noticed before. Also his skin has a grayish cast, as if he has given up washing even with his special all-purpose soap, or as if he is molting. "And here I thought you were a self-made Jew," he says.

Mona says that she is; but that somehow her experiment has turned into his experiment.

"Is that my fault?"

She claims yes. Gray-of-face listens carefully, growing grayer. She waits for him to say something sardonic. And indeed he begins to argue with her, only to stop himself. He thinks again. He apologizes.

"Guilty as charged." He had not dreamed, he had not realized, he had never figured, he says. And certainly he never meant to pull a Professor Higgins. He really had thought her more radical than she realized, a kind of Jewish Yoko Ono. But how convenient of him to believe that. He offers to make amends, or at least to try; and in offering, he sounds more or less sincere. He admits misjudgment, he admits insensitivity, he offers to take her on a ninety-mile bike ride in which she rides on the handlebars. To any place she names, he says. Anything to prove how sorry he is, and to what lengths he will go (literally) to make it up to her.

And part of Mona knows how hard all this is for someone like Seth to say; he might as well be admitting himself to be wrong. But instead of thinking about that, Mona thinks, Ninety miles on someone's handlebars! How uncomfortable! In short, she clutches her certainty to her like the sort of itty-bitty terry wrap that barely makes it around your bosom. Having never broken up with anyone before, she is determined to do it right, which is to say heartlessly. How liberating to be mean! All her life she has been funny; she has tried too to be sweet. Never has she been powerful. She could be Popeye, popping open spinach cans with her bare hands. Who needs a can opener? Mona has not started this deadly game, but now that she understands there can be victory between people, she is bent on avoiding defeat. She has always thought fear a hot emotion; now she knows it to be cool. Now she knows how it turns to vengeance. She is unmovable. She is the Rock of Gibraltar, a strategic fortification with which any Mandel must reckon.

Seth begins to cry. He has his hands in his hair; if it were long enough to get a grip on, he would probably tear it out.

"Are you all right?" asks the spinach-fed Rock of Gibraltar. And she sees what a stringy pleasure has been hers. For she has never seen Seth cry before, and it is a surprise how unnatural the process seems to be for him. He does not cry the way Barbara and Mona do, with wails of virtuoso facility. He cries as though each tear contradicts his very nature; watching him is like watching an animal cry, except that he wipes his eyes with his black turtleneck sleeve. Also the crying seems to be giving him stomach cramps: His whole body is doubled over in the manner of an out-of-use gym mat.

"No," he replies. "I am not all right. Jesus, how I've fucked up." And then he says that he loves her.

Of course, there is a rider to this statement—namely, that he's thought a lot about what those words mean, and that he is not exactly sure he has settled on a definition. However, he does think he indeed means whatever it is that he doesn't yet understand that he means.

"How romantic." Mona stands, full of dignity. "Now you can go have an affair with Barbara."

"Barbara?"

It is too late. Mona is already making her grand exit. And if she does peek back to be sure he gets up eventually and can at least walk, she makes sure he doesn't see her. For let it here be said that she truly fully expects him to turn around and apply to Barbara for some huggery, as he used to call it. She is surprised when he does not; and furthermore, it seems that Barbara is surprised too, although less than entirely disappointed—her thoughts having boomeranged home to Andy Kaplan.

A most unexpected turn of events: Seth develops a fixation. Maybe this can happen to anyone in the world. Maybe in everyone there are parts that can turn mushy, leaving the person substantially pudding. So thinks Mona. Or else maybe Seth was meshugga from the start, she should've known—all that soul searching, it just wasn't normal. Also the teepee. In any case, he sends her letters, to which she does not respond. These are long and closely argued, line after line of the kind of cramped inky black script you associate with the discovery of paramecium and other cellular wonders. She moves her shifts around at the restaurant; he moves his too, giving chase, and is fired. (He would have been fired anyway, says Ralph; Helen was set on it.) Seth tries to see Mona in other ways, and when those fail too, he tries to at least get her attention. Various sources report: Did Mona know Seth has stopped eating because of her? Did she know Seth has stopped using gas-powered transportation? Did she know he has shaved off his beard? Eaten two frogs? Jumped off a house?

"He jumped off a house?" Mona says.

It was only a ranch, it turns out, and there were soft spots in the lawn where the roots of an old tree stump were rotting. He did jump off the roof, though, saying that he hoped she got the reference to a well-known Russian play involving a cherry orchard. Luckily, he was unhurt.

"Tell him not to do that anymore," Mona says.

But he does, exactly because it worries her. Mona tries to ignore this, even if it is like a bright light exploding at the edge of her field of vision, or like a certain farmy perfume arising from a baby's diaper. In short, a challenge. So that when the news comes round that Seth has secretly applied to colleges, and that he has at the last minute decided to go, Mona is relieved. She and Barbara shake their heads together. *Leave it to Seth.* To which college has Seth consigned himself? No one knows, but presumably it is one on the trimester system, seeing as he is starting in late October. Also one that allows its students to live in teepees.

Predictably, he takes his leave Seth style, which is to say by leaving behind a most enigmatic note. This is written on the back of the fortune from a Chinese fortune cookie. On one side, there is the official message: *Expectation is a light shining in the eyes.* The other side is equally obscure. In Seth's minute scrawl, it reads: *Watch for the return of a most mannerly fellow.*

Meaning what? Barbara and Mona consider and consider.

"That Seth!" says Barbara, finally.

"Typical!" Mona crumples the note up.

Thankfully, they're too busy to mull over such things, having entered the year that is focused like a railroad tunnel on its end. Seniors! Every day they say that word, every day they imagine June. June! They can already see their new luggage—frameless backpacks for travel in the summer, army-navy trunks for college in the fall. First, though, there are the SATs to contend with. Again! At least for poor

Barbara. Then there are college applications. Barbara is already drafting her essays, which she's going to have her father's secretary type up on an IBM Selectric. Never mind that she hasn't decided what colleges she's going to apply to yet; she figures she can always just wait and see what Andy Kaplan does.

Meanwhile, Eloise stops by Mona's locker one day to say she's decided to apply to all of the Ivies, plus the Seven Sisters, plus Hampshire.

"Hampshire?" says Mona. "The hippie school? You?"

If she can't get into any of the real schools, replies Eloise, she might as well at least learn to throw a Frisbee. She says this wistfully, as if she would genuinely like not to have to challenge her way up the tennis ladder. Sitting cross-legged on the floor, they swap admissions stories: About the kid who sent Harvard a violin he made from scratch. About the kid whose application demonstrated some principle when you opened it.

"You have to get their attention," says Eloise.

"Are you sure?" Mona says. "Callie got in on an essay about how she was like a peanut butter and jelly sandwich."

"Did she send a sandwich?"

"No."

Says Eloise, "Perhaps if she had, she'd have gotten a scholarship." She winks. "Are you applying to Harvard too?"

Mona shakes her head, only to have Barbara jump on her.

"I know," she says. "You're convinced you'll be a failure if you don't get in like Callie. But (*a*) you could very well get in. And (*b*) it's better to be a failure than a dropout. That's what my dad says."

Then she launches into an exposition so lengthy that Eloise finally stands and excuses herself—only to have her red-laced, Vibram-soled hiking boots replaced by the blue-laced, Vibram-soled hiking boots of someone who bears a distinct resemblance to Sherman Matsumoto.

"Sherman!" Mona says, looking up.

"Mona?"

Sherman is so changed that Mona is not sure how she recognized him. Gone the little-boy innocence. Now he is wearing a Chouinard T-shirt, and a red flannel button-down, and carpenter pants. The carpenter pants are appropriately washing-machine worn; the T-shirt looks as though it has done time as a moth community center. He is wearing a string of beads, perhaps a source of mystic power. His hair, in related fashion, is black as ever—so thick and stallionate that it puts Mona in mind of certain Walter Farley books. Yet it is his face most of all that has changed. Gone the baby-fat upholstery, and the poky pink flush. His face is kite-shaped, a bit pale, distinctly planar—a face that bespeaks testosterone. As for the old hole in his left eyebrow, that has grown over without a trace; his eyebrows are veritable slashes now.

Mona scrambles to her feet. How much Sherman has grown! He is taller than Seth easily, however with the shortest legs and longest torso of anyone she's ever seen. If he and she turned out to wear the same size pants, she wouldn't be surprised.

"Hey, man," he says.

"Sherman!" she says again. "I can't believe it."

"I know what you mean," he says, coolly enough. But with that, he turns and flees.

Later that same day, Mona gets a telephone call.

"Sherman?" Mona says.

It is like old times, except that Sherman's English is so greatly improved that his voice itself seems somehow to have improved along with it. Apparently that's what immersion in another culture will do; it's sort of like what Mona's French teacher used to tell her—that if she lived in France who knows, even she might pick up some *je ne sais quoi*. Also Mona finds that being able to picture Sherman makes for a whole different listening experience. How much sexier he sounds— how much more like someone on whose account she would have to take eighty showers.

However, some things remain the same. To wit, she does not ask the questions that are foremost on her mind—namely, why he ran off on her that way, and what it means that he came to look her up, and whether he's still meaning to marry her. She does not even ask where he is living, or how he got her phone number. Instead they talk about Bar Harbor, Maine. They agree that the shoreline there is very beautiful, although perhaps somewhat dangerous. They discuss what they think would happen to someone who fell off the rocks into the water—whether the person would get smashed against the boulders, or pulled out to sea.

"Maybe people shouldn't be out on the rocks to begin with," Mona says. "Maybe land animals should stay on land."

She says this expecting Sherman to agree. However, he doesn't. Would the person die of hypothermia? Mona tells Sherman about the prisoners on Alcatraz. They were not allowed to take cold showers, she says, because by exposing themselves to the cold they could build up their brown fat. And brown fat is so much more insulating than regular fat, she explains, that with it they might have been able to swim to freedom without freezing to death.

"That's called adaptation," Mona says. "It's a healthy process. And Alcatraz is an island that is also a prison that was once in a famous movie. It's in California."

"San Francisco," says Sherman, surprising her.

They discuss lobster. Whether the big ones really are too tough to eat; also how old they are, and how the fishermen know. Do lobster shells have rings, like trees? Mona knows someone who once caught a lobster so big it had to be cooked in a garbage can. This is, in her view, an interesting fact. However, Sherman thinks it's a shame to eat lobsters that old; it's not very respectful. And Mona agrees.

"So how come you're back from Japan again?" she asks.

Silence. Then he does not answer except to explain that he has most recently been living in Hawaii. Also that he now considers himself not Japanese, but Hawaiian.

"Hawaiian!" Mona says.

He hangs up.

A few days later, he calls back, and this time Mona gets more of the story. It turns out his father is in the hotel-buying business; hence all the visits to Pleasant American Beauty Spots. But it also turns out that after living abroad, the Matsumotos had some difficulty going back to their old life. So much difficulty, in fact, that they were more or less forced to become expatriates.

Mona finds this out after an hour of discussing whether the Great Lakes are really all that great. There is therefore not a lot of time left for the subject of how Sherman got sent to a special returnee school, much less how that was related to his not keeping up his Japanese. What is it about Japanese that requires keeping up? Mona doesn't get a chance to ask before Sherman has gone on to mention how also there were incidents. As for what kind of incidents, who knows? Sherman is more forthcoming than he used to be, but his new manner seems tied up with his new life. He tells her how he has a car now, a green Mustang, and how he likes to drink beer.

"Are you a jock?" Mona says.

"Yes," he says.

"Not a hippie? I thought you looked like a hippie."

Are they edging toward the subject of why he ran away from her? She wonders, especially as this subject might naturally lead to another subject. Namely, are they ever going to see each other in person, or are they going to get married on the phone?

"No," he says simply. "I am a jock." He goes on to describe how he's given up judo for baseball. This, it turns out, is a big sport not only in Japan, but in Hawaii too. He calls Hawaii "Hawah-eee."

"Are you American now?" Mona asks. "Have you switched?"

"One hundred percent. Are you surprised?"

Barbara and Mona are prowling a used car lot, on the lookout for the van. This, Barbara's parents have traded in on her. Barbara, though, is determined to get it back.

Through the dealership window, the salesman at the first desk gives them the eye. He is, it seems, all about brown. Brown hair, brown shirt, brown tie, brown jacket, brown desk. From reading *Babbitt*, Mona knows he is leading a life of quiet desperation. However, he doesn't look it. If anything, quite the opposite—he looks utterly at home in his universe, at one with his brownness.

"Think he's going to call the police?" asks Barbara.

"Flash him your checkbook," says Mona.

They check out a van that looks just like Barbara's but isn't—Barbara can tell by the mileage. Although maybe the odometer's been set back? Barbara stares out at the road traffic, thinking. Then she says, "I could probably get my parents to buy it back for me for graduation, assuming my dad doesn't get fired."

"What?"

"You heard me."

"I heard you say fired."

"That's what I said."

"As in, it begins with an *F* and is sort of like retired?"

Says Barbara, "Have you ever thought why you always have to be funny?"

Investigation, authorities, loophole, elaborates Barbara. She's not supposed to know, but she overheard her parents talking. Her dad didn't even do anything. It was some new guy working for some guy working for him who was shorting the stock of bankrupt companies—who knows where the guy found the winning buyers, but he did. The people thought they were investing in a corporate restructure; they had no idea no new stock would be issued. Now they only wished their certificates were tissue paper, at least they could use them to wipe their eyes. Especially since they can't even sue, though they're trying to—hence the scandal—what the broker did being, it seems, legal enough. Mr. Gugelstein didn't even know about it, how could he? He was on the Vineyard at the time. But the consensus of the higher-ups was that someone should step down, in order to restore the good name of the firm.

"So they asked him to resign. But he said, What if no one stepped down? They'd already fired the selling broker, after all. Why the ritual purification? But his questions just went to prove that he didn't put the good of the firm first. Proving to him that Gugelstein was never how you spelled Popularity to begin with."

"Wait. Wait! This doesn't have to do with Eloise Ingle's dad, does it?" says Mona. And she describes with great excitement the conversation she overheard in Rhode Island. She describes Mrs. Ingle's objection, Mr. Ingle's reticence.

"How very interesting." Barbara sweeps her hair off her neck. "Mr. Ingle must be one of the people who want to hang my dad. But where does that get us?"

"It's got to get us somewhere," says Mona. "Maybe your dad can sue."

But to know the truth of what goes on isn't worth as much as you'd think.

"Yeah, right." Barbara circles some more around the van that does look so exactly like hers.

. . .

The new Sherman wants to hear about Mona, a surprise. And so she tells him about Seth, and Barbara, and Rabbi Horowitz, and the hot line; also about Eloise Ingle, and Andy Kaplan. And then there's the restaurant, and Alfred, and the mod squad, not to say Evie, and Callie, and Naomi, and Ralph, and Helen. Sherman seems to slightly remember some of these people; also he recalls, of course, the hot line. For the most part, though, he just listens. Mona expects him to be jealous of Seth, and indeed, Seth is enough of a topic of interest that she's careful to leave out the teepee. She concentrates instead on Seth's bike riding—just the sort of thing to tell a guy with a Mustang, she figures. Also she tells him (by way of switching the subject) what it's like to be not Wasp, and not black, and not as Jewish as Jewish can be; and not from Chinatown, either.

"You are a sore thumb," says Sherman. "Sticking out by yourself."

She says, "I'm never at home."

He says he knows how she feels; he's in the same ship. She tells him about her family. The fights. And Harvard, Harvard, Harvard! Of course, Barbara Gugelstein's parents want her to go to Harvard too.

"But for my parents, it's the whole point of life," she says. "Jews believe in the here and now; Catholics believe in heaven; the Chinese believe in the next generation."

"You are their everything."

"Exactly!" When Mona was a child that was okay, she says, but now that she's older and has a mind of her own, she doesn't want to be their everything anymore.

Sherman knows what she means. He talks about how things are in Japan—about education mamas. The competition. The pressure. Examination hell really is hell.

"Jeez," Mona says, "it must be great not to be Japanese anymore."

"I'm Hawaiian now," Sherman says—agreeing, but with a disconcerted note in his voice, as if he had almost forgotten this himself.

The restaurant is quieter these days, what with Seth gone, and Barbara. As for Alfred, rumor has it that he's gotten himself a job in a steakhouse where he's allowed to eat off the menu. How such a restaurant can stay in business is not clear. All the same, Mona pictures Alfred with a T-bone a day, and is glad for him.

Staff turnover has led to a distinct change in atmosphere. This is not only because all the openings have been filled with friends of Cedric's; also, two of the friends have ended up waiting table. There are now males, plural, in the dining room. Not that Ralph has completely abandoned his notions about who makes a proper serving figure. Seth may have broken down some barriers, but if there's one thing Ralph now knows, it is *No more smart aleck*. He hires only *people have proper attitude*, like these new waiters. Who are both legal, and of course, two males in a room is not a lot of males. Yet being both from China, they make an impression on everyone. The customers leave comments in the comment box: They have never seen so many Chinese waiters outside of a Chinese restaurant, they say. As for the non-Chinese help, they have comments too.

Mona likes the new waiters. Edward and Richard, they call themselves; they're from Hong Kong. They wear their hair neat, and somehow it seems to suit the formality of their names that they have unearthed a supply of paper doilies, on which they have been serving dessert. Other improvements: They've taken to folding the napkins so they stand up on the plate. Also they notch the edges of the lemon slices in a fancy way.

Hong Kong style, Cedric calls this. "Everything in Hong Kong is for show," he says. "Everything is for try to look nice. Hong Kong people just like some fancy schmancy."

But as much care as they lavish on dining room presentation, they seem to have drawn some line at the dishwashers. They don't usually have to bus their own tables. However, when they do, they throw their dishes as if over a cliff. It's how they save face, Cedric says (even as he scolds them for the chipping and breaking). Something has to be beneath them. It has nothing to do with the dishwashers being one of them black and the other Puerto Rican; if they were Chinese, claims Cedric, things would be the same.

Is that right? Mona isn't sure until one of the dishwashers quits, and Russell from Taiwan takes his place. But then, sure enough, Richard and Edward throw plates at him too. The only difference is that Russell seems to expect this. He doesn't bother to get mad—except, that is, to point out to Ralph how Richard and Edward swear so loudly in the kitchen that they can be heard clear out in the dining room. And in Chinese too. Isn't this a breach of the No Chinese Out Front rule?

Storm weather. Mona tries to talk with Richard and Edward about the dish throwing, which seems to her the First Cause of the trouble. This makes her feel very young and very old at the same time.

"Sure sure sure," says Richard.

"No problem," says Edward.

Then they go on throwing the dishes, either as if they know she's only the boss's daughter, a person with no real power, or as if they haven't even bothered to calculate whether they should listen to her or not.

Meanwhile, Callie comes home for the weekend, also with no intention of listening. This is because Ralph and Helen have something to discuss with her—namely, the dread subject, Medical School. They discuss this in their various ways. Helen concentrates heavily on filial piety. Here her parents slave all day to pay tuition, think of that, she says. Also think of how her poor parents have no son to send instead. Ralph goes with a more philosophical, nature-of-the-world approach: *You got to have a meal ticket,* he says. And, an interesting argument: *You got to earn your own money, otherwise your husband treat you like a slave.*

"Medical school is sure," he says now. "Other way, you never know what's happen."

"But I'm not really interested in medicine," argues Callie.

Says Helen, more or less, *Medicine is very interesting.*

Says Ralph, more or less, *Life is about work, and since when is work supposed to be interesting?*

They comb over the fine example of Auntie Theresa, who is such a good doctor many round eyes go to see her, not just Chinese. They regale Callie with stories about children of friends of theirs. Many of these have gone to medical school and now are earning good money. One child even has a pool. Never mind that he does not know how to swim. Every day he practices. Every day he does one stroke more, before you know it he's going to be able to swim from the beginning of the pool to the end.

"Hmm," says Callie.

Also he is a great help to his parents, say Ralph and Helen. His father had some trouble with his heart, and you know, that son, he arranged everything for the operation. Gave the father a peaceful mind. Otherwise, he would have been so worried, you know. These doctors, they just like to operate, sometimes the whole thing isn't even necessary.

"Hmm," says Callie.

But here's the difference between her and Mona: Even while she's giving them a hard time, Callie's taking in the parents' point of view—especially the taking-care-of-them-when-they're-sick part.

She says, "It *is* nice to have a doctor in the family. Mom and Dad are right. You can't really trust anyone else."

"That's Chinese thinking," says Mona. "In America, a lot of doctors don't even take care of their own families. They consider that they're not objective enough."

"Hmm," concedes Callie.

But a few days later, she seems to have made up her mind. "Someone has to take care of them, and I can tell it's not going to be you," she says. "Plus I think medicine is interesting."

"Maybe you should talk to somebody. Isn't there a student adviser up there?"

"Not really. I mean, they give you people like Rabbi Horowitz."

"Rabbi Horowitz?" Mona sits up.

"He was the sub-in freshman adviser last year. The first one had a nervous breakdown." Callie shuffles her Chinese vocabulary cards. "By the way, Horowitz isn't even a rabbi anymore. Now he's a grad student."

"Are you kidding? Oh, you should go talk to him!"

"I have no interest in talking to him," says Callie. "Plus I'm not a freshman."

Mona explains to Sherman about her sister, and also about Richard and Edward. Has she ever done this before, shared with him her preoccupations? She has not. But with their solid old format broken up like ice floes, she simply starts talking; and so easily open is she that she almost does not know who is this Mona Chang. Or for that matter, who is this Sherman Matsumoto: For no sooner does she raise the topics of Callie and Richard and Edward than Sherman begins to talk about boundaries. This is a kind of talk Sherman has never engaged in before; and yet it has been coming, she can see, along with his car and his beer drinking. A moment later, it seems natural enough. A moment later, what seem unnatural are their former habits of conversation. Beauty spots! Lobsters!

Sherman says he's read a book about the American personality and the Japanese personality; this is because he's not a tourist anymore. Now that he's American, he's been thinking more about what it means to be Japanese.

"But wait," says Mona. "Now that you're American, shouldn't you be thinking about what it means to be American?"

He says that's right, he is indeed thinking about what it means to be American. He's thinking about that by thinking about what it means to be Japanese.

"I see," says Mona, though she does not see. And for a moment there is that familiar longish silence between them. "Don't hang up," she says.

He doesn't. Instead he proceeds to apply his reading to Richard and Edward and Callie, never mind that they are Chinese. All three of them have drawn certain boundaries, he says, and within the boundaries each has done far more than a run-of-the-mill American would have done. What with the doilies, and the lemon slices, and so on.

"You mean, run-of-the-mill Americans do not become doctors in order to be able to take care of their parents," says Mona.

And Sherman says that is also a good example. As for outside the boundary, though, Richard and Edward have done less. He understands why they do less; he himself doesn't exactly see why dining room waiters should have to concern themselves with dishwashers.

"But that is Japanese thinking." He says that according to the book, Americans do not distinguish so sharply between who they should concern themselves with and who not. "Americans are all the time talk about civic duty. Public spirit. As if they consider the public is their family too. The book says Americans do not distinguish so clearly between who they have a relationship with, and who they do not, and what that relationship is.

"With the Japanese people, everything is circles. The family is inside; next maybe comes the office circle, or the school circle. And next comes the town circle, the country circle. Everybody else is everybody else."

"Hmm," says Mona.

And later in life, she will catalog the ways in which the Chinese and the Japanese are as opposite as their geographies. They are land and sea, large and small, open and closed, continent and island. Later in life, she will go antiquing, and marvel that anyone could ever have lumped these cultures together—the Chinese with their love of symmetry, and things matched; the Japanese with their love of asymmetry, and things juxtaposed.

But as for the similarities: Sherman and Mona talk about the line Edward and Richard have drawn.

"They will have to study a long time for the citizenship exam," says Sherman. "Participation. Democracy. They will have to study a long time to understand that question."

Says Mona, "The Jews they should look at! Now, we Jews, we participate."

"America is not like Japan," Sherman says.

"Or China. My mom says that in China, people mostly try to stay out of trouble. Keep their heads down. The tallest tree catches all the wind, they say. Sweep the snow from your own doorstep. If families take care of themselves, society will take care of itself."

And what about the circle beyond the town, and beyond the country? Beyond the town, and beyond the country, there is no circle. There is outer space. Nothing to be concerned about—nothing with which anyone has a relationship. Mona and Sherman agree: In outer space there are no rules.

On the other hand, within the circles there are so many rules that the Japanese have a word for them—*tatame*. *Tatame*, says Sherman, is like the world of what the Changs call *keqi*—the world of politeness and obligation. But then there is another word too, in Japanese, for the world inside that world: *honne*, the world of true feeling, and intimacy—the world without words.

Is *honne* like the Chinese word *xin*, the world of what is hidden in the heart? Later Mona will wonder. And later too she will wonder where the line between duty and real feeling lies in Japan—whether it lies only between society and the family, or whether there may be a line between the family and the individual too.

A story: A friend who grew up in China complains that you never feel truly inside a home in America. In China, there is a compound wall; in America, there is lawn. It makes Americans seem so friendly, so approachable. But where does the world end? Where does the family begin? And how is it that the family allows everything to come out? People have stories in America, that's just like in China; but how is it they are willing to tell them on *The Newlywed Game*? It is as if they are not real family members, says this friend.

Is Mona a real family member? And if she is not—if she is a member of the world concerned about her civic duty—how is it that she still finds a truth of her own in Sherman's next words, which are not that to have a public face and a private face is to be two-faced; but rather that without the world of outer politeness, you cannot have a world of inner richness.

What is not hidden cannot be the flower, says Sherman. A quote from someone or another, he can't remember. Some monk.

And Mona says, *Hmm*, startled; or maybe she says nothing, there being nothing to say.

Barbara's nose runs extraordinarily when she cries, another medical impossibility. Her doctor has said that nose-running in times of weepiness is a universal phenomenon governed by forces divine. He claims that the most skillful of surgeons could not alter the mucal flow for all the insurance coverage in the world. But Barbara maintains her nose didn't used to do this; certainly not so copiously. And whether she is right or wrong, it certainly is true that if there is a share of world Kleenex to which each human is entitled, she is claiming her birthright with a vengeance.

Her father is indeed being fired.

"I don't know why anyone would want to be Jewish," she sobs. "I mean, who wasn't already."

Mona agrees this is a mystery.

"If only he could sue!" says Barbara. "But what can he prove? That no one there turned out to be his friend?"

CHAPTER 12

A Stay of Execution

Mr. Gugelstein cannot sue, but Alfred can. Mona comes home to find Ralph looking as though he's just seen his SAT scores and didn't even get the two hundred points you're supposed to earn for spelling your name right. In his hand is the Chinese-English dictionary, but it's closed. After all, how to translate New York State Division of Human Rights? What means Executive Branch?

"For firing him," says Ralph, grasping with one hand a letter with attached official complaint form. His other hand is on his stomach. "So-called racial discrimination."

Helen is less shaken than Ralph, more convinced. For this is the difference between a listening mind and a telling mind: Helen's is the kind of mind to which stories occur in itchy enough detail to make her want to scratch. For example, she is not surprised when Mona explains about Alfred's friend Luther, who may have goaded Alfred on. Of course! A crazy person arranged this! She says that it wasn't their fault, the firing. Alfred brought it on himself.

Why does Mona try to tell some other truth?

"You have nothing to say," says Helen, turning on the vacuum cleaner.

Mona, though, refusing to be drowned out, shouts, "You wouldn't have promoted Alfred! You were prejudiced!"

Whereupon Helen raises her hand, and for a moment Mona thinks she is going to slap her the way she used to slap Callie. But instead she hands the vacuum over with what looks to be sadness veined with satisfaction. It is as if despite years of checking the stove at night, she finally has woken, just as she always predicted, to the smell of everything burning.

"We did not trust him the way we trust Cedric," she concedes evenly, when the living room is done and all is quiet again. "But that's not the reason why we fired Alfred. Alfred we fired because he made trouble at your friend's house. You don't think your friend Barbara's parents are racist? What do you think they were upset about?"

"And so what if they were racist?" counters Mona. "Would that make it okay for you to be racist too?"

"Our trouble is that we are in the middle," Helen goes on. "Alfred is mad; he would like to sue your friend Barbara's family. But he cannot sue them, so he sue us."

"That's because they didn't do anything illegal."

"As if we did?" Helen says airily. And when Mona starts to argue, Helen explains more vigorously. "Just remember why we work so hard, always try to do our best. Just remember why we struggle to make money."

"In order to send me and Callie to college," says Mona.

"That's right!" Helen, quick, picks up a newspaper, claiming a pop victory; and though she does not look at Ralph when he comes in, he too quickly picks up a section of the paper, as if catching his cue. Or maybe he has his own reasons for wanting to disappear behind a handy curtain of news: For business in the restaurant seems to be slowly but surely falling off. In the beginning it seemed like a wavering in the numbers, a wee inexplicable dip. But now it appears a ditch, unfortunately attributable to the staffing. Namely, Richard and Edward. Why should people not come to a restaurant just because the help is Chinese? But they don't. It's a simple fact of contemporary society, like babies needing their picture taken. And what should Ralph do now? Fire Richard? Fire Edward? Helen doesn't think that he should any more than he does. However, it makes her furious that Ralph thinks he can't, especially when he points out how this might be like firing Alfred, mysteriously illegal. *Impossible!* says Helen. *As if Richard and Edward are going to sue anyone!* She says, *Chinese people don't sue.* Still he refuses to do anything about this or any other problem. Sometimes it seems to him that the restaurant is his business, and that he should be able to do whatever he wants. But other times he's not at all sure about this. Other times it seems to him only natural that people should have to consider other people in everything they do.

"Everyone except your wife!" says Helen later. "You consider everyone except your family!"

Is that true? Ralph puzzles as Helen cries, "Why don't you do something? Why don't you say something?"

Aunt Theresa is coming to visit. Nobody says this is because of the lawsuit; officially, they are still waiting for the matter to blow over. Officially, they are one hundred percent sure that it will. Theresa is simply suddenly coming for a holiday. Ralph and Helen may have to call a lawyer soon, after all; and having never had this kind of trouble before, they are apprehensive. How will they find the right lawyer? How will they know if the lawyer is good? Someone has told them that lawyers charge for every minute of their time, including just picking up the telephone. According to this source, lawyers charge even if they have a cold and spend most of their time blowing their nose. Is that true? And should Helen and Ralph tell everything to the lawyer? Say nothing to anyone, that was the rule in China. Know nothing, say nothing, do nothing. Of course, things are different here. Still, before they do anything, they first want to hear what Theresa will say. She is the smart one in the family, they are just *make-money guys*. And the matter being so serious, they didn't want to discuss too much on the phone. Not that they exactly believe their line is bugged. However, they don't quite trust the phone either.

There is a lot of talk about operators. It begins to seem to them that they can hear, past the operators' perfect phone voices, traces of their real voices. These are nowhere near so pleasant, and maybe even foreign. The way Helen in particular says the word *foreign*, Mona has to roll her eyes.

Mona says, "How can you of all people think having an accent makes you a spy?"

But so unshakable is Helen on the subject of the accents that she could be the bedrock on which nestles Manhattan. Who knows, she says, they might be Russians.

"Mom," Mona says. "The Russians aren't suing you."

"That's enough!" Helen says. "I don't want to hear that word again."

"What word?"

Helen doesn't want to say.

"Suing?"

"Grounded! One week, no long phone calls either."

"But, Ma," Mona says. "There's nothing the matter with the *word*. Plus you *are* being sued."

"Two weeks!" Helen says.

Is she really superstitious? Mona has never been able to figure out whether Helen is serious or not about things bringing bad luck. However, it's true that the one time Ralph had to go on a plane trip, Mona and Callie were absolutely not allowed to mention accidents of any kind. Helen whacked the girls if they so much as mentioned a flat tire, never mind a fiery, big boom–type crash. They weren't allowed to mention dryer fires, either, even if there really was one in Callie's classmate's house. How could Helen have passed up such a prime educational opportunity? *You see how important to clean out that lint filter.* But no; she really didn't want to hear one word on the subject. Not with Ralph on a plane; no.

Of course, this only made the girls whisper and giggle all the more—as they would these days too, if Callie were home. If Callie were home, she would roll her eyes with Mona, they would do roller coasters. Their chatter would be the foreground of their lives, the bicker of their parents the kind of low-interest backdrop you associate with drama club plays held in cafeterias. But with Callie away, there is mostly just fighting, so many nights of fighting that it is beginning to seem the true sound of the night itself—a sound, say, you normally cannot hear for the crickets. Mona can't actually understand a word of what the parents are saying—they're fighting in Chinese—and yet she gets the gist just fine: *If you hadn't, if you had. So you tell me whose fault it is.* And of course, *One thing I can tell you, she is your daughter, not mine.*

The import of Theresa's visit is somewhat obscured by her manner of arrival, which is fresh from the vegetable kingdom. She is wearing an Oakland A's baseball cap, and carrying a large straw backpack full of surprises. *Look!* A Hawaiian florist neighbor has made these herself, leis for everyone; Mona alone has three—one of purple orchids, one of pink, and one of yellow and white, alternating. The flowers weigh heavy as a horse collar on her shoulders, and she can feel the petals piled soft against her earlobes. A nimbus of smell surrounds her; it's like hearing stereo speakers for the first time, only with her nose. Also Theresa has bags of figs from her fig tree; she has lemons from a neighbor's lemon tree. She has special vegetables she has grown in her garden—heads of garlic the size of baseballs, and beautiful bright-violet finger eggplants that look as though they belong in a bouquet.

But of everything, she herself is the most blue-ribbon specimen. She is wiry and tan and sweetly befreckled, and when she takes off her baseball hat you can see that she's given up her bun, and is wearing her brown hair all loose now. Except, that is, for a single skinny braid. She's managed to gather almost all white hairs for this braid, so that it shines like liquid silver. As for clothes, she is wearing blue jeans like a hippie, only new-looking and fresh-pressed, with a crease down the front of each leg. The jeans go with a lightly starched work shirt, on which has been embroidered chain after chain of daisies and—in a little half-moon around the shirt tag in the back—her name, only without the *h*: *Teresa.*

This H is not the only one that is missing. Most conspicuously absent is Uncle Henry. But since Theresa and Uncle Henry are not married, he is not missed. Everyone talks instead, over tea in the backyard, about the World Series, and about Theresa's cats, Barbie and Ken. Also about how Theresa likes living on the beach. In English this is—Theresa's preferred language when either of the girls is around. Doesn't sand get tracked into the house? Helen asks. And what about ocean storms? Theresa tells them about a big flood they had. *Not so bad,* she says. And cool as can be, she reports that she's given away everything she doesn't absolutely need—anything she couldn't help but worry about, but didn't think worth the concern. Everything really important, she keeps on the second floor.

"What kind of things you gave away?" asks Helen, in a casually quavering voice. She is so shocked that she does not seem to hear the inventory at all: the hi-fi cabinet, the Statue of Liberty lamp, everything cut crystal, that white flokati rug full of cat hair . . . It is as if she is seeing her own house being swept out to sea.

". . . also some other things." Mona can tell her aunt's not really done, that really she's winding up as a minor act of mercy.

"Clean house is always good," says Ralph blithely. "Fact is, why we need so much stuff? Just make us crazy. . . ."

"I'll tell you who's crazy," Helen starts to say. But then she doesn't tell anybody anything.

Everyone has some more tea. Ralph tries a fig, pronounces it delicious. They reminisce about persimmons they have eaten, and pomegranates. There is some talk about a hurricane they had right in New York.

"And what about mildew?" Helen asks finally.

Theresa explains how she leaves lights on in the closets. "You'd be amazed. Just one lightbulb can dry everything out."

"Mildew can be serious problem," says Helen, apparently relieved that Theresa at least takes fungal growth seriously. They go on to discuss dry-cleaning bags, and whether they are, in combination with the lightbulbs, a fire hazard. What wattage does she use? And is there a shade on the bulb?

"No such thing as too careful," says Ralph, helping himself to another fig. "Even you are very very careful, you never know what will happen." He shakes his head. "Fate."

"Fate! Our trouble has nothing to do with fate," says Helen.

"What? Everything is I abdicated responsibility? Everything is I do not care?"

And so begins the subject of the lawsuit. Helen and Ralph vie with each other in their efforts to be reasonable. However, there is energy in need of discharge; everything seeks the ground, crackling. They begin; then try to begin again, at the beginning, only to discover that there is no beginning. They fear there will be no end. Still they explain to Theresa everything they can—including in their explanation some facts Mona knew but didn't know. For example, how Ralph hired Alfred despite his having a police record. Apparently he was recommended by Theresa's parish priest in such a way as left Ralph no choice. For the priest said first of all, that Alfred was innocent; and second of all, that Ralph of all people should have a heart for someone trying to start over. Helen contests the and-so-we-had-no-choice part of the story. She says the priest was just making a recommendation. She says only someone like Ralph lets other people decide his business as if he is still in China. No wonder he has trouble with his stomach!

Meanwhile, Theresa listens carefully. For all that she had seemed a dubious authority on the subject of oceanfront property, as they talk on she seems to somehow rise in stature, never mind that she remains sitting down. She seems to be subtly straightening, aligning herself with the stripe of her folding chair. Helen explains about Barbara Gugelstein's house, and about how they had to fire Alfred. Though in general they have more choice than Ralph thinks, she says, in this case they didn't. Also she explains about Mona—how she was led astray by bad elements, especially this good-for-nothing Seth, but how at least she has atoned by breaking up with the good-for-nothing. Helen says they didn't even have to ask her to do it; Mona realized herself that this would make her parents happy, and went ahead on her own.

Is that what happened?

"She's still a good girl," finishes Helen. "Sometimes she likes to have a big mouth, but then she looks in her heart and realizes she is still our nice Chinese daughter."

"In the morning, we hear her, she is like a bird," says Ralph. "So sweet and nice, at the restaurant, she is the best hostess you can find. You cannot hire someone smile at the customers like that. Make everyone feel good."

Theresa nods thoughtfully, considering with a profound look her thong sandals. These are a little cool for New York—lucky thing she's sitting with her long feet in the sun—though these are not sandals Helen would ever wear even if it were summer. These are sandals that not only bare all ten toes, but seem to take their inspiration from the loincloth. However, on Auntie Theresa, they look somehow elegant; maybe it's just the contrast with the rest of her outfit. A smile seems to flit across her face, but then she reenters the role of presiding elder and says, after an elder-like pause, that it doesn't sound to her as if Alfred has much of a case. Naturally, she's no lawyer, and clearly Alfred's dismissal had something to do with race. But what?

"If Cedric went to live in Mona's friend's house, you would fire him too," she says.

General relief. "That's right! We would fire Cedric too. Of course, Chinese people would not move into someone's house to begin with."

More happy agreement. What discrimination could Alfred be talking about?

Mona brings up, as delicately as she can, all about her mom and dad not being willing to promote Alfred the way they did Cedric. And why? Because he wasn't Chinese.

Helen says, admiring the sky, "We do not know who is this big mouth or where she got it from."

"Well," says Theresa, "maybe that's not quite right, about the promotion. In China, is one thing. But here in the United States, that's not the way to think. You cannot think all the time about relationship. You have to think about the law."

"How could be?" says Ralph. "America is supposed to be the land of the free."

"That's why we have laws, to make sure that everybody is free," explains Theresa. "But anyway, say you are racist. I don't mean that you are. Let's just consider that case. Even if you are, how could Alfred know that? How could he know you are thinking to promote Cedric? How could he know you are not going to promote him? And how could he know why?"

"There's no way he can find out," says Ralph.

Says Helen, "After all, he doesn't have that—what is it called? EST." Everyone laughs with relief.

"ESP," Mona says.

Everyone laughs again.

And Mona, sitting on the milk box, tries to laugh too, wishing she did not have to tell them not only how she told Seth and Barbara, but how, during a camp rap session—trying to be up front, figuring the truth never hurt—she even told Alfred himself, and Luther.

The news is received calmly at first. Theresa sets the tone by praising her niece for being so forthcoming. Theresa sees this as proof of her loyalty to the family, that Mona would not think of holding such a thing back. Everyone agrees that Mona was under a lot of peer pressure, especially from that good-for-nothing Seth; and that Mona is, after all, not a full-grown adult but still a child, who does not quite know how to talk. They conclude that she still needs her parents to tell her what to do. They agree they should never have let her near that Seth Mandel to begin with; that was Ralph's fault. Helen wanted to make them break up, she says, it was Ralph who said to let Mona learn her lesson by herself.

"He said we could ask Magdalena and Cedric to watch them," complains Helen. "As if they are the same as parents!" She vows that they will be stricter in the future, so that they will not have to blame themselves again.

"We have abdicated our responsibility," says Helen.

And Ralph, who knows who she means when she says *we*, admits, "Pay too much attention to the restaurant, it's not right. Make our children suffer."

"No more go out, go out," says Helen. "From now on, Mona stay home."

Everyone nods.

"No more drive family car. From now on, ride bicycle." Ralph has an odd expression on his face that may or may not be a smile.

"Walk," says Helen.

"Crawl," Mona says.

Ralph smiles again without smiling.

"No more jokes, either," says Helen. "You think everything is funny. That's the beginning of your trouble."

"Wrong attitude," says Ralph, winking.

"He is not this way all the time," Helen says to Theresa. "Only because you are here."

Both women look down.

"Just want to laugh and have fun," continues Helen.

"But, Ma," Mona says.

"No *Ma*," says Helen.

"I thought you guys liked it that I was always laughing about something. Didn't you tell Auntie how I was just like a bird, so gay and everything?"

"We must think about our duty as parents." Ralph is serious now. "We laugh when you laugh, that's just encourage you. We are wrong that way. Abdicate our responsibility!"

"No more typical American parents," agrees Helen. "No more let the kids run wild. From now on we are Chinese parents."

"You know what you guys sound like?" Mona says. "You sound like the Puritans."

Helen frowns.

"You know," Mona says. "The Puritans. The guys with the funny buckles on their shoes?"

Helen says, "Is that the family, all their five kids got scholarship to Yale?"

Ralph whistles. "All five kids!"

"Not all five got full scholarship," explains Helen. "Two just got so-called work study aid, have to work in the dining hall."

A moment of silence, during which everyone contemplates just what the Puritans' secret could be.

Says Ralph, "Their parents must do some good job, kids turn out like that."

"No more go out," starts Helen again.

"No more fool around," echoes Ralph, sternly.

Through all this, Auntie Theresa diligently nods her head. Her eyes do not narrow in shrewd discerning fashion, but rather seem preternaturally wide open, accepting of all; she could be a rain barrel left out in the backyard. Does she really think Ralph and Helen remiss, does she really think a parental crackdown in order? Or does she simply think Mona is better off having them blame themselves than blame her?

Later Mona will think the latter, and credit her aunt for her prescience. Because, all too soon, Theresa leaves—she most unfortunately has nonrefundable tickets for a deluxe cruise of the Hawaiian Islands. Before she hurries home to pack her bikinis, though, she finds the time to hang a hammock up in the backyard with Mona. Naturally, this is not a regular old hammock. This is a special hammock from California, made of many colors, and with a built-in pillow. They test it out together. The sky rocks above them.

"One thing very important in life," says Theresa, "is to know how to make yourself at home."

"I didn't mean to make so much trouble," says Mona. "Really I didn't."

"No one could make so much trouble by themselves," says Theresa. "Do you like the beach?"

"Sure."

"Good. You are welcome to come to California anytime. Anytime you like, you can come make yourself at home."

"Maybe I really will come visit you."

Theresa straightens her legs, kicks her feet a little. Today she is wearing regular shoes and regular pants. However, her shirt is red-checked like a tablecloth. "Before you know it, it will be your home away from home."

"It's that nice, huh."

"Very comfortable," says Theresa, still swinging. "Just remember, you are invited."

"Okay," says Mona.

"Just remember," insists Theresa. "Don't forget."

"I won't forget."

"No matter what, you're invited. Remember."

"No matter what."

Theresa repeats her invitation one more time, in the airport; in the cavernous lobby, under the hard fluorescent lights, though, her generosity resounds in an Old Testament manner. *Thou shalt not forget to come visit.*

"All right already," says Mona. "I'll start saving for my plane ticket tomorrow."

Theresa clasps Mona's hand as if she's been granted an audience with the Pope. "Shalom," she says. "The cheapest way is standby." And with that she turns into the walkway, stops to wave five or six times, and is gone.

It's the War of the H's—Helen versus the High Holy Days.

"That's enough Jewish," she says. "Forget about services. Not funny anymore. You know where all the trouble started? All the trouble started from you become Jewish."

"Mom," Mona says. "It's a free country. I can go to temple if I want. In fact, if I wanted to, I could go to a mosque."

Mona expects her mother to say, What's a mosque? But Helen knows which counter she is headed for; she is not about to be distracted by any discount special.

"Forget about free country," she says.

"What do you mean? This is America. I can remember what I want, I can be what I want, I can—"

"You want to be something, you can leave this house, don't come back," says Helen.

They are putting their summer clothes away, taking out their winter things. The latter are quaintly woolly—scratchy, bulky. Prehistoric. Does it really ever get that cold around here? Certainly it's cooler and cooler out, and clear; some days the air is almost metallic, like tinware. Still it's hard to believe anyone with a normal fat level would ever need to wrap herself up in all that. So thinks Mona.

Helen, though, packs as if summer is the season without compelling reality—as if this year the winter will, quite possibly, not end. She uses so many mothballs that the wastebasket cannot hold all the empty boxes, they have to start a bag for overflow.

"It says here you only have to use one box of balls for every ten cubic feet," Mona says.

"Forget about what it says. You listen to your mother."

"I'm just reading the directions."

Helen takes the box she has just opened and upends it onto the floor. Her motions are undramatic, yet the balls scatter excitedly, noisily making her point. "If you Jewish people so smart," she says, "you can do it by yourself."

"That's a stereotype!" Mona says. "We're not any smarter than the Chinese."

Helen is not listening.

Mona does not go to services; the temple is kind enough to re-sell her ticket. But no sooner does this skirmish end than Helen and Mona fight over whether it is safe to put chopsticks in the dishwasher. One day a chopstick slips down near the heating element and gets charred. This to Helen is a sign that Mona is going to burn the house down.

"First of all, there's nothing the matter with washing chopsticks by hand. Not a big deal. Only Americans have to wash everything use machine," she says. "Second of all, we are not racist."

Mona continues to demonstrate her special method of jamming the chopsticks into the silverware drainer. "You just have to put them in sideways, like this."

"How could you say that to outside people?" Helen says. "What kind of daughter talks that way? Tell them your parents are racist."

"Mom," Mona says. "You were never going to promote Alfred. Because he was black."

"First of all, we hired Alfred when no one would give him a job. He should thank us instead of sue us! And how do you think he got to be cook if we didn't promote him? As for new promotion, since when do we owe someone promotion? We don't owe him anything."

"But Alfred could only go so far, when it came to—"

"Second of all," continues Helen, "parents are racist, parents are not racist, even parents are Communist, a daughter has no business talk like that. You talk like that is like slap your own mother in the face!"

"I didn't mean to slap you in the face, Ma. We were just having a discussion about racism, which happens to be an important social problem, and in that context—"

"Context! Social problem! What kind of talk is that?"

Mona closes up the dishwasher. "It's a free country, I can talk however I want. It's my right."

"Free country! Right! In this house, no such thing!"

More social analysis: "That's exactly the problem! Everywhere else is America, but in this house it's China!"

"That's right! No America here! In this house, children listen to parents!"

And the inevitable conclusion.

"Okay," Mona says. "I'm leaving. I'm going to pack up my backpack and check out a train schedule and take all the money out of my bank account."

"Go ahead," Helen says.

Mona hesitates. "I'm not even going to get traveler's checks, I'm just going to carry cash," she says.

It's what she thinks of as an invitation to motherhood; this is what children have to do every now and then, give their parents a chance to play the boss. But Helen is too mad even to rise to the bait. Of course, never having had much faith in credit, she has always carried around a lot of cash herself.

She slaps Mona in the face.

"Mom." Mona straightens her glasses. "Mom. I'm not Callie." She feels her cheek; she knows the skin is hot by how cool her hand feels against it, an iceberg. She says, as clearly and mightily as she can, "If you ever do that again, I'm going to slap you right back."

Helen slaps her again, then calmly picks up a mug of cold tea. Her face looks like a plaster cast of itself. She says, "You think you are so smart, you think you know everything. But let me tell you something: Once you leave this house you can never come back." And with that, she marches upstairs to her bedroom, cradling the cold liquid as if she fully intends to drink it.

CHAPTER 13

Mona's Life
as Callie

Mona is not the one who usually runs away. It's true that once, when she was little, she packed a suitcase and wrote a note and hid under the bed; and it's true that she was disappointed when no one collapsed with shock and grief upon reading that she had removed herself to another clime, she knew not whither. She bade her family farewell and forgave them their foibles and sincerely hoped they came to recognize the sorry error of their ways, for their own sake; then she fell asleep and woke up with a dust ball in her mouth. This was nowhere near so gross as almost anything you see in the movies. However, it was perhaps one of the grossest things ever to happen to her.

She hasn't forgotten it. Still, in general, it has been Callie the Achiever who has walked out into the snow or rain, grim intention in every step. For example, after they moved to Scarshill and Helen told her she would get the small dark room with the leaky ceiling, while Mona would get the large yellow one with the windows on two walls. Callie thought then that Helen should at least flip a coin. She said it wasn't right for mothers to play favorites; she said it had been going on almost her whole life, and she wasn't going to take it anymore. Big words. But she said them in a Callie-like way—as if she wanted to run away from her own working mouth—and perhaps that is why Helen slapped her, because she was cowering already. Helen hated it that she made Callie cower. Or so she said. *Like a servant.* Slap. *My own daughter!* And that made Callie threaten to slap her back. She was wild as a squirrel in a corner, the kind of squirrel with half its fur bitten off, and nothing to call its own except twitches. Helen slapped her again; and when

Callie slapped her back sure enough, they ended up on the floor, yanking each other's hair out. Then Callie went out into the sleet without a coat, and when she came back, after hours of Helen claiming *nothing wrong*, it was with a policeman, and a coat someone had given her, a total stranger. And even before Callie took it off, anyone could see why a total stranger in a car would stop and give Callie the coat off her own back. Callie was drenched and thin and shaking, and her ears were white with what Mona thought must be frostbite.

All the same, Mona kept the room. The favorite daughter pinned peace pins on her curtains, hung a hat rack on the closet door. On one wall she taped pretty packages, gum wrappers, fortune cookie fortunes, making them into a kind of collage; here and there, she placed Coke bottles full of peacock feathers, very artistic. Also Mateus wine bottles with different-colored candle wax dripped all over them. She spent hours figuring out what color to burn next, and how to make dripless candles drip.

Meanwhile, Callie studied. For that's what hysterics did, when they were being perfect. When they were being perfect, they practiced their posture and got themselves into Harvard-Radcliffe and looked askance at the decorating efforts of others. They made mildly snide comments. *I earn my keep.*

Mona wonders now at how strongly she feels about all this. It feels, in memory, as if she were the one who walked out into the storm— as if she were Callie all along, even as she was Mona. Is this what it means to be sisters? Mona wishes she had given Callie the big room; or at least that they had tossed a coin, the two of them. She wonders what she thought at the time. Did she think, *Of course, I am the favorite, this room is mine*? Did she think, *Please let them stop*? Did she think, *That is not my mother, that cannot be my mother*?

Even now it is unthinkable, how she grew up by day while her sister grew up by night. She can no more imagine this than she can imagine why she chose to enter the night herself, Callie's night; or at least to leave the day. Someone once told her a story about Callie: about how teased Callie was by her math teacher on account of being smart. This was when Callie was in eighth grade. The teacher did things like snap her bra strap during exams, this friend said; she knew because her brother was two rows back and saw the whole thing. How the teacher pulled Callie's strap and laughed—really it was a sign that she was his favorite—and how Callie did nothing at all. How she sat there, and worked out the problems, and handed her exam in early—some people said without even checking it over.

Mona knows this about her sister; and she knows too how Callie became the kind of person these things happened to. She wonders: Do favorite children in China feel guilty? Or do they simply accept their spot in the hierarchy—*How lucky am I!* Perhaps only a New World daughter would wonder about the fairness of it all. Mona can hear her mother's voice: *Fair! As if there is such a thing.* A voice not unlike Mr. Ingle's: *You've got to know how the game is played.* In the background, Mrs. Ingle tinkles, *It's just not right.* But her voice is nowhere near so loud as her husband's, or Helen's. *Fair! Fair!*

Perhaps this is why Mona allied herself with the Jews, with their booming belief in doing right, with their calling and their crying out. *Justice!* But then again, maybe she would have turned into anything no daughter of her mother could be; maybe it was just that simple. Adolescent rebellion, just like Rabbi Horowitz said, maybe certain urges come shrink-wrapped with your first bottle of pHisoHex.

She finds herself first at their local train station, and then in the city, alone. She considers who she might call. She would call Barbara, except for Mrs. Gugelstein. She would call Aunt Theresa, except that she is at sea. She would call Callie, except that Callie is Callie. And she would call Sherman, except that she doesn't know his phone number, and what would he say that Mona would want him to say? She would want him to say, *Why don't you come on over, I'd love to talk in person and even do mushy stuff.* Instead she would probably get more Zen wisdom: *What talks back cannot be the flower.* Maybe she shouldn't have broken up with Seth the sex maniac; in truth, she practically misses him, teepee and all.

Grand Central is large and, in one room, full of benches, like a church. She would say temple, except that around the corner there are ticket windows, lined up like confessionals. These are mostly closed, just like in church, and the air is still, and voluminous—a palpable, roller rink of an expanse like the charged, curved space between the hands of a god. There was a time when this is what Mona would have imagined—a god as big as King Kong. Someone able to reach all those high windows and, if he was in the mood, able to give them a nice wipe such as would let the sun shine in on poor earthlings like herself. So pale! So lost! There was a time she would have looked up with frail hope and felt what a pittance she was. She would have felt her smallness of consequence like a wrinkled-up name tag at the back of her collar.

But today, before she sees herself in perspective, she feels, quite unexpectedly, as though she stands in the Garden of Eden. Just for a moment. The wind of apprehension, as always, will blow. But between gusts, she feels it—not even that she is standing in, but as though she is herself the Garden of Eden. A place that will remain a place of sun even after the poor forked whatever have been banished. She feels as though she stands at the pointy start of time. Behind her, no history. Before her—everything. How arrogant! *As if you have no mother! As if you come out of thin air!* She can hear Helen's voice. Still Mona feels it—something opening within herself, big as the train station, streaming with sappy light. And feeling this, she is almost not surprised to find next to her—she is sitting, it seems, on a bench—a lady. This lady has laid herself down, stretched herself out—and now, sure enough, is making herself comfortable. One of her legs dangles over the bench edge, foot almost touching the floor; her other leg extends straight up into the air. The lady is wearing yellow fishnet stockings; her garters show; the leg descends through the air with the willy-nilly grandeur of a felled tree.

Heads up! Mona watches with amazement. This is not something that could ever happen at home. For one thing, fishnet stockings have gone out of style. Down to bench level. The lady's foot looks as though it is going to land inches from Mona's thigh, but doesn't. Instead it lands smack square in Mona's lap. Is this life outside of high school? Mona clutches her backpack. She makes sure the zippered compartment is zipped, even though the lady seems harmless enough. Blue pumps she is wearing, with a red leather tassel, and also a piece of green ribbon. The ribbon is tied around the bottom of the shoe, into a glorious bow on top; she seems to have just put it on, for it is perfectly clean and apparently un-walked on. Should Mona say something to her? *Excuse me, your foot is sort of in my lap.* If Mona were her mother, she would certainly extricate herself from the situation. But so removed is Mona from her everyday ways that she finds a strange small comfort in this contact. And so she takes the lady in: oldish, the color of cherry bark, evidently asleep. Short matted hair. One might surmise her zip dress no longer zips, for she is wearing safety pins all down her front. Big silver ones, little gold ones, oddly spaced; the dress is certainly in no danger of coming off. Her skin, though, is another story. Once Mona read in a book about how ladies in the Old South put wax on their faces for makeup, and how that wax would come off if they sat too close to a fire; this lady too looks as if her outer layers are softening. Mona fears for her—not that the lady seems afflicted with any such worry herself. Soft ratchety snores slip away from her like truant ghosts. Mona considers the lady's shoes a little longer—how the seams appear to be straining; how they appear, in fact, under that green ribbon, to be split. The heels are so worn that the leatherette alongside curls up in a little froth; and yet, behold the scoop of man-made material on the underside of her arch. This is fresh and shiny black, with the shoe size crisply incised. Nine and a half B. Too big for Mona to give the lady her own shoes. Schizophrenia? thinks Mona. Drugs? She wonders how she ever could have worked on a hot line, she feels so helpless. The lady stirs a little; the dangling leg loses its mooring, threatening to drag her whole weight down. What to do? Mona considers the higher windows of the station, then reaches for the lady's other foot. For a moment the lady jerks, as if about to kick. But no; it is just a deep-sleep twitch. Mona closes her eyes too. She clasps her hands on the lady's slim ankles, and holds on.

"So what's this? A homeless waif? A runaway?"

Mona opens her eyes, adjusts her glasses. The safety pin lady is gone, and sitting next to her is Bea, smelling of almonds. Mona feels for her backpack—still there. She blinks. Bea is still there too. Bea is likewise holding on to her bag, in the immortal manner of ladies out in public, except that hers is not a lady's bag. It is, rather, the kind of beaded pouch that is most properly stuffed with wampum. And perhaps it is, for Bea is dressed to a theme. This is to say that she is mostly soft fabrics, knits and fuzz and stretch pants. However, she is also sporting a Stetson hat, a fringed suede jacket, and cowboy boots. If it weren't for her fall oh-so-touchables, she could be Buffalo Bill.

"You were asleep." Bea takes Mona's chin in her hand. "Is something wrong? Something is wrong, I can see it. You're all puffy."

"What are you doing here?" says Mona.

"I'll tell you what I'm doing here if you'll tell me what you're doing here."

Mona doesn't know what to say.

Bea nods comprehendingly. "I see." Adding, as if to keep her side of the bargain, "I'm here to pick up the branding irons for my roundup. You would think I'd be going to Wyoming for these, but actually I went to Lincoln Center." She indicates two enormous packages, wrapped for the ages in brown paper and masking tape. "Do you know where you are going?"

"No."

Bea nods again. "We all have to go through this; it must be the water. Every one of my kids did exactly the same thing, all that differed was the particulars: This one hitchhiked; that one took planes; Seth, as you know, moved into a teepee. That wasn't so bad—at least we didn't have to worry about tropical diseases. I tell you what. Why don't you move into our yard for a while? Seth took the teepee, but we're doing a corral for the roundup anyway. How about if we add a little stable? I'll call your parents and let them know where you are, and you can have your rebellion in peace."

Mona frowns.

"Are you pregnant?"

Mona shakes her head.

"Then what is it? Share with me this state secret."

Mona tries to explain, but mostly she asks: What if she were Bea's daughter and had done something awful? Something that really hurt her parents? Can she imagine that?

"Well, of course, I do not have a daughter," says Bea. "Only boys, boys, boys. Not that I didn't love having boys. But they certainly were boys. And the particular kind of boys I had seemed to specialize at a certain age in saying the absolute meanest things possible. For example, my dear stepson Seth." There is a slight catch in her throat; she runs a light hand over her wrapped-up branding irons. "Seth has spent this year calling me a hypocrite. All my do-gooding, says my dear stepson, is just a way of maintaining my social status."

"He *said* that to you?" Mona is wide-eyed.

"He did, and I tell you, it was not so easy to hear. And I would be lying if I did not admit that I argued with him, and threatened to lock him out of the house, or at least to revoke his laundry privileges. But every time of life has its job, and that is his job right now, to say the thing that will hurt me most. It is how he is becoming his own person, by pointing out the truth."

"Is it the truth?"

Bea sighs and looks at her hands. These are freckled, with pale-colored nail polish and a number of rings Seth says she cannot bear to take off—every one reminds her of something. "Life is more complicated than he thinks. And what's the matter with liberal guilt anyway? Better to feel guilty than to feel nothing, that's my opinion. I write my letters, I'm doing my best. The rest I'll have to leave to the great leaders of our age. Anyway, insulting me was Seth's job, and my job as a stepmother was to let him do his job. That's what I agreed when I married like a fool his adorable father, Phil."

"Even if it meant letting Seth not go to college?"

"We couldn't force him. He's an adult. It was his decision."

An adult! His decision! Mona cannot help but hear what another voice would say in the same situation: *What do you mean, not going to college? You kill your parents, you talk like that.*

Bea worries a hangnail. "You watch, he'll end up on the straight and narrow yet. It's the talented ones you have to worry about. Especially the ones who can sing, or play something—with them you have to worry about rock bands. Seth, luckily, has no talents. That leaves law school."

"You must be relieved that he changed his mind."

"Changed his mind?"

"Didn't he tell you? He's gone to college after all. That's what I heard."

"Is that where he is!" says Bea. "We've been getting postcards from him, but he doesn't seem to be anywhere near where they're postmarked. His father is worried sick. Do you know what school he went to?"

"I don't know. We broke up."

"No kidding."

Track announcements come over the PA system. A lady with six children struggles by.

"My parents think people like you don't care about your kids, that's how come you let them do what they want," says Mona. "They think you're abdicating your responsibility."

"How interesting."

"In fact, they think that's the exact job of the parents, to make sure the kids go to college."

"Really."

"And the kids' job is to go and not hack off. Our job is to remember how hard our parents worked, and to get all A's to make it up to them."

"Sounds like a good deal all around," Bea says, but she's frowning. "Do you have any money?"

"I do."

Bea rummages in her wampum pouch. "Here's more."

A hundred dollars!

"Oh, no," says Mona. "I can't—"

"For your project. A charitable contribution. Don't stay in any fleabag motels, they're dangerous."

Mona looks at the money as if it is a foreign currency with a funny bill size she isn't sure is going to fit in her wallet.

"Oops! That's my train they're announcing," says Bea.

"Thanks so much," says Mona.

"Have fun! Think Paris! London!"

"Maybe I can stow away."

"Stow away! Great idea. When you come back you can advise me. Maybe we can get a fund-raiser out of it."

Mona laughs.

"In the meantime, I'll call your parents." Bea hoists up the branding irons, one package in each arm. She swivels, wobbles, hoists them up a bit more.

"Do you need a hand?"

"I need four more hands." She walks off just fine, her cowboy boots clicking. "Bon voyage!" she calls from between her giant blinders. "If you hear from Seth, call me!"

"I will," promises Mona.

"And have a good time! That's important!" Bea turns completely around to make this point.

"You're going to miss your train."

"I am," Bea agrees, and starts to trot backward. That's when she hits someone, and drops both her packages, only to discover that the someone is her train's engineer. A sweet man, this is, not to say a most able one; he very nicely holds the train until they're both on it.

Call the parents! Mona is not sure she wants Bea to do any such thing. What a stomachache it is going to give her father! If he doesn't have one already. Still, an hour and a half later, Mona is disembarking in New Haven. Bea would laugh if she knew, but this really is what Mona wants to do—her parents having thought it unnecessary for her to go on a college tour. *What is there to look about?* They knew what colleges Mona should apply to already—it was obvious. Mona should apply to the same colleges as Callie. *Go to Harvard if you get in, Yale second choice, Princeton also nice.* Harvard was better than Yale because it was so close to MIT—how much more likely she was to find a husband there! They saw it as a kind of twofer. As for other schools—if they are all Mona can get into, say her parents, that is one hundred percent all right, nobody has to know.

But all of Mona's friends have gone looking, and so this is what Mona does now too, pretend she has a choice.

Yale. Brown. UMass. Smith.

In the beginning, the tour is fun. Now, though, she worries about worrying her parents. She trusts that Bea remembered to call. All the same, Should she call herself? and Why should she call? twinkle alternately in her mind like a pair of Christmas lights. Didn't her mother more or less dare her to leave? If they are truly worried, she decides, they will put out a search. A compromise: Mona begins eating lunch in front of campus police stations. She gives her real name everywhere. She stops in at the city police for directions. "I'm Mona Chang. I wonder if you can help me." She checks the pictures on the wall, to see if she is perchance included, but no. She is missing among the missing.

Cambridge. Staying with Callie is practically turning herself in, and after only three days. This is not the action of a self-respecting renegade. Still she stands outside of what she thinks is Callie's door, and leaves a note. Callie's suite is something of a rabbit warren, right down to the two different entrances; one of these used to be a fire door, but now is Naomi's door. Mona leaves a note there too. She does this again later. And again, later still. Where is her sister? She is tiring of cafés, and what with all the coffee she's had, her heart is thumping like a prisoner in a car trunk. Also her hands shake, and she is developing an odd headache at the top of her nose; it feels like an acorn implant. Somehow she had not imagined that Callie would truly be in classes all day, even though she is just the wonk type to take five courses a semester instead of four. And where is Naomi? The only person who eventually shows up is Phoebe, the like-it-or-lump-it floater Callie and Naomi couldn't get rid of.

Phoebe is so miniature that even short Mona's first reaction is to gentle down, as if she had just happened on a bird in the woods. It is therefore a surprise to discover that Phoebe is, personality-wise, all elbows. As she is carrying a megaphone, she is managing the stuck suite door one-handed; she hurls her weight against it as if she has taken more than enough truck from these hinges already.

"Um, excuse me," says Mona. "I'm looking for my sister."

"Are you talking to me?" Phoebe swings around abruptly, blindsiding Mona with the megaphone.

"Yes." Mona reseats her glasses.

"Well?"

Mona reaches for the megaphone, so surprising Phoebe that she lets go. Mona holds it up to her lips. "I'm looking for my sister."

"Give me that back."

Mona holds on. "Do you know where she is?"

"She's out of town."

"Out of town?" Mona drops the megaphone down. In a normal voice: "How can she be out of town?"

"I'm not your sister's keeper, and you'll have to excuse me, but I'm late." Phoebe reclaims her mouthpiece.

"Late for what?"

"Crew practice."

"Are you a coxswain?"

"I'm late," she says again. "Callie and Naomi went hitchhiking somewhere."

"They're not at some resort in Rhode Island, are they?"

"Excuse me," says Phoebe.

"You're late, right?"

Phoebe gives her a look that is distinctly menacing, in a miniature way.

"Listen. I wonder if I can stay in Callie's room for a while. I came all the way up here to visit her, and now I don't even have any place to stay."

"I don't know why you ask when you're going to do what you want anyway," says Phoebe.

It turns out Mona doesn't even need a key; locking doors is against Naomi's politics. Phoebe hurries out, Mona settles in.

Long gone are the olden golden days when each student had not only his own separate bedroom, but also a separate living room in which to park his splendidly smelliferous pipe stand. Now the students stack themselves in bunk beds. That is, unless the group as a whole is able to drive out a roommate or two, and/or is willing to give up the living room. Naomi and Callie have managed to do both. They are still stuck with the spindly Phoebe Me-Me, as they call her, after her obvious first interest. But the other floater unaccountably opted to move off campus after only two and a half weeks of rooming bliss; and so it is that with Callie living in what used to be a living room, each roommate has her very own habitat.

They are not the first roommate group to use the suite as three bedrooms instead of two bedrooms and a common room. Part of the living room has been walled off to form a common hallway; the main suite door opens into this, as does Phoebe's door, and also a hollow-core door brightened with a blowup of Angela Davis. This is Naomi's door—the original connecting door between her room and the living room being locked up. Callie's room doesn't really have a door, only an Indian-print bedspread turned into a curtain. It's the least private.

But Callie, Mona knows, loved the living room as soon as she saw it, because of the fireplace—working or not, she didn't care. She was happy to have the extra molding too, and the peeling mystery medallion on the ceiling, even if it was just there to hide some cracking plaster. And she was happy to have the big three-part window that looked like the Holy Mystery of the Trinity come to roost right at Harvard (especially in the morning, before a person put her glasses on). Never mind that there was no closet, meaning that she had to have two trunks and a big hamper; this room was nothing like Callie's room at home. Naomi wanted the room with the three doors; it was a room that would never make her feel trapped. Phoebe wanted the conventional room. But so far as Callie was concerned, the living room was the big room, the light room, the best room, even if the partition wall was covered with dark-brown cork squares. This Callie has creatively turned into a collage wall—tacking onto it a sweet mishmash of odds and ends, in the exact same way as Mona has at home. Postcards. Packages of freeze-dried food. Book jackets. Peacock feathers.

Copycat! On another wall, more brazen theft: Callie has heisted wholesale Mona's propensity to decorate with clothes. This may in fact be honestly related to the absence of a closet. All the same, Mona wonders if Callie really had to hang on the locked-up door leading to Naomi's room a hat rack just like Mona's at home; or if she had to drape the nearby plant holder with a scarf so like a scarf of Mona's that she has to wonder if it is not indeed hers. Mona climbs up on a big stuffed chair to see.

No sooner does she commence inspection, however, than the phone ding-lings. Should she pick it up? Probably she shouldn't. Anyway, she does. This is not meant to be an act of dissemblance. It is entirely in observance of standard behavioral custom that Mona says, "Hello?"

"Hello, Callie?" says Helen.

"Hi, Mom," Mona says.

"Did she call you yet?"

"You mean Mona?"

"Of course, Mona. Who else?"

"Hmm," says Mona.

"Since when do you have such a big mouth too?"

Mona isn't sure what to say.

"Did she call you again?"

"I talked to her today."

"So what happened? Did you tell her Auntie Theresa should make her call us, after all we are the ones she is making worry sick?"

"Oh, no. She's not with Auntie Theresa."

"What do you mean? Last time you said—"

"I thought she was."

"You said she called and that's where she was. With Auntie Theresa in Hawaii, the two of them both crazy."

"That's what she said. But this time she said she's having a great time, she just wishes she'd paid more attention in French."

"French! What? Don't tell me she went to France!"

Mona doesn't tell her.

"How could be? As if Hawaii is not bad enough. Oh! She is one hundred percent crazy."

Mona flinches but goes on. "It's where she always wanted to go. She said she's always wanted to go around topless."

"Topless means what?"

"It's a kind of French bathing suit."

"Forget about bathing suit, when is she coming home?"

"She didn't say. But she said to tell you not to worry."

"Not to worry! Is she going to call you again?"

"I don't know."

"If she calls," says Helen, "make sure you call me. Make report."

"Yes, ma'am."

"And tell her . . ."

"Tell her what?"

"Tell her she can stay in France! Tell her she is crazy!" A moment of hesitation. "Is she turn something else while she is there?"

"You mean?"

"She is not turn French, is she, or . . ."

"No. She said she didn't have the figure for it."

"Tell her she should think about her parents instead of about some bathing suit!"

"I'll tell her."

"And tell her come home right now. Tell her she is our daughter, she cannot just run away as if she has no parents."

"Okay."

"Tell her if she wants to leave the house, she has to ask parents to kick her out. Not just one day leave by herself."

"I'll tell her." Mona hesitates. "Don't you want to tell her you love her or something? You know, to soften her up. I mean, if you want her to call." She says this even though her parents have never been the type to talk drippy talk; that's what her friends' parents do. Mona's are more likely to express their deep unalienable affection by yelling. "Or maybe she should talk to Dad?"

"Tell her she is good-for-nothing pain in the neck," says Helen. "And why should she talk to Dad? So she can send him to the hospital with ulcer?"

When Helen was exasperated, she used to say that Callie always seemed to be expecting someone to yell at her; and that made Helen yell at her. Helen ordered her around, she asked nothing of Mona. Everything was Callie do this, Callie do that. And Callie did it, that was the amazing thing. That was the thing that made Helen unable to stop.

She's just like Ralph, Helen said sometimes, with a sigh. Other times she said, with the same exact sigh, *She's a good Chinese girl. Just like I was.*

But how could Callie be just like Ralph if she was also just like Helen? And would she have had to be like either if Ralph and Helen had been happy together? Which daughter is the good daughter now, which one the bad? And what would Helen think if she realized that Mona is no longer missing—that the one unaccounted for is her very own Harvard matriculate?

When the phone rings again, Mona almost does not answer. But what if it is Callie, calling to say where she is? Mona picks up the receiver, and to her stupefaction discovers it is Sherman.

"Callie?" he says.

Mona draws in her breath. "Yes," she says.

"You sound funny."

"You do too."

"Did you find her yet?"

"You mean Mona?"

"Of course Mona."

"No news yet."

Silence. "Oh!" he says finally. "They're never going to find her!"

"You sound funny," Mona says.

"You sound funny too." He hesitates. "Callie?"

"Yes?"

"Are you Mona?" he says.

"We've always sounded a lot the same. Our own mother can't tell us apart on the phone."

"A little the same. Today you sound exactly like Mona."

Mona hangs up, and when the phone rings again, she does not answer it.

Mona sleeps in Callie's bed, in Callie's nightshirt. She washes her face with Callie's soap, she brushes her teeth with Callie's toothbrush. She consults Callie's schedule. Maybe I'll sit in on some classes, Mona thinks. For example, Bio 16: Developmental Biology. Why not? Mona walks over to the new science building, the one that looks as though a giant mutant spider got stuck in its roofing tar. On the way, there is golden leafy extravagance of a nonimmigrant sort—if these trees were kids, what a scolding they would get! *All that nice green chlorophyll their parents save up for them, and what do they do? Throw it all away! As if chlorophyll grows on trees.*

"Callie?"

Mona has never thought she looked at all like her sister, especially now that Callie wears contacts. And yet about a dozen people wave hello, only to startle when they get closer. "Oh," they say. "Sorry. I thought you were . . ."

Apparently it's their profiles that are similar, those distinctive flat noses you can hang a spoon on. Also Mona has her hair up, so you can't see how much longer it is than Callie's; and she is, after all, wearing Callie's clothes.

Mona says, "I'm her sister. She's out of town."

No one asks where Callie's gone. People are getting to their classes, getting to their seats, getting out their notebooks. Mona opens Callie's; she thinks there's no harm in trying to take notes for her sister. Not that she's exactly sure what developmental biology is. However, better developmental than full-blown biology. She figures she'll simply write down everything the professor says. If the writing's too sloppy, Callie can rip the pages out; in the meantime, Mona will have had the kind of experience that every admissions office has been struggling to provide. Here she is finally! Beyond the Campus Tour.

Mona listens. Nature, nurture. Ontogeny, phylogeny. RNA, DNA. Proteins, many -ases. She had not realized college to involve such a multitude of arrows. This professor draws big double-barreled thrusters; if they were in a museum, you would think, Oh, how quaint, that a primitive should draw penises everywhere and not even realize his libido was showing. Poor biologically determined creature that he is. So she thinks, even as she endeavors to understand what he's saying about biological determination; and that's the surprise, that she does indeed want to know what genes and proteins and -ases have to do with a person. And where does it come from, the will to make yourself into something more than your endowment? Is that just inherited too? There are Chinese Jews in China, Mona knows. Will she one day discover them to be her long-lost relatives? Auntie Leah! Uncle Irwin! She listens, listens, as if for their names; somehow she had not imagined this, that college would have to do with matters of interest.

With considerable enthusiasm, at the end of the hour, Mona consults Callie's schedule, ready for another adventure in learning; only to discover that she has a break. Already! Mona supposes it is time to return to her favorite basement café—a tiny place with tiny tables. However, with giant intellects. Or, well, a fair number of giant intellects anyway, with what appear to be some giant egos mixed in.

A tap at her elbow.

"Callie?" It's a man with a handlebar mustache.

"I'm her sister," Mona begins to explain—then realizes that before her is Rabbi Horowitz!

"Dan!" he says. "Call me Dan! I'm not a rabbi anymore." He winks. "I've converted."

"Converted!"

"Only joking. But it's true I'm not a rabbi anymore. And how is that possible? Because I married another rabbi."

"I heard she was a goy."

"Forget about a goy; she could be a leper, that's the kind of welcome she gets sometimes. And all because of what? Some long hair and hips."

The Big R.H. is wearing a tweed sport jacket with his jeans, and carrying a dark-green book bag—the grad student look, complete with political buttons all over the book bag. Also he is wearing a Mickey Mouse watch with a macramé watchband. This seems to go, somehow, with the mustache. No beard, but in its place there is plenty of sandpaper; it obviously hasn't been so easy to get rid of.

"You couldn't both be rabbis?"

"I couldn't find a job. Everyone knows I got"—he stage-whispers, cracking his knuckles—"fired."

He is more theatrical than he used to be, a bit of a character—Mona surmises this to be a kind of shell he's had to grow, and is sad for him.

"But that's not fair! You were such a great rabbi."

"Next time I apply for a position, I'll ask you for a recommendation." More knuckle-cracking. Then, thoughtfully: "It hasn't been so easy, getting used to this change."

"It's the lesson of a lifetime."

"Who said that?" He winks. "A man of great wisdom. For this is the truth: It's not so easy to get rid of your old self. On the other hand, nothing stands still. All growth involves change, all change involves loss. It's not fair to have had to pay a price for love; and yet I'm a richer person for it. A paradox." Knuckles. "Now I'm at the school of government, thinking maybe I'll do something about the world, seeing as how I'm mad at it. But tell me. How are you doing these days? You really were a terrific student, you know. A real mensch."

"I've run away from home," Mona says.

"No kidding."

"Everyone's upset."

"Do they know where you are?"

"They think I'm in France, turning French."

He laughs but insists they sit down immediately and have coffee, so that he can hear the whole story. (How much larger he seems in a bistro than in an office! His legs do not begin to fit under the table-top, especially with their Frye boots attached.) She explains and explains. Dan wants to know everything, though he does not seem so much worried as interested. He downs five cups of coffee. She explains some more.

"Some families are like that," he says in a philosophical voice. Except for the coffee-drinking, he seems to be reassuming a rabbinical posture. "Some have a brick wall around them, some a picket fence. Let me ask you. If you drew a picture of your family, what would it look like?"

"A fort," says Mona, after a moment. "Fort Chang."

"But with one vocal Jew, shouting from the ramparts. Perhaps even entirely escaped. Although to leave is to betray, is it not? In the eyes of your parents. Are you still practicing?"

"I am."

"Good for you. Though with your learning curve, pretty soon you're going to be on the lookout for a rabbi willing to marry you to a goy. And then it will start all over again, like a new batch of pancakes from your father's pancake house. Your children will seek out the proper authorities. Who am I? they'll want to know. One parent Jewish, the other a goy, and that's not even including the rest of the story." He worries his Adam's apple.

"You think I'm going to marry a goy?"

"I'm not predicting. I have simply observed this occasional generational phenomenon."

"And will you do the ceremony if I do?"

"I would say yes if I could say yes." Dan gives a big shrug, with upturned palms. "But for this, I'm afraid you'll have to ask the wife."

"I can't believe you took my notebook!" says Callie. "What are you doing here? My room is a mess, you took my schedule, you even used my toothbrush."

"*I* can't believe you check your toothbrush first thing when you come home," says Mona. "Plus you stole all my decorating ideas, and where have you been, anyway?"

It turns out Naomi and Callie have just returned from New York, where they had gone as a result of the project. They had originally intended to write a term paper based on their notes from the summer—a kind of narrative account *cum* vague thesis and impressive bibliography, complete with charts, and tables, and diagrams. The plan was to have the kind of footnotes that took up three quarters of the page each, and they weren't going to have too many *ibid*s; those just made you look as though you had only actually read one or two of the biblio books, instead of all of them. Except that lo and behold, the professor was actually more excited about the account than the enhancements—so excited, in fact, that she mentioned it to a sharpshooting New York editor. With the result that, before you could say Shit me not, Naomi and Callie were doing up a book proposal. ("It was just like you always hear," says Callie. "These Harvard profs are connected every which way.") Naomi's boyfriend Ed escorted them down to New York, but now they are back to reality, Callie especially. For delicately enough, it seems, over a lunch in squishy chairs, the editor suggested that the more personal the account the better. Meaning it should be one person's—namely, Naomi's.

"We're not book material," Callie says. "Naomi's experience has an import ours just doesn't. After all, blacks are the majority minority. Also they've been slaves and everything."

"Is that what the editor said?"

"She said I probably have a book in me too. People are interested in China, she said."

"But you've never been to China."

Callie shrugs. "She said I'm a natural ambassador."

"I thought you wanted to be a doctor."

"I think it would be cool to write a book." The next time she goes to New York, Callie says, she's going to wear a Chinese dress.

"But you've never worn one in your life," Mona says.

"I have a book in me," Callie sings in reply. "I have a book! I have a book!" and already it sounds like a song Mona has been hearing nonstop.

Helen is relieved to hear that Mona is fine. However, she is furious about Hawaii, even if Mona hasn't been there. Also she is furious about France.

"Do you want me to come back?" Mona asks finally. "It doesn't sound like you want me to come back."

She says this knowing that probably her mother does—which is exactly why, she realizes later, she should not have asked. For how could Helen say so? It would be like slapping herself in the face.

And sure enough, given no choice, Helen hangs up.

This at least renders Callie more understanding. After all, she has an inkling of what it's like to tangle with their mother. *Being on the outs,* she calls it. *On the outskirts of the skirts.* She tries to listen in appropriate big-sister fashion, and even Mona has to admit that for once she manages to ask the right questions without having the right answers. Also Callie provides helpful information. For example, that she is not surprised that Mona picked up the phone and got Sherman Matsumoto. For Sherman, she says, has called three or four times already.

"How did he get your phone number?" Mona asks.

"Beats me."

Inquires Naomi, from atop the character-building comfort of one of Callie's trunks, "Is he really your fiancé?"

"Who told you that?" says Mona.

Naomi eyes the ceiling medallion. "The marriage fairy. She said you promised yourself to him when you were eleven."

"Thirteen. The fink was exaggerating."

"He called and introduced himself as your friend," Callie says.

"Now, there's a surprise," says Mona.

"And why a surprise?" inquires Naomi.

"We never see each other in person. It's all just talk on the telephone." Mona tries to explain. "He's very shy."

"Sounds like the platonic bullshit story to me," says Naomi.

Says Callie the helpful sister, when Sherman next calls: "She's at death's door. In fact, she's dead."

"Dead?" says Sherman.

"There's been a car accident."

"But she doesn't have a car."

"She was in a bus."

"Who is this?"

"This is Callie," says Callie.

Says Sherman, "I think this is someone making some joke."

"Anyway, I know she'd love it if you came."

"But if she is dead . . ."

"You meant so much to her. I know she'd want you to be at her service. You should come to my dorm. We're sitting shiva." She pronounces this *shee-veh*, which means rice gruel in Shanghainese. She gives the address.

"This kind of joke is very bad luck," says Sherman.

"You always were a terrible liar," says Mona.

Callie agrees. They agree that Naomi should have handled the call. They agree there should have been a better plan, this one had the inspiration of an overcooked pea pod. No one imagines Sherman is going to come up to Cambridge after the gala invitation issued. Still, the next day, Mona hangs around the room in funereal style. She tries calling home again. No answer. She tries the pancake house. No answer there, either, a surprise; Ralph must be shorthanded.

She thinks about what she would say to Sherman if he did show up. Hello? The few times she met Naomi's boyfriend Ed, she was struck by how he and Naomi seemed to touch the whole time. It was as if they were a single organism that only divided up for debates. *Take the South,* he would say, or *Take the Knicks,* or *Take the ancient instruments of astronomy.* And without further ado, they would be off and arguing, Naomi's proud alto holding its rich own against his profundo bass.

Doesn't that just go to prove?

But the statistics say otherwise.

If I may clarify.

Therein lies the fallacy.

Finally he would hold up his fine-boned hands in surrender; and there came an end to the pointing and the making of points. All the straightened fingers would curl. Peaceably, they would intermingle again.

Mona sighs. She figures Sherman must in his own way be in love. Probably madly. Why else would he go to the trouble of tracking her down? But when she imagines what he will do if he comes, as much as she can hope is that he will run out of the room after ten words this time, instead of five. She supposes this would be progress. However, at that rate it could be some time before they advance to full face-to-face conversation, she might as well be teaching him to speak English all over again. Not to say how to hold hands: She indulges in fantasies involving passionate forms of palm and finger contact, and so real are these scenes, so affecting the interplay of cuticle and hangnail, that Mona almost does not hear Sherman's voice on the other side of the door.

This is the blocked-off door to Naomi's room—the one with a hat rack attached to it, in front of Callie's armchair. The armchair is of the high stuffed variety, distinctly related to the wing chair. However, it is what bordello red is to Harvard crimson, or the Addams family to the Adams family. In short, a comfortable chair, but one that you might well imagine to be haunted. And so it is that when Mona first hears a tiny knocking and a "Mona?" she jumps as if something had sprung out of the stuffing.

"Mona?"

"Sherman! Is that you?"

"It is," he says.

"How did you get in?"

"Someone told me, Go in. Make myself at home, she said."

"Naomi?"

"I don't know. She told me you were behind this door."

"Was she black?"

"Yes, black."

"Naomi," says Mona.

"How come you told me you were dead?"

"That was Callie."

"How can you let people say such a thing? It's very bad luck."

"Well, it worked anyway. We were trying to get you to come up here, and sure enough, here you are."

Silence. "Why did you want me to come?"

"Oh," Mona says. "I guess I was just thinking it would be nice if we could have a conversation in person sometime."

"I am very shy," he says.

"I know." As Mona talks, she starts to move the chair. There's a bolt on the door near the top; continuing to talk, Mona attempts to finagle this open. This is not so easy, what with the peg rack full of hats in the way. Still she tries. "But why?" she says as she works. "I won't hurt you."

"I don't think you will like the way I look."

"I saw you, remember? And I thought you looked fine."

"That's not how I look anymore."

"What do you mean?"

Silence.

"What could make me not like the way you look?"

"Oh," he says. "Maybe my nose."

Mona laughs.

"Or maybe my eyes."

"I don't think so. And so sure am I of this that—" She yanks on the door.

But the door does not open; it must be bolted on the other side too.

"Sherman?" Mona says.

No answer.

"I'm sorry I tried to open the door," Mona says. "Really, I am. That would have been a dirty trick."

Silence.

"Sherman?" She bangs on the door. "Sherman? Are you there? Will you say something?"

But still there is no answer; and sure enough, by the time Mona has run around the wall and into Naomi's room, he is gone. She opens Naomi's hall door. No one. She wants to cry.

A knock on the main suite door.

"Hello?" she calls.

"Mona?"

"Sherman?"

CHAPTER 14

A Most
Mannerly Fellow

And Mona yanks open the ever-sticky door to welcome who else but Seth Mandel. In voice he is Sherman Matsumoto. In person he is the person he always was, only thinner. He is growing his hair back, also his beard. Still through the bristle Mona can behold for the first time the true curves of his face, which are sweeter than she would have expected, and include a surprise cleft chin. Also she beholds something she has no doubt witnessed before, but somehow without perceiving it—the rising flush of emotion. She would have imagined him to be wearing in this situation a most satisfied grin—the grin of a boy who has after concerted tinkering gotten all the switches of his train set to work. Instead he looks more like an engineer finally in sight of his home station—frankly just happy to see her.

"Are you surprised?" says Seth/Sherman.

"Well, let us just say that you're right," says Mona. "Yours is not the nose of my dreams."

"Maybe I should give Barbara's doc a call?"

Mona smiles despite herself. Seth may be Sherman, but still he is Seth. A Seth who moves differently, though. At another time, he would have been leaning on the door molding, one hand on either side of the frame, like a human slingshot. He would have appeared just about ready to launch himself into the room. Now he stands square in the doorway without laying claim to it. This is so unlike Seth that for a moment Mona cannot imagine what he is waiting for. What is he, shy? But no: He is simply waiting, patiently, for an invitation to enter.

And it is this pause that enables her to feel her own presence in the room—something that does not end at her skin but radiates modestly around it. It is this pause that enables her to say, with warm ambivalence, "Since when are you so polite? Come in."

He enters. He settles himself on the very chair that had not long ago seemed a talking chair; it seems for all the world to have gotten its voice back. Next comes quite a conversation. What happened to Sherman Matsumoto? it begins. Didn't Mona meet him one day in the hallway at school?

Seth explains how Sherman wasn't Sherman from the start—how in the beginning it really was Andy Kaplan on the phone. Barbara Gugelstein was right. As for why Andy did it, "It was a joke. It was a project, like growing dope in the basement."

Mona tries to keep her tone light. "Ha ha ha." She is not surprised to hear a skin of ice in her voice, though; and in a way, this is what breaks her heart, to hear her own bitterness. Bitterness—the very word so bitter to utter, what with that *b* and double *t*, not to say its associations: Decrepitude. Bunions. Gout.

Seth allows them both a moment of reflection. He still likes to match up the fingertips of his hands; that hasn't changed. He continues: As time went on, Andy got hooked. "I think he liked the challenge of it. You know how his father is a Japan expert and everything."

And did Seth help?

"Not until a lot later. No one was trying to dupe you, exactly. It wasn't a conspiracy. And I tried to tell you once, but I'd sworn on my *cojones* that I wouldn't."

Was he not telling her now?

"I've changed my mind."

Sweet reasoning. And why did Andy stop?

"He worried it was mean. Also it was getting too weird. It was weird how much he liked having an alter ego. And the secrecy. He said the secrecy had a life of its own."

In Sherman's second incarnation, Seth took over the role, to Andy's relief. Andy coached him, but Seth couldn't get the voice quite right. Ergo, Sherman turned Hawaiian.

And the Sherman Mona met?

"That was a real live Hawaiian exchange student from Larchmont High, who agreed to pretend to be Sherman on a dare. His last name really is Matsumoto, but his first name is Trevor. He was supposed to hang in there a little longer. However, he chickened out."

Mona thinks about calling him when she gets back, apologizing for her friends.

How did Seth know she was here?

"I guessed. Bea told me you were running away. She didn't think you had any money. So I figured, where could you go with no money?"

He talked to Bea?

"I called so she and Dad wouldn't worry."

Is he really going to school?

"Don't worry, I'm not taking anything for credit." He hesitates. "You know," he says, "this is the big recognition scene. If we were in a Shakespeare play, this would be the happy ending."

She should be delighted to be duped.

"You're supposed to be happy to have discovered your own true love."

And Seth is supposed to be that? Her own true love?

"Your one and only."

This is supposed to be some kind of comedy?

Though Mona really is perfectly comfortable on the floor, Callie volunteers to go stay elsewhere for the night. She does not volunteer where that elsewhere might be—a mystery apparently related to her owning two toothbrushes. It is only lucky for her that Mona is in no mood to sleuth, having plenty enough to think about already. For instance, Sherman-Andy-Seth. From the standard-issue comfort of Callie's narrow bed, Mona considers them all; then not Sherman, and not Seth, but just Andy. How thrilled Barbara will be to hear all that's transpired! And in a way, Mona looks forward to telling her, to sharing with her friend this great feast. For a feast it will surely become in conversation, a regular Thanksgiving turkey rather than a dead warty bird. In the meantime, though, alone with the *clat-clat* of typewriters and the dueling volumes of other people's music—how noisy college is!—what is Mona to make of him? Andy. Whatever it is, she will be making it; that's the only thing that's sure. It will be the kind of long-shot conjecture you associate with the origin of the universe. For Mona could write to Andy; she could sweetly or sharply inquire of him this thing or that. She could, in a word, *nudge,* and perhaps he would answer to the best of his ability. But what really will she know for it?

She can still hear the real Sherman of years and years ago: *This is a chair.* But so very much louder is the Sherman of the hot line: *If he loved her he should leave her alone.*

Is there a word for someone like Andy? Is there a name for their brand of relationship?

In fact, he is the first of many loves that will crowd her official life—unofficial plantings that will thrive for their neglect. And eventually she will learn a name for them, a word for plants that spring up on their own. Volunteers. He is like one of these—plants she will in time learn to appreciate, even as she lets them go to seed.

As for Sherman: *One thing becomes another.* That's according to Hegel according to Seth. Here too Mona tries to learn from nature. *The apple rots that the tree may grow.*

Another day, another matter: warm-blooded Seth. The ever-knocking fact of him! By the time he touches his knuckles to the suite door, wondering if Mona might like to continue their chat, she is rent asunder by the choice of which to discuss first: Topic A—Is Seth a low-down out-and-out liar? Or Topic B—How did he get to be so good at it?

Seth says he's been reading about Japan, and culture, and Zen, even though Sherman as Seth understood him was more a guy than a monk. He says it's only American hippies who think that everyone in Japan is a Zen master. And maybe the real Sherman sleeps on a bed, who knows? Still, by way of getting into his part, Seth has been sleeping on a futon. Gone are the smoky-smelling sheepskins; he's covered his teepee floor with tatami mats. He's been using chopsticks. Of course, he had been sitting on the floor to eat already. But the long hot baths have taken some getting used to, and it hasn't been easy trying to learn to cherish a certain exquisite melancholy. However, through all of this, he's begun to feel, actually, sort of Japanese. Or at least, that the Japanese manner corresponds to something in him.

"Hot baths," mulls Mona. "Melancholy. Tatami mats."

This feeling was so strong, continues Seth, that he would almost not be surprised to discover that in a previous life he had been Japanese. But then again, maybe it was something else Eastern he used to be. Just in case, he has bought himself a Nehru jacket, and some sitar tapes.

"But Seth," Mona says. "You don't believe in an afterlife, forget about a former life. Remember? You only believe in this life. You're Jewish, for Christ's sake!"

"Am I?"

They back up to Topic A.

"Things got away from us," says Seth, hands in his pockets. "Plus it's just what you always used to say—things aren't so straightforward. Sometimes deception is necessary. Even Nietzsche says that there is truth through masks."

"You were two-faced! Dishonest! You were wily and underhanded!" Mona says this knowing that she can never forgive Seth, and that his deception spells the end of their relationship. Which, she reminds him, was already ended to begin with.

"I think there's a way of being honestly insincere," he says simply. "Or do I mean sincerely dishonest? Anyway, we were stuck. We were no longer one-thing-becoming-another. You had filled in the blank, and that was that." He says, "You have to at least give me credit for commitment."

Mona stares past him—not as if he is not there, for this is not possible, but as if trying to sidestep this man.

"Maybe I should call you on the telephone?" He assumes his Sherman voice. "Is this Mona?"

She starts to cry even as she starts to laugh. "I can't believe you told me you drank beer and had a green Mustang. Maine! Lobsters!"

"Brown fat," smiles Seth. "Do you mind if I come in?"

Mona—suddenly realizing that they are still standing in the doorway—says no. Of course she does not mind, she says. And complicated as the air is between them, the simply polite thing proves to be the right thing to do. The right thing to do is to invite him to come in, and also to make himself comfortable, and even, a little later, to stay awhile with her.

So it is that Seth is all too comfortable when Ralph and Helen pay their surprise visit. Phoebe automatically shows them to Callie's bedspread, then goes back to her mirror, pencil in hand; for her Visual

Studies class, she is working most absorbedly on a portrait of herself. Seth politely stands when the Changs enter, but as he is only half dressed, his new-found manners are somewhat lost on them.

"I'm so sorry," he says. "I seem to have removed my pants." He sits back down quickly, situating a large red textbook in his lap. Unfortunately, it does not seem large enough. He opens it.

"Very studious," says Ralph distantly. "Always work hard in the restaurant. Never give us any trouble."

Everyone swallows, including Mona, who is hiding behind Seth. She has pulled the covers over her head, and is trying to make herself look like a pile of bedding.

"Just as long as Mona is okay," whispers Helen, turning to leave.

"Of course she is," says Seth warmly, reaching back toward the bedding pile and giving it a pat. The bedding pile hits him. Bedsprings creak.

Ralph helps Helen out of the room.

"I should open the door for you, but perhaps I shouldn't," says Seth.

"Thank you," says Ralph.

Did Helen see Mona? Seth thinks Helen's back was already turned when Mona delivered the fateful whack. But when Mona looks out the window, she knows what her mother knows. For Helen has always taught Mona to walk properly. Helen has always taught Mona never to drag her feet, especially in a place where people might look down on you. But there Helen is, shuffling as if she doesn't care who sees. Around her looms mighty Harvard. Enormous trees rise, the kind of trees that make you think what means girth. Their boughs reach toward some higher fraternity; they shoulder in with the brick and ivy buildings, a club. Normally, Helen would be making her way along the path with a certain polite defiance. *I am as good as any ivy plant. I am as good as any tree. Forget about girth.*

But instead her head is bent. She is holding firmly her pocketbook—Helen is never in public without her pocketbook—but the belt of her London Fog raincoat is hanging from one loop. This is an all-weather coat with zip-out lining that she's wearing; Helen bought it for half off, but would've paid full price if she'd had to, that's how well it fit. A special petite size; she hadn't had to alter a thing. She intended to wear it for the rest of her life, and maybe she will. But in the meantime, there is the belt, dangling, getting full of mud. Mona hopes her parents have parked nearby; otherwise, she's afraid, that belt's as good as lost.

Time to return to Scarshill. Mona's missed an entire week of school already; it's a little early in the year for a senior slump. Also Seth needs to get back. He's interested in his political philosophy class, and doesn't want to miss the rise of the nation-state. But Mona can't go home yet, Helen needs time to cool down. So where to stay? Until Mona has in mind someplace in particular, Seth is determined to stay with her. This being what geese do, he jokes, at least according to Konrad Lorenz.

The plan, therefore, is to fetch Seth's teepee from school, and set it back up in Seth's trusty backyard. This is preferable to leaving it where it is because while Mona needs to go to school every day, Seth has only two days of classes a week; and what is a thirty-mile bike ride to Big Chief Thunder Thighs? However, they do have misgivings about this plan. The first being Bea. What a position to put her in! Will she not feel obliged to inform Mona's mother? Then there will be a scene such as no one is exactly prepared for. And what if Bea keeps mum, and Helen finds out on her own? (As she is bound to, Scarshill being not so big a town.) Then poor Bea will have the dickens to pay too. All this they discuss with Barbara Gugelstein on the phone. (Seth has done the calling, so as to bypass Barbara's mom.) Barbara promises to mull the problem over, and by the time she picks them up at the train station in her parents' car, she has for unveiling Plan Alfred. Id est, why don't they go live in her house? For this, it turns out, is now her ex-house.

"We've moved," says Barbara.

"So fast!" says Mona.

Barbara, wearing sunglasses, explains how the house turned out to have been leased.

"Is that like rented?" Mona asks.

"It wasn't ever even really ours; all we owned was an option to buy. My dad had to beg to be allowed to break the contract. Beg and pay, I should say." Barbara laughs unnaturally. It seems Mr. Gugelstein is now officially unemployed. "Usually people are out of work a month for every ten thousand dollars of salary. That's what my dad says. That's the rule of thumb."

"Oh! I'm so sorry," says Mona. "I mean, that he made so much money."

Barbara seems to sink into herself. "We were just lucky we still had our original house to move back into. There was an offer on it, but the people didn't get their financing, and the deal fell through." She goes on to say that there's no new occupant in the house as of yet, and while a broker might come by every now and then, so what? Aren't there are a million places to hide, not to say the tunnel?

The grounds are being kept up, but Mona can tell even from the driveway that no one is home. For one thing, there are no curtains on the windows, meaning that from certain angles you can see right through the house. Mona finds this somehow indecent; maybe living with Seth the sex maniac is making her think like a sex maniac too. Or maybe this is just what happens when you start using in conversation words like *innuendo*—a word she formerly could've gotten right on a multiple-choice question, but not one she actually employed every day. With her and Seth happily interpenetrating, however, she finds she reaches for it as she would for a ketchup bottle.

The electricity is still on, but Mona and Seth hesitate to use the lights for fear of giving themselves away; and it is surprising how long the evening trails on as a result. No wonder Alfred wanted a radio! They wish they had one too, and that's even with each other for diversion. They zip together their zipper-compatible sleeping bags. They huddle into each other, grateful for the thin comfort of their foam sleeping pads. Fugitives, they are. Homesteaders.

Nothing, though, stretches on so long as Mona's first day back at high school. How strange it all seems! The desks, the bells, the overhead projectors; even the parking lot seems strange. She sees people circling, looking for a good spot, hoping to avoid having to park all the way down the muddy road by the stream, and she remembers harboring such hopes herself. Though why should she have been afraid of a little mud? Seeing as how she was wearing hiking boots. How ridiculous seem these concerns now; and how much easier to exit this world than she ever would have dreamed. She writes herself a sick note. She tells her classmates she was out with a stomach bug, she must've lost five pounds. Envious sympathy. People compliment her; Mona feels positively svelte. No one seems to notice that Mona is wearing Callie's clothes. And outside of Barbara Gugelstein, no one seems to have the least idea about Mona's other life except Rachel Cohen. Several times she has tried to call, Rachel says, only to get hung up on. Is something the matter? Has Mona been grounded? Mona does not answer, but only stands in the jewelry shop like a big locked-up supply closet.

The house stays warm by itself, a mysterious phenomenon no doubt linked to its authentic Norman-style walls; through some equally mysterious technology, it generates dust balls of a mansionate scale. Barbara comes to visit. This is a pleasant if sobering interlude; one thing she forgot to mention, she says, is that her family had been having trouble with disappearing objects. *Right before we moved. Nothing too serious, but maybe the tunnel.* Mona and Seth should be spooked by this information. Who would break in now, though, to a house full of nothing? It is just one more thing, they agree, like the cavernous rooms, the air of palpable desertion, the whole ghost town feel. Those should spook them too.

Instead they are coming to feel at home in the emptiness. *Very Zen,* says Seth, and Mona can feel what he means. The rooms no longer cry out for furniture, or rugs, or tchotchkes; they no longer seem to be missing anything. In fact, there are things that could yet be removed— for example, the milkmaid murals. Garish as billboards these look, perhaps because Mona and Seth are at peace.

It is as if they have finally taken that trip to the Cascades together— as if they are catching fish for dinner, and melting snow for water, and repitching their tent at night because of the wind. Seth says if they really lived together, it wouldn't be so idyllic, and Mona knows he's right. She knows they would write in each other's books, and scratch each other's records, and put clothes in the dryer that said Hang Dry right on their labels. But so sweet is this present life that Mona wishes it could go on forever—a sweet background, say, to backpacking forays in various sub-continents. As for which subcontinents and in what order, they debate this lustily, employing without hesitation the lowest tactics available.

What with the threat of brokers, they don't cook, exactly; in fact, all they eat are sardine sandwiches (with Tabasco sauce and lemon juice, this is—Seth's specialty), and they wash their dishes immediately. Mostly they use the tunnel to come and go. Still there are scares. For example, one day someone comes to view the house. Mona and Seth squirrel themselves away, listening as the realtor opens every closet door; apparently the customers have complex storage needs. These needs are discussed at length. Then on to further complications. In egalitarian fashion, the customers, a couple, have one each. The man's being his gym equipment. There is much discussion about where best to locate the bar bells and stationary bike, and if it would be possible to enclose the outdoor pool. The woman's concern is drafts. She worries that if they were to simply move the greenhouse so as to house the pool, the result would be drafty. Also several of the larger rooms look as though they would have drafts.

"I've an absolute horror of colds," says the woman.

"We spent two years in Scotland," explains the man.

"The worst years of our life," says the woman.

"A most unfortunate assignment," says the man.

"We only barely survived," says the woman. "And that was thanks to boiled wool."

Seth and Mona are barely able to make it down the back steps without laughing; and for the next several days, they too give thanks to boiled wool. How is it that, way back when, they happened to both sign up for the hot line? Was it or was it not thanks to boiled wool? And how was it that Seth happened to save Mona from the attacker? What would they have done if it weren't for boiled wool!

The phone rings. Should they pick it up? The sound glances off the walls, an edged noise. Ten times, a pause, then ten times again. Then twenty times. Wasn't phone service cut off? Did someone order it back on?

"If I didn't know better," says Mona, "I'd think it was Sherman Matsumoto."

More realtors.

And yet another day, squeaking. By this time, they are used to emergencies, their hearts do not palpitate. Neither do their palms sweat or their stomachs secrete stomach acid such as produces security-threatening burps. This is a scrambling under the floorboards that sounds distinctly like claws.

"Squirrels," guesses Seth.

Is he right? *Scratch, scratch,* they hear, but also a *thump thump thump.*

"That must be the daddy squirrel. Someone has taken his boiled wool."

More thumping; more woolly jokes. The thumping approaches.

"Closet time," says Seth.

"Let's just hope it's not someone with complex storage needs," says Mona.

They manage to sequester themselves just as the footsteps approach. Another realtor? They figure it must be, even though this person does not turn any of the lights on—an odd thing at dusk. The realtors always turn the lights on, even in broad daylight, so that the house seems as bright as possible. It's a trick everyone knows, but they do it anyway. Whereas this person prefers dark. From their hiding place, Mona and Seth hear him scrape along. Swearing.

"Peekaboo," wheedles the voice. "I see you."

He is standing right outside the closet door. Mona's calf muscles pull, but she doesn't dare move except to put her hand down for balance. A mansionate dust ball; the floor through its diaphanous heft is gritty. With her other hand she cups Seth's kneecap. Seth loops his arm around her shoulder—leaning on her more than she'd like, or is that just the weight of his arm? He smells as if there is peppermint soap still left in his shirt. She watches the dim line of light at the bottom of the door.

"Come out, come out, wherever you are."

"Drunk," whispers Seth. And of course, Mona's attention lists his way, so that she almost does not hear the man outside the closet say something very like "Oh, Mona."

Did he really say her name?

"Skinny monkey."

"That's what Cedric used to call us," whispers Mona.

"What?" says Seth.

Mona does not dare repeat herself.

"Skinny monkey."

Cedric sounds nothing like himself.

"Did you say Cedric?" says Seth. Even in the dark, Mona can see him lighting up. Delight is dawning, the whole scene about to become an improbable joke.

"Shh," she says.

Still his arm drops down her back; they're out of their huddle. *"Cedric?!"* So loudly, there seems to be an echo.

"Cedric!" she says then, even louder, figuring the gig to be up. "Are you drunk?" And she bursts into the room, occasioning with the closet door a collision.

The burglar reels. For it is indeed a burglar, complete with royal-blue winter gloves and a matching cold-weather face mask. He holds his hand up to his head, twisting the mask out of alignment.

"Fuck," he says.

"You're not Cedric," says Mona.

"Fuck." The burglar tries to adjust his mask so that the eyeholes are back over his eyes, but this is not so easy with winter gloves on. Also he is not so steady on his feet. He is a meaty man in a jacket with no zipper; his mechanic-blue pants have no hem at the bottom. His fly is open.

Seth emerges. "Who are you? And what are you doing here?"

"Fuck," says the burglar again, still working on his mask.

"Vocabulary is the better part of grammar," observes Seth. "How did you get in here?"

When the burglar doesn't answer, Seth and Mona exchange glances.

"Anyway," she says, "I think we know his answer to that question, don't we?"

"The tunnel?" says Seth.

"No, 'Fuck,' " says Mona.

"Fuck you!" says the burglar, struggling to stay on his feet. He glares at them with the one eye he has finally managed to line up with an eyehole; also he breathes aggressively, as if realizing his breath to be his most potent weapon.

"Why don't you just take that thing off," says Mona. "You'll be able to see better."

"It's my mask," he says thickly.

"Hmm," says Mona, "And how did you discover the tunnel?"

"A groundhog showed me."

"But it's camouflaged," says Seth. "It's not so easy to see."

Says the man, tottering, "From the right place, you can see anything." And with this he slumps conveniently to the floor.

Discoveries

Fernando! The cook who put a curse on the house of pancakes—now a burglar! And possibly the attacker of yore—Seth thinks he must be.

"Can't you see," insists Seth. "He's been stalking you."

And how elegant it would be for that to be true! Two large-man experiences, made into bookends.

"The attacker was hairy, Fernando is hairy," allows Mona. "But you are hairy too."

So she says. For already she knows this symmetry will elude them; and this is one of the many things they discuss on their way to Alfred's apartment in Barbara's new van (which she finally just went and bought for herself, believing it to be actually her old van). Map in hand, they discuss coincidence, and pattern, and the sorts of synchronicities such as are no more than you can expect from novels, but that in real life do give you the heebie-jeebies. Also Mona and Seth discuss whether they were right to leave Fernando lying there. Can a passed-out person come to harm? (They think not.) And will he come after Mona again? They probably should have called the police. They probably should not have simply penned a longish note, expecting him to be touched by the power of words. What youthful folly! They agree about this.

And, of course, they discuss their great discovery—namely, that in Fernando's jacket pocket was tucked Mr. Gugelstein's silver flask. Is this truly a discovery? They recognize this moment, naturally: The false cupboard back, the clue in the courtyard. *Her heart beat faster.* Then what? Mystery solved, end of book. Except what have Seth and Mona found? For all they know, someone else stole the flask. For all they know, Fernando bought it in a pawnshop. For all they know, this is not Mr. Gugelstein's flask at all, but a fake, maybe even the fake they themselves made.

They know only that they should not have drawn conclusions about the mod squad. Also that they don't know by what stony path the old Fernando has come to be the new.

"He was a great cook," says Mona.

"Alfred?" says Seth.

"Fernando. Alfred was a great cook too. But Fernando was a perfectionist. He was always on time. He dressed up on his days off in these shiny shoes, and he had a shiny car to match. You've never seen such hubcaps."

"But he punched Cedric."

"That's why he was fired."

"And he stole something, right?"

"A case of minute steaks," says Mona. "Or so we thought. In fact, we don't know what happened. Let's face it, The Silver Flask Incident is nothing but a remake of The Minute Steak Case."

"Pun forgiven."

"Fernando thought he would lose his job to people like Cedric, and what do you know? He did." Mona says again, "He was a great cook. I'm sure we didn't single-handedly ruin him. On the other hand . . ." She pulls the van over, waves down a pedestrian, asks directions.

Andy, the attacker, Fernando, and who knows who else?—each with an unofficial contribution to her life. Little packages she never ordered but that arrived in the mail all the same. *Sender unknown.*

And she, and her family, with their unofficial contributions. They send out packages too. *Addressee forgotten. Package returned. Curses due.*

How to right the wrong? Can teshuvah ever be made?

Are Seth and Mona in the right place at all? They are looking for garden apartments, but see only six low brick buildings, distinctly gardenless; in fact, distinguished mostly by how burnt is the grass patch before them. The north-facing buildings boast assorted live weeds. The south-facing buildings boast grass of the extreme low-maintenance kind. *Kentucky brown grass,* jokes Seth. *Westchester ex-grass.* The patches are separated by a grid of concrete walkways. Of course, it is fall here, as it is elsewhere in the greater metropolitan area; the walkways are littered with curled-up dead leaves. At the same time, this courtyard feels like summer—there being, mysteriously, not only no trees of girth, but no trees at all, only an onslaught of sun. A ceiling of sun, it seems, an immovable radiant slab. The entries have concrete stoops with gap-toothed railings, and striped metal awnings that afford hankies of shade; these fall wide of the stoops and the people, but do provide trapezoids of respite for the litter-flowered prickle bushes. The most hospitable shade is cast by a bright-blue dumpster at the end of the brick horseshoe; a couple of kids hog this, they've even set up lounge chairs. From these they stare, like the adults on the stoops, at the visitors.

"Ain't no Alfred 'round here," a large man announces, rucking up his mouth. "No Alfred, no Knickerbocker. Never was none, either."

But even as the man makes this declaration, Alfred leans out a sec-ond-story window like a surprise Juliet. In place of a ring of roses or other spriggy hairdress, he is wearing a chef's hat in full pouf.

"It's all right," he says. "These are my friends." He makes a swing-ing gesture with his hand, like Ed Sullivan giving a big welcome: "That girl there, see, I'm suing her daddy."

"Ah so!" the man says then. He puts his hands together as if in prayer, and gives a little bow. Then, with a mock-Oriental accent: "You mean A-fled! Why you no say so?" He calls, "Ahh-fled! Ahhh-fled!"

People laugh. No one moves, but something seems to roll back as Mona and Seth make their way down the walkway; something allows them passage.

Alfred's apartment is small but brightly lit; the decor is wood-grain electronic. There are speakers the size of easy chairs; a tower of other circuitry; records; a TV with an enormous rabbit-ear antenna. For fur-niture, there is a red leatherette Mediterranean couch; two folding chairs of no particular background; and a Spanish coffee table shaped like a guitar. The metal scrollwork of the last is propped up with cinder block, and in its sound hole is a bowl full of cigarette butts. Bottle caps. A Roach Motel. Packages of gum. Altogether, it presents the picture of bachelorhood to Mona, only Seth could discern a resemblance to the Gugelsteins' place. Still he launches into a description of *our Zen pad,* as he calls it, and as he segues into the comparison, Mona finds herself seeing the Zen in Alfred's pad too. Not that she is convinced. She is sim-ply looking again.

As, it appears, is Alfred. His face, when they first entered, was fur-rowed with wariness; she'd never seen him so horizontal of aspect.

Now he seems reoriented toward the vertical. He throws his head back, he is positively animated. His chef's hat languishes on a counter-top like a half-collapsed soufflé.

"You're shitting me, man!" He offers Mona and Seth beers. "You mean you're hanging around all night with no bed and no lights on and no radio, either? How come you don't get that Miss B. to correct the situation, now? How come you don't ask her to bring you something nice?"

Alfred lights a cigarette; Mona and Seth explain and explain. But it's like trying to beat dust out of a rug—the more they beat, the more dust there seems to be. Among other things, they try to convey why Mona can't move home, and also about what most unfortunately happened to Mr. Gugelstein.

Alfred is outraged. "The motherfuckers!" he says, cigarette in mouth. "You mean, they fucking crossed our Jew-daddy?"

"They did, they fucking did!" exclaims Mona. She wants to say *our Jew-daddy* in group-affirming style—it's what they learned in hot-line training, to echo the person they're talking to—but she can't bring herself to do it. Seth, though, as if reading her mind, supplies, "Can you believe it? To our very own Jew-daddy, this happened! It could've been my daddy!"

They continue with the story. At the word *sue*, Alfred seems to puff harder; his outrage on Mr. Gugelstein's behalf explodes again. "Somebody messes with you, you've got to pay them back," he says. "Otherwise, they're just going to mess with you again, man. What's he going to do now? Nothing? You're telling me a rich bastard like him is going to punk out?"

Alfred listens some more, then it's his turn to talk about what's happened since the firing. "See," he says, twice, but doesn't go on until Mona asks him about a little golden chef's hat atop one of the speakers in the corner.

"That's my award," he says with satisfaction.

Not only does Alfred have a new job in a steakhouse, he's won this award; it's one of the nice things about working for a big-time outfit, that they have awards and softball teams, shit like that. Plus he's training other cooks now. "I'm getting over all right," he says. Also, a surprise: He's back in touch with Evie.

"Eee-vie," he says, grinning. "That girl's crazy as a clock with one hand. Can't tell her nothing, see, without she's going to tell you what time it is. Time for us to have a talk. Time for us to try something else. Time for us to think creative. I told her a million times, You're dealing in zeroes, babe. But that girl's got wax in her ears. She even called up Charlene, man. Called her on the telephone."

"And?" says Mona.

But there's no elaboration. He's looking down, thinking of something, and when he looks back up, he could be the Cheshire cat crossed with the Mona Lisa. Once again there is something he's keeping from them, maybe just a certain satisfaction. Is it on account of the word *telephone*? As in, *I-done-used-the-tel-e-phone*—?

Still Mona says, "We have something for you," and presents him with the flask. "We apologize," she says. "We sincerely apologize. Please tell the rest of the gang too."

"This is the flask the Jew-daddy lost?"

"This is it."

Alfred takes the flask, then looks away. Mona expects him to ask where they found it, but he doesn't.

"Luther got beat up," he reports instead. "He went down to the protest, and got beat just about dead."

Mona's heart blows open. "Is he okay?"

"That Luther's always all right in the end," says Alfred carefully. It's as if he's keeping even his doubt to himself. Then, as if to change the subject, he looks hard at Seth, and even harder at Mona. "Knew soon as you showed up you'd be wanting me and the Race Man to drop that suit against your daddy," he says.

On the way home, Mona imagines her mother's face, lit with relief. She had not dared imagine Alfred would drop the suit; she wasn't even convinced that he should. In a way, she would have liked to apologize without receiving anything in return. At the same time, she imagines the in-suck of her mother's body as it straightens—a little lighter, a little younger—and this makes Mona feel similarly floaty. She has rarely seen Helen take a deep breath, but those few times she's remarked on a certain gasp in the middle. It is as if Helen drew the air through some cinch; as if her lungs were, quite uniquely, shaped like an hourglass. Mona imagines the hourglass full. Her mother most certainly does not stoop as she walks; and why would she let the belt of her raincoat drag on the ground? Instead she is smiling; she is standing behind Mona on the front steps. *No problem! No problem!*

"Mom? Mom? I'm home!" Mona bursts into the kitchen. The metal screen door wheezes almost shut behind her—that pneumatic tube—she reaches out automatically. A familiar click.

How different the kitchen air feels from the air outside! It smells different too, of course—like sesame oil today. But mostly she notices how enveloping it is, how moist, and warm. She feels as though she breathes differently in this house, her home; certainly she moves differently through its atmosphere. More slowly. All this is familiar.

And yet what she sees, she sees for the first time—namely what a veritable jumble is the kitchen, it's as if all the years her family has spent shopping the bargain basement have inspired them to re-create it right in their own home. Everything is in piles; piles could almost be a design element, a kind of unifying theme. Then there is the walnut sheet paneling they put up themselves, with the still unfilled nail holes; there the authentic Swiss cuckoo clock, with its fancy-cut hands and pine cone weights. There is the suspended grid ceiling with its fluorescent light panels; and there too are the Mediterranean-look cabinets crammed full of cans and bottles, rolls of things, years of stuff. So many of her friends had organized cabinets; and maybe Mona would too, one day. Cabinets with swing-out features—with lazy Susans, and pot-lid holders. Maybe Mona would one day have the kind of kitchen where leftovers get whisked into zip-lock bags, and there are no refrigerator odors. At Barbara's house, you can actually see to the back of the refrigerator; the whole thing's lit up like a hospital corridor. It's not jam-packed with glass and clay and plastic containers full of shrively, pickley, primordial foods, all of them pungent, and unlabeled, and probably unlabelable, seeing as you can hardly even say what color they are. Brownish, greenish, blackish. Maybe one day Mona would have the kind of kitchen that bespoke law and order and recipes you can write down.

But then again, maybe her kitchen would be exactly like this. A bargain basement, hardly elegant, hardly a place where you could execute with efficiency your culinary intentions; but where you might start out making one thing, only to end up, miraculously, with a most delicious *dish du jour*.

"Mom?"

No answer.

"Mom?"

Mona starts up the stairs, only to have Helen appear at the top. Even though it is daytime, Helen is wearing her old quilted bathrobe, which features squarish diamond buttons. These look as if they were designed to light night games at Yankee Stadium. As three of them are missing, however, Helen is using safety pins in their stead. Mona shudders. Helen looks as though she has just woken up. Her hair is disheveled, longer than Mona remembers; it almost touches her shoulders. Can Mona really have been away that long? But, no—Helen's hair only seems long on account of her failure to set it the way she usually does, with her medieval pink rollers. This is what Naomi would call her natural, however unnatural it looks. Helen is not wearing her glasses, either, and this gives her a look of sudden age. Flesh seems strangely collected around her eyes. It is as if after so many years of wearing glasses, her face has evolved an answering structure—its own soft-sculpture frames, which return her gaze to an inner focal point.

"Who is this?" she says.

"Me," says Mona. "It's me, Mona."

The carpet of the stairs seems to mute her words; that absorbent plush. Helen retreats to her room, her backless slippers softly clopping. Whereas Mona has never been a slipper wearer, her mother's slippers seem part of her feet, and the sound of them too seems the sound of her mother, they're like horseshoes on a horse.

Mona dogs Helen pathetically, also knocks on Helen's door pathetically. The knocks are strangely loud and rapping—the door, though not hollow, is not as solid as she remembered.

"Mom?" She calls through the wood. "Mom?" No answer. Still she continues hopefully. "We talked to Alfred. He's going to drop the suit!"

Helen emerges on cue. "Who is this?" she says, opening the door. "Is this my daughter?"

"It is!" Mona tries to keep up the pathetic air despite her enthusiasm. "And guess what? Alfred is dropping the suit! We talked to him!"

"What are you talking about, talked to Alfred?" says Helen, mildly. "And who is this *we*?"

Helen returns to her bedroom; and this time she doesn't even close the door, she doesn't have to. For it's as if this is what she's seen with her glasses off, operating on inner sight—that this disturbance can be trusted to leave by herself. Finally she's big enough not to need to be told.

Epilogue

Some years later, Mona is visiting Aunt Theresa. She is now sort of married to Seth; they're going to be more married soon. Meaning that there have been extrarelationship lovers along the way—little vista points off a generally scenic highway—and also they never did have any kind of ceremony, much less a getaway car trailing tin cans. However, they're common-law married, like it or not—the kind of married that arrives like a Welcome Wagon gift from your friendly federal government if you share a bed and bath for more than long enough.

And finally, Mona the Uncommitted has agreed to stand up in a room full of folding chairs. No huppah, no glass, a most modest reception. She and Seth will kiss. Presumably there will be clapping. They've said no presents, but are secretly regretting their nobility.

For witnesses they have trusty Barbara Gugelstein, who's flying out for the nonevent, and a friend of Seth's from ed school—Dave, his name is. The two of them both still sport beards, but Mona is the one with a ponytail now; she's too busy to wear her hair any way but out of the way. Mona could also have asked a friend from college or grad school. All-play Maureen, for example, or no-play Louise. But Barbara was the first person who came to mind—Barbara, who these days spritzes her hair to frizz it up more, and who immediately agreed to *be there for them*. After all, Mona's been a bridesmaid for her twice. First when she married Andy Kaplan, and then when she married him again, and who knows but there may be a third time? She and Andy are the longest-running show off Broadway, maybe it wouldn't have been so bad if they didn't both work for the airlines. But as it is, they seem to be endlessly circling some control tower, being denied permission to land.

To be honest, Barbara thinks Mona should ask Eloise Ingle instead;

it would be better luck. Charmed, matronly Eloise, after all, has forged on with her foundation work despite two sets of twins. (Her only life mistake has been getting married on a beach full of greenheads.) Or what about Rachel Cohen, who lives right in the area these days? The epitome of stability, and quite the success as a sculptor—big, ungainly, clattering contraptions she makes, all the while remaining seamlessly self-contained herself. Perfectly, contentedly attachment-free. Or no, no, no—the obvious choice! Alfred and Evie, the love bugs, Mr. and Mrs. Community Organization. They've marched, they've cooked, they've given up denying that she married him to assuage her own guilt, or that he's a white-bitch-lover who shouldn't have needed her to get him through college. They figure every marriage involves some horse trade; at least theirs worked. They don't beat on each other; they pay their bills; and they pay the bills of their friends in need—for instance, that Luther. Also they're attentive parents to their three death-defying tree-dwellers. Everyone's expecting the Knickerbocker clan to be made into a TV show, and what with Naomi now an author and her main man a producer, who knows but that they won't? Naomi says she's ready to stop playing the superwoman. She's going to rest on her laurels, no more high-profile projects; she says she's going to bake bread and make applesauce, and that lately she's been thinking a lot about ginger. Also babies, and the old neighborhood. She's thinking about volunteering in a youth program.

Still everyone can see the full-color production.

And of course, there is also Callie. You can always ask, says Barbara. You never know.

But Mona doesn't see why she should ask someone who's going to be ambivalent. Barbara is her first choice, and as for the presiding authority, that will be the authorities two—Rabbi Horowitz and Rabbi Horowitz. The latter being also known as Mrs. Horowitz—a most learned, exuberant, voluminous woman, whom Mona used to admire in all ways except one. Namely, why did she change her name? Mona couldn't help but wonder. Libby truly was a libber, after all—the only person Mona ever met who really did once burn a bra. (She said it half burned, half melted, and that she never would have done it without a fire extinguisher right there.) But then it turned out that her name was already Horowitz before she met the Big R.H. And what was she going to do, change it to something else? Of course, it did cause some confusion when Dan found a new job and became the other Rabbi Horowitz. But then, as he likes to say, every love has something in it to put up with. *I put up with this Rabbi Horowitz like I put up with myself.*

Such a production, this wedding, for a non-production! Mona and Seth could have opted to do the deed more privately; and sometimes they discuss this option still, even though Mona has her dress, and the baker's lined up. For really, they are marrying for money. What they have on their minds is mostly their major medical. But what the hell, they were going to throw a one-year birthday party anyway, for little Io. Their toddler trundler has just learned to walk; she holds her arms in the air as if determined to surrender to the first sheriff she meets.

"Two birds with one cake," said Seth when the idea first arose. "I like that."

All three of them are going to adorn the top tier. This will be on the outside, butter cream, on the inside, zwieback crackers.

Quips Mona, still an active mouth: "How easy to tie the knot, once you've cut the cord."

"That's my Mona," says Seth. "Still yolking after all these years."

In truth, they still experience their share of relationship difficulties. Seth's become a professor and generally noble type, meaning that he is married to his tenure prospects. Mona the second wife is thinking about going back to work too—she left a real almost-paying freelance job at B'nai B'rith, researching ethnic cartoons—but how will they divvy up the child-care duties? "I feel like a heel," says Seth, "if that makes you feel any better." And sometimes it does. Other times, though, when they are discussing what means job, and ambition, and manhood, Mona wishes that she could open a door and discover, not Sherman turned into Seth, but—to her utter stupefaction and relief—Sherman turned into a woman.

By now she takes it for granted that she and her mother do not speak to each other. When Io was born, she thought surely her parents would relent, never mind that she and Seth weren't married. She looked at her pink-prune child with her many sweet reflexes and imagined that at any moment her parents were going to burst through the door, if only so that her mother could judge for herself whether Io could pass for pure Chinese with that nose. She imagined that Theresa would talk them into it; or how could they resist honey from the Bea? Seth and Mona had an agreement: If her mother came to the hospital, they would name the baby Helen. In fact, they almost did not pick a backup name. For how could her parents stay away?

And indeed, her father came, bearing a teddy bear the size of a small couch.

But Io became Io, and Mona's whole gory story is no longer even an active topic of conversation. There is no why or what-if talk anymore—only how to scare up the airfare to California. For Mona has come to take for granted that this is how she spends her holidays, at the beach.

The beach: This is not so bad. Auntie Theresa's fold-out couch is the most rickety imaginable, but in anticipation of fashion, Seth has dug out his old futon—his mattressmoto, he calls it. This is their backsaver. Io, luckily, still fits in a drawer. The endless leave and return of the water restores in them a sense of rhythm—a balance of cycle and reach—and Mona enjoys the cats. She enjoys too the tales Auntie Theresa and Uncle Henry tell about the West Coast—all about how eucalyptus trees came to California, and snails. Mona has not heard such delicious stories about greed gone wrong since she turned Jewish; it might as well have been the pharaoh who imported this completely useless tree for timber, or brought on this gastropod plague. Mona thought she'd never get used to the latter. But now she steps around those escargots no problem, just as she does the truly gross banana slugs.

Theresa and Henry tell tales about the family too, which Mona could not bear to hear in the beginning. But now she is happy to consider her sadness in new ways; it's sort of a sick hobby. Theresa includes in her stories all kinds of things no one else would consider worth telling. For instance, how Helen used to measure out the water for washing the floor; also the Spic and Span. This is a Helen Mona never knew—a young woman not sure what mattered, someone a little like Mona herself, except quiet, and full of secrets. Secrets? What secrets? Mona wants to know. But Theresa will never say what they were, though she knows everything. She knows what size girdle

Helen wore, and that Helen once cried because her shoes and pocketbook didn't match. She knows how Helen learned to play bridge with a bridge-a-matic. And how much she hated old cars! All that overheating. Mona remembers the overheating herself, just as she remembers Helen's shopping habits—how expertly she picked fruit in the supermarket. And she remembers how soft her mother's skin was. She remembers being allowed to touch her mother's stomach once. And indeed her mother's skin was the softest thing she ever felt— softer than any silk, any chick, any moss.

She imagines this soft-skinned woman, reading magazines. This soft-skinned woman, learning to cook. She imagines her mother, still soft-skinned, writing to her family, year after year, only one day— finally!—to get a reply, and the news that her parents were dead.

This has happened since Mona's break with her mother. Mona put a yellow ribbon in her hair, just like Callie, as a sign of mourning. She wrote her mother a note.

But of course, it is now she who writes, and does not hear back, and wonders.

Her dad: Mona knows that Helen knows that Mona is in touch with Ralph. Still there is an air of complicity to their rendezvous. Ralph is aging gracefully, things are going well—he's found an herb medicine for his stomach, for one thing. For another, he's bought that second restaurant after all, and is resisting halfheartedly a third. After all, he knows he can make it work, having just the man to put in charge. Namely, Moses, a black cook and a good friend to Julio Alvarez, who replaced Cedric when he and Richard and Edward decided to open their own business. (This last being an ice cream store where you can have your ice cream warmed up if it's too cold, and where, if you change your mind, you can have some sesame noodles or moon cakes instead.) By Ralph's own admission, Julio and Moses are people he probably would have overlooked ten years ago; they take some getting used to, is his explanation for the change. "Before I was not used to it." (*Used to it* still being a big phrase in his thinking, maybe even bigger than *make sure*.) Of course, relying on blacks is not the only thing Ralph's learned. He's also learned to keep the Chinese help in back. *Dining room is about make the customers happy,* he shrugs. And then he quotes Moses: *Some things just be's that way.*

As for having a common-law son-in-law, who could get used to that? Yet Ralph has. Nowadays Ralph even boasts to his friends about Seth. *My son-in-law, he eats everything,* he says. *Even the leftovers he eats. Right out the refrigerator. He does not even use the microwave oven, that's what kind of son-in-law I have.* And Ralph's friends are impressed. *Eats everything,* they say. *Not even Chinese, but he eats everything.* This is in contrast to some of their sons-in-law, who *don't eat this, don't eat that.* These are *picky guys,* according to Ralph. *Those guys soft. Those guys good for nothing. Never get anywhere.*

As for where Seth will get as a result of his eating habits, Ralph doesn't say; he leaves it for Mona to predict, *The hospital.* For Seth eats even the fat on Auntie Theresa's red cooked pork—the fat that sits atop each piece of meat like a shiny square sponge layer. Mona sets hers aside; and she never cooks it this way herself, with the fat as thick as your thumb. For in her view, people in China can afford to eat that sort of thing, but it is another thing altogether for people in America. People in America having, after all, too many sources of calories already. For example, *latkes.* (These Mona deep-fries in a wok that Bea gave her.)

Callie: Ralph is not the only one who has changed, Callie has too. She loves being a pediatrician, even if it means endlessly discussing *ehh-ehh*—BMs she calls them now. Moreover, she has turned more Chinese than Seth—so Chinese that Ralph and Helen think there is something wrong with her. Why does she wear those Chinese padded jackets, for example? They themselves now wear down parkas, much warmer. And cloth shoes! Even in China, they never wore cloth shoes, they always had nice imported leather. And why does she call herself Kailan? So much trouble to find her a nice English name, why does she have to call herself something no one can spell? She says she's proud to be Asian American, that's why she's using her Chinese name. (Her original name, she calls it.) But what in the world is an Asian American? That's what Ralph and Helen want to know. And how can she lump herself together with the Japanese? The Japanese *Americans,* insists Callie/Kailan. After what they did during the war! complain Ralph and Helen. And what, friends with the Koreans too? And the Indians? The parents shake their heads. Better to turn Jewish than Asian American, that's their opinion these days. At least Jews don't walk around with their midriffs showing!

Or so Callie reports. Mona thinks she exaggerates a little—wanting to feel like she isn't only about the straight and narrow, even if she does lead a straight A life, what with the two beautiful children and the big-success husband, and the single-family house with double-dug flower beds. *I left home too,* she says sometimes. *I'm my own person. I made my own choices.* The truth is, she would stand up for Mona and Seth in a minute, if Mona asked. But Mona isn't sure she wants to ask someone who also says, *You did what you wanted, someone had to pick up the pieces.* And: *It would have killed Mom if we'd both been like you. It might kill her yet.*

The big day minus one: Is that right, that Mona might be the death of her mother? Mona has heard all about Helen's heart problems; it hasn't sounded so very bad. Still she worries.

At least Callie is coming to the wedding, there's that much good news. For a while it was maybe she will, maybe she won't; Mona probably shouldn't have made such a big deal of how it was no big deal. In any case, Callie will be arriving in a few hours. Ralph will be here soon too; and Auntie Theresa, of course, is already here, as are Bea, and Seth's dad, Phil, and Seth's infamous three half-brothers. Isn't that enough family?

"What's the matter?" Auntie Theresa wants to know.

Mona is trying on her dress. She's not sure how appropriate it is for a mother to wear white to her wedding. However, this is the plan. She and Seth happened one day on something long and antique, with a billowing skirt; it had seemed like fun in the store. Now, though, she thinks she looks like a tent display. She thinks she might as well have decided to get married in a huppah instead of under one. "Maybe I'll wear something else," she says.

"Like what something else?"

"My purple suit."

"You could." Theresa has been extra patient these days; she just goes around opening the shut windows and shutting the open ones. "Is it clean?"

Mona frowns. Io spit up on it last week. "Maybe I should rethink the flowers."

"You could," says Theresa again. And again: "Is something the matter?"

Mona doesn't say, except to ask what Theresa thinks of the veil. Mona doesn't have to wear it; someone just lent it to her in case she wanted to do the whole corny shebang. And what about her name? Should she change it in this wedding tomorrow?

"To Mandel?" says Theresa, surprised. "No more women's lib? Mona Mandel. Mona Mandel." She tries it out. "It sounds very nice. Like a river."

"No, no. To Changowitz," says Mona. "I was thinking that Seth would change his name to match."

"You could," says Theresa bravely. "Though what about Io? Will she become Changowitz too?"

"Of course," says Mona. For how could she leave Io out—bright Io! Who Mona only hopes will grow up knowing a Zeus when she sees one. For now she's a plump, noisy, busy little girl, who loves nothing more than to tear up telephone books. Or no—there is one thing she loves more. She loves to eat. *Mam! Mam!* she says, meaning *Mange! Mange!* For what else would be the favorite cuisine of a child part Jewish, part Chinese, barely off breast milk? But of course, Italian. She even got to the spice rack the other day and dumped out a whole bottle of oregano.

Mona smiles. She thinks how she really could change her name if she wanted to; and she thinks how at one point in her life that was what mattered more than anything. But now when Theresa asks her if she's serious, she answers, "Nes and Yo," and winks—almost missing, as a result, a certain four-legged creature now creepy-crawling up the oleander-lined walk. Half of the creature she recognizes: That's her father in his wing-tip shoes. He is carrying an airline tote bag, and a folding umbrella, even though there's a drought on. As for the other half, she recognizes that too, even as she takes a deep breath—she does this just the way her mother does, in two stages. The steps stop; it's the shuffle before the doorbell rings. Mona glimpses through the greenery, Helen's good pocketbook, which is navy-blue leather with a full leather lining—a classic style that, sure enough, has yet to go totally out of fashion. Mona was with her mother when she got it—on sale, of course. The doorbell rings.

"It's open," Mona calls; Io has already crawled over to investigate. Now she pulls herself up and bangs on the screen. Helen exclaims as Mona turns, adjusting her illusion veil—and even before she sees her mother, she's glad she finally got contact lenses; also that she doesn't wear mascara. For the way she's crying, anyone would think that Helen is the person Mona's taking in sickness or in health—is it really her mother, so tiny? The way Mona's crying, anyone would think that she's being taken too—finally!—for better or for worse. *Until death do us part,* she thinks, and rushes forward, just as Io falls down. Io's arms shoot into the air; her cheeks wobble; everyone expects her to start crying like Mona. But instead she stands right back up on her own two feet, and like a fine little witness, claps.

ACKNOWLEDGMENTS

Many thanks to the Guggenheim Foundation for its most generous support; also to Florence Ladd and the Bunting Institute, once again.

I have relied on many readers for their wisdom, including my editor, Ann Close; my agent, Maxine Groffsky; and my dear friends Rosanna, Alyssa, Maxine, Kimberly, Rachel, Leila, Mignonne, and Jill.

I thank Luke for sharing me with my work; and I thank David, as always, for his endless love and good sense.

From the highly praised author of *Mona in the Promised Land* and *Who's Irish?*—a generous, funny, explosive novel about the new "half-half" American family.

THE
LOVE WIFE

A NOVEL

BY GISH JEN

Praise

"Galpin traces the challenges she has overcome, from a rape in her twenties, to her fund-raising efforts for a girls' schools in Afghanistan, to her div tain2Mountain, hile a sin comes in challenging the limitations girls and women face in Afghanistan." —*The Boston Globe*

"Really Good Read . . . Five years ago, Colorado native Shannon Galpin broke the gender barrier by becoming the first woman to mountain bike in war-torn Afghanistan. Galpin's memoir, *Mountain to Mountain*, recounts her journey toward female empowerment and shares how her tangerine singlespeed became a vehicle for social change." —*SELF*

"[Shannon's] story makes a convincing case that interactions like the ones she has had in Afghanistan matter. Individual encounters can alter the lives of the individuals, and the members of their families, and the members of their communities. Just by being an open, adventurous, compassionate woman in Afghanistan, Shannon Galpin has encouraged people there to understand that not everybody from the U.S. wears a uniform and carries a weapon." —NPR, *Only a Game*

"Galpin's honest prose chronicles moment by moment, the event that changed her life forever and the victories, failures, and challenges she faced in trying to make a difference. *Mountain to Mountain* is about life, adventure, personal growth, and how a love for mountain biking and adventure can be used 'as a vehicle for social change and justice to support a country where women don't have the right to ride a bike.'" —*MountainFlyer Magazine*

"When Galpin writes about the moments that were most poignant to her—bombs erupting just blocks from her guesthouse, listening to the stories of female prisoners, and the 'honorary male status' that comes with being a foreign woman in a patriarchal society—the pages practically turn themselves. And when she peels back the curtain on her own loss of voice at age eighteen when she was raped in a park, readers come to understand why she fights so hard to help other women." —*5280*

"*Mountain to Mountain* is an inspiring look at how one woman can become a pioneering voice for women's equality." —*Bicycling*

"She sweeps you in, right from the beginning. And there is no exit. Shannon makes Afghanistan come alive on a personal level that no news story can ever replicate . . . This book is a winner . . . and so is Shannon." —Rita Golden Gelman, author of
Tales of a Female Nomad: Living at Large in the World

"Shannon is as brave as they come. For almost a decade she has battled the odds to empower Afghanistan's dispossessed and disabled populations. Now, at a time when women's rights are again under attack across South Asia, she provides a poignant story of how education and sport can overcome Taliban attacks and social neglect. Inspiring as only a real doer can be."
—Parag Khanna, author of *The Second World:
Empires and Influence in the New Global Order*

"Read this touching story from Shannon Galpin, who utilizes her unique position as a western woman to immerse herself in Afghan culture. She had the courage to leave everything behind and use the bike to as a tool to lead a physical and political movement—a way towards freedom for the women of Afghanistan."

—Marianne Vos, champion road-bicycle racer
and Olympic gold medalist

"*Mountain to Mountain* is nothing short of phenomenal. This captivating, inspiring, and heartwarming memoir shows us all that, with unbounded and unwavering passion, determination and courage, change can happen and mountains can be moved, one pedal stroke at a time. Shannon Galpin and the women of Afghanistan, I salute you and your illimitable strength." —Chrissie Wellington MBE,

four-time Ironman World Champion

Mountain to Mountain

A JOURNEY OF ADVENTURE
AND ACTIVISM FOR THE WOMEN
OF AFGHANISTAN

Shannon Galpin

ST. MARTIN'S GRIFFIN
NEW YORK

MOUNTAIN TO MOUNTAIN. Copyright © 2014 by Shannon Galpin. All rights reserved. Printed in the United States of America. For information, address St. Martin's Press, 175 Fifth Avenue, New York, N.Y. 10010.

www.stmartins.com

Map by Jeff Ward

The Library of Congress has cataloged the hardcover edition as follows:

Galpin, Shannon.
    Mountain to mountain : a journey of adventure and activism for the women of Afghanistan / Shannon Galpin.
        p. cm.
    ISBN 978-1-250-04664-2 (hardcover)
    ISBN 978-1-4668-4705-7 (e-book)
    1. Galpin, Shannon.   2. Women—Services for—Afghanistan.
3. Women—Afghanistan—Social conditions.   4. Women—
Violence against—Afghanistan.   5. Women's rights—Afghanistan.
6. Cycling—Afghanistan.   7. Women social reformers—United
States.   8. Women political activists—United States.   I. Title.
    HV1448.A3G35 2014
    362.83092—dc23

                                                    2014016897

ISBN 978-1-250-06993-1 (trade paperback)

Our books may be purchased in bulk for promotional, educational, or business use. Please contact your local bookseller or the Macmillan Corporate and Premium Sales Department at (800) 221-7945, extension 5442, or by e-mail at MacmillanSpecialMarkets@macmillan.com.

First St. Martin's Griffin Edition: December 2015

10   9   8   7   6   5   4   3   2   1

FOR DEVON,

you are my reason for everything.

Contents

x   Contents

No matter how high the mountain, there is always a road.

—AFGHAN PROVERB

UZBEKISTAN

TURKMENISTAN

JOWZJAN
PROVINCE

Sheberghan •   Mazar i Sharif •

BALKH
PROVINCE

Maimana •

FARYAB
PROVINCE

IRAN

Herat •

AFGHANISTAN

Kandahar •

KANDAHAR
PROVINCE

© 2014 Jeffrey L. Ward

Mountain to Mountain

Single-Speeds in a War Zone

Afghanistan 2009

This *is a bad idea.*

Breathe. Just breathe. Steady.

Just let go of the brakes and ride through. You got this. You know how to ride a bike.

Damn, these rocks are sliding! Worst trail ever. Don't crash. Please, please, please. Not here.

The mountainside was more rock strewn than it had appeared. These barren slopes were not like those I was used to biking in Colorado. Devoid of trees, the slopes looked like someone had dynamited the mountain and left the rubble where it had fallen. My bike was rolling down what had started out as a narrow goat path farther up the mountain. Almost immediately the path disappeared, and there was no clear way up or down, just rocks in all directions.

The ground slid, and small stones sprayed underneath my tires. I tensed.

Whose idea was this?

Yours, my brain replied.

There's no path!

Yeah, well, there could be land mines if you ride off the path.

My heart pounded. I focused downhill. Picking a line through the rubble, I steadied my nerves and took a deep breath. I gripped my handlebars and tried to keep my bike upright. The school and the open courtyard sat at the base of the mountain, a small white oasis in the sea of brown. I shifted my weight over the back tire. I let go of the brakes and let the speed take me through. Shades of brown rushed by in a blur as I picked up speed. I bent my elbows deeper to allow my arms to absorb the bouncing. My teeth chattered with the vibrations. My tires slid more than they rolled, searching for solid ground.

You're almost down. Relax. Breathe. Just ride. You know how to do this. Breathe! Dust stung my eyes. My hair was sweaty and plastered to my head under my checkered head scarf. My heart pounded even harder—whether from fear, exertion, or the layers of clothing I wore that felt like a sauna, I wasn't entirely sure.

Suddenly the tires stopped sliding and I was on level, solid ground. The mountain had spat me out alive. As if a mute button was released, sound flooded my ears: cheering. Six hundred boys were cheering. I looked up for the first time since I'd started my descent and smiled in relief through the cloud of dust. Six hundred Afghan boys smiled back. And one threw a rock. Six hundred to one? I'll take those odds.

Travis was smiling at me from behind the sea of faces. "Nice job, mate. They loved it. They can't believe you didn't crash. It would have been more entertaining if you had, though."

I wanted to punch him, but in Afghanistan women don't punch

men, playfully or not. But, in Afghanistan, women also don't ride bikes.

In a remote village, in the heart of the Panjshir mountains, six hundred boys, their teachers, and a few random villagers who wandered over, had just watched a woman ride a mountain bike behind their schoolyard. This was the first time any of them had seen a girl ride a bike. What they maybe didn't realize was that they had just witnessed the first time *any* woman had mountain biked in Afghanistan.

I didn't go to Afghanistan planning to ride a mountain bike. Does anyone travel to a war zone and say to themselves, "I wish I had remembered to pack my mountain bike, helmet, and lycra! This would be an awesome place to ride." No, they probably don't.

But on my fourth trip in 2009, I decided to bring my tangerine Niner 29er single-speed and challenge the gender barrier that prevents women from riding bikes. Afghanistan is one of the few countries in the world that doesn't allow its women or girls to ride. But I'm not Afghan. Standing tall at five foot nine, with long blond hair, I am clearly not a local. While many back home assume being so obviously a foreigner is an inherent risk, it has become my biggest asset. A foreign woman here is a hybrid gender. An honorary man. A status that often allows me a unique insight into a complicated region.

Afghan men recognize me as a woman, but as a foreign woman. I am often treated as a man would be. I sit with the men, eat with the men, dip snuff with the men. I have fished with them. They have let me ride buzkashi horses. All while their women are often shut away in the family home, not to be seen or heard. I'm in a fascinating position, being able to speak freely with the men who make the decisions, while having full access to the women because, despite my honorary male status, I *am* a woman. It allows me a unique insight into both sides of the gender equation, which often have extremely divergent perspectives.

I have discussed this with other foreign women I know who live and work in Afghanistan and Pakistan—journalists, photographers, writers, and aid workers—and they all have the same experience. They are most often met with curiosity and a willingness to talk as equals. Unfortunately, too often they are also faced with overly flirtatious Afghan men. More than once I have been groped in close quarters by a man who thought he could get away with it because I'm American. The assumption that American women are promiscuous is an unfortunate and deep-seated stereotype that has preceded me in many countries throughout the Middle East and Central Asia. It has led to more than one unwanted advancement, and the occasional marriage proposal. Thanks to globalization, the only consistent exposure many cultures have to American women is through movies, television, and music videos. Do we realize that our gender is judged on the standards of rap videos, Miley Cyrus, and the Kardashians?

Shaima, a friend I met on my first visit, illustrated the gender issue succinctly. Shaima was an American from Boulder, Colorado, and was half Afghan and half Costa Rican. She was in the country for several months to work with an Afghan nonprofit. Because she looked Afghan, she often encountered men who wouldn't speak to her. She would be at a meeting discussing next steps with the program they were working on, a program she was in charge of, and Afghan men often wouldn't shake her hand or speak to her directly. They would speak to her male colleagues as if she were invisible.

Over time I began to embrace the access that my honorary male status allowed. I was frustrated by the double standard, but I soon recognized the opportunity to challenge the gender barriers as a foreign woman in ways that might not have been tolerated if I were an Afghan woman. My theory was that beyond illustrating what a woman was capable of to Afghans, I would also be able to experience Afghanistan in a way few others had before me. By sharing my experiences and stories back home, perhaps I could challenge perceptions in both countries.

So it was on October 3, 2009, that I first put the rubber side down on a dry riverbed in the Panjshir Valley. It was part of the small but strategic Panjshir province, its mountains so steep that they'd kept the Taliban out—one of the few areas able to do so.

Travis, Hamid, Shah Mohammad, and I were driving through the province on the main road that followed the Panjshir River. Our driver, Shah Mohammad, was a sweet man I'd met on my first visit. Short and stout, he had a solemn face framed by a neatly trimmed beard and an ever-present embroidered white taqiyah prayer cap. We had seen some goat trails and a truck path on the other side of the river, so we were keeping our eyes peeled for a bridge large enough for our car. When we spotted one that seemed safe enough, Shah Mohammad drove through a small village and over the water. He opened the hatchback of the white Toyota Corolla so we could unload our gear.

Travis Beard and I had also met on my first visit a year prior. He'd become a trusted friend and an advisor to my fledgling non-profit organization, Mountain2Mountain. Focused on women's rights projects, it was what had brought me to Afghanistan in the first place. Travis was an Australian photojournalist, rock musician, motorcycle tourer, and aspiring filmmaker, and he was on hand to document the trip. I trusted his opinions and advice, if not necessarily sharing his comfort level of assumed risk. As he spent a lot of time traveling through Afghanistan on a motorcycle, he supported my desire to ride and had encouraged me in previous discussions. Trav came across as a brash and cynical war journo, but he nonetheless cared deeply about Afghanistan. He's done more for mentoring young Afghan photographers, artists, and musicians than anyone else I knew. Unlike most aid organizations and embassies, he's done it without the stamp of approval or the desire for credit, and often out of his own pocket.

Also along with us was Hamid, Travis's Afghan "brother." Hamid was working for me on this trip as my translator. He looked like a young Lenny Kravitz, circa "Fly Away," with a short curly fro and killer good looks. He would break hearts wide open if he lived somewhere where dating was acceptable. Not only was he always up for adventures, but his family was also Panjshiri. It was important to have someone with us who was local and considered part of the province's social fabric.

On this visit to Afghanistan, I was staying with Travis and Hamid, along with their other housemates, Nabil and Parweez, in their large private house in Kabul's central Taimani district. Living with a group of young Afghan men for several weeks was proving to be interesting. When I arrived with my bike, Hamid and Parweez were curious about my plan to ride it, and they watched the assembly as I took it out of the Thule bike box in pieces. We discussed the components, the tools, and what did what. Both of them rode motorcycles, but neither rode bicycles, and they thought I was a little crazy to want to ride a mountain bike instead of something with a motor. We talked in broad strokes about my plan, potential obstacles, and what to wear on a bike to keep from offending people in a country where women don't ride. The beauty of staying with them was that their house, like most in Kabul, had a walled courtyard, and I could take off my head scarf and dress as Western as I liked. And so, wearing my halter dress and jeans, I pulled on my cleats and took the bike outside into the courtyard, to see if my reassembly was adequate or if I'd forgotten something important.

Their courtyard was small and contained a car, three motorbikes, and one frisky stray cat they'd adopted named Mojo. So it was a bit like a small BMX course for three-year-olds. My handling skills are poor at best and I'm not great with tight corners and switchbacks, so this was actually a challenging environment. I soon realized I needed more air in my front shock and my rear tire, and my seat was too low, but the brakes worked, and I thought I'd done a damn fine job at the first-time assembly. This coming from a girl who rarely washes the mud off her bike and whose only maintenance is occasionally remembering to oil her chain. Very occasionally.

More important, in the courtyard I discovered that I could, in fact, ride in jeans and a skirt. Not ideal in the heat, but feasibly rideable and socially respectable. I had a few Patagonia halter dresses that I liked to wear over pants and under a tunic around town, and the combination proved comfortable for riding—a big start toward figuring out cycling attire that wouldn't offend in rural villages on or off the bike. So I continued playing around, coming up with a little clockwise courtyard circuit, round the garden, through the carport, under the clothesline, over the grass, up the concrete porch, and down the other side over the loose pile of bricks. I got more confident on the loop and picked up speed.

The trouble came as I reversed direction. Not paying attention, I rode toward the carport between the pillars that supported the clothesline I'd been ducking under. From this angle, I could get more speed but also had to go up the curb rather than down. I rode toward it, focused on the curb and lifting my bike up it, forgetting about the clothesline. It cut me across my right eye and the bridge of my nose, whipping my head back. I swore loudly as I instinctively took my feet off the pedals to keep my balance and put them on the ground, on either side of my bike. I doubled over and tentatively felt above my eye.

It was official. In my desire to be the first woman to mountain bike in Afghanistan, I had injured myself on day one, in a private courtyard, with a clothesline.

My eye hurt, but one of the housemates, Nabil, was on the porch watching, so as I got off my bike to go inside, I felt obliged to chat with him. My eye was starting to throb, so I excused myself, and Najib said, "Oh, yeah, your eye is bleeding quite a bit. You should go clean that."

Uh, thanks?

How about telling me that ten minutes ago when I was trying to pretend that I'm okay and could have a coherent conversation with you?

So I went upstairs to take a look and sure enough—I had gashed the bridge of my nose and my eyelid and they were already swelling. Nice. Really smooth, Shannon. My penchant for clumsiness was front and center in Afghanistan.

I decided that I'd had enough humiliation for one day, so I went back downstairs to put my bike away in the front room.

Three days later, I was unpacking it from the hatchback of Shah Mohammad's Corolla, beside a dry riverbed in the Panjshir Valley. Behind my sunglasses, my eye was still sore.

While I put the wheels on the bike, Travis went up the road and perched on a small hill to shoot some video from above. Hamid hung back with me while I attached the wheels. Shah Mohammad watched quietly, obviously curious as to what I was going to do next.

I considered my bike helmet. Wear it over my head scarf? No head scarf? What if I had to take my helmet off? Did I even need my helmet? How do I do this with the least amount of offensiveness and the least amount of awkwardness? I was already wearing many layers: long pants under my long dress under a long-sleeved tunic. The helmet seemed to fit over the head scarf, which I pulled down and wrapped around my neck and tied behind it—checking the length of drape so it wouldn't kill me Isadora Duncan–style by getting caught in the back wheel and breaking my neck.

I did a quick once-over . . . all seemed to be in order. Glasses. Bike gloves. Two wheels. By this point a healthy crowd of men had gathered around, mostly workmen from the construction trucks we'd passed. Since we were off the main road, I'd assumed we would be mostly alone. Nope. Word spreads like wildfire when something unusual is going on. Great, no pressure.

A stormy gray sky was developing, but the clouds hadn't yet covered the sun. I looked around. The rugged mountains rose up on all sides, and ahead of me a dry riverbed offered a rocky path that I could navigate. When I got the signal from Travis that he was ready, I took a deep breath and started pedaling. And, voilà! I was riding my bike. In Afghanistan. On my thirty-fifth birthday. A huge, goofy grin pasted itself to my face.

The path was strewn with boulders and was bumpy as hell. Since construction trucks came through here regularly, we knew this area was clear of land mines. I played around, hopping my bike over rocks, just enjoying the experience, and riding around to see what the terrain was like, how it felt to ride it, and what sort of reaction I created among the men who saw me. I had to go through runoffs that crisscrossed the ground as I picked my way through the riverbed. Each crossing sprayed water as I splashed through like a kid, trying not to slide on the slippery rocks just under the surface. It felt almost like riding back home, where I hit puddles and water at every chance, much to the horror of friends who try to keep their bikes clean.

Many of the men who were working in the area shouted "*Salaam*" when they saw me, but most simply watched curiously. I was riding back and forth along one section that was smooth and fun to play on when I noticed a mother and young girl sitting quietly, almost hidden, under a tree watching me. I immediately thought of my daughter, Devon, four years old and half the world away. I wished she could be here with me. As I rode past them I waved shyly, and they both smiled and waved back. I smiled and put my hand to my heart, the way Afghans do when they are saying "*Salaam*" to show respect, and they did the same.

My heart happy and my pants muddy, I arrived back at the car boiling hot under the layers of clothing. I couldn't stop grinning. I took off my helmet and grabbed a bottle of water. Hamid and I talked to a few of the local men who had gathered around. They asked where I was from and what I was doing there. I asked about their work and families. One young man shyly asked if he could ride my bike. I smiled and offered it to him, nodding. "Bale"—*Yes*. He smiled back more confidently as he took my bike. He pedaled around in wide circles while the men laughed and joked with one another.

The clouds rolled in, blotting out the sun, so we said our good-byes, and I quickly took off the wheels to put the bike back in the car. We were heading to the village of Dashty Rewat and didn't want to arrive in the dark. We still had a few hours of driving ahead of us, much of it on dodgy dirt roads. Until now we'd been on paved or relatively smooth dirt roads just inside the entrance to the valley, and we'd made good time.

Unfortunately, when we hit the dirt roads, it became apparent that Shah Mohammad should not be driving outside Kabul. He couldn't see the numerous crudely constructed concrete speed bumps made to slow down traffic through the villages that dot the main road. His ancient Corolla was not meant to take on these things at high speed, yet he seemingly couldn't see them until it was too late. The lack of shocks in the car rattled our bodies each time the car made contact with the speed bumps. The problem came to a head as we were driving around the hill of Massoud's tomb. It sat in the middle of the valley overlooking the river. As we rounded a bend, Shah Mohammad overcooked the turn and suddenly the car was careening straight toward the cliff.

Travis had been sleeping in the seat next to me, holding his camera in his lap, when I screamed.

Luckily for us, a few months prior, as part of the ongoing construction work being done on the road, and on Massoud's tomb above us, rock barriers had been built along the cliff. I hadn't noticed them the last time I visited. Even more luckily, the barriers were solidly built. We busted off a chunk when the Corolla made impact, but the car didn't follow the rocks tumbling down the cliff side. Shah Mohammad quickly tried to reverse the Corolla so he could keep driving. We all shouted for him to stop so we could check the car, the barrier, and collect ourselves.

I looked over at Travis, he looked at me, and we both leaned forward to look into the front seat to check on Hamid. He appeared stunned. None of us had been wearing seat belts. I wasn't even sure there were any functioning in the car. We'd come inches from death, and I realized that in a so-called near-death experience your life doesn't flash before your eyes. You just think, "Oh, shit!" and everything else is blank.

Without saying a word, we all got out to look at the car and the barrier.

"What the hell, dude?" said Hamid in a low voice to Travis.

His years as an English translator for American troops and hanging around expats like Travis had honed his slang and timing, and I often forgot that Dari was his first language. The fender and wheel panel were smashed in, but there was far less damage than I'd expected. Judging from the rectangular barriers on either side, I guessed that the one we'd hit had lost half of its concrete. We looked at one another again, and then we all started laughing, the adrenaline leaving our bodies. Hamid and Travis peered over the edge. "*Daaaamn*," said Hamid.

"Uh, guys? You gotta look at this." They turned around. I pointed at the car.

Shah Mohammad had gotten a crowbar out and, as if to prove that Corollas were as resilient as the Afghans themselves, he hooked the curved end of the crowbar under the fender and pulled it back into place. He did the same with the wheel panel. Good as new! Sort of. Hamid shook his head in disbelief.

We piled back into the car and continued onward as if nothing out of the ordinary had happened. We got about an hour or so farther down the road, which had quickly become bumpy, rock strewn, gutted out, and four-by-four worthy. It was around this time that Shah Mohammad started complaining. He wasn't happy he had to drive so far, on such bad roads. Hamid, who sat beside him and was the only one of us fluent in Dari, one of Afghanistan's two national languages, took the brunt of it. About fifteen minutes from Dashty Rewat, we encountered a massive rock pile that we had to navigate across. Shah Mohammad told Hamid he wouldn't go any farther. The discussion became a bit of a kerfuffle, and I said I wouldn't pay the full day's rate if he turned around. I told Hamid to explain that we had hired him for the day to go to Panjshir. If he had a problem with the distance or the roads, he should have said so and we could have hired another driver. He continued to complain but he also continued to drive. I didn't blame him really. We were all getting cranky, hungry, and tired. The road was battering our bodies as well as our moods. But Travis continued to sleep, his camera cradled in his lap like a small cat.

Travis and Hamid had spent time in Dashty Rewat on their first attempt to summit the Anjuman Pass, which borders the back end of the Panjshir Valley. They traveled there by motorcycle with their good friend and fellow adventurer Jeremy Kelly. They'd randomly stopped here at dusk to ask if any of the villagers knew where they could spend the night. Idi Mohammad, one of the villagers, had immediately offered his home. In the time-honored tradition of Muslim hospitality, all three had received a warm meal and a place to sleep. It turned out that Idi Mohammad was the principal of the boys' school and Travis told him about me and the work I was looking to do with my organization, Mountain2Mountain. Travis, Hamid, and Jeremy were unsuccessful on their first attempt to summit the Anjuman Pass, and were stopped by the local police in Parion and forced to spend a night in their custody. They returned a few weeks later with a letter of introduction from the Panjshir governor to complete the ride, and again stayed with Idi Mohammad's family. Knowing I would be interested in meeting Idi and discussing education in a rural community, Travis had promised to introduce me to him the next time I was in Afghanistan.

Dashty Rewat looked much the same as any of the other villages we'd been driving through—crumbling mud walls and shipping containers that housed various shops along the dirt road. It had the general look of a village recently used for bombing practice. The only distinguishing feature was its remoteness and a new structure being built. Two men were on the roof of a two-story white building. One turned out to be Idi Mohammad, in a light-brown pakol hat, the type favored by the Northern Alliance mujahideen leader and Panjshiri hero, Ahmad Shah Massoud.

Panjshir is known as the Valley of the Five Lions, and Massoud was often referred to as the Lion of Panjshir. He was a powerful figure not just in Panjshir but throughout Afghanistan, a rare Che Guevara type, with iconic photographs on buildings, roadside banners, and even in the windows of cars. He was not just beloved by his own Panjshiris, but potentially had the ability to unite Afghanistan. He rose to fame as a mujahideen leader fighting the Soviet-backed central government. After the Soviets withdrew, the Afghan government collapsed. Civil war erupted and Kabul became the battleground for mujahideen factions fighting for control of the city and the country. Eventually, the Taliban took Kabul, and Panjshir became a key staging ground in the fight against the Taliban under Massoud's leadership of the Northern Alliance. The high mountains surrounding the narrow province create a natural defense, and Panjshir was not taken by the Taliban. Massoud was assassinated on September 9, 2001, by posing as a news crew under the orders of Osama bin Laden. When the United States was attacked two days later on 9/11, many analysts made the connection to the major terrorist attack Massoud had warned against several months earlier in a speech to the European Parliament. The United States soon found itself in Afghanistan, hunting Bin Laden, and fighting the Taliban on the side of Massoud's Northern Alliance. Revered in life, he is still revered in death. The tomb under construction on the hillside overlooking the valley is a symbol of the people's love, as are the men that still serve him and his cause. There is a pride and independence in Panjshir that comes from their love of their commander and his love of Panjshir, which is still plainly visible in every village.

Idi's face lit up when he saw Travis and Hamid stepping out of the car, and he shouted down at us, "*Salaam! Salaam!*" He quickly climbed down from the roof, beaming broadly, while we walked around back, gathering a crowd of children and men. Travis shouted up, "*Salaam,*" in his Aussie drawl, waving up at the men. "*Salaam,*

salaam," he said to the children, smiling and high-fiving some of them as we walked through the crowd.

After Travis, Hamid, Idi, and the second man, Idi's brother Fardin, embraced and shook hands, I was introduced and found myself, once again, mesmerized by the handsome features of Panjshiri men. Photos of Massoud highlight his charisma, and my Panjshiri friends are all striking. Idi Mohammad was no different. Idi was genuinely happy to see the guys and asked how their motorbike trip went. He'd been worried about them. There was no cell phone service, so he had no way of knowing if they'd encountered problems, if they'd been successful, or even if they'd gotten back alive.

The men were disappointed that Jeremy was not with us. Travis explained to me that they'd loved his red hair and beard. Hamid explained to Idi in Dari that Jeremy was working in Kabul, but that he was healthy and sent his best to everyone.

Idi asked us to come inside and join his family for dinner and to spend the night, since the sun was already behind the mountains. Hamid explained to him that we'd wanted to drive out to Dashty Rewat so that they could introduce me, but that we had to go back tonight, especially now as our driver was being such a pain in the ass. Idi Mohammad looked concerned and unhappy that we couldn't stay. He offered a second time in case we were simply being polite in declining, but we explained that our driver was the main issue and that we would come back next week and plan to stay longer. Idi agreed and we sat down to talk on a stone wall overlooking the road and the mountains as the entire village watched, or at least the men and the children. Not one woman was to be seen.

Idi explained to me that he was a teacher, and like many Afghans during the civil war, he'd spent years as a refugee with his family across the border in Pakistan. In Pakistan, he received an education, and when he returned to his village, he started up a school for the local boys with a few other teachers. It expanded as more and more families sent their boys, and they now had a school that provided education through high school. He was the principal and while they had a school and teachers, they lacked supplies. This was something I could potentially help with. We discussed the immediate need for paper and pens. Ironically, the simple lack of supplies is the unfortunate reason many children do not attend school in countries like Afghanistan. Families are often too poor to afford the twenty cents for a notebook. The school housed six hundred students on average. Amazingly, their other need was computers. I was surprised and asked why. Idi Mohammad explained that it could connect them to the rest of the world and allow their remote village to provide a better education. They already had a teacher trained in computer science, so it was simply a matter of machines. Many of their boys hoped to get into Kabul University, and basic computer skills could help.

When I asked about the girls' education, he replied that there was no school in the village or nearby.

"Would the village be open to the idea of a girls' school?" I asked.

"Yes, we would allow our girls to go to school. It is a very necessary thing for all children. Boys and girls."

"Is there land that could be used, or a building that could be improved? Are there any female teachers in the area?"

"Yes, we can discuss that more. There is a piece of land that used to be a girls' school before the Russians. There are no female teachers. But if it was just through year five, we could use male teachers."

"Could we discuss this more when I return?"

"I would be most honored to discuss it further, and I will help in any way I can."

During the last few minutes of the talk, we heard banging. Behind us, in the street, Shah Mohammad was striking the front fender with the crowbar. Was this passive aggressive behavior to get us moving along, or did he really think it would further improve the dents?

I shook my head in disbelief, but I reluctantly stood. I shook Idi's hand and the hands of many others in the crowd. *"Tashakur, Idi. Khoda al fez."* Thank you. Good-bye. We all said good-bye, and I promised to come back the next week with school supplies as a start, and we'd stay for a few days.

Back in the car I was positively giddy. I was fully aware that this meeting wouldn't have been possible without the previous visits and cups of tea drunk by Travis and Hamid—opening the door for me to step in with solid connections already in place.

"Thank you, thank you, Trav. I am so grateful. You have made this the best birthday ever." He smiled amusedly and muttered in his dry Aussie drawl, "Yeah, yeah," and promptly fell asleep again.

I leaned back and sighed with contentment as we began the long drive home, dusk already setting in as Shah Mohammad bitched to an uninterested Hamid, who continued playing his role as seeing-eye dog in the front seat, pointing out speed bumps and upcoming curves. Strangely enough, Shah Mohammad was now wearing a pair of glasses. *Perhaps they could have been of use a few hours ago when we nearly died?* I thought to myself.

Five days later we drove back to Dashty Rewat in a rented four-by-four. We left Shah Mohammad in Kabul. Hamid was at the wheel. The back was filled with a thousand dollars' worth of school supplies and my bike, which I hoped to ride some more. We had a five-song playlist of American hip-hop in the tape deck and another tape with five Bollywood songs. "In Da Club" by 50 Cent bumped loudly on repeat halfway through the trip while Hamid sang along gangsta-like in his new black sunglasses we'd bought at Bagram's black market that morning. Travis was in front of us on his Honda dirt bike.

Once we got inside the Panjshir gates and completed the security check-in with the guards, we stopped at several places we'd spotted on the last visit where I'd wanted to bike but hadn't had time. Four or five times along the route, I unpacked the bike with Hamid's help. None of the paths connected, so I couldn't ride far, but I explored different areas and had discussions with new groups of men. On each ride, I gained more confidence and was soon enjoying the interactions with the men that gathered. Hamid answered questions while I rode and when I returned, he made introductions and the discussions continued. I was met with curiosity about who I was and why I was there. I answered and asked my own questions: Did their kids go to school? Girls and boys? Could girls play sports? Would they allow their girls to ride bikes? If not, why not? Impromptu discussions by the side of the road naturally unfolded and progressed down different rabbit holes. Each time, I had to tear myself away and decline offers of tea or dinner at their homes.

Several hours later, as we pulled into Dashty Rewat, night was falling. Idi Mohammad's brother, Fardin, welcomed us back. Thirty seconds after our arrival, flashlights came out of the courtyard and we were led back into the home. We'd let Idi Mohammad know when we were coming, but he was in Kabul for a few days to buy supplies for the guesthouse he was building. His brothers made us feel more than welcome. We were led into a large rectangular room, with traditional dark-red toshaks lining the floor and three sea-foam green walls. While seated on the toshaks and pillows, we were fed, watered, and introduced to a few neighbors who came to check out the foreign visitors. One in particular was a real comic. Older, missing a few teeth, he wore a traditional pakol hat and a pale-green shalwar kameez that matched the walls. He had the look of a real outdoorsman, Afghanstyle. He brought an old boom box—circa 1970s. It was encased inside a burgundy velvet "purse" brocaded with mirrors.

"So Afghan," Travis said with a lazy smile, shaking his head in wonder at the scene that was unfolding. Laughing at the unexpected entertainment, I glanced over at him. Chuckling, Travis winked at me and stood up. He put the velvet-encased boom box on his shoulder to demonstrate how they were carried in the hood. As the entire room clapped and sang, Hamid perked up from his toshak, where he had been quietly watching. Travis handed the boom box back, grinning, and sat down to the appreciative laughter of the entire room. Our visitor was a natural comic. He left the room, and when he came back in, he strutted through the doorway with the boom box on one shoulder and his hat cocked over an eye—another Afghan gangsta. He sat with a big smile, and I took his photo, laughing so hard my iPhone shook. The entire room had erupted in laughter.

The family lived together in this compound, three brothers, four wives, two grandmothers, and approximately fourteen children, although I never got an accurate count. The women stayed in a separate part of the home. The young boys served dinner, so the women were still not seen. After dinner I was invited to go back and have tea and talk with them, but was told no camera, and no translator, since Hamid was a man. One of Idi's boys came along and offered to translate. His English was very basic and my Dari was even worse— but it was sufficient for niceties and general questions. The four wives were beautiful and the two grandmothers had heavily lined faces, full of character and with smiling eyes that made me feel welcome. Children ran around and were allowed free rein through the compound. They were curious, having never met a foreign woman before, and they gestured for me to sit on the floor. The oldest girl, maybe thirteen, brought me green tea and placed a dish of dried berries and walnuts in front of me. They sat, surrounding me on all sides—four wives, two grandmothers, and about a dozen children.

Only three men lived here so I assumed one had two wives, but didn't feel it was appropriate to ask so soon after meeting them. With the confusion my young translator had with family words— brother, cousin, mother, sister all interchanged randomly—I figured that I wouldn't understand the answer even if I asked. I didn't know if this was a case of two wives for one brother, or if perhaps one was a sister whose husband had died. Instead, I asked less complicated questions, mostly about the family. I complimented the children and learned how to sit quietly, smile, and drink tea with twenty silent faces watching me. I offered to answer their questions as well, but they didn't have many, were too shy, or didn't understand what I'd said. Sometimes I want to share that I, too, have a daughter, but then there's the husband question. Where is my husband? Why do you only have one daughter? Are you barren? I have learned to avoid this question simply by saying that he lives in the United States and takes care of my daughter while I'm in Afghanistan. This is essentially true, and the subject is dropped, but with the people I am building relationships with, it sometimes feels like a falsehood not to explain that I'm divorced and to allow them to think what they will. Divorce is rarely an option here, and women who are divorced are typically looked upon dishonorably. Family is everything in Afghanistan. Men may take many wives, but rarely will they request a divorce. It is rarer still for a woman to be granted one should she choose to request it. When a Muslim man decides he wants a divorce, he can just say the words, "I divorce you," and it is official under Islamic law. The courts are starting to hear women's divorce cases, but it is still rare. Yet, as with many other things, like riding a bike and motorcycle, or sitting with the men, I am a foreign woman and divorce isn't so shocking. But without the ability to communicate well, I didn't want to risk delving into this subject.

Despite my desire to sit and talk with the women all night—as I would in the United States—I'm much more comfortable with the men. I said good night to the ladies after an hour or so, and asked if I could come back in the morning to take photos. They told me that photos of the children and grandmothers would be okay, but the older girls and the wives were off limits. I wondered if it was an issue of simply not liking their photo taken, or if it was forbidden by the men. But the gorgeous wife of Idi Mohammad mimed getting slapped if I took her photo. It was forbidden. This still surprises me when I meet the wives of men I think of as more progressive, or at least less conservative. Idi Mohammad was a principal and teacher; he valued education, including girls' education. He treated me as an equal and yet had these deep-seated cultural restrictions firmly in place with his own women—always hidden away. That's not to say they weren't treated well by Afghan standards, or were even unhappy. That I couldn't answer. But they were not free. They did not have the same rights as men. Their lives were controlled by men, and often even by the sons they'd raised. And that was not freedom, nor could I believe that anyone could be truly happy without it.

Amid hugs, handshakes, and smiles, I again promised to come back in the morning to take photos. I walked through the inner courtyard to the men's side. I ducked under the low doorway and found Travis and Hamid laughing. One of the neighbors, the toothless one with the Afghan boom box, had expressed interest in purchasing me as a second wife. Prices had been discussed, half-jokingly. No harm or unease apparently, just a laugh on the boys' part. Apparently, they talked him up to $120,000. They were quite pleased with the amount and figured they could retire on the beach somewhere cheap. I played along halfheartedly, joking about selling women wasn't as rib splitting to me as it was to them. I told Hamid that I'm worth at least half a million. *Good luck raising that kind of cash in the rural mountains of Afghanistan*, I thought. Still, we were sitting in the heart of the emerald mining region, so who knew what was possible?

As we got ready for bed, I realized I had no idea where the bathroom was. Bathroom facilities are always an interesting experience in the developing world and seem to be a source of much discussion and comparison by travelers. In Afghanistan, they cover the entire spectrum: from the luxury of a flush toilet in foreign guesthouses and cafés, to porcelain squat toilets on the floor in restaurants and government buildings, to a concrete floor with a hole cut in it Porta-Potty style, to the horror of a facility that involves any of the above three, reeking of urine and with nothing but a watering can to clean up with. No toilet paper, coupled with no running water or soap.

Here, the outhouse was like many in rural areas, a small raised mud structure with a hole in the floor through which everything simply dropped on the ground below. I had a group of children following me everywhere to make sure I was okay, and that I had everything I needed. When I asked, *"Tashnab kujas?"* they offered me a small shared roll of pink toilet paper and even gave me their slip-on sandals so that I didn't have to put on my cumbersome motorcycle boots. It is a little unnerving to be the center of attention and the recipient of so much curiosity in the best of times, but to be the center of attention for a trip to the bathroom is more than a little awkward. We walked to the outhouse as a procession, and I smiled and thanked them as I went up the step and inside. Eight or so children waited for me. I closed the warped wooden door and blocked it with the rock placed there for that purpose. I hoped I wouldn't have performance anxiety as I could hear the kids chattering excitedly while they waited for me. When I emerged, eight smiles greeted me, and I couldn't help but smile back. I let them lead me to a pump where I washed my hands, and then they escorted me back to the main room.

Hamid, Travis, and I were invited to sleep there on the toshaks. Big heavy blankets were brought out from the corner where they'd been stacked neatly, and the men literally tucked us all in—even Travis and Hamid. It was possibly the strangest bedtime ritual ever, but quite sweet. I felt like a little kid and wondered if I'd get read a bedtime story. We slept in our clothes. I'd been mountain biking in mine all day and would be wearing them for two more—day and night. The men made sure we had a flashlight and everything else we needed and bade us good night. A couple of the older boys slept with us on the other side of the room, either out of curiosity or for security.

Travis and I woke up at a predawn six o'clock to do some biking in the village. I wanted to ride without attracting so much attention. I should have known better. Even at this early hour, we were the talk of the town. All the village men came out to watch and chat, and many invited me to breakfast. Throughout it all there was a lot of curiosity and no animosity. An old man in a traditional brown blanket worn as a shawl and a matching pakol hat stopped me in the street to talk. He mimed pedaling, and I understood that he wanted to know how I clipped my feet in, so I showed him the cleats on the bottom of my cycling shoes and how they clipped into the pedals on the bike. Several young men took turns riding my bike around the village street. One man who I stopped to chat with—and by "chat" I mean mime and speak with in my limited Dari since Hamid was still sleeping—apparently worked in the emerald mines in the mountains behind the boys' school. He mimed necklaces and bracelets and invited me to breakfast. Maybe I'd found Afghan husband number two? I explained that I had plans to visit the school and thanked him. A few minutes later, I was stopped by an older man with a striking long white beard, a kind wrinkled face, and twinkling eyes. He was strolling through the early morning in his traditional green striped Afghan coat, the ones with the long, skinny arms that aren't used but instead hang down the back; the coat itself is draped from the shoulders like a cloak. He asked if I was cold, and we commented on the weather and the beautiful mountains in the sunrise. He had the sort of face that spoke of stories to be shared, and I cursed Hamid in his bed for preventing me from a deeper conversation. Then I cursed myself for my dependence on a translator. I vowed to make learning Dari a priority. Whether from lack of focus and time, or simple laziness, I have struggled with foreign languages, despite having lived overseas for a decade prior to Afghanistan.

Many people peeked out of windows and came down from the fields to watch the crazy woman on the bike. Amazingly—just like on yesterday's ride—no one was hostile, offended, or annoyed. There were just smiles, laughter, joking, simple curiosity, and the desire to chat. "What is your name? Why are you here? Why are you riding a bike?" In exchange I got to share about myself—my love of bikes, my work with Mountain2Mountain, my desire to see Afghanistan and learn about its people. Men nodded and smiled, and invited me to have tea with their families. I asked questions about girls playing sports, if that was acceptable, and if so, which sports? Soccer and basketball were the most common answers, both sports that could be done in privacy, at school or behind courtyard walls.

I rode through rocky, dried-up fields, empty after the early fall harvest. I had to navigate piles of dirt as solid as concrete and practiced bunny hops, working hard to avoid crashing. I had a first aid kit, but I'd have preferred not to break it out. My future husband was there, this time strutting through town to show off his hunting rifle and prove his prowess as a skillful provider. He'd told us last night that he was a proficient deer hunter. Apparently, there were several hundred deer in the area, but he was in need of binoculars to spot their grazing areas. I smiled weakly, took a few photos, and when he saw I had the camera out, he again hammed it up, tilting his hat like a French beret and strutting, the rifle jauntily held over his shoulder. He then stopped and offered to take us fishing after we visited the boys' school. I knew that both Travis and Hamid would be keen to go after the school visit, and I was curious to check out the local fishing techniques. I had seen Afghans throw sticks of dynamite into the river to get fish. Another friend had watched RPGs launched into the river to catch dinner. Hoping for something less dangerous and more sustainable, I agreed that we'd come along. Fishing would be another experience that continued to link my life and work in mountain communities here to the mountain community where I lived in Breckenridge, Colorado.

I discovered a much better way to bike with the men's kaffiyeh scarves, which was what I began to wear on the motorcycle to look like a man. These were black-and-white patterned scarves often worn around the neck or wrapped around the head like a turban. I wrapped it around my head and my face, leaving only my eyes peeking out when I was traveling by motorcycle. It helped keep the dust out of my nose and mouth, and disguised my gender. It was perfect for the bike, but instead of wearing it like a full-face turban, I wore it like a hadji from the nineties, or the politically incorrectly named "cancer patient" style, and then I simply added another scarf around my neck. If I could get away with it, I'd wear them all the time. They're much more my style than the women's head scarves, still respectful but edgy and much more functional. My walk is even different when I wear men's scarves. Women's scarves blow off in the wind, and I have to constantly hold them, so I tend to look down more to keep them in place and as a result I don't make eye contact with others. I wear the men's, and I'm actually more covered up—my blond hair all tucked away, the scarf so tight it doesn't slip like the women's, and my neck covered completely. Yet I walk like me, big strides, head up, athletic, with a more confident, almost defiant, demeanor. I stand out because women don't wear men's scarves, but I stand out anyway in the women's scarves that show much more blond hair and constantly fall back off my head. So it's a crapshoot. The men's scarves wouldn't work in the south or in more conservative areas, or for formal meetings, but for around Kabul and Panjshir they're perfect. Hell, with my reputation for forgetting to wash my hair in Colorado, they'd be perfect back home!

We went back to the house after an hour or so of biking and making friends. Immediately, Travis crawled back into bed, laying down on the toshak next to Hamid, who hadn't yet stirred. I needed the bathroom and a wash after two days of wearing the same clothes while biking in the Afghan dust. The bathroom processional followed me to the outhouse and again I listened to them giggle and chatter on the other side of the door. I walked back to the main room, and my young translator from the night before asked if I would like to wash up. He pointed to the door across from the room where we were sleeping. Inside was a small concrete cubicle the size of a Western shower but without a drain. A broken mirror was propped against a tiny window that let in a few rays of early morning light. I nodded gratefully with a "*Bale, lotfon.*" Yes, please.

He brought me a jug of blissfully warm water that the wives had warmed up. He placed it on the floor, and I closed the door with a "*tashakur.*" I washed my face and my feet but couldn't bear to take off all my clothes in the cold air just to put them back on again dirty. I would get a full shower soon enough. The warm water and the cold air on my face refreshed me, and I felt ready for the full day ahead.

We'd passed by the boys' school during the bike ride through town and discovered that we would have to cross a narrow bridge to get there. This made delivery of the school supplies more complex. After a quick breakfast of naan, fresh cream, and cherry jam with the men of the house, we drove the four-by-four along the road to the path that led down the hill to the bridge. As we unpacked the supplies and stacked them on the ground, various men gathered around to watch and help us unload. When the four-by-four was empty, the villagers stopped the young boys walking by on their way to school and had them help carry boxes. The young boys each took a small box, and the teachers and older boys took the heavier loads. We walked as a long procession down the steep path to the bridge.

The boys led the way across, and we walked up concrete stairs into an enclosed dirt courtyard at the foot of a mountain. I hung back as the boys went inside and took their seats in the classrooms, the courtyard briefly quiet. It was such a small gesture, giving school supplies. But if it meant these boys, who might have the chance and opportunity to go on to university, felt that others were valuing their education, then perhaps they would feel more valued in return and understand that an American woman cared whether or not they went to school. Or maybe they just thought, "Hey, you crazy infidel, thanks for nothing!" Hopefully, it was the former.

I knew some people might wonder why I would help a boys' school when my focus was on girls' and women's rights. This was a simple first step, a drop in the bucket, that could help the children at the school where Idi Mohammad and his brother worked. When I made this first step and then opened up a discussion of their views on girls' education and potential sites for future schools, they understood that my intention was sincere. I wanted to help the children of this area get an education. Educating boys often leads to more understanding of the value of education and can open the doors to educating girls. I continued to discuss land potentially available for a girls' school. Building a school was perhaps not necessary if we could find available rooms in the village. The real issue is that there simply aren't enough female teachers in Afghanistan. Doing a little bit to support the boys and visiting the school would give me more leverage to say, "The boys already have a school, teachers, and education through high school, but the girls have nothing right now." Both Idi Mohammad and his brother had girls—none of whom were in school. I wanted to ask them bluntly, "If you believe in education so much, then why aren't you working to get your girls in school? Why aren't you teaching them at home? Why are they worth less than your sons?" But I didn't. Instead I looked for a back door into that discussion.

Distributing the supplies was bizarre. I wanted to get photos and film a little so that I could show the images to donors back in the United States. But trying to get the teachers and administration to "do it for the camera" was hilarious. I hated having to do these things for the camera. It felt false, and I was sure they were wondering, "Why are we pretending to unpack the boxes here when we want to do it over there?" Though I'd like to do the work without fanfare and let the work speak for itself, I needed to document it to build support for Mountain2Mountain back home so that I could fund future projects. The video camera is a powerful tool to share stories and engage supporters.

Distributing the supplies in a second-grade room, I encountered a stern teacher in camo fatigues. He didn't smile or shake my hand when we greeted each other, and I wasn't sure what he thought of me or the situation. We were led to a fourth-grade class. As I began to distribute supplies with a couple of the teachers, the room quickly became chaotic, with notebooks, pens, and pencils being passed in all directions, one gruff teacher shouting at the boys. They looked dumbfounded, as if they were wondering what was going on. No one had made an introduction or an announcement to explain what we were doing there.

Down the hall, we visited a twelfth-year class with their English teacher. He was very interested in getting computers for the school. He'd studied in Pakistan and recently returned to Dashty Rewat. He stood at the front with me, and we talked to the boys. When I asked how many wanted to go on to university, all of them raised their hands. Most wanted to study to be doctors and engineers, but there was a journalist as well. I asked how many thought they would need to use computers to reach their career goals. All of them raised their hands, but when I asked how many had used a computer before, only one raised his hand.

After visiting several classrooms, I sat down to interview the head of the teachers, but the conversation was stilted, and I struggled to get answers from him. The English teacher was also there and replied to a few more questions. Sitting next to him was the Islamic teacher, who said nothing. He didn't smile and was impossible to read. Oh, the questions I had for him . . . but most of them were inappropriate for a first meeting and too deep for an informal discussion. I couldn't think of any questions for him that weren't controversial. During these trips to Afghanistan, I was often stepping into the shoes of a journalist. I was excited by the opportunity to have conversations with remote villagers, government officials, school teachers, members of Parliament, and prisoners, but I'm not a trained journalist. I'd prefer to have meandering conversations inspired by my curiousity about their lives, families, communities, and thoughts.

Outside, the students gathered in the courtyard to sing for us while the teacher in camo fatigues tried to bully them into some form of order. After they finished, I let a few of the older boys take turns riding my bike. They rode it around the courtyard, narrowly missing the younger boys, scattering them like bowling pins.

We said our good-byes and walked back across the bridge to the four-by-four. Idi Mohammad's youngest child was in the backseat. He'd been there since we started to unload more than an hour ago. He was sitting quietly, looking as if he'd been left there as a gift or a bodyguard. As we unloaded the boy and loaded up my bike, men gathered around to discuss the day's events thus far, and as if on cue, my future husband turned up to take us fishing.

Travis, Hamid, and I walked with our personal fishing guide through town, and went down a small path that led behind his house. We stopped in the patch of yard behind his house and watched him don green waders and matching rubber boots. He grabbed his weighted net and nodded at us with a mischievious smile. We followed him to the river just below his house. He had a large Afghan dog with pale blond fur and black markings on its face, and it followed us to the water's edge. I reached down to scratch his head. Our guide waded to the middle of the river and expertly threw his net. On the second throw, he aimed into the current and pulled the net back with a fish. He smiled triumphantly at us. He threw the fish onto the beach where a young man, maybe his son, picked it up and speared it on a stick. He caught six fish in about half an hour, and I was presented with them all strung up on the bendy stick, some of them still thrashing. I was unsure whether by accepting I would be accepting more than just the fish, but as no money had exchanged hands and I didn't see Travis and Hamid high-fiving or discussing vacation plans, I assumed that I was still a free and single woman.

We walked back to our house, and when the men saw the fish, they took them to the wives, who cleaned them and packed them in plastic for our journey to Kabul. I would have been happy to leave them there as a gift, but alas, they were returning with us in the four-by-four.

We stayed for lunch—not that we had a choice. It was already planned so we gratefully sat down and stretched out on toshaks. While we waited, we chatted aimlessly, and the men pulled out tins of naswar and shaped small balls that they then slipped into their mouths. Naswar is essentially snuff. The ball of powdered tobacco sits against your gums for a while and then gets spit out. Travis said it was like a really intense cigarette, and the men offered some to me. After checking that it was straight tobacco, not mixed with hashish or opium, I accepted.

Fardin handed me the tin, and Hamid used the lid to section out a small amount that he put into my hand. The technique is to use the forefinger and thumb of the other hand to squeeze the powder into a tiny ball and place it into the crease of the bottom lip. Hamid laughed as I tried, unsuccessfully, to make a ball like Fardin's. He poured a little more into my hand, and this time I squeezed it properly. I pulled my lip down and placed it where they showed me, and sat back. The men smiled and nodded, and Travis and Hamid were laughing. A slight burning began at my gumline then spread; my entire bottom jaw became somewhat numb. Travis told me about being given a large portion of naswar by a villager last year. It was so strong he had to run to the toilet and vomit—this coming from a man who smoked cigarettes and marijuana regularly. I laughed, then realized my head was spinning. I felt very mellow and a little sleepy. Hamid joked that we'd get home faster this way since I'd be sleeping in the car and we wouldn't have to stop to bike or take photos. I would have laughed out loud if my head wasn't so woozy.

After about five minutes, I discarded the little wad into the spittoon as directed and spat a few times. The naswar tasted awful, and I didn't want to swallow any.

I sat back. I was starting to break out in a cold sweat. I decided I should go to the outhouse. I stood up—a little wobbly—and immediately realized I needed to move quickly. I thrust my feet into my motorcycle boots and hurried to open the front door. Two big rocks were blocking it, and the children were all signaling that I should duck under the other door that led to the inner courtyard of the women's area to get to the outhouse. One handed me the pink roll of toilet paper, and they all followed. I felt the bile rising and was desperate to figure out which direction was the correct one, never having been this way in the daylight. I burped, the taste of bile in my mouth, but I controlled myself. I saw the outhouse and raced inside, barely having time to put the stone in place before I hurled into the hole.

Vomiting is unpleasant enough into a clean toilet. Vomiting into a hole with a mound of feces so high that my face was mere inches away took things to another level. I spat a few times, then slowly stood up. I steadied myself with a hand on the wall and looked out the open hole at the chickens wandering around the dirt courtyard. One of the little girls was chasing them with high-pitched squeals. I wished my head would stop swimming. I breathed deeply but immediately regretted it as the stench alone was enough to bring on another round of vomiting. I slid the rock out of the way with my foot and stepped down into the courtyard. The women and the children were all waiting to see how I was. They waved me over to the water pump so I could rinse my hands. I smiled weakly in gratitude, then splashed my face.

"*Tashakur, tashakur,*" I said, thanking them. Two of the wives came over to the water pump and started talking quickly. They were either miming eating, washing my face, or vomiting. I tried to keep up, but my head was still fuzzy, and I didn't have my little translator with me to fill in the gaps. I mumbled, "*Naswar?*" and they mimed

the mouth action again. I took it to mean vomiting. I nodded, and
they giggled, and I nodded some more, said *tashakur* one more time,
and turned to leave.

As I walked slowly back, I wished I could just find a quiet corner
and sit down for a few minutes alone. The emotions and experiences were swirling around. The constant yin-yanging of fear and
exhilaration was playing havoc with my emotions. The constant
questioning and the feeling of being a specimen under a microscope,
being examined and judged, was more overwhelming than I had anticipated. I just wanted a little space to get grounded and absorb
everything that was happening. I was experiencing Afghanistan in a
way few get a chance to, and it was opening up so much. I wanted to
do so much, but the learning curve was still wickedly steep—much
like the mountains I tried to conquer on my bike.

As I explored rural Afghanistan, the bike was proving to be a
valuable tool. I'd wanted to engage here in unique ways. I wanted to
share the beauty of the land and its people back home. But more
than that, the bike had become an icebreaker among the Afghans I
met in ways I could never have imagined. The idea that I could ride a
bike—something that symbolizes personal freedom and mobility—
in a place known for war and oppression was amazing. It was even
more amazing that I could challenge this particular gender barrier
as a foreign woman. I was struggling to reconcile that joy with the
knowledge that the women here were still confined to the back part
of the home and couldn't leave without wearing a burqa.

I took a deep breath to steady myself and reminded myself that
each step brought me a little closer to understanding what I wanted
to do here.

I entered the room where the men were all still seated, feeling
sheepish, and sat back down.

Just in time for lunch.

2

Genesis

A week later I was back home, cuddling on the couch with my daughter, Devon, while we watched *Ratatouille*, a movie about a rat who dreams of being a chef in Paris. Of the children's movies we had, it was one of my favorites. I was struggling to keep my eyes open. Jet lag made it hard to stay awake past 6:00 P.M., so we were curled up on the couch under a blanket, and I dozed with my arms around her, her hair smelling sweetly of her sweat from a day of playing outside. I was exhausted but happy. Devon didn't mind I had fallen asleep. When it was over, she turned her face up and kissed my cheek, and I squeezed her. I was so tired.

"Okay, chica. Let's get you to bed. And me. Go brush your teeth, okay?"

"Okay, mommy," she replied, kissed me again on the nose, and crab-walked down the hall. I listened for the sound of running water to signal she was actually brushing her teeth. Feeling like a zombie,

I sat up and stared numbly into space as I waited for her return. A few minutes later she came back and crawled onto my lap.

"Come on, Mommy!"

"Okay, I'm up. I'm up." I laughed. She slid down and grabbed my hand pretending to help me stand up. Then she reached up and I held out my arms in prep for her to jump up. I carried her to bed, luckily only a few feet away from the living room.

"You're heavy!" I groaned, half serious.

She giggled.

"What did you eat while I was away?" I joked, and she giggled more.

"Cheese!"

"Shocker. No wonder you're heavy. You must have eaten fifty pounds of cheese. I think you got taller, too. Did Daddy stretch you out each night?"

"Yup!"

I hugged her close as I staggered into her room, and then I laid her down heavily on her bed with a bounce, and she dove under her turquoise fleece blanket.

I sat on the edge of her bed, and her head popped back up from underneath her blanket. She sat up for a big hug, and as I squeezed her, I said, "I love you, chica."

"I love you more," she replied, squeezing me hard and pulling me on top of her.

"Nope, not possible. I'm bigger. Therefore, I have more room to love you with." I squeezed her hard and then sat up and smiled tiredly, loving our nightly tuck-in banter.

"I love *you* more because I'm smaller." I laughed. You can't argue logic with a five-year-old.

"*You* are awesome. Good night, sweetie. Sleep tight." I stood up to leave and kissed her on the forehead. "See you in the morning. Okay?"

"Okay. Good night, Mommy."

"Sweet dreams, princess," I said as I shut the door.

I walked to my room two doors down the hallway and crawled, fully clothed, into bed and pulled the down duvet over me, closing my eyes with a sigh as exhaustion overwhelmed me. I took the contact lenses out of my eyes and flicked them to the floor. Ten seconds later, I was out cold.

The two ends of the spectrum in my world are extreme. Mountain biking and activism in Afghanistan and being a single mother in Breckenridge, Colorado. I didn't set out to build a life around extremes or seemingly divergent paths, but when you allow life to unfold, it has a flow that invites you in. Soon you find yourself living day by day in ways that from the outside seem insane but to you feel as normal as a nine-to-five and a white picket fence do to other people.

I didn't always want to work in Afghanistan, though. Originally, I wanted to be a modern dancer. So determined was I to pursue this path that I didn't even bother taking the SAT or ACT. I'd filled out applications to colleges with strong dance programs, but I didn't send them in. I knew that wasn't for me. I saw my life, and it didn't involve me living in a college dorm. I couldn't explain why, but I knew that going to college wasn't my first step. During my senior year in high school, I auditioned for a placement as an apprentice at Zenon Dance Company in Minneapolis. I got a spot and applied for a job at the Gap in the downtown. Three months later, I was living in a studio apartment in a brownstone just off Nicollet Avenue, while everyone else I knew was starting their freshman orientations.

I had no idea that fourteen years later I would have given up dancing, lived in Europe for ten years, worked as an outdoor guide, become a sports trainer, had a daughter, married and divorced, raced mountain bikes, started my own nonprofit, and begun to work and travel throughout Afghanistan. Years filled with mistakes, triumphs, fuck-ups, and victories, heartache, heartbreak, love, and laughs, and joy. Life reveals itself in fascinating ways when you let it do its thing.

It was Thanksgiving week in 2006, and I was visiting my parents in Bismarck, North Dakota, with my soon-to-be ex-husband, Pete, and nearly two-year-old Devon. Sitting in the living room of my childhood, I announced to family and childhood friends that I was starting a nonprofit organization, and I was naming it Mountain2Mountain. Its first baby step was to raise money for the Central Asia Institute, a nonprofit organization founded by Greg Mortenson that focused on education for girls as a way to facilitate peace in Afghanistan and Pakistan. I had read his book *Three Cups of Tea*. Intrigued by the cover—a photograph of three young girls in head scarves reading books—I'd bought the hardcover on a whim from my local bookstore and finished it in a few days. Soon after that I read John Wood's *Leaving Microsoft to Change the World*, and Rory Stewart's *The Places in Between*. I was inspired by the willingness of these men to experience countries many choose to avoid and to focus their lives on helping them. But more than that, I was struck by the perspective of men working for women's rights, and until I read *The Blue Sweater* by Jacqueline Novogratz, I was struck by the lack of female voices.

This was before Nicholas Kristof's *Half the Sky*, before organizations such as Girl Up, UN Women, and the Girl Effect. The idea that investing in the education of women and girls was not only the right thing morally and a human rights issue, but that it could also lead to greater overall community viability and stability, was not yet so widespread. Investing in women and girls as the key to economic growth and peace was not being looked at seriously by the mainstream public or media.

Something sparked, and almost overnight I was discussing the idea of raising money to help an organization whose work inspired me. It could be my first step while I figured out how far I wanted to travel down the rabbit hole I was looking into. Could I rally my own mountain community to care about building a school for girls in rural Pakistan? Could one mountain community come together to support another half the world away? This wasn't Nepal where many Coloradans travel to climb and explore. This was a country known for terrorism, not tourism.

Yet, rally the community did, and quickly. During a seven-month period, we put on two events, an author event with Greg Mortenson attended by more than six hundred people, and a trail running race I dubbed Race for the Mountains. I had no event planning experience but did have the ability to envision and put together an event. Thanks to the logistical skills of my friend, Tara Kusumoto, and the support of the Breckenridge community, we raised over $105,000 for Central Asia Institute to build two schools for girls in Pakistan. I was overjoyed, encouraged, and motivated.

I immediately leaped into another partnership with an organization that worked in Nepal and India, hoping to replicate what had been accomplished in the first attempt. But those seven months I'd spent fund-raising for CAI—coupled with continuing to run my own business, a Pilates and wellness center, raising a toddler, and moving out of my home as I started the process of divorcing Pete— had left me severely burnt out. My efforts and my energy stalled, and we raised $20,000 for the organization—nothing to sneeze at, but their expectations were that we could at least match the effort I'd made for Central Asia Institute, and they were disappointed and frustrated. They were not willing to recognize that Mortenson's then rocketing star power, book sales, and compelling story were a huge factor in the success of the initial fund-raising initiative.

My energy and creativity in the tank, I found refuge on a mountain bike. For years, I'd been a runner. I'd started running in Germany around the same time I began working as a sports trainer and outdoor guide, and soon I started racing to see what I was capable of. I'd gotten the idea that I wanted to run a half marathon, and thanks to the network of forest trails in the Odenwald, only a few minutes of jogging from my apartment in central Darmstadt, I quickly built up mileage and speed. My first half marathon was in Trier, a beautiful German town with cobblestone streets and stunning architecture. My second half of the race was faster than my first, and I finished close to my goal of 1:30, with 1:33. I was energized and euphoric, hooked on running, if not racing. I did half marathons, 10k, and local 5k races—mostly to push myself further and as a way to see nearby towns and villages differently. But it was my evening runs, surrounded by the forest's beauty, that fueled my spirit and gave me a sense of peace. Running stuck with me when I moved to the mountains of Colorado, and I took to the trails as a way to lose myself in the mountains and in myself. I learned to embrace the pain that came with the uphills and the altitude.

Running was put temporarily on hold when I showed up for my first pregnancy doctor's appointment on crutches. I'd twisted my ankle running with Pete on the trail behind our house earlier that morning. My doctor asked me to stop trail running but said that I could continue on the road if I wore a heart rate monitor.

"Have you used a heart rate monitor before?"

"Yes," I replied. "I'm a sports trainer, but I've never used one on myself."

"Okay, well, you'll need to wear one for any physical activity. Running, hiking, etc. I'd prefer you don't bike, but that's entirely your call. Essentially, I'd like you to work out with sports that don't elevate your potential to fall and hurt yourself or the baby."

"Okay, got it."

He looked at me, holding my gaze. "I'm serious about the heart rate monitor. The higher your heart rate, the higher your internal core temperature rises. Let me put it simply: you don't want to cook your baby."

"No microwaving my baby. Got it." This put a whole other spin on "bun in the oven."

I tried to road run for the first month or so, but it was just too hard to keep my heart rate down to the acceptable non-baby-cooking level. So I starting hiking every day with our dog Bergen, a German shepherd–chow mix we had gotten two years earlier from the pound.

After I had Devon, I quickly regained strength and speed thanks to the resistance training that jog strollers, bike trailers, and nordic sleds provide. I raced on dirt trails in the summer and on snowshoes in the winter. I did well. I podiumed often and won occasionally. Running made me feel strong, and I loved the challenge of going longer, farther, faster, as well as the seemingly endless options for trails in Breckenridge. But I didn't realize that running was also a means of escape. Lately, it was an escape from marriage. Never an early morning riser, I found myself getting up early to run, which eliminated the chance of morning intimacy. Looking back, I realize that it allowed me to escape all sorts of things: monotony, weakness, fear, and my past.

Then I was challenged to ride a single-speed bike. Brent approached me after a late-season snowshoe race in Frisco. We'd both finished at the head of the pack, and he asked if I wanted to ride bikes sometime. I was in the chaos of the Mountain2Mountain fund-raisers, and I was leaving Pete, but we stayed in touch. After my two fund-raising events were done for Central Asia Institute, I took him up on the offer to ride. I needed a challenge and a distraction from the chaos in my life, and I wanted to try something new.

So in June 2007, I drove up to Boulder, and Brent loaded two DEAN custom titanium single-speeds and we headed to Hall Ranch in Lyons. A little apprehensively, I mounted the 29er frame and clipped in. I had grown up riding bikes around the neighborhood, and in Europe I rode a bike for commuting and for weekend rides along the forest trails in Germany and France. But mountain biking, particularly mountain biking in Colorado, is something altogether different. The trail was narrow and winding, carved into a hill scattered with clusters of boulders and stones called rock gardens. Here was a new kind of riding that was a world away from the wide, dirt-packed forest trails I'd ridden with friends throughout Germany and France. It was more akin to riding through a trail of sharp objects determined to draw my blood. The only bike I owned was a heavy Cannondale, with grip shifts, that cost me $350 new in Garmisch, Germany. It was perfectly suited for forest trails and rides to beer gardens, but not for steep inclines and rock gardens that begged for a lighter, more agile ride, and an altitude that begged for bigger lungs.

It took me at least thirty minutes to get up the front side of Hall Ranch through its infamous rock garden of boulders and puzzle-like rock formation "problems" that riders better than I tried to "solve" in an attempt to get through without dismounting. My right shoe didn't release smoothly from the clipless pedals and more than once I found myself fighting and failing to unclip fast enough to put my foot down, leading to many bruises, some blood, and a few cactus needles embedded in various parts of my body. Not to mention having to dismount every few yards to hike, lift, or crawl over massive boulders or around tight switchbacks. I finally got to the top, exhausted but smiling at the challenge. Brent was sitting on a park bench, helmet off. He'd obviously been there awhile. I rode over, red-faced and panting. My helmet was slightly askew as I hadn't tightened it enough. I took it off and fully expected steam to release from my head. I drank water, assessed the congealed blood on my knees and shin, pulled out a cactus needle, and wondered aloud if I had much more of this ahead. I felt more than a little embarrassed, but I wasn't defeated; I was determined for more. This was definitely not like the forest roads in Germany.

"You did remember that this is the first time I've ridden a single-speed when you picked this trail, right?" I asked in between gulps of water.

"Yes. But my car has been at the mechanic's for the past couple of weeks, and I've been itching to ride out here. Since you had a car that could carry the bikes, I figured I'd seize the opportunity."

"And, you didn't think this would be a little over my head?" I was slightly incredulous at his reasoning. It was akin to taking your non-skier friend (whose car you needed to get to the slopes) to the top of a double–black diamond run, and telling him to just point his skis downward.

"You seemed tough enough to handle it."

"Yeah, whatever. Fine. Are you ready to roll yet?" I joked.

Brent glanced at me. "You sure you want to continue?"

Indignant, I replied, "Are you kidding me? Yeah, I'm sure. I didn't come here for a thirty-minute ride. Hike. Whatever."

"Okay then, tough girl. Well, that was the tough part. This section is smoother, and you can probably stay on your bike."

"That's a novel idea, a bike ride where I actually ride my bike," I replied, and punched him in the arm.

"Just follow me, smart-ass. You should be good at this section. You're built like a hill climber, and you've got the lungs from running."

I took a deep breath. "Okay, let's do it." I put my helmet back on, and Brent looked over at me.

"What are you, twelve? This thing is huge on you!" He tightened it up the best he could.

"Yeah, yeah, yeah." I brushed him off. "Let's go."

Ten minutes later, I was still on his wheel, keeping up with his pace, and starting to climb. He was right: *this* I was good at. I sat until I couldn't push the pedals smoothly, and then I stood, and it wasn't that different from running. The simplicity of a single-speed appealed to my running nature. I could concentrate on pushing my body hard to climb the hills, and when small rock piles emerged, I didn't have to think about what gear to use. I just rode my bike. I was in love.

We stopped briefly for me to catch my breath at a little bench, at the start of a short loop that would take us to the top of the hill. The climb was harder, and it was now hot as hell, but if I pushed myself, I could keep Brent in my sight. We started to head back down to the car. Brent had a surprise for me.

"Let's go down the backside. You'll like it more than trying to get down the rock garden."

"There's a backside?"

"Yeah, it's pretty fun. Rolling switchbacks."

"You mean we could have come up a different way?"

"Yeah, but my grandmother rides the rock garden. In her wheelchair. So I figured you could, too."

"Fuck off." I shook my head, trying not to laugh.

He was right again. It was tough to negotiate the switchback turns as my bike-handling skills were less than stellar, but the roller-coaster swoops and turns were smooth, rideable, and fun as hell. When we hit the pavement to ride back to the car through the town of Lyons, I was chattering away nonstop about building up my own bike, the wind rushing in my ears.

Two weeks later, I found myself purchasing a tangerine Niner 29er single-speed frame at the Golden Bike Shop. Brent had written out a list of parts I needed to build it up. Instead of purchasing a fully assembled bike with stock parts, I would assemble it myself, which would allow me to get better-quality parts that suited the style of riding I was doing—things such as a seat post, lighter wheels, stronger brakes, a front suspension fork, and handlebars were self-explanatory. But the list was also full of things less obvious: bottom bracket, stem, spacers, and seat clamp. I didn't even consider gears; the simplicity and the challenge of the single-speed fit me like a glove. I couldn't imagine riding anything else. Little did I realize what an important role the bike would play in my life and how it was a metaphor for everything that was changing.

I spent that summer riding trails in Boulder and Breckenridge, building my stamina and my confidence. Beyond the physical challenge, I loved the mental reprieve. Unlike running, where my mind could wander, mountain biking required my full concentration. The mental attention each ride demanded allowed my brain to rest. I felt sparks of creativity punch through my burnout. The strength and confidence I felt building in my body allowed me to continue down the path I'd started on. But my path often felt so empty that I often wondered if I'd ever see anyone else on it.

In my typical "all or nothing" approach to life, two months after my first ride, I entered my very first mountain bike race at Winter Park, the Tipperary Creek race. Thirty-three miles of cross-country racing over single-track and steep fire roads. Lining up at the start, I was petrified. What had I gotten into? I had a better-fitting helmet now, and mountain biking baggies over my chamois, and a camelback. I looked like a mountain biker. Actually, I looked like a single-speeder. Instead of matching lycra jersey and shorts, covered in sponsors, like most racers were wearing, I wore skull-and-crossbone black knee-high socks and a bright purple top. Even the male single-speeders look different than the other racers. Instead of a race jersey, some had mechanic's shirts on. Brent was wearing pink, striped knee-highs and a Tinkerbell T-shirt, insisting that pink was the new black. I was petrified with all the riders in lycra surrounding me. I didn't want to be "that girl," the one that held up better, faster riders, or be stuck behind a slow train of granny gears. I didn't want to crash. I didn't want to make a fool of myself.

I looked around the lineup. Single-speed women lined up with the semi-pro and expert women. I looked down at their bikes to see how many were single-speeders. I saw one, then another, the knee-highs giving many of them away. Two minutes later it became obvious: the long hill climb separated the geared semi-pro and expert women and our small clump of single-speeders. The other girls took the time to say hi as we climbed, since they knew one another from previous races. Once we hit the trail, two of us separated from the rest, and we found ourselves in a friendly game of cat and mouse. She was a fast and competent downhiller, but I was a stronger climber. Riders passed me, and I passed riders, to a constant theme of "Hey single-speed, go get 'em," "Hey Niner, nice work." The welcome camaraderie on the trail kept a smile on my dirt-covered face and made me feel part of the community of riders. By the time we were on one of the last fire road climbs, I was nearing my redline—there was nothing left in the tank. I got off my bike and hiked, alongside many others who were also defeated by the long procession of steep climbs. I found I could hike it up pretty fast and catch my breath. At the moment I was in front. What if I could just stay in front for the upcoming descent?

Coming across the finish line, I was elated, and my front wheel was rattling. . . . Apparently, my skewer was coming loose. I may have come in first, but I was chided by Brent to remember to check rattles so that I didn't end up a bloody heap on the side of the trail when my front wheel flew off.

I kept pushing my own boundaries and conquering my fear on the trail into the fall, with my first trip to Moab, Utah. The trip was an example of the strength and determination I had to "not be a girl" and be tough as nails. I drove out with a group of guys, all strong riders who invited me to join for a one-day ride of the White Rim, a hundred-plus-mile trail inside the Canyonlands National Park. The trip started with a stopover in Fruita to ride Mary's Loop/Horsethief, a trail that has become my go-to ride to and from Moab every spring and fall—a trail that makes me smile from the moment I start climbing the rock at the trailhead to the dirt road traverse back to the car at the end. It's a trail that has taken more than its fair share of blood, my first flat tire, and hamburgered my entire forearm on a descent. A few hours later I found myself on my first "double" as we added in a second ride of the day—a seemingly endless sufferfest in Moab on the Golden Spike jeep trail, with deep sand and endless climbing on a wide slab of slickrock that led to the top of the cliffs high above town. Day two, we rode Amasa Back, another trail that is now a go-to ride that I've never skipped on a Moab trip. Instead of an afternoon ride, we rested our legs while packing and shopping for supplies. Day three was the one-day unsupported ride of White Rim: more than a hundred miles of slickrock, single-track, and dirt climbs with no potable water. Looking up the description for the trail before I left, I found this online: most riders spend three or four days to ride this trail, spending the night at campgrounds. (Two days = Monster. One day = Lunatic.)

Great, I thought, *that's fitting.*

In the end, it was the most-challenging three days of desert riding I could have imagined, in an otherworldy terrain unlike anything I'd ever seen—striated rock formations that looked like the movie set for a science fiction movie. Throughout the four epic rides, I emerged relatively blood-free despite descending rock gardens and drops I had no business attempting, but being the only girl in a group of guys, I wasn't going to let inexperience dictate my choices. Thanks to the strength and skills I'd built during a summer of intense single-speed riding, I was always near the front of the group. I was hooked. The bike was my new love and possibly my sanity.

The following spring I was still feeling the full effects of a mental and physical burnout from my fund-raising efforts for the second nonprofit I'd been supporting, the one that worked in Nepal. Against my better judgment, I'd agreed to do a fund-raiser for it only weeks after wrapping up the two fund-raisers that I'd spent six months creating for Central Asia Institute. I was running on adrenaline and passion, with no foundation underneath me to support my energy, and no amount of biking was going to offset the emotional drain. My work may have stalled there, and I would have gone back to full-time sports training and Pilates had it not been for a fortunate cup of coffee in Breckenridge that I had with one of CAI's staff members, Christiane Leitinger, a few months earlier. Christiane had driven to Breckenridge to meet and discuss the author event I was creating as a fund-raiser. She was the director for the Pennies for Peace program that engaged students and schools in a service learning program that benefitted CAI's programming in Pakistan and Afghanistan. She was also the only staff member who wasn't in Bozeman. She lived nearby in Evergreen, Colorado, and wanted to discuss the event and how to maximize the community's involvement so that it would be a success.

My friend Tara and I met her at Cool River Café in Breckenridge. Christiane arrived in a cobalt blue Patagonia puffy jacket that matched her large blue eyes. Her long brown hair was pulled back in a ponytail, and she had a graceful look illuminated by the lack of makeup, her bone structure much like that of a ballerina. She pulled out her laptop and began to discuss what we were planning and how she and CAI could help. Throughout the next seven months, she checked in periodically, and she was at the event itself to handle the two book signings we'd planned for Mortenson as well as his schedule, which was starting to become chaotic.

Months later, we met for coffee as friends, and when Mortenson was speaking at Colorado University's Mackey Auditorium, Christiane invited Tara and me to come. Short on volunteers for an event in Evergreen, she asked if I could help out. Her thin frame seemed even thinner than before, and after a late-night event, she was supposed to drive to Telluride with her two girls the next day to speak at two schools. I asked if there was anything I could do to help her.

She looked at me, her blue eyes tired, and said, "Any chance you could drive me to Telluride in the morning? I am not sure I should be driving."

I paused, looked at her, and found myself wanting to help her and take something off her plate.

"I have to pick up Devon, but if your girls and Devon can get along in the backseat for five hours, I think we could make that happen." I was half kidding, half serious. I had very few female friends, none with children, and never arranged play dates.

Christiane's eyes lit up. "Really? Do you think you could?" Her husband, Charley, came over ten minutes later and gave me a huge hug—the type of hug that I learned to love and appreciate in the years that followed, the kind that makes you feel like you are family. "Thank you for helping out Christiane. You have no idea how worried I was about her making the drive."

I smiled, slightly embarrassed. "It's the least I can do, she seems so tired, and I have the weekend free. I'd love to help."

We made plans. I drove back to Breckenridge, and the next morning I picked up Devon from Pete at my old house. I met Christiane and her two girls, Isabel and Eva Sophia, in Frisco to combine cars. For five-plus hours, we talked like old friends while the girls read to one another and played games in the backseat. We spent two nights in Telluride and turned around. It was during the drive home that the lightbulb flickered.

I'd been telling Christiane about my frustration with the organization I was fund-raising for. I'd created a photography exhibition that I'd named *Views of the Himalaya*. The exhibit was a collaboration of world-renowned photographers famous for their work and insight into this region of the world from varying perspectives. Among them, Nevada Wier, Beth Wald, Jimmy Chin, and even the trust that managed the late Galen Rowell's photography contributed images to create an exhibition that could serve to inspire and educate viewers. I'd reached out to the photographers involved to ask for a contribution of images, and local photographer Kate Lapides had offered to advise with the printing and framing—something I knew next to nothing about.

I was beyond thrilled with how the exhibition had developed, and I loved using photography to tell the story of the region we were fund-raising for. Beyond the exhibition itself, I'd created a book online to complement the exhibit with its photos and an artist statement from everyone involved. Yet the founder of the organization I was working to support was more focused on the dollars used to support effective programs, not the vision of storytelling. Understandably, this is the norm; the end goal is money in most organizations, as more money equals more projects and growth. I felt frustrated at every conversation and just wanted to get through the events we'd committed to and move on. My heart wasn't in it.

All of a sudden, Christiane spoke up. "There's a silver lining here, don't you think?"

I looked at her incredulously. "Oh, yeah?" I smiled. "Do tell."

"Well, you know what you don't want to do now. You realize what you don't want to be. That's almost as important as realizing what you *do* want to do because it's more specific."

"Yeah, I don't want to be *that* guy. I don't want to be focused on the 'sale.' I want to be focused on the stories, the connection, the change of perspectives. I think I'm more passionate about the shift of perspectives that can create a bigger ripple than I am about a traditional sticks-and-bricks approach."

"No, you're right. And you know that you want to be creative in how you engage people."

"Yeah, it's weird. It's like I want to connect the people here to the people I want to work with over there in a visceral way. I want them to be inspired to get involved. I don't want to just raise money. I'm sure a fancy event with thousand-dollar-plate dinners would be more effective at that, but I'd blow my brains out. That sounds boring and staid. If I am choosing to do this, I'm going to do it my way. Otherwise, why bother?"

I was getting riled up. "Why can't I work in ways that inspire change, that inspire communities, and do good work? I mean, there are a gazillion organizations much larger than me that can focus on the big stuff. Why can't I focus on ways that engage people and communities—that challenge stereotypes and perception? Engaging people and inspiring individuals could create a bigger ripple effect than just writing a check."

"Exactly," Christiane said with a big smile. "*That's* exactly it. You see the power in storytelling as a way to connect people to a cause. So do *that*. Do what matters to you. If you are going to put your drop in the bucket, make it yours."

I watched the white lines go past as we continued to drive back to Breckenridge. The rabbit hole was opening up wider, and I saw myself diving in headfirst.

Back home, I mulled over all that we'd talked about: starting my own nonprofit, rallying the masses to care, working for girls and women in conflict zones *as* a woman, sharing their stories in unique ways, connecting communities and cultures.

Throughout the months and years that followed, Christiane became my soul sister, the big sister I never had. An advisor, a confidante, and family. The single best thing that came out of my initial decision to raise money for Central Asia Institute was the friendship that was forged with her and her family. Her friendship would allow me to tap into a sisterhood of amazing women and open up my deeply buried vulnerability to my own sister and daughter. This would change my life profoundly, in a myriad of subtle ways.

And I rode my bike. A lot.

3

Inshallah

Afghanistan 2008

I looked over at Tony sitting beside me and then back out the window again. The airplane was losing elevation and the gridwork of mud walls below revealed themselves through the haze of thin clouds. The expanse of jagged peaks we'd been passing over retreated, and one snakelike road led across the mud-colored grid toward square patches of green. The first color I'd seen since we left Dubai. It was not until we were practically skimming the rooftops of single-story houses that colors emerged below in turquoise blue, red, green, and yellow, and began to take shape as fences, gates, shops, and cars.

I tugged at my scarlet head scarf, feeling as though the silk covering my hair was less a sign of modesty and more like the *A* the heroine was forced to wear in *The Scarlet Letter*. Rather than helping me blend in, it felt like a harlot's cry for attention. I craned my neck to look at the other two foreign women on the plane. One wore black, the other white. Damn. I pulled the front of the scarf farther down my forehead, as if I could crawl inside.

The photographer and friend, Tony Di Zinno, was with me for my first trip. This was 2008, one year before I would become the first woman to mountain bike in Afghanistan. He'd joined me to document the journey and bring back images that could help rally support for our yet-to-be-determined projects. Tony was a sensitive soul with an eye for seeing things and the ability to capture them through his lens. We'd been friends for a few years, and the ease with which he traveled the world, his excitement and pride in what I was setting out to do, and his desire to see Afghanistan firsthand, made it a no-brainer to bring him along. In addition to being my documenter, Tony would be my shadow and companion for this foray. The fact that he was a large, bearlike man of Irish-Italian descent didn't hurt. After a couple of weeks without shaving, he blended in so well that most Afghans assumed he was Turkish. I had my own personal Mafioso strongman watching my back, albeit a nonviolent, Buddhism-practicing one.

The plane touched down, and as soon as the brakes kicked in, seat belts were being unclipped. Turbaned men were standing and opening overhead bins, the plane still speeding down the runway. Chatter erupted around us as cell phones were pulled out of pockets and bags. By the time the plane came to a stop, the aisle was blocked with men and bags. I wouldn't have been surprised if a goat or two jumped out of the overhead bins.

We'd arrived from Dubai, and the juxtaposition of wealth and poverty had never felt so extreme to me as it did between the two terminals. Arriving on Emirates into the fabulously ostentatious Terminal 3 was like entering the Las Vegas of the Arab world, minus the tassels. We collected our luggage and spent an hour trying to find out where our connecting flight was departing. We got at least three different suggestions from airport information staff. No one seemed to have heard of our connecting airline, Kam Air. We left the glitz and glamour of Terminal 3, and when the sliding glass doors opened to let us outside, the heat and humidity slammed into us. We took the shuttle to Terminal 1—the international terminal on the other side. It was 8:00 P.M. and well over ninety-five degrees.

After wandering around Terminal 1, I asked at the information desk out of where Kam Air was flying. I was then finally directed to the third and final terminal—Terminal 2—which was surprisingly a substantial cab drive away. Why isn't it just called a separate airport with a different name? Why doesn't anyone know how to give us directions? This is insane. Calling it Terminal 2 implies it lies somewhere between Terminal 1 and 3. With a sigh, I changed some money into Dirhams, and we climbed into a cab for a twenty-minute drive through Dubai at night to the terminal that time forgot.

A more dreary and empty airport terminal I'd never seen. Far from the hustle and bustle of Dubai's other terminals, this one seemed like a different country: one barren corridor, a bathroom, an information counter, and no food or drink to speak of, as the lone newsstand was closed at this hour. We settled in for the ten-hour layover. As far as I could tell, I was the only female, and Tony and I were among three Westerners crowded around an ancient television mounted on the wall that by some miracle was broadcasting the U.S. election results as they came in on BBC World. The entire world was watching, it seemed, to see if Barack Obama would become the next president of the United States. As the election results trickled in, the departure gates opened and we were allowed to go through security and check-in. I looked up at the departure list on the screens above us and laughed. It was the departure list to hell: Baghdad, Kabul, Kandahar, Kuwait, Fallujah. As we joined the crowd queuing to board, mostly Afghans, mostly men, I felt my excitement building.

We emerged from the airport in Kabul with our bags in hand and no idea of where to go next. We followed the crowd that was walking across a deserted parking lot toward a gate. I kept my head down so the head scarf wouldn't slide back, my hands constantly checking it. We went through the narrow doorway and saw in the crowd a small man with thick glasses holding a sign with my name on it. Najibullah—my fixer, translator, and guide for this visit. "Good morning, Shannon. You are most welcome to Kabul. Your new president is Barack Obama," he informed me with a smile. I sighed with relief, knowing that from here on out, I was in his hands.

Our guesthouse was in a remote area of town, run by the NGO Afghans 4 Tomorrow. It was accessible only after going through a double barricaded checkpoint on either end of the street. The guards recognized Najibullah and waved us on. Our driver, Shah Mohammad, the same one who would nearly drive myself, Travis, and Hamid off a cliff a year later, slowly maneuvered the white Corolla through. Inside, we were greeted by the severe face of the housekeeper, a man dressed all in black. The stone floors echoed as we made our way through to our rooms and were told that there was only one other guest. We dropped our bags, then followed Najibullah outside.

Najibullah walked us to the breakfast room, a separate structure at the back of the courtyard. We sat down to discuss our plans and goals for the weeks ahead over a pot of green tea.

Shah Mohammad, Najibullah told us, was an ex-military commander. Ironically, he'd been in the transportation department, but it took the help of Najibullah's guidance and directions to steer be-

tween buses and around donkey carts and pedestrians in the complete and utter chaos of the Kabul streets. It was a free-for-all in
every direction, people crossing between cars and buses that came
at each as if in a high-speed game of chicken. Drivers didn't yield to
anyone: human, donkey, bicycle, tank, or bus. Yet the littlest car
would confidently pull in front of oncoming vehicles, the wrong
way, calmly beep his horn, and somehow melt into the multiple
lanes of traffic.

What I hadn't expected when I arrived was the city's deteriorated infrastructure—one hundred times worse than what I'd seen
living in Beirut. Buildings were gutted and crumbling, without
rooms, windows, or complete walls, often with people and businesses
still occupying them in some fashion. There was only one paved
road we'd been on thus far, the newly fixed one from the airport; the
rest required off-road driving skills. This was six years after the
Taliban had been pushed out. If this was the capital city, where
most of the money was concentrated and most of the reconstruction
was focused, what did the rest of the country look like?

Everything in Afghanistan is done on the streets. Need to
change money? There's a guy at a roundabout that changes my $200
dollars into the local currency, Afghanis, or Afs—not to be confused with Afghans as a people. Afghani—money; Afghans—
people. The rate was fifty-one to one which reminded me of working
in currencies like Lebanese pounds that required more head space
when I switched back and forth. You can use U.S. dollars or Afs to
pay for things, and you may get either back in return, or a combination of the two, depending on the establishment. Currencies are like
the New York Times crossword puzzle—a frustrating but effective
brain exercise to stave off Alzheimer's.

Need to buy a phone card for the cell phone? There's a guy on
the side of the road at a busy intersection with whichever phone

card you need: Rohsan, Etisalat, or MTN. The markets are street-side. Carts with apples, bananas, nuts, fresh-squeezed lemonade, balloons and children's toys, scarves, construction materials, and pretty much anything else you could need are set up each morning inches from the traffic.

It was quickly apparent that Najibullah was well connected and that any meeting I requested was possible, from school tours to visits with members of Parliament. I made a mental note to send photographer Beth Wald a thank-you. Beth had worked with Najibullah several times and generously shared Najibullah's information with me when I met with her for coffee to discuss my upcoming plans for Afghanistan. Najibullah also offered great advice and direction, but he did lean to the conservative side with security, to the point that I got a little claustrophobic at times.

We quickly settled into a routine. Each morning I returned to consciousness with the local Imam's call to prayer through the loudspeakers of the neighborhood mosque. His warbling voice was a cultural alarm clock that put a smile on my face despite the predawn hour. I grabbed my contacts and pulled a blanket off the bed to wrap around me in the drafty, cold room. I turned on my computer and sat in the dark, checking e-mails and writing thoughts and observations from the previous day.

After a chilly shower to remove the previous days' Kabul dust, I greeted TLC and grabbed breakfast in an outbuilding across the courtyard. I'd dubbed our guesthouses's resident puppy TLC, "Tastes Like Chicken." He was sweet and needed TLC, but I held a suspicion that our cold-hearted housekeeper was tolerating him only to fatten him up for a cold winter night's feast.

Breakfast was a crapshoot. The first day it included naan bread, spreadable cheese, jams, peanut butter, and, if we asked, runny eggs.

Day by day, it became scarcer and more unusual. The naan was always there, but the cheese varied and then disappeared, and once jars of jam or peanut butter were finished, they weren't replaced. The only constant was the giant thermos of green tea. The cook and the guesthouse manager didn't communicate well, it seemed, so if things ran out, everyone waited for someone else to replace them. Pretty soon we were down to naan and the occasional runny eggs.

TLC typically followed us back to the guesthouse where we shut down computers and grabbed our stuff in time for Najibullah to ring the bell. Greetings were passed back and forth in Dari, each day getting a little smoother. We loaded bags and camera gear into the back of Shah Mohammad's car and then it was time for round two of endless Dari greetings. Shah Mohammad liked to mix it up, which kept us on our toes for the rapid-fire greetings and replies that were issued in quick succession. *Salaam Alekum, Hubisti, Chitoristi, Jonnyjuras, Tashakur.* He grinned when he threw in a new phrase or simply changed up the order to see our furrowed brows as we concentrated to keep up and respond appropriately.

The days varied in purpose and activity, but not in the nonstop pace. From the moment we hit the road, eyes and ears were trained on the scenes that unfolded before us. Najibullah pointed out landmarks and let us know the current Afghan news on the radio. Many mornings we were discussing the latest attack in the southern provinces, a kidnapping at the school around the corner from our guesthouse, or a recent foiled bombing attempt. I hardly missed my morning coffee, but the adrenaline shot Najibullah delivered was more effective than any espresso shot.

One morning we heard that a group of girls were attacked walking to school in Kandahar. Eleven girls and four teachers were splashed with acid by three men on motorcycles. Months before the attack, there had been posters placed around local mosques stating,

"Don't Let Your Daughters Go to School." My thoughts immediately went to Devon. What would I do if my daughter risked an acid attack just for walking to school?

Full mornings, adrenaline, and the randomness of our breakfast worked up an appetite, and that meant kebabs, fresh yogurt, Kabuli rice with lamb and shredded carrots and grapes, and a meat dumpling called mantu. Sometimes we were seated cross-legged around the meal in traditional Afghan style, and sometimes at a table. The meal was always delicious. Shah Mohammad would join us and smile broadly as Najibullah schooled us with impromptu Dari lessons, connecting thoughts and phrases from the morning's work.

I wrote the phrases and words in my notebook phonetically so I could try to commit them to memory. Languages had never been my strength. I lived in Germany for six years, and I wasn't even close to being fluent in German. I took three years of French in high school, and spent years visiting various areas of France, and several months living in Paris and Beirut, and my French remained abysmal at best. I found myself wishing I could upload languages directly to my brain via a Matrix-like database.

Tony and I came up quickly with a shorthand for photos and descriptions. It started with the blue burqas worn by many women in Kabul. We called them bluebirds—as if they were free to fly about if we thought of them that way, making the burqa a thing of beauty. We came to refer to the Afghan police as the parrots, since they were green and squawked loudly. The white burqas were doves, symbols of peace as they swirled around the dust-covered city. The badass private security, spilling out of jeeps dressed all in black, with their mirrored sunglasses and extensive firepower, were the blackbirds. Ever present, flitting about the city looking for spare crumbs were the sparrows, the street children that swarmed around asking for money, offering to shine your shoes, sell you a map, or waving their smoky cans of "good luck." Street children often wander between cars in slow traffic waving cans of burning incense meant to ward off evil in exchange for a few Afs.

The sparrows hung out by the doors of several kebab houses we frequented for lunch, and afterward we handed them leftovers that Najibullah had wrapped up. He unfailingly had several small bills of ten or twenty Afs—a few cents worth—that he would hand out. Occasionally, we bought their gum or pencils. Najibullah took us to several schools, including one specifically for street children. He was always generous and patient with those that gathered around us.

In the afternoon, the pace ramped up until dark, when Najibullah tried to have us home for security reasons. We took a different route each night and entered the first of two security gates guarding both ends of our street. After a few days, I realized that Najibullah still had a long drive home to his family and that his days were at least two hours longer than ours with his commute both ways. Yet he always arrived bright-eyed and ready to work.

We dropped our bags and headed straight to the outbuilding again for dinner. The saving grace was the fresh naan bread, as the main course varied in its sparseness and sliminess. Praise Allah for the incredible lunches at kebab shops and teahouses that fueled us and kept us going!

After dinner, the work continued. Tony retreated to his room to download and back up the day's captured images, and I went upstairs to organize interview notes, write blogs, and interpret new layers of cultural understanding. The first few nights I attempted to light a fire in the little metal stove in the middle of the room, the only source of heat, but the fuel briquettes smoldered more than burned. I gave up and put on a few extra layers of clothes instead. The room grew colder and colder as I worked, with the solar generators giving their warning bell around ten o'clock. There were two beds in my room, and after I shivered and froze on the first night with no heat, I stripped the extra bed to pile on more warmth to mine. I had a few hours to work off my computer's battery and turn on my headlamp for a last-call bathroom run. Then sometime around midnight, when the room was dark and cold, I crawled under the layers of covers, already dreaming before my head hit the pillow.

I wasn't looking at buying real estate, but despite the chaos, stress, and security threats, I was exactly where I wanted to be.

One of the first meetings, and the only one I'd specifically planned ahead of time, was with AINA Photo Agency. For decades, the people of Afghanistan had endured war and chaos. In 1996, the Taliban gained complete control and placed the Afghan people under Sharia law. Citizens were forbidden to participate in a free press, and it was considered a crime to take or even possess photographs. Truth and communication were suppressed. After the Taliban were pushed out of power in 2002, AINA, Afghanistan's Independent Media and Culture Center, was established by Reza Deghati. This foundation was born out of the desire to develop photojournalism from within Afghanistan and to find outlets to allow the truth to be seen. The offices shared space with *Kabul Weekly*, a trilingual newspaper run by Faheem Dashty who also served as the president of AINA Photo.

AINA was a key part of my decision to go to Kabul. Through filmmaking, photography, radio, journalism, and design, AINA trained, produced, and empowered individuals and communities to speak out and make sustainable changes in civil society. This was Afghanistan's first and only Afghan-owned and -run photography agency. Now, a group of talented men and women photojournalists were developing AINA's talent pool to further the country's ability to tell its own stories.

I hoped to support the work of AINA Photo and reach out to local Afghan photographers so that I could include their work alongside that of Western photographers in a cultural exhibition I wanted to create. *Streets of Afghanistan* would showcase the country from a variety of perspectives.

We met Faheem Dashty in his office to discuss the project and learn more about AINA, freedom of the press and artistic expression, and in the process get a history lesson dating back to the time of Massoud. He told me of death threats, some subtle, others more blatant due to the unbiased content of *Kabul Weekly*. He worked hard to maintain his job as editor in chief and not be swayed by politicians, leaders, and warlords. His office wall was taken up by an imposing life-size portrait of Massoud, the leader of the Northern Alliance, who fought the Taliban and inspired a nation. The Lion of Panjshir served as a moral compass for Dashty, who referred to him as "Chief." If not for journalists and editors such as Dashty in countries like Afghanistan, corrupt and violent groups and individuals would run rampant without fear.

Around the world, the work of journalists and photographers serves to tell stories that would otherwise remain hidden—whether atrocities normally swept under the rug or individual bravery and kindness that can inspire others. Yet telling such stories often puts the storytellers at great risk. Corrupt governments, bribed policy makers, and others don't want their story told. And Afghanistan has no shortage of corruption, violence, and atrocities. But it also has its share of brave souls, storytellers, and artists.

Beyond storytelling and the ability to educate and inspire, media can be a powerful weapon against tyranny and violence. Photography takes that one step further. It reaches us on a visceral level. It can combat the apathy and tell stories in ways words often cannot. The idea of the *Streets of Afghanistan* exhibition was to use photography to galvanize individuals and communities to believe that change is possible in Afghanistan. It aimed to build support for projects that could help the next generation of storytellers.

Faheem pointed to the portrait of Massoud behind him. He explained that he'd served as his press secretary. Three days before 9/11, Massoud had been assassinated by Tunisians posing as a television crew. The bomb was in the camera. Faheem was nearly killed as well, and he was still haunted by his decision to grant access to the false media team that killed a great leader. He continued to work as an editor for *Kabul Weekly*, despite the threats, so that the truth could emerge, so that corruption could be fought, and so that Afghans could hope for a better future.

We were soon joined by the majority of the AINA photographers, mostly men, but two women attended the meeting. We had been speaking in English with Faheem, but now we reverted to Dari, and I asked Najibullah to explain to the room what we were doing and what I hoped to accomplish.

Fifteen minutes into the meeting, the door opened and in strode Travis, who I'd only communicated with by e-mail. He was assisting and mentoring at AINA, and was my first line of communication in setting up the meeting to discuss the exhibition. He was dressed in a black North Face puffy coat, black pants, and a black-and-white checkered keffiyeh scarf. I didn't know what I'd expected but not someone that looked as if he'd just climbed off a motorcycle.

He listened while we discussed the project and suggested that the photographers each pull their top ten images for me to look at the following week. I could then get a better sense of their work since the agency database was slow at best and nearly impossible to use. I could negotiate image use fees with AINA after I decided how many I wanted. Travis would also put me in touch with Farzana Wahidy, a female photographer that was originally with AINA Photo but was now represented by Agence Française, a French photo agency.

After the meeting, Faheem invited us to have lunch with him and his family in the Panjshir Valley, to see more than Kabul and meet his father. I agreed enthusiastically, though at that time I had no idea how prominent a role the Panjshir province would come to play in my life.

Afghanistan is visually heartbreaking in both its beauty and its devastation. The Afghans have endured hardship with incredible resiliency, and it's easy to fall into the trap of looking through rose-colored glasses at the ancient aspects of the country, from the herders along the busy streets of Kabul, their goats intermingling with the cars, to the elaborate turbans and timeless faces lined with history. Often, it feels as if you've stepped back in time to the days of the silk roads and camel caravans. But the security restrictions soon temper that. Suicide bombs, kidnappings, and acid attacks occurred during our visit—a harsh reminder that this is a war zone and a warning to stay alert. The tendency to romanticize the dust, the call to prayer, and the mountains is quelled when you meet women living as modern-day slaves, kids forced to beg in the street, and men hobbling along, one of their legs having been blown off. The violence and oppression is as overpowering as the beauty.

Tony captured the image that perfectly illustrates the beauty in the heartbreak. We were driving to Panjshir province to meet General Dashty, Faheem's father, at their home in the Panjshir Valley for lunch. As we were leaving Kabul, we saw a woman in a burqa with her baby begging in the middle of the street. The woman was directly in the line of fire from traffic in both directions, but she sat there unflinching as traffic whizzed by, peaceful in the eye of the storm. Dust swirled, and Tony grabbed his camera at my request to shoot through the windshield, catching this bluebird in the road.

That image is the one that has stuck with me throughout numerous visits to Afghanistan. The haunting quality of the woman and child is offset by the blurred line of Shah Mohammad's hand on the steering wheel giving a real sense of impending conflict. It's an image that I used years later as a cornerstone of the photography exhibition *Streets of Afghanistan*. There was heartbreak and beauty combined in one beautiful frame.

Then I pushed my luck and asked Tony to get a shot of the road behind us as we passed. Bearing in mind that Najibullah had warned him not to shoot photos from the car—at least not when there were police around—Tony had been uber stealthy. My big-mouthed request meant that he lifted his camera just in time to get us waved down by the police. I shrunk in the backseat and apologized to Najibullah. Luckily, they let us off with a warning and didn't confiscate anything. Tony laughed at me and my big mouth and shook his head ruefully. "You are supposed to be keeping a look out, not getting us in trouble."

I shrugged my shoulders sheepishly. "Sorry!"

The rest of the drive passed without incident, and as we drove north out of Kabul, we went under a checkpoint with a large sign that arched across the road. It had been put there by the Ministry of Health, and Najibullah explained that it referred to family planning and said that space between children was good for both the mother and child. "In other words, don't try to knock up your wife a couple of days after she gives birth," I joked to Tony. I may have a dark sense of humor, one that has gotten darker after years of working in Afghanistan, almost to a point of inappropriateness, but we were talking about a country with one of the highest rates of maternal and infant mortality. I had to crack jokes to keep from wallowing in the insanity around me. Commonsense practices surrounding family planning weren't common sense. Over the years that followed, I often met young women with six and seven children. The mothers were missing teeth and malnourished, their bodies exhausted from the constant demands of feeding newborns while pregnant and living in rural communities already lacking food and resources.

As we continued north, the Shomali Plain spread out in front of us, a brief landscape of wide open views. We arrived at the gateway to the mountains several hours later. We saw land mine clearing on the left and stopped to buy some grapes from one of about twenty or so men selling them. They stood in a line at the side of the road, with small gnarled grape vines spreading out behind them into fields I hoped were free of land mines. A couple of hours later, the mountains closed in as the valley narrowed and followed the river, and we came to the entrance to the Panjshir Valley.

Najibullah asked Shah Mohammad to slow down. On the right-hand side of the road was a small shack, about the size of a police checkpoint. An old man with red hair was standing there. Najibullah rolled down his window and exchanged greetings with him, then handed him some Afs. The old man looked inside the car, then put his hand on his heart and nodded when he saw Tony and me. I did the same in return with a smile.

"Who is he?" I asked Najibullah as we drove off.

"He is one of Massoud's men. He still stands guard every day at that little hut as a first watch before the gates of Panjshir. Everyone who comes to Panjshir gives him a few Afs. He's almost seventy years old now."

The gates of Panjshir are not just a metaphor for the narrow valley opening where the Panjshir River runs through the mountain ranges that surround this narrow province just a mile or so past the old man's checkpoint. The proverbial gates have a literal gate, an official police checkpoint that the Panjshiri still maintain to see who is coming in and leaving. This checkpoint was manned by a serious-looking bunch of uniformed men. They peered through the driver's window and asked a few questions. I put my right hand on my heart, nodded, and said, "Salaam." One of them responded in kind and smiled, allowing Tony to take his photo. He told us he'd been a commander under Massoud and now worked this checkpoint to continue his loyal service to Panjshir. The guards invited us to join them for tea, but Najibullah explained that we didn't have time as we were expected for lunch farther down the road. I was a bit disappointed. How often was one invited for a roadside cup of tea by ex-mujahideen fighters?

The dirt road, interspersed with short sections of pavement, followed the river through the valley while the mountains looked down on us from both sides. We periodically munched on the slightly wrinkled, anemic-looking grapes in the pink plastic bag. Suddenly, we arrived at a village that screamed, "You're not in Kansas anymore." The road narrowed and market stalls pressed in tightly on either side. A cow was getting cut up on the street in front of the butcher shop. *Can't ask for fresher than that,* I thought as my stomach growled at the thought of lunch. The Corolla wove through the crowds of animals and people, and all I could think was what I would give to get out of the damn car. I was aching to stretch my legs and get closer to this experience. Stands selling liter bottles of Coca-Cola, fresh yogurt in clear plastic bags, butchered animals, fruit, and clothing had their wares hanging by strings and ropes tied to the low roofs of the metal shacks.

Slowly the neutral, dusty landscape we'd been driving through since Kabul developed some splashes of color as trees with golden yellow leaves appeared in great clusters along the sides of the mountain across the river. We'd caught the last few days of autumn in Panjshir. The foliage was a welcome sight after the muted shades of brown we'd become accustomed to.

We arrived at Faheem Dashty's family home by way of a narrow alley off the road. On both sides were steep rock walls, and I couldn't see any other houses nearby, but I could hear the river raging. Faheem welcomed us at the gate and directed us to the garden, where a table and chairs were set on the lawn. The house had mountains on both sides and a flowering garden overlooking the river. It was hard to believe that this was the stronghold of Massoud's resistance against the Taliban. It was too peaceful—an oasis, really.

Faheem's father, introduced to us as simply the General, came out. Compared to the slightness of Faheem, his father was large, with a kind, grandfatherly face. He greeted us and warmly shook my hand between both of his, welcoming us to his home.

We sat in the garden, my eyes drinking in the color. A servant brought freshly pressed apple juice from their own trees in the orchard out back. Thick and pulpy, the juice was the first I'd had in days and it tasted as though I'd just bitten into a sweet yellow apple. A refreshing break from the constant stream of watery green tea.

Faheem and the General shared many stories of the family home, the Panjshir Valley, life during the Soviet occupation, and their relationship with Massoud. Faheem still referred to Massoud as the Chief and smiled mischievously, recounting a story about getting caught smoking after the Chief had forbidden it.

The General told us how Massoud asked him to blow up the road near the valley entrance when the Taliban were trying to enter. The road collapsed into the river, boulders and rubble making it impassable for vehicles. The Taliban that survived were either captured or killed, or they fled back to Kabul. Ironically, the General's government job was road building for the Ministry of Transportation.

After a couple of hours sharing stories, the General guided us to a small outbuilding on the other side of the garden for lunch. We entered a tiny foyer with a red afghan rug just large enough for us to slip out of our shoes, and we walked into a small rectangular room with cobalt blue pillows lining the four walls. We sat cross-legged on the floor, and a tablecloth was spread in the middle of the empty space. Food and water were brought in from the kitchen, and Faheem passed along plates, then platters of food. I sat next to the General, and he gestured that I should serve myself first.

I adore Afghan food. It is a great joy to be invited to a private home for a home-cooked meal, no matter where you are in the world. My favorite meals in Paris, Beirut, and Germany were served in the intimacy and familiarity of a private home. Here it was all the more special as so few foreigners experienced the hospitality in such an intimate way. On the floor in front of us was an array of dishes that the General's wife had cooked. Rice mixed with raisins and carrots covered tender hunks of lamb. Another platter was stacked with fresh-baked naan bread. A bowl was filled with quorma, a slightly spicy Afghan stew of lamb chunks and potatoes. A tiny condiment bowl contained spicy green peppers crushed with garlic, and yet another bowl contained tomatoes, onions, and fresh basil. Lastly, there was yogurt, freshly made that day. Everything from meat to vegetable to naan bread had been produced on the family land.

I was in heaven as the General gestured for us to "eat more, eat more!" Tony joked with Faheem that his mother's cooking would be famous tomorrow as I would surely write about it. I suggested that perhaps I should simply return for some cooking lessons.

After a post-lunch walk around the garden with the family dog, a gorgeous German shepherd, we said good-bye to the General who insisted firmly, but with a wide smile, that I must return to see him. Faheem offered to drive us to visit Massoud's grave to pay respects, so we walked through the inner courtyard and piled into the General's Toyota four-by-four. We stopped first at Massoud's family home. The driveway was blocked by a thin chain that a child removed when we pulled up, and we drove up the steep dirt driveway. Faheem showed us around the house of the most famous Afghan in recent times.

The grave was not much farther, and as we got closer, we could see construction in progress on a large marble structure around Massoud's grave. This was the same hillside where I would almost meet my demise when Shah Mohammad crashed his Corolla a year later. It overlooked the Panjshir Valley in all directions, a unique vantage point and one that was chosen to allow the Lion of Panjshir to continue to look over his flock. People had been coming here since 2001 to pay respects or to picnic.

Faheem stopped to say hello to a group of workers, and I pressed my right hand to my heart and said "*Salaam*" quietly to each of them. We followed Faheem toward a covered casket under the roof of the uncompleted tomb. I hung back in respect as he bowed his head for several minutes while Najibullah and Shah Mohammad prayed silently across from him. The mood was somber as we walked slowly to the car.

Two days later in Kabul, the somber mood was replaced with nervous excitement. Najibullah set up two "interviews" for Tony and me with two prominent female leaders and activists. The first was with the former minister of Women's Affairs, Dr. Massouda Jalal. She ran for president against Hamid Karzai in the first post-Taliban elections in 2002. As we drove to the meeting at Dr. Jalal's home,

I looked over at Tony and said quietly, almost whispering, "What the hell am I doing? This is the equivalent of sitting down for a meeting with a cabinet member and senator back in the United States. I'm seriously out of my element here."

"You are going to be great. Just let her do the talking. You want answers. Here's someone who may have them. Just breathe and be yourself."

"Lame," I joked, smiling over at him while rolling my eyes.

"Nope, not lame. You want to know what's really going on here? You want to show others what Afghan women are capable of? This is exactly the sort of woman you've been looking for."

I nodded and looked down over the hastily scribbled questions in my notebook.

I needn't have worried. Dr. Massouda Jalal was not a wallflower. Dubbed the Mother of Afghanistan, she set an example for women looking to challenge their position in Afghan society and promote the role of women in government. After exchanging pleasantries in her living room over tea, we started in. Her answer to my first question about her work as minister of Women's Affairs took over fifteen minutes. The second, about her run for president against Karzai, another twenty. This part was fascinating. Though she didn't have the international support or financial backing that Karzai had, she came in a relatively close second. She talked a lot about the role that women could have in politics. "Women are peacemakers. Men are the fighters. Men hold grudges and work on ethnic boundaries that go back generations. Women don't have the same grievances and generational resentments. We can negotiate and build alliances better than men." Her English was fluent, so Najibullah excused himself to pray in the corner. Five or six questions later, I had said very little but had gotten a solid overview of her life and government work. I asked a few follow-up questions about her newly established organization, the Jalal Foundation, and its work with women's issues, and then we were finished.

Relief poured out of me as Tony and I ate kebabs afterward. I steeled myself for an interview with a female member of Parliament, Dr. Roshanak Wardak.

Dr. Wardak was not an easy interview. Here was a woman who had stared down the Taliban. Even now, in Parliament, she worked alongside warlords who preferred not to see women in politics. I got a heady dose of how intense her gaze can be, perhaps made more so by the Parliamentary room we were meeting in. Red leather chairs surrounded four long, polished dark-wood tables arranged to form a large square. The Afghan flag stood solemnly in the corner. Where Dr. Jalal was motherly and animated, Dr. Wardak was tough and blunt. She represented the tumultuous province from which her family took its name: Wardak. Fighting and violence is ongoing there, with a large number of Taliban in the region. Wardak neighbors Kabul, and the difference in security between the two provinces is almost incomprehensible.

Dr. Wardak was the province's only female OB/GYN. During the Taliban's reign, most women wore the burqa, but she insisted she could not do her job covered up and simply wore her black head scarf so that her face was covered except for her eyes. She worked throughout those difficult years, and when the Taliban were pushed out and elections held, the people of Wardak encouraged her to run as a candidate for Parliament. With seemingly little effort, she won.

As she sat across from me, her eyes probed mine, silently questioning my interest, my knowledge, and probably my intentions. Her eyes continued to search and probe as we talked, and when silences came, they were not for me to fill. They were there for her to decide if she would continue, and when she did, it was with direct honesty. This was a woman with no time for games. Her mantra, "politics is lying," was repeated often throughout our conversation. She hated politics and said so openly. She was a doctor, and loved her work, and loved her people. "A doctor must be honest and direct at all times," she told me. As a politician, she saw the falsehood and manipulation, and had no patience for it.

We discussed women in politics, gender equality, the political climate, and most important, given her unique insight, the Taliban's role in the future of Afghanistan. Her point of view was unique because she'd had no rights under the Taliban. She'd been forced to cover her face. She'd not have been allowed to vote, much less run as a candidate herself, had the Taliban held elections. Yet, she realized that the Taliban were Afghan, and as such, should be allowed their place in society under the Afghan constitution. Like Hamas and Hezbollah, the Taliban were part of the country and represented a great number of people. Wardak believed that they needed to be part of the process to bring peace, and others like President Karzai and the American government were coming to the same conclusion.

"Let them run candidates if they wish, the same as anyone else. If they win seats, then we must honor that," she said. "But the trick is that they have to abide by the 'rules' and accept women as their counterparts, perhaps even as their new president. Yet, if they are given the chance to run amok, isolated from the political system and peace process, it will be to the destruction of the country and will put Afghanistan in the center of the war on terror."

When I asked about her most important work in Parliament, her answer was immediate and concise. "Security. It is the *only* priority for progress. Achieving it is another story. Yet the Parliament, ministers, and the people of Afghanistan need to work toward a peace process conducted with all of Afghanistan represented as a complete way to end the violent spiral."

Staring back into Wardak's tough gaze, I realized that while she may hate being a politician, she was perhaps the kind of politician this, and every, country needs.

Wazhma Frogh, an Afghan female activist and writer, echoed that sentiment three years later, after ex-president and head of the High Peace Council, Burhanuddin Rabbani, was assassinated in September 2011 by a Taliban emissary. She stated her belief that the High Peace Council needed women involved if the country was ever to truly be at peace, then added: "Women in Afghanistan had to fight to have representation in the High Peace Council. They have been able to make headway where the men could not. For example, some of the women at the High Peace Council were able to make contacts with some of the families of one of the armed opposition groups and were welcomed in their homes. Not one of the men in the High Peace Council has been able to enter the house of an armed opposition group commander."

She then compared the situation to the women in South Africa going door to door, in essence, selling the newly formed Constitution.

"I am sure the world remembers how South African women went around the country uniting every South African in favor of their new Constitution at the end of apartheid. It was actually the South African women who prevented a bloodbath by giving everyone a voice during the Constitution-making process."

Women have an important role in Afghanistan, whether the Afghan men realize it or not. Without the full participation of society, a country cannot be unified. Studies continue to link a society's economic progress and overall stability with gender equality. The viral digital campaign that launched in 2007, the Girl Effect, illustrates simply and powerfully how educating girls directly affects a society's overall progress. The world is beginning to recognize the power women have, and the importance that gender equality and women's rights have in the health of a nation.

As if Najibullah knew that I could use a day off, we spent the next day exploring the older side of Kabul—an outing that could have been scripted for my father.

My father is an architect and loves restoration projects, the preservation of historic buildings in particular. I have fond memories of walks around numerous job sites with him as a young girl, collecting odd bits of wood for my "workshop" at home. I remember the smell of sawdust and the sound of hammers and circular saws, the maze of a framed-out building, and seeing from one room to the next through the two-by-fours.

Tony and I were fortunate to be guided around the oldest preservation project in Kabul, Murad Khane, by the lead engineer. This is a project that falls under the guidance of Turquoise Mountain, a nonprofit focused on restoring traditional Afghan art and culture. Murad Khane is at the heart of old Kabul and was once a bustling commercial center. The area has fallen into disrepair over the last century. It has no sewage, and buildings collapse weekly. We were shown photos of garbage piled eight feet high across this area, the removal of which was an enormous first step toward reconstruction.

Walking through the job site, I felt at home, even if the cessation of work and extensive staring illustrated the point that I was the only woman there. These buildings were all made of clay and mud, and great piles of it were on the ground. Men shoveled it to keep it moist and properly mixed, the smell mingling with that from the open sewers and the sawdust from the woodwork restoration.

Suddenly, my head scarf wasn't a burden as I pulled one end of it across my nose and mouth.

The construction coordinator and project engineer showed me around, up and down narrow stairwells, through rooms and onto balconies. The bazaar's buildings were built around three separate courtyards but were mostly interconnected. Then we ascended one last narrow spiral stone staircase, and I found myself on the roof. All of Kabul stretched out before me, just three stories up. The maze of the bazaar and the restoration project itself became clearer as we walked from rooftop to rooftop, looking down into the courtyards. I was free to watch instead of moving through scenes, trying to take everything in at a brisk pace. Below us, the daily routines of Kabul unfolded. Children fought with a small dog. Women in head scarves hustled through streets. Others in burqas picked their way more slowly as they shopped, occasionally lifting them over their heads to talk or simply to get some oxygen. Men prayed inside an open window. Others pissed in the alley. It was all there to be taken in from above, and I loved being able to watch the scene without disturbing it with my presence.

Najibullah had brought his son, Mustafa, with us, and he'd waited patiently in the car with Shah Mohammad all day during my meetings. The reward? We bought two kites and some string and headed up to Nadir Shah Hill, commonly called Kite Hill, overlooking Kabul.

My father loves kites. He had trick kites and the great big ones that resembled those used for kite boarding and that could drag you along for miles if the wind was strong. I imagined he would be as excited as Mustafa at the prospect of catching some wind. Afghanistan's national pastime is kite flying, and most boys grow up flying them or running them down during kite fights. Every Friday, families come to this spot on the hill where the wind is strong and the space is open. Many will coat their strings with a powdered glass for kite fighting. Kids will duel in the air and aim to cut the other's string with their own. If the string is cut, the kite is lost and "finders keepers." This is where the runners come in, chasing down the kites through the neighborhoods.

Najibullah had introduced us a few days prior to one of Kabul's master kite makers. He'd shown us how he fashioned the delicate and often elaborate kites out of pieces of tissue paper, glue, and thin strips of wood. I'd been surprised that the kites didn't disintegrate upon flight when we tested one in our courtyard.

I watched Najibullah and his son fly the kite from the top of the dusty hill, surrounded by young children, a few horses, and the ongoing reconstruction of King Nadir Shah's tomb, which like everything else, had been damaged during the war. The tomb was an imposing marble structure, topped by a metal dome and covered in scaffolding. The king had been assassinated in 1933, one more in a long line of Afghan leaders removed from office by violence.

I wished Devon could be with me. She was too young to fly a kite by herself, but at four, she would have loved to watch the kites dancing through the sky as much as my father.

On one of my final nights in Afghanistan, I bent the security rules I'd been living under. I upset Tony, and worried Najibullah unnecessarily, but as Katharine Hepburn once put it, "If you obey all the rules, you'll miss all the fun." And seeing Kabul from the back of a motorbike is worth breaking a rule for.

I'd made plans to meet up with Travis at the AINA offices, to talk more about the exhibition and his own experiences living in Kabul. When we set a date and time, he asked if I was "allowed" to go for a motorcycle ride. "Allowed" is such an inflammatory word to me. It immediately puts me on the defensive. *What am I, a child?* In Kabul, though, Travis's question wasn't unusual, as many aid workers and NGO employees must abide by certain security rules involving curfews and drivers. Many are not allowed to go out at night or, if they are, only to certain restaurants on a list that changes based on security reports. One woman I knew was required to carry a GPS tracker in her bag wherever she went. I was under no such restrictions other than the extraordinary care of Najibullah. He and Tony were going to visit the land mine museum while I met with Travis, and we made plans for them to pick me up a few hours later.

Unfortunately for Najibullah's sensibilities, seeing Kabul on the back of a bike was *exactly* what the doctor ordered after three weeks of head scarves, locked car doors, and being home by 6:00 P.M. Not that my trip hadn't been an adventure or that Najibullah hadn't been an amazing guide, but I needed a bit more freedom—a bit more wind in my face. I wanted to see Afghanistan from the perspective of someone who lived there full-time.

The obvious challenge was riding the motorbike with a head scarf. It was difficult to keep it in place when walking down the street and a near impossibility on the back of a motorbike. I attracted second looks in the car, so I'd definitely stand out on the back of a motorbike. Travis told me that women in Afghanistan rode side-saddle, if at all. So when I straddled the seat, I was already clearly a foreigner, regardless of my blond hair blowing out of a billowing head scarf. I tucked the ends into my coat and hoped the Taliban weren't watching.

This was an old bike—more a glorified dirt bike than a motor-cycle, dubbed the Super Kabul. Travis revved the engine as I climbed on, and I felt the wave of calmness I always get when I am happy to be exactly where I am. A small burst of adrenaline replaced the calm as the freedom from cars and locked doors and security hit with the first gust of wind.

I quickly realized the head scarf staying put would in fact be an issue, as I couldn't hold on to the bike with just one hand on these streets and I wasn't wearing a helmet. Gutted out, muddy, and worthy of a four-by-four or a full suspension mountain bike, the roads posed serious obstacles: rocks, deep puddles, and enormous potholes, not to mention the traffic. In a car, you see the chaos. On a motorbike, you feel it. So I pulled the side of my head scarf to my face and held the fabric between my teeth. As I did, Travis mentioned casually the rumor that the roads were purposely not fixed to keep traffic slow and give suicide bombers a tougher time. A comforting thought.

There were few, if any, actual traffic rules in this country. There were two stoplights in the entire city. At roundabouts and intersections, people had a general sense of rules, but if you needed to go left and the roundabout traffic flowed to the right, you just weaved between oncoming traffic to make the shortcut. One-way streets? No such thing—often we were the only vehicle going against three lanes of traffic. Lanes were nonexistent. Each road had a varying number of lanes at a given time, from two to four or even five on the same stretch, depending on the time of day. Bikers and pedestrians crossed at will, and at their own risk. On a motorbike you abided by all the non-rules of the road, times ten, plus you had access to the sidewalks.

We climbed a steep dirt road up TV Hill, named for the hundreds of antennae that covered its top. The city of Kabul spread out below us, and the overpowering smell of diesel, dust, and rotting garbage began to fade. Typically, lights dotted Kabul in the early dusk, but that night rolling blackouts had darkened swaths of

Riding my bike past the boys' school in Dashty Rewat in 2009. The first time these boys have ever seen a girl ride a bike. (PHOTO CREDIT: TRAVIS BEARD)

Looking over Kabul's old town from the rooftops of Murad Khane with Najibullah in 2008. (PHOTO CREDIT: TONY DI ZINNO)

Riding the Desert Eagle on my first night ride in Kabul. (PHOTO CREDIT: BARRY MISENHEIMER)

Q&A at the A4T girls' school in Kabul in 2008. (PHOTO CREDIT: TONY DI ZINNO)

Early morning traffic in Bamiyan. (PHOTO CREDIT: DENI BECHARD)

Riding past a Soviet tank graveyard in the Panjshir Valley. (PHOTO CREDIT: TRAVIS BEARD)

Unloading school supplies in Dashty Rewat. (PHOTO CREDIT: TRAVIS BEARD)

Speaking with village men in the mountains of Panjshir, trying to keep warm under an Afghan sandalee. (PHOTO CREDIT: TRAVIS BEARD)

Woman begging in the street with her child in Kabul—this became the cover photo for the *Streets of Afghanistan* exhibition. (PHOTO CREDIT: TONY DI ZINNO)

Learning to fly kites in my guesthouse courtyard with one of Kabul's master kite makers. (PHOTO CREDIT: TONY DI ZINNO)

Hamid and Travis getting ready to film in the Panjshir Valley, Tour de France style, during one of my first bike rides in 2009. (PHOTO CREDIT: SHANNON GALPIN)

Posing with my "prize" after learning to fish with nets in the Panjshir River. (PHOTO CREDIT: TRAVIS BEARD)

Crossing the river, twice, near the turnaround point of the ride across the Panjshir Valley in 2010. (PHOTO CREDIT: TRAVIS BEARD)

Delivering laptop computers to the A4T girls' school in Kabul with Travis in 2009. (Photo credit: Travis Beard)

Standing at the Venue with local graffiti artist, Shamsia, in front of one of her unfinished pieces. (Photo credit: Anna Brones)

the city. We stopped briefly to take in the view, allowing a few of
the small children chasing us to catch up. One little boy didn't respond when I offered a few words in Dari, but his dirty face lit up
with a big, shy smile. He hung around like a sparrow, scrutiniz-
ing us while Travis pointed out the landmarks and I finally got
my head wrapped around the lay of the land. Travis indicated
another large hill directly across from us and said that was stop
number two.

Fifteen minutes later, we arrived at the infamous Olympic diving pool, built during the Soviet era but never used for its intended
purpose. The pool was a stark rectangular hole in the ground with
three concrete diving boards, rusty ladders running up their sides.
During the nineties, it was the site of Taliban executions. The accused were pushed from the top diving board into the empty pool.
Those who survived were deemed innocent. Most, not surprisingly,
were found guilty. Now Afghans used the pool for dog fighting, a
popular sport, and impromptu football games. We stood underneath the high dives watching a group playing soccer below us.
Voices ricocheted around the inside of the concrete pool along with
the ball. A full moon rose behind us, illuminating the men while the
dusty air added a strange softness to the scene. I felt as if I were
watching a moving painting.

I inwardly cursed my luck as I was used to having my photographer-
at-large with me at all times to document these classic moments.
I knew Tony would kill to see this as well, and I vowed to ask
Najibullah to drive us up here Friday morning before we left.

In the course of our conversation, I told Travis that I raced
mountain bikes. As we started back down, he promptly said that
he'd been driving cautiously so as not to scare me, but now all bets
were off. We tore down the hill, my head scarf gripped tightly

between my teeth and the exhilaration of this temporary freedom pulsating in my bones.

When we got back, Tony was upset because he and Najibullah hadn't been sure where I'd been when they showed up at the AINA offices to pick me up. They knew I was meeting Travis, but as I didn't have a phone here and was utterly dependent on Najibullah and others, I couldn't let them know I would be a few minutes late. Tony's outrage was amplified slightly. Maybe he was jealous of the ride—of my temporary freedom—or of Travis's influence, or maybe a little of both. I apologized to Najibullah for any worry I'd caused him, but I was angry at Tony for overreacting, knowing he'd have made the same choice given the opportunity. But the next morning's activities pushed my so-called security infraction to the back of both our minds. On our last day in Afghanistan, Najibullah informed us that there was a buzkashi match near Kabul and we could go.

I'd dreamed of one day seeing a buzkashi game, and had hoped a match would take place near enough for us to watch. Buzkashi was an iconic sport that epitomizes the Afghan spirit, featuring Afghan warriors on horseback. The director of the Buzkashi Federation happened to be a friend of Najibullah, and he invited us to attend the match as his guests, an honor that not only eliminated complicated issues of checkpoints and security, but also provided a few other unexpected perks.

We met Tashili in the dusty field behind Kabul Stadium where the horses for the Kabul team were housed. As we arrived, horses were being loaded into trucks and several were still tethered in the field waiting their turn. Tashili welcomed us warmly and asked me if I liked buzkashi. I replied that it was a great honor to watch a game and a lifelong dream. He showed us the horses, and stopping

in front of a large white one, asked if I would like to get on. I thought
he was joking, that there was no way they'd let a woman on one of
these treasured animals. There was even an old Afghan wives' tale
saying that if a bride rode on a buzkashi horse it would never compete again, and I wondered what would happen if a foreign female
rode one. Nonetheless, I was fairly bursting with excitement and
told him I would be greatly honored. He smiled broadly and gestured for one of the stable boys to remove the blanket covering the
saddle, then allowed me to mount. A crowd materialized, all of the
faces with an air of disbelief.

Not waiting to see if Tashili was pulling my leg, I hoisted up my
long skirt (I was wearing jeans underneath) so that my foot could
reach high enough to slide into the stirrup, and prayed I could make
this look graceful. I was thankful for the strength built up in my
legs from a summer of mountain bike riding. The crowd grew larger
to witness the foreigner accepting the challenge of mounting one of
their prized horses. A grin spread across my face as I felt the
strength of the animal beneath me. I knew that I would see this
horse compete under the skill of one of Kabul's chapandaz, the
burly riders that competed in this iconic sport. It was a dream come
true.

Regretfully, I dismounted, wishing I could ride it around the
field. I handed off the horse to a young man who led it to the trucks.
Tashili led me over to meet the president of the Federation, Aji
Abdul Rashed. This man could have been a professional wrestler in
another life. Heavyset and looking every bit as strong as the horses,
he grinned broadly and clapped my hand in both of his with a powerful grip. "You love buzkashi? You must buy some horses, and we
will keep them for you," he said in a booming voice that practically
echoed through the stables.

"You can help us find sponsorship, and we will make you secretary general of Buzkashi," he continued loudly.

I laughed and said it would be a great honor to own some buzkashi horses, but alas, I was in no position to afford one.

"Not today, maybe in the future," he insisted.

"*Inshallah*," I replied, and with that we shook hands again.

He was obviously enjoying the exchange, and we talked about the state of the sport in Afghanistan, the horses, and of course, the legendary chapandaz themselves. He would be riding himself today and I promised to follow his horse throughout the game.

We watched as the horses got loaded into flatbed trucks, then we all walked back to the cars. Tashili was riding with us for the hour-long drive north of Kabul to an empty field on the Shomali Plain, which was owned by Marshal Fahim, an avid buzkashi supporter who sponsored one of the top buzkashi players Aziz Ahmad.

Marshal Fahim was the vice president of Afghanistan, a former defense minister, a military commander, and overall, a controversial figure. He'd survived many assassination attempts, and when we arrived we were led through tight security. We walked across the muddy field through horses and riders warming up and making adjustments to their mounts. Stone bleachers lined one side, and I realized we would be sitting just inches away from the action.

Guards with guns stood by a private covered seating area slightly above us and separated from the stone bleachers. Najibullah told me that Marshal Fahim would sit there with his friends and heavy security. Shivering slightly, I wondered if they were inside somewhere, staying warm and drinking pots of tea. Then the gates we'd entered reopened and four black Land Cruisers with tinted windows roared across the pitch. Marshal Fahim and his entourage had arrived and now the game could begin.

The riders had been warming up their horses, riding around the field, and talking with one another for the better part of an hour. Slowly, the four teams lined up across the back of the field to introduce themselves to the crowd. Then, suddenly, the game started. As is typical in Central Asian versions of buzkashi played throughout the region, the "object" is a headless sheep, lamb, or calf carcass. In Afghanistan, it was often a small calf. The carcass was tossed onto the field near the winner's circle, and the "rodeo clown" blew the whistle. Riders surged forward to gain position, the members of a team creating a safe pocket for a rider to grab the carcass while on horseback. Leaning over into a crowd of charging horses to pick the carcass off the ground required skill as well as the strength to lift it onto the saddle in one fluid motion. The rider also needed the courage to face getting crushed in the mayhem. He then had to race to the green flag at the end of the field before he could attempt to race back and drop the calf in the circle. But the calf was heavy and difficult to hold on to, and the rider had forty or more riders chasing to steal it, block him, or simply force him off course.

To say that this game was controlled chaos would be an understatement. It was like a rugby scrum with horses surging into the pack, jockeying for position, blocking and maneuvering, until someone, somehow secured the calf and broke free. More chapandaz scored than I would have thought possible and each time the calf was released into the circle, cheers of "Hallal" went round the field. The rider then collected his cash prize from the stands and headed back out to try again.

As a sports photographer, Tony was in his element. He entered the scrum to the delight of the crowd and befriended the "rodeo clown/referee." His new friend encouragingly shoved Tony right into the action and quickly backpedaled out of the melee. Caught up in the spectacle of thundering hooves and acrobatic acts from the riders, Najibullah and I quickly forgot that Tony was in among the players. He emerged periodically to catch his breath and get his bearings, before diving back in.

Three and a half hours later, the third calf was thrown in (the first two had disintegrated under the constant tug-of-war). Tony showed me a frame he'd captured, a portrait of one of the black stallions rearing up. He had the unmistakable cat-that-got-the-canary look. He was pretty sure he'd gotten some good stuff. It was freezing cold as we walked quickly back across the field toward the gate. One of the chapandaz rode over and gestured that I could get on for a ride back to the gate. This drew a few cheers from the crowd, and it was with regret that I declined, as I saw there was no space on top of the horse due to the size of this sturdy chapandaz. He shrugged with a good-natured grin and rode past.

On the way back to Kabul, we had just enough time to detour to the hillside diving pool to show Tony before Najibullah dropped us off at the airport to begin the long journey home. The sky was blue, and several kites dotted the horizon. It was a fitting end to the visit, nostalgic and heartwarming.

Back home, sitting at my kitchen table in a four-in-the-morning jet lag haze, I realized how important the past three weeks had been.

"I found myself in Afghanistan." I said these words to Christiane when I finally got to see her in person. "Does that sound corny?" I was inwardly cringing at the Pollyannaish sound of the statement.

Christiane smiled, wrapped her arms around me, and said, "It would if I hadn't been reading your blogs while you were over there. It's totally obvious you were home."

Tony saw this, too, and understood my fear of being perceived as a so-called do-gooder. "Shannon, you are the anti-Pollyanna."

And he was right. There were no rose-colored glasses when I

looked at Afghanistan. It was simply that it was there, in a war zone, that I stepped up to the plate and accepted that I did, in fact, want to "save the world." Citizen diplomats are needed across the globe, connecting communities and cultures, looking at individuals as agents of change. This was essential if any real change was to be possible in countries like Afghanistan. I needed to be part of something bigger than myself. Devon deserved a mother who was willing to enter the fight. Girls around the world deserved it.

4

Turning Point

Colorado 2004

The phone rang and I picked it up to hear my sister's normally boisterous voice quietly say my name. "Hi, Shan." My instincts pricked.
Something was wrong.

Holding the cordless phone close to my good ear, my right one
being nearly deaf after an accident canyoning in Austria when I was
twenty, I paced the wooden floor in my living room as I heard
phrases thud my consciousness. *Last night. Walking home. Campus.
Attacked. Raped.*

I sat down on the black steamer trunk in front of the windows
that looked out the back of my house into the open expanse of bea-
ver ponds. My mind struggled to process what I was hearing. Snow
still covered the ground, despite the onset of spring, and I wondered
how much longer winter could hold on at ten thousand feet.

Larissa said she hadn't seen a doctor yet but had called the campus police with her roommates. There was a strange twist to her

story, something about a man pretending to be a police officer coming to her door and asking for evidence after the episode. All of it confused me, worried me, and I felt a dull ache in the pit of my stomach as I listened. She was scared but safe, and she wanted to finish out the last few weeks of school to get through her finals.

We hung up with a promise I'd call her back after talking with Mom and Dad. Someone needed to go down to the college and be with her. Adams State was in the small town of Alamosa, three hours south of Breckenridge. Immediately, my parents offered to fly down, but I insisted on going instead. I was closer, I could leave in the morning, and I wouldn't try to take over. I was also much too familiar with this story.

I stared mindlessly out the window, my gaze unfocused, my mind blank.

"Shan?"

I refocused and looked around. The phone was still in my hand. Pete was in the kitchen, looking at me from across the counter. "What's going on? Is everything okay?"

"That was Ris." Ris, Rissa, Lis—all pet names used by my family for my younger sister, Larissa. "She's been attacked. She was walking home, across campus. Some guy attacked her."

"Jesus, is she all right?"

"Yeah, no. Not so much. She was attacked. Raped." I stood up and walked over to the brown leather couch and wished the fire was going in the fireplace. It was so cold in this big house. I was always cold, but this was much worse. "I don't understand the details. . . . I don't know if even Ris understands them yet. It doesn't make sense. But she's with her roommates now. I think she's called campus police. Mom and Dad want me to go down. She needs one of us."

"Do you want a cup of tea?" he said, filling the kettle.

"Yeah, sure," I said distractedly. Tea, I thought, the British symbol of comfort. Or perhaps the British proxy for therapy. Right now the warmth and the distraction were welcome. My mind was reeling.

A long pause, then, "Would you be all right with that—if I drove down to Alamosa to see her, I mean? She needs someone to take her to the police station tomorrow, and I should be there."

"Doesn't she have her roommates who could help out?"

"Of course, but she should have family there. Mom and Dad want to check in on her. Make sure she's coping, has everything she needs, you know—how is she dealing? Plus she's got finals coming up and wants to stay to finish the end of the school year. . . ." I trailed off. "But she's pretty freaked out. So am I, frankly."

Pete poured water over two bags of PG Tips. He looked across the room at me, before turning to get the milk out of the fridge. "So what happened exactly?"

I wanted to ask him to say something more than just a series of one-sentence questions. It felt so cold. I wanted him to leave the tea, sit down, and hold me, and have a real conversation about what was going on. Why couldn't he just wrap me up in his arms, ask if there was anything he could do, or just ask how I was? My tolerance of his British reserve was wearing thin. I needed some emotion, some reaction beyond a cup of tea, some love.

"Exactly? I'm not sure. Other than she was attacked walking home across campus. The asshole raped her, and left her there, and she was able to get back to her apartment. The creepy thing is that a fake police officer showed up at her door asking for evidence."

"Fake? What do you mean?"

"Well apparently he showed up in uniform, said he'd been sent over by campus police to collect evidence. She gave him her underwear in a plastic bag and he asked a few questions and left. Apparently, the police never sent anyone to her, and if they had and the officer had collected any evidence on site, then protocol states using a paper bag, not plastic. It means 'he' knows where she lives, or that there are a couple of guys working together. It's beyond creepy."

"So, when are you thinking of going down there?" He set a mug of milky tea on the kitchen counter for me and took a sip of his, still standing in the kitchen, the horrible pink-hued wooden cabinets behind him. Who put pink wooden cabinets in a house like this? I couldn't help my mind from wandering as I digested what I had just heard.

"I was thinking tomorrow morning first thing."

He sighed. "Do you have any money to make the trip?"

I took a sip of tea, my gaze lowered to a familiar pattern of exposed knotholes on the surface of the table. I absently took one hand away from the mug, and with my fingernail I scraped out some of the dust and food particles that always gathered in the deeper crevasses. My heart sank a little with the disappointing turn this conversation was taking. Was this really the priority for every discussion we had? This wasn't the time for logistics or finances. This was the time for emotion, for compassion, empathy, love. I retreated further inside myself.

"No, not really, would you mind helping? My father said he'd cover the costs, but it's a little silly to ask him for something like this. It's just gas, and a night or two at a hotel to get her back on track and give her some support."

This was a recent and ongoing bone of contention: money. More precisely, the disparity of income between the two of us, despite having been married for six years.

I stood up from the table and went to our bedroom to pack a bag, and Pete walked upstairs to finish some work in his office. As I packed, I couldn't help but feel rage building at the injustice of what I was processing. My only sister, nearly ten years younger than me, brutally violated. Deeply buried thoughts clawed at the edges of consciousness, but I refused to acknowledge them. Now was the time to focus on Larissa, but my mind kept wandering backward over a decade earlier.

Eleven years had passed and not once had I talked to Larissa about my own attack. Now here we were. She had just turned twenty. I had been eighteen. The similarity of the situations, our ages, nearly a decade apart, was disturbing. I hadn't talked to anyone about what had happened to me so many years ago, and now it was bubbling just underneath the surface, threatening to boil over. I crawled underneath the covers, exhausted and scared.

The next morning, I awoke feeling as if I had a wicked hangover, despite having drunk nothing but a mug of tea the night before. A glass of whiskey may have been a better choice for once, perhaps deadening my thoughts and allowing a modicum of peace in what was a restless night wrestling with my own nightmares and imagining those of my sister's. The reality was, I was pregnant. We had found out only last month, and I wasn't even showing yet. Pete and my family knew but it was still so new that I hadn't processed it yet.

I made a bowl of oatmeal and boiled the kettle for tea and sat down at the table, my attention focused on the same knothole from the night before while my mind was elsewhere. Pete came in to make some cereal, and after a few strained pleasantries, went upstairs to work. I grabbed my bag from the bedroom and got ready to leave with the weird tension still between us. He didn't think I really needed to go. I knew that I did but was scared to. I looked up at the ceiling as though I could will him to come back down and thaw the ice that was forming. Instead, I sighed and shook my head as though my feelings and thoughts functioned like an Etch A

Sketch. I walked down the stairs to the garage below, still shivering in the chilly house.

Pulling into the small town of Alamosa, I was struck again by how grim this corner of Colorado was. Colorado was known as an outdoor playground. Snowboarders, skiers, mountain bikers, kayakers, and hikers all streamed into the state. Amateur photographers swarmed the trails, inspired by the stunning beauty of the mountains. Yet a few hours south was a flat, barren land of strip malls and alligator farms that made you wonder if there were any architects in the entire forty-mile radius, or zoning codes for that matter. When my father encouraged my sister to attend Adams State in southern Colorado three years prior, thoughts of Durango or Crested Butte came to mind—charmingly rustic mountain towns with a cool college campus vibe mixed in. I was psyched to visit her the first time to see where her formative years would be spent, getting a taste of something different than what she would have experienced had she stayed in the Midwest. But as we drove in, on a lonely road, more akin to rural North Dakota than Colorado, past an alligator farm and numerous forlorn homesteads with rusted-out cars and kitchen appliances in the yards, I gulped and hoped against hope that Alamosa was an oasis, or at least a diamond in the rough.

It wasn't. It was the rough without the diamond. The small campus of Adams State just off Main Street was the only thing that looked encouraging in the entire town. Alamosa was essentially one long main street with a series of hotels and strip malls, and it was immediately obvious that the town was financially dependent on the small college, the students, and their families that came to visit.

Nothing much had changed since that initial visit to watch one of her college soccer games three years prior. I drove through town and past the campus to the Hampton Inn on the edge of town, and I waited for Larissa to get out of class. I paced the room, nervous to see her.

She was quiet when we met up. Her long hair was in its soccer-chic messy bun, her face typically devoid of any makeup. I smiled when I saw her and gathered her up in a big hug. We had always laughed that we were built so differently as sisters. I was five nine, weighed 125, and built like a lanky boy. She was five six and curvaceous, with D cups and hips. She was the powerful soccer player, and I was the ex-ballerina. She looked like Rissa. I didn't know what I'd expected to see. There was no visible damage, thank God, but I knew what lurked beneath the surface. I was at a loss of what to say or do. Act normal? Cry? Rage?

Eat.

"Do you want to get some lunch first?" I asked, thinking a little downtime together would be nice before we headed straight to the police station.

"Sure," she said. She smiled, but her voice was wavering.

We had lunch at the local Chinese restaurant Hunan, and talked a bit about her classes and upcoming finals.

Then I asked the key question that was bothering me. "So what's the situation with the fake police guy at your door? That's just so weird."

"I know. We found out from the campus police that it's apparently been done in a few different college towns. Basically, the person who attacked you, or someone working with him, follows you home and knocks on your door pretending to be the police and collect the evidence. Pretty smart actually."

"Pretty fucking scary. How do you feel about staying there for the rest of the term?"

"My roommates and I made arrangements so no one is ever there alone, and it's only a couple of weeks until we are done for the year."

"But do you feel safe there?"

"No. But I don't know if I'd feel safe anywhere."

I looked down at my plate. I knew exactly how she felt. I paid the bill, and we both stood up, bracing ourselves for the next step. "Okay then, let the fun begin," I said sarcastically. "Where do we need to go?"

"Just head back to the campus and I'll direct you from there. Let's get this over with." We got into the Subaru and rode a few blocks in silence.

We pulled up and stepped out of the car in front of a small police station off a side street. The officer on duty was expecting us, having already talked to Larissa and my father on the phone. He asked us to sit down in his office and went over her report again. He then asked her if she would try to look at a few faces in a book of mug shots. She flipped it blankly. Page after page, she flipped, the faces blurring together, indistinct to the casual observer. Nothing.

The officer then asked if she would work with a police artist to attempt to reconstruct the attacker's face. Larissa agreed, and I watched silently as the artist asked her questions to start the sketch. "Is his nose large or small? Pointed or rounded? Straight or crooked? Did it look like it had been broken?"

Larissa answered in a monotone the best she could.

"Were his eyes close together or set apart? Do you know what color they were? Big or small?"

It was soon apparent that Larissa was overwhelmed and unable to describe her attacker's face in any way that could lead to a picture of him. Sitting there listening, I realized how hard it would be to describe my own mother in such terms, much less a man who attacked me in the dark and who I would much rather forget.

Leaving the police station, I had a feeling of helplessness and déjà vu. There was little to no chance that her attacker would be caught, much less identified. It felt like a useless exercise that kept the policeman informed but did little to bring justice to the situation. Larissa seemed to feel more frustrated than anything else.

In an effort to lighten the mood and create a distraction, we drove to Dairy Queen the next town over. The warm weather and sunshine was a welcome change from the current winter storms in the mountains that I'd just left, and I rolled down the windows, letting the warm breeze breathe new life into the car. I hadn't gone to DQ in years, decades maybe. Memories of walking to Dairy Queen with my father on warm summer nights when I was growing up entered my thoughts. He'd put on his flip-flops and we'd walked the four blocks down Washington Street to get an ice-cream cone dipped in cherry, or a lime slushy, and then walked through the park across the street, mosquitoes buzzing through the evening air around us. It was always warm, and slightly humid, and we could hear crickets and mosquitoes. It was definitely one of my best and strongest memories of him from growing up.

We walked a little on the gravel path past the Dairy Queen, eating our blizzards in quiet thought.

"How's Dad dealing with all of this?"

"I don't know. He doesn't really say much."

"He doesn't really know how, probably. I don't think we've ever talked about my attack."

"I didn't even know you were attacked until last year."

"Really?"

"Well, I was only eight or nine when it happened, right? I remember I heard you guys talking about it at the kitchen table and you were crying, and when I asked what was wrong, they told me you had been mugged in Minneapolis. It wasn't until last year that I found out. I remember I was so mad at them for not telling me."

"Well you could be mad at me, too. . . . It's my fault, too. I just never ever talked about it after it happened, still haven't really, so I never thought to bring it up to you once you were old enough. Not even when you came to visit me last year in Germany. The safe-sex talk, yeah, condoms, college and career, sure. But not the rape. That's just not something I've even thought about sharing."

" 'Til now?"

"Well, yeah, 'til now. Makes me kick myself that I didn't tell you about my experience. Like somehow it could have helped prevent it happening to you if you had been more aware. Like you would have had better radar, or been extra-cautious, or some such nonsense. Why didn't you confront me when you found out?"

"I didn't want to bring it up if you didn't want to talk about it, and I think I was just mad I didn't know. Like it was hidden from me. But regardless, it's not an easy topic to bring up when we only see each other once a year."

Larissa came back to my hotel room to hang out and do her homework so that she could be with someone until her roommates were home. We sat on the two queen beds, watching random TV while she studied and I worked. A strange mood hovered over both of us. I worked on my laptop, but was thinking of my parents.

They had two daughters, born nearly ten years apart. No sons. Both daughters were raped. That must have been devastating. The saddest part is I remember my mother being strongly against my move to Minneapolis. She sat on the edge of my bed, and told me how worried she was that something bad would happen. I assured her with all of my seventeen-year-old invincibility that she was being silly—I'd be fine. I was almost embarrassed that she was making such a fuss about it. How much guilt I harbored in the years that followed, that I'd proved her protective instincts right.

I talked with my mother several times throughout the trip. I was having a hard time believing that it had happened to Ris. I was trying to find proof it hadn't happened, because it couldn't have really happened to her. Months later I was so mad at myself for not being more comforting, more mothering. Instead I had felt almost scared to get too close, and kept her at arms' length. The wall that had protected my emotions was becoming a wedge between us, and I felt it and yet couldn't do anything to lower it. I was simply unable to comprehend that my only sister could have been violated in such a way.

A year and a half later, I found myself announcing to my family over Thanksgiving dinner my plans to start an organization to be called Mountain2Mountain. Devon was not quite two years old, my sister graduated college in the spring, and I wanted a change. Haunted by what had happened to my sister and immersed in Devon's development, I felt a pull to change my course. Despite the success I had in my career, I didn't feel challenged or fulfilled as a sports trainer. I didn't care about training individuals or preventing injuries anymore. I was sick of the apathy I saw in the world. I was sick of the violence, some of which had affected both me and my only sister. I was tired of the status quo. What would the world be like for Devon? I could spend the rest of my life ranting about the injustices I saw, or I could step up to the plate and do something about it. How could I raise Devon in a world that I wasn't fighting to make a better place, be it for her, or for her counterparts?

Pete once said after we separated, "Fund-raising for CAI isn't going to be enough is it? You're going to go over there." "There," being Afghanistan. I pooh-poohed him, suppressing the urge to say, "Yes. I have had enough of men treating women like they are disposable playthings they can just abuse and leave behind. Why can't you understand that I want to do more? I have to do more. What if this was Devon?" It was bad enough that it was Larissa, but Devon, too? Perhaps I felt I needed to pay some sort of karmic penance to ensure that this couldn't happen to anyone else I cared for. As much as I hated to admit it, Pete knew me better than I knew myself at the time. He saw what I was afraid to voice. I was too afraid he'd say no, or laugh, or worse, try to talk me out of it. I wanted to change the world and nothing was going to stop me from trying. The stakes were too high.

5

Speakeasies and Motorcycles

Afghanistan 2009

"Open this box," the security guard sitting behind the conveyor belt of the X-ray machine demanded. He pointed at a large cardboard box that I just put through, along with my bike box and duffel bag. I inwardly groaned.

"Why?"

"What is inside this box?"

"Computers for a girls' school here in Kabul." I had arrived at the Kabul International Airport's sole terminal and was standing at the final step before clearing the chaos. To be fair, it was a modern-day marvel compared to the old terminal next door where you searched for your luggage among the rest piled up on the concrete floor willy-nilly.

"You must pay tax."

"No—these are old computers, not new. These are donated. For a girls' school, here in Kabul."

"Open the box!" he barked. His colleague stopped gazing blankly at the bags still coming through the conveyor belt and took interest in the exchange, as did several other onlookers.

"With what?" I barked back. I had no intention of paying a tax on old computers and stood my ground. Besides, what's with the X-ray to enter Afghanistan? What could it have possibly picked up that the United States and Dubai X-rays hadn't already?

"*Open!*" People shoved past me gathering their luggage that was continuing to pour out of the X-ray.

"*With what?*" I shouted back. I pointed to the layers of duct tape surrounding every inch of the box, making it impossible to open without a sharp knife. I was making a scene and hardly cared what I looked like. I felt some locks of blond hair escaping from my head scarf, and I shoved them back in. We both waited to see who blinked first.

A middle-aged Afghan, in a gray business suit, standing behind me gathered his luggage from the conveyor belt and asked what was going on. I explained I was bringing these computers over for a girls' school and they wanted me to open the box so they could "tax" me.

He stepped forward, leaned over the conveyor belt, chastised them rapidly in Dari, and then switched to English more slowly. "This woman is bringing computers for our girls, and you are trying to take her money? No, you must let her go. Enough." He grabbed his luggage, nodded at me curtly, and squeezed past the crowd.

The security guard threw his hands up, scowled at me, then waved me out with a brisk, "*Burro burro,*" as if I was the one holding up the line.

Working in Afghanistan had forced me to develop an entirely different set of skills: bargaining, patience, and an assertive nature that bordered on rude when I was challenged. Two years ago I was concerned about falling into the "ugly American" stereotype—the one that shouts English slower and louder instead of learning the local language, the one that won't eat suspicious-looking food offered to her, fearing it will cause gastric issues. Afghanistan broke me of that. Don't get me wrong—I was learning the language, and I'd eat anything locals served me, even if it meant I'd be chasing the last bite with Immodium and Cipro for dessert. But when you are in the right, and someone has decided you aren't, no amount of politeness and explanation will change their mind. Often it's only sheer stubbornness and an increase in volume that gets the job done. The blond hair usually catches them off guard as well.

I smiled sweetly at the security guard and gathered my luggage and boxes. "*Tashakur,*" I said, knowing that my sarcastic tone wouldn't be understood but not caring. Having won this round, I stacked the awkward load onto a cart and maneuvered my way through the airport and parking lots to find my driver and Najibullah.

I walked outside alone, pushing my overfull luggage cart across the front of the airport toward the metal gate where my driver was to pick me up. But he wasn't there. Nor was anyone else holding a sign with my name. I wondered what to do. Several taxi drivers walked up and asked if I needed a ride, and I started to wonder if there'd been an accident. He'd never been late before. My phone was dead, so I couldn't call Najibullah to check. I decided to wait and if I needed to, I could double back and grab a taxi driver to take me to my guesthouse. I turned around and, standing right behind the guards, was the short figure of Najibullah, who beamed when he saw me. Relief flooded my veins and I beamed back.

"*Salaam, Najibullah. Hubisti? Chituristi?*"

"*Salaam,* Shannon. Thank you, I am very fine."

Najibullah brought Habibe as a driver. I smiled warmly and

shook their hands heartily while exchanging the litany of greetings to both of them. Habibe smiled at me and then turned his face and said something to Najibullah who nodded in return.

Najibullah smiled and said, "Welcome back, Shannon. We are both very pleased to see you in Afghanistan again."

We headed out into the dusty city in a loaded Toyota Corolla hatchback, down the familiar road that led to my guesthouse. A smile of joy crossed my face as I inhaled the distinctive smell of dust and diesel that, more than anything else, told me I was back in Kabul.

Najibullah and Habibe dropped me off so I could get settled into my guesthouse in the center of town. This one was much more social and accessible than the others I'd stayed at. There were about forty rooms, and at times the breakfast room was packed with men and women from all over: Indians, Pakistanis, Afghans, Canadians, Americans, Germans, French, and Belgians mingling at the buffet each morning. It was much more pleasant than feeling isolated in a building with only one or two other guests. The guesthouse was also located centrally enough that I could walk or call private taxis to get around when I wasn't working with Najibullah. It was a slice of freedom that felt much more normal.

I arrived on a Thursday, so we wouldn't start working until Saturday, as Friday was the Afghan day of rest. This meant that Thursday nights were the new Friday—the big night to go out for the ex-pat community that wasn't on security lockdown. In a dry country where alcohol was forbidden, Thursday nights often meant private house parties or defying security warnings to party at one of the local bars.

Drinking in Kabul invoked the feeling of a 1920's speakeasy, minus the flapper girls. Nondescript unmarked doors with heavily armed security guards greeted us when I pulled up on a motorcycle

with Travis. He'd asked if I wanted to join him and the Kabul
Knights Motorcycle Club for a motorcycle road trip to Panjshir in
the morning. I didn't need to be asked twice. But first we were to
drink and mingle with the ex-pat community at L'atmosphere, the
infamous Kabul watering hole.

We were let inside door number one. Here, Travis shook hands
and hugged the guard who asked us to check our weapons. The
guard obviously knew him well and joked with him. We continued
down a hallway to door number two. A knock. A peephole slid open
at eye level and immediately shut again as the door opened.

We entered a large courtyard with a path that led to a bar and a
large open area to drink outside. I took off my scarf and stashed it in
my coat pocket for the remainder of the night.

We went inside the crowded bar, filled with foreign aid workers,
photographers, journalists, and a few beefy, thick-necked contractors (hired killers, not house builders). All nationalities were represented, including Afghan, and it all felt comfortingly familiar—this
ex-pat existence was similar the world over, and after nearly ten
years of living in Europe it fit like an old glove. The bar was replete
with Heineken, Kronenbourg, wine, and enough generic hard liquor
to make one rapidly forget it was illegal here. But at seven dollars a
beer, I started to wonder who the real criminals were. To put it into
context: two drinks cost me a little more than the equivalent of a
hearty multicourse lunch for four at a local *chaikhanna*, or Afghan
teahouse.

After introductions to several of Travis's friends and acquain-
tances, we wandered back outside with Kronenbourgs in hand. We
entered the courtyard to gather around a large fire pit with many
others who were escaping the noisy crowd inside and taking advantage of a clear night to drink under the stars. It was much the same
as ex-pat communities I'd known in Germany and Beirut, where

different nationalities bonded over shared work and in common languages. Except that here conversations ranged from local security measures, assignments and projects, and general story sharing from those who'd made this life in a conflict zone their own. Those covering the war here had done so in other conflict zones. People discussed flak jackets and their quality, kidnappings in Colombia, the desire to move to Somalia as the next probable hot spot, and other risky endeavors. Each story led to another, laughed-at retelling of a similar experience in a dodgier locale. A tension-reducing one-up-manship played out over many more drinks.

Eventually, 2:00 A.M. rolled around. The crowd had thinned dramatically, but many were still entrenched, enjoying the last hours of alcohol and flirting before it was back to reality. Travis was talking to a pretty young French photojournalist by the fire pit. Gloria Estefan's "Conga" was playing inside and more than a few inebriated people were making attempts at salsa dancing, which served as entertainment for those of us outside who watched through the floor-to-ceiling windows. I found myself next to a charming conversationalist, a British photojournalist wearing traditional Afghan clothing—a pakol hat and long shalwar kameez—who claimed he was famous for his salsa dancing. I was tempted to ask for proof, but I was too scared he'd drag me along with him.

Two of the thick-necked contractors got into a little scuffle, a signal that it was time to head home. I had an early morning date with a motorcycle gang.

Kabul Knights Motorcycle Club was formed by three friends, including Travis. Members came and went, all brought together by a mutual love of adventure, but no matter who was riding, the core group had the same goal: to experience and explore the real Afghanistan on the back of a bike. They'd ridden many of the main roads, the endless back roads, and hoped to one day ride the ring road that ran the perimeter of the country, but much of it was too dangerous to attempt. The number of Taliban checkpoints and controlled areas continued to increase, making traveling by road more difficult. Overall security had been deteriorating since 2008.

The road north of Kabul into the Panjshir Valley remained relatively safe, as long as you avoided the convoys and heart-stopping traffic on one of the main arteries out of the city.

Travis picked me up at my guesthouse and took me back to his place to meet everyone. Travis's Afghan roommate Hamid was ready to go on Travis's first motorcycle, the Super Kabul. I had met him at AINA the previous fall when Travis and I went for a ride around Kabul. He was speaking with Andreas, a Swede who'd procured a beautiful, albeit old, Triumph from another ex-pat who recently left Kabul. Travis handed me a spare helmet. It was miles too big but allowed plenty of room to arrange my head scarf underneath.

Their friend Jeremy was the last to arrive with Lianne, an English freelance journalist. Lianne had worked with Jeremy previously and knew the crew as part of the extended ex-pat community, although this was her first motorcycle ride with the guys.

Four bikes, six riders headed out of town, stopping only to regroup at a petrol station to do a last-chance health check for the bikes. We had two Chinese motorbikes, one Japanese dirt bike, and the Triumph.

Riders took turns at the lead, making sure that everyone stayed together. One hour into the ride, we had our first breakdown: the Super Kabul. We regrouped by the side of the road, across from a tiny Afghan police outpost. Less than five minutes passed, and we'd attracted quite the crowd. The policemen came over and offered their help tinkering with the bike in between posing happily for photos. Children were soon hanging out around the edges, watching the scene. The riders tried the "Afghan jump-start" while Andreas posed with the Kalashnikovs on his Triumph. Running alongside the bike and leaping onto the seat sideways often jumped the engine to life. This time it did little more than tire out the runners.

After much debate in Dari and English, the decision was made to leave the Super Kabul. Hamid would ride behind Andreas on the Triumph. Surrounding us were snowcapped mountains, mountain bike–worthy hills, and the now–vibrant green Shomali Plain, lush with the spring thaw, stretching out in front of us. It wasn't hard to imagine what it would have been like to travel here in the sixties when it was part of the Hippie Trail. Not for the first time I found my mind wandering to the potential for exploration and adventure here. This could be an adventure travel paradise in more peaceful times: mountain biking, kayaking, hiking, mountaineering, yak trekking to nomad yurts, not to mention the obvious bit of motorcycle touring.

The back roads we rode were deeply rutted, muddy from the recent rains, and they required the drivers to pay close attention to the road. There was no straight line. The bikes wove back and forth, from one side of the road to the other, avoiding obstacles and trying to find the smoothest way through the rubble, much like a mountain biker finding a line through a rock garden. I was riding behind Travis on the dirt bike, but it was not exactly meant for touring with two people. There were two small pegs for my feet but no rail behind the seat to hold on to. I was sitting above the shock, which meant that to keep myself from getting bucked off, I had to hold on to Travis with one hand and use my left to hold the fender behind me, careful not to let my fingers get shredded by the spinning wheel. It proved a serious workout just to stay on.

After twenty minutes of navigating possibly the worst road of the trip, we pulled into Bagram—an Afghan village that also "hosts" Bagram Air Force Base. Makeshift stalls, stores, and repair shops lined streets with the usual chaos of people driving, walking, and biking in multiple directions. We pulled off the side of the road in front of a *bolone* stand, a delicious fried dough stuffed with potatoes and spices. Kids and men gathered to look at the foreigners and their bikes. I took off my helmet, and Hamid laughed when he saw my face. He asked for my camera and took a photo, then showed me a face two shades darker from dust and with a distinct monobrow of dirt between my eyebrows. I laughed and tasted Afghanistan in my mouth thanks to the dust I had ingested and the gritty film coating my teeth. We all shared a few pieces of *bolone*. We dipped the hot, oily dough in a spicy tomato sauce, much like a salsa. I chased it down with a warm can of Pepsi, and I followed Travis and Hamid to the black market. There you can get military knockoffs of all kinds: flak jackets, combat boots, American shampoo, soap, sunglasses, and even iPods. Guns are apparently off limits, but it was hard to believe there wasn't some dark corner in the back of one of the shops where you could purchase a weapon with enough money.

Meanwhile, it seemed that the Triumph's headlight hadn't been working, so we stopped at a stall at the end of the market. As we waited, a swarm of twenty or more people gathered to watch, but unlike in Kabul, when kids surround you here, there was no *baksheesh* plea for money; it was simple curiosity. Fifteen minutes later, though, a policeman came by and threw a few small stones to break up the crowd. The owner of the repair stall showed off his air rifle and fired a few shots for good measure. The Triumph proved a difficult match for parts, and black electrical tape was used to put everything back together as a short-term solution.

Riding again, we hit motorcycle nirvana on a road as smooth as a baby's bottom, courtesy of the American military. Travis opened up the bike and we flew ahead, only to regroup minutes later as the Triumph seemed to be operating on one cylinder now. But after a little more roadside tinkering, Andreas and Hamid turned back to Kabul on the ailing Triumph. Running the bike on one cylinder with two riders was taking its toll. Two bikes down.

Four riders and two bikes continued on toward the narrow river valley entrance that marked the beginning of Panjshir province, where General Dashty regaled me months earlier with tales of Massoud and his own part in blowing up roads to thwart the Taliban's attempts to reach this Northern Alliance stronghold. We were greeted at the guarded checkpoint and waved through with smiles.

The goal was to ride deep into the valley and visit Massoud's tomb, but the multiple bike delays had eaten up a lot of time. We stopped about an hour past the gates and got off the bikes to take a few photos and stretch our legs before turning around. Children streamed out of the fields and houses to watch us. A little boy riding a donkey proved to be a comedian in training. He hammed it up for the camera, and Travis let him try on his helmet. He paraded around on his donkey wearing the helmet and a huge grin, cracking jokes to the rest of the children who laughed at his antics. It was like a sketch out of Monty Python and a fitting end for the ride.

We headed back out of the valley and made our way toward the main road to Kabul with the setting sun casting a golden light as the scenery flashed by. We stopped briefly to fill the tanks with "fresh" petrol, which in Afghanistan typically involved an ancient can of petrol poured into a funnel, sold by an old man at a roadside stall. We purchased bottles of warm Sprite and Fanta at the stall next door. We'd been riding for six hours, and everyone was parched and tired. Travis called Andreas to see if he and Hamid had made it back all right. Men walked over to have a look at the bikes and the foreigners. One man brought out a warhead he'd apparently found somewhere in the fields behind us. When we backed away, he tried to reassure us all was well by showing us that the tip of the dusty warhead was unscrewed, but that was hardly comforting.

Check please!

"Uh, seriously, can we get out of here?" someone said. We were all laughing at the absurdity, and I was torn between the curiosity of wanting to see it closer, and getting as much distance as I could between myself and a possible explosion.

He posed with his prize find for a few photos, and we left, shaking our heads in disbelief and anxious to put some distance between us and the warhead show-and-tell.

Darkness fell as we got close to Kabul, and cars clogged the wide road, but the bikes wove in and out of traffic and along the side of the road, passing neatly through the lines of headlights.

It was late when Travis dropped me off at my guesthouse gate to the surprise and mirth of the security guards who weren't accustomed to seeing foreign women climb off motorcycles. I leaned over to give Travis a hug and thank-you for the incredible day, but as I moved forward he warned me, "Afghanistan." I quickly changed direction mid-lean-in and shook his hand instead. As I walked through the gates and greeted the night guards on the other side, I realized how happy I felt. On each visit, I had the opportunity to experience Afghanistan in a unique way, and to share that back home to those who see this country only as a war zone, destined to remain in the dark ages.

That fall I returned, and I forwent the guesthouse accommodations and accepted Travis's offer to stay at his house with his roommates since they had an empty room at the moment. And so it was that I found myself a temporary resident of the Rock House, named for the sound studio that had been soundproofed in the maid's quarters where the ex-pat band *White City* played. The current incarnation included Travis on guitar, Andreas on drums, and a new lead singer, a British woman named Ruth, who also played bass. Travis and the Afghan "boys"—Hamid, Parweez, and Nabil—all called the Rock House home. English journalist and photographer Gilly rented one of the rooms as an office, and Nabil's grumpy German girlfriend lived there as well, although all I saw of her was the occasional stink-eye in the morning when I went down to make tea and met her in the kitchen on her way to work.

Living at the Rock House brought a whole host of entertaining experiences with the "boys" and a unique insight into living in Afghanistan through the eyes of young Afghan men.

First up was a trip to Chicken Street for a burqa. For a tall girl like me, this caused a bit of humor in the shops and in particular with Hamid and Parweez, who was holding his stomach laughing at the idea of me wearing a burqa that would hit just below my knees, defeating the point of the oppressive garment.

When we got back, we held an impromptu burqa fitting in the living room. My black Dansko clogs were deemed too ugly to be Afghan. The boys decided that I needed to go back shopping for a pair of Afghan shoes—which are completely impractical. In Kabul, women frequently wore high-heeled sandals, deftly negotiating ditches, potholes, open sewers, and speed bumps. Even in the rainy season, they wore heels and open-toed sandals whereas I would choose boots or my clogs. But the shoes were a dead giveaway that I was foreign. The burqa could be lengthened, another panel added to the bottom quite easily to rectify the height issue, but the shoes and my stride were deemed to need some work. We discussed burqa etiquette, and Hamid told me that wearing your hair in a bun under a burqa was a potential sign of a prostitute. Ankle flirting, especially during Taliban times, was often the only way to judge attractiveness. But, let's face it, pretty ankles do not necessarily equate to a beautiful face. So there was essentially no foolproof way to assess beauty until the burqa was lifted and the face could be seen. I'd purchased a traditional bluebird burqa, as it was the most common in Kabul. But there were other colors throughout the country. Mazari-Sharif was known for its dove white burqas, Kandahar for brown, sage green, and eggplant, and Herat for vibrant purple along with the neighboring, Iranian-influenced black chadors.

While I was out burqa shopping, the Afghan boys had been cooking dinner for everyone. Massoud and Parweez were in the kitchen, and a delicious smell emanated from the pots, but when I asked what was cooking, Massoud laughed. "We don't have a name for it. It's an experiment." I went upstairs to tell Travis that dinner was almost ready, and he laughed too when I told him that I didn't know what it was. He explained that while he'd been trying to teach the boys to cook for themselves, and they were starting to try and were getting better, meals were still a crapshoot. In this case, it was perfectly edible: a kind of hybrid beef stroganoff with lamb and rice instead of beef and pasta. Two young women, sisters, joined us for dinner. They seemed to be sixteen to eighteen years old, were very pretty, and acted very modern. Both of them were dressed in modern clothes and wore dark kohl eyeliner and bright red lipstick. One of them was Hamid's girlfriend, and the other seemed to be with everyone else or no one at all—I wasn't sure yet. It was very unusual for Afghan women to date, so it was interesting to observe the interactions over dinner and talk to them during their visits. They appeared comfortable with the guys romantically, like American college-age couples, but in a way that was unusual to see even with married Afghan couples. They sat close, their familiarity apparent. While the boys served dinner, the girls poured tea for all of us, and when dinner was over, they helped the boys clean up. They explained that their families were in Canada and they would be leaving for there soon.

Post dinner, the discussion moved into the territory of Afghan and Western superstitions: Friday the Thirteenth, black cats, ladders, and the like. The Afghan number thirty-nine is the equivalent of our unlucky thirteen, but it had gone beyond unlucky into the realm of taboo in the past few years; it now implied a connection with being a pimp, though no one knew why or how that had developed. Cars with the number thirty-nine on the license plate were to be avoided like the plague, to the point that drivers covered their license plates. Parweez was a lanky, tall Afghan who'd been living part-time with his extended family in Austria. He provided a lot of the household humor, and after dinner he retold hilarious Wardak jokes—hilarious because they weren't funny in the least. The jokes focused on the stereotype of Wardak people being simple and a little stupid. Apparently, you couldn't just substitute a different province into the joke. Kandahar jokes revolved around homosexuality, for example. Parweez swore that the jokes lost a lot in translation. Hamid shook his head and said that they just weren't funny.

I was getting sleepy but couldn't help laughing when the discussion took an unexpected turn to the subject of balls—as in the family jewels, the veg in the meat and two veg. Afghan men apparently couldn't leave their junk alone. They were always fiddling down there, in public, at home—it didn't matter. They loved to move the things around. I assumed this was the result of their loose-fitting shalwar kameez, but apparently they did the same when ensconced in jeans. The discussion "evolved" into the subject of the shaking technique post-piss. Travis stood up to simulate proper shaking technique and soon everyone was rolling on the tashaks. Apparently, toilet humor wasn't reserved for the British. I called it quits and headed up to my room before I fell asleep, leaving them to carry on. I heard occasional bursts of laughter and smiled.

The next day I had a free morning and decided to go for a walk. I hadn't yet gone off exploring on my own, and I kept telling myself as I got ready that the first step was the hardest. I felt this way when I lived briefly in Beirut. The first morning that I walked to work was the hardest. Like diving into a cold pool, you just had to steel your-self, and then *do it*.

Part of the apprehension was the lack of maps or street names. I needed to count streets and focus on landmarks to navigate the city. So, donning my head scarf, I took a deep breath and said good-bye to the chowkidor who "guarded" the Rock House. He was a young man from Logar and looked surprised to see me leaving alone and without a car. I told him I'd be back in a couple of hours, and set off, more nervous than I had thought. The large steel door noisily clanked shut behind me, and my heart jumped a little. The dusty streets in the Taimani neighborhood were quiet and peaceful, and by the time I got to the main road that led into the city center, I was feeling more relaxed and confident. More people were around, and while I still stuck out, I blended more easily than on empty streets. The energy around the main streets and markets distracted most pedestrians from noticing me.

I headed back toward Chicken Street to find a bookstore. I needed a Dari-English dictionary, and that felt like a good goal for the first excursion. As I got closer, the cars, bikes, pedestrians, and kids crisscrossed in a myriad of directions on the main road. The street kids here were ruthless and would follow you for blocks and blocks repeating the same phrase, but you couldn't give them money or twenty more would join the fray. Once, I gave fifty Afs to a little girl who grabbed my hand to walk with me, and I saw her again when I was running errands to buy the burqa and she did the same. This time I smiled and practiced my Dari with her and received the biggest smile in return. Her name was Madina and she was adorable. She was petite, with large brown eyes and the perfect face to encourage people to open their wallets or simply to sweep her up and take her home to feed her a decent meal. Unfortunately, when I gave her a dollar, I was immediately joined by five others. I finally just turned and started walking home toward the empty streets away from the busy center of town. One young boy stuck with me for fifteen minutes, repeating "one dollar miss" over and over. I needed to pick up shampoo so I stopped into a shop. When I came back out, he was waiting and started up again. Losing patience, I shouted "No" and he left. Let's face it—it's heartbreaking to tell any street kid no anywhere in the world. These kids were often working the streets to help support their families. There were lessons to be learned here. One: if you are going to give money to street children, have it ready in a pocket so you can grab it without drawing attention. Two: be firm when you are not going to give money. Avoid eye contact and walk away. Pretending you don't hear them or ignoring them doesn't work; they will hang with you for blocks if they think you'll give in. I watched Najibullah for guidance with this. He always had a stash of twenty-Af bills in his coat pocket to distribute. Twenty Afs was approximately forty cents. Whenever we saw a group of children, he gave something to all of them quickly, and he always bought the gum or pencils that many of them were selling.

Another thing I wanted to pick up was some fresh naan and *mohst*—fresh yogurt. Naan was easy. I could purchase fresh bread from any number of bakers in the area. *Mohst* I had trouble with. A small corner shop had a refrigerator case and some yogurt. I was excited and carried everything home. But when I tore the sealed container open, I saw that it was moldy inside. A few days later, our *chowkidor* pointed me in the right direction. He explained in broken English and Dari that many stands sold fresh *mohst* by weight. A block behind the house, on the corner, there was one with Fanta and Coke stacked outside. Inside, the vendor had a large container of *mohst* in a cooler. When I told him how much I wanted in kilos, he put a plastic bag on the scale and measured it out. Then he tied it and double-bagged it to prevent leaks. I carried my baggie of yogurt home like a prize. The small victories often meant the most.

The decision had been made and now it was time to think about logistics. How did a woman purchase a motorcycle in a country where women didn't ride bikes?

I sent two Afghan housemates to pave the way. Parweez and Hamid went down to the motorcycle shop in Shar-e-nau and talked with the owner. I'd already decided that I wanted a low rider Chinese-made bike called the Desert Eagle. So they were there to haggle and spin the story that the bike was for Hamid, and his "boss"—me— was coming to pay for it. Cue the blond infidel.

I walked in, and they'd already secured the price of $700 for a brand-new Chinese bike—not exactly high quality but perfect for learning the streets of Kabul. Once we handed over the money, the mechanics put some fuel in the tank and checked that everything was working. Immediately, fuel started leaking from the bottom. No worries, they told me—they just hadn't connected the fuel line to the engine. The battery was installed. Twice. Then a variety of tools came out to tighten bolts or simply bang a few things into place.

I stepped into the back of the dark shop to sign some papers and get the registration to show ownership. I had my first experience with using my thumbprint as my signature on official papers. I remembered seeing a document in passing the previous year that had at least twenty thumbprints. The owner was starting to suspect that the bike might be for me rather than Hamid, but he played along since he was making a sale.

Everything checked out. The fuel leak was fixed, and another guy took the bike for a quick test drive. Ironically, the only thing *not* removed was the plastic coverings over the headlights, seat, and handlebars. This was a real Afghan obsession. The plastic stayed on to show that the bike was new. It reminded me of my grandmother's couch when I was a kid. Even the bubble wrap around one turn signal would typically stay. I found it safer to have my headlights and turn signals fully exposed, so I removed it all.

Hamid was driving the bike back to complete the ruse, but before we left, I had to give the customary *chirany*—a bizarre Afghan concept. Hamid told me I had to give a "gift" to a few members of the staff and also bring candy home for the two chowkidors. We stopped at the market to buy several bags of candy and chocolate. Sure enough, when we pulled up with the new bike, the first words out of the chowkidors' mouths were "Where's my *chirany?*" Essentially, custom dictated that if one had the means to buy something like a motorcycle, then that person should share the wealth.

We parked it in the courtyard next to the assortment of other motorcycles. I sat on the Desert Eagle with a glass of smuggled single malt I'd brought for the house from Dubai, and I toasted the boys—grateful for their help, bargaining skills, and guidance. Tomorrow, I would learn to ride!

The boys took me out around 8:00 P.M. It was dark, especially without streetlights, but there was a full moon high in the sky, casting its light and perfect for learning to ride incognito. Hamid tied a men's kaffiyeh scarf around my head and face, and I borrowed Travis's oversized hoodie to disguise my gender. We drove toward the airport, me in the car with Parweez while Hamid rode the Super Kabul. His friend Shams, who worked with Skateistan, rode his motorcycle. We took out the Super Kabul instead of my Desert Eagle, which was bigger, with wider handlebars and a new clutch that was still very tight. The Super Kabul was perfect to learn on. It was a bit smaller, and I felt I could control it without getting too freaked out. The three vehicles played cat and mouse on the nearly empty roads all the way there, driving way too fast considering no one was wearing helmets or seat belts.

We arrived at the long stretch of empty frontage road that paralleled the main road to the airport, and we switched up the riders. The lights were kept off on the bikes to keep our profile as low as possible. Hamid took my scarf and wrapped it like a man's turban, covering the lower half of my face, only my eyes and nose exposed. He rode behind Shams and coached me. After a few runs, back and forth, with the other bike beside me and the car behind us lighting the way, Hamid took over the second bike. He told me to follow him and do what he did: swerving, slowing down, taking on the numerous speed bumps and potholes. My legs were shaking in my motorcycle boots, but following made it easier to relax. It was hard to do something for the first time with an audience—harder still when you are a woman doing something no other woman does in front of a group of men.

Hamid was a surprisingly awesome teacher, patient and relaxed. He didn't say much but told me to do some drills, then let me go. When we decided to leave, he didn't give me the option to ride in the car. He just said, "Follow me. We're going home." We rode the whole way with no problems, even over the muddy, four-by-four demolition-style dirt road by their house that I was dreading. The potholes, deep ruts, and slick mud were less foreboding obstacles than I'd feared. The roaming packs of wild dogs that came out at night proved to be much worse on my nighttime excursions than the road conditions ever were.

Hamid smiled at me when we got back to the house and said, "You're a natural." I couldn't stop grinning and high-fived him. I thanked Parweez and Shams, who smiled good-naturedly.

The next morning, I texted Travis, who was away for a few days working. "I can ride!" He texted back. "Yeahhhhhh!! Bike chicks rock!"

The next morning, I was sitting outside on the balcony in the early morning light, looking at the hillsides and listening to the city come to life. I heard a far off *thump* and a plume of smoke rose in the distance. Something had just gotten bombed. A few minutes later, Hamid knocked on my door.

"Bomber," he said, and walked back out, probably to go back to sleep—completely nonplussed.

Thirty minutes or so later, Hamid knocked on the door again and told me to come down for breakfast. Food was set on the table— eggs cooked the way I adored, with a spicy mixture of cooked tomatoes, onions, and way too much oil. On a plate next to the eggs was Iranian feta, black olives, some seeds I was unfamiliar with, and a stack of fresh naan bread to mop up everything. I'd learned that it was much easier to eat with the bread when you split each piece by peeling off the top layer of bread. This made grabbing food, especially eggs, much easier. Parweez joined us, and I got a better taste of the camaraderie these men share, though I was spared another round of Wardak jokes. I cleared the dishes and announced I was heading into town.

Not yet trusting my bike skills on my own, I walked down the narrow alleyway that led from the house. A few blocks later I reached the main road and heard a loud sound, like a broken horn.

It was a young, black calf tied outside a butcher shop. I realized that if I came back tonight or the next morning, I'd most likely see the head, hide, and entrails in a steaming pile by the curb. The same was true of the goats. When I'd gone for early morning walks, a few streets were quite wet, the blood washed away and a neat pile of "extras" near the road. I assumed they just got washed into the open sewers.

My phone beeped. It was a text from Travis: "Reports of second, roaming suicide bomber and abductions. Lay low."

I was walking toward City Center, so I turned and started home. I texted back: "Shit. Walking into town—heading home now."

He replied immediately: "Get taxi."

I saw on the news later that the morning target was the Indian Embassy. In the end, eighteen were dead and seventy-plus injured, depending on the report. The Taliban took responsibility.

A few days later, after another nighttime practice session, I rode my bike alone to the City Center shopping mall to get a coffee. The basement coffee shop was a great place to people watch. It wasn't like going to Flower Street Cafe or the other ex-pat coffeehouses that were usually filled with foreign NGO and aid workers, contractors, and journalists. I circled the street twice, looking for a place to park that wouldn't involve hoisting the bike onto the sidewalk or leaving it too remote and unattended. I found a spot on the street, on the corner of City Center, and figured it would be fine there. After parking, I did a quick gender change. I let my black skirt down over my jeans, undid my turban and changed its position into a traditional head scarf. Voila! A woman. Once I got a little farther I pulled out my women's head scarf and draped it over the men's, which I then slid out from underneath. My transformation complete, I walked into the City Center for the requisite security check and bag search. Once inside, I went through the mall and into the basement area.

Waiting for my cappuccino, I looked around. There was a unique combination of Afghan businessmen, the occasional ex-pat contractor, and young Afghans. I noticed the last time I'd visited that at a few tables, young men and women were sitting and chatting. This was harmless enough, but in Afghanistan, dating wasn't done. One couple in particular, at the table across from me, caught my attention. Both were dressed in modern attire. He was in black acidwashed jeans with black leather "pimp" shoes and a long-sleeved black T-shirt. She was also dressed all in black, her gauzy head scarf edged with rhinestones, and a large black purse resting on her lap. Her eyes were lined in black kohl, and she was wearing a vibrant rose lipstick. Perhaps they were just brother and sister, or relatives? I gave them the benefit of the doubt, not wanting to assume, until I watched the tension between them develop. They stared into each other's eyes, smiling but never breaking the acceptable distance. There was no hand holding or foot nudging. It was still obvious that they were flirting and very much enamored with each other. The girl began to dab at her eyes with a tissue, her kohl-rimmed eyes turning red. Still, neither closed the distance. She collected herself and smiled, and they resumed their pattern of alternating between chatting and staring endlessly at each other for full minutes at a time.

I drank my cappuccino and got ready to go back to my bike. I did the head scarf shuffle in reverse once I was outside. To my right was a phone card salesman, so I bought a new phone card as I was almost out of credit. Immediately, one of the street children with his pail of spiritual good-luck smoke was on me. I had ten Afs in my side pocket, and I slid it to him, but immediately I had a crowd again. They followed me to my bike, surrounding me as I got on.

They realized I was a woman, and their reactions drew more attention than I liked.

Unfortunately, my bike wouldn't start. Apparently, my good
luck smoke karma didn't cover motorcycle issues. I'd conveniently
parked near the motorcycle shop where I'd bought it. The kids
tried to help, moving the choke switch. But this didn't help at all
when they were all trying different buttons. I sat back and sighed.
Frustrated, I put the bike in neutral and walked to the shop. I explained to one of the guys there that the bike wouldn't start. He
nodded and motioned for me to bring it closer. I did and one of the
young kids who worked at the shop jumped on. He moved a button,
the red one that I didn't know anything about, and the bike roared
to life. Sheepishly I smiled—to which I was sure the guy was thinking, *Dumb woman, what's she doing riding a motorbike anyways?* I gave
out the last of my ten-Af bills to the kids that helped, and I hit the
road. I reminded myself to ask Trav about the red button.

I made my way into the now-heaving traffic and inched across
the four-plus lanes of cars to the Shar-e-nau petrol station. I had
some petrol, but without a gauge, I didn't want to run out, especially
on my own, so I filled it up. Again, the pump attendants recognized
me as a woman as soon as I spoke, and they showed their surprise
and curiosity. I thanked them and rejoined the fray. Next stop: Le
Bistro for some croissants to bring home to the boys.

I needed to get to the right side of the street again, so I cut my
way across and turned right down the bumpy road that ran parallel
to the main road and led straight to Le Bistro. I had to get past the
security gate, which again meant that my voice gave away my disguise.
The guards' eyes went wide when they realized I was a woman, and
they laughed good-naturedly, then raised the barrier while smiling.
I smiled, nodded, and headed down the road. I parked my steed on
the corner. The guard looked at me suspiciously, and I lowered my

face scarf and said, "Le Bistro." More surprise and laughter followed, and he waved me to a space catty-corner to where I was to park my bike instead. I dismounted and left the turban on as I went inside the restaurant where I wouldn't need any head covering. The four or five security guards were all smiling and jovial as I walked by. "Nice job," they said in English as I passed. What? Nice job how I parked my bike? Hilarious. I headed inside the two sets of security doors and removed my turban completely.

Fresh fig croissants were piled on a platter. Baked fresh every day, they looked like pain au chocolat but filled with fresh fig. I got the last four for 260 Afs.

I went back outside, turban in place again, a bag of yumminess in my backpack, and the guards were still smiling. They waved me over to chat, and one of the younger ones pointed to his bike; it was a Desert Eagle just like mine. His was all pimped out, Afghan style, with a small Afghan rug on the seat, the *Chips*-style windshield, and some tassels. Proudly, he teased, "You want to trade?" I admired his bike and smiled but shook my head. I turned to get back on mine, very much aware of the many eyes watching to see if I could, in fact, ride. Praying that the damn thing would start, I backed it up and around a UN vehicle whose driver had decided that he should stop right in the middle of the narrow street. I started it up. It roared to life, and the security guards cheered. I smiled and waved and headed off, back down the bumpy road.

6

Motherhood

Boarding the plane to DC en route to Kabul, I saw my window seat was next to a mother and child. The little girl beamed up at me, holding a Ziplock bag with sliced star fruit. She happily informed me, "My fruit is shaped like stars and tastes like the Bahamas."

I couldn't help but smile and agree with surprise.

"Is that right? I've never eaten star fruit before or been to the Bahamas. That is *very* cool!"

She beamed wider and put a piece in her mouth.

"How old are you?" I asked.

"I'm five," she said, proudly holding up her right hand to show me her fingers.

"Wow," I replied, "a whole hand?"

"Yup," she responded proudly. Her dark brown eyes twinkled with the spirit of a happy girl excited to be on an adventure. She was the same age as Devon, and she had the tray table folded down with a pile of Tinkerbell valentines spread out. She was putting stickers on them and writing her friends' names on the invites, while her mom spelled out the names to her. It was such a familiar scene I felt my heart ache as I thought of Devon and wished she could be coming with me.

When Devon was born, something shifted. I had been petrified of being a mother. I can remember sitting on the floor of our bedroom, crying to Pete that I didn't have any maternal instincts and "what if they never kicked in?" I didn't want to be a bad mother. To top it off, I was scared of the label "mother." I also hated the labels "husband" and "wife" even though I had been one for nearly a decade. It brought back antiquated images of the 1950s, or worse, that of my parents' relationship when I grew up, which was the traditional model of the father who worked, the mother who stayed home, and the inevitable inequity in the perceived roles. Parents who grew apart and stayed together for the kids, but seemed to make each other miserable in the process didn't set a better example for their children than parents who divorced. It was terrifying and daunting, yet I was seven months' pregnant. Terrifying or not, I was going to be a mother.

When Devon was born, she opened a place in my heart I never knew existed. I wanted nothing more than to make sure she grew up happy, healthy, and full of joy. So why, I am so often asked, when you adore your daughter, when you want to see her grow up— perform in ballet recitals, go camping, meet her first boyfriend, meet her first love, and find out who she is—would you risk your financial and physical security by working in Afghanistan?

What if these Afghan or Cambodian or Pakistani girls were Devon? What if these women's fate was her fate? It's really just a matter of geography, the uncontrollable act of being born in one country versus another that can dictate so much of your future.

Why are their lives worth less than hers, or mine? Someone needs to fight for them. Someone needs to speak for them when they are unable, and someone needs to share their stories. Someone needs to combat the apathy that prevents change. What if that was Devon? I would want someone to fight for her if I couldn't.

It's not an easy decision to leave Devon for periods of time to work in one of the most dangerous places in the world. She was three when I first went to Afghanistan and it was heartbreaking to leave her. It was the first time I'd been apart from her for any length of time, and she was too young to really understand why I was gone for so long or to talk on the phone while I was away. I felt a physical ache throughout the time and distance we were apart, and it made me think long and hard about the path I was embarking on. Luckily, that trip coincided with a trip Pete wanted to take with Devon back to England to see family. So she was having the time of her life with cousins and grandparents and making memories with her father on their first trip alone together. This made my first trip to Afghanistan so much easier.

Now, years later, the trips are easier, as she knows why I am going and understands that I will be coming home. She thinks I am going to "build schools for other kids," and this is safe and easy for a six-year-old to digest. She gives presentations at her preschool and kindergarten, showing the photos from my trips that she likes, as well as Afghan money, burqas, head scarves, and buzkashi hats. She teaches them, "*Salaam Alekum*," a traditional Afghan greeting, and "*Hubisti?*" "How are you?" She's at an age now that she thinks it's pretty cool, but each time I drop her off at Pete's house for a long trip, I feel as if I'm leaving a piece of myself behind. My excitement about the impending trip back to Afghanistan and the next step in project development is tinged with the regret that it is at the expense of being with Devon.

This is the subject that is most difficult for others to understand. How could a mother leave her daughter to work in a war zone? The controversy really boils down to the fact that I'm leaving my daughter for Afghanistan, not Nebraska. If I was working in California, it probably wouldn't elicit so much commentary. The maddening part is how different that commentary is depending on gender. I look at men in my field, and in adventure sports, like mountaineering, adventure filmmaking, and journalism. I rarely read commentary about a man's responsibility to stay at home and avoid potential risk because he is a father—or that being a father negates his right to follow his passions and build a different future for the next generation if it involves risk. I never see men degraded as parents due to their career choices or risky hobbies. But for women, all of the above are commonplace in media questioning and in online commentary. The most biting critiques of the choices I make are the anonymous comments on news articles. One in particular was a reader's response in my own local paper, *The Summit Daily*, cut deep, even though I knew it was bullshit and cowardly. "Who does this woman think she is, galavanting around Afghanistan in a head scarf, putting our soldiers at risk?"

For weeks, I came back to this comment. It hurt because I knew it wasn't true, and because I knew others might read it, too. This person didn't know me any better than the people who blindly give me their support, or the occasional ones who call me a hero, and yet it's the negative stuff that sticks, challenging my equilibrium and calling into question my choices.

I had this discussion with Christiane, who'd worked with climbers and mountaineers, and Charley, who was the president of the Alpine Rescue Team and had been the executive director of the American Alpine Club for many years. Christiane compared the gender discussion to mountain climbing and the different perceptions of fathers and mothers who choose to climb big mountains. One example she shared was the accomplished British climber Alison Hargreaves, who summited Everest without Sherpas or bottled oxygen, the north face of the Eiger, and Ama Dablam, among other impressive climbs. Alison was also the first climber ever to solo climb all the great north faces of the Alps in one season. She did many of her major climbs while pregnant. She died in a storm while coming down after summiting the infamous K2. The subsequent controversy in the climbing community and press, including many female journalists who publicly questioned the ethics of a mother engaging in such a dangerous sport, was an obvious double standard. Why is the same questioning and post-mortem commentary not done of fathers who climb, take risks, and often perish in their pursuits? Fathers are not pilloried for having left their children fatherless, as mothers typically are. Instead, they are often praised for their intrepid adventurism and lauded for their daring and courage in attempting to break new boundaries and scale new heights.

The chances of dying during an unassisted climb up mountains such as K2 and Everest are around one in four. In an interview with the *Guardian* in 2002, Alison's husband, James Ballard, now a widower and father of two young children, was asked why he'd let her go in the first place. "How could I have stopped her? I loved Alison because she wanted to climb the highest peak her skills would allow her to. That's who she was."

Would that journalist have asked Alison the same question if it had been her husband who'd died on a mountain pursuing what he loved, despite being a husband and father?

Women adventurers and athletes have just as much right to pursue their goals, dreams, passions, and pursuits as men. They should not have to repress who and what they are simply because they become a parent. How many fathers attempt to climb Everest every year? How many skydive, base jump, and freedive? Why, in a country where women have had the right to vote for almost a century, are we still debating gender roles so ignorantly?

Mothers are simply not allowed to take the same risks as fathers according to the public conversation, and those that do are judged harshly. Gender stereotypes continue to skew our perception of the risk equation. Because I am a mother, should I not be working in Afghanistan? That subject is up for debate, with solid arguments on both sides in regards to responsibility, risk, security, and identity. And I welcome it. But we shouldn't be basing it on gender. Unfortunately, we don't debate this in the public forum—we cast judgment based on gender and perceived parenting roles. It's one-sided, and unfair, and frustrating as hell. I know this: Devon is the only one who can judge what kind of mother I am to her. I want her to see her mother fully embracing who she is, and I am setting the example of a woman who followed her path, as I would want her to do. She is the only one whose opinion on this subject matters. The risks I choose to take are measured through the prism of her, and while my level of risk may seem too high for some, it is a personal decision that regards only me and my family.

Being a single parent that coparents can be difficult and frustrating at times. Decisions regarding what's best for the child are mutually shared, but shared with someone you've chosen to break ties with. In my particular case, the fact that I have chosen to make my work in Afghanistan is still a sore point. It probably always will be. But I am grateful for the amicable relationship that Devon's father and I have. It allows great flexibility for both of us and gives Devon the stability of two happy households.

Yet I find myself pondering for the first time in my adult life, "If I were a man, this wouldn't even be an issue." It wouldn't. Fathers travel for work all the time. Fathers often make their careers the priority over family. My ex traveled extensively and for long periods of time from the moment our daughter entered our lives, and still does. He is not criticized or questioned for his choices spent away from Devon.

I look at the example I'm trying to set for Devon. Through my actions, I am showing her that involvement in the global community is important, and that one person can make a difference. I am raising a daughter who will have a strong sense of self. I hope that when she becomes a mother, she will continue to follow her dreams and stick to her ideals rather than give them up when she has her own children; the two are not mutually exclusive.

Part of my preparations for each trip includes writing Devon an "insurance" letter. It's a letter that my sister will give her when she's older if the worst should occur. It's insurance against her not having a written reminder that her mother loved her and how very sorry I am that I'm not there. In some bizarre way, I view that letter as insurance against the worst happening. A karmic token—that if I write the letter, it will never need to be delivered. I also bought two lockets. One is for her and has a photo of me and our old dog, Bergen, in it. It's pink with an elephant riding a bicycle. Her favorite animal is an elephant, and she knows that I love to ride bikes. The second locket is for me. It's green and has a different elephant. It contains two photos of her, and I wear it daily, like a talisman, while we are apart.

Christiane calls her the Elephant Princess, and to this day, if she sees a small item that has elephants on it, she buys it and sends it to Devon, addressing all her letters to the Elephant Princess. Devon has a small drawing that Christiane bought her on the street during a walk the two of us took together in SoHo. Now at age nine, her favorite animal is the snow leopard. She is interested in endangered species, and yet she will always be the Elephant Princess to me and Christiane, even if she has moved on to champion another animal.

I also write her letters on her birthday, each year documenting the year in a few pages of her likes and dislikes, what we did, who her friends are, and the details that make up the amazing little girl she is. Then I seal it and label the front with "Devon—1st birthday," and so on. I've written down why her father and I divorced in words that lay no blame, but simply express my regret that we couldn't stay together for her sake; in the end, my hope is that she would grow up with two loving and happy homes, surrounded by people who love her unconditionally. I've written down her first words, favorite games and toys, and what she likes to eat. When she turns eighteen, I'll give them all to her. Who knows? Maybe I'll continue past then, each year writing a letter to my daughter on paper, hoping she never forgets how amazing she is to me—how she cracked open a place in my heart that I had kept guarded, and how, because of her, I learned to love unconditionally and without expectations.

I don't know what she will think when she grows up. Will she resent the risks I took once she understands them? Will she be proud of me? Will she want to do the same? I hope that she grows up seeing a mother who fought for change. For human rights. For women's rights. That she sees a mother who fought to make the world a better place for her and for girls on the other side of the planet. I hope she understands that you cannot sit on the sidelines of life and wish things were different. It is your responsibility to be involved whether it's in some far-flung corner of the Earth, or in your own backyard: for animals, the environment, human rights—whatever inspires you to take action and enter the fight and contribute in some small, or huge, way.

During a previous visit to Kabul, I'd donated computers for a girls' school. This was a school in Kabul run by Afghans 4 Tomorrow.

The organization had the small guesthouse where Tony and I had stayed during my first visit to Afghanistan, and Najibullah had taken us to visit one of the girls' schools they operated. These were girls who had a real chance to follow their dreams. They were living in the capital, where there was much less resistance to girls' education than in other parts of the country. They had the support of their families and an NGO's commitment to help them finish school. They had the potential to continue on to Kabul University should they choose to. Najibullah continued to work with and help Afghans 4 Tomorrow, and he reached out via e-mail in between my visits to see if I could help with a school computer lab.

I gathered more information about what they needed. Laptops were better than desktops, easier to keep secure and dust-free, and they used less power. I reached out to the Mountain2Mountain community to see if anyone had computer contacts, and eventually a woman with Dell was able to get us six laptops at cost with Microsoft software. A couple of months later, I brought over the laptops for the computer lab, paid for a backup generator, and covered the salary for a teacher for one year. Basic computer skills with Word and Excel would increase the girls' ability to attend university. Many of them, around the age of thirteen, had never turned on a computer. Internet cafés were opening in Kabul, computer programming and business training were important areas of growth, and if any of the girls wanted a chance to study overseas in a student exchange, computer skills were necessary.

After we set up the computers, turned them on, and talked with the teachers, I got the chance to ask the girls some questions. I recognized a few faces from my visit to the classrooms a year prior, and I told them so, not sure if they recognized me. They shyly smiled back and said they remembered. When I asked what they wanted to be when they grew up, they answered, "Doctor, lawyer, engineer, journalist, teacher, and artist"—not any different from the answers you would expect back home. They wanted normalcy and had the desire to go to college, to have a career. They'd grown up with the knowledge that these things were possible in post-Taliban times. Only eight years after the fall of the Taliban, this was a clear sign of progress.

Then the girls asked me, "How did you learn about us over here? Why are you helping us?"

I was momentarily tongue-tied. How could I explain why I wanted to help, even if it was only in some small way? Any answer I could think of sounded inauthentic and trite.

"I have a young daughter back in the United States. Her name is Devon and she is five years old. She can go to school and even to university if she wants, just like most American girls. You deserve to have the same opportunities that she has. I hope that each of you can continue your education and follow your dreams and be an important part of your community."

They smiled shyly, but a small girl who'd told me she wanted to be a doctor had a radiant smile, and said, "Thank you for saying that we are as important as your own daughter."

I gulped hard, not wanting to show how overwhelmed I was. Instead I smiled, put my hand over my heart, and said, "*Hush Amandine, shoma tashakur.*" You're welcome, thank *you*. Another drop in the bucket, but a drop that had the potential to create some ripples.

Past Mother's Days make me think hard about my role as a mother, not because the Hallmark holiday hits me emotionally. It hardly registers as anything to celebrate. The day is typically spent like any other—hanging out with the Elephant Princess, going for a hike if it's not too snowy, making pumpkin pancakes, and squeezing in some work on the laptop. One of my most memorable Mother's Days was spent watching Devon at age four creating her own elephant sign language. This kept me on my toes, considering I was still trying to find time to learn Dari and some basic sign language since I'd been supporting a deaf school in Kabul—having secured a land donation of nearly five acres in a remote, undeveloped area of Kabul for the school's future home.

Where in the "motherhood manual" does one find the rules? Where does it say that I am not allowed to embrace my true path in life? Where does it state that the best role model you can be is to suppress who you are?

Those who know me well see the opposite—that by carving my path I am doing my utmost to raise a daughter who will have the confidence in herself to find her own path and courageously follow it. Her needs remain my priority, and that tempers my choices. Putting her first in the heavy list of priorities doesn't replace my needs, wants, desires; it simply bumps them down the list, not off the list entirely.

As a mother, my daughter comes first. As a woman, I must remain true to myself and the things that are important in my life. Let's not forget that one must work in order to provide. Men continue to work, and oftentimes we view them as heroes because of their sacrifices for their families. My father owned a business, and this required long hours at the office and travel away from us. It wasn't viewed as selfish. It was necessary. It was work.

Why Afghanistan? Why take the risk? Because my daughter is born in a country that ensures her right to choose. She is promised an education. She can ride a bike, ski, or simply walk down the street with little risk other than that which she causes herself with the genetic clumsiness she inherited from me. She can choose when,

who, and if she wants to marry. She has every opportunity thanks
to the genetic passport she was gifted at birth—that of a U.S. citizen. I had and have those same rights, and I realize how lucky I am.
Young girls in Afghanistan shouldn't be afforded less opportunity
just because of where they live. I can only hope my daughter feels
the same way as she matures into the woman she chooses to become.

7

Road Trips and Prisons

Afghanistan 2009–2010

Sitting in the back of yet another white Toyota Corolla, I looked into the front seat at my driver, Habibe. He was a kind man who practiced his English as I practiced my Dari. He was always smiling, and we shared stilted stories about our children and family. He enthusiastically agreed to drive me to the northern city of Mazar-i-Sharif so that I could visit a women's prison. It had become clear that I couldn't go by plane. Flights were running only once a week, and I didn't have that kind of time to spend in one place. I wanted to visit two women's prisons in the northern provinces to better understand the situation from a women's rights perspective and to look at potential programs that I could create. Habibe's one condition was that his seventy-year-old father-in-law could come along as "protection." Mahmahdoud, aka John, looked as though he weighed a hundred pounds wet and, like many his age, was missing several teeth. His eyesight was also poor. I'm not sure who was protecting whom on this road trip, but having a respected elder in the car couldn't be a bad thing if we found ourselves in trouble.

It would take us eight or nine hours to get to Mazar, assuming that the Salang Pass wasn't snowed in. I became a little apprehensive when Habibe asked me to please pull my scarf further forward, entirely covering my hair and creating a shadowy hood to hide my face—the first of many signs that this road trip was not like a family excursion to the Grand Canyon. There would be no roadside picnics and corny photo ops. My main concern was not bandits, checkpoints, or the Taliban; it was the car. We were traveling in the same car that broke down three times in one day last week while running errands in Kabul. Though Habibe assured me repeatedly that it was travel-worthy, I had my doubts.

We left Kabul on the road toward Panjshir with snow-covered mountains on the left and smaller rolling hills to the right that paralleled the road out onto the Shomali Plain. We went straight through the large roundabout that led to Bagram, and past Charikar. We passed a jeep filled beyond capacity with Afghan men. Three were hanging on the back and one sat on the hood like a comical ornament.

On our left, the river was raging and we followed it for the next twenty miles as we climbed the switchbacks to Salang Pass. These mountains were part of the Hindu Kush, and the road was a major trucking route. Heavily painted and bejeweled trucks clogged the lanes in both directions. As the landscape turned white with snow, we followed the trucks into a series of tunnels built to protect the narrow roadway from avalanches and heavy snowfall. They were all unlit, but many had natural light coming through at regular intervals—all but the last and longest. We entered the dark cavern, the walls and road wet. Enormous potholes spread out across the road, creating obstacles in addition to the complete darkness. To make matters worse, many Afghan cars have very dim lights, and many motorbikes have none. Often you didn't see another car until you were right on top of it. Majority ruled here, much like in the streets of Kabul, and whichever team had more cars spread out side by side across the road, won.

Surprisingly, we emerged unscathed on the other side of the tunnel. The scenery here was among the most spectacular I'd ever seen. As we descended the switchbacks, cars of men and burqa-covered women stopped for impromptu picnics, and I wished I could join them to enjoy the view and be part of the experience. John needed a bathroom break, so we pulled over. He got out slowly, and he drew his brown shawl around himself for a little privacy as he conducted his business in the snow. When he returned, he told Habibe to tell me that if I needed to go, I could borrow his shawl. I considered that he said that to all the young women he played body-guard for. I smiled graciously and said, "*tashakur*" to John. He smiled sweetly at me and nodded in return.

The snow receded as we drove farther, and now the mountains were covered in lush spring grass and wildflowers. Beside us on the left, the river continued to rage with snowmelt. The landscape was dotted with sheepherders, red flowers, and the occasional horse. The game trails that crisscrossed this area screamed for lengthy trail running and mountain biking. I wondered how badly land mined this area was and if I could perhaps arrange a little excursion on future visits with my bike or even my trail-running shoes. I daydreamed for miles about riding the goat paths, which surely, I decided, must be clear if goat herders and goats walked them regularly.

Hours later, I was sitting with my legs crossed in the backseat, contemplating John's offer of his shawl. The hunt was on for a *tashnab*, a bathroom. Habibe didn't want me to squat on the side of the road, but the one village large enough to have a public bathroom,

Pul e Khumri, Habibe deemed too unsafe for a stop. And so, twenty minutes later, off the side of the smooth road to Samagran, I found myself squatting in the rain behind a crumbling mud wall, in a field of red poppies like the ones Dorothy fell asleep among in the *Wizard of Oz*.

As we got closer to Mazar-i-Sharif, the landscape flattened dramatically into empty plains, reminiscent of my home state of North Dakota. Amazingly, the car had made it nine full hours to Mazar, but as we entered the city, I realized that my phone had stopped working. It had been fully charged that morning, so there was absolutely no reason for this. But here I was, in an unknown corner of Afghanistan for the first time, with no communication link. I fought the urge to panic. *This wasn't a big deal*, I told myself. *You can figure something out.* I explained to Habibe where I was staying and figured I could sort the problem out once I was settled. I sat back and within a few minutes we were driving past the Blue Mosque and my phone worries faded as I marveled at the beautiful aquamarine tilework that decorated the famous structure.

We pulled up to the Mazar Hotel on the other side of the mosque, and at first glance it seemed normal enough, a solid structure of bland concrete Russian architecture and Afghan flags. Once inside, I realized that I'd entered some sort of time warp or perhaps simply a bizarro alternate reality. The hotel staff wasn't sure what to do with me as the only foreigner in the hotel and an unaccompanied female to boot. The reception area was full of Afghan men of varying ages lounging around talking. Eventually, all eyes fixated on me. The staff led me through a maze of hallways and staircases to my room, 206. While I waited for a key to be brought to me, a small group of young men gathered to watch. I groaned. I was hot, dusty, slightly annoyed, and in dire need of my Dari dictionary, which I just then realized I had forgotten in Kabul. I was handed off to the manager, Mohammad Karim. Extremely friendly and perhaps more than a little lonely, Mohammad Karim spent the next forty-eight hours trying to be my new best friend. He was slightly goofy in his appearance, his white shirt tucked into his pants that were belted high above his waist. He had a childlike face, which proved to match his innocent demeanor. He came in to change the sheets on the beds (which perhaps should have been done before I checked in?), fixed my door's lock (a bit worrying), and brought me tea. When I requested a towel so that I could shower—having not realized that I needed to bring my own since the guesthouses I stay at in Kabul typically have at least one thin towel—he scrounged up a ratty orange towel with two holes that seemed relatively clean. The bathroom was down the hall, and when I opened the door, I immediately had the queasy sensation of entering a humid animal den. The musky smell was overpowering. The concrete room was larger than my hotel room and consisted of a bathtub shower with no curtain, a toilet, a sink, and a small mirror. No toilet paper or soap was available. The floor was almost entirely flooded. And the hot water tank was empty. Perhaps I could wait a bit. Perhaps the entire trip?

I peeked into the bathroom directly next door and found a veritable paradise in comparison. The floor was only slightly damp, and it lacked the heady zoo aroma, but when I walked in, I was immediately shooed out by Mohammad Karim. He guided me back to the other door. I was going to have to use commando skills to sneak into the enemy bathroom!

My room had a concrete floor covered with a worn Afghan rug and two twin beds that were basically wood platforms with a sleeping mat—thinner and lumpier than most camping mats. The coatrack stood at such an angle that it looked poised to attack unwary guests. Each time I unlocked my door and peeked out to use the

forbidden bathroom, Mohammad Karim came pitter-pattering over
to say hello, clasp my hand, or try to rub my cheek and tell me how
happy he was to meet me—to which I smiled, said, "*Tashakur,*
Mohammad," and retreated into my room to unpack. Thirty minutes
or so later, he knocked and brought in a pot of green tea, then left. I
plugged in my phone, hoping against hope that the charge was simply out, but the electricity wasn't working. Mohammad knocked on
my door again and delivered a small plate of cookies to go with my
tea. I thanked him sweetly and then ushered him back to the door,
where he shook my hand longer than necessary. "You are so lovely. I
love you." Yikes.

"*Tashakur, xoda al fez.*" Thank you, good-bye.

The saving grace to the comedy unfolding was a balcony overlooking a small garden where I could sit on the end of the concrete
ledge and be outside with my head uncovered. I worked on my laptop and watched the swallows chase one another as dusk fell and the
evening call to prayer filled the air, content at my own Afghan-styled
Hotel California.

Travis arrived that evening, and I couldn't stop laughing when I
heard Mohammad Karim accost him in the hallway and follow him
inside the room. Travis was on the phone and in a flurry of uncon-
tainable energy. He strode through my room and headed straight
onto the balcony to sit outside in the fresh air. I could barely see
through my tears of laughter as I shared with him the eccentricities
of the hotel and of Mohammad Karim.

The next night, we walked into town toward the Blue Mosque,
stopping on the way for a little snack of Afghan burgers, something
I'd consciously avoided until now: a small plate filled with soggy
French fries cooked in none-too-fresh cooking oil in sidewalk vats,
garnished with some shredded cabbage and hot sauce, and rolled up
in thin falafel bread. It reminded me of late-night runs to the chippy

in England with Pete—greasy chips, doused with malt vinegar and then rolled in several layers of newspaper, the oil leaking through the newsprint as we walked home with a meat pie on top. Ours was topped with a dodgy-looking chicken drumstick that screamed salmonella on a stick. But life was for living, so we took our bounty to the gardens outside the mosque and dug in, daring each other to try the chicken. But seeing as the chicken and the fries were cooked in the same grease, and the chicken had been sitting on the rest of the pile of food, whatever the chicken had, so did the rest of our meal. So down the hatch it went, my fingers crossed that I wouldn't be spending the evening in the toilet-paperless bathroom, swallowing Cipro tablets.

The Blue Mosque was incredibly beautiful, and if this architectural wonder resided in any town other than an Afghan one, it would be the epicenter of tourist activity. In this case, we were the only foreigners among throngs of Afghans. The call to prayer emptied the area of worshippers as they flocked to the open prayer rooms. The bizarre part came as the light began to fade and I realized that the mosque was covered with multicolored neon lights, including a bright neon sign flashing "Allah" in Farsi—turning the centuries-old cultural gem into a 1970s Las Vegas act.

We walked around the mosque until dark, then headed back to the guesthouse, stopping on the way to buy a container of fresh yogurt from a young boy for twenty Afs—about fifty cents. It was covered with a plastic bag so it wouldn't spill. We walked a little farther and bought two fresh round loaves of naan in the traditional Uzbek style Mazar-i-Sharif was famous for. Then we picked a random kebab shop out of the many that lined the street, ordered a few lamb kebabs to go, and took our bounty back to the hotel porch. Mohammad heard us walking up the stairs. He'd probably been waiting the entire time, and he followed us to our rooms. Travis and I went onto the balcony to eat, and within three minutes Mohammad knocked. He brought in some tea. When his cat followed us out to the balcony so did he. I smiled, trying to hide my exasperation, and I shooed both of them out and locked the door. He knocked only once or twice more before bed.

The next morning, Mohammad woke me with a knock on my door. He feigned a look of surprise when I sleepily opened it. In his hand was the key for 207 (I was in room 206), and he explained that he'd made a mistake. I mustered a smile as fake as his excuse and closed the door. Awake, I dressed and walked into town to buy a few supplies as well as breakfast. I was also on the hunt for the fabled Mecca compass to see if it really existed. It was a compass that supposedly always pointed to Mecca instead of north. Thanks to my broken Dari and the wonders of charades, I got shampoo, breakfast, bottled water, and biscuits for emergency snacking, but alas, no toilet paper. I was simply unwilling to play charades for that one.

Again, I was headed off at the stairs by Hotel California's manchild, when I returned from the market. He looked hurt that I hadn't asked him to get me breakfast. I assured him I'd wanted to go for a walk. He said he'd been watching me sleep this morning and wondered if I was okay. Suddenly, the meaning of the 207 key became clear. The room next to mine shared my balcony, and he'd entered it and peered in through my large French door windows. Though this was creepy and more than a little off-putting, I decided he was harmless, as he acted much the same with Travis. He tried to follow me into my room to talk more, but I firmly shook his hand and said bye-bye! But my lock was stuck again, so Mohammad got his tools back out and knelt by my door to "fix" it.

When he was done, I attempted a shower. I entered the still-reeking bathroom, avoided the flood plain, and stripped by the edge of the tub so I could keep all my clothes off the floor. The water heater was plugged in now. The water came out of the faucet hot, but no more than a trickle left the showerhead. So I took the world's wimpiest shower to get the worst of the dust off me. I felt as if I were in an Afghan version of a *Fawlty Towers* episode.

Mohammad must have been waiting outside my door, because when it was time for me to leave for my meeting at the women's prison, he was right there to ask me when I would return.

Security at the women's prison in Mazar-i-Sharif was not much more enforced than the security check at the gates of most Kabul NGO offices. It was completely unlike security at the Kabul prison. I had visited it several times, but the erratic commander had made access and interviewing the women a nightmare. Travis was working in Mazar-i-Sharif for another project, and I'd arranged this trip to coincide with his trip so that he could document some of the stories I wanted to share.

Women and men shared the same prison compound, but the women's section was behind a locked metal door just off the main courtyard. Behind this door were forty women and fourteen young children. Whereas Kabul's women's prison looked like what I expected of a prison block, housing more than a hundred women and children, this prison was nothing more than a small courtyard and two small rooms where the convicted prisoners and their children lived. This multipurpose communal space was all these women saw for the duration of their sentence. It served as their sleeping quarters, daycare, dining hall, and classroom. We walked through a small doorway out of the rain and into the larger of the two rooms where a sea of multicolored head scarves filled the space. Women of all ages and several young children and babies were learning to read and write. The sea of women turned their heads to find out who had arrived and miraculously parted to allow us space to enter.

These women comprised the entire female prison population

for the whole of Balkh province. They'd been convicted of murder, robbery, prostitution, and the ever-ambiguous crime of adultery. Recent studies estimate that nearly 80 percent of the female prison population in Afghanistan have been convicted of morality crimes. Many of the women in jail were trying to escape an arranged marriage or assisted another woman trying to escape one. Many accused of the crime of adultery were actually raped by a male family member—an uncle, brother-in-law, or friend of the family, and they were accused of adultery to save family honor. In Taliban-controlled areas of the country, where prison isn't an option or Sharia law takes precedence, accused women are still stoned to death, beheaded, or—as seen recently in the case of Bibi Aisha whose face graced the cover of *Time* magazine—have their ears and nose cut off to punish them and warn others in the community. This isn't as rare as you'd like to think or relegated to the southern Taliban-controlled provinces of Helmand and Kandahar. In the rural, mostly peaceful province of Parwan, located on the route between Kabul and Panjshir, the Taliban executed eleven women in the district of Shinwari in 2012 alone. Only one execution, that of twenty-two-year-old Najiba—accused of adultery—was covered by the media. An amateur video, posted on YouTube in July 2012, shows her gruesome execution in the street.

The experience of sitting with the women and their children on the concrete floor where the women and children slept and led their entire existence was humbling enough. Two of the women served me tea and offered me a small tin of chocolates, surprisingly gracious—as if I were a guest in their home.

As we began to talk, one woman emerged as the de facto leader of the group. Sitting near the back of the crowd in a thin white head scarf, Maidezel was a fiery woman with an easy laugh and a strong gaze. She freely admitted that she was guilty of murder, and the translator explained to me that Maidezel was accused of murdering her husband's son. But because of the translation, I wasn't sure whether the son was her own or that of another wife, as many Afghan men have multiple wives who all raise their children together. Regardless, Maidezel said she was sentenced to eighteen years. A fellow prisoner nudged her and asked, "Why did you say that? You should have lied!" Maidezel just laughed good-naturedly and got up to sit directly in front of us.

The room was filled to capacity with women sitting cross-legged on the floor facing me, many with children in their laps. Once the children were school age, they would either join their other siblings at home, if that was an option, or become temporary wardens of the government at an orphanage set up for children of prisoners.

These women spent twenty-four hours a day within a few feet of one another, but rather than turn against one another, they'd built a sisterhood, taking care of one another and the children. As if to prove the point, Maidezel was passed one of the younger babies, which she placed in her lap as though the baby were her own.

Several of the women in Afghan prisons were convicted of murdering their husbands. Many of these women were sold or forced into marriages with much older men, beaten, and raped. Divorce was rarely an option for them, because their husbands had to agree to it, and running away wasn't possible. Regardless of the crime the women were accused of, and regardless of the truth behind the accusations, they were often disowned by their families and, as convicted criminals, became outcasts in Afghan society. The social workers helping the prisoners focused on educating their families and creating bonds with them so that the women didn't end up on the street after they were released. At the same time, literacy and vocational programming were one key to giving the women the tools they needed to build a better life for themselves after they'd served their time.

Maidezel grabbed my hand and led me into the other room. There were several sewing machines, and she promptly sat down at one and started making something out of a cream-colored gauze. I sat on the floor to watch, and soon another woman started working on the machine next to her.

Occasionally, Maidezel looked up at me and smiled, clearly proud to show off her handicraft. I was fascinated as I watched a woman so powerful and strong-willed soften as she sewed in front of me, the layers of human nature slowly exposing themselves. Children migrated in from the other room and from the courtyard, and gathered around me. They took turns sitting on my lap, all except for one sweet little girl in a red dress who shyly watched from the lap of her mother. She looked to be two or three years old, but her mother appeared to be in her fifties. I often found it hard to estimate age in Afghanistan. War and poverty coupled with the lack of health care aged faces prematurely. This mother could be as young as me despite her weathered face.

It wasn't any easier to guess the children's ages. They'd had to grow up quicker in this harsh environment, and I often thought they were a couple of years older than they were. Throughout Afghanistan, many kids Devon's age were working instead of attending school, and the kids sitting in my lap, laughing at my silly faces and playing peek-a-boo, were in a tough spot. While the state and culture believed they were best served staying with their mothers, they were deprived of anything related to childhood. Stuck in the same bare courtyard prison as their mothers, they had no playground, no books, no toys, and harldy any stimulation. Even the poverty-stricken street children had daily experiences and a changing environment to stimulate their brains and spur development.

I felt humbled to have been trusted so openly and to get a rare glimpse into their lives. I listened to them talk for hours. The current prison situation for women in Afghanistan would prove tougher to navigate and even tougher to tolerate the more I learned during my various visits. I would find myself becoming more enraged and more determined to do something. Yet I was constantly stonewalled by the whims of the rotating prison commanders. One step forward, two steps back became the two-step the prison system intended for me. I realized over time that it was an arena I needed to leave to human rights and justice organizations with bigger teams and a stronger presence on the ground. I decided to focus on sharing their stories and highlighting the issue so that people understood the difficulties women faced throughout the country.

The next day, Travis and I headed to Sheberghan, the capital of Jowzjan province, eighty miles west of Mazar-i-Sharif. As we drove, camels dotted the fields, and we passed several camel trains on the roadside. We would be staying in a remote area, in a home that housed the organization Travis was working with. I was hitching a ride with him so that we could visit another women's prison a couple of hours past Sheberghan in the neighboring province on his day off.

I spent two days cooling my heels, working on my computer and watching Afghan rural life from the rooftop of the house. One night, the chief of security took us out for a walk around a local park where Afghans picnicked with their families. It had a small swimming pool and was in a beautiful area of walking trails surrounded by trees and flowers. Travis and I posed for pictures on the diving board much to the amusement of our guide. We walked around looking at flowers, a favorite Afghan pastime. I learned a few of their names along with a local history lesson from the security chief.

Sheberghan was once a flourishing city along the Silk Road, and in the thirteenth century, Marco Polo wrote about its honey-sweet melons. Sheberghan is also where Soviet archaeologists discovered the famous Bactrian gold, an enormous treasure cache buried under a hill for two thousand years. The collection of Bactrian gold—a collection of about twenty thousand gold ornaments, including coins, crowns, jeweled necklaces, and medallions—went on exhibit at the National Gallery in D.C. It is a true national treasure of Afghanistan, and a special museum is now being built in Kabul to house the gold so that it can be shared with Afghans.

The region is mostly agricultural and as such is very green. The town itself is now known as the stronghold of the infamous Uzbek warlord General Abdul Rashid Dostum. We drove past his home—a heavily reinforced compound—on the way back from the park. He was currently in exile in Turkey but would be returning to help President Karzai with his reelection bid in the upcoming months.

On the third day, Travis arranged for a driver to take us to neighboring Fayrab province, to the capital city of Maimana, where I was going to visit another women's prison. My alarm was set for 5:30 so we could get an early start. I woke up a few times in the night with my digestive system in chaos. I decided to take a Cipro and kill whatever strain of nastiness I'd ingested. I was lucky to be relatively pain-free, but intestinal liquifaction didn't make for great road tripping. Maimana was a three-hour drive from Sheberghan and not a place to be squatting by the roadside. Rumors of Taliban checkpoints reemerging in the northern provinces had reinforced my dislike for road trips. I had my burqa just in case, as well as toilet paper, and I hoped the Cipro/Immodium cocktail would kick in.

The morning light as we drove was incredible, and even Travis, who wasn't a morning person, commented that once in a while it was worth getting up early for the light. The green landscape remained flat, with numerous camels, donkeys, and goats, and the morning routines of its inhabitants added a timelessness to the scenery. Large, turban-wearing Turkmen sat straight and proud atop tiny donkeys trotting along the roadside. Donkeys and camels alike were loaded with stacks of cloth bags and bundles to transport, while young boys tended to the herds of goats. There were more motorbikes and rickshaws than cars and trucks. The mud houses had a uniquely domed shape that reminded me of desert nomadic tribes. The journey to Maimana was a hundred miles or so, and we both catnapped during the more than two-hour drive. When I opened my eyes again, twenty minutes or so later, the landscape had turned into stunning rolling hills covered in red golala poppies and pale lavender flowers. The colorful carpeted patterns covered the hills, interrupted only by more goat herds. All I wanted was to stop and take photos—all I wanted, that is, until I spied the array of trails winding through the hills and realized that *this* was where I could possibly go mountain biking. No land mines, little traffic, few people to create an audience save for a couple of goat herders. And the area was gorgeous. I broached the subject with Travis, and he thought he could take his motorbike off road on these trails. Perhaps a joint trip would be in order with some dirt bikers and mountain bikers, he joked. I sat back, seriously contemplating it for a future visit.

The beauty continued all the way to Maimana—a thriving Afghan market town. We drove past a bustling goat market, and nearly every woman here wore a white or bluebird burqa. The only ones not wearing burqas were Turkmen women with traditional head coverings in vibrant reds and purples. The men had faces worthy of portraits, and all wore elaborate and colorful turbans. There were no street beggars that I could see, and the only real traffic came from donkeys, motorbikes, and elaborately decorated rickshaws.

Men in traditional emerald-striped coats mingled with the blue-birds and doves everywhere. Even Travis was spellbound. I could easily have stayed here for weeks.

We had plans to meet with the director of a women's organization that works with the prisoners, AWEC, Afghan Women's Education Center. Rashed met us at the corner of a street to guide us. He discussed their programs as we headed over to the women's prison. Security was similar if not even more laid-back than in Mazar. Guards allowed us to duck under the barrier and waved us in. The deputy commander of the prison, Mohammad Akbar, met us at the entrance and led us back with the commander of the women's section. The inside of the compound looked like a small rural farm, and only the telltale barbed wire and men in orange jumpsuits rebuilding a wall revealed that this was a prison. A small blue building to the right of the field was the women's prison. It housed all the female prisoners in the province—currently twelve women and two children (both ten months' old). We entered the building and walked through it, past a tiny courtyard to a large room set up with a loom and sewing machines for the women's vocational training. The freshly painted space doubled as the literacy classroom, but unlike in Mazar, the women slept elsewhere, in pairs in the small rooms across the courtyard. A large bathroom, cleaner and nicer than many I'd used in Afghan guesthouses, was behind the last door in the little compound. The women appeared to be treated well, and their quarters, while still a prison, were less visually depressing than at the Mazar prison. On the surface, the building felt more like a hostel.

We sat down on white plastic chairs that lined the wall in the classroom while the women sat on the floor facing us. The deputy commander, the women's commander, and the teachers joined us. I wondered how open the women would be in the presence of the authority that kept them locked up. We started with an older woman in a pale blue head scarf who seemed interested in speaking and who, as in the Mazar prison, might have been the voice of the group by right of age and time served. At sixty-three, she was two years into a twelve-year sentence for murdering her husband. She had three girls and one son who came to visit once a week. The meeting felt awkward sitting above the women. It was too formal and slightly authoritative. I was acutely aware of the guards' presence on the chairs next to us, as were the women. I asked Rashed if we could sit on the floor with the women, and he nodded and joined me to sit cross-legged among them. I again tried to engage them, this time speaking to a young woman directly in front of me. She wore a black head scarf decorated with silver sequins and held a gorgeous little girl. When I asked Rashed to ask her for her name and story, she smiled shyly and tried to explain her crime. Najilia, age twenty, was originally from Logar province but married a man in Maimana. Her ten-month-old daughter, Basilla, lived with her in prison. Najilia was accused of instigating a plan to help her neighbor and her boyfriend run away. They were caught, and she was jailed for helping, as was the young boy for running away with a girl promised to another. The girl avoided prison but was married off to an uncle. Najilia's husband was supportive of her and knew that she didn't do anything wrong. She said she hoped that when she left she could continue the literacy education she'd begun in prison.

Most disturbing was the story of eighteen-year-old Mahria, a Turkmen woman also living in prison with a ten-month-old son. Mahria had a sweet round face and wore a striking yellow patterned Turkmen-style head scarf. Her husband had gone to Iran for work, and she was left behind at the family home. Her brother-in-law raped her during this time, and—as I was learning happened all too often—instead of the rapist going to jail, Mahria was accused of adultery to save face for the family. She had a two-year prison term with her baby. When I asked if she would have family support when she was released, she replied that she would live with her mother. She added that her husband was still in Iran and had said that when she was released, he would kill her.

This prison was run with the oversight of the Norwegian Provincial Reconstruction Team (PRT). Each province had PRTs related to the local international forces, and they oversaw public projects, reconstruction, and community building. In Fayrab province, this came mainly under the Norwegian directive. Prisons in Norway are radically different from prisons in other countries. Inmates are treated humanely, their living conditions are luxurious by other standards, and they have fewer walls and more space. Norway also has the lowest rate of recidivism in Europe. Here was a prison whose commanders were taught to respect their detainees and treat them with dignity. The prisoners were allowed to go outside, into the courtyard, whenever they chose. They appeared to be treated humanely, and they had female guards. The current commander, Hadj Sadr, came to work here seven years earlier after escaping the Taliban. He had recently returned from Washington, D.C., where he toured American jails and had also visited a prison in Norway. He said he'd been shocked by the level of freedom there in comparison to U.S. or Afghan prisons. He seemed to value the softer, more humane approach. This was refreshing to witness, though I would have liked to have more time to see it in action. Rashed told me that several years ago there were many problems in this and other prisons with the women and the male guards. Guards sexually harassing and raping women was commonplace. This was another example of crimes that were nearly impossible to track, as the women were not likely to speak out and had no incentive to do so because, even if they did, the perpetrator was unlikely to be punished. Since the

Afghan Women's Education Center had begun working there in 2007, there had been fewer, if any, such incidents.

As in the Mazar-i-Sharif prison, the children had no toys or playthings. Sensing the possibility of outside involvement here, I asked Rashed if the commander would allow me to go to the market and buy toys and clothing for the children. The commander agreed. With a smile, he showed us a small brightly painted room with murals that could be used as a kindergarten. He told Rashed that if we returned later today, we could deliver what we bought to the women. Rashed took us to the bazaar, to a shop owned by Afghanistan's most flamboyant Afghan, Humayan. Humayan ran a shop for women, full of sequined dresses, undergarments, and toiletries. He seemed overjoyed to meet us. Rashed explained that he was Humayan's English teacher, and Humayan went to great lengths to make us welcome. He sent for tea next door, and when he found out that we were in the market for toys, he had his assistant run across the street to find some and bring them over. He shared that he had recently vacationed in India, and he pulled out photos of himself at the Taj Mahal—sunglasses, hip jeans, and black pointy boots— looking quite the fashionista.

Locals heard that foreign visitors were at Humayan's, and several came in to say hi and meet us—introductions, more tea, and photos. I picked out some clothes for the children. He wrapped each in plastic, and bundled them into shopping bags. My environmental sensibilities internally battled my awareness of the cultural need to wrap items that were special.

We drove back to the prison, dropped off the bundles and headed to AWEC for lunch. Lunch consisted of Uzbek pilau— basically Kabuli rice, but a bit tastier—or so the Uzbeks claim. I was happy to accept that claim as the dish was by far my favorite in Afghanistan, and I had to restrain myself from moaning happily while I ate—it was so good. The Cipro and Immodium combo I took a few days ago had kicked in, and I was not racing from *tashnab* to *tashnab* anymore. Rashed was surprised to see me eating with my hand rather than with silverware (everyone else was using their hand, but since I was a Western guest, silverware had been brought for me). I explained that as I was in Afghanistan I would happily eat like an Afghan. He seemed pleased, and I worked my way through the bowl of rice and lamb with my right hand, occasionally using the bread to help scoop up the food more neatly. After lunch, we said our good-byes and I thanked Rashed for all his help and hospitality. Wanting to see more of the town before our return to Sherberghan, Travis asked Wahid, our driver, to take the long way around the city.

On the outskirts, Wahid pulled over for gas, and Travis and I got out to walk ahead on the road, surrounded by lush green hills. I saw a herd of donkeys, some motorcycles, and an old Turkmen man riding another donkey converge. It was photography nirvana. Travis and I scoped out potential trails and just when I was considering walking all the way back to Sherberghan, our taxi pulled up. Alternating fields of grass and wildflowers blanketed the hillsides, and we felt content with the short walk and the day's visit.

But sure enough, it was time for a reality check. Two men waved down our car, and Wahid amazingly stopped and got out even as Travis pulled on his arm and shouted at him not to. Focus snapped back to crystalline, and we watched helplessly as he crossed the road. One of the men started slapping and hitting him. Travis jumped into the driver's seat as I rolled up windows and locked the doors.

"If we have to go, we'll have to go. Understand?" he said quietly to me, not taking his eyes off the driver outside.

"Okay, I understand." I pulled the head scarf farther around my face, trying to hide my features without drawing too much attention to the car. It was too late for the burqa. I looked at Travis. How would I feel if we had to leave Wahid behind? *Shit. Shit. Shit.* What in the hell was happening?

Amazingly, the men stopped hitting Wahid and turned to leave. Wahid came back and got in the driver's seat as Travis slid out of the way. I looked out the window to see the men walking back to our car.

"Travis!" I shouted.

Travis looked out and told Wahid to drive away, but for some reason he refused as the men stood at our window and shouted at him. Suddenly, they turned and walked off. Wahid put the car into gear. He tried to make a U-turn to follow them, but Travis grabbed the wheel and told him to drive us home. A little power pull on the steering wheel occurred, and the driver conceded.

We sat in silence while Travis tried to find out from our driver what happened, but he wouldn't talk. Ten minutes later, we were stopped at a police checkpoint. They insisted that the road wasn't safe. No shit. They took Travis's name and asked if I was his wife, he said yes for ease of explanation, and gave them my first name. They didn't question him or bother to look back at me. They said that the Taliban were in the area the day before, and we should be careful. This was relatively unexpected. The north had been essentially void of Taliban for years. Taliban raids and false checkpoints were a recent development and a worrying sign of things to come. The rumors we had been hearing were apparently true. The policeman allowed us to continue on but asked us to send word when we made it back to the guesthouse. I vowed to give our driver a hefty tip.

Exhausted and more than a little freaked out, I curled up in the backseat with my head scarf draped over my face and tried to close my eyes. But not longer after, the taxi screeched to a halt in front of two enormous armored vehicles, their guns pointed at us.

"What the hell?" I shouted loudly.

Travis looked back at me. "It's okay, mate, just a convoy. Looks like they have a mechanical."

"Seriously?" I laughed nervously. "What are the odds?"

Sure enough, a Swedish convoy had broken down and was preventing traffic from passing, keeping its guns trained on the stopped vehicles. I'd have preferred that they scouted the landscape instead of us as they—and we—were sitting ducks if the Taliban was in the area. Within ten or fifteen minutes, they got their vehicle running, and we were all moving. I sighed once we were back up to highway speed. The rest of the trip passed without incident, and when we got back to the guesthouse, Travis asked one of the NGO staff who spoke better Dari than he did to find out what had happened with the driver. They talked with the driver quietly then explained that he'd gotten smacked around for traveling with two *xoragees* (foreigners) in his car—and something about a checkpoint.

Over dinner that night, we recounted the story with the other staff. Travis confessed, " Yeah, it could have been a real problem. I don't know how to drive a stick."

"*What?*" I shouted at him.

"I never learned to drive a stick. Not sure how well that would have worked out had the shit really gone down."

"Are you serious? I know how to drive a stick. I could have jumped over the seat."

"If it came to that, I'm sure I would have figured it out."

"Oh, yeah, because an attack is a *great* time to learn how a clutch works. No pressure."

"Maybe I should put that on the to-do list of life skills?"

"Ya think?" I laughed sarcastically. "Thank God, you didn't have to figure it out today."

While there are pockets of instability even in Afghanistan's so-called safe provinces, such as the ones I visited during my trip to the north, the southern and eastern provinces were simply too dangerous for traveling by car. These are areas that are under Taliban control or being fought over. Commercial airlines travel only to the bigger cities. After the attack on my driver in a relatively calm area of Afghanistan, I was more aware of how I traveled and with whom.

I had been invited for lunch at the home of the female member of Parliament, Sahera Sharif, and her family, to discuss the situation of girls' education in Khost province. She'd then asked me to join her on a visit to Khost City to visit the girls' high school and meet the staff. Visiting Khost was a little trickier than other places. There were no commercial flights, and the road from Kabul was too unsafe. The roads to the southern provinces were notoriously insecure, and businessmen, government officials, and foreigners were kidnapping targets.

Luckily, the Afghan National Army, the ANA, often takes parliamentarians between home provinces on routine helicopter flights for security reasons and timing. Some of the roads weren't just unsafe but remote, and the journey by car could take days. After two attempts to align our schedules, we finally were ready to make the trip together.

Sahera went this route often and arranged the journey with the flight commander. They made plans to confirm the flight one hour before departure, and if it was confirmed, we were to meet at Massoud's square to drive into the ANA flight area together with her security. We would spend the day in Khost City, visiting a girls' high school, a women's group, and another clinic project that Sahera was working on, and then catch the return flight home before dark.

But the trip didn't go as smoothly as we had hoped. Once again, Afghan scheduling wreaked havoc on a simple plan. Sahera, her driver, Travis, and myself all met from different areas of Kabul at the traffic circle near the airport. Several lanes converge and no stopping was allowed due to security—not the easiest of meeting points. Yet I pulled up and sure enough, Sahera was waiting with her driver. I got out of the taxi and jumped in her car to drive onto the airfield. Unfortunately, it became apparent that her driver wasn't sure which entrance to use. Cue some back and forth driving, U-turns, and stopping in the middle of the road to ask directions with random people walking by.

There were two struggles that appeared inherent in Afghan society: timekeeping and information sharing. Afghans will wait and wait when a simple question could solve the situation. Example? We waited outside the security gates of the ANA airfield for nearly half an hour, making us exactly half an hour late for our flight. Neither the driver nor the MP asked the guards for more information or explained who they were. We just waited.

I finally stepped out of the car to get some air. Let's just say we were all a few showers overdue, some of us more than others. The entrance guard saw me and came over to inquire why we were there. Never mind that we'd been parked a few feet in front of him the entire time. I introduced Sahera and explained about our flight to Khost. "Come in, come in," he said. "I didn't realize who you were." *Of course, you didn't. You didn't ask, and we didn't offer.* An Afghan standstill.

The flight hadn't left without us, but it was now not flying directly to Khost. It was flying to Bagram, Ghazni, and *then* Khost. The Afghan flight command had made some changes and that meant that not only had we not missed our flight, but we wouldn't take off for another forty-five minutes. One-and-a-half hours late plus two extra stops? Right on schedule.

There was no point in getting worked up. If I'd learned anything in years of travel, it was the need for patience and the acceptance that things could be frustrating, slow, and inefficient. But plans tended to work out however they were supposed to in the end.

We walked around the airfield to load up. The beast was a MI8, a solid Russian helicopter that rattled a bit, but the crew assured me confidently she was air-worthy. An American copilot joined the Afghan pilot and told me that the Americans were mentoring the Afghan pilots with new flight technology. A large, serious-looking man in a pristine white shalwar kameez and a large black turban arrived with a bodyguard. Both checked their guns with the crew who, finally assembled, passed around earplugs. It was my first flight in a helicopter, and I was excited to get an aerial view of the country. Through the circular windows, I saw the hills that dot Kabul recede as the wide expanse of the Shomali Plain spread out below in muted shades of brown.

At our first stop, in Bagram, Sahera looked nervous. She hadn't heard that we were stopping in Bagram and Ghazni since she'd been on her phone. I couldn't explain the situation to her until the engine was shut down, and when I did, she worried that we wouldn't arrive before the girls were out of school. We had to wait to pick something up in Bagram, and then we traveled another forty minutes to Ghazni. The crew member who'd been sitting by the open door mounted a gun for this leg of the trip. I watched as he loaded ammunition—another reminder that this wasn't a pleasure ride. But fifteen minutes into the flight he was dozing, his forehead on his arm, which rested on the rifle. I relaxed. If the gunner was sleeping, an attack was probably unlikely. But later, when I told a friend the story, she said, "Nah, he'd probably wake up when the first bullet hit."

Bullet-free in Ghazni, we refueled and waited to reboard for another thirty-minute flight to Khost. American soldiers at the base met us. They kindly pointed out a Porta-Potty and brought us food from the mess hall for an impromptu picnic on the airstrip. The man in white pulled out a small rug to pray by the side of the plane. I hoped he was praying that this Russian bird didn't rattle apart in the air—or get shot at. The forty-minute ride from Kabul to Khost was going to end up taking three hours. This would give us just two-and-a-half hours on the ground if we wanted to catch a ride back that day, which I definitely did.

When we landed in Khost City, we quickly piled into a car sent for Sahera and drove to the girls' school. The province is lush, green, and warm. En route, Sahera pointed out the site of the recent Taliban suicide bomber attack that had been all over the news a few days earlier and that had targeted a police checkpoint and killed eleven.

We arrived at the girls' school fifteen minutes later to find everyone had indeed gone home, but a women's group had gathered in the back courtyard to wait for Sahera. Fifty women, many in burqas, swarmed around us in a flurry of introductions, hugs, and a general outpouring of enthusiasm. It was touching to witness, and they were obviously thrilled with their female MP. As she held court in Pashto, I hung back with several young children, trading names in Dari, which amused them greatly. I took photos with my iPhone and showed them, wishing I had a Polaroid, as sharing photos was still the one true barrier breaker the world over. There was nothing quite like being able to take a photo and give it to the person immediately, and I always felt frustrated that I could show people the photos but not give them copies. It would be a powerful connection between photographer and subject in a country where so much was taken and so little given back in human connection. We then passed the time learning how to play Afghan marbles. One of the boys had four marbles: three green and one silver shooter. In the rocks, we huddled and he showed me how to shoot. I was all thumbs, not having played since I was a little girl, and he laughed appreciatively and encouraged me until I started to improve.

One of the women tapped me on the shoulder, and I turned to see that several men had arrived. I stood up and wiped the dust from my hands on my skirt as I smiled and thanked her. The head of school, the director of teachers, and a general gathering of all men interested in the goings-on introduced themselves. We talked about the school, the province, and the state of education while Sahera continued to speak to the assembled women. Tea arrived exactly at the time we needed to be heading back to the helicopter. I groaned inwardly. Sahera joined us, and despite the clock ticking, no one was in a hurry. Not wishing to play the role of the rude American rushing people, I finally interjected that I was incredibly sorry but we really *had to go*. The helicopter wouldn't fly after dark, and we would be left here.

Sahera nodded distractedly as if to say, "Yes, yes, but first another cup of tea," and when someone brought her a plate with bread on it, I stood to gather my things, protocol be damned. I knew that Sahera had family here, and that if we were stranded, we could probably stay with them, but I had no desire to spend an unplanned night here. I started shaking hands with the men who'd gathered and expressed my sincere apology that we had to go and explained that the helicopter was waiting and I would love to stay longer next time. I assured them I wanted to return and see the school with the girls. I walked out to the car. The chopper was leaving at 4:30. It was now 4:25, and we still had to drive through town. Sahera sauntered out with her entourage. As she got in the car, the Afghan police turned up to provide escort, so at least we would have a clear path to the airfield. Women were still saying good-bye and holding her hand as we started to drive off.

We arrived ten minutes late, but the chopper was still there, much to my relief.

"We weren't going to leave without you," the pilot said, and chuckled. "You had five more minutes at least."

"A whole five minutes, eh?"

"Did you get what you needed?" asked the American pilot.

"Not even close," I said, and smiled tiredly.

"Sorry to hear it."

"Me, too . . . Afghanistan, never easy, right?"

We piled into the machine as it was grinding to life. Forty minutes straight back to Kabul should get us there just as night was falling—in time to battle Kabul's epic rush hour. I sighed.

I wasn't sure what had been accomplished on this trip, other than more insight into the workings of the country, the pace of things, and the unexpected turns. At the end of the day, I had my first helicopter ride and made a journey to Khost. It wasn't bad if you looked at the trip as an adventure. It was a chance to see the country in ways others rarely do and a reminder of how lucky I was to get this sort of insight and access. More important, the last few trips illustrated to me that I needed to let go of my initial limited focus on girls' education. My projects over the previous three years— supporting schools and literacy programs, starting computer labs and kindergartens, securing land donations and working to build a deaf school—had taught me an enormous amount about Afghanistan. But there were bigger organizations that could tackle these types of projects more effectively, with large budgets and a team of staff. Trips like this one to Khost, and to the women's prisons around the country, allowed me unparalleled access to a variety of Afghan women. Meeting women in prisons, female members of Parliament, teachers, students, activists—in both urban and rural settings—was giving me a broader understanding than I could have ever imagined of the country and the issues surrounding women's rights.

I was realizing that I needed to keep my focus on the projects that I could support with the limited resources I had, and that inspired me. I was dialing in on projects that worked in nontraditional ways through storytelling, arts, and sports. Projects that were culturally sustainable. Projects that could flourish with limited funds and oversight, engage young Afghans, and that built community in unique ways.

As if to prove the point, about ten minutes into the flight, the pilot called me up to the cockpit and said, "People pay a lot of money to do this in the States. Would you like to sit up here with us? It may help take the sting out of the frustration."

"Seriously? Uh, yes please!" I grinned.

He smiled and gestured to the jump seat between him and Maqsood, the Afghan pilot. I watched the scenery through the curved glass window. We swooped through the mountains southeast of Kabul, everything below us looking peaceful. The details were blurred at this height, snowcapped mountains morphing into green hillsides, with dots of mud houses and crisscrossing roads. Closer to Kabul, Maqsood pointed out the Queen's palace underneath us, tucked into the landscape. I marveled at how easy it was to forget we were in a conflict zone, and that there was a gunner in the helicopter door watching for RPGs below.

8

Financial Fear

Colorado 2010

Several weeks later, I took Devon to get groceries, and for the first time in a long time, I was truly scared. I had $42 in cash and $21 in my bank account. We were out of almost everything, including toilet paper, milk, bread—the necessities. How had I gotten this close to the wire? As we pulled into the City Market parking lot, I told her brightly, "Sweetie, we are only going to grab a few things, okay? So please, let's just get the things we need, and we'll come back later for the other stuff. Okay?"

I opened the back of the Element to get the shopping bags, and she grabbed my hand. "Okay, Mommy. I just want to get my gummy vitamins."

At eighteen bucks a bottle, that would be nearly half our grocery money.

"Sorry, baby, not today, we'll get them next trip okay?"

"But I'm out. We need to get these."

I sighed and grabbed her for a hug. "I know, sweetie. Next trip, okay? Can you just come with and help me get the other stuff for now?"

"Okay," she said, frowning slightly as she took my hand. This was not what I had in mind when I said I wanted to do the best for Devon. My nerves were fried, and I could feel myself becoming short and distracted with her—something I needed to rectify. None of this was her fault.

"Race you?" I challenged her, smiling. We ran across the parking lot, her rain boots stomping through puddles of melting snow, and her infectious giggle made me laugh out loud. My heart pounding, I bent down before we entered the store. I gave her a kiss as I told her, "I love you so so so much."

"All the way to the moon?" she asked.

"All the way to the moon *and* back again!" I assured her. "Now, let's go buy some toilet paper."

As I stood in the checkout line, I went through my mental survival checklist. I had meetings in Denver this week, important ones with potential donors that I couldn't miss. I had several projects ready to launch but as of yet hadn't secured the funding to put them into action. Luckily I had half a tank of gas, so if I conserved, which meant staying close to home this weekend with Devon, I should be good to go.

I'd been here before when I first separated from Pete. I left the marriage with a couple hundred dollars in my bank account. He was not in a mindset to help me with the logistics of separation, and since we had our own accounts, I had no cushion to fall back on to help me break away. He had insisted that if I wanted out, I was free to go, but he wasn't going to support it or make it easier for me to leave.

So I took out a personal loan using the only possession I could take freely from the marriage until our divorce went through—my car. Leveraging it as collateral, I was able to get a loan for $17,000, enough to help me pay rent and supplement the money I earned teaching Pilates. It also allowed me to focus on launching Mountain2Mountain, to get to Afghanistan in the first place, and survive until our joint assets were divvied up nearly a year later.

The settlement we reached over my half of our house was not insubstantial, albeit a fraction of what I could have asked for under the law. I hadn't been willing to battle. Something I, at times, look back on with regret. I felt it was more important to coordinate and focus on Devon's shared schedule than fight over financial issues. I didn't have the stomach for it, and it may have allowed us the understanding that we have today, where we can raise Devon in tandem with very little drama, and share special occasions and the occasional dinner together as an extended family.

Instead of using the money to give me and Devon the stability of a home, savings for vacations together, and the semblance of security, I used it to build our future in a different, some may say riskier, way. I paid off that initial loan, funded multiple trips to Afghanistan, started several of my smaller projects, and more important, worked sixty hours a week solely to build M2M without taking time from Devon. Each night, after she went to bed, I cranked out a solid five hours. The rest of the work was done when she was at preschool or with her dad. The settlement supported us for the past four years while I worked to build our future and create something both she, and I, could be proud of.

On the flip side, I stopped racing because of the time commitment, entry fees, and focus, and I forewent any vacations other than my trips to Afghanistan. I gave up health insurance, occasionally went without car insurance, and often was a month in arrears with rent.

But this day was especially tough. I went to the PO Box, fingers crossed that there would be some checks I could deposit. Nothing.

My eye doctor left me a voice mail that my new contacts were in, but I couldn't afford to go pick them up. My cell phone bill was due. Rent and Dev's ballet class tuition were due in three days. I looked down at the silver ring on my right index finger. It was a gift from my father and sister at the beginning of my M2M journey and was engraved with the words of Longfellow: *The lowest ebb is at the turn of the tide.* My life definitely felt like low tide.

There was only one item in the PO Box: a package from Vail Mountain School, a private school forty-five minutes away. I drove home and once we put the groceries away and Devon was busy building a fort out of our pillows, I opened it. To my surprise, it contained a stack of cards, each of them a thank-you from a child in the fifth grade in a class I'd spoken to a month ago about Afghanistan. They had been reading a book *Parvana's Journey*, by Deborah Ellis, about a young girl in Taliban times who disguised herself as a boy. The children had a lot of good questions. I opened the first card. "Dear Ms. Galpin. Thank you so much for telling us all about Afghanistan. It was really cool to put on a burqa."

I smiled and opened another. "Dear Ms. Galpin. Thank you so much for talking about Afghanistan. I love how so many people like you are trying to change the world one step at a time."

Another had a picture drawn of a globe shaped like a heart. Most of them mentioned the burqas I'd brought to their classroom and wished me good luck in Afghanistan. Many hoped they could go there when they were older. Others wanted me to say hello to Afghan kids for them. I felt my heart swell. This didn't put food in my fridge, but it was a lovely reminder of why I was doing this.

"Who are all these cards from, Mommy?" Devon asked, walking over to the kitchen table and opening the various cards to look at the drawings and pictures.

"These are from a group of kids in Vail that I visited to talk about Afghanistan. They sent me these notes to say thank-you."

"Can you come talk at my school?"

I looked up at her from the pile of cards. "Yes, if you want me to, of course I can. You should help though. What would you like to show the kids in your class?"

"We could show them the Afghan money and the flag!"

"We could do that. . . . How about a burqa and buzkashi hat?"

"Yeah! And can we show them the picture of you riding a horse!"

"If you want to. Why don't you pick out some of your favorite photos. I'll print them, and you can glue them on a piece of foam board. I think I've also got a map we can use. Then you can talk about the photos, and I'll talk about what I do in Afghanistan."

"Okay, but first can I have a snack?"

"Snack first. Afghanistan second. Deal."

That conversation sparked the realization that perhaps I was trying too hard to explain myself and Mountain2Mountain through the lens that others used to view me. I was passionate about working as a woman *for* women in conflict zones where women often didn't have a voice. But I was also interested in how art and storytelling could amplify those voices and challenge the apathy that so often prevented action on the U.S. side of the equation. I didn't want to focus on building schools or clinics or infrastructure or vocational training. These were all necessary and vital steps in a country like Afghanistan, but they weren't my skillset. I didn't have the education, experience, resources, or financial backing to tackle these large sticks-and-bricks projects. Yet time and time again, this was what advisors or board members clung to as though I should model myself on Greg Mortenson. But I wasn't him. I didn't want to be him. I wanted to focus on what women could do *with* an education. I wanted to focus on projects with the next generation that sparked voices, that inspired change, and that could challenge stereotypes. I wanted to transform the way people viewed women and the way Americans viewed Afghans, and the way the public viewed humanitarian work—a goal much less tangible than building a school, and much harder to rally the masses and raise money for. Creating a computer lab or trying to build a school for the deaf was not where I wanted to put my passions going forward. Supporting graffiti and street art projects, working with female activists, and creating other programs that challenged perceptions and empowered voices were.

I was tired of banging my head against a wall. I was tired of living on a tightrope all by myself. I was tired of feeling the weight of the risk of the choices I had made. Yet other than my immediate family, which now included Christiane, I was reminded daily that I was out on that tightrope by choice, and no one else was going to join me willingly.

The area that caused the most conflict from the beginning was the formation of the board of directors and the subsequent incarnations of it that followed. Good people do strange things when they sit on the board of a nonprofit. I've talked to several other founders who led nonprofits and they all say the same thing. Boards are often the most frustrating part of running a nonprofit.

If I could do it all again, I'd consider creating a for-profit entity and steer the profits to the projects I wanted to do. The skewed mentality associated with nonprofits is astounding. Part of the problem is in the name: nonprofit. As if making money is evil. Yet without money, nothing can get done.

I've seen nonprofits, including Mountain2Mountain, which has a tiny budget, barely $100,000 a year on average, held to a completely different set of operating rules than for-profits. For-profits are judged on the work they do. Nonprofits are judged on their frugality. For-profits hire adequate, qualified staff and pay them a competitive salary. Nonprofits often operate on a bare-bones staff, severely underpaid compared to their for-profit counterparts doing the same job. They rely on volunteers and interns to make up the difference. But it's difficult to expect the same level of competence and expertise from staff who aren't paid competitive salaries. For-profits can spend money to make money. They can create innovative marketing campaigns in order to make a much larger profit. Non-profits are criticized if they spend money on marketing or fund-raisers. I see founders of nonprofits get attacked for taking a modest salary, as though running a nonprofit should be a volunteer position done out of goodwill. But that isn't sustainable for building a solid foundation for goals and accountability.

Dan Pallotta gave a great example in a 2013 TED talk about how nonprofits are judged by their frugality rather than their effectiveness. The limitations put on nonprofits create an inability, or unwillingness, to take risks. If you try and fail with a nonprofit project—even if you learn from it to improve other projects, programs, and approaches for the future—you are judged much more harshly than if you have a failure in a for-profit company. If we are trying to shift paradigms of poverty, abuse, and human rights, we can't always play it safe. This is exactly the space where we *need* to think outside the box, where creativity and the ability to take risks are your best assets. Government organizations and large NGOs have too much structure and red tape to be nimble, flexible, and creative with how they tackle issues. But small nonprofits can develop unique and groundbreaking approaches to serious issues. Small organizations, individual risk-takers, and start-ups are in a great position to tackle many of these problems, but the public perceptions and judgments of nonprofit often don't allow it. Getting work done costs money—end of story. It's not evil to have operational costs. It's evil to waste money and not accomplish your goals.

Adding to the dysfunctional nature of nonprofits is the public's obsession with creating heroes out of humanitarians. There is an unrealistic paradigm of the hero's journey, based on the mythology that has developed: a nonprofit is deemed worthy only if its founder has significantly martyred him- or herself with extreme financial and personal sacrifice. Does this unhealthy cycle manifest itself in unrealistic expectations that the public holds toward those trying to do good work? Did I make unhealthy choices in my own life, financially and physically, in order to be more worthy? And does that discourage others from putting their drop in the bucket because it seems too small in comparison? That is not the example I want set.

Did Greg Mortenson feel the need to exaggerate, or perhaps even lie, to sell his story and fund his nonprofit, as writer Jon Krakauer and 60 Minutes have suggested when they accused him of repeatedly lying in his memoir, Three Cups of Tea, and mismanaging donors' funds? Did others feel that need to exaggerate? Would I? Is that the only way to make a small, start-up nonprofit financially viable in today's social media era? Could Mortenson have created such a successful multimillion dollar organization without embellishing the details of his story? Was he just a climber wanting to do something good for a rural Pakistani village and who got frustrated by the lack of support? Was he a man with a hero complex? Or was he something in between—neither the hero as the public wanted him to be, nor the villain portrayed on 60 Minutes and through Jon Krakauer's evisceration?

Who knows? But by insisting on making heroes out of those wanting to do good work, do we create an environment much like the current celebrity culture in which those sacrificing for the greater good drink the Kool Aid and start to believe they *are* heroes—that they are beloved and deserve to be treated as such? A Kardashian in humanitarian clothing? Beyond the ick factor of a celebrity and humanitarian collision, the unholy union creates an unhealthy model for start-ups to base themselves on and for young people to aspire to. You aren't supposed to want to save the world in order to get famous. Yet in a world where people strive to be famous for fame's sake, altruism seems to be getting kicked aside for feature stories.

I often found the constant comparison of my work to that of Greg Mortenson frustrating and misleading. I never wanted to be Greg Mortenson. Yet time and time again, the comparison was applied as though the only way to tell my story was to filter it first through him.

One advisor wanted me to be the next Greg Mortenson, or at least get his endorsement to put on our Web site. "You raised over a hundred thousand dollars and a lot of publicity for his organization."

"I did, and I did that without expecting anything in return. That was a chance to dip my toe in the fund-raising waters and see if we could inspire a community to support another community half the world away."

"Yes, but a note from him on the Web site could really help legitimize what you are doing."

"But he doesn't know what I'm doing. He's doing his thing, and I'm doing mine. I started M2M to develop my own approach. It's not about me replicating what he's doing. It's about tackling the issues that others aren't or won't, or that they are addressing in different ways." The suggestion that I should essentially ride his coattails because he was famous and I had once raised money for his organization seemed absurd and insulting to both of us. Mortenson owed me nothing, nor did he owe anyone else who donated to his organization or spearheaded fund-raisers. That would be like donating money for building a school and insisting to have a plaque with your name on it.

Yet articles, news stories, and magazine features would continue to describe my work with at least one reference to Mortenson, despite my insistence to writers that I shouldn't be compared to him. I wasn't building schools. I wasn't focused solely on girls' education, and I wasn't a climber. There are other humanitarians and activists I was probably more similar to, but *Three Cups of Tea* was a phenomenon and Mortenson was a household name. I worked in Afghanistan; he worked in Afghanistan and Pakistan. I'd raised money for his organization. We both lived in mountain towns. Educating women and girls was at the heart of our organizations, although we had completely different approaches to how we wanted to tackle the issue. My goals were starting to define themselves with artists, activists, and athletes. The more time I spent in Afghanistan, the more I evolved my goals; as my network expanded, I got more exposure to the emerging group of young Afghans. These were young people growing up with Facebook and Twitter, and embracing the opportunities that the post-Taliban era allowed.

At every one of my speaking events, at least one audience member asked me about Mortenson. I fielded the questions diplomatically. I wanted to create a voice, combat apathy, and build a virtual army of women who could tackle the issues of women's rights, gender violence, and inequity *as women* and in culturally sustainable ways. I wanted to focus on changing and inspiring individuals, not just building things. I didn't want to create more international aid dependence. I didn't want to model the "great white hope" approach to aid work that in many ways caused more harm than good. I

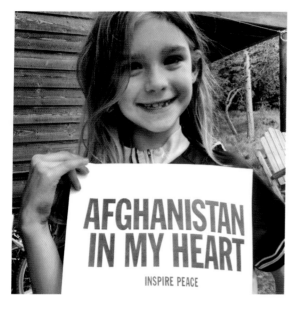

Devon showing her support of the #inspirepeace project and her desire to go to Afghanistan. (PHOTO CREDIT: SHANNON GALPIN)

My two favorite women in the whole world: My sister, Larissa, goofing around with Devon in Denver. (PHOTO CREDIT: SHANNON GALPIN)

The furry addition of the "Bear" to our family, as we bring home a Bernese Mountain puppy. (Photo credit: Mark Wiggins)

Larissa and Devon reading the first copy of the *Streets of Afghanistan* book at our local bookstore, The Next Page. (Photo credit: Shannon Galpin)

Standing in front of the United check-in desk at Denver International Airport with Anna Brones with the entire *Streets of Afghanistan* exhibition ready to transport. (PHOTO CREDIT: MARK WIGGINS)

Setting up the *Streets of Afghanistan* exhibition in the village of Istalif (PHOTO CREDIT: TONY DI ZINNO)

Setting up one of Paula Bronstein's images as part of the *Streets of Afghanistan* exhibition against Soviet tanks at the top of Massoud's tomb in Panjshir. (Photo CREDIT: Tony Di Zinno)

Men walk by the *Streets of Afghanistan* exhibition on the streets in Istalif. (Photo CREDIT: Tony Di Zinno)

Riding a buzkashi horse at Kabul Stadium before loading up the horses for a match in the Shomali Plain. (PHOTO CREDIT: TONY DI ZINNO)

Village life in Bamiyan on two wheels. (PHOTO CREDIT: DENI BECHARD)

Talking bikes and Afghan history with the gardener of Darul Amon Palace in Kabul. (PHOTO CREDIT: WARREN BUTTERY)

Teaching Coach Seddiq to fist-bump during a training session break on the side of the road. (PHOTO CREDIT: SARAH MENZIES)

Getting permission from and making friends with members of the Afghan National Army at Qargha Lake. (Photo credit: Deni Bechard)

The Afghan Cycles documentary film crew in April 2013 in front of Darul Amon Palace in Kabul. (Photo credit: Najibullah Sedeqe)

Lining up with a few members of the women's national cycling team during a training ride. (Photo credit: Sarah menzies)

Joining Mariam and other members of the Afghan National Team at the end of a long day of filming the Afghan Cycles documentary. (Photo credit: Sarah Menzies)

wanted to use my gender to challenge gender barriers in unique ways, even if it created only a ripple.

The irony was that, years later—when Mortenson's star fell unexpectedly and publicly—I and many others felt the backlash of public distrust. Here I was, having never taken a penny from Mortenson and yet having to answer questions about him and his organization. News reporters called me to ask questions. But neither myself nor Mountain2Mountain had any relationship with him or his organization beyond the initial fund-raiser before we became an independent 501c3 nonprofit. But the public lost a hero. It felt betrayed and foolish, and wanted answers.

It was interesting to look back and see lessons emerging. I learned that nonprofits needed to be as open about mistakes as about successes. Founders had to build strong teams of people smarter and more experienced than they were, and trust them for advice and knowledge. Founders had to let go of control of the organization, especially financial control, to ensure transparency and public trust.

I have always worked for myself, and as an entrepreneur, I have different skills.

I can imagine, conceptualize, and implement projects half a world away, even in a war zone. I am one half of an effective organization, but in order to be successful, I know I need to find the yin to my yang, a business-minded, financially savvy manager to take over the operations for Mountain2Mountain. The trick is to find a person who has a mutual trust in my abilities to continue to create and inspire and evolve without putting a harness on me—and who I can in turn trust to lead my organization onto a solid foundation of financial stability that will allow me to do what I do best.

With the lessons learned and the search begun, I continued to operate my one-woman show and focus on what I believed in. I lived on the tightrope, believing that people would rally behind ideas like mine—behind creativity, activism, risk taking, individual voices, and the changing of perceptions, not just traditional humanitarian models.

It took five years of work and exploration until a lightbulb went off. I was talking to my friend and Mountain2Mountain advisor Heidi Volpe on the phone. She was describing the guilt one can feel after returning from war zones or impoverished countries—paying $4 for a latte at Starbucks after meeting people who earn $1 a day. How do you reconcile that?

Another woman at a fund-raiser had told me how difficult she thought it would be to leave all those orphaned children behind; she'd want to scoop them all up and bring them home.

In both instances, I understood, but I didn't feel that way. I chalked it up to being well suited for the job. I could separate my realities and my emotions, and comfortably cross over time and time again between two worlds. But after the call with Heidi, I realized that I wasn't just right for the job per se; rather, I recognized how lucky I was to be born in this country and era. Through no choice of my own, I was born to a middle-class family in the 1970s in the United States. That gave me more opportunities and basic human rights than women born in Afghanistan. By dumb luck, I'd been issued a geographic passport to a country that allowed me a myriad of expectations and opportunities. This passport shouldn't be wasted. My life shouldn't be spent suffering or sacrificing at the expense of experiencing joy, following my passions, and exploring the world. My desire to create change, to put my drop in the bucket in hopes of starting a ripple, shouldn't overshadow the opportunities I'd received in the lottery of life. That night I wrote these thoughts while I was in bed. I spent days pondering the choices I was making.

Why did I feel guilty at the idea of planning a vacation? Why was making no money and working insane hours more important than mountain biking on my lunch break and taking a paycheck as the director of a nonprofit? Why was a bleeding ulcer just an inevitable side effect of the stress and pace I was keeping? How would this affect Devon as she became more aware? Is this the example I wanted to set?

The decade I had spent living in Europe, traveling, exploring, experiencing new tastes, new smells, and new cultures in my twenties had been replaced with sacrifice and guilt. I knew a happy medium was possible. Balance was needed: joy in daily boosts, more laughter, more 7:00 A.M. dance parties with Devon, more midnight hikes, and space for a real relationship with an amazing man. It felt like an insult to the women I met around the world who didn't have the opportunities I did to just throw them away or bury them under a giant to-do list that would never be completed. I am so lucky and blessed to have this life, and I should be setting the example to Devon to make every day count. I can't waste what I was given because I am outraged by the injustices I see in the world. Be outraged. Fight. But don't forget to play. Make time for friends, family, and love. Remember what is important.

The significance of the bike re-emerged. It had been my source of play and of strength, a metaphor for how I lived. With a single-speed, I had to embrace the suffering. There were no gears. I sat, stood, or walked. That was all I got. But I loved its simplicity. I may not love the suffering, but I do love the challenge. I embrace the suffering for the return I get back in spades. Mountain biking requires some blood and skin donation beyond the expected sweat and tears. If I wanted to become a stronger rider, it wasn't just a matter of muscle and lungs. It was about confidence alongside trial and error. I fell, a lot. I bruised. I hoped there was nothing worse, but it was always possible. Yet, despite that knowledge, the expectation even, that I would be hurt, I continued to ride. Why?

Because of the joy I felt on two wheels—dirt in my face, my teeth, mud on my legs, the wind in my face making me feel alive. The exhilaration of bombing down singletrack or the challenge of riding up a steep, rocky climb are the epitome of conquering fear and building mental and physical strength. I couldn't be indecisive. Indecision on a mountain bike—should I go over the rock or around the rock?—would draw blood. I had to let go of the brakes, ride through the rock garden, or I would get stuck. It was all there—life lessons in cheesy, two-wheeled metaphors. The bike was freedom of movement, of individual choice. Nothing was more important than that.

Maria Ward, the author of *Bicycling for Ladies*, published in 1896, stated it best: "Riding the wheel, our powers are revealed to us." That gets to the heart of how I feel every time I ride. It's why I have a ridiculous grin on my face when I ride through mud puddles and why I seek out exploration of new places on dirt trails and back roads. Riding a bike, I'm strong, I'm free, and I'm filled with joy.

What if I could harness that joy and that strength with other women? Could I encourage women who have survived the worst of gender violence—rape, sexual trafficking, and domestic abuse—to get involved in the fight for women worldwide? People seem to put women like this in a box labeled "victim." This label can completely disempower them, as though by being victimized, they are weak. I know different. Survivors are stronger than people think. I believe one woman can make a difference—that one voice matters. I wouldn't have set off on this journey if I didn't believe change was possible with the voice and willpower of a single individual. But I also believe that our strength is in our numbers. If I could inspire more women to use their voice, to stand up for those that are voiceless, I could create more than a ripple. I could create a tsunami of change that couldn't be ignored.

I needed to separate Shannon Galpin, the individual, from Mountain2Mountain, the organization. I had no idea how to accomplish that with zero money in the bank, but I knew that realizing the need for separation and the search for more balance in my life was a first step.

9

The Barrette

Afghanistan 2010

My first morning back in Afghanistan started off with a bang. Literally. I'd slept fitfully through the night. The heavy spring rain echoed down a drainpipe that emptied noisily outside the door of my room. I awoke to an explosion. I thought it might be thunder because of the rain. As I jumped up to look out the windows, they blew open from the delayed force of the blast. Luckily, the latches were loose so the glass didn't break under the pressure. A telltale plume of smoke and dust rose on the other side of the courtyard perimeter wall, maybe a block away—the same kind I'd seen the previous year when the Indian Embassy was attacked.

Gunfire ricocheted outside, and the guesthouse guards started running past my window. Shocked, I stepped back, my heart banging in my chest. I grabbed my phone and my backpack, and quickly shoved my passport, emergency contacts, and money stash inside. I called my friend Mike who was staying in another room of the guesthouse to see if he was aware of what was going on. He was an American cameraman from Colorado who worked for NBC and freelanced, and was also one of Christiane's closest friends; she'd introduced us when we were both in Kabul at the same time a year prior.

The security guards were standing on the wall that ran the perimeter of the guesthouse. They were shooting down, and gunmen below that I couldn't see were returning fire. Whatever had blown up wasn't the only target.

Mike didn't answer. My clumsy fingers refused to work the phone and figure out the number of his Afghan cell. I called Travis. Amazingly, he was awake, and he answered on the second ring.

"I know all about it. You okay?"

"Yeah, except the gunfight is outside my window."

I could hear gunfire through his phone and outside my window, almost in stereo, except that I'm deaf in one ear. Two guards ran past my window.

"Okay," he said distractedly. "I've got to go." *Click.*

I wasn't sure what to do. I was too antsy to sit still. I had my bag with my passport and money in my hand. The guards had moved from the wall across from me. I opened my door and stepped out. A guard came toward me, motioning me back inside. "Go, go." I ducked back inside.

I was staying in a room that was in a separate building from the main house. I wanted to know what was going on. I turned on the news, but of course nothing had been reported yet. It had just happened—it was happening now! The BBC was talking about the devastation left by the Chilean earthquake. For about twenty minutes, I alternated between watching the news and pacing the small room. Mike still wasn't answering his phone. Finally, I decided to make a run for the main building to check on him and see what the hotel staff were hearing. There was also a safe room there if the situation got really bad.

With my laptop and my backpack, I ran down the narrow outdoor passage toward the main house and through the courtyard. More guards rushed past me in the opposite direction. I bolted through the door of the guesthouse lobby, where the staff was gathered at the desk watching the news unfold on Al Jazeera. I exchanged pleasantries. They looked concerned but calm. I took deep breaths and tried to appear calmer than I felt. I walked down the hall to knock on Mike's door. No answer. I knocked again. Nothing. Had he simply slept through it? Maybe he used earplugs or sleeping pills. My hands were steadier, so I looked for his Afghan number in my phone and called him. I could hear it ringing on the other side of the door. He picked up.

"Where are you?" he said quietly into the phone.

"Outside your door." I replied. The door opened, and I hung up.

He was dressed in a pale cream shalwar kameez, with his curly light brown hair looking a little wild as though he'd been running his hands through it.

"Let's get some tea," he said. We walked across the hall to the breakfast room for a cup of tea and news coverage on Al Jazeera with several other guests already sitting at tables. Gunfire still rang out occasionally, prompting looks around to read the reaction of the staff and each other.

We ate, drank tea, and discussed what was unfolding. The majority of the news on Al Jazeera was still focused on the Chilean earthquake. There was no news yet on the attack.

"Why didn't you answer the door when I knocked?"

"Do you remember the big attack in Mumbai a couple of years ago?"

"Yes."

"Well, there were several coordinated attacks. One of them was at a large hotel."

"I vaguely remember—huge death toll, right?"

"It was big. During that attack on the hotel, the gunmen went door to door, knocking, and when the guests answered, they shot them."

"Oh."

Mike got up for a second cup of tea, and when he sat down, he began to share a few things he'd learned in a security training class for media he'd taken through the news network he worked for.

"Look, the overall goal in situations like this, or in a kidnapping, is to stay alive for as long as possible—not necessarily to get away."

He used a few mistakes I'd made as examples of what he'd learned in the security training.

"The first thing you did wrong is going to the window when the explosion hit. If gunmen had been inside the compound, they would have seen you. Or you could have been injured by glass shattering from the force of the blast. You were lucky that your latches gave way on these weak windows." I gulped and took a sip of tea.

"The second mistake you made was going outside. You heard gunfire, you saw guards, but you were too anxious to wait it out. But outside, you could get hit by a stray bullet, or kidnapped if gunmen had gotten inside."

It was pretty obvious when it's laid out like that.

"I understand wanting to know what's going on and wanting to be near hotel staff or in a public area, so you should make it a point to consider location when you choose your room in the future. You also should always find a hiding place and an escape route from your room whenever you first get settled. Sometimes, the bathroom windows are big enough for someone small like you to squeeze through. Your size is also good for hiding so that if gunmen break into rooms and you can't escape, you can make it look empty so they don't search the room."

Travis called my cell to check in with Mike, who he was supposed to be helping out with some filming. He wanted to know what the plan was with this unexpected turn of events. He was getting footage from the bomb site and was calling me from the motorcycle. He abruptly hung up, and two minutes later he called back.

"Hey, you okay?" I asked.

"Sorry. There was a body in the street and I almost ran it over."

"Seriously? You okay?"

"Yeah, I'm going to get some more footage, and I'll come by the guesthouse after I'm done."

"All right, be careful."

"No worries, mate." Sure, no worries, mate. Except carnage, bodies in the street, and a big-ass explosion.

He joined us for breakfast an hour or so later. The news on the television in the breakfast room was still piecing it together, but the gunfire in the streets had stopped. He showed us some of the footage from the bomb site—essentially a giant crater—and from the gunfight near the City Center. He'd been standing behind a pole, holding his camera out to the side of his face at eye level, when a tracer whizzed by, with a flash of red and an unmistakable sound.

"Holy crap, Trav. That's a little close!"

"Yeah, I know, but I've already got a news agency that wants to buy the footage. I'm glad I went. I don't usually cover bombings. It was really ugly down there. Going to be a lot of casualties. Anything on the news yet?"

"No, it's still mostly the Chilean earthquake. Al Jazeera had a quick update that a car bomb went off. That's it so far. But it's going off on Twitter."

"Yeah, it will take awhile for the news agencies to report."

Travis and Mike drank some tea while they planned the filming schedule. They had only communicated via e-mail until this morning. Mike had needed someone local to be a second cameraman with some street smarts. He remembered meeting Travis on an earlier trip, and I'd reconnected them. They were going to work together for a few days of filming in some rural communities with a nonprofit that had hired Mike to document.

Najibullah came by an hour later to check in with me as we'd originally planned, but we canceled the scheduled meeting he'd made for that afternoon. He said hello to Travis while I made him a cup of tea and introduced him to Mike.

Throughout the afternoon, the city's inhabitants began to emerge to tackle the cleanup. I offered to pick up kebabs for Mike who was getting ready to film an interview at the guesthouse.

"Sure, but take Travis. I'd feel better considering this morning's events. I don't need him right now."

Travis grabbed his jacket and tossed me my keys. "You drive. Your bike's outside."

I caught them nervously. It was the first time back on my bike since I'd arrived and it had been raining all morning. We drove a few blocks through roads flooded by spring rains. The intersections by the guesthouse had notoriously bad drainage. Puddles got so deep that I nearly submerged the tailpipe. There were pools of blood that splashed up on my jeans as we rode through.

I pulled over. "You drive. I'm too sketched out. Please?"

I knew he'd had a rougher morning than I had, literally dodging bullets, but he also rode a motorcycle every day. I hadn't ridden at all since my last visit in the fall, and I felt twitchy from the blood I'd driven through. A month or so later, I would randomly read in a friend's blog that someone had slaughtered a cow there and that was probably the source of the blood.

Travis took over, and we drove the few blocks toward the City Center building. The multilevel tower that housed a hotel and shopping center had its windows blown out. Glass was everywhere, and the police were out in force. On every street, Afghans were sweeping up glass and boarding up blown-out windows. Travis pointed out the pole in the traffic circle he'd been hiding behind during the gunfight he'd filmed.

Throughout the day, news stations pieced together more of the attack. A car bomb had targeted the Park Residence guesthouse, just a few blocks away from my guesthouse. Seventeen were dead and thirty-four injured—a stark reminder not to take anything for granted. My heart went out to all those who hadn't survived. That night, I sat up in bed late, thinking about my choices and the risks I was taking, and how that might affect Devon and my family.

It was cold. The electricity was out, and therefore so was my heat. I got out of bed and put my insulated jacket on over my yoga pants and sweatshirt, kept on my wool socks, and crawled back into bed, burrowing deep under the thin blanket.

A few hours later I was awakened by my bed shaking. My first thought was, *Seriously? Again?* I assumed it was another attack and struggled to figure out why my bed was rocking. The sound of a headboard banging against a wall confused me. *Are my neighbors shagging next door?* But there was no moaning from the other side of the wall, and I was in Kabul; it was unlikely that my guesthouse neighbors were getting it on.

Hmmm . . . What else makes the bed rock?

Oh, yeah, Earthquake.

But I'm not near Chile! My four-in-the-morning mental fog made it difficult for me to tell whether I was awake or having a dream resulting from a stint watching *BBC World News*. Most of the day's news had focused around the Chilean earthquake, and maybe it had infiltrated my subconscious. The shaking stopped, and I reached down in the dark and grabbed my laptop off the floor. I sat up, placing the laptop on my bed, and turned it on. It was too soon for any news, but Twitter revealed in less than five minutes that I hadn't been the only one woken up by a shakefest. Someone posted a link explaining there had been an earthquake with an epicenter in the Hindu Kush.

I'd been back in Kabul only forty-eight hours and my nerves were already fried.

Three days later, I left for Kandahar with the security report update from a friend that my guesthouse was on the Taliban hit list. I wasn't surprised per se. Any foreigner-occupied guesthouse would be a potential target, but the official knowledge unnerved me. I was still a little edgy from my "welcome back." Now came a NDIS report that ten Kandahari suicide bombers had entered Kabul two days ago.

I'd again hired Travis to document this trip though we both knew it was a long shot that he'd be able to video inside the prison. I was glad for the company, although perhaps he'd been living in a war zone for too long—four or five years now—or perhaps he needed a vacation; his mood over the past two trips was increasingly foul. Still, it was easier to hire and work with him rather than searching for someone I didn't know. I also trusted him more than anyone else I knew in Afghanistan. He was the most reliable travel companion and advisor I had, and I was grateful to be able to hire him for projects like this one. His advice and gut instincts were crucial.

After an hour-and-a-half commercial flight out of Kabul, we exited the plane on the Kandahar airfield and walked to the main terminal. The Kandahar airport's architecture was distinctly dated.

Unlike the typical concrete blocks that many public buildings in Afghanistan resembled, this terminal was built in the sixties and suggested a uniquely modernistic view of the future. Sweeping arches framed large windows that looked out on the airfield and beyond, reminding me of Tomorrowland at Disney World. Outside the terminal was a small "garden," a bizarre patch of grass with plastic wood scattered throughout. Images of an Afghan theme park popped into my head. I almost wanted to take a posed photo with Travis as though we were just happy tourists on vacation.

For the rest of our public appearances until we were back on the plane to Kabul, we assumed the attitudes of husband and wife. We went past the plastic garden and down the gravel road to the main security gates. The March chill and rain of Kabul were a distant memory as a warm breeze and full sun greeted us. We walked about a mile down the road to a parking area where our fixer, Sharif, was waiting beside—surprise, surprise—a white Toyota Corolla. Sharif was shorter than me, around five foot five, and had a very traditional Pashtun face with dark skin and large dark brown eyes framed with black lashes. When he greeted us, he exuded a gentleness that put me immediately at ease.

"*Salaam Alekum*, Shannon. It is very nice to meet you. You are most welcome in Kandahar," he said with smiling eyes.

"*Salaam*, Sharif," I replied. "*Tashakur.*" Then I realized that my Dari was relatively useless in Kandahar. I knew two words of Pashto.

"Now, for the drive into Kandahar City, it is not far, but I must request you to put on your burqa."

"I understand. Thank you, Sharif," I replied. I pulled the bluebird burqa out of my backpack.

It was just ten miles from the airport to Kandahar City, but it was one of the most dangerous roads in the province. It connected not just the airport but the U.S. military airfield and base to the city. Because it was the only road into Kandahar City, it was convoy central and thus one hell of a target area to hit both foreigners and military—two birds, one bomb.

Just the previous week, the bridge on the road had been hit with a car bomb when an American military convoy went past. As we drove across the bridge, Sharif pointed to where one entire lane was missing, the gaping expanse showing the ground far below.

As we spoke with Sharif, he quickly moved past formal niceties to the harsher realities and safety precautions he wanted me to take while working with him.

"The burqa for you is a necessity not just for culture, but for preventing a kidnapping. A Taliban attack is not necessarily the biggest danger for you. Kidnapping is. There have been thirty-eight kidnappings in the past thirty days—mostly wealthy businessmen and foreigners kidnapped for a ransom. For money." Kidnappings by both Taliban and criminals were increasing around Afghanistan, but Kandahar was worse simply because security there was far worse. We agreed that I'd wear the burqa anywhere outside the airport or hotel so that I would go unnoticed in the backseat of the Corolla, like any other invisible woman.

Forty-five minutes later, I was relieved to arrive at our guesthouse, not just because of the dangerous drive but because being seated in the backseat of a warm car in a burqa, I was quickly running out of oxygen. I kept lifting the bottom of the front flap and waving it back and forth to circulate some air. Focusing my vision through the mesh also took some getting used to. It was one thing to do so for a short period of time, but quite another when trying to see what was happening outside the window. Men in brown shalwar kameez, large shawls, and turbans whizzed by on motorcycles, the wind billowing their shawls dramatically, like a scene out of

Mad Max. I saw no women until we got closer to the city outskirts. There were women in burqas of all colors—a palette of sage green, pale green, a deep eggplant, and light brown took precedence over the bluebirds and doves I was used to seeing throughout Kabul and the north. The most obvious difference was that there were no female faces anywhere on the street; women wore burqas without exception, their eyes barely visible behind the mesh.

At the guesthouse, the registration desk explained to Sharif that we were the only guests. As we walked to the block of rooms overlooking a garden surrounded by high walls, we discovered that half of the building was completely destroyed. Perhaps this explained the lack of guests? Sharif said that a couple of weeks earlier the guesthouse had been bombed. The Taliban had launched rockets over the wall since it was one of the few foreign guesthouses still operating in Kandahar. It was the only option we'd found. Most foreigners now stayed on the military base or in private NGO compounds. On one side, our set of rooms looked perfectly suitable. On the other, next to the perimeter wall, a similar set of rooms was all but destroyed.

Sharif also said that the road along our guesthouse was regularly attacked because of a girls' school that was behind our building. Locals had found three mines there in one day. Sharif had several nieces going to the school and was visibly concerned as we talked about the violence that the Taliban directed toward it and the Afghan people in general.

I found the juxtaposition of that violence and the current serenity in the guesthouse courtyard hard to comprehend: sunshine, a lush patch of green grass, flowers blooming, and a warm breeze. It didn't feel like one of the most dangerous cities in Afghanistan, even with the bombed-out section.

But this was the province where, in November 2008, during my first visit to Afghanistan with Tony, several girls were attacked with acid as they walked to school. The story had been covered in *The New York Times* by Dexter Filkins, and it had made headlines in Kabul. This was the province where the Afghans believed "he who controls Kandahar, controls Afghanistan." It was the key to the country, and a fierce battle was brewing. Educating anyone, boy or girl, was met with fierce resistance in most of the province. Only in city centers were there schools, accessible health care, and Internet cafés, albeit with great risks. Rural areas were a wasteland of opportunity due to the lack of jobs, resources, and education, as well as the extreme poverty and ongoing battle for territory between the Taliban and international forces. Women had few or no rights, girls couldn't attend school, and boys' education was typically limited to religious studies at madrassas.

It surprised me that the Taliban could retain power and control while putting the lives of their people in the crossfire of their ideology. Sharif talked about the irony of the terrorists calling themselves Taliban. He explained that Taliban were originally religious scholars, and in fact the word Taliban means "student" in Dari. Today the majority of the Taliban community were common people—illiterate, unable to read the holy book they were so vested in. Instead, religious leaders interpreted the original teachings as they liked and instilled that interpretation, however mutated, into the heads of young boys They were polluting already muddy waters, stunting Afghanistan's growth, ensuring that its people remained the helpless victims of their militant countrymen.

Sharif quickly proved himself to be not only a capable fixer and trustworthy advisor, but a wonderful storyteller. Over a pot of milky tea brewed with cardamom in Travis's room, Sharif told us that during Taliban times, he'd been in Pakistan and graduated from the university in Peshawar with a degree in agriculture, though he'd never used it. He returned and worked as an English teacher at a boys' school in his village while the Taliban were still in charge. He showed us a photo ID of himself with a long beard and an elaborate black silk turban—a dead ringer for any one on a Taliban watch list. His solemn expression, long beard, and turban made him nearly unrecognizable from the kind man sitting before me. I asked if I could take a photo of the ID and a portrait of him now. He still wore a thick beard, but much shorter, maybe only an inch long instead of the Taliban's required fist length, and his eyes were kinder than in the ID photo. It was fascinating to see the simple difference a beard, turban, and stern look could make.

Sharif admitted to me that his family didn't know he was working for us. He used to work regularly as a translator and fixer with foreign journalists, but his wife had become increasingly worried about his safety. Sharif explained that he liked the work. It was often interesting, he was exposed to many different nationalities, and it supported his family. He said he also felt he was helping in a small way by making sure others could tell stories of Kandahar to the world. But even though he continued, he took fewer risks than before and didn't tell his wife.

The only family member who knew what he was up to was a nephew. Sharif called the young boy in to do a little shopping for us. Sharif had decided that I needed a new burqa before we visited the prison. He'd deemed my blue burqa from Kabul too "risqué" for the Kandahar scene. Too short? Too blue? Who knew? Sharif couldn't explain exactly, so I simply acquiesced. It's a pretty telling sign of the culture when you can feel whorish in a burqa.

The nephew came to the guesthouse with a brown burqa. It was also too short for me, but it wouldn't be seen other than in a car and inside the prison as I wasn't allowed to walk in the streets or visit the market. He'd also purchased several phone cards for us to give as gifts to the deputy and his guards at the prison. This should allow us more access and hopefully allow Travis to film. He said the cards were better than cash because they gave the appearance of gifts rather than bribes.

Sharif handed me a beautiful cream-colored scarf embroidered with different tones of gold and brown—a perfect complement to the colors of Kandahar.

"A gift from me to you," he said.

"Thank you, Sharif. It's beautiful, I am honored." I immediately swapped my plain black head scarf for it.

He smiled back warmly. "I hope you will wear it and think of Kandahar."

Next, he handed Travis a men's kaffiyeh scarf in local colors. Travis was also visibly touched by the gift and wore it for the rest of the trip.

Sharif got a call that the Canadians were currently doing a routine inspection at the prison. As in Maimana with the Norwegians, here in Kandahar the Canadians were in charge of reconstruction projects and that included the prison. We couldn't show up during their visit, and as the daylight hours were ticking away, I worried that we'd miss our opportunity to meet with the commander. If we did, we'd have to wait a couple of days. I was especially keen not to stay indefinitely in a guesthouse that had already been half destroyed. I requested another pot of milky tea, and we settled into Travis's room to escape the sun. Sharif sat at the desk, I sat crosslegged at the foot of the bed, and Travis sat at its head, propped against the wall with a pillow. Sharif helped us pass the hours by talking about Kandahar, the city, and the Taliban. Sharif was a beautiful storyteller and knowledgeable historian. He shared much about his own life and those of his family alongside the region's history. When we finally got the call that we were clear to go, I was almost sorry to interrupt storytime.

The commander of Kandahar's prison was by far the most accessible and friendly official I'd yet encountered. Not only did he grant us access with nothing more than a cursory glance at my Ministry of Justice introduction papers, he allowed a video camera inside. Travis grinned at me and winked, then started unpacking his equipment. We had yet to get permission to film or take photos in any of the prisons we'd visited. Occasionally, once we were in, we could take some portraits of the women with their permission. We had been kicked out of the Kabul prison before for carrying a camera.

We went into his office for the requisite tea to discuss what we'd like to accomplish by visiting the women. Once seated, he thanked me for wearing the burqa for culture and security, but then said, "I realize this is not your culture, so please, make yourself at home. You do not need to wear this inside."

I was happy to remove the brown burqa, but I was mortified that I'd forgotten to bring a head scarf. I felt naked without it and was self-conscious of going from one extreme to the other, my blond hair messily pulled back in a ponytail. But no one seemed at all concerned, so I tried to relax and focus on what needed to get done.

Travis asked the commander if he could video the meeting. The commander immediately nodded and put on his hat and proceeded to hold court, playing to the camera. He seemed sincerely proud of what he and the Canadian PRT were doing to improve conditions in the prison. He told us he was originally from Wardak, the same province that Parweez made the awful dinner jokes about and where Parliamentarian Dr. Wardak was from. It was another predominantly Pashtun province close to Kabul where the Taliban was reemerging. He'd previously been the deputy commander at Kabul's infamous Pul-e-Charkhi prison, notorious for torture and executions, with frequent prison breaks and riots as recently as 2008. The living conditions of the prison have been criticized by several human rights groups due to overcrowding and subpar living conditions. After forty minutes of tea drinking and questions, the commander stood. "Come, I will show you around now."

Inside the door, I immediately heard the laughter of children. There was a small playground. Two swings and a slide took up a large part of the dirt courtyard. I smiled at the children playing there, and they bashfully came over as I crouched to shake their little hands. They giggled and raced off to find their mothers. The commander gestured for me to sit on a swing, then proceeded to push me as if this were a summer day at the park. I fully expected him to buy me an ice-cream cone next. Surreal didn't begin to cover it.

Travis set his camera and tripod up in an unobtrusive spot to film. Surprised to be able to film, he was incredibly kind with the curious children and women who emerged to talk with me, fully aware that some may not want to be on film. He filmed so discreetly that soon even I forgot he was there.

Beyond the playground was a small building that contained the women's rooms where they ate, slept, and studied. It felt more like the Mazar-i-Sharif prison—communal rooms and dirt courtyards but in slightly better condition. I realized that I'd expected it to be much worse simply because it was in Kandahar. I'd expected this visit to be one of the most depressing in terms of conditions and commanders, and yet it was well run, at least on the surface.

The commander told us he'd recently completed a training exchange at a prison in South Carolina, courtesy of the American Embassy—just as the commander we'd met in Maimana had done an exchange in the United States and Norway. Such exchanges appeared to be extremely beneficial to the prisoners under their care.

Afghan women's prisons in particular had been infamous for the high rate of rape by male prison guards. Most women's prisons now had female guards, which lessened the level of abuse, though there were still babies born in prison. When I asked about this in front of guards or commanders around the country, they often replied simply, "You should not ask such difficult questions."

It was hard enough to imagine being raped and then thrown in jail for it, charged with adultery while the attacker lived out his life freely, with no repercussions. But to then face systematic rape from your jailers? Only an estimated 6 percent of rapists faced jail time in the United States, but at least the victims weren't subject to the double atrocity of being jailed.

As we walked to the back courtyard, women gathered and several pulled on my sleeve to tell me their stories. They clustered around me and described escaping arranged marriages, murdering their husbands, rape by male family members, and on and on. All of these stories were similar to those I'd heard in other prisons—the women incarcerated with little knowledge of their sentence. Many didn't know how long they would be there. Few had received legal representation to plead their case in court. When facing an accuser in front of a male judge, what chance did any of them have if a woman's voice was worth only two-thirds or in other cases, only half of a man's? Examples of this abound throughout Islamic law, or Sharia law, which states that two women would need to testify against one man. Sharia is the basis for personal status laws in most Islamic majority nations. These personal status laws determine rights of women in matters of marriage, divorce, and child custody. A 2011 UNICEF report concluded that Sharia law provisions were discriminatory against women from a human rights perspective. In legal proceedings under Sharia law, a woman's testimony is worth half of a man's before a court. Pakistani scholar Javed Ahmad Ghamidi has written that Islam asks for two women witnesses against one male because this responsibility is not very suited to their temperament, sphere of interest, and usual environment.

I'd met with a deputy minister of justice in Kabul six months prior and asked him about the judicial system in regards to women's rights. He spoke openly about the rights technically afforded to women in the current constitution. His opinion was that the issue was not in the affordance of their rights under the judicial system but in the implementation of the justice system—not enough lawyers, too many corrupt officials, and longstanding cultural norms. Most of the women were illiterate, lacked access to money to afford a lawyer or pay necessary bribes, and most lacked even the knowledge of their rights or of what to ask for.

Rape most often fell under the crime of adultery and landed women in jail—that is, if anyone actually learned about it. Many women, especially those in conservative provinces, were simply dealt with through Sharia law or "cultural courts" within families and communities: shot, beheaded, stoned to death, or simply beaten and disowned by their family. On the helicopter ride to Khost with Sahera Sharif, I'd asked if Khost City had a women's prison. She smiled wryly and replied, "We are Pashtun. Our women do not need prisons. We deal with our crimes ourselves." Irony was heavy in her voice—frustration and defeat apparent even through the helicopter noise.

Kandahar prison was where I met Nooria, a woman who has become a symbol of everything I strive for. Nooria was accused of killing the son of her husband's other wife. He blamed her, she denied it—a game of he said, she said. Regardless, she was the fifth wife of her husband. He was sixty-five and she was twenty, and she'd been his wife for four years—married off to him when she was sixteen.

She told me that his first three wives were dead—all killed by his beatings and fond use of knives. She shyly pulled up her sleeves and showed me multiple slash scars, as if someone had used her arms as a knife sharpener.

She told me that she felt safer in prison, away from her husband. The women, like in many of the prisons I'd visited, seemed to have formed a sisterhood. They slept, ate, and, when allowed, studied together, and they raised their children communally. I'd asked several women if they felt safer in prison, and many replied that they did. While I couldn't imagine the oppressive loss of freedom as anything less than a death sentence, these women often had very few freedoms outside of prison, so the loss of freedom perhaps wasn't much of a loss when compared to the protection from their husbands. The hardest part of prison for many women was the separation from their children, as only very young children typically remained with the mothers. That, too, I keenly felt, the notion of not being able to see Devon because I'd been raped was mind blowing.

After I'd spoken with the women for a couple of hours, dusk settled in. I knew the commander and his team were waiting to have dinner. I asked Sharif to please tell the women I wished them all the best, that I was grateful for their willingness to speak with me, and that my heart was with them. Then I moved through the crowd, clasping their hands in mine and thanking them individually in Pashto and occasionally in my scant Dari. Nooria pressed a silvery jeweled hair barrette into my hand. She'd taken it from her hair to give to me. I smiled and gently refused, not wanting to take anything from these women, but she insisted. The commander took the barrette from her and tried to put it in my hair but couldn't figure out the clasp. The women laughed at his clumsy fingers, and

Nooria took it back with a small smile and the women turned me around, their hands lightly on my shoulders. I could feel one of the women slide the rubber band out of my long ponytail, then another combing my dirty blond hair roughly with a small plastic comb. A third clipped it neatly together again with the silver barrette. They handed me back my black rubber band, laughing and smiling while Nooria smoothed back a few loose strands from my face and kissed me on the cheek.

I was glad for the cover of darkness as I felt tears building. I smiled, holding back the wave of emotion, and turned to leave with the commander. I paused once to wave and say good-bye again. At the door, Nooria was there waiting for me alone. She clasped my hands tightly, speaking softly in Pashto and not letting go—thanking me for taking the time to visit them, for listening, and for giving them a chance to talk and share. No translation was needed. Sharif recognized the moment and held back, waiting for me to ask for his help. I held her hand for as long as she let me, squeezing lightly, hoping she could sense how much emotion I felt for her. As I turned away from her, the tears released and coursed down my dusty cheeks unchecked.

As we left, I put my burqa back on, seeing for the first and only time its benefit by covering up my overflowing emotions. The commander walked us out and invited us to stay for dinner. We politely declined as it was already late, and we wanted to get back to the guesthouse. He was worried for our safety and insisted on sending us away with a heavily armed escort. A pickup with four armed men in the back followed us to the hotel. Their spotlight shone into the car, illuminating us like a high-profile target in the backseat. I was lost in my thoughts as we drove, hidden under the brown burqa, bouncing along the otherwise dark and empty roads. As we arrived at the hotel and parked in the empty lot, I raised the front of the burqa from my face and thanked Sharif for all he'd done for us that day.

Travis and I walked through the quiet lobby and through the inner courtyard to the back of the hotel. I tried to ignore the bombed-out section that reminded me how risky it was to be there. I went straight to the intact section of the guesthouse rooms.

Travis looked over. "Are you okay?"

I kept facing the door, looking down at my key. "Yeah. Well, no. But I'll be fine." While it was great working with Travis on trips like these, having him document and give advice, his cynicism could be tough at times. I knew he'd think I was ridiculous for getting so upset over a silly barrette. I walked back to my room, dropped my bag, and curled up on my bed. I bawled, uncontrollably, for ten minutes.

Spent, I felt released. I went outside to sit on the concrete stoop outside my door that overlooked the garden in the cool night air. The clear evening sky was filled with the sound of the last call to prayer. I stared into the garden, my mind empty. This place would be beautiful if only it wasn't so damn dangerous.

Dinner arrived ten minutes later and was served in Travis's room. I sat at the bottom of his bed cross-legged, my face blotchy and my eyes red. He appeared to notice but didn't ask any questions, and I didn't offer, but his tone for the rest of the trip was gentler than usual. I stared at the bizarre meat on my plate that looked like lamb with some sort of rubbery skin and fat. At first, I thought it might be the eggplant from lunch until I realized it was all attached. I was hungry enough to dissect it and not think twice about it until my mind wandered to our friend Gilly's recent run-in with dodgy meat in Kandahar. He'd had a rare case of botulism, something I'd actually had to Google the day before to learn its symptoms and how it was contracted. Tainted meat and contaminated canned food was the leading cause apparently. Botulism contained the same toxin used in botox—a poison women spent large amounts of money to inject into their faces to get rid of wrinkles. I crossed my fingers with each bite, though maybe the silver lining would be a reduction of my newly formed crow's feet from the inside out?

To get my mind off the botulism and other such thoughts, I asked Travis what time we were leaving with Sharif to go back to the airport. The road was so dangerous that Sharif wasn't keen to do it again, so he charged an extra $100 just for the drive. I was happy to pay it considering the risk for him and us, and I was more than a little concerned. The feeling that I was tempting fate had been with me this whole trip, ever since the Kabul explosion woke me up a week prior.

With thoughts of botulism and convoy bombers dancing around in my head, I said good night and headed back to my room. My nerves were on edge but I was exhausted—a bit as if I'd had a Red Bull and vodka—and I fell asleep with the lights on, fully dressed. I used my eye mask to create darkness, as though the light would keep the boogeyman away like it did when I was a kid.

Thankfully, it was a peaceful night. I awoke to the call to prayer. The muezzin sounded as if right outside the window, and birds chirped madly. I washed my face. As I was drying it, Sharif knocked. He announced his arrival and that of breakfast, again served in Travis's room.

Travis had just woken, and Sharif and I poured the wonderful milky tea from a brown thermos. It was so much more comforting than the ever-present weak green tea served elsewhere in the country. He took his previous seat at the desk, and I again placed myself cross-legged at the foot of the bed for some fresh naan and fried eggs. Sharif was a bit distracted. I could tell he was not looking forward to the drive since the heaviest convoy traffic took place throughout the morning.

After a tense drive to the airport, skirting around the missing chunk of bridge and pulling off the road when a convoy drove past in the opposite direction, we arrived back at the parking lot where Sharif had picked us up two days prior.

We said good-bye, and I tried to tell Sharif how much I appreciated the risk he'd taken by working with me and asked him to text us later to let us know he'd gotten back safely. I was worried about him, knowing that the Americans had declared the recent offensive in Marjah a success and that an upcoming offensive in Kandahar would be next, increasing the daily risk to him and his family.

Security at the Kandahar airport was much more thorough than in Kabul for its domestic flights. Sniffer dogs walked throughout the men's bags, the main security checks taking place when passengers got inside the terminal.

As soon as we were seated on the plane, Travis was asleep with his headphones in his ears. The desert morphed into snowcapped mountains outside my window while I considered the past few days and wondered what awaited me back in Kabul.

My guesthouse was still standing when I got out of my taxi. At the gate, I smiled at the guards. Sandbagging efforts out front revealed increased security. I grabbed my key at the front desk and asked the new guy working how everyone was.

"Everyone is fine—not to worry. We are fine. No problem," he replied.

I dropped my bags in my room, grabbed my messenger bag and helmet, and took my motorcycle out for a spin to clear the cobwebs and get a coffee and a botox-free lunch.

An hour later, a fig croissant was in my belly, and I was slowly sipping a second cappuccino while sitting in a red plastic chair. My table on the stone patio overlooked the garden at Le Bistro. My thoughts kept returning to Nooria and my reaction to her gift. Why had I reacted so emotionally when we left? I'd visited many prisons in Afghanistan, all of them heartbreaking in their own way. All of them tugged at my soul, threatening to harden it with cynicism so that I could keep the strength to continue hearing these stories without losing myself in them. I couldn't remember the last time I'd cried about anything. Had my heart already hardened? If it had, it was long before Afghanistan.

10

Whore

New York and Afghanistan 2009

My skeleton finally came out of the closet in a very public way one
sunny spring day in 2009, before an audience of millions. I was taping an interview with NBC's Ann Curry for *Dateline*. We were sitting
in a small darkened office in Rockefeller Center, spotlights illuminating us and blinding me to everything in my periphery. I'd presented to Ann a key point about the backbone of my work and
efforts with Mountain2Mountain. I was telling her that I believed
we needed to transform the perception of victimhood, both as individuals and globally if we were ever to combat the apathy that
prevented action.

I'd met Ann two weeks prior to this interview at a women's heroin rehab clinic on the outskirts of Kabul. I was doing initial research with the staff and founder to see if I could do some work
with the women there—literacy classes or establish safe houses for
those who had no home to go back to. I was also considering what

could be done for the children living on site with them. I'd brought toys and supplies for a kindergarten and discussed what could be done post-rehab with the women to ensure they had options. Like those in prisons, many here were disowned by their families. The stigma of drugs and prison was such that even when I'd talked to educated women in the government, they spoke as if these women were beyond help and would forever be victims relegated to the streets.

Ann's cameraman was my friend Mike, and he invited me for a drink to the Serena Hotel, where many of the major news teams holed up in Kabul. I arrived at the gates of the country's only five-star hotel on the back of Travis's motorcycle. I'd just ridden to the other side of town to visit an orphanage run by an Australian woman who Travis thought I might like to meet. I invited him to come with me to the Serena since we were running late. Given that he was a freelance photographer and insider, I also considered that he and Mike should meet.

As I walked through the glass doors into the opulent lobby covered in dust from head to toe, I became aware that I was, as usual, a complete mess. My long pale blue skirt that I wore over my jeans and motorcycle boots was more brown than blue. My head scarf was dusty, and I caught a waft of gasoline as I pulled it back. I smoothed my hair that had escaped its ponytail. My face, it seemed, had absorbed the brunt of the dusty ride, and when I removed my sunglasses, Mike laughed loudly.

"Would you like to use the bathroom to clean up a bit?" he asked quietly.

I glanced at Travis, and he said in his ever-cool Melbourne accent, "Um, yeah, you'd best get cleaned up a little, dahling." I raised my eyebrow questioning.

I walked down the hallway to a bathroom. I barely recognized myself. I had a dark monobrow, dust having covered the empty space around my sunglasses. My face was a different color altogether, and my two front teeth had a smudge of gritty dust across them.

"Good lord!" I exclaimed, grabbing a towel and turning on the faucet.

Mike had forwarded on a couple of my blog posts to Ann's producer, who would also be on the trip. Unbeknownst to me, I was having dinner with the entire production crew. Mike had figured if we were going to meet in Kabul, the crew may as well meet me, too, in case there was any interest in what I was doing. They'd arrived several days ahead of Ann to research and chase down potential stories. Over a buffet dinner that could rival Vegas, I shared what I was working on in Afghanistan. We discussed how my approach to working there was different from that of many NGO's: my lack of professional security, my friendship and trust with the Afghans I worked with, my interest in projects that focused on individuals over sticks-and-bricks projects, and my focus on youth activists and female leaders. We also discussed my desire to travel the country and really see it in unique ways, although I hardly needed to explain that as they were all privy to my motorcycle entrance.

Having Travis there proved useful as he was one of many freelance journalists who'd lived in Afghanistan long-term, without security, among the Afghans. He traveled mostly by motorcycle, for freedom and fun, and because it cut through Kabul's crippling traffic. He shared his own view of the country from the perspective of one who lived a real life there outside of a compound. His inside views of Afghanistan gave weight to how I presented my own work there, minimizing the risk of having a cynical news crew label me a Pollyanna or a stereotypical do-gooder.

Talk moved to my work in the women's prisons and the women's heroin rehab center. They were intrigued, and by the time coffee rolled around, they asked if they could tag along.

It soon became apparent after a couple of meetings the next day that the crew wouldn't be allowed to accompany me into the Kabul prison. No filming was allowed, and news crews weren't generally welcomed. But the rehab center had no such restrictions, and they came along to my first meeting with the director who ran the center out of passion for the women and their plight, and with very little funding. They filmed me interviewing several of the women and followed me later to the market where I bought toys and supplies for the children in the kindergarten and brought them back to distribute. I also discussed plans for a playground and a part-time preschool teacher with the director.

A few days later, when Ann arrived in Kabul, the team developed the footage into a story about children addicted to heroin for the *Today Show*. Ann met with several street children and addicts, and followed the story to the clinic. She asked to interview me briefly at the rehab center about my work with women and children and my views on drug addiction.

We met outside the clinic in the front garden on a particularly beautiful spring day before the heat and the dust really kicked in. Mike wired me for sound and told me to stay relaxed and have a conversation with Ann. After some small talk, we got into the interview, and I got my first taste of Ann's penetrating gaze. Her black eyes searched deeply, and I found it a little destabilizing at first to be speaking with someone so intensely focused on what I was saying.

When we finished, I got on my motorcycle, and they got into their two-vehicle convoy with security guards, and we parted.

A week later, I was sitting at my desk at the Park Palace, listening to Al Jazeera English and wondering why the bathroom drains always smelled so toxic, when I got a call from Justin Balding, Ann Curry's producer who I'd met at the Serena.

"Hi, Shannon, this is Justin Balding from NBC."

"Hi, Justin, how you? Are you guys still in Kabul?"

"No, we are back in New York. How are things?"

"Pretty good, considering. What's going on?"

"Well, the reason I called is I wondered, is there any chance you could fly home via New York? We would like to interview you in the studio with Ann."

"Seriously?"

"Seriously. We would like to do a story on your efforts. It's a good story."

"Wow. Thank you, Justin. I'd be thrilled for the opportunity. Thank you."

"No worries. I'll call you in a few days to check in, and I'll get our production assistant to figure out flights with you. She'll handle all the logistics for you. Be safe."

So eight days later, there I was, in this small darkened office, sitting on a chair across from Ann with bright spotlights illuminating us and making it impossible to see Justin and the rest of the crew watching on the couch and in the doorway.

Ann started getting personal. She wanted answers. She wanted to know why—why did I risk my life in Afghanistan when back home I was a single mother to a young daughter? Why at the age of thirty-two had I given up financial stability to work in a war zone? And why did I work in such an unorthodox and potentially dangerous way for a woman, traveling around Afghanistan alone, without security, often by motorcycle?

"Because," I said. "Because I have to." I paused, waiting for Ann to jump in, but she didn't. Her eyes searched mine. "Because if I don't, who will?"

Ann's dark eyes held my own and made it difficult to concentrate. Softly but firmly, she said, "That's not good enough."

It's not good enough? I thought frustrated. Well, shit, what was "good enough?" I had no idea *why*. I was just doing what I was doing.

I laughed nervously, trying to buy time, not sure *what* to say, worried about what was going to come out of my mouth.

"Is this going to be a Barbara Walters moment?" I joked, suddenly more aware that the cameras were rolling.

"No," she said, still holding my gaze intently, "but if you're saying that we have to be transformed, then we have to be honest about what transformed you."

Something shifted inside me. She was right. It wasn't good enough. Not anymore. My closest friends didn't know the truth, and my family didn't know the details. For more than a decade, I hadn't spoken about what happened to me that dark, frigid Minneapolis night. I had rarely even thought about it. And yet now, on national television, it came to me in a rush that my own personal catastrophe, my own victimization, defined everything I had become and was motivating everything I was doing in life. An epiphany caught on camera.

"Okay," I said, looking straight back into her gaze. I'd avoided the real answers for so long I'd nearly forgotten what they were.

I closed my eyes, took a deep breath, and remembered a saying I'd heard many times in the past—the truth will set you free.

"Okay," I said again, and again looked into her eyes. "When I was eighteen, I was raped and nearly killed."

It was late Spring of 1993, and I had come to Minneapolis to pursue my dream as a modern dancer. I had taken the wrong bus home late from work, which meant I had to walk the darkly lit paths through Loring Park to reach my apartment on the other side. I was lost in my thoughts, hunkered down in the cold with my hands in my pockets, considering my chosen path as a modern dancer and whether it was the correct decision for me after all. Suddenly, a hand reached from behind me and clasped me around my mouth. Another powerful hand grabbed me around the chest and forced me backward along the path to uneven dirt and grass, my feet tripping over themselves. I struggled until I felt the cold, sharp edge of a knife against my throat.

I fell face first as my attacker shoved me into the dirt. He applied his boot to my head, pinning me in place, the pressure threatening to crush my skull. Dirt filled my nostrils and mouth, making it hard to breathe. "Don't move," he said in a low, menacing voice.

I heard his belt buckle clank and his zipper being undone, and I panicked, struggling under the pressure from his boot. *He's going to have to take his foot off my head to do anything*, I thought, so I would lash out when the pressure let up, and then I would roll away, scream, and run for help. I felt for all my limbs so as to get my bearings, and I tried to brace myself on the ground. I waited for what felt like an eternity, tense, like a sprinter listening for the starting gun.

I felt him remove his boot and I thought, *Go! Go now!* Yet with the same foot that he had just used to pin my head, he kicked me hard in my ribs, causing me to instead curl into the fetal position. Again the boot made contact. And again. And again. I lay there pathetically in the dirt wincing at each kick, trying to protect myself. Thoughts of bolting evaporated as I struggled to simply breathe. Then he grabbed me and forced me onto my back. Before I could uncurl, kick back, or even take a breath, the knife was at my throat again. I froze and looked up to see his eyes boring into me through his ski mask. "I told you, don't move!"

He pinned my legs with his knees and applied his full weight to my body, crushing me. His free hand punched me again and again, the force of his punches causing him to inadvertently dig the knife into my skin with his other hand. He grabbed my hair and slammed my head back into the dirt. The knife remained, pressing in hard, but he let go of my hair and fumbled with my pants. The knife made small cuts along my throat as his hand bounced around, his body weight cutting off circulation in my limbs. I tried to say no, but it came out as more of a whimper. Hot tears coursed down my cheeks as he punched me again in the face. I felt his knife slice a new cut, warm blood running down the side of my neck.

His hand was inside my underwear now. Taking off his glove with his teeth, he pulled and tore my underwear, his nails goring my skin, ripping at the most sensitive parts of me. He plunged into me and it felt like he was ripping me in two from the inside. He grunted and the knife cut into my throat, and then he put his bare hand on my mouth and nose, nearly suffocating me and pressing my head into the ground again. I nearly passed out from the pain. As he thrust inside me, his hand pressing harder into my face, I could feel myself drifting away. More grunting and a sharp cut across my lower abdomen brought me back. He would thrust a few times and then cut me, thrust a few times and then cut me again—as though to keep me alert, or because he liked the sight of my blood, or because he could.

Eventually, he stopped the cutting and sped up his thrusting. I felt my head sliding back and forth in the dirt. *Stupid, stupid, stupid*, I thought hazily. It became a sort of mantra. *Stupid, stupid, stupid*. How could I have let this happen? Why had I cut through the park? Why hadn't I taken the right bus? Why hadn't I walked with my head up and my hands out of my pockets?

Three slow deep thrusts, and he mercifully groaned, shuddered, and stopped. Blood dripped down my belly and my neck, mixing with the stream of hot tears into the dirt below. Warm liquid stung my insides and dripped to the ground as he pulled out of me. I closed my eyes, unable to move, my tears and blood intermingling in the dirt beneath me. Was he going to slit my throat?

Keeping his hand over my nose and mouth, he pushed himself up to his feet. He bent over, kicked me twice again, and replaced his hand with his boot. He needn't have bothered; I didn't have the lung power to breathe, much less scream. He pulled up his pants and looked down at me, his eyes dark behind the ski mask. "Whore," he said, practically spitting the word. And then he left.

I lay there. I waited for whatever was coming next, not believing he was gone. But nothing happened. I listened to the sound of the leaves rustling in the wind. Keeping my eyes closed, I tried bending my knees, placing my feet on the ground, and rolling onto my side. The pain coupled with the realization of what had just happened caused me to vomit violently. The heaving wracked my bruised abdomen and possibly broken ribs, and I started crying again. My hair was matted with dirt and blood, and when I gently touched the back of my head to inspect the damage, I nearly passed out.

Somehow I eventually staggered to my feet, pulled up my pants, and rearranged my clothes as best I could. I stumbled onto the path and looked around. I squinted under the glare of the street lamp, my head swimming. I willed myself to put one foot in front of the other, just wanting to get home, but the path never seemed to get any closer to the sidewalk on the other side of the park.

I had been praying that someone would find me, see me, hear something. Now, finally, someone turned up. A man in a suit and overcoat walked toward me and, upon seeing what a state I was in, tried to grab me to help.

I recoiled, and he stepped back.

"Miss," he asked, "what happened? Are you okay? What can I do?"

I shook my head and tears began to pour anew. He tried to touch me and again I backed away like a frightened animal. He removed his overcoat and held it out.

"Please," he said, "take it."

I shook my head, just wanting to get home.

"Where are you going?" he asked. "Can I help you?"

I nodded and pointed down the street.

"You live down here?"

I nodded again.

"Can I take you to the hospital? Please. Can I call the police?"

I shook my head. "Please, I just want to go home."

He seemed unsure. Watching my face for signs of fear or resistance, he gently put the coat around my shoulders. It covered me down to my calves and felt like a warm blanket. He walked me to the door of my brownstone a block away. When I reached the door, it occurred to me that I might not have my keys or money. By a small miracle, I had my keys. I felt a wave of relief wash over me to not have to return to the park.

The man waited as I unlocked the main door. He made no move to step closer.

"Please, miss, can I call someone? Anyone?"

I shook my head again and took off his coat. Handing it back to him, I felt sorry that I had probably gotten blood and dirt on it.

"Thank you. Thank you," I mouthed softly as I turned to go inside the lobby.

Upstairs in my apartment, I pushed the bookcase in front of my door and turned on the shower. I spent hours sitting on the bottom of my bathtub under a warm shower, soap and water stinging my cuts and wounds. I tried to clean myself but found everything was just too painful, and I simply plugged the drain and let the water course over me from above and fill up underneath me. When the bath was full, I sat there until the water went cold. The depth of the old clawfoot tub allowed me to stay nearly completely submerged. At some point, I got out and crawled into bed. I stayed there for days. Blood stained through my clothes and the bedclothes. The cuts on my throat and abdomen were too crisscrossed and long to cover with Band-Aids and they were shallow enough that I didn't worry about them. The wound and swelling on the back of my head, my bruised ribs, and my torn up insides were the worst. I lay in bed for several days, in the dark, in a blessed state of fog.

I often think back to that man. Not *that* man. But the one who gave me his coat. That act of kindness. I wonder if our paths have or will cross again. If he knows how much that kindness he showed me has resonated with me, even if I could do little more than grunt and point at the time. How many others would have seen me coming and crossed the road, avoided my gaze as I was avoiding theirs, and just walked past, shaking their heads and wondering what trouble I had gotten into, not wanting to get involved, or not be late for an appointment? But this man saw me, tried to help and tried to comfort me. I will always be grateful for that. It was a welcome contrast to the injustice just done to me by another.

When I made my first call, after coming out of my self-imposed cave, it was to my aunt and uncle in nearby Shakopee, south of Minneapolis. Upon hearing I had been attacked, they drove into the city to get me and take me home with them. I don't remember much about the period that followed. I do know that after several days in Shakopee under their watchful eyes, I moved back home for several months with my family in Bismarck, North Dakota. I told everyone that I had been attacked, not raped. My mother, who'd initially battled my decision to move to Minneapolis, was the first person, and for a while the only one, to know the truth. She figured it out when I made an appointment to visit my OB/GYN to get tested for STDs. I had been too upset and disoriented to go immediately after the rape, but I needed to get an all-clear for my sanity. I was so scared at the doctor's office that I passed out in the chair when the nurses took my blood for the AIDS test.

I dealt with the trauma by trying to push it back into the farthest reaches of my mind. I did whatever I could to act as though nothing had happened. When a close family friend found out I had been raped, she commented to my mother that I "wasn't acting like a rape victim." I briefly started up again with my boyfriend from high school. It felt safe and normal, and yet I pushed him away when things got too familiar, scared he'd never look at me the same if he knew everything. I was afraid to show any vulnerability, yet I also failed to bury what happened so deeply that it wouldn't spill out.

I worked that summer as a maid at a Days Inn, and briefly as a flagger on a road construction crew. I didn't dance once. Not anywhere. Not at a studio. Not at a bar. Not even in my head. I dated. Superficial flirtations that allowed me to pretend to be normal. When autumn came, I moved back to Minneapolis. My mother accompanied me. We stayed together at my aunt and uncle's house in Shakopee.

The first day there, I asked my mom if I could borrow the car to drive into the city.

"I want to drive to the park," I said.

She knew immediately which park I meant, and she simply nodded and gave me the keys. "Take care of you."

I almost cried when she didn't question me or ask to come along. She understood that I needed this and that I needed to do it alone. It was one of the most sensitive things I could remember her doing. I drove to my old apartment and looked for a parking spot. The park was just ahead. I walked to a bench on the outskirts of the park. The sun was high in the sky, and people were bustling around the sidewalks, going about their day. I sat at the edge of the bench, ready to bolt at the slightest hint of a threat. After a minute or two, I took a deep breath and sat back against the bench, willing myself to stay. I sat there for an hour or more in the sunlight, unfocused, just being present in the place that tried to break me. Then I stood up, determined to leave this place behind.

And for most of my entire adult life I did leave it behind. It bubbled to the surface for the first time when I tried to help Larissa. But the pace and juggle of my life, the distance between Pete and me that was leading toward divorce, and my focus on raising Devon, ensured that it was a passing thought, nothing more. But looking back, the guilt of Larissa's attack and my fear of the same happening to Devon allowed what I had repressed to bubble up, slowly, one bubble at a time, over a decade, as though it was an oil slick.

But it was Ann Curry's insistence on voicing the truth to better understand my motivations that broke through the final barriers. I realized that I was not ashamed of what happened. What had happened to me had also happened to my sister. We were two strong, independent women. We were not victims. It happened to women around the world daily. In the United States alone, a woman is raped every two minutes. Why wasn't I talking about it? Why wasn't everyone talking about it?

But it wasn't until I met Nooria that the dam broke—the personal connection we made, the barrette, the unique situation of talking alone with the women, without security guards listening in. I saw myself in her. In all of them. I could be any of them. Because I was born to two American parents in the Midwest, in the 1970s, my life was very different than the ones these women led. As a rape victim, if I had been born in Afghanistan instead of the United States, I might be in jail under the crime of adultery or prostitution.

The injustice felt all the more sharp knowing we were interchangeable if not for geography.

The question I am most often asked is "Why?" Strangely, it's the simplest but the hardest question to answer. I wrestle with words to find a simple explanation.

Afghanistan is a country that begs for understanding and for compassion. It's a country where women have been routinely stoned to death for morality crimes where the Taliban took hold, but the people prove their resilience daily, fighting tooth and nail to regain their land, their freedom, and their future.

It's a place I'm inexplicably drawn to—wanting to understand it in hopes that I may understand myself. It's a place most Americans view through a very narrow lens because terrorism, poverty, and oppression are all the media tend to focus on. When the media do focus on the individual stories, they often do so through a skewed lens of victimhood that encourages Americans to think that these horrors are limited to "those" people: Those poor women, those poor victims. What about myself, would I be considered one of those poor women? Someone to be pitied? Someone forever defined as a victim and thereby limited by all that it implied?

Getty photographer Paula Bronstein took a powerful portrait of a self-immolation victim that I chose for the photography exhibition I'd created with the Afghan photographers, *Streets of Afghanistan*. I printed up the portrait seven-feet-tall so that viewers would be confronted with her face, larger than life. Heartbreaking and difficult though the subject is, her beautiful face is revealed underneath a drawn-back burqa and her burnt hands crossed in front of her reveal the beauty in the heartbreak that I see throughout Afghanistan. She has been victimized, but her resilience and her soul come through in her eyes. She is more than someone to be pitied.

I believe a large part of my "why" is my desire to understand the misunderstood. To see the beauty in the heartbreak. To see beyond the guns and bloodshed, the fear and apathy, and to connect with the underlying spirit of a people. To see the beauty that resides in all of us and share that back to others as a way to change perceptions and inspire action by connecting our stories through our common humanity.

11

Panjshir Valley

Afghanistan 2010.

The eve of my attempt to ride across the Panjshir Valley served as a reminder that what I was attempting wasn't a bike ride across Kansas.

Mike Simon and I had again been staying at the same guesthouse near the center of Kabul, but he was evacuated the previous night at 10:30 P.M. by the UN, prompting him to inform me that he wouldn't ever stay there again and neither should I. Two stays, in two years, and two major security situations. Mike was in the country to film the author Khalid Hosseini who was a spokesperson for the United Nation's Refugee Council. This meant that Mike fell under UN security protocols that are among the highest of any organization working in Afghanistan. He was given three minutes to pack and leave, and as he did, he tried to call me to get me out as well.

I didn't get his repeated calls because I was at a rock concert at

L'Atmosphere and couldn't hear the phone ring. Travis's band White City was playing with two other ex-pat bands, one of them supposedly made up of British spies. The night felt akin to a college party, long lines for $8 warm cans of Kronenbourg beer and no-name hard liquor, which ran out within a couple of hours. The entertainment-starved crowd cheered and danced, while the low-quality speakers and amps crackled. It was a great night out in Kabul, and it wasn't until after midnight that I took my phone out to call a private taxi and saw all the missed calls.

My friend Kate called about the UN report first thing in the morning, confirming what Mike had been told. She worked for a large Australian NGO and had better access to security reports than I did. There was a security warning about another imminent threat against our guesthouse during the next forty-eight hours.

Throughout the day, it appeared that it was a false threat. The UN was understandably hypersensitive to any perceived threats after the attack that killed eight a year before at a UN guesthouse not far away. Mike said he told the UN security who collected him that he wanted me to come with him, but when he couldn't get hold of me, the security team told him, "Look, she's not our responsibility." He sounded shaken and was going to be staying at a UN guesthouse for the remainder of the trip. I was scheduled to leave early in the morning for Panjshir but, depending on the situation, we considered staying elsewhere just for the night. Travis and Kate had both offered up floor space at their places if I needed a safe place to crash.

This was complicated by my shadow. Nick Heil, a freelance writer, author, and former editor for *Outside* magazine, was with me on this trip. For three weeks, Nick had been following me, observing, interviewing, and documenting what I did, and hopefully bringing clarity to the "why" for a feature in *Outside*. He was also a biker and the backbone of this story was a ride I was planning across the Panjshir Valley. From a mutual friend, he'd heard about my previous rides in Panjshir the year before, when I'd gone with Travis and Hamid, as well as about my plans for this adventure. After talking with me at length and gaining my trust, he pitched the story to *Outside*, and it was accepted.

Unfortunately I found out that some of Nick's colleagues felt that what I was doing was controversial simply because I'm a woman, because I'm a mother, and that the ride was some sort of ego trip to get *Outside* magazine to write about me. It hurt deeply hearing that and put me on the defensive. I had thought that *Outside* would get it—that they would understand what I was doing more than anyone else. They wrote about Greg Mortenson multiple times with glowing accolades, as well as numerous adventurers and humanitarians, but mostly they featured men. Was it as simple as that? Gender? Or was it something else?

After my first ride in Panjshir a year earlier—testing the waters in villages and on goat paths to gauge reactions and open conversations—the people's curiosity and openness gave me the idea and the confidence to try something more ambitious. I wanted to ride across the province and attempt to summit the 14,000-foot Anjuman Pass that marked the border with Badakhshan. Travis, Hamid, and Jeremy had ridden this stretch on their motorcycles, and it had taken them two attempts. They'd completed the ride, summited, and circled around the back side into the neighboring province to make a big loop. On both occasions, they'd spent the night at Idi Mohammad's home in Dashty Rewat. I'd asked Travis if he thought the climb would be possible by bike. He said he doubted it but it would be a hell of an adventure. As always, his was the perfect blend of cynicism and adventurous spirit. I hired him right there and then to come with me and document the trip.

At the same time, I thought about connecting a series of community rides back home to my ride in Afghanistan. Since girls couldn't ride bikes in Afghanistan, I would ride my bike across the Panjshir Valley one year from the date that I became the first woman to mountain bike in Afghanistan. At the same time, communities back home would ride their bikes and raise money for our projects that benefited women and girls. I dubbed it the Panjshir Tour.

A few months later, after numerous e-mails and phone calls, Nick and I met face-to-face for the first time in Dubai. As I'd requested, he'd let his hair and beard grow in. When I'd initially asked him to start growing a beard for the trip, he'd replied, "Okay, I'll try," in a voice that sounded like he seriously doubted his face's ability to sprout more than a few stray hairs. But the beard appeared to be filling in nicely except for two small round patches on either cheek.

We arrived in Kabul the day before the latest parliamentary elections. There was scattered violence throughout the country, targeting election officials and candidates, particularly female candidates. That day, two candidates and eighteen election officials and campaign workers had reportedly been kidnapped in three separate incidents. Election violence was notorious in Afghanistan. Intimidation, kidnapping, and murder of candidates, campaign workers, and election officials made campaigning nearly impossible in Taliban-controlled provinces.

Election-related violence had started back in July when a shopkeeper in Logar province was killed when he put up a campaign poster in his window. This was a warning to local residents not to participate in the upcoming elections. In nearby Khost province, Sayedullah Sayed, a candidate for Parliament, was fatally wounded—losing both his legs—when a bomb planted in the mosque he was attending exploded.

The past few weeks had seen more of the same across the country, with the worst still focused in Taliban-controlled Pashtun provinces in the south and east. That particular morning, fifteen districts had declared their polling stations would be closed due to an inability to secure them.

Al Jazeera English had posted an interactive map to track electoral violence. It broke down threats into three categories related to their sources. The map also contained blue markers for each of Afghanistan's thirty-four provinces, indicating whether the number of female candidates had increased or decreased since the last parliamentary election in 2005. Though the total number of female candidates had risen from 335 to 413, this gain had been largely limited to Kabul province where security was strongest.

Under President Karzai's amendments to the electoral law made earlier that year, sixty-eight seats were reserved for female candidates. That would suggest that there would be little point in intimidating women for running as they would be technically running against one another for guaranteed seats. Yet the reserved seats in provinces that did not have female candidates would not sit empty. They would go to male candidates under electoral law, thereby increasing the risk to women running for office; intimidation or assassination could equal an extra male seat.

Female candidates were accused of being prostitutes and un-Islamic, their campaign workers kidnapped, and their families threatened. This increased risk hadn't deterred women like Naheed Ahmadi Farid, a twenty-four-year-old in Herat. "I want to be a voice for women," she said when an ABC reporter asked why she was running for office. "Because there was about thirty years, thirty-one years that women didn't have any voice. I think we have to change the situation for women, and I want to be a member for that reason."

Journalist Alexander Lobov wrote, "At this point, hopes aren't high and all parties are concerned with maintaining the status quo. As long as both corruption and violence are kept in relative check, the elections will still serve as a moderate PR victory and the country will continue on its present course."

It was a lot of risk to take for a so-called moderate PR victory, but in Afghanistan, continuing on the present course was actually a step forward, especially for women's rights. Countrywide security had deteriorated over the past five years, and yet more female candidates were taking part in this election than the one in 2005. People were coming out to vote, and there was the feeling that the elections, however flawed, had to continue if Afghanistan was to survive.

Around midnight on our first night in Kabul, the walls started shaking. I hadn't been able to sleep, so I was sitting in bed writing. I'd just e-mailed Nick the election map link I'd found on Al Jazeera's Web site.

Nick was awake, too, and replied, "Hey, thanks. Um, did I just feel the building shake?"

"Yup, earthquake. I wasn't sure if you were sleeping through it. :)"

"Well, I was sleeping, but not through it! I got up to check it out and the dude in the hall with a gun just reassured me and waved me back into my room, saying, 'Everything ok. Relax. I have six men on patrol.'"

We woke up to the news of a rocket attack in Kabul around seven o'clock. Earthquakes and rockets—a great start to Nick's first experience in Afghanistan. It was nothing unusual, but what I hadn't accounted for when planning this trip was the heightened levels of violence and protests across the country resulting from one ignorant man in Florida, a minister who'd threatened to burn the Koran on 9/11. The threat of a 9/11 Koran burning wasn't just ignorant from the perspective of tolerance, religious freedom, and respect. It wasn't just tasteless to take the focus on 9/11 off those who'd lost loved ones and turn it into a sideshow, making a day of mourning and remembrance into a twisted Islamaphobic protest. It wasn't just dangerous to fan the fire between Christians and Muslims worldwide. It was also bigoted, reckless, and nauseating. Our country is great because of the freedoms we have. People of all religions and races and nationalities have traveled from afar to call America home because of these freedoms. This is not something anyone, of any faith, should take lightly. *All* beliefs deserve respect and are afforded the freedom to be practiced under our constitution. That's the beauty of it.

The Florida minister had the freedom to burn the Koran should he wish, as others had the freedom to destroy the Bible or Torah under the same laws. But actions have consequences. Proof in point? Another anti-American riot exploded in Kabul in protest to his publicized plan.

Threats degrading Islam, like Koran burning, play into the hands of the Taliban by fueling the belief that this is a war against Islam and not a war against terrorism. Fueling this fire puts our troops and international forces further at risk. It also puts journalists, humanitarian organizations, and development aid workers in greater danger. Those like me, who choose to work in Afghanistan to help rebuild, educate, and create stability, get thrown into the fire as well. I watched the news before flying into Afghanistan, with growing anger at what a small-minded bigot with some media attention could do to rock an already unstable boat.

Luckily, the elections took place with limited violence, and Kabul escaped mostly unscathed this time around.

Meanwhile, once we made our decision to stay at the guesthouse, we got to work. The bikes needed to be assembled, and we met in my room to do the assembly and talk about the ride logistics. We chattered on about single-speeds. This would be Nick's first time riding one, also at my request, so that we would be riding similar bikes and would, in theory, have a similar experience on the journey. I made piles of clothes, food, and bike tools that I would reduce to the bare essentials so that Nick and I didn't carry more than we needed. I had a bag of easy-to-eat snacks, power gels, bars, and packets of honey almond butter for quick fuel on the bike, as well as my café latte-flavored hydration powder and water filter. Most importantly, I added the key item for the ride—the silver barrette Nooria had given to me in the Kandahar prison. I opened one of the small pockets in my hydration pack and placed the barrette inside next to the locket with Devon's photo. A piece of Nooria would be with me on this ride, a piece of her free, and a reminder to myself of why I was doing this and who I was doing this for.

On the news that evening, we heard updates on other provinces as we were packing—two attacks in northern Afghanistan: one in Balkh province where I was headed after the Panjshir trip to revisit the women's prison, and the other on a military base.

It would be a relief to ride in the remote mountains of Panjshir for a few days.

Neither Nick nor I slept particularly well. He said he'd had dreams about a ship getting attacked.

Our driver picked us up at the guesthouse—a sweet man named Najibullah, recommended by my fixer and translator, Najibullah. He was a small, plump, smiling man from Panjshir, since it was always key to have someone local with us. I was often amazed at how many Afghan men I'd met named Najibullah or Mohammad, or both! Najibullah was actually Najibullah Mohammad. The driver Najibullah—Najibullah 2—as I thought of him, showed up in a rented Toyota four-by-four whose back door didn't open, so we had to load the bikes over the backseats, which didn't fold down. This was a complete pain in the ass and made me long for Shah Mohammad's Toyota Corolla hatchback, though not his driving skills. Amazingly, our Panjshiri translator for this journey was yet another Najibullah who'd also been recommended by "my" Najibullah. I referred to him in my head as Najibullah 3. It was a warped version of the old "Who's-on-third" comedy routine.

Najibullah 3 was dressed in a freshly pressed suit and shiny black leather shoes. He was friendly, but quiet, and extremely formal considering we were on a three-day trip to the mountains. Unfortunately, his English wasn't very strong. He looked a little overwhelmed when I laid out our plans and asked more than once if I could speak more slowly. I wondered if he was overwhelmed by the speed at which I was speaking or petrified by the idea of what I was proposing. I considered dialing up Najibullah just to make sure he knew what we were up to and could, if necessary, explain it to Najibullah 3.

Our first stop was to pick up Travis as well as a few supplies I'd left there. He let me keep my motorcycle and a storage trunk at his house between visits. The trunk was stocked with a few clothes and extra bike gear from the ride the year before so that I didn't have to schlep it back and forth each time I came to Afghanistan. The trunk sat in the corner of his courtyard alongside the collection of motorcycles. It was coated in dust, but when I lifted the lid, I felt as if I was receiving a little Christmas surprise. Inside were my bike shoes, gloves, and a number of things I'd forgotten about, like my extra helmet inside my favorite Osprey backpack and other road trip necessities: toilet paper, duct tape, tampons, industrial military-grade wet-wipes I'd picked up at the Bagram black market on the last trip. At the bottom of the bag was my first aid kit stocked with

Cipro, Immodium, Vicoden, Band-Aids, saline spray, and Neosporin. Game on. What more could a girl need to venture on a mountain bike across the Panjshir Valley?

Travis had obviously just woken up and looked haggard. No big surprise there. He'd probably had a late night after the rock concert. I suspected there would be a lot of napping behind sunglasses en route. There was also a new girl wandering around—Travis's latest conquest or one of the boys', or simply a temporary roommate crashing in the living room. I didn't ask.

"You ready?"

"Rock on, mate," he replied hoarsely.

Travis blearily grabbed his stuff, and we loaded it into the back. I noticed that the four-by-four was already packed to the gills and we still needed to pick up more supplies, including bottled water and snacks. As we were driving to the shop, Travis asked, "Hey, do you still want a female translator?"

I nearly punched him. I'd been searching for a decent translator for this trip for the past month and just secured Najibullah 3 two days before, in the nick of time thanks to the help of Najibullah 1.

"Well, we could pick up Fatima. She'd be great. Her English is perfect, and you wouldn't have to pay her. I told her about what you are doing, and she'd love to come with us."

I searched his face and something clicked.

"There isn't going to be any drama if she comes, is there?" I looked directly at him, trying to read his features. He probably didn't have a strictly professional relationship with her.

"Nah. She's cool." He smiled, an evil twinkle in his eye.

"I'm sure she is," I replied, smiling and rolling my eyes.

I was torn, as I'd be thrilled to have a female translator for the first time. It was hard to find female translators who were able to travel and stay overnight with a group of foreigners. Most of their families wouldn't approve. With her, we could sit with the wives in Dashty Rewat and really converse instead of using broken English-Dari exchanges brokered by the elder sons. At the same time, I felt bad about letting Najibullah go, despite his poor English. Travis suggested I simply offer to pay him a full day's fee. No harm, no foul.

I explained to Najibullah, slowly, that we'd found a female translator who was going to join us unexpectedly, and I asked if he would mind if we didn't use him after all. I apologized for the change of plans. He nodded, not really understanding, and I called the original Najibullah 1 to explain properly, then passed the phone over. Najibullah was happy with a full day's salary and no need to road-trip in an overpacked four-by-four of foreigners planning to ride bikes in the mountains.

Najibullah stepped out of the car to grab a taxi, and within five minutes, Fatima joined our motley crew. She smiled widely and introduced herself, then excitedly jumped in back next to Nick and me while Travis moved up to the front. We were off!

Our four-by-four was a right-hand drive, like a British car. Travis sat on the left side, and as soon as we were out of Kabul, heading north on the highway, he became Najibullah's eyes for passing. The highway was notorious for high speeds and bad drivers, and though it was one of the safest in Afghanistan in terms of IEDs and kidnappings, it was one of the most dangerous in terms of car crashes. As Najibullah was on the right-hand side, he couldn't see if he could pass until the car was almost entirely in the lane of oncoming traffic. This put Travis directly in the line of fire of the trucks coming at us at full speed. The result was a wild game of chicken, a comedy act that the three of us in the backseat enjoyed immensely. Tears were rolling down my face until Travis and Najibullah settled into a comfortable rhythm for traffic navigation.

We stopped at our highway bolone stand as per Panjshir road trip tradition. It was my fifth or sixth time there, but Nick's first. It felt different without Hamid along. He and Travis had a brotherly banter that I missed.

I was desperate to go to the bathroom, and while the bolone was cooking in the dark, murky vat of reused oil that most likely hadn't been changed in months, if ever, I snuck out back to find a discreet place in the surrounding fields. But every time I thought I was in the clear, a solitary Afghan would emerge from one direction or the other. Eventually, I went back to the stand and grabbed my bag. Inside was a Go Girl, a vibrant pink flexible funnel that was created for women to pee standing up. I had it for emergencies like this, and so I undid my jeans and simply turned my back and peed like a man. No need to bare my ass and squat, attracting attention. In fact, no one was the wiser, and I considered how lucky men were. The world was literally their urinal.

When I rejoined the group, Nick's eyes were wide, taking everything in as we made ourselves at home. We were seated on green plastic chairs at a table with a red-and-white checkered plastic table-cloth, on the side of the dusty highway. Market stalls lined both sides, and we were the only foreigners here. Bags of fresh *mohst* hung from the sides of stalls, along with stacks of Coca-Cola bottles and the requisite piles of red plastic jugs used for collecting water. Piles of bolone and a pot of green tea arrived at the table, served by one of the owner's sons. We dabbed the freshly fried dough with the newspaper to absorb the artery-clogging amounts of dirty oil while Fatima rinsed out the teacups with hot tea before pouring a full cup for each of us.

Full of fried dough and potato, we finished our tea and loaded back up for the best part of the drive, leaving the flat landscape of the Shomali Plain outside of Kabul for the mountains of Panjshir.

Travis continued to direct traffic for Najibullah, but the chaos of the first two hours abated.

Jeremy called Travis to check if we were en route. Jeremy and Travis had a $500 bet that Jeremy couldn't stop smoking for six months and Jeremy was due to collect it. He told Travis he'd donate it to Mountain2Mountain if we made it to the top of Anjuman Pass. He was extremely doubtful that we could, and was confident his money was safe. I felt the familiar thrill of a challenge and a strong desire to prove him wrong.

We arrived at the Gates of Panjshir, and for the first time since I'd been going there, Massoud's seventy-year-old red-haired guard was not at his self-appointed post. I wondered if he was okay and if I would see him again. We checked with the guards at the official entrance and drove around the corner to set up the bikes out of their view to avoid questioning or delays.

We unpacked by the side of the road, just past the bridge where I first mountain biked the previous year. The Panjshir River was raging alongside us, and there couldn't have been a more stunning scene to start this ride.

Nick and I assembled the bikes and put on our shoes and gloves as Najibullah watched amusedly. He, like Jeremy, was doubtful of this endeavor's success.

We took off together on the newly paved asphalt road, and immediately, the ride was harder than I thought it would be. I'd only traveled here by car or motorcycle in the past, and after two weeks in Afghanistan with little exercise, my legs felt leaden. The road would be a gradual climb along the entire valley floor until we reached the Anjuman Pass and took on the mountain itself. It was a beautiful sunny day but a bit too warm for my conservative riding outfit. This was hardly the place to wear racing lycra or bare my legs. I had on a variation of my outfit from the year before—padded bike shorts under a long pair of loose, black Prana yoga pants, my ever-present black Patagonia halter dress, and a blue long-sleeved tunic over that. I'd tied a men's black-and-white checkered head scarf around my head and another around my neck. The outfit was topped off with my Osprey hydration pack, biking gloves, and my well-broken-in Sidi bike shoes. Though they had holes, they fit like gloves. A rubber band around my right pant leg kept it out of my chain, and I skipped the helmet entirely. I thought about the barrette and locket inside my pack, and my Longfellow ring under my gloves, and I remembered how lucky I was to be doing this no matter how uncomfortable it would be and already was.

I soon realized that the worst part about the ride wasn't the climbing or the security concerns, but not being able to get enough air to keep my body cool. Nick had rolled up his khaki pants and his shirt sleeves, which was at least something. Big sweat patches appeared under his arms and on his chest, his blue button-up hiking shirt not quite up to the job of absorbing the amount of sweat he was generating. This was not a scenic excursion, as much as I wished it was, so I was trying to drive a fast pace so we could complete this safely and quickly.

The initial climbs weren't particularly extended other than Nick's aptly named L'Alpe D'Huez climb that kicked both of our asses. Most were short and punchy, and I stood and easily outpaced Nick on each one. While I pretended not to notice, my inner pride was beaming just a little.

Nick pulled up beside me after an hour or so. "This isn't flat!"

I looked over at him, smiling. "Who said it was flat?"

"Well, Panjshir Valley. Valley floor—flat. This isn't flat."

"I told you it was a steady incline the whole ride until we reached Anjuman Pass, and then it's a climb, most likely on foot pushing the bikes."

"I don't remember you saying that."

"Oh, well, it's too late now. Let's ride!" I laughed. It didn't matter what the terrain was or would be. We were biking across an insanely beautiful corner of the world. What more did we need?

The reaction of those who saw us was apparent in the first few miles: surprise, curiosity, and a lot of double-takes. Periodically, boys and men joined us, riding alongside, asking questions, and occasionally challenging us to a race. One man in traditional shalwar kameez and a pakol hat rode along for a couple of miles. He was commuting to the neighboring village, from his day job as a teacher at a boys' school to an office job in the afternoon. As we rode together, we talked in my basic Dari about his work and his family.

An hour or so later, Nick and I were alone again, and I saw the hill in front of us that housed Massoud's now-completed tomb. When we reached the top, we stopped to allow the four-by-four to catch up. I sat on top of "our" barrier, and as Travis got out of the car, I smiled, pointing at my seat—the barrier Shah Mohammad almost took out exactly one year ago on my first attempt to mountain bike here. It was easy to spot, as it was the only one whose concrete had been distinctly redone. We looked down the cliff into the green valley, and I shared the story with Nick, laughing at the memory of Travis's abrupt awakening from one of his many road trip naps to see us careening toward certain death.

We enjoyed the cruise from the hilltop into the village below and headed toward the capital of Bazarak, a small village that served as the seat of the provincial government. I waved down the four-by-four and asked if Najibullah could stop in Dashtak or another village before we were too far back into the valley, and get us some extra cases of bottled water for the ride tomorrow as well as some meat for our family in Dashty Rewat.

Nick was obviously stunned by the beauty of the landscape, and more than once we discussed how many people would pay large amounts of money to have this experience, to ride through this unexplored region. It was wonderful to see this region I'd visited many times now through his eyes for the first time. He was a mountain man at heart, based on what I knew of him, and it was obvious he connected with the rugged landscape surrounding us, and perhaps understood for the first time one part of why I was doing what I was doing.

Occasionally, a motorcycle or carload of young men tailed us for a while, and it unnerved me a bit. But Nick and I soon discovered that it dissuaded them when I rode inside of Nick, side-by-side. Nick effectively took a protective stance as a blocker. A firm *"xoda al fez"* made our intention clear. *Bye-bye!* Move along. Nothing to see here.

We pulled into Bazarak, and I was disappointed that we didn't have time to stop in to say hello to some of the public officials I had visited on previous visits, or to eat lamb kebabs at my favorite *chai-hanna*. We wanted to get to Dashty Rewat by nightfall, so we kept pushing through after refilling our water bottles from the four-by-four. Fatima told me that Najibullah also doubted we could get to the Anjuman Pass. "But," she said, smiling broadly, "he also thinks Dashty Rewat is too far for you and that you will have to get in the car to get there by nightfall."

I laughed appreciatively at the extra goading from our good-natured driver. He'd proved accommodating with this crazy expedition, even allowing Travis to climb through the sunroof to film from the top of the four-by-four as Nick and I pedaled along.

Despite the extra incentive to prove Najibullah wrong and take Jeremy's money, I could feel myself getting tired. The roads became dirt, and we spent more time navigating ruts and bumps. Before long, though, I recognized the sweeping road that overlooked the river basin, and the construction crews below signaled to me that

Dashty Rewat wasn't far around the next bend. We would make it
before nightfall—a relief, as dusk was settling in.

We rounded the final turn. On the edge of town, the new building and security gate of Idi Mohammad's family was in stark contrast to the dilapidated mud houses and corrugated steel stalls that
made up most of these villages. Idi wasn't home. He was in Kabul
and since cell phones didn't work this far into the mountains, we
couldn't let him know we were arriving. As usual, we were showing
up unannounced.

His brother, Fardin, greeted us in his stead and welcomed us
inside. I gratefully got off the bike and noticed the fatigue on Nick's
face. His beard was dusty, but it had filled in much more since I'd
first seen him three weeks ago in the Dubai airport. While he didn't
look Afghan, he also didn't look American. We'd been riding hard
for five or six hours, and when we climbed the stairs to the guesthouse's upper level, my knees ached with each step. This was the
first time I'd climbed these stairs in the guesthouse that I'd paid to
help decorate a year and a half ago as thanks for the family's ongoing
hospitality. There was also now a porcelain squat toilet inside, a
welcome addition to the outhouse.

We were dirty and sweaty. Nick's cotton button-down shirt was
soaked through, but we sat on the toshaks on the floor to wait for tea.
We rifled through our supplies to eat biscuits, chips, almond butter—
anything to get fuel into our bodies. I offered the various bags around
to the kids who'd followed us in, and to Fardin. The Prince biscuits
I'd brought from Kabul—chocolate paste sandwiched between two
pale biscuits—were the winner. Both Nick and I stretched out our
tired legs. My usual respectful pose of sitting cross-legged was too
uncomfortable and caused my hips to cramp. We quietly and methodically shoved food into our mouths, and I noticed two of Idi's
brothers were looking curiously at Fatima.

Fardin asked Fatima questions in Dari, and after her long exchange, I asked her to explain.

Fatima looked Hazara, from the Pul-e-Charkhi area, but she'd been raised in Iran after her father died. She had a more modern and global view of her birthplace. She was also brutally honest and frank, a trait that I took a shine to immediately. Her mannerisms and demeanor were decidedly Western, as most of her social group in Afghanistan was the ex-pat community.

She explained in English, "They probably think I'm a prostitute."

"What? Did he say that? Why? Because you aren't married?"

"They know Travis isn't married, and as an Afghan woman traveling alone, and with my looks, they think I'm maybe Uzbek, not Afghan at all. The real question is the propriety of a single woman traveling with a group of foreigners without a male escort."

"Shit, we should have said you and Nick were married." I laughed. Nick looked over with a blank stare. Fatigue had been settling in around him like a cloud until he heard his name.

Fatima laughed and said, "Or Travis."

"No way, not Travis. They may see him a few more times in the future, and we'll have to maintain that lie. But they'll never see Nick again."

At that moment, the door opened and one of the younger boys came in with a tray bearing the tea and glasses. He clearly took pride in being the one to serve us.

Nick perked up after our bellies were full, and he downed a second cup of tea. Talking through Fatima, he asked Fardin some questions.

"What do you think about Shannon riding a bike through the valley?"

I smiled at Fardin and interjected, "I can leave the room if you would like to talk openly without offending me."

As Fatima translated, I watched Fardin wave his hands and shake his head at me. "No, no, no, you should stay. It's no problem." To Nick, he said, "I respect Shannon and the work she is trying to do. I have no problem with her riding a bike. She is very sporty and strong. When she came last time with a bike to the boys' school, she walked up a narrow path with her bike and rode down behind the school. The boys were all amazed a woman could do this."

Nick grinned. "Do you think there is any man in Panjshir faster than Shannon?" I wondered if the "joke" would translate.

Fardin laughed with a big smile, getting the joke. "No, there is no man in the valley as fast as Shannon." I laughed loudly when Fatima translated this and smiled at Fardin. He had a twinkle in his eye as he smiled back, acknowledging the banter.

"We are going to try to ride to the top of the Anjuman Pass," Nick said. "Do you think we will make it to Anjuman?"

Fardin replied, and all the men started laughing. There was a flurry of words back and forth between Fardin and Fatima.

"We think that yes, Shannon can do it," Fatima translated to Nick in a deadpan voice, "but that you will not. You are too fat."

I burst out laughing despite myself and looked at Nick, who was hardly fat. I wondered how he'd respond. "It's true, it's true." He sighed and nodded self-deprecatingly. He nodded some more and shrugged at the men as if to say, "What can I do? You are right."

The children laughed uproariously.

Changing the tone, Nick asked, "Can Afghan women ride bikes?"

Fardin responded seriously. "No, it's not part of our culture."

I sat back and wondered once again why it was that foreign women and Afghan women were treated so differently. A woman was a woman. Why was I allowed to get away with this? In Saudi Arabia, for example, being a foreign woman didn't give you any more leeway. Rules and customs were to be observed by everyone, regardless of nationality.

I excused myself to go to the bathroom. I took off my bike chamois and dressed again with a clean tunic and pants. I'd be sleeping in this, too, and in the morning, would simply put on my clean chamois under the pants. I used the wet wipes to remove the layers of dirt and grime and sweat as best I could. I felt tired but strong, and more confident than ever that we could do this.

Soon, one of the other children came in with the red plastic tablecloth to unfold across the space between the toshaks, signaling that dinner was on the way. A large flat naan was thrown down in front of each of us and plates of mysterious and slightly gray meat covered in suspicious-looking sauce on beds of rice arrived, along with tomato and onion salads. I looked sideways at Travis, who'd gotten dysentery after every meal we'd had here, and winked. He groaned quietly in response but took a hunk of naan to scoop up some rice and meat, knowing what he was in for.

Nick had yet to eat in true Afghan style. Seated on the toshaks across from me, he'd crossed his long legs and was watching me scoop food into my hand to eat or use hunks of naan as a food-to-mouth utensil.

The men and children watched Nick with amusement as he scooped some food with his hand and rice spilled everywhere.

"I have the same skills as a five-year-old," he lamented.

After dinner, Fardin took a tin of naswar from his pocket. He smiled at me, a twinkle in his eye again as he offered it to me. I laughed but declined. I told Nick the story of the first time I'd tried naswar with Fardin, encouraged by Travis and Hamid, and that it had led to flu-like chills, me turning a dark shade of green, and a rapid run to vomit in the outhouse.

Fardin now poured some into his hand and pressed it into a little ball. Once he had it wedged against his gum, he asked about Devon. I pulled out my iPhone. I had a folder of photos just of her for these occasions. Most of the family now knew to use their fingers to slide each photo to the next, and as usual, the phone went around the room. I wondered if Steve Jobs realized how innate his technology really was.

A couple of villagers joined us, but my "betrothed"—the Afghan comedian with the stereo we met on our first visit to Dashty Rewat— was fishing at a lake on Anjuman Pass. I laughed when I heard this. Great, we would make it to the top of the pass just in time to run into him. He'd probably interpret this as a huge gesture on my part that I was willing to climb a mountain just to be with him.

Things quieted down, and I took my cue to have tea with the women in the other part of the compound. Fatima came with me, and I was again grateful she was along to translate. We entered, stooping through the half door that divided the compound from the new building and courtyard. The wives and grandmas were excited to see me and ushered us into a room I hadn't yet visited. They gathered around, along with all the children, but for the first time, the older boys weren't in attendance since they weren't needed to translate. There were women only, a girls' night in, so to speak.

Immediately, the questions started as Fatima and I sat drinking tea in front of ten or more faces.

I asked how they were. The last time I was there, Idi Mohammad's gorgeous wife, Huma, had a new baby, and I got to meet him. Adorable, he was now one year old and had been named Mohammad. I was thrilled to see he'd survived his initial harsh winter. I also met the newest member of the family. This time, Fardin's wife, Massouda, had the newborn. I saw that she'd lost two of her teeth to malnutrition and the stresses of multiple pregnancies so close together.

The women asked about Devon, and again the iPhone made

the rounds, starting with my favorite member of the family, Idi Mohammad's mother. She asked, for what seemed the twentieth time, "Why don't you have more children? Don't you want a son?"

I smiled and nodded, and for perhaps the twentieth time responded, "No, I still only have my daughter, Devon, and I love her as much as any son. I'm very lucky to have her."

Grandma smiled knowingly at me, assuming I was barren, and said, "I'll pray for you that Allah grants you a strong baby boy."

Great, I thought. *You do that, and I'm going to double up my protection.*

The talk immediately turned to birth control when one of the wives asked me directly, "Do you use birth control?" The iPhone was still circulating around the room, and I was so surprised that I had to ask Fatima if she'd translated correctly. She had, and so the first topic of conversation at the girls' night in was about birth control. I turned the question of whether I was on birth control around and asked if any of them were and what they knew about it.

Massouda replied that she was now on birth control, a form of the pill, that the local doctor gave her after her most recent baby. She'd been told that she could be on it safely only for one year. Clearly, the campaign to convince men to give their wives space between babies for the health of the mother and the child was being heard in some form. She pointed to where her teeth had fallen out and said she hoped that it would prevent more tooth loss.

I couldn't speak to that but was intrigued at the direction of the conversation. They asked why I never came back to train midwives— something I'd discussed with the men a couple of years ago. I explained that a training in Dashty Rewat wasn't possible because there were no women who were literate. The new midwife now working with the doctor at the village clinic was a welcome addition, and I was relieved to hear that some maternal care had finally arrived.

Idi's oldest daughter, Ariana, was to be married in a few months. The women talked about this proudly, and Ariana smiled softly. It would be a big celebration for the family—the first of the children to be married.

Then the women shared that they couldn't leave the house except under a burqa at night or on special family occasions. I was shocked. I knew I shouldn't have been. But this region of Afghanistan, and this family in particular, had always struck me as more progressive or simply less conservative than other rural provinces. Panjshir was the bastion of Massoud, the Lion of Panjshir, who'd been a proponent of girls' education and the iconic leader of a free Afghanistan.

I asked if they knew about the girls' school I'd discussed building here with Idi Mohammad. Huma said that the village had laughed at Idi when he'd proposed it. The local mullah was against it. Even though there was a school in a neighboring village, the girls here weren't allowed to attend.

Speechless, I decided not to broach the subject with the men tonight about progress on the village land donation for a future girls' school in Dashty Rewat. I was devastated, but this explained the delays and suspicions I'd had during prior visits. I swallowed the lump of disappointment and frustration building in my throat.

After a few more questions, Fatima and I said good night and wished them all good health and for the babies to grow up big and strong. Nick and Travis had been hanging out with the locals, and both appeared mellow and sleepy. Tomorrow was going to be another long day in the saddle, so I got ready for the ritual tuck-in. The young boys pulled down the blankets and pillows from the corner stack, and Fardin came around to tuck us all in, Nick, Travis, Fatima, and me at one end of the room around the toshaks. Najibullah slept at the other end, next to the entrance, along with Idi's oldest son and a few of the youngest—our protectors perhaps.

I slept so hard that I wasn't sure I'd even moved. I opened my eyes, stretched my legs, and woke to several of the younger boys watching me. I sat up and smiled at them, then searched for the little bag I kept beside me with my contact lenses. Nick and Fatima were stirring as well. Travis just groaned and rolled over, trying to avoid the daylight. Once we were upright and had rubbed the sleep out of our eyes, the room was filled with tea and our hosts.

The red tablecloth came back in, and a breakfast of naan, fresh cream, and a cherry preserve was served along with plates of fried eggs. It was the perfect way to fuel up for the day, and I was grateful for something solid to put in my belly as I'd discovered the Dashty Rewat curse got me yet again and had already liquefied last night's dinner. Needless to say, I was even more grateful for the squat toilet and the pink toilet paper they now stocked for special visitors.

After breakfast, we discussed the logistics for completing the pass. Beyond Parion, there would be no more villages. We'd have to ride for a few more hours before we got to the start of the arduous climb. This could take a few more hours, and we'd possibly have to walk our bikes a good portion of the way. We couldn't ride to the pass and get up and down before nightfall. I suggested sleeping in the car, but that was met with dubious looks. Frankly, I couldn't see any other option unless we rode as far as we could, doubled back to Parion in the car, and restarted the next morning. Safety was a huge issue. This wasn't like bike touring across the United States or Europe. We couldn't just set up camp by the roadside or in the hills because of land mines, kidnapping, or assassination. Ten medical aid workers had been killed a few weeks before on the other side of the pass. It was a lawless area back there. We didn't even know if the four-by-four would make it all the way, as it had to be turned off several times the day before so the radiator could cool down. We agreed that we'd make a run for the pass as best we could and leave Parion open as our potential option to do a double-back if we needed to.

The fact was we really didn't know what to expect beyond Dashty Rewat. When Travis, Jeremy, and Hamid did this trip on motorcycles the year before, it took them all day from Dashty Rewat to get over the pass by nightfall. We would be about three times slower than the motorcycles. We didn't even fully know what the road condition would be as construction crews had been working on sections of it for the past few years. Stretches that had been dirt in the spring were now smooth pavement, interspersed with boulder-ridden, rocky areas that were so torn up we had to pick our way through. It could be faster riding or much slower than we anticipated.

The other concern that unexpectedly greeted us that morning was water. We couldn't buy bottled water here, and Travis and Najibullah hadn't bought any in Bazarak as I'd asked. Travis had of course assured me it would be "no problem, mate," but I should have known better and stocked up with more than we needed in Kabul. This was a major problem. He suggested river water as an option, and Nick and I looked at each other incredulously, knowing it could literally kill us. Travis seemingly had no concept of these kinds of things. Livestock and human waste as well as mining pollution were all dumped into the river. I wouldn't eat the fish caught in this river without a Cipro chaser, much less drink the water. I wasn't even willing to put my water purifier to that challenge. Nick was seriously not amused and wrongly assumed that I was considering the river solution as a viable option. I tried to assure him I was not.

We headed downstairs and brainstormed. I asked the family to boil enough water to fill all the empty water and Sprite bottles we could dig out of the truck. Meanwhile, I walked across the street to check out Fardin's little shop and see if there was something that would work. I bought a full case of individual juice boxes on the bottom shelf, covered in dust, but still within the sell-by date. I also bought several Afghan prepackaged cakes, biscuits, and tea. They might be stale, but they never seemed to expire. Idi's brother had also packaged the remaining naan from breakfast for us and loaned us four blankets, a tea kettle, and a little fuel tank (which was empty) for our potential overnight in the car, if it came to that.

A crowd gathered outside when we finally got our show on the road. We waved good-bye, and several kids chased us as we started riding. My ass felt sore, but my spirit was happy. Nick and I eased into a gentle pace to coax the legs back into what was going to be a long, tough day in the saddle.

Thirty minutes or so out of Dashty Rewat we came across a Kuchi camp off the side of the road. The Kuchis are Afghanistan's nomadic people. Kuchi literally means "nomad" in Dari, but they are typically Pashtun in ethnicity. Camel caravans, brightly colored tents and clothing in vibrant purples, fuchsias, and emerald greens made me feel as though I'd stepped back in time. Every view was postcard perfect, and Nick was also visibly blown away. My awe quickly took another course a few miles later as we encountered a gnarly set of switchbacks—steep, loosely graveled, and seemingly unending. After grinding our way up a couple of them, we started walking to conserve energy. I considered switching out my rear cog for an easier gearing if this was how the rest of the day was going to play out. Travis and crew pulled up in the four-by-four. He had a huge grin. "Don't worry. It levels off in a bit, and you'll be able to ride again."

"Thank God for that," I said, gasping. My calves were cramping from walking on my toes in bike cleats up the incline.

When we got to the top, we pulled over next to the four-by-four and had an impromptu snack and chat. Fatima sat down beside me.

"I'm so proud of you," she said. "You are really doing this. This is really great."

I smiled broadly, feeling and tasting the grit in my teeth, and I leaned over to give her a hug. I was touched and so glad she was with us. I only wished she knew how to ride a bike as I was certain she'd join us in a heartbeat. Having another female presence along, especially an Afghan, made this ride resonate all the more deeply for me. I offered to teach her how to ride when we got back to Kabul and she nodded enthusiastically.

At each hill, I left Nick in the dust—a good feeling, as I'd worried before we left that he might find the pace too slow. I had the advantage of riding my single-speed in the mountains of Breckenridge, which sits at 9,600 feet, so the long climbs that forced us out of the saddle didn't faze me. Nick was used to gears, although the altitude in his home of Santa Fe almost identically matched the elevation in the Panjshir Valley—around 6,000 feet. As we rode, we were steadily climbing and would continue until we reached the summit of the Anjuman at 14,534 feet.

I vacillated between tiredness and feeling the pain, to euphoria at the beauty back here and the positive reaction from the locals. Nick seemed to be trudging through in survival mode.

Before we arrived at the last outpost of Parion, Travis pulled up next to us and said to just ride past, ignore the checkpoint, and see if we could evade the police who'd delayed him, Hamid, and Jeremy on their first attempt with motorcycles. They pulled ahead and went through, and we followed. It only took about ten minutes before a police jeep pulled up beside us. The four-by-four was long gone ahead with my translator. The police were insistent that we return with them to check in. I tried to explain that our papers were in the truck with the driver—the familiar duel of broken English and broken Dari as we tried to communicate. They finally understood and told us to wait while they went ahead to find our crew. We sat on the roadside and before long, the police returned with Travis and Fatima, who offered to go back to register us.

Travis said, "They will allow you to wait here and rest, but as soon as we're gone, start pedaling and we'll catch up with you when we're all clear."

Once they were out of sight, we pedaled off to make up some miles and keep on schedule. An hour or so later, we stopped. The road was getting very desolate, and we didn't want to go much farther in case they didn't turn up and we had to ride back to Parion.

Soon Najibullah pulled up with a note from Travis to sit tight and that they were just waiting for the commander to arrive and sign the papers. We unloaded some food and supplies from the truck for an impromptu picnic and wrote a reply to Travis and Fatima. Our personal Pony Express turned the four-by-four around and headed back to Parion.

One $250 "donation" later, the crew arrived at our picnic area with an all-clear. I'd never paid a bribe and certainly didn't want to start now, but we were in the clear, along with a proposal from the commander to Fatima. The police had warned Travis about Nooristanis with guns up by Anjuman, and they wanted to send a police escort with us—hence the bribe. We got off easy, as the previous year Travis and his friends had to pay $500 for permission to continue *and* each took a police officer with them on the backs of their motorcycles. Fatima was a little worried about the proposal. The commander was very insistent and had taken a serious liking to her. Travis said it was worrying enough that he would advise against staying in Parion for the night for Fatima's safety.

At this point, several elderly men walking down the road offered us tea and food should we need it. This was incredibly kind, and I wished I could take them up on the offer, but we needed to press on.

We came across a small bridge construction and a road crew. As we rode close, they practically swarmed up to stop us and chat and ask what we were doing. We were probably the most interesting thing they'd seen all week, and several asked if they could ride our bikes. For fifteen minutes or more we watched and laughed as the men took turns on our bikes. They wished us luck and strength as we set off again.

As we continued, the roads became steeper, rougher, and more remote. The mountains that surrounded us on all sides started to feel like the badlands from an old Western movie. I imagined Afghan snipers on the mountaintops above. There was a noticeable energetic shift in the atmosphere, the sense of being watched and the awareness of the vast emptiness around us made my skin tingle. As Nick and I biked through a couple of small river runoffs that crossed the dirt road, he commented on the shift as well.

When we were walking our bikes up a major incline, an old man in a white turban came down with two donkeys and stopped us. He asked where we were going, and when we replied "Anjuman," he started shaking his head and mimed a rifle. He kept saying we shouldn't go up there—men with guns, not good. Dari and sign language made everything pretty clear, but we explained that our driver and translator were in the truck coming up behind us—would he explain more to them?

We continued on as the old man spoke with the crew. Nick expressed his unease, and soon Najibullah pulled up and Travis got out. Travis pointed ahead, and we had our first clear view of the Anjuman itself. The mountain's jagged silhouette was in full view, with a few small snow fields tucked into the saddle that dipped between two peaks.

"Nooristani gunrunners," Travis confirmed. "The old man is talking about Nooristani gunrunners around the pass. Apparently it's been an issue for a while now. It's not Taliban, just criminals. Drugs and guns."

"Well, shit." Defeat was heavy in my voice. "That's a definite no for staying the night up there." And I had to face it—a strong argument against even venturing up there at all. "Could we maybe just ride a bit farther while we think? Maybe ask someone else?" I was grasping at straws.

We decided to ride a bit farther as I preferred to think about this while I pedaled. The others drove ahead to see if they could find anyone else to speak with. Nick and I discussed the palpable change in atmosphere, tension, and risk.

"It's starting to feel like a rigged game of Russian roulette, don't you think?" he said. I had to agree. I knew he wanted to turn around, and while my head was in agreement, my heart needed a few more pedal strokes to come to terms with the news.

I was disappointed. Seeing the pass in front of us made it all the more tempting. So close. I understood why mountain climbers talk about the descent from a climb being more dangerous than the ascent. You can push through and get there, but you still need to survive in the danger zone long enough to get down. Our danger zone wasn't extreme elevation and lack of oxygen, but men with guns.

We were both riding at a steady pace, feeling the tiredness but pedaling strong. I didn't want to turn back because of this sort of stuff, but it *was* Afghanistan after all. Gunrunners of any sort were to be avoided, no matter the country, but in the remote, desolate badlands of Panjshir, their presence was an unfortunate reality. The trip had just turned from a challenge and exploration to potential suicide. This wasn't even a real choice, especially when I had Devon to think about.

I had to remember that the goal was not the summit—this was simply a logical end point. We'd already achieved the real goal: riding for two days across the entire valley as a woman, challenging perceptions, asking questions, racing young boys and men on their bikes, and connecting this ride to a series of rides back home to raise money for projects in one of the few countries in the world where women couldn't ride bikes. Even in the sixties when Afghanistan was a tourist destination—and Afghan women in urban areas like Kabul attended university alongside men and wore short skirts and no head scarves—biking was still a deep-seated taboo.

I knew we couldn't use the backup option and double back and stay in Parion with the police chief taking such a shine to Fatima. It wasn't safe, and I wouldn't put her life at risk just to do a third day of riding, which was already feeling too dangerous even in the daylight. We couldn't do the pass safely regardless of where we spent the night, so the decision was made for us.

Travis suggested that we ride up to the major river crossing, cross it if we could and ride the little incline for a proper look again at the Anjuman. He said that there was a large grassy field with a stunning view of the surroundings. It would be a nice place to sit and contemplate what we'd done before we turned around.

The river crossing was knee-deep and freezing cold, with a strong current that threatened to push me over. Staying upright on the slippery rocks was nearly impossible in bike cleats. We would get to do it twice, of course. But on the other side was one of the most incredible spots I'd seen in Afghanistan. We sat in the field with our bikes, my legs wet up to my knees, and I quietly cried for the second time in Afghanistan. I took out the barrette and held it in my hand while I digested my disappointment and my elation that we'd gotten this far.

The afternoon sun was fading, and Nick and I decided to enjoy a little of the incline in reverse. We got back on our bikes and cruised toward home, the light golden and soft with all the dust in the air.

We kept riding for an hour or so, enjoying the "free miles" of pedal-free descents.

Coming up to a lengthy incline, legs tired, and the cold air of nightfall settling in, I stopped. I waved the truck up and said, "Okay."

"Enough?" Travis asked.

"Yup, it's time to go home."

He smiled gently.

"Come on then, let's get you in."

Najibullah pulled over to the roadside, and we gingerly stepped off our bikes. Fatima got out of the car to give me a hug.

"I'm so proud of you, Shannon. This is really amazing," she said as she squeezed me harder.

We took the wheels off the bikes, stuffed them in the back, which was now strewn with empty Sprite bottles, snacks, and Travis's camera equipment. We piled into the car and headed back to Dashty Rewat to return the stuff we'd borrowed. I was quiet in the back, tired, hungry, and disappointed, my legs cramping. Nick joked that the way to do this ride would be to drive up the Anjuman Pass, jump out with the bikes, and ride the entire pass and valley downhill—totally doable in two days and way easier, though the symbolism of climbing the mountain would be lost. Either way, I was in no mood to talk about a redux, yet.

A couple of hours later, we arrived at Dashty Rewat in the dark and despite the offer of warm food and a bed where we could stretch out, we made the unwise decision to press on. The consensus was that we might as well get back to Kabul tonight, Travis's dysentery and my mood being deciding factors.

Travis, Fatima, and I were in the backseat so that Nick, the tallest, could stretch his legs next to Najibullah in the front. We were all bouncing around with the bumps and Najibullah's increased speed to get us home. It was a four- or five-hour drive, and Nick got the ride of his life. In the front seat, Najibullah played "dodge the trucks" from the right-hand drive position, which left Nick staring wide-eyed at oncoming truck traffic. He decided it would be a money-making video game: Afghan Highway. Travis ran with it and created a spontaneous game from the backseat that assigned Nick five points for calling out the correct passing intervals for Najibullah.

"Zero points if you get dead, mate," he said dryly.

The drive led to several high-pitched screams from Nick, who was gripping the dashboard. This inspired raucous, slap-happy laughter from the three of us in the backseat, and certainly kept us entertained for an hour or so despite the increasingly uncomfortable ride.

When we stopped to get some fresh naan at a late-night bakery, I took my head scarves off and tied them around the "oh shit" handle in an effort to traction up my legs. I leaned back, slipped both feet through, and let my legs swing free as we went over the bumps. My ass was falling asleep, but getting my legs up helped enormously. *I could be stretched out on a toshak right now,* I thought more than once. It had been a rash decision to press on. We should have stayed, spent more time with the family, then taken Nick to see Massoud's tomb on the way home.

We got back after ten o'clock and drove straight to the guest-house, which again—like it was after the Kandahar trip—was still standing despite the threat warnings. We unloaded our gear, said good night to Fatima and Travis, and thanked Najibullah for his help and phenomenal support.

When we got inside, we realized that all the restaurants were already closed. We hadn't had anything solid to eat since breakfast other than a piece of plain naan when we'd stopped in Panjshir. I was ravenous for some real food. I explained to the front desk staff the situation, and they kindly fixed us a plate of reheated leftovers from dinner that we could take back to my room to eat. Nick and I devoured everything, still in our filthy clothes. I took out my little two-shot bottle of single malt that Mike, another Scotch drinker, had given me—not nearly adequate to mark the occasion, but still, it was something. We each took a swig and then, exhausted, we said good night.

Alone, I took off my Longfellow ring, pausing to read the inscription for the thousandth time: "The lowest ebb is at the turn of the tide." I walked into the bathroom and turned on the shower. As I let the lukewarm water wash over me, I watched the dirt and dust turn the water around my feet a muddy brown. My mind empty of thoughts, I stayed there until the water became cold. Then I dried myself off and layered myself up in the warmest clothes I could find. I took out the silver barrette and Devon's locket from my hydration pack, and placed them beside the Longfellow ring. My talismans and spirits with me, I climbed into bed with an exhausted smile.

12

Strength in Numbers

London, Colorado, Afghanistan 2010–2012

Three days later, I was a world away in London Heathrow's brand-new Terminal 5. After searching high and low for an outlet to charge my laptop, I was sitting in a quiet area of the terminal checking e-mails.

My thoughts were heavy, as if the culmination of the ride, the three weeks of interviews, conversations, and probing from Nick, and the relief of the trip being completed had stirred all sorts of emotions and memories up. Sitting there, I realized I wanted to share a thought that had been revolving in my head on the plane from Dubai, where Nick and I parted ways on different flights back home.

He was the first person I'd talked to about my rape in any detail, ever. Talks over cups of tea each night in Kabul, specific conversations about my work, and my motivations became more and more intimate as the trip wore on. At one point, Nick said, "You know,

I'm really surprised at how much you've shared with me throughout this trip. I anticipated you being more guarded from our initial phone conversations."

"I guess I realized at some point that once I made the leap to allow you to join me, I'd better be okay with sharing. I don't have any control over what you write. You can write whatever you want, and I can't do a thing about it. The only control I have is to be completely open. The way I see it, if I'm open about everything, then it gives you a better chance of understanding how I think and how I feel and why I do what I do."

So for some reason, I felt I wanted to share what was going through my head with him. Maybe he'd understand what I was feeling; maybe he'd understand me better and therefore tell a more accurate and honest story.

Nick sent me an e-mail while I was in transit. In it was a quote from the book he'd been reading on the trip, Ernest Hemingway's *A Call to Arms*: "The world breaks everyone and afterward many are strong in the broken places." I sat there, my eyes focused on the words, reading and rereading the quote for a full ten minutes. My world narrowed into focus. A chill ran down my spine, and a heaviness of realization settled in my heart.

Could the rape have a silver lining? Was that even acceptable to consider? Could it be the root of my courage and drive? If so, then I would be saying that the rape was what allowed me to have the courage to work in Afghanistan the way I did. If that was indeed the case, then I had to realize the irony that I had a rapist to thank for my courage and passion and bullheadedness. And that was potentially the way I could forgive him. If that was even possible.

For a girl who didn't want the rape to define her, it defined me more than I ever thought was possible.

I am stronger in the places that were broken. Sometimes to a fault.

I remembered how the last guy I'd dated had said on more than one occasion, "Why do you have to be *so* strong?" Perhaps more his own feelings of weakness than my strength were at fault. My previous boyfriend, Mark, who remains a dear friend, hadn't complained about my strength per se, but had commented after we broke up that I wasn't particularly "soft." Lord knows Pete would agree that my strength was front and center in our relationship. Was it an overcompensation?

Perhaps my real strength was in my vulnerability . . . and if that were true, I was much weaker than I wanted to admit. Perhaps my strength was less about my inner strength but more like an armor, worn to protect myself but impenetrable to those who wanted to get closer to me.

My mind racing, I called Christiane, international charges be damned.

She answered on the first ring. "Hi, sweetie! Where are you?"

"I'm in London."

I could hear the relief in her voice. "I'm so glad. How are you?"

"I'm good. Safe. Confused, though. I need to talk."

"Is it about Nick? You sounded tired and overwhelmed in your e-mails. Emotionally spent."

"Oh man, you have no idea. It was tough—him being there, me feeling like I was under a microscope half the time, and then becoming friends as we were spending so much time together—then remembering that everything I said was 'on record' and up to his interpretation and his editor's direction."

"Do you think he'll do a good job?"

"I think so, but that's subjective, isn't it? It was hard knowing that some of his colleagues were unsupportive of this story and thought I was a narcissist, like I was a little girl playing dress up as an activist. My work shouldn't be controversial. It wouldn't be if they were writing about a man. If I hadn't known, it would have been easier to relax and be myself. Instead, I felt on the defensive for most of the trip."

I took a deep breath. This wasn't why I'd called.

"So, here's the deal. What if my rape had a silver lining?"

I paused, not sure how that sounded.

"I'm listening."

"I am who I am because of all the things that have happened to me, right? So that means that the good and the bad define me. Would I be the woman I am today if he hadn't attacked me? If I hadn't thought I was going to be killed, would I see the world the way I do today? Is my strength, in part, due to him? And if so . . . then in a really fucked up way, I have him to thank for who I am today. I like who I am. But I wouldn't be here, wouldn't be doing what I do, wouldn't think the way I think, wouldn't fight for what I believe is right, in the same way."

I paused, thinking, and Christiane let the silence wait.

"I will never forgive 'him.' Never. Fuck him. But perhaps I can come to terms with this in a different way. Maybe by admitting that that night *did* define me, then it no longer does. Does that even make sense?"

"It does, sweetie. It does. You are the woman you are because of all that you have endured, but you aren't broken—you are strong, but you are also compassionate, and loving, and beautiful. I am so sad that you had to go through this. You didn't deserve it. No one does. But maybe you are letting go of the final hold that experience has over you. Maybe this makes you whole in a way you never knew you weren't."

"I don't have the right words. It comes out all wrong, saying my rape has a silver lining. That's insulting to everyone who's ever been raped. But I don't know how else to say it."

"Don't worry about saying the wrong thing to me. You have been through so much on this trip. Much more than you ever anticipated. And following the last trip to Kandahar, it's a lot to begin to process, and you haven't taken the time to do that."

"How can I? I'm too busy trying to survive day by day. Pay my bills, keep a roof over my head and Devon's. Feed her. I don't know how much longer I can keep this up, Christiane. Why am I doing this? I'm sacrificing everything to make this work, and now I'm sacrificing my personal life to an audience that is already judging me before they know me. I'm not sure I'm strong enough for this. I'm exhausted. I'm broke. This trip was *so* hard. Seriously, enough. I don't need to be processing this decades later on top of everything else."

"I know, I know," she said softly. "But right now isn't the time. You just need to get home. Cuddle up with your Elephant Princess, and just rest. You need to find some time for yourself."

That Hemingway quote integrated itself into my life, and the life of Mountain2Mountain, in the years that followed. It became something I periodically pondered, until eventually it became the heart of my first TEDx talk with TEDxMileHigh in January 2012, which highlighted the backbone of everything I believed and wanted Mountain2Mountain to represent—*The Perception of Victimhood and the Power of Voice*.

I took the stage, standing on the infamous red dot, and looked out at the crowd. I took a deep breath, and the first image came up on the screens on either side of me. "What do you see when you look at this photo?" It was from my first visit to Afghanistan—the photo Tony had taken of the woman in the burqa sitting in the middle of the road, begging with her young child.

"Do you see potential? Possibility? A change-maker?"

During the talk, I challenged the audience to think about how they viewed victims, individuals, and countries, and how difficult it was not to become apathetic to the injustices we were assaulted with daily in the media.

Then I put up a photo of me riding a buzkashi horse in Kabul.

"Now, what do you see when you see this photo? Do you see an adventurer? An athlete? An activist, a fighter, a mother, a daughter?"

I looked out into the crowd, voicing my biggest fear.

"Or do you see a victim?

"You see, many years ago when I was walking home from work, I was brutally attacked, raped, and left for dead. A victim at eighteen.

"But I was only one of over two hundred thousand women raped in the United States every year. That's one woman every two minutes. Had I believed I was a victim, had my friends and family treated me as one, had I been born in a country like Afghanistan, perhaps things would have turned out differently. But in fact I was petrified of that label . . . victim. The finality of it."

In a matter of minutes, I was through the hardest part, and my voice got stronger as I reached the heart of my talk, what I had come to realize since I'd first spoken to Ann Curry, and what had become the backbone of all Mountain2Mountain's work going forward.

"It starts with *voice*. Yours, Ours, and *theirs*. I would start with looking at a different model of philanthropy altogether, where the victims we want to 'fix' are instead the solutions to the problem itself. Giving victims a voice creates a much more powerful ripple than a handout. Empowering them to use their voice can change their lives, their communities, and their countries from within— organically and sustainably creating change with the individual, which acts as a catalytic spark through the entire community.

"So as we leave here tonight, I implore you to change your perception not only of victimhood but of risk. Risk doesn't mean you have to start your own organization in a war zone. It's a risk to use your voice to stand up for someone who doesn't have one. It's a risk to say no. It's a risk to say yes. But that is life—life is a series of risks, of opportunities, and if we want to see a world without oppression, without conflict, without victimization, we have to take risks. Change doesn't happen by playing safe.

"So leave here, use your voice, implore others to use theirs, and assess the risks of doing nothing in your own life. Then look outside yourself into your community, and look at how you can speak for children, for abused women, for refugees, for the homeless, because you can see them as more than victims. You can see them as catalysts for a better world."

Thus a few months later, Strength in Numbers was born, although I didn't realize the full extent to which it would emerge and allow me to evolve into my truest self—an activist, not an aid worker. I was on the verge of creating a sustainable global program, using the bike as a vehicle for social justice with women who'd previously been labeled victims. I would build an army of women who could change the world, stronger in the places that were broken and therefore more capable of taking on the challenges ahead.

In a blink, I was done. The audience was applauding, and I walked off the stage, for the first time aware that Afghanistan may have changed me more than I could ever hope to change Afghanistan. Afghanistan allowed me to be fearless and to be vulnerable and to realize that both were sources of my strength. Now it was time to use my voice and encourage other women to use theirs. One woman can create change, yes. But I also realized that our strength was in our numbers, and together, as individuals, we could pedal a revolution. I knew what I wanted to do. Now it was time to get to work.

But first I had one last big project in Afghanistan.

In November 2012, I returned to Afghanistan with a photography exhibition, exactly four years after meeting the Afghan photographers at AINA. The *Streets of Afghanistan* photo exhibition had launched in the United States at an event at the Denver Art Museum. Five Western and five of the original AINA-trained Afghan photographers had contributed images, and I had blown them up ten feet tall by seventeen feet wide on collapsible frames. The images could be set up anywhere, in any configuration, to allow the viewer a unique interaction in a variety of locations. My goal was to take photography off the walls of a gallery and surround the viewer. Instead of viewers staring at a wall, they had to walk among the images, contemplate the face—larger than life—of a young girl. They imagined themselves in the streets of Kabul, the rolling green hills of Badakshan, or contemplated the empty caves in Bamiyan where the giant Buddhas had once stood before the Taliban blew them up.

I had also created a series of black-and-white photography from Afghanistan in the 1960s and displayed it on easels to showcase Kabul as a progressive and peaceful city: women in miniskirts at a record store in Kabul; women and men studying side by side at Kabul University. This series showed that Afghanistan was much more than what Americans saw in the news and media today. It gave a sense of hope for what could be based on what had been. Too often I heard people talk of countries like Afghanistan as deep dark holes of terrorism, poverty, and oppression that had never escaped the fourth century. Looking back just a few generations to see that Afghanistan *had* been a modern Islamic country shocked many who saw the photographs. Sometimes we have to look back in order to know what is possible in the future. If men and women went to school side by side, if women walked freely in the streets of Kabul without head scarves, perhaps they could do so again. Forty years of occupation, civil war, and unrest changes a society for the worse, but this doesn't mean that it can't right itself given the opportunity.

While I'd originally wanted to use the exhibition to challenge perceptions of Afghanistan, I realized that it would be even more powerful in the literal streets of Afghanistan.

I had funded a graffiti art project in Kabul created by Travis and Gilly under their moniker of Combat Communications. They'd brought in the street artist Chu from England and gathered artists from Kabul University to learn about the history, culture, and techniques of street art and graffiti. This was a statement on the power of public art and the power of art as activism. One young woman in particular took what she learned in the workshop and embraced it wholeheartedly. Shamsia developed into a talented graffiti artist who focused on the bluebird burqas as her trademark. Images of fish and bubbles intertwined throughout her images as though the burqas were underwater, representing the words that Afghan women say but that no one hears. The community engagement of public art inspired and created conversation, which was what made street art so powerful. Art as activism, not just through its subject but through the very nature of its application and audience.

I wanted to take the entire exhibit to Afghanistan and set it up as a series of public art installations for Afghans. Unlike the art exhibitions that reside in embassies or secure locations, I wanted to explore the idea of making the exhibition accessible to everyone. Public art doesn't belong only in secure environments; it belongs on the streets. If art is voice, then voice needs to be public. Furthermore, of the photos taken from Afghanistan every day by journalists, photographers, and travelers, how many are seen by Afghans? How often are these taken images returned?

I launched a Kickstarter campaign to raise the funds to take the exhibition over to Kabul. Knowing I couldn't execute this endeavor solo, I enlisted the help of good friend and writer Anna Brones. In the spirit of her "say yes to everything" policy she'd adopted for the upcoming year, she gulped and said, "Hell, yes." Tony was a no-brainer. I knew he wanted to return to Afghanistan, and it felt synergistic to have him along to document the finished exhibition, which included several of his prints from our first trip together.

We departed Denver International Airport with thirty-one black duffel bags containing the *Streets of Afghanistan* exhibition, thanks to the three-truck convoy of friends who dropped us and our gear outside of United Airlines. Miraculously, all thirty-one bags, twenty-nine photographs, and two bags of luggage arrived in Kabul after three flights, two delays, and forty-nine hours of travel. It took five porters to help maneuver our luggage through Kabul International Airport and one confrontation with the customs agents.

"What is in the bags?"

"It's a photo exhibition." They looked at the bags, then at me, not comprehending.

"Do you have a letter?"

I sighed. *Here we go again.*

"No, I don't have a letter. This is a photo exhibition we are setting up in villages around Afghanistan."

I understood the confusion. What photo exhibition fits into thirty-one duffel bags? I could imagine how the aluminum collapsible frames looked on the screens of the X-rays they'd just gone through.

"These are photos taken by Afghan photographers to show Afghans."

"You need a letter."

"I don't have a letter."

"You must have a letter."

"I don't have one."

"These are not photos."

Aha, the problem is the bags.

"Okay, fine." I raised my voice slightly with frustration and exhaustion. I walked over to one of the porters and grabbed a bag. I hoisted it onto the metal desk and unzipped it. The agent's eyes went wide, and he backed up. I pulled a photo out and put it upright on the desk and started to open it like an accordion, the image expanding across the desk, all ten by seventeen feet of it.

"See? It's a photograph."

"Okay, okay. You go now."

I looked down as I pushed the enormous image back together so the agents couldn't see my triumphant smile. I put it back in the bag, zipped it up halfway, and dragged it to the porter who helped lift it on top of his cart.

Anna's face was aghast.

"All right," I said, "let's roll." I grinned as I circled my finger in the air. The porters grinned back, and off we rolled to find my friend and fixer Najibullah, who would be waiting outside as he was nearly every time I arrived.

"What about low profile?" she asked, thinking back to the conversations we'd had about security and such.

"This is different. Gotta surprise them. We got over forty bags in total to Kabul. I'm not getting stopped by customs in the final stage!"

We walked outside into the dusty air of Kabul. Najibullah was at the exterior gate to meet us with a minivan and a smile to welcome us back to Afghanistan.

"*Salaam*, Shannon."

"*Salaam*, Najibullah. *Hubisti?*"

"Thank you. I am very well."

He looked over at Tony, his smile widening. "*Salaam*, Tony. It is very good to see you again." For four years, Najibullah had asked how Tony was, and he was clearly pleased to see him again.

Smiling, Tony grasped Najibullah's small hand in both of his. "*Salaam*, Najib, I am very happy to be back."

"Najibullah, this is my dear friend Anna. She is going to help us with the project."

Najibullah looked at the bags and the porters, and smiled at all of us. "That is very good. I think we have a lot of work to do."

I laughed and nodded. "Yup, you're going to love this, Najib."

"Do you like our vehicle?" Najibullah pointed to a blue and white minibus. Standing in the doorway was a small man with Uzbek features, in a cream shalwar kameez and light brown vest. "This is Mohammad. This is his minibus."

"Najibullah, it's perfect. Thank you for arranging everything."

I shook Mohammad's hand, and he smiled in return. We'd gone back and forth via e-mail about how big of a vehicle we'd need for transporting the exhibition, and us, around Afghanistan. I'd eventually told him to imagine thirty to forty large duffel bags plus people, and I left the logistics to him.

Once in our guesthouse, we stacked the bags by the security gate so that the guards could search them. While we unzipped them, and as if on cue, one of the guards asked me where my motorcycle was. Home away from home—it was good to see some familiar faces. As storage for the exhibition, the staff gave us an empty room on the second level, overlooking the street and the security bunker that was sometimes used for banquets. Every day, we had to carry the heavy images—each an awkward forty pounds—up and down narrow staircases, avoiding barbed wire, and loading them into the awaiting minibus. Anna and I were going to get as strong as bulls.

I let Anna and Tony hang at the guesthouse to get settled while Najibullah and I made a visit to the Kabul police commander, General Salangi. This wasn't required, but it was recommended to let him know what we were planning, as the exhibition would be in public places under his jurisdiction. Sitting behind an enormous desk at the far end of the room, the general was an imposing figure, built like a bear. His enormous frame made it easy to imagine him bare-knuckle fighting. We sat on the chairs that lined the wall near his desk while he spoke into his cell phone. He was watching a television that allowed him to view security cameras at street level around Kabul. A traffic accident was getting cleared, and he was advising the police on the ground where to go. He hung up, handed the phone back to his colleague, then turned to us. Najibullah had met him many times before, and after greetings, he introduced me and explained what I would be doing in Afghanistan on this trip.

After some discussion, General Salangi thanked us for informing him. Najibullah told him that in a couple of days we planned to set up the exhibition north of Kabul in the village of Istalif and asked if there was anything we should be aware of. The general said things had been quiet and that he would alert the Istalif police that we were coming and that we should be treated as guests.

"They will allow us to set up the exhibition without any trouble," Najibullah informed me.

The next day, we loaded up the minibus and headed to Kabul's historic Darul Aman Palace ten miles south of the city center for our first test run.

As we drove toward the palace, its solemn structure emerged, residing stoically on top of one of the many small hills that dot Kabul. Najibullah explained to Anna and Tony that decades of war had not been kind to the palace. It had been set on fire twice and had sustained heavy gunfire and shelling from rival mujahideen forces that battled for control of Kabul during the civil war. We turned onto the narrow road winding up the hill itself, the palace rising in front of us and its damage becoming visible. The roof had caved in, and the walls were riddled with bullet holes, but even in its ravaged state—or perhaps because of it—the palace was astonishingly beautiful. History lined its walls like wrinkles in an old man's face, each bullet hole affirming its place in history. The palace was surrounded by barbed wire and guarded by a small group of Afghan National Army soldiers who watched us from behind their gate as we got out of the minivan. Najibullah went over to talk with them.

Najibullah walked back over to us with two of the Afghan soldiers who guarded the building. Below us, there was a field with boys playing football, their shouts rising up.

"They will allow us to set up the exhibition here," Najibullah said.

I nodded my head to each solider with my hand on my heart in gratitude. They nodded in return.

Our goal here was to discover how easily we could transport and set up the images in public, and to test the reactions of the people who watched, so that we could troubleshoot potential problems with the full exhibition. Darul Aman was a very public place, but due to its placement on the hilltop, it limited the car and foot traffic that mostly kept to the main roads wrapping the bottom of the hill. We unpacked eight of the enormous images, and soon a small crowd of men and boys had gathered, curious about what we were doing, as were the soldiers. Out of each bag, Anna and I pulled the bulky, collapsible frames. Two people were required to unfold and lock each frame into place, the cloth photographs stretching taut to reveal their images and vibrant colors. We moved them, selecting locations and experimenting with different layouts and spacing. Each image was freestanding, but if we had a windy day, we would have to get creative to keep them from blowing over due to their large sizes. The palace presented a dramatic backdrop with which to frame the images, and when I finally stepped back to take in the scene, I smiled widely. The palace, and the golden dust lit by the setting sun created a timeless backdrop to the exhibition. The project had taken four years, but now here it was, larger than life and more beautiful than I could have imagined. Afghanistan in Afghanistan.

We stood back and watched the reactions. Curious schoolboys on their bikes and men wandering past stopped and gathered around each photo. Many took photos of themselves in front of the landscape images with their phones. Photos in front of photos as though they could step into the giant landscapes through a transporter. Tony documented the process and the interactions. I was planning to create a book about the exhibition and its return to Afghanistan. We stayed for several hours, talking with the soldiers and the men who asked us questions.

As the sun set on the images in front of the palace, I took a breath. Exhilaration coursed through me. I'd pulled off our first public exhibition in Afghanistan. This was the first real taste of the ephemeral nature of street art installations—the impermanence. Over the course of this trip, we would set up these images and take them down six more times, and each time I found myself disappointed at how empty the space felt without the images at the end of each day.

The next day was the first of Eid celebrations. We left Kabul early to drive an hour and a half north into the Shomali Plain, to the village of Istalif. Istalif is a quiet place known for traditional handmade turquoise-glazed pottery. We arrived in time to unload the exhibition while the majority of the village was walking toward the small blue-and-white tiled mosque for Eid prayers. The women would mostly likely be at home preparing the Eid feast.

I looked around, working through the puzzle of the landscape to figure out how best to set up the photographs. One long dirt road led through the entire village straight to the mosque. Normally, it would be lined with market stalls, but they were closed for the holiday. We could literally line the street with the exhibition so that as everyone came out of the mosque and walked back through the village, they would pass it.

Najibullah and our minibus driver, Mohammad, helped unload the exhibition. Anna and I unzipped each bag and pulled the heavy frames out and stacked them carefully on the dirt road. There were twenty-nine photographs in total. The local police showed up in a green jeep, just as the call to prayer rang through the village. As Najibullah made introductions, they smiled at Anna and me, and shook our hands. Najibullah explained to them and the gathering crowd what we were planning. One of the policemen explained that General Salangi had called and they were planning to stay with us to make sure we were safe. They curiously watched as we began unfolding the images in the dusty street. As each one expanded on the accordion frames, the crowd closed in to look at the emerging image. We set the images up one by one against the empty market stalls. Within an hour, we'd created a walkway of photos leading to the mosque. Slowly, men filled the street as they finished praying and headed toward their homes.

The surprise on their faces was clear—smiles, curious looks, and laughter—as groups gathered around images. Anna and I walked the length of the exhibit road several times, watching villagers viewing and interacting with the art. Most amazing was watching the young kids who stood for ten minutes or more in front of the photo of a Kabul market street, pointing out individual people and buildings while discussing the photo with one another. Young girls in vibrant emerald green and ruby red walked by the images, running their fingers across them.

A young man rode his bike close to us, keeping pace and observing us, but maintaining his distance. After a couple of laps, I turned and walked over to him. I pointed at his bike, "*Makbul ast.*" It's beautiful. This was no ordinary bike. This was a bike with pinwheels, multiple horns, and a plastic flower vase containing a single plastic flower mounted on the handlebars. There was some sort of fur wrapped around the front of the bike, tied with a pink satin bow. He smiled with pride and spun the pinwheel. I laughed. He stepped off and handed the bike to me. He spoke quietly but I heard, "*Shoma?*" You?

"I can ride your bike?" I asked in English. He nodded vigorously.

"You're sure?" He nodded again. I looked at Anna. How could I say no?

"I'm going for it."

"Hell yeah, you are." She laughed.

I accepted the bike and sat down. The seat was way too low, and I immediately discovered the brakes were barely working, but I certainly wasn't going to complain. I rode up and down the bumpy road, avoiding the worst of the potholes and piles of rubble, not daring to go very fast as I was unsure of my ability to stop. Laughter erupted from the men around me, and small kids chased after me.

I rode the bedazzled bike back to the man who was now standing next to Anna. I motioned to her questioningly. "Can she ride the bike, too?" He understood and nodded with a huge grin.

"You wanna ride?" I teased, knowing her love of bikes was nearly equal to mine.

"Are you kidding?" She laughed. "Holy shit, yes!"

While she was riding up and down the dusty road, one of the villagers spoke to me in English in awe, "It takes a lot of intelligence to ride a bike, I've never seen a woman do it." Perhaps the most significant statement any Afghan man had made to me about women riding bikes—equating intelligence with the action of riding, as though that was the reason women didn't do it. This showed me that even though I was a foreign woman, my riding in these areas and my welcoming the curiosity and the conversations could create a small shift in the overall perception of a woman's ability and her worth.

Over the course of the next week, we set up four more public exhibitions. We set up the next day, the second day of Eid celebrations, in the inner courtyard at Kabul's historic Babur Gardens. Hundreds of families came to picnic on the grass and by the end of the day we were told by the head of the gardens that almost two thousand people had come through. The next day was the final day of Eid and the most unusual venue we had chosen—the Kabul Zoo. We competed among the bear and monkey cages for wall spaces. It made for an unusual exhibition in a space that many Afghans like to visit. The last Kabul show was at the Women's Garden, an area open only to women, where they can relax without men around. Inside, there was also a driving school, training and educational workshops, and a small market for the women. The garden felt like an oasis after the intensity of the previous three exhibitions. It was the first time we got to sit and watch and talk to one another and to the Afghan women who walked through. Normally, we were surrounded by men, having our pictures taken or simply stared at.

At the gardens, I first met Mary, a woman who'd lived in Kabul nonstop since she first moved there in the 1960s. My friend Warren, who joined us for the Darul Aman bike ride, introduced her to me because Mary had ridden her bike around Kabul nearly every day and continued to today, even now, in her eighties. She shared some amazing stories of living in Kabul during the civil war and the Taliban time. She worked for a small women's rights organization, and when the Taliban kept harassing her at the office, she stood her ground and complained to anyone who would listen. Apparently it worked because Mullah Omar himself, in Kandahar, wrote a letter and sent it to Kabul saying she was to be left alone. She ate lunch with us in the garden and shared more stories. I told her that someone should write her story, and she replied that she was attempting to but it was very difficult. I hoped she wrote it or that someone else did before her incredible stories and experiences were lost forever.

The final exhibition was the most powerful. We drove out to Panjshir to set up a small staging at the top of Massoud's hill. Panjshir had become incredibly significant to me, and I wanted to set these images up there at least once. I chose the hillside of Massoud's tomb, as it was not only the first place I'd visited four years prior with Faheem Dashty, the fearless leader of AINA Photo who'd nearly been killed alongside Massoud—and who'd introduced me to Afghan photographers for the exhibition—but also because it overlooked the entire Panjshir Valley.

The tomb was completed, and this was the first time I'd seen it without scaffolding or workers. It was quiet except for a few of Massoud's soldiers who stood guard. Najibullah explained what we were doing and asked permission to set up the photographs for a few hours. The guards tentatively agreed, and I asked Anna to help me unzip the various bags. I wanted the first image we pulled out to be the shot Tony had taken at Kabul's Olympic Stadium four years earlier, with the billboard of Massoud looking down at the runners on the track below. We found it and set it up near the edge of the hill overlooking the valley.

In the shadow of his own marble tomb, Massoud's face gazed over his valley. One of the men looked at the photo and then at me, and smiled broadly, nodding in approval. I put my hand on my heart and smiled back. He called one of the other soldiers and together they looked at the photo and then curiously at the others we were unpacking: Beth Wald's beautiful rolling green hills; her landscape of the Buddha caves from Bamiyan; Tony's photo of the burqa-covered mother and child in the Kabul street; and Paula Bronstein's vivid portrait of a young girl peering at the camera surrounded by a sea of lapis blue burqas. As we lifted each one out of its bag and unfolded the enormous frame, the image emerged, met with curiosity from the soldiers and the visitors who'd come to pay their respects to Massoud.

It was windy at the top of the hill, so I asked Anna to help me carry some of the photos over to the old Soviet tanks that rested at the side of the hill. As "frames," the tanks made for a stunning backdrop to the images, and it was a disappointment that we couldn't leave them up, since they would blow away overnight. Instead, we set up the exhibition like we did at Darul Aman, a limited staging with the soldiers in a historic place. As the light started to fade, we packed the images back up, thanked the soldiers, and headed home. We stopped briefly at a kebab house along the Panjshir River to celebrate the finale of the exhibition I'd dreamed up exactly four years prior, now come to life in the country I'd come to love.

The final show occurred the day after we flew home, at the U.S. Embassy, in conjunction with a rooftop rock concert with the Afghan metal band *District Unknown*, and the first female Afghan rap-per, Susan Firooz, to celebrate the life of Daniel Pearl. The embassy liaison had agreed to keep the exhibition for me until I returned.

In the end, my goal was to show that art had a place in conflict zones—to showcase the work of Afghan photographers and to bring the images "taken" in Afghanistan home to the Afghans. They deserve the same access to art and beauty that we all crave. Public art isn't limited to the urban cultural centers of New York or London. Shows like this one can be done safely and publicly in Afghanistan, and should. Art has the power to inspire and create a ripple of change that resonates through communities. Public art serves the purpose of bringing art out of private places and into public spaces among the people who are least likely to engage with art.

While Afghanistan is not the place that many think of for emerging artists and activist culture, few countries in the world are more ripe for an artistic scene. In the time since I started working in Afghanistan—a period of approximately six years—a space has emerged for modern and edgier artistic voices and an activist movement. Today all you have to do is look on the billboards and concrete walls around Kabul to see how contemporary art is emerging in public spaces. Banksy-inspired artists, like Kabir, have embraced graffiti art as a public statement on peace. His stencil art silhouettes feature intertwined hearts. Billboards around town were sporting a collection of street art; machine guns shooting rainbows, a tank with a rainbow of colored pencils erupting from the cannon, and another with a row of grenades interspersed with a heart. One of my favorites is a map of Afghanistan with a giant Band-Aid across it. There is space for art to emerge in Kabul, and amazing Afghan artists, musicians, poets, and photographers are using art as their voice, and as that goes more public, their voices amplify.

In Kabul, I took Anna to one of the newer coffee shops, Venue, a coffee shop turned artist refuge that was opened by my friend Humayun. Sitting in the outdoor courtyard, we were surrounded by the work of emerging graffiti artists like Shamsia and Kabir. The pulse of an artistic heartbeat was clear. Just inside the entrance was the artist statement spray painted on the steel doors. "Beware of Artists: They mix with all classes of society and are therefore the most dangerous."

We had come to meet up with my friend Warren and a few friends spearheading an incredible street art initiative, part of the visionary, yet anonymous, street artist JR's global public art project, *Inside Out*. The project was the result of JR winning the renowned TED prize as a way of illustrating the power of photography and street art to represent community and illustrate the faces that make up our global neighborhoods. The group was meeting to discuss the logistics of putting up hundreds of poster-sized, black-and-white portraits around the city. Sitting around the table in the courtyard were members of District Unknown, visiting Swiss artists Shaykla and Shervin who were spearheading the Kabul *Inside Out* project, and emerging graffiti artist, Shamsia, and her friend, another talented artist, Nabila.

To great excitement, Shaykla put two large mailing tubes on the table. Each one contained a roll of a hundred or more large poster-sized black-and-white portraits of Afghan men, women, and children. Locations were discussed for maximum impact—those that were accessible and still relatively safe for the art to be stationed at for an extended period of time. Someone had brought a sample of the glue they planned on using, and everyone agreed that a test was necessary to check how the glue would react with the ink. A space on the courtyard wall was chosen, next to a large in-progress mural by Shamsia and one of Kabir's stencil art pieces of a young boy carrying buckets of hearts. An old man in a pakol hat was chosen as the poster, and five minutes later, it was deemed a success, and plans resumed for large-scale logistics of hundreds of portraits. It was beautiful to bear witness to and exciting to envision.

Three days later, on an early morning bike ride through Kabul, I got to see the images close up on the walls of Kabul. I had made plans to ride to Darul Aman Palace with a friend of mine, Mikhail Galustov, a Georgian photographer who lives in Kabul and loves to ride. Mikhail told me about the men's national cycling team, the first I'd ever heard about them. He'd introduced me to one of the young men on the team, Ashraf Ghani, who worked as a waiter at Design Café, a few doors down from Venue. Ashraf and I spoke at length about biking, the men's team, and racing. Ashraf had asked if I wanted to ride with the team, and I enthusiastically agreed. We made plans to ride the next morning at six o'clock. I invited Mikhail to come with us. When I woke at 5:30, there was a light rain, and ten minutes later a text from Ashraf cancelling due to weather. Mikhail was already en route to meet me at our guesthouse and was more than happy to ride as the rain looked to be clearing by the time we set out a little after six. We decided to ride to Darul Aman as the roads should be quiet this early in the morning.

Tony, Anna, and Warren came along to play and take photos. They wanted to meet the men's team and watch a training ride. Warren also wanted to see the finished *Inside Out* project while the streets were quiet. When we told them that the team cancelled, they decided to come along anyway since everyone was already awake and assembled at the guesthouse. Mikhail and I took off, the roads empty but relatively dry. I was on my brand-new Alchemy 29er single-speed mountain bike, and Mikhail rode his Cannondale 29er fully geared bike looking ever the European in a fashionable sweater over a shirt and fitted khaki pants, a kaffiyeh scarf around his neck. I was in my usual layered getup: long black pants under my black halter dress, tunic, and a thin puffy jacket. I had a kaffiyeh scarf tied around my head and another around my neck. With no more than an occasional car passing, we chatted amiably as we pedaled side by side, mostly about bikes. As we rode past a mosque and a long stretch of wall, the series of portraits emerged. Tony, Anna, and Warren cheered out the bus door, taking photos and celebrating as we rode by. I laughed out loud at the absurdity of keeping a low profile biking through Kabul with a minibus of photo-taking, cheering friends.

Twenty minutes or so later we turned right onto the dirt road in front of the hill where Darul Aman Palace sat. It was probably just after seven o'clock, and traffic was getting busier. Kids were walking and biking to school. I blinked hard and realized there was a girl on a mountain bike in front of me—on a bike miles too big for her, wearing a backpack, but it was definitely a girl.

"Mikhail, did you see that?" Disbelief mingled with excitement.

He nodded. "This is a Hazara neighborhood. They are a little more progressive here. Occasionally, you see something like that."

"Holy shit! That's the first girl I've ever seen on a bike here."

His Georgian personality showed little emotion. "It is pretty cool."

"I didn't realize this area was Hazara." Hazara is an ethnic group, like the Tajik who predominate in the north and Pashtun in the south. Bamiyan province is predominantly Hazara and is one of the safest in the country and one of the most progressive in terms of sports, youth radio, tourism, and apparently their women. It was where the Taliban blew up the Buddhas. It was also where, for the past three years, a ski competition had taken place as ski tourism developed. Girls had been allowed to learn to ski, and the

Band-e Amir lakes in that area had been designated Afghanistan's first national park. Bamiyan also had a female governor, Habiba Sarobi, who had been in charge since 2005.

My mind blown, we rode down a bumpy road and toward the hill to the palace. Mikhail's chain broke, so he walked back to the minibus at the bottom of Darul Aman to see if our driver Mohammad could help. Meanwhile, a group of young boys on their way to school joined me, and together we rode laps like a biker gang. They turned out to be avid football fans.

"Who plays football?" I pointed to each in turn and asked in Dari, "*Shoma?*" You? And each replied "*Bale.*" Yes.

"Are you proud of the Afghan football team? They just played at Kabul Stadium, right?"

"Yes," one of them replied in English, "but I like AC Milan better."

"Really? What about you?" I pointed to another boy. "What team do you like?"

"I like Barcelona."

"Wow, a lot of European teams.

"What about you two?" I pointed at the two shyer boys at the back.

"Barcelona."

"Bayern Munich."

"Well, all right then." I laughed as they shouted out their favorite teams.

"Where are you from?" the leader of the gang asked.

"I'm American."

"What are you doing here?"

"I work in Kabul. I have a nonprofit."

"Do you always ride your bike in Kabul?"

"No, not always. But I wish I could. I love riding bikes. What about you? Do you like riding bikes?"

He smiled big. "Yes, I love riding bikes."

"Very cool. Follow me."

We rode up to the top of the hill where Warren was already talking to the guards. Anna and Tony were talking with Najibullah, and Mikhail soon joined us, the chain repaired. We all chatted for a while. An old man, with a long white beard and a black turban with white stripes, pushed a bike up to me and asked what was going on. I exchanged greetings with him and told him my name, then I called Najibullah over to help translate. He talked for a few minutes with the man.

"'This is the gardener. He has been working here at the palace since he was a small boy.'"

"Seriously? Please tell him we are honored to meet him."

For twenty minutes or so we listened to stories about the palace, his childhood, the civil war, and his family. Then he asked me about my bike, and I asked about his. Bike bonding in Kabul—nothing unusual there, right? In hopes of getting us access, Warren had been buttering up the soldiers who guarded the palace and who were curious about what was going on. They were insisting we weren't allowed, mostly because it was unsafe.

"What if I ask them if they want to ride my bike?"

"Definitely." He nodded. "They'll love it."

I walked over to the barbed wire gate with my bike and offered it up with a smile. "Anyone want to ride a bike?" Two of the guards smiled and nodded. They walked out, and I tried to explain "disc brakes"—basically saying "softly softly" while pointing at the brake levers, hoping that this translated somehow. Brakes on Afghan bikes take serious grip strength to engage, and these were brand-new Avid disc brakes that barely had to be touched with one finger. Squeeze too hard, and someone would be flying over the handlebars. I didn't need an Afghan soldier face planting on my bike and getting pissed off.

With a large grin, and to the cheers of his fellow soldiers, one mounted my bike in his fatigues and plastic sandals. He pedaled in circles around the large stone courtyard in front of the palace. Everyone was cheering and laughing, and I glanced at Tony to see if he had his camera out. Of course he did, but before I could turn back, I heard a collective intake of breath and a "Oooohhhhhhhh." Shit, a crash? I swung around, and sure enough the soldier was righting himself and my bike, having squeezed the front brake too hard. He'd somehow leaped off and landed on his feet like a cat. Relief flooded me, and we all cheered again as he rode over with a sheepish grin into a crush of hugs from the other soldiers, Warren, and Tony.

He stepped off with a shy smile and walked over to me, but before he could hand the bike back, his commander, a much sterner looking man with a beard and stocky build, took it. He glanced at me mischievously and off he rode. The soldiers had a turn, and the gardener and the biker gang watched while Tony and Warren took photos. Warren was shaking his iPhone each time he took a photo, and I realized he was taking photos with the Hipstamatic app set on random. I grabbed my bike and rode some circles, and the boys followed me, a little train of bikes cruising. A few minutes later, while the gardener spoke with the guards, I asked the boys if they needed to get to school. I assumed we had delayed them en route since they were all wearing backpacks. They nodded reluctantly, and with waves to our crew and many "*khoda hafez*," they pedaled off down the other side of the hill.

Najibullah walked over. "If you want, they will let us inside the palace."

"Really? Yes, please!" I nearly hugged Najibullah with excitement, but over the past four years I'd learned how to celebrate solo so that I didn't embarrass him. Usually, I gave a little high five to whatever female was nearest and did a little jig on my own—much to the amusement of Najib. I shouted over to Warren, Mikhail, Tony, and Anna. "Guys, they are going to let us inside!"

Najibullah continued. "They said you can bring your bikes inside, too."

"Can we ride in there?" I hardly dared to believe things could get any better.

"They say yes, but to be careful. There are places that are not safe."

Without further ado, we got a personal tour of the palace. The soldiers weren't wrong. There were sections of missing floors, collapsed ceilings, and piles of rubble lined every corridor. Graffiti writing covered a lot of walls, and bullet holes were scattered throughout. We gingerly carried our bikes up the exposed, disintegrating staircases to the second and third floors, where open windows and missing walls gave stunning views in all directions across the city. Mikhail, Anna, and I took turns riding down the rubble-strewn corridors, exploring, and giggling like school children at the serendipity—the doors that open when you ride a bike.

As if the universe was conspiring to support my work and give a stamp of legitimacy to all that I'd done so far, I woke the next morning to the public announcement that I'd been chosen as one of National Geographic's Adventurers of the Year. This wasn't just because I was the first woman to mountain bike in Afghanistan and all the sorts of things that are typically labeled "adventurous," but the profile on the *National Geographic Adventure* Web site focused on the overall work I was doing in Afghanistan as an activist, with women and voice, and in particular with the *Streets of Afghanistan* exhibition. Seeing my name with the group of explorers and adventurers I admired under the umbrella of National Geographic

Adventurer of the Year strengthened my resolve to continue to explore, use my voice, and push boundaries.

Before we left Kabul, I tried one more time to ride with the men's team. Ashraf had told me to meet the team at 6:30 A.M. at a petrol station on the road to Panjshir. I pulled up with Najibullah, Anna, and Tony. Ashraf introduced the team, and we discussed the ride I would join on the highway to Bagram. They were a motley crew of riders in assorted clothing and bike gear. They reminded me of the group I used to ride with in Germany—garish cycling clothing in neon colors, a mix of tennis shoes and cycling shoes, and various styles and mismatched gear. Most of the guys were on legitimate road bikes of varying ages and materials, but they could all have done with a basic bike fit; some had their seats too low, and others were too far away from their handlebars. As we waited for two more riders to arrive, a car pulled up and a man and young woman stepped out. He saw me, looked at my bike, and started shouting at the boys. I backed up and stood with Najibullah, waiting to hear what was going on.

"This is their coach," Najibullah said quietly as he listened.

"He wasn't told about their plans for a training ride, and he is upset."

No shit, I thought. He was shouting his head off. The young woman was quietly standing beside him. She was wearing black high heels and was very put together. I noticed her angular face accentuated with strong black eyebrows and bright red lipstick. Beautiful but tough.

"Who's the young woman?"

"Let's wait and we'll talk to him."

As if on cue, the coach turned to us, got right up in my face and continued in a louder than normal voice, although he had toned down the shouting. Najibullah calmly introduced us all and explained what we were doing there. Coach shouted; Najibullah listened.

"This is Coach Seddiq. He is upset that the team is arranging a ride with a foreigner without telling him. They disrespected him by not asking his permission. The fact that you are a woman is a concern to him as he is afraid something could happen to you and it would reflect badly on the team. He was driving to Mazar to meet with some other riders when he noticed his team meeting here. That's why he pulled over."

"Coach, it is an honor to meet you. I am sorry you were not made aware that I was joining the team. I was invited by one of the riders for a fun ride since I ride and race in the States. I simply wanted to ride with them and experience what it is like for them to train in Afghanistan. I meant no disrespect to you."

Coach listened and then shook his head. "No problem, no problem," he said in English. Then he told Najibullah that I was most welcome to Afghanistan and he was at my service.

"Who is the woman?" I asked. Najibullah spoke with the coach, and the young woman looked up as the conversation turned to her. I smiled at her, and she shyly smiled back.

"The young woman is Mariam. She is assistant to the coach. She helps with the woman's team."

"Wait. What?" *Women's team?*

More talking.

"Yes, she is on the woman's team and helps the coach as his assistant. He coaches the men's and the women's national cycling team."

My mind was reeling. No one I knew had ever heard of a woman's team. No one I had talked to in Kabul besides Mikhail had even heard of the men's team.

"Can the coach tell me more about the women's team? Tell him I am a bike rider and I have been looking to find Afghan women who are allowed to ride bikes."

"The coach says that he started coaching a woman's team because his daughter wanted to ride. They have competed in Pakistan and hope to race more outside of Afghanistan. He is going to Mazar because he heard about a group of women who want to learn to ride bikes."

"Holy cow. Can you explain to him that we are leaving, but we would love to find a way to help the teams? I will be back in a few months and would like to meet with him and meet the women's team."

Najibullah translated, and the coach smiled at me and started nodding his head excitedly. His demeanor softened, and he grabbed my hand. "Thank you, thank you," he said in English. He continued to Najibullah in Dari.

"Coach says that you are most welcome to come back and ride with the women's team. It would be an honor. We can all sit down and discuss with him when you return, and you can ride with the men's and women's team. No problem." Najibullah continued to me, "Coach was just upset to be disrespected by the boys."

Ashraf was embarrassed and was hiding off to the side, his swagger long gone after having been chastised in front of us. He'd brought us there, as the de facto leader of the team, and his ego had taken a bruising.

"Coach, I look forward to meeting with you when I return and riding with the teams. I will see what I can do to help both teams, and I wish you and your team all the very best. Najibullah can stay in touch while I am back home. I will be hoping that all your riders stay safe, *inshallah*."

My mind was already thinking of the donated bikes and clothing we could rally as an initial first step.

We said our good-byes and loaded into the minibus to get some breakfast. I was bummed to miss riding with them but excited to discover women riding, in public, and doing so as part of the national cycling federation. This was huge! These women were the first Afghan women to ride bikes. I babbled nonstop all the way to breakfast, my mind still reeling with the possibilities and already plotting my return. Here were women challenging the status quo and taboos that prevented other women and girls from riding. My heart swelled with pride at what they were both accomplishing and risking. Coach Seddiq was another example of an Afghan man like Faheem Dashty, Najibullah, and the myriad of male teachers and doctors I'd encountered who were fighting for the rights of women and girls—men who realized that Afghanistan cannot truly succeed unless all of its citizens had access to the same opportunities for education, training, and sports.

I'd been gifted a book, *Wheels of Change*, by a woman who'd read about my mountain biking adventures in Afghanistan and my disappointment with the cultural barriers that prevent Afghan women from riding. The book illustrated the cultural shift when American women began riding bikes at the turn of the century. As in Afghanistan, women who rode were considered immoral and promiscuous, in part because of straddling a bike seat in public, and in part because of the individual freedom the bike allowed. The bike became more than a hobby or sport; it became a vehicle for change and an integral symbol of the women's suffrage movement. The bicycle gave women true freedom of physical mobility so that they no longer depended on male family members for transportation. It truly expanded their world. Bicycling gave a woman the freedom to go off on her own, as far as she could pedal, unaccompanied by a chaperone.

The women's rights activist Susan B. Anthony famously stated in 1896, "I think the bicycle has done more to emancipate women than anything else in the world. . . ." It gives a woman a feeling of freedom and self-reliance. The moment she takes her seat she knows she can't get into harm unless she gets off her bicycle, and away she goes, the picture of free, untrammeled womanhood."

The bike sparked a change in women's fashion as well. Riding in petticoats was cumbersome and difficult, so split skirts or pantaloons were invented, heralding a new era in women's fashion. As a woman who is happiest in a pair of jeans, I, for one, am grateful. But these changes weren't without controversy, as one famous quote I found stated, "The wearers of the bloomers are usually young women who have minds of their own and tongues that know how to talk."

It wasn't long before those independent minds and talking tongues were changing the entire idea of feminism, fashion, and sports in the United States. Although even in the United States, where we tend to view women's rights as progressive, it wasn't until 1984, the year my sister was born, that women were allowed to cycle in the Olympics. It took nearly a hundred years from the time American women started riding before it became acceptable for them to compete in the Olympics alongside their male counterparts.

Today, the bike is used as a tool for change around the world, and organizations like World Bicycle Relief and 88 Bikes use the bikes directly with girls as a vehicle to change lives. In communities throughout Africa and Southeast Asia, the bike increases the access to school for boys and girls alike by simply reducing the commute they have to make on foot. In rural Cambodia, school typically ends at the primary level for many girls simply because the nearest secondary school is too far to commute to by foot. Typically, the commute is not just long but increasingly dangerous as rape and gender violence have reached near epidemic proportions in the countryside. The vast majority of underage rape victims were assaulted while walking home from school. But with access to a bicycle, one of the key barriers to education disappears, as do the attacks against girls.

In Afghanistan, girls on bikes—despite bikes being a logical and affordable tool—are just not culturally acceptable. Time and time again, men who accept me as a foreigner riding a bike admit freely that they wouldn't allow their girls to do so. Constantly, I have questioned the men I met—Why? What if? There is a women's boxing team and women skateboarders, but what is it that makes the bike so taboo in Afghanistan? Yet these young women like Mariam were riding as part of a national cycling team, for the simple joy of learning a new sport and hobby—the same as women anywhere else. This was unimaginable ten years ago but a sign of progress in the post-Taliban era. These were the first Afghan women to pedal bicycles. Change is slow, often generational at best, and when I consider the parallels between the women riding bikes in Afghanistan and the women who started to pedal a revolution in the United States, I can't help but get excited at the spark that has begun—even if it's a slow burn.

Human Rights Watch employee Heather Barr stated in *The New York Times* that, on the morality ladder, riding bikes is just one step above the morality crimes that Afghan women are jailed for. That in itself sums up the courage and the controversy these women embody when they dare to ride. These are young revolutionaries on two wheels, even if they don't realize it. They are revolutionary simply by the very nature of the taboo they are breaking every time they pedal. Many may say, "Well, it's just a bike." But I see it's another drop in the bucket. It's one more way women are illustrating their equality and making that equality the norm, not the exception.

I sensed that my work in Afghanistan was about to ramp up rather than wind down as I'd envisioned at the beginning of the trip. If anyone embodied Strength in Numbers and the power of the bike to create change, it was these women. Was it a coincidence that I'd just decided to create Strength in Numbers as a vehicle for women to use their voice and become agents of change a few months before finding Afghan women riding, after years of riding my bike there? Or was life simply unfolding organically, revealing to me what I needed to see at its own pace?

Things unfold in a way that we often can't see until we take the time to look back at all the steps that have led up to the present, as if a road map had been laid out. I never planned to work in Afghanistan or to become an activist for women's rights. I never thought I'd be a mountain biker, much less the first woman to mountain bike in Afghanistan. But things were set in motion decades ago that led to me standing at a dusty petrol station on the outskirts of Kabul, speaking with the coach of the women's national team and plotting a two-wheeled revolution.

Twenty years ago, I lost my voice, somewhere in the dirt, behind a bush. Perhaps it simply ran out with my blood.

How was I to know it would be in Afghanistan that I found it again?

In a strange way, I have my own attacker to thank. He tried to break me, to kill my spirit and possibly my body, to leave me less than whole. He nearly succeeded. I've just started to realize how much it affected me and my relationships with the men and women in my life over the years. But when I became ready to face it and the horrors of that night, I became fearless. I realized that I wasn't scared. Of anything. Except maybe of doing nothing, of turning a blind eye to the injustices I saw in the world, of becoming apathetic and desensitized.

I took the wrong bus. That simple act created a domino effect that rippled through the rest of my life and led me to a dusty, war-torn corner of the world where women who are raped are often jailed. Where women aren't allowed to drive, or ride bikes, and in some cases are not allowed to even leave the home without their faces covered and a male escort. Where girls have acid thrown on their faces to scare them away from school. Where women set themselves on fire to escape their husbands. To a country where women's rights aren't just trampled—they're crushed into a fine dust that blows across the country.

Yet this place, whose pollution turns my nose black and fills my lungs with a cough that impedes my mountain biking each time I return home, is the place I chose to risk everything and fully commit to be an active participant in the world that surrounds me. It is the place that showed the best of humanity in the worst of circumstances. It is the place that showed me hope is always stronger than fear; that my vulnerability could be my biggest source of strength rather than my weakness; that a bicycle can be a vehicle for social justice; and that a two-wheeled revolution is possible. By doing so, Afghanistan illustrated for me the parallel situation for women in my own country, and how sparking a two-wheeled revolution in the United States was perhaps my next step and the evolution of Mountain2Mountain.

Every day has become a reminder to never forget how fortunate I am to have the freedom to ride my bike, anywhere I wish, dressed however I like—a reminder that I should never take for granted the life I have, and the opportunities that unfold. This life is a ride, and I am so very glad I'm on it, balancing on two wheels, trying not to crash, but pedaling as hard as I can, with the wind in my face, and a smile as big as the sun. As a dear friend always says, "Just ride. Just ride. Just ride."

Epilogue

A Two-Wheeled Revolution

Afghanistan 2013

The final day of filming the Afghan National Women's Cycling Team was one of the best days of my most recent trip and an unexpected culmination of my own years of biking in Afghanistan. We met up with Coach Seddiq whose white Land Cruiser held four members of the women's team, their bikes strapped to the roof. We drove outside of Kabul to start their ride. Heavily loaded, brightly painted, Pakistani trucks thundered by as the team prepared their bikes and the coach spoke with them.

After meeting the coach and some of the girls in October, I'd returned home to Breckenridge. That January, I'd lunch with two girlfriends, Anna Brones and Sarah Menzies. I told Sarah about these girls and what an amazing film their story would make. As Anna had been with me on the previous visit to Afghanistan and had met the coach and the girls, she added her thoughts. By the end of lunch, our decision was made—Sarah would join me in Afghanistan to make a film about the women who dare to ride. We'd figure out the details, but for now, we have three and a half months to do logistics and preproduction, and get funding secured.

I had set up a gear drive with local bike shops, and I reached out to my friend Claudia Lopez. A fiery Colombian photographer, she was living in Boulder and we'd met several times for coffee and chats about travel, photography, art as activism, and the power of voice through different mediums. When I explained the project and proposed that she joined as a photographer to document it, she immediately said yes.

Sarah brought on board Whitney Connor Clapper as codirector. Whitney was another Anna type—a woman who simply "gets shit done." She was affable, smart, and ready for anything. More important, as I discovered throughout our time in Afghanistan, she created a safe space for everyone to collaborate and create without ego—allowing the best of everyone to shine. With four passionate, high-energy creatives working together for the first time, our crew's synergy may not have gelled the way it did without her subtle influence and incredible tirelessness.

The crew complete, we made plans in the months leading up to the trip about logistics, filming, and the arc of the story. I worked hard to get yet another crew of first-timers up to speed on all things Afghan. I collected four hundred pounds of cycling gear and soon had a storage unit full of bikes and gear that we packed up to bring over to Kabul to distribute to the cycling federation for the men's and women's teams. Three months later, all four of us were standing on the side of the highway leading north out of Kabul, watching a train of girls on bikes pedaling away for the first time.

For the following two weeks, we filmed daily: training rides, b-roll of daily life and scenery in the city, and interviews—hours and hours of interviews. We interviewed the coach and four of the team riders, Mariam, Nazifa, Sadaf, and Farzana. We also secured an interview with a female member of Parliament and women's rights activist Fawzia Koofi, to give us her perspectives on progress for women's rights in Afghanistan, the uncertain future of these gains over the past ten years, and her thoughts on this team of women cyclists. Fawzia helped put into context the risk these girls undertake by challenging the taboo against women riding bikes. She'd been left outside in the sun to die by her family at birth when they discovered she was "just" another girl. To her family's surprise, she survived the exposure but had burns on her skin that remain today. They took her inside and raised her as part of the family. She survived the era of the Taliban regime, married a man she loved, had two daughters with him, and eventually became a member of Parliament, an author of the bestselling memoir *The Favored Daughter*, and a strong political force who seriously considered making a run for president in the 2014 elections. She freely admitted that these girls were on the front line, risking their lives to challenge the status quo, but that without women willing to take on those risks, change would never occur.

While it's hard to imagine these young women having to fight that fight, the truth is that all Afghan women have to fight that fight. Young girls my daughter's age who walk to school and risk harassment, threats, and acid attacks have to fight that fight. Women forced into arranged marriages with men forty years their senior have to fight that fight. Women who risk their lives and their honor to run for political office in order to fight for their rights and the future of their country are fighting that fight. If no one takes on the risk to make a stand, to use their voices, and to fight against the norms that oppress them, change will never occur. Change doesn't happen without risk.

Risk was a key theme we examined in the interviews with the girls and their families. They ride with their families' permission, something their coach himself insists upon. Each time we spoke with the girls, they acknowledged the risks they were exposed to, whether it be traffic or harassment. While they downplayed that it was controversial, they also admitted the frustration of the logistics of being a female cyclist. The girls couldn't meet up on their own for a group ride or even venture out by themselves. Sadaf and Farzana talked about riding with a brother or father occasionally, but the inability to train without their coach providing safe logistics was extremely limiting. The girls still tended to focus on the opportunities that cycling had provided, namely travel. Being part of the national cycling team had allowed them to acquire passports and travel outside Afghanistan for the first time. Exposed to other female cyclists at races in Pakistan and India, they were able to interact with their regional counterparts and learn from them.

One rider, Nazifa, inspired the entire crew during her interviews. Nazifa was one of the smallest riders but had exhibited some of the deepest drive and strength as a rider. She completely opened up to us and bonded particularly with Sarah. Her large smile and tinkling laughter was a constant source of joy during filming with her. She had lost her father, and so her uncle was the main source of support for the family. He'd obviously instilled a sense of national pride in her, and this came out when she spoke of her desire to represent her country in the Olympics, to "show the world that Afghanistan is not just a drug country."

These girls are the next generation, the first to have access to computers and the Internet—and therefore the first to know more broadly what is happening in the rest of the world. All that they are doing—going to university, riding bikes, racing, working outside the home, traveling outside of Afghanistan—are risks, challenges to the status quo that most Afghan women have found themselves living under for at least the past forty years. Yet each time they are asked, they willingly accept the risks, in order to gain the opportunities.

As Fawzia Koofi reiterated often in our interviews, "The time has come to stop referring to Afghan women as 'poor Afghan women.' That changes nothing. It is time to start calling them 'strong Afghan women' because that's the only way to change the perception of Afghan women, and encourage them to succeed."

So there we were, standing on the side of a highway leading out of Kabul, watching the girls get their bikes off the roof of the coach's white Land Cruiser for a training ride. We watched them pull out on the highway with apprehension. Men stared at the girls from all directions, cars honked, trucks swerved around one another in typical Afghan mayhem. The girls seemed so vulnerable on their skinny tires entering the fray. Standing on the side of the road, I felt the mayhem as dust swirled, and the wind gusts challenged the girls to hold their line. There was a sense from the crew of heavy responsibility, and we all gut-checked ourselves as they pedaled off. None of us felt good about watching them ride here. This was seriously dangerous riding, not just because they were girls doing something Afghan women didn't do, but because it was a trucking highway where driving a car was dangerous enough. The brightly painted, intricately decorated Pakistani trucks roared down the highways, creating huge gusts of dusty wind as they passed. I reminded myself that the girls weren't doing this for us; this was their training ground and they faced these risks every time they pedaled. We just needed to document and share their incredible story.

Standing on the side of an Afghan highway, I thought back to all the things that led me to this place: my rape, Larissa's rape, Devon's birth, ten years working as a sports trainer, a life lived in multiple countries, my love of mountain biking and exploration—all bricks in the foundation that brought me to Afghanistan and brought me deeper into my truest self. Working here, I began to realize that my deeper motivations could be a simple desire to believe that my own beauty could emerge through my heartbreak; that women's voices matter; and my own need to express and thus be understood through my own layers of complexity. The hope that reconciliation and forgiveness can be found within me for those who tried to break me. That if I can find forgiveness for the man that raped me and nearly killed me, I can find compassion in humanity itself.

The young women who dare to ride their bikes are pedaling a revolution. They train on some of the most dangerous highways in the world, in a country where their existence is a challenge to the status quo, breaking a major cultural taboo. Like the American women who dared to ride in the late 1800s in America, they are refusing tradition in the post-Taliban era, taking advantage of all the opportunities before them. They serve as inspiration to women around the world, and to me. My hope is that the gains made for women in the past decade aren't lost in the upcoming one as the international focus shifts, international support wanes, and the Afghans take on more control of their country. As they work to ready themselves for international competitions—with their eyes set on representing their country in a future Olympics—they are already demonstrating to the world the strength of Afghan women. They are the best possible example of the heart and soul behind Strength in Numbers—showing the world a different view of women in Afghanistan while showing Afghans the strength of women. One pedal stroke at a time.

Acknowledgments

First and foremost: Devon, you are my reason for everything. Not one day goes by that I am not grateful beyond measure that you came into my life, and I am honored to be your mom. I love you, I love you, I love you. To the moon and back a million times over.

Larissa, we grew up ten years apart, and half a world away for much of it. I am so blown away by our relationship now. Sisters, best friends, neighbors, and you're the best aunt that Devon could ask for. Thank you for believing in me and for allowing me to share the part of your story that intertwines with mine. Silver linings out of violent histories.

Christiane Leitinger, my soul sister and the woman that believed in me through the toughest of times, when everyone thought I was crazy, including myself, for continuing down this path.

Mom and Dad, thank you for believing in me and supporting the work I chose to dedicate my life to, for making me believe from a very early age that a young girl from North Dakota could do anything she wanted.

A huge thanks to Dede Cummings for coming on as my agent, pitching my book to St. Martin's Press, and firmly getting behind the project. And to my editor, Daniela Rapp, who understood what I wanted this book to be, and supported me throughout!

Jason Dilg, for challenging me to speak not once, but twice at TEDxMileHigh, which helped me to find my voice and stand up for those that don't know how to use theirs yet. For your friendship, your advice, and mind blowing brainstorming sessions! #giveashit.

Allen Lim, for reminding me that suffering is part of the journey and letting me cry on your couch when I wasn't sure I could keep doing this alone. And for believing in the power of bikes to transform the world! "Just ride, just ride, just ride."

Travis Beard, the man, the myth, the legend. Thank you for your years of friendship, advice, and inspiration. You kick serious ass and have done far more for mentoring and inspiring the next generation of artists and musicians than anyone I know. You are Afghanistan's best-kept secret and I am grateful for your sarcasm, your support, and your assistance. Rock on.

Hamid, for teaching me to ride a motorcycle, being my translator on many trips to Panjshir, and endless laughs, many of them at my expense, and the best nickname I've ever been given. CIB.

Najibullah Sedeqe, my translator and fixer extraordinaire. Thank you for the initial introduction into Afghanistan, the friendship, and the advice when I continued to encounter unknown situations. Six years we have worked together, and I hope that we have many more years working together.

Tony Di Zinno, the photo sherpa. Thank you for the photos and the support, documenting my first trip, and coming back four years later to see the *Streets* exhibition in the streets, parks, and villages of Afghanistan.

Justin Balding, for believing in my work and my story enough to introduce me to Ann Curry, an interview that unexpectedly sparked so much change, personally and professionally. Even more important, you became a dear and trusted friend and I hope I can return the favor someday.

James Edward Mills, for believing in me from the beginning, continuing to publicly share my work and my story, and for calling me Blondie, which always makes me smile.

Sarah Menzies, Whitney Connor Clapper, and Claudia Lopez, for showing me how amazing creative women can be and what a powerful force we can become when we drop our respective egos and collaborate our asses off. So proud and humbled to work with you on Afghan Cycles, and most important, honored to call you friends.

Anna Brones, you fabulous woman, you! I dub thee, the woman who "gets shit done." Thank you for joining me in Afghanistan on the promise of kebabs and pomegranate juice and not once complaining after setting up the Streets exhibition about a billion times.

Mark Wiggins, for years of new trails on two wheels. You are an amazing friend, and I will always love riding single-speeds with you!

This book, and many of my ongoing efforts, wouldn't be possible without the kindness and patience of Ket McSparin. Thank you for being the best landlord ever. Devon and I are grateful beyond words.

To all the Afghans who opened their homes, their lives, and shared their stories and their tea with me. It has been my greatest honor to work in and explore your country. Thank you for your friendship, your advice, and your patience.

Last but not least, Deni Béchard, for your incredible patience and help in the last-minute push with the editing while I was in Kabul. In particular, your cleanup of my wayward grammar and liberal sprinkling of random punctuation. I promise I was paying attention. Sort of.

Glossary of Dari Words and Phrases

aks. *photograph*

anor. *pomegranate*

bale. *yes*

bolone. *fried dough stuffed with potatoes*

burro. *go*

baisekel. *bicycle*

buzkashi. *traditional horse polo played with headless calf or goat*

chaikador. *watchman or gatekeeper*

chaihanna. *tea house*

chai. *tea*

chirany. *gift*

Dari. *national language of Afghanistan*

Hazara. *ethnic group of Mongol descent from central Afghanistan*

hosh mekanam. *you're welcome*

hubas. *good*

imam. *Muslim religious leader*

jihad. *holy struggle or holy war*

jirga. *council of community elders and leaders*

kharajee. *foreigner*

khoda hafez. *good-bye*

koh. *mountain*

Kuchi. *nomad*

kojaa. *where*

lotfan. *please*

madrassa. *Islamic school*

makbul. *beautiful*

mazadoras. *delicious*

muezzin. *the one who calls Muslims to prayer*

na. *no*

pakol. *flat hat worn by Afghan men*

Pashto. *second language of Afghanistan*

Pashtun. *dominant ethnic group, predominately from southern Afghanistan*

pilau. *meal of rice and meat*

Quran. *the holy book of Islam*

salaam. *hello*

shalwar kameez. *traditional male garments made up of knee-length shirt and baggy trousers*

sher chai. *milky tea*

shoma. *you*

Tajik. *second-largest ethnic group, predominantly from northern Afghanistan*

tashakur. *thank you*

tashnab. *bathroom*

toshaks. *sitting/sleeping mattress*

Uzbek. *ethnic group concentrated in northwest Afghanistan*